Y0-CAX-956

TEST OF COMMAND

"Do not attack those ships!" Caitlin ordered. She could hear Pyr speaking passionately into a microphone, putting her message out.

Dannet stiffened and turned to face her, but before she could speak one of the sensor techs spoke up.

"More ships coming around from the opposite face of the planet. Looks like...at least another twelve ships."

"Orders to *Arjuna*," the fleet commander snapped, not looking away from Caitlin. "Move to intercept and interdict those ships. Orders to *Pool Buntyam* and *Ban Chao*: maneuver to the flank of the ships from the moon, and prepare to fire."

"Do not attack those ships!" Caitlin said again firmly, her body positioned in the angles of *adamant-purpose*.

Dannet's body shifted to *ultimate-responsibility*. "They are enemy. They are attacking us. We must defeat them to be safe."

DISCARD

Caitlin let her body's posture shift to pure *adamant*. "They are not Ekhat, Fleet Commander. They are no threat to us. Their missiles are too small to be anything much more than smart rockets, and they are too slow to be mass-heavy projectiles that could punch through us. Your lasers will take care of them, and if anything slips through, that's why the ship designers put armor on these ships."

Dannet's angles slipped for a moment, and Caitlin laughed in reply; laughed with an edge, but laughed. "I read the reports, Fleet Commander. I know something of what we're facing here. They're not that much farther ahead of Earth than you think."

Caitlin let her angles move to *command-from-superior*. "I have *oudh* over this search, and I say you will not destroy the only chance we've had to find new allies because of a lack of restraint. You will not repeat the mistake that was made with the Lleix!" She stared at Dannet, daring her to cross that line.

BAEN BOOKS by ERIC FLINT

JAO EMPIRE SERIES:
The Course of Empire with K.D. Wentworth
The Crucible of Empire with K.D. Wentworth
The Span of Empire with David Carrico

THE RING OF FIRE SERIES: *1632* • *1633* with David Weber • *1634: The Baltic War* with David Weber • *1634: The Galileo Affair* with Andrew Dennis • *1634: The Bavarian Crisis* with Virginia DeMarce • *1635: The Ram Rebellion* with Virginia DeMarce et al • *1635: The Cannon Law* with Andrew Dennis • *1635: The Dreeson Incident* with Virginia DeMarce • *1635: The Eastern Front* • *1636: The Papal Stakes* with Charles E. Gannon • *1636: The Saxon Uprising* • *1636: The Kremlin Games* with Gorg Huff & Paula Goodlett • *1636: The Devil's Opera* with David Carrico • *1636: Commander Cantrell in the West Indies* with Charles E. Gannon • *1636: The Viennese Waltz* with Gorg Huff & Paula Goodlett • *1636: The Cardinal Virtues* with Walter Hunt • *1635: A Parcel of Rogues* with Andrew Dennis • *1636: The Ottoman Onslaught* • *1636: Mission to the Mughals* with Griffin Barber • *1636: The Vatican Sanction* with Charles E. Gannon • *1637: The Volga Rules* with Gorg Huff & Paula Goodlett • *Grantville Gazette I–V*, ed. by Eric Flint, and *VI–VII*, ed. by Eric Flint & Paula Goodlett • *Ring of Fire I–IV* ed. by Eric Flint

MORE BAEN BOOKS SERIES by ERIC FLINT

ASSITI SHARDS SERIES • RATS, BATS & VATS SERIES • THE HEIRS OF ALEXANDRIA • BELISARIUS SAGA • JOE'S WORLD SERIES • CROWN OF SLAVES SERIES • THE BOUNDARY SERIES • THE PYRAMID SERIES

To purchase these and all other Baen Book titles in e-book format, please go to www.baen.com.

THE SPAN OF EMPIRE

ERIC FLINT
DAVID CARRICO
with
K.D. WENTWORTH

THE SPAN OF EMPIRE

This is a work of fiction. All the characters and events portrayed in this book are fictional, and any resemblance to real people or incidents is purely coincidental.

Copyright © 2016 by Eric Flint and David Carrico

All rights reserved, including the right to reproduce this book or portions thereof in any form.

A Baen Books Original

Baen Publishing Enterprises
P.O. Box 1403
Riverdale, NY 10471
www.baen.com

ISBN: 978-1-4814-8292-9

Cover art by Bob Eggleton

First paperback printing, April 2018

Library of Congress Control Number: 2016022584

Distributed by Simon & Schuster
1230 Avenue of the Americas
New York, NY 10020

Pages by Joy Freeman (www.pagesbyjoy.com)
Printed in the United States of America

CONTENTS

PART I
Reconnaissance

CHAPTER 1

The gray moon still held a few ruins, mostly extending beneath the surface, while the once habitable planet visible overhead in the airless sky had been scoured lifeless with solar plasma in that gruesome way the Ekhat had so long ago perfected. Suited up against the vacuum, Caitlin Kralik stepped down carefully from the shuttle and rotated her body to get a better view. Inside the helmet, her breathing rasped in her ears and she felt awkward in the low gravity, which was only about a fifth of that of her home world, Earth.

The Ekhat plasma strikes had not been aimed only at the planet. Caitlin had to watch the placement of her feet, because the shuttle had landed at the edge of a strike here on the moon, and the nearby surface was marred by ribbons of solidified molten splash from that attack. She picked her way across the flow until she reached her destination, a structure that was just far enough away from the center of the plasma strike that it had survived, albeit with serious damage.

The pitiful remains of the moon's former inhabitants, mummified by exposure to vacuum, were scattered across what had once probably been the observation deck of an eating establishment. Thick glass lay shattered in the moon dust, the shards reflecting the starlight like discarded diamonds. Metal struts that had formed the supporting structure had been melted into formless slag that had puddled, then solidified on the ground.

These nameless people, listed nowhere in the Jao database, had been diminutive with long sinuous arms and a multitude of digits that resembled tentacles far more than fingers. Their hairless heads were narrow, their eyes small and recessed deeply into their skulls. They had apparently loved color because red, purple, orange, and blue clothing draped their shriveled torsos.

Many of the mummified corpses were tiny and had fallen clutching one another. Small figures made of a plasticlike substance lay scattered about, most of them crushed, broken, or melted. Caitlin picked one up and turned it over in her gloved hand. It was iridescent blue and seemed to be some sort of animal with an oversized skull and three slender trunks.

Then she realized—they were probably *toys*. Dear God, these small bodies were most likely children. Had this been some sort of daycare or a creche for the raising of the next generation?

Her eyes felt damp, but Caitlin resisted the urge to weep for these lost people. If she gave into her emotions now, she would have to cry for the rest of her life because the damned Ekhat had apparently been everywhere in this arm of the galaxy, working their way out from the galactic center and killing every sentient being in their path except for those they enslaved. The Ekhat had done their maniac worst here long ago and moved on, seeking more victims.

"These people have obviously been dead for millennia," she said. "Could even be a million years, who knows? The Ekhat are ancient." Her fists knotted in frustration. "There's no way we could ever have gotten here in time to help."

"We will take measurements," Kaln krinnu ava Krant said, responding to Caitlin's rhetorical statement with Jao literalness. "At least, the information will fill out the database and allow our calculations to be more accurate."

The Jao tech had joined the landing party from the *Lexington*-class ship that the Krant kochan had contributed to the fleet. Caitlin's shuttle had contained techs from all over the fleet, since it was obvious soon after they had jumped in that the system was lifeless. Kaln wouldn't be needed on her ship for now and had joined the others to make herself of use by helping with forensics instead of preparing for battle. That of course was the way of things when working with Jao. For them, making oneself of use at all times was of the highest priority.

The Jao stared at her, body *neutral*, waiting, and Caitlin realized that her statement had actually been a request for direction. Caitlin had *oudh*, as the Jao termed it, in this search for sentient life and new allies. It was for her to decide how to proceed.

"Yes," she said. "Please collect samples and take the proper readings." For all the good it will do these poor lost devils, or even us, for that matter, she told herself.

This was the second dead civilization they had found since they had left Earth almost a year ago out of eighty-one systems visited, working their way by frame gate travel along the Orion Arm of the galaxy toward the center. The first one hadn't been technologically advanced enough to spread beyond their own planet, though.

There might have been sentient populations on two other planets, but if so, they'd been too technologically primitive to have left traces after the Ekhat scoured the planets with plasma balls. The expedition had also passed by many more solar systems than they'd investigated, because they'd been able to determine that they didn't have habitable planets. It was possible that a few survivors of a ravaged species might have been hiding in one of those systems, if they had the technological capability. But the likelihood was remote and they couldn't check every possibility.

And if they did, they probably wouldn't have detected anything anyway. Such a species would have to be very well hidden, if they'd been able to escape Ekhat attention.

Caitlin had known the Ekhat were fiercely efficient exterminators. But it was one thing to know it with the logical part of her brain, and another altogether to stand over the remains of slaughtered children and their broken toys.

Kaln's arms moved in a choppy version of the Jao posture signifying *orders-acknowledged*. The Jao kochan of Krant, though tough and reliable, was not much taken with fancy body-styling. The Jao was taller than Caitlin, taller even than her husband, Ed, built broad and stocky with heavy bones. Her dark-russet face with its nearly invisible black facial markings, or *vai camiti*, blinked at her with green-laced black eyes, then Kaln gestured to one of the tech teams emerging from the shuttle with their equipment.

Captain Caewithe Miller, commander of Caitlin's bodyguard, picked her way through the debris into the shattered observation deck and stared down at the corpses. "We have to stop the Ekhat," she said. "Things cannot go on like this."

Caitlin nodded, though the gesture felt foolish in the stiff spacesuit. Someone did need to stop the insane Ekhat in their quest to exterminate all sentient life in the universe. She just wasn't sure it could be their Jao/Human/Lleix alliance. The Ekhat were an incredibly old and vicious species, and successful at killing far beyond anything humans had ever imagined before the Jao had conquered Earth.

When the Jao had arrived on her world, over twenty-five years ago, they had defeated Earth's armies after a short but savage war and then installed their own government. They had informed their new subjects about the dangers of the Ekhat, but humans had not believed them. Even her father, who had been vice president of the United States at the time of the initial invasion, then later puppet ruler of North America for the Jao, had not credited the stories about the fiendish bogeyman aliens who wanted nothing more than to be alone in the universe with their own perfection.

What they had not understood in those early days was that the Jao, though consummate warriors and gifted techs, had no capacity for imagination or prevarication. They had been uplifted into sentience long ago by a faction of the Ekhat to serve as warrior-slaves in the ongoing slaughter of all intelligent life. The ability to picture that-which-did-not-exist, what they called *ollnat*, had been bred out of them long before they finally freed themselves from their terrible masters. They did not make things up because they couldn't.

When the Ekhat had later attacked Earth, humans realized that the Ekhat were far more terrible than the Jao had ever been able to make them understand. The reality of the Ekhat was a hundred times worse than any tale ever told, no matter how gruesome.

Gabe Tully emerged from the shuttle, a gun slung across his shoulder, although there was no one left to fight here in this depressing moonscape. He had accompanied a squad of his soldiers; not that anyone expected there to be any dangerous Ekhat or other aliens lurking in dark vacuum corners. Still, the occasional need for strong backs still arose, even in this day of starships and solar plasma balls. He hopped toward them, using long gliding strides in the low gravity. "Didn't leave much, did they?" he said, plowing to a stop just short of Captain Miller.

His tanned face beneath his gold hair surveyed the wreckage and dead bodies. He looked a little green beneath the tan. Caitlin knew he didn't like space travel and would have much rather remained back on Earth, cajoling the remaining scattered pockets of the human resistance to come out and use their fierce will to help in the fight against the Ekhat.

"They didn't leave anything," Caitlin replied in a grim tone. "It's beginning to seem utterly hopeless. I think they've already scoured this galactic arm from here on in."

"We found the Lleix," Tully said. He bent to pick

up a shard of shattered observation window and turned it over in his gloved hand. "They survived, so there must be more species out there."

"The Lleix had been fleeing and hiding for over a thousand years," Caitlin said, "and even so the Ekhat found them again and again. If we hadn't come along when we did, they would have exterminated them at Valeron in that last raid."

Which would have been a terrible loss, Caitlin acknowledged to herself, picking her way through the rest of the debris. The Lleix, with their amazing capacity to adapt and learn new languages and concepts, were staunch and valued allies now. The Jao/Human taif that ruled Earth had allotted them temporary living space on the Colorado high plains and promised to relocate them to a new world all their own. But so far, on this exploratory expedition, the only habitable worlds they'd found that might have once harbored intelligent life had already been savaged by the Ekhat, every one of them reduced to lifeless cinders like the one overhead at the moment.

Tully turned back to her. "What now, Madam Director?"

What now, indeed? she thought. She was in charge of this disheartening and fruitless chase. What had seemed an exciting opportunity to acquire new allies back on Earth when Preceptor Ronz first approached her now was only tedious, often depressing duty, just going through the motions until they could justify giving up and returning home.

"Document what we can," she said, resisting the urge to sigh. "Wrot has taken a shuttle and tech crew to the planet, but I don't think they'll find even this much there. From the readings we took in orbit, it doesn't even have a proper atmosphere left, just a bit of outgassing from its interior."

"It's not your fault," Tully said. "The Bond laid this course out for us. We're acting on the best information we have."

"I know," she said. "We'll gather as much data as we can here, then move on to the next system."

"Even though there most likely won't be anyone home?" Miller asked.

"It will just take one inhabited world to make this expedition a success," she said, though she feared she was right, and it was so heartbreaking to follow the scourged trail left by the Ekhat, finding nothing but once verdant planets burned to ashes, a holocaust of dreams, and slaughtered children. "If we can discover even one advanced species, we'll increase our own chances of prevailing against the Ekhat."

"And we just might save one more planet and one more people from becoming nothing more than a haunted memorial," Tully said in a remarkably poetic utterance.

Caitlin looked at him in surprise. "We can try."

That was reason enough to go on, she decided. To try and keep one more planet from becoming nothing more than an orbiting gravestone for a nameless race.

Senior Tech Kaln krinnu ava Krant prowled the surface of the dusty moon, taking samples and readings while others penetrated the building and its lower levels. Her nap crawled with distaste. Waterless environments always affected her like that. The Jao had evolved in the seas of some now-nameless world and always felt most at home when swimming. She gazed out at the arid, dead landscape. No one had ever swum here, even before the Ekhat had blasted this outpost to ashes. She could not understand a species that could be happy under such circumstances.

But then the Lleix were not swimmers either, yet they had made good lives for themselves, despite the pursuit of the Ekhat. One of the great unstated truths of the universe was that there was no one way to live best. You only had to look at humans and Lleix to understand that. Even the many Jao clans, called kochan, varied in their approach to life and living well. And now that her kochan, Krant, was becoming more prosperous, their two homeworlds were changing. Jao, who did not adapt well to change, were being challenged by the alliance to stretch their minds, to see possibilities where none had occurred before. That was mostly the influence of the humans, who pursued *ollnat* as rigorously as Jao had always pursued pragmatism.

It was her secret that she was attracted to *ollnat*, that doing things in a new way made life more interesting. She had kept that part of herself hidden with some difficulty until Krant had come in contact with humans and their way of thinking. Humans valued *ollnat* with the same devotion that Jao strove to be of use. She actually felt at ease among them, since she had come to understand that.

Kaln collected samples of the blasted buildings with her gloved hands, stowing them in her pouch, then recording images on her scanner. This had been a frivolous establishment, set out here on the surface, when it would have been much more efficient to locate all facilities under the moon's surface, but she supposed, like humans, the view had beguiled them—back when there was a living planet above them in the sky and not a lifeless ball of scorched rock.

She directed Giln, one of her underlings, to retrieve several corpses from the structure, including one of the apparent young as well as adults. They would be stored on the *Lexington*, command ship of their fleet, for eventual transport back to Terra where scientists could pore over them and glean what could be learned from the dead flesh of these victims. She wondered if they had even seen the Ekhat coming. She chewed on that as her subordinate, aided by a couple of Colonel Tully's jinau troops, carefully loaded the corpses into body bags. Or had the world just ended for them between one heartbeat and the next in savage blasts of solar plasma?

She had fought in two major battles against the Ekhat, the first destroying or critically damaging three of Krant's treasured ships and killing most of their crews; then in a second, in the magnificent *Lexington* captained by then Terra-Captain Dannet krinnu ava Terra herself. Against all odds, Dannet had prevailed against five Ekhat ships in a single battle, an amazing feat, never before equaled. Now, like Kaln, Dannet was assigned to this expedition. The Terra-captain's new rank was fleet commander, putting her in command of the entire flotilla—more like a small fleet, if you counted all the auxiliary ships—that had been assigned to the expedition. The fleet commander was still on the *Lexington*, but no longer as the captain. Instead, in the human way of phrasing it, the big ship now served as the commander's flagship.

Dannet was all Jao in her devotion to duty and being

of use. She had been a gift to Terra from the great kochan of Narvo, in recompense for the actions of a crazed scion who had abused his authority as Terra's first Jao governor, and she had since proved a valuable one indeed. Her attitudes concerning duty and service provided an exemplar to both Jao and humans within Terra taif. And her astounding combat record as the captain of the *Lexington* only increased her stature.

Kaln broke off her thoughts when the body bagging was completed. She motioned to Giln and the two of them followed the other techs into the wrecked facility to record additional images and see what little was left of these unfortunate beings. There would not be much, she feared. There never was. The Ekhat were dreadfully efficient. It occurred to her that this was almost Jao-like.

Back on board the *Lexington*, Caitlin called a meeting in one of the conference rooms on the same deck as her stateroom. They'd been at this for almost a year, visiting dead system after system, but she still felt like a fraud whenever she gave orders in her role as the official holder of *oudh* on the expedition. Three years before, when the *Lexington* had made first contact with the Lleix, a misunderstanding instigated first by Kaln and then perpetuated by Wrot had fraudulently presented her as "Queen of the Universe," in charge of all humans and Jao. That had been embarrassing enough; but now her responsibilities were real and she often felt like a child playing dress-up.

One by one the senior members of the fleet entered the room and sat down. The mood was somber as the room filled. Fleet Commander Dannet krinnu ava Terra entered first, followed by the captains of all four of the *Lexington*-class battleships and the commander of the support ship fleet. Among these was Krant-Captain Mallu krinnu ava Krant, captain of the Krant warship. It was officially listed in Krant's shiplists as Krant Ship 3547, but to everyone except perhaps Fleet Commander Dannet it was known as *Pool Buntyam*. The humans had even christened it so when its construction was complete. Its sister ship, another *Lexington*-class battleship, in the shiplists as Krant Ship 3548, was *Bab the Green Ox*. This was also the legacy of the same moment of low humor perpetuated by Kaln that had resulted in Caitlin's regal title.

Behind the fleet commander stood a very tall, very lean human, Lieutenant Fflewdwr Vaughan. It hadn't taken long after attaining her new position for Dannet to realize that she would need assistants, a staff of sorts. Her position in Terra taif was not sufficient to take individuals into service, that almost feudal relationship between the highest of the individual Jao and those who were gathered around them; and being who she was, she would undoubtedly refuse to take humans into service even if she could. But Terra taif's elders had all but ordered her to make use of those humans who would be of service to the taif. And the one who made it past her disdain and bristly attitude was a certain dour young Welshman from Caernarvon. Caitlin hadn't had much contact with him yet, but from all accounts he was a good match for the fleet commander in personality and temperament.

Also present were Colonel Gabe Tully, the ground forces commander of the fleet, accompanied by the

Ban Chao's First Sergeant, Adrian Luff; Wrot krinnu ava Terra, one of Terra taif's elders and her primary assistant (a wily old devil, for a Jao); Brakan and Matto of the Lleix Starsifters *elian*; Ramt of the Lleix Ekhatlore *elian*, and Pyr and Lim of the Lleix Terralore *elian*.

Completing the roster, and standing against a wall flanking the door, were Caitlin's personal bodyguards.

For many years Caitlin had been assigned a Jao bodyguard; first Banle krinnu ava Narvo, a terrible wretch who had abused her and held her hostage to ensure her father's cooperation with the occupying Jao, then later Tamt, a staunch ally who stood between her charge and certain death more than once. After it was determined that Caitlin needed more than the single guard, she selected Miller, a jinau veteran of the Lleix campaign, who was unexpectedly amusing as well as efficient. Tamt now officially reported to Miller, but remained assigned to being Caitlin's closest companion. Her body-shield, as it were. The two were almost inseparable.

Caitlin had never had a close female friend before. Though she had attended college, Caitlin's father's status at that time as a notorious Jao collaborator had prevented development of those sorts of relationships. Her close association, first with Tamt and subsequently with Miller, had proven unexpectedly welcome.

Special benches had been provided for the Lleix as their dimensions were rather broader than even the Jao. The four silver-skinned Lleix gazed at her with upswept expectant black eyes, their fleshy aureoles standing at attention like crowns worn over the head on edge from ear to ear. Taller than humans, their vividly brocaded robes were draped properly, which was always of paramount concern to a Lleix, their hands folded in the proscribed most polite fashion. No one outside the Lleix would ever know now, Caitlin thought, that Lim and Pyr had been thoroughly disenfranchised when the *Lexington* had first come calling, long-time impoverished denizens of the Lleix slum known as the *dochaya*.

"We have to make a decision," she said, once everyone was seated.

Across the table from her, Wrot's eyes danced with enigmatic green fire. One of his ears signaled *slight-error*.

She sighed. "Or rather, *I* have to make a decision, but I want your input." She gazed around the table, gathering their attention, human, Jao, and Lleix. "So far, this expedition has been a failure. We have found nothing but the ashes left behind by the Ekhat. I worry that it won't get any better if we continue on this heading. The Ekhat have been working their way out along this arm of the galaxy for unknown thousands of years. Quite possibly hundreds of thousands of years. I have to consider the possibility that it might just be best to cut our losses and return to Terra."

"We have supplies enough to go on for many months still," Dannet said. She adjusted an already flawlessly placed strap of her Terra-blue harness, then her face with its bold *vai camiti*, characteristic of her Narvo origins, turned to Caitlin. That Narvo face always gave Caitlin a bit of a pause, reminding her as it did of mad Oppuk krinnu ava Narvo who had killed her brother and ruled Earth with an iron fist for most of her childhood.

Dannet's head and ears were canted at the angles

which communicated *unafraid-of-challenge* to anyone versed in Jao body-speak. "There are millions of stars in the Orion Arm of the galaxy. We have examined only a tiny percentage of them. Sampled, it would be better to say."

Caitlin flushed and let her own angles answer with the Jao posture *bold-intentions*. "Yes," she said clearly, "but we cannot visit any significant portion of them in the time allotted by the Bond for this expedition."

"You believe they are all dead," Lim of Terralore said. She bowed her head on its long graceful neck. Her voice was a piping lilt, incongruous for a creature so tall and sturdy. "That is correct?"

"They have all been dead so far," Caitlin said. Heartbreakingly so, she thought, though a Jao would have trouble making sense of that emotion. They were far too practical. Dead was dead and therefore of no use. Move along to the next world.

"We cannot ally with the dead, and available resources are limited," she said, trying to think like a Jao so they would understand her reasoning. "We cannot afford to waste time exploring systems unlikely to contain sentient civilizations."

"Since you want input, I say let's not give up just yet," Gabe Tully said, sitting back in his chair and running his hands through his shaggy blond hair. "The Bond gave us a mandate to explore. Despite the odds, we can't just go skulking back with nothing to show for it."

He was right, she thought. They needed something to justify this expenditure of resources and manpower. Jao respected results. Mere trying counted for nothing with them.

"We have found two worlds so far that were clearly inhabited by intelligent technology-using species," Wrot said, "including this latest one where the inhabitants developed spacegoing technology." His head with its many service marks nodded. "The probabilities are that other civilizations are definitely out there somewhere. I say we give it a few more tries, and step up the pace so that we look at twenty or more additional systems, jumping, then moving on the moment it appears hopeless, not lingering to take samples and recordings. Out of millions of stars, the Ekhat must have overlooked at least a few."

"Is it possible the species we saw today is hiding somewhere in this system?" Tully said. "Like the Lleix did?"

"No," Dannet said. "A large outpost was located by our sensors on the next planet out from the sun, which is too cold to sustain life as we know it without environmental provisions. The blasted remains of their settlement were detected. There's no sign of any energy signatures or survivors."

She could dispatch a squad there to check in person, Caitlin thought, but it would just waste more time, and they had none to waste. The Ekhat would attack Earth again as soon as they were ready, one of the Harmony factions, the Melody faction, or even the fanatical Interdict. She had boarded an Ekhat ship once, seen the monsters with her own eyes, which was more than most people on Earth or even Jao could say. She knew firsthand how totally insane—no, unsane—they were. The two that had spoken with her group had killed themselves before their visitors were permitted to leave because contact with lower life forms had rendered them subsequently unfit to exist.

The monsters had tried to exterminate all life on Earth once already. They would be back, in much fuller force the next time. Their last attack had incinerated a million people and rendered a good chunk of China uninhabitable. The next time, Earth might not survive unless they had extra resources to bring to the fight.

Resources it was her responsibility to secure.

"We will go on," she heard herself say. "We can't give up until we find what we have come for."

"More people," Pyr said. His aureole stood on end. He inclined his sturdy body toward her. His silver skin gleamed with oil.

"More people," Caitlin agreed. "To stand with us against the Ekhat. To ally with Jao, humans, and Lleix. To exterminate the Ekhat as completely as they seek to do away with us."

"That is desirable," Lim said. She inclined her head respectfully. "But is it likely?"

"Not likely," Wrot said, "but then how likely was it that humans and Jao should come to the Lleix in the hour of their greatest need?"

"Not likely at all," Pyr said, "but much appreciated."

"Together, we are stronger," Caitlin said. She spread her fingers on the gleaming wood table and stared down at them as though they could give her sorely needed answers. "We will find another species and convince them to work with us, and then another after that, and another, until, united, we can stand strong against the Ekhat."

Wrot placed his hands on the table across from hers. "On to the next framepoint then."

Heads nodded around the table. Even the Jao had picked that mannerism from the human as a substitute for their *affirmation/readiness-to-perform* bipartite posture.

Caitlin looked to Dannet. "How long until we can jump?"

"We will jump when we are ready, Director Kralik," Dannet said with a sly crackle of green in her eyes. One of her ears flicked with *repressed-amusement*.

A smile quirked at Caitlin's lips. Dannet was referring to the infamous Jao time sense. Jao always knew how long something would take or when it would happen. They had no need to chop time into tiny pieces and then obsessively count them as they maintained humans did. Strangely, after years of association with Jao, sometimes she thought she could feel it too.

"But in human values," the fleet commander continued, "probably not long."

"Good. Until then," Caitlin said and stood, signifying that the meeting was adjourned. "Batten down the hatches. We're heading on."

"I do not know those words, Madam Director," Dannet said, rising to her lean muscled height and gazing down at Caitlin. "What are 'hatches,' and how, as well as why, are we to 'batten' them?"

"It's a nautical Terran term," Caitlin said. "It means secure everything and ready the ship for action."

"Then I see no reason why you did not simply say so," Dannet said with an impatient wrinkle of her muzzle. The four Lleix stumbled back to make room as the big Jao strode out of the conference room, her body stiff with simple *irritation*.

The door slid open, then closed. "You shouldn't

tease her," Tully said, gazing after Dannet, though his green eyes twinkled. "I don't care what color harness she wears now, that one is always going to be pure Narvo at heart. She might snap one day and tear off your head."

"I know," Caitlin said. "But it's just so tempting."

Wrot took a posture of unabashed *amusement-at-the-expense-of-others*. "Well," he said, with an undecipherable twitch of his whiskers, "there is that."

Caitlin Kralik stopped at the door to her suite. "Caewithe, you and Tamt take off and get some rest. I'll be in my room all evening. These guys," she nodded at the two Terra taif jinau who stood beside the door, "will take care of me tonight."

"No midnight expeditions without us," Caewithe said.

"You'll be the first I call if something comes up," Caitlin said, holding up a hand as if swearing an oath.

Caewithe made a brushing motion with her hand. "All right, hit the sack, then. See you mañana."

Caitlin gave a tired wave and ducked through her door. Caewithe gave the two bodyguards, one human and one Jao, the eye.

"We've got it, Captain," the human said with a grin. The Jao just wrinkled his nose in the barest sketch of *assent*.

"Call me if she leaves," she ordered.

"Yes, sir."

Caewithe and Tamt headed down the hall side by side. Sailors and soldiers of both races ducked around them. As chief bodyguards to Caitlin, even though their ranks were nominal, their status among the Jao was high. Caitlin was a member of the service of Aille krinnu ava Terra, governor of Terra and first kochan-father of Terra taif, so her personal status was about as high as it got among the Jao; plus she had *oudh* over the fleet's mission, which meant that she was essentially in command over them all. All that status reflected on her bodyguards. As a person in service, Caitlin could not take people in service to herself, but her bodyguards came closest to that status in the eyes of the Jao, and the humans of the mission didn't think much less of her than the Jao did.

The two bodyguards drew near to a mess room, and Caewithe looked up at Tamt. "You up for some tea?"

The Jao grunted. "Swim first. My skin is so dry that it's about to powder."

"Right. Later, then."

Tamt said nothing, just continued down the hall headed for the nearest pool.

Caewithe ducked into the mess room and walked over to a beverage dispenser, where she punched the buttons for Tea, Earl Grey, Hot, Decaf. She did want to sleep tonight, after all. Collecting her cup, she parked at a table and pulled out her com pad to check the next day's schedule.

She had finished that review and was about to open a report sent to her by one of her sergeants when someone else came in the mess. She looked up to see Lieutenant Fflewdwr Vaughan coming in the room, reading his com pad as he walked. He made his way over to a beverage dispenser and seemingly punched buttons by feel, never looking up. Caewithe decided he had really good peripheral vision as he collected his cup without a fumble and brought it to his lips.

Caewithe hadn't had a lot of contact with the

lieutenant, yet, but what little she had seen had impressed her. He was smart, sharp, quick on the uptake; and it didn't hurt any that he was easy on the eyes. Ever since her relationship with Gabe Tully had cooled to the point where they admitted it wasn't going to work between them, she'd kind of had an eye out for a possible companion. Vaughan had recently been added to the short—too short—list. So her ears perked up, figuratively speaking.

One sip, and Vaughan frowned. "We can fly between the bloody stars," he pronounced, "but we can't program a machine to make a cup of bloody tea."

"Oh, I don't know," Caewithe said. "I think it's pretty good."

Vaughan looked up in surprise.

"Oh, Captain Miller, I didn't see you."

"I didn't think you had," she replied, "the way your eyes were glued to your pad."

"Sorry." Vaughan took another sip of the tea, and grimaced.

"Is it really that bad?" Caewithe laughed.

"I've drunk worse," Vaughan said, "but not willingly. You, however, being an American, have undoubtedly been abusing your taste buds with generic coffee ever since you were big enough to reach your mother's cup."

"Guilty as charged, Lieutenant. Have a seat." She waved at a chair at her table, and Vaughan folded his tall frame onto it. "Can I ask you a couple of questions?"

"Ask away." Vaughan took another swig of tea, this time repressing his grimace of distaste.

"How do you pronounce your first name? My best guess is Flewdwer but I doubt that's right."

He smiled. "Not bad, actually, for someone who's not Welsh. But you can save yourself a lot of grief since I generally go by 'Flue.' What's your second question?"

"Just what do you do for Fleet Commander Dannet?"

Vaughan snorted, then said, "Whatever I can. In a human navy, she'd be a commodore at least, or more likely an admiral, and I'd be a flag lieutenant. But Dannet's Jao, and they don't have that concept."

Caewithe thought for a moment. "But actually, wouldn't a flag lieutenant be kind of like being in service, like Caitlin Kralik is to Aille?"

"We had hoped that she would see it that way," Vaughan replied. "But Dannet's not high enough up in the taif ranks to be allowed to take people into service, so I don't think I fit into that slot in her mind. And she's still struggling with what to do with a staff member who doesn't automatically feel what it is he's supposed to be doing. Almost as much as I am, that is," he ended in a disgruntled tone.

"We?"

Vaughan looked discomfited. "Well, Lieutenant General Kralik and Wrot. They asked me to volunteer along with some others when Dannet asked for a staff. She chose me, and we talked again."

"And?"

"And?" Vaughan repeated.

"And if Wrot's involved, something sneaky is probably going on. Give."

Vaughan laid his cup and com pad down, placed his hands on the table, and leaned forward. When he spoke, his voice was low.

"I really am on her staff, and I really am trying to

learn to be a flag lieutenant to a Jao. But I'm also her tactical shadow." Caewithe gave him a skeptical look, and he nodded vigorously. "'Strue."

"So what's a tactical shadow?"

"I'm supposed to record everything she says and does during combat situations, audio and visual, with time ticks and running commentary and every impression I can give. At some point we," gesturing to the two of them, "are going to want to see humans in the command seat of a *Lexington*-class ship, right?"

Caewithe nodded.

"Well, then, Dannet's about the best we can learn from. She was Narvo, after all."

Of all the Jao kochans, Narvo was the most combat oriented, particularly in spaceborne conflict. Only the Bond of Ebezon compared favorably to them, and the Bond drew the best from all the kochans.

Dannet had joined Terra taif willingly, but no one forgot where she came from. No one.

"That explains why her," Caewithe said, "but why shadow?"

"She's Jao," Vaughan said. "How good are any of them discussing anything that has to do with their 'flow' sense?"

"Point."

At that moment, Vaughan's pad beeped. "Crap! I'm supposed to be on the command deck in three minutes! Bye!" He slurped his tea and was gone.

An intense young man, Caewithe decided. But she liked intense.

CHAPTER 2

The five Lleix strode back through the ship's corridors to their common room, aureoles quivering. It was so strange, Lim of Terralore thought, to sit in the presence of human and Jao, to see two species who processed information in such different ways still able to find common purpose.

"So we will go on to the next star system," the young Lleix said.

Brakan and Matto of the ancient and highly respected *elian* the Starsifters, forged ahead and did not look back. The two, both much taller, who had quite properly been accepted by the Starsifters during their Festivals of Choosing, did not approve of "*dochaya* trash," such as Lim and Pyr, believing themselves on an equal footing with real *elian* members.

No matter what Tully and the other humans had tried to teach them about rights and justice, traditional Lleix continued to find comfort in *sensho*, in doing things as they always had been done. They believed one either found an *elian* at the proper moment in his or her life or was quite correctly turned away and worked forever as a lowly unassigned. You did not make up a name for a new *elian* and then prance about with new purpose in the face of your betters, expecting their respect.

Oddly, despite belonging to the equally august Ekhatlore *elian,* Ramt did not join them. She lagged behind, not quite walking alongside Lim and Pyr but remaining close enough to avoid being openly rude the way the two Starsifters were being.

Pyr looked at Lim as they passed a knot of humans working on a conduit. "Each time we 'jump,' as they call it," he said, "I fear *they* will be there on the other end, waiting for us, the great devils who eat the universe."

Brakan and Matto increased their pace as though even hearing the two Terralore speak was polluting their ears, then entered the Starsifters' quarters. The door slid shut as the three remaining Lleix passed.

"We may encounter them again," Lim said, "but this is a mighty ship; the great *Lexington* itself, which took our people to safety. *Lexington* defeated all the Ekhat who came to kill us that day. And now it is joined by two other ships just as powerful. Four *Lexingtons* all told, if we count the Krant kochan's *Pool Buntyam.*"

They reached the quarters of Ekhatlore. Nodding at them politely, Ramt passed within. Lim and Pyr continued on a short distance until they reached their own quarters.

"Our benefactors fear the Ekhat," Pyr said, turning into Terralore's quarters. "At least as much as ever the Lleix did."

"Because they are wise," Lim said. "Only the very foolish or ignorant would not fear them."

Director Kralik had requested strong representation from both the Starsifters and the Ekhatlore *elians* for the expedition, as they had records of the Lleix travels throughout the galaxy and their own form of framepoint travel.

She had asked members of Terralore to accompany the expedition as well. The official explanation was to function as translators, should another living civilization be found. Lleix were naturally gifted linguists compared to their new-found allies. Apparently, in humans and Jao, the portion of the brain which allowed babies and children to easily acquire language switched off at some point in their early development. That same facility in the Lleix brain, however, remained active all their lives.

Lim and Pyr were quite sure that explanation was a polite fiction. The Starsifters and Ekhatlore Lleix could have served as translators just as well. They thought the real reason they'd been asked was that the humans deliberately tried to bolster the status of the newly formed *elian* created by the *dochaya*.

Unfortunately, polite fiction or not, translation was their only official function on this voyage—and there was no translation to be done when all that was found were the long-dead ashes of those for whom they'd be translating.

"So far, we are useless here," Lim said, "unless another inhabited world is found."

"I learn more about humans and Jao every day from the records," Pyr said, "which will enrich Terralore when we return." He settled onto a bench and turned to a viewing station hooked into the ship's information database. He keyed it on and the screen lit up with a brilliantly colored picture of the Colorado mountains. "Both have a most astonishingly violent history, and it seems that humans perpetually fought among themselves whenever the least disagreement occurred, never letting their eldests sort matters out."

Lim was so astonished, she had to support herself against the wall. "They fight *each other*?" On Valeron, children who showed early and constant aggression had been quickly ejected from the Children's Court and barred from taking part in the Festival of Choosing, doomed forever to labor as common workers in the *dochaya*.

This wasn't because violence and combat were in and of themselves in some manner unacceptable for the Lleix. They had armed spaceships, after all, and had fought the Ekhat and their Jao slaves as bravely as they could for much of their history. But the actual combat was supposed to be performed only by members of the Weaponsmakers *elian*, and had been limited to desperate defensive measures.

Violence and fighting among the ranks of the other *elians* was simply not acceptable among the chosen. It was not *sensho*, acceptable behavior. Or at least, it was never recorded in the records they still had of their racial history.

"They did," Pyr said. "I do not think they do now, at least not very much, though it is apparently one of the reasons why the Jao were able to conquer them."

Lim tried to imagine Caitlin or Tully striking one another and failed. "They are an—an energetic species," she said, "for ones so short." She used the word not only to indicate a deficiency of height, but in the Lleix manner referring to a lack of experience and wisdom, as well.

She had grown a bit herself since leaving Valeron and gaining access to better nutrition. No matter how long she lived, though, she would never be a tallest. Early malnutrition had stunted her growth, but her skin had brightened into a passable silver and her aureole thickened. She appeared somewhat more respectable now, so that she did not automatically shame her *elian*.

"I was disappointed we did not find them here," she said. "The *Boh*. They have not been anywhere we have visited so far."

Pyr looked up from the viewer where he was examining the ship's records. "These people most likely had other gods," he said. "Not the *Boh*. There was no reason you should expect to find them here."

"Their gods are dead," she said, "because all who knew their name are gone."

Pyr's aureole sagged. "But the *Boh* yet live," he said, "because the Lleix do not forget."

"Their memory is safe on Terra," she said, "for now."

Pyr did not answer this time, seeming absorbed in something he had called up to his screen. She settled then at her own data station, missing her *elian*. So much of her short life had been spent in misery in the *dochaya*, going out each day as she sought work at the fabled *elian* in the city, hoping for a chance to work as a servant and, in that capacity, spend time in one of the great houses where her betters ran the city.

She remembered seeing the elongated *Boh*-faces carved into the fronts of many of the *elian*-houses, reminders of what they had lost. They had been so beautiful and so sad, forever left behind when the Lleix had fled the Ekhat and gone into hiding. They had tugged at her every time she saw them. What would it be like to actually experience the presence of the *Boh*?

Humans had "churches" and "temples," actual land and buildings where they experienced their gods. Lim had investigated those whenever she got the chance, but felt no sense that the *Boh* were there either. They were gone, with all their wonder and wisdom, and Lim found herself aching for them. The universe was so large and the Lleix had left the *Boh* behind such a long time ago. How would they ever find them again?

"I will go and speak to Tully," she said to Pyr's back. It was Tully who had first taught her English, coming to the *dochaya* day after day, telling her and everyone else who lived there in long endured misery that they could have a better life, but they would have to make it for themselves and not wait for the elders in the *elian* to simply give it to them.

"Let me know when the ship is ready to jump," Pyr said without turning around.

"Yes," she said and slipped out of the room.

"Did that go as you expected, Colonel?" Tully's companion asked after they exited the meeting.

"Pretty much, Sergeant Luff, pretty much," Gabe replied. "The director isn't going to give up after this, even if she did talk like that was one of the options. Not after finding those dead worlds. All that does is make her more determined to find other civilizations."

"I can see that," the sergeant said. They hit a

T-junction in the hallway, and paused. "Sir, we've got a little over half an hour before the shuttle leaves. I'd like to check in with the lead sergeant from *Lexington*'s jinau detachment. Last I heard, he had a suggestion about training that sounded good."

"Go to it, Top," Tully responded. He tapped one of his pockets. "I'm going to find a cup of coffee and a table somewhere and see if I can make a dent in this month's paperwork before returning back to the *Ban Chao.*"

"Very good, sir," the other said. "Meet you back at the shuttle."

The first sergeant took off down one angle of the hall, and Tully went down the other. Before long he found one of the *Lexington*'s officers' messes and stepped in. He pulled a cup of coffee from the appropriate machine, settled at a mess table, and took an appreciative sip of the dark liquid. *Lexington* had picked up a few traditions from some of the United States Navy personnel who had survived the conquest and made themselves of use in the new era following the establishment of Terra taif. One of their traditions was having strong coffee.

Tully propped his pad up and opened up the next in an interminable series of reports that he needed to read and approve. If he'd realized just how much paperwork being a colonel involved, he'd have turned down the promotion when General Kralik offered it.

Of course, he wasn't sure that the general would have let him say no. He still recalled that conversation rather well.

He'd been called to the general's office not long after the Valeron expedition had returned with all the

Lleix refugees that would come with them. "Take a seat, Tully," Kralik had said before he was two steps in the door. The general's voice was brusque; his face was showing lines that Tully hadn't remembered being there. Above all, the normally unflappable Kralik seemed to have an air of harried patience.

"Tully, I've got a job for you," the general began.

"Back to dickering with resistance groups?" he'd asked.

"No. We pulled in the last of the effective ones while you were gone, and the others are evaporating now that jobs are available again. No, I need you to take a command."

That had set Tully back a bit. He'd figured he'd stay with his assault company on *Lexington* if the resistance work was going well.

"What kind of command?"

"All the ground forces in Caitlin's flotilla."

He remembered his jaw dropping as he looked at Kralik in shock.

"You're making me a freakin' general?"

Kralik had chuckled, and a few of the lines on his face had eased.

"No, I'm making you a freakin' colonel. Mind you, I could almost justify a general, because by the time we put a full assault group on the *Ban Chao* and fill all the companies on the battleships, you'll have close to an old-time brigade's worth of bodies. But neither one of us are ready for you to be a general. It's enough of a stretch giving you the eagles of a colonel."

"But why me?" He remembered the moment of panic he'd felt. Truth be told, some days the echoes of that panic still were felt. "Don't you have real colonels you could use? Someone with experience at the job? What about Rob Wiley? He was on the *Lexington*, too."

Kralik had leaned back in his chair and interlaced his fingers over his flat stomach. "Yep. And General Wiley and the others are all going to more important, more high-profile positions. You haven't been back long enough to catch on to what's happening. Aille has us expanding the jinau forces as rapidly as we can; space, air, and ground. We weren't much more than sepoy troops before, mostly just keeping order and occasionally dealing with the resistance. Now we're adding new companies every month, organizing new battalions every quarter. We've got three new divisions formed up while you were gone.

"We've learned the Ekhat lesson, Gabe. They've got our attention. China alone has mounted two of those new divisions, even after the diversion of resources to deal with the aftermath of the plasma bombing. We have recruits from all over the world. And Aille will see to it that they are 'of use' in the war against the Ekhat.

"We can train them—barely," the general had said as he sat back up straight. "We can shove the best of them through quickie officer training and get embryo company officers, enough to keep things organized. And between us, the Europeans and the Chinese, we've been able to find enough—barely—effective senior officers to get by. What we don't have is the middle—we don't have anywhere near enough experienced field-grade officers, even using the simplified organizational structures the Jao have mandated for the jinau. That's where the casualties of the conquest have really hurt us. You'd have been put to work months ago if you'd been here instead of haring off in the *Lexington.*"

"So why me?" he'd repeated his question. "Why for this one?"

Kralik started counting items on his fingertips. "One: you have a reputation as a fighter, of not backing down from anybody. The humans respect that, and even more importantly, the Jao respect that. You will have a lot more Jao troops under your command than you've had before, so that respect is important.

"Two: right now you are one of a unique—and very, very small—group of humans. You have fought Ekhat up close and personal and survived, and brought most of your troops back as well. You have no idea what your reputation among the troops is like because of that. That kind of track record is invaluable.

"Three: the fleet commander will be Jao, no two ways about it. It will be years—decades probably—before we have enough sufficiently experienced human ship captains to even consider putting a human in that position. But because Terra taif and Krant kochan contributed almost all the ground troops for the fleet, we can put you in as ground forces commander, which means that you will counterbalance the fleet commander, as well as giving Caitlin someone she can rely on with no hesitation."

"Politics," he'd muttered. "I hate that."

"Time to grow up, Tully. The Jao—or at least Pluthrak kochan—could have taught Machiavelli a thing or two, and Preceptor Ronz could have tutored Sun Tzu and Miyamoto Musashi. You're going to deal with it for the rest of your life; you might as well get good at it."

Kralik had ticked off one more finger. "Four: you not only have a reputation of being a fighter, you're a damn good one. If it comes down to hand-to-hand combat for any part of the fleet, I can't think of anyone better to have on hand."

The general had folded his arms on the desk and leaned forward. "I'm not going to leave you hanging totally out to dry, Tully. We'll find some good sergeants and Jao equivalents for you. They may be more valuable to you than a bunch of new officers."

And Tully had to admit that the general had delivered on that one. Every detachment on the battleships had at least two experienced sergeants, and the assault group had experienced men in three out of every four non-officer leadership slots. The Jao were just as good. And First Sergeant Luff, crusty as he might be at times, was pure gold. He'd come out of the preconquest United States Marines, where he'd been a gunnery sergeant. There wasn't anything that anyone, Jao or human, could pull that he hadn't seen (or done) worse. There wasn't a problem that anyone could think of that he didn't have a suggestion or two about how to deal with it. And Tully had learned that if the first sergeant said, "If I might suggest, sir . . ." that he'd best pay attention. He'd learned that the hard way after one monumental goof, and Luff had saved his official colonel-type backside for him more than once since then.

Kralik had ended their talk with, "But get this straight, Gabe. Caitlin's mission is what we used to call a reconnaissance in force. You may or may not end up conducting ship-to-ship actions, and maybe some raids along the way. But your purpose is to defend the fleet and the director. This is not an invasion force. You will not have enough troops and resources to take and hold ground against what the Ekhat could bring. So be smart. Be very smart. Not because of Yaut, or even Aille. You risk the fleet unnecessarily, you waste this command, and *I'll* shred you. Yaut will get to sweep up the pieces."

Tully came out of the haze of memory. "Gotcha, boss."

He took another sip of coffee, and dove into the reports on his pad, skimming and thumb-printing as quickly as he could. Before long he was so deep in the routine that he was startled to hear his name.

"Gabe Tully," a familiar voice said.

"Lim?" He looked to find the young Lleix standing before his table. She gazed at him with those narrow black eyes, her body very straight, and so utterly still; as the Jao, with all their fancy body-postures, never were.

"I would speak with you," she said clearly.

"Fine," Tully said, waving a hand at an armless chair. "Take a seat." His pad chimed, and he looked at it. "Never mind," he said, standing up and sliding the pad into a pocket. "I've got to head for my shuttle. Walk with me."

Tully was fond of this particular Lleix, who had been among the first in the *dochaya* to believe him when he said the unassigned did not have to just give up and be second-class citizens all their lives.

"Do you need something?" he said, looking up into her silver face for a moment. Tully was not a short human, but even short Lleix topped him, with long graceful necks, upswept black eyes, a dished face with very little nose, and stocky slightly pear-shaped bodies.

She twitched at her robes, though they'd already seemed just fine to him. "I have no purpose on this voyage," she said, matching her pace to his. Her black eyes glittered. "I am useless."

They turned a corner. "During explorations, most of us in the fleet have no purpose," Tully said, "and will not, unless or until we find another species or get into a battle with the Ekhat."

She was silent for a moment, her fleshy aureole rippling across her head. "I am not accustomed to being useless," she said finally. "All my life, I am working hard, cleaning *elian*-houses, fetching supplies, weeding and cooking and repairing, not just sitting around and—waiting—for something that may never occur. This—" Her black eyes gazed around at the ship. "This being unneeded is too hard. Studying Terralore is not enough. I require something to do—now."

They stepped through a set of heavy blast-proof doors and turned another corner. It was clear to Tully that the poor kid was bored out of her mind. He could certainly sympathize with that. He studied her from the corner of his eye. "What would you like to do?"

Lim stopped and twisted her fingers together, shifting her weight restlessly from foot to foot as Lleix often did when uncertain. "What is needed on the ship?"

"All jobs are currently filled," he said, "but you could train for one of them anyway as a backup. What are you interested in? Engines? Communications equipment? Food service?"

She was silent then, as though she wanted to say something but did not know how to bring it up. "Pyr said humans used to fight one another," she said finally.

"Yes," he said, "we used to be very quarrelsome

among ourselves, but now we use that energy to fight the Ekhat."

His pad chimed again, reminding him of the shuttle. "Walk with me," he said again.

"The Lleix tried to fight the Ekhat," she said as they started down the passage, "especially at first, but they always just killed us, so mostly we ran away."

Tully wasn't sure where this conversation was going. "There's no shame in refusing to fight a battle you're sure to lose if you can avoid it."

"The Ekhat drove us from our homes," she said, "from lush beautiful worlds with perfect climates, soaring mountains, deep swift rivers. Every time this happened we left behind gardens that had been tended for a thousand years, great houses whose every room had been perfected over many lifetimes, and *elian* containing knowledge that has never been recreated." She was silent for a moment, blinking. "We even left behind the *Boh*. The Ekhat took everything from us, including most of who we are." She was quiet for several steps, then said in a low voice, "But we *let* them."

"I have been in an Ekhat ship," Tully said. "I have fought against the crazy devils myself. They have endless resources, and are scary crazy, mad to destroy. I am sure that the Lleix did the best that they could under the circumstances."

They took a turn into a wider passage.

Lim's fathomless black eyes regarded him. "Did they?"

He didn't know what to say then. The Lleix, with their emphasis on *sensho*, which ranked individuals according to age and height, viewed life very differently from humans. Even Lim and Pyr, who had been remanded to a slum solely because of their failure to meet Lleix standards of beauty, aspired to be old and tall, as though those qualities really mattered. Frankly, Tully was not surprised that, in the end, the Ekhat had pretty much kicked the Lleix's collective ass, though he kept that opinion to himself.

"I am wishing to no longer be helpless," Lim said. "I am wishing to learn to fight so that if we encounter the Ekhat again, I do not have to cower in my quarters and wait for others to save us."

Tully regarded the young Lleix. "Isn't there an *elian* that fights? Aren't they building a *Lexington* for them?"

"The Weaponsmakers." Lim adjusted her robes again. "But they were—are—not very good. Not effective." The last almost sounded like a curse in her mouth.

The Lleix were not cowards, certainly. But it dawned on Tully that they had nothing in the way of a martial tradition as humans and Jao did. There was no separate function for soldiers in their society; nothing even close to a warrior *elian*. Instead, when the Lleix had been forced in the past to fight back against the Ekhat and Jao, they had turned the work over to the Weaponsmakers *elian*. From what Tully could tell, it was as if, in human terms, fighting World War II had been turned over to Rosie the Riveter and the engineers who designed the B-17s and the Sherman tanks. And Tully knew better than anyone that there was a world of difference between being able to make or service a weapon and being really good at using it.

The Lleix had no tradition at all, so far as Tully knew, of fighting hand-to-hand or at close range. For Lleix, "combat" was something that geeks did at a distance, using geek methods. If the enemy managed to get close, they were as helpless as so many lambs. Big lambs, but still lambs.

Tully spent a bit more time studying the young Lleix as they moved through the big doors to one of the *Lexington*'s shuttle bays. Lim had grown sturdy with better food and living quarters, and she was certainly intelligent, having learned English and other Terran languages with a rapacious ferocity that spoke volumes about her will. Her desire to learn combat was perhaps an unusual attitude for her people, but her determination was not—at least, not among those who had not been part of the elite. She had clawed her way out of the *dochaya*, and she wasn't the only one who had when their one opportunity to do so had arrived, courtesy of Caitlin Kralik and one Gabe Tully. There was no doubt in Tully's mind that she could accomplish anything she set her mind to.

They came to a stop by the lift to his shuttle.

"So what do you want?" he asked.

"To not be afraid," Lim answered simply.

"Learning to fight will not kill your fear," Tully said. She looked at him in silence. "But it might teach you to work beyond your fear."

Lim nodded. "Teach me."

Tully looked at her. With her recent growth, she was now taller than Tully and had longer arms. She had mass. With some training, she just might be able to hold her own in a battle. It was worth exploring, anyway.

"That's not a bad idea," Tully said. "If you like, you can drill with my troops. I think everyone should know how to protect herself."

The Lleix's black eyes gleamed. "When shall I be starting?" Lim said.

"Now is fine with me—well, let's make it after the next framepoint transfer," he said. "Unless you have something better to do. Come to the *Ban Chao* and we'll see what we can do."

"Until we find a new species with whom we need to communicate, I have nothing to do," Lim said. "I am much wanting it to be otherwise."

Caitlin entered the bridge of the *Lexington*, or the command deck, as the Jao preferred to call it. Caewithe Miller came with her and Tamt followed them, a silent shadow who took up a stance beside the lift.

Fleet Commander Dannet herself, in the days when she was Terra-Captain Dannet, had not approved of superfluous personnel in her command space on the *Lexington*. She had allowed it during the mission to Valeron, because Wrot krinnu ava Terra had possessed *oudh* over that mission and he had wanted others there.

The new captain of the *Lexington* seemed to be a little more tolerant than Dannet had been. Terra-Captain Uldra krinnu ava Terra had been born Uldra krinnu Ptok vau Binnat, scion of a lesser associated kochan of a mid-tier kochan, according to the briefing Caitlin had received. The Jao, of course, would never have described the relationships that way. They would have instead said that Binnat was a kochan of lesser associations to the great kochans of Pluthrak, Narvo, or perhaps the scarcely lesser Dano, Hij, and Jak. Not as lesser as Krant had been before their Krant-Captain Mallu and his crew had become entwined with the affairs of Terra taif and its guardian, the

Bond of Ebezon, the one Jao organization that was apolitical, standing aside from the constant association maneuvering and shifting that was normal existence among the kochans. But lesser, undisputedly.

Binnat and Ptok had sent troops for the conquest of Terra, perhaps more than they could rightly afford to risk; and more still for the long struggle to maintain Jao control of the restive planet. Uldra had been among the first of them. He had survived the conquest. He had survived the long grinding aftermath to the conquest, and finally had taken the bauta and retired from service on Terra, much as Wrot had done. But perhaps most importantly, he had come out of retirement to pilot one of the hastily modified Terran submarines that battled the Ekhat ships in the interior of the Sun; one of the two surviving pilots who had done so with some skill. As Wrot had put it recently to Caitlin with one of the human phrases he loved to collect, Uldra "had seen the elephant, up close and personal."

At the founding of Terra taif, Uldra had joined the overwhelming majority of the veterans of the Terran wars in shifting allegiance to the new taif. Now, in the Jao manner, Uldra was of use as the captain of one of the greatest warships Jao warriors had ever manned, greater even than the *Harrier*-class warships of the Bond of Ebezon, as well as serving as what the humans would have called the "flag captain" of the fleet under Fleet Commander Dannet.

So far Caitlin had found him to be even-tempered. Given her experiences under Oppuk, the crazed-and-now-mercifully-dead Narvo governor, she chalked that up as a big mark in the plus column.

At the moment, the mood on the bridge was industrious, voices murmuring, heads bent low over displays, crewmen consulting one another in low voices. Dannet krinnu ava Terra was up there too, standing and gazing down at a readout, her body communicating uncomplicated *steady-interest*. Her golden-brown nap was still damp. Evidently she had come straight from one of the *Lexington*'s many pools. Lieutenant Vaughan was seated at a station to the rear of the deck, focused on multiple screens all streaming data, oblivious to everything going on around him.

Caitlin drifted around the bridge. She still didn't understand a lot of the details of what was going on, but she had been on the bridge often enough in the last two years to know whether things were in their normal flow. No problems yet today, it seemed.

The mood subtly shifted. Crew, both Jao and human, settled deeper into their seats and bent over their screens. Voices did not grow so much louder as more intense.

It was getting close to the time for the jump, she thought, and her stomach gave a lurch. Personally, she found frame travel extremely uncomfortable. It wasn't that it hurt. The experience was more that she felt like she was being forced to exist for the duration of the jump in dimensions that did not support human life. Or life of any sort. Like she was being folded and stretched at the same time, existing both *here* and *there*, turned inside out and upside down. She shuddered. She'd tried to explain it to her father, after they'd returned from the Valeron mission, but words had simply failed her.

Dannet looked up at her with green fire blazing in her black eyes. "You feel it," the fleet commander said.

Caitlin nodded. "Yes," she said, "I don't know how, but I do."

"Not entirely unexpected," Dannet said with a *satisfied* flick of one ear. "After all, you were associated with one of Narvo's best."

I guess you could call it that, Caitlin thought. She'd always thought the word "tormented"—or perhaps "terrorized"—closer to the reality of the situation. But she knew now that Jao were also tough on their own progeny, demanding a lot and not babying them. She'd seen that much for herself after visiting one of the Terra kochan-houses, so perhaps her upbringing at the rough hands of Banle krinnu ava Narvo had not been as vicious in the eyes of a Jao as it had seemed to her. But Caitlin wasn't Jao.

A low hum built as the great jump engines charged. The ship seemed suddenly more *alive*. Uldra was now all business, up out of his captain's chair and striding from station to station, making corrections here and there, approving readouts and moving on. His ears were flattened in unabashed *focus*.

Caewithe Miller came over to her. "Are we close to jump?"

"I think so," she said, as her heartbeat accelerated. "Not that anyone tells me anything." Of course, they didn't need to. To be fair, that was not her function, all the details that went into the running of the great ship. They would turn to her when it was appropriate for her input.

"Maybe this time will be the charm," Caewithe said with a smile. "We're due for some luck."

"Maybe." She made herself return the smile, though her heart was racing. It was just as likely they would find ten Ekhat ships on the other end of this jump as an inhabited world filled with agreeable aliens and highly developed tech that they would be absolutely delighted to put at the Human/Jao/Lleix's disposal.

An alarm sounded, not a strident bell, but a clear ringing chime that was being relayed throughout the great ship. "Stations," Uldra's deep voice said over the ship com in his capacity as Terra-Captain of the *Lexington*. "Jump preparation has been initiated. All personnel take appropriate action."

That meant hold onto your proverbial hat, Caitlin thought. No matter how many times they jumped, she never got used to it.

The bridge doors opened again and Wrot krinnu ava Terra walked through. She motioned for him to join her. The old Jao was both wily and wise, but what she often liked most about him was his sense of humor.

Close by, Fleet Commander Dannet looked up over her shoulder at Caitlin. The black eyes danced with green fire. Dannet's ears canted to an angle that communicated *disapproval*. "You should take a seat, Director Kralik. It would not do to have you injured on the jump." She turned back to the console she was monitoring. "That would create a lot of fuss over your well-being at a moment when we could least afford to have our attention diverted from what really matters."

Wrot took her arm. "Just what I was going to say," he murmured in Caitlin's ear, "sort of." He settled her into a seat before a vacant station next to Lieutenant Vaughan. She fastened her harness.

The screen crawled with figures that she supposed no one needed to know at the moment.

"First framepoint generator set," a voice said.

The ship trembled beneath her feet like an eager hound about to be released on the hunt.

Uldra checked one screen, then another, his ears pitched at a mostly *approving* angle, though occasionally lowering in *dissatisfaction* as he pointed out an error that needed to be corrected. He was a calmer captain than Dannet had been, Caitlin thought, remembering how the big Jao had stalked about the command deck, cuffing those who were slow to handle their responsibilities, even throwing one to the deck and taking over the station herself. Of course, to be fair, Dannet had been working with an unfamiliar and mixed crew of Jao and humans, not those from Narvo, her former kochan.

That, of course, was the norm for this fleet two-plus years later. Only the Krant ship *Pool Buntyam* was crewed solely by a Jao crew. Even Dannet seemed to be resigned to the integrated crews these days, although one could still see flashes of *irritation* in her posture from time to time.

"Second framepoint generator set," a different voice said with no more excitement that someone reading the choices for dinner off a menu board.

The vibration increased, so that the ship herself seemed eager to get on with the jump, which all the Jao present mostly found a thoroughly ridiculous notion, she thought.

"We're getting close," Wrot said.

She took a deep breath. They had jumped the *Lexington* many times now. The crew knew what it was doing. They would come out into a new system and hope that this time they would find what—and who—they were looking for.

The shaking increased. Wrot seemed to settle somehow into a *waiting-for-necessity* position that gave the air of being as solid as a mountain.

"Third framepoint generator set," another crewman said, and this time there was just the slightest hint of excitement in his tone.

Uldra's posture said *calm-acceptance.* Caitlin looked over at Dannet, whose body was angled to communicate *disdain*. One did not surrender to crude excitement when merely doing one's job, at least one did not if one was Narvo, which Dannet would always be, no matter that she had been gifted to Terra Taif like a prize heifer to make up for Oppuk's crimes.

"Fourth framepoint generator set," a female voice said.

The ship was lurching beneath their feet now. Caitlin hastily checked the harness that would keep her from being ejected from the seat. "I hate this part," she said, just loudly enough for her guards to hear.

"Amen," Captain Miller muttered back from where she grasped the station console for balance. She looked pale, but resigned. "I don't hate it as much as the thought of what could be waiting for us on the other end, though," she finished.

It could be something wonderful or something terrible, Caitlin thought. The only way to know was to jump and take a look.

"Fifth set!" a male voice said.

The ship rocked beneath their feet as though buffeted by five monstrous opposing tidal waves, all trying to wash it out to sea in a different direction.

"You may jump, Navigator Annen," Uldra said.

The great ship *leaped.*

As always, Caitlin's stomach was left behind. She gritted her teeth, feeling distinctly unwell, as though being torn apart and compressed into exotic matter at the same time. She tasted *blue* on the back of her tongue, saw the strange gleam of *bittersweet* behind her eyes, felt the rasp of *fear* along her spine.

It will be over in a heartbeat, Caitlin told herself. Jao endured this all the time and had for centuries now. She could not let herself be seen to be weak.

Captain Miller was swearing under her breath. Her face was very pale. Her grip on the console showed white knuckles at every joint.

On and on they went, traveling and not-traveling, propelling themselves through something that simply was *not-there*, striding across the galaxy with seven-league boots like some preposterous fairy tale character.

Then, with a jerk, they arrived, existing at least *somewhere* again, when only a second ago they had been both nowhere and everywhere. Caitlin's breath blew out. She hadn't even been aware she was trying to hold it.

"I will never get used to that!" Caewithe muttered with a gulp.

"Amen." This time it was Caitlin who replied.

The viewscreen blazed with light, the local view of the photosphere of this system's star that surrounded them. "I guess we made it," Caitlin murmured.

Terra-Captain Uldra strode from screen to screen, checking readouts, his body showing *cautious-approval* with every step. Caitlin looked over to the lift. Tamt flicked an ear of inquiry at her. She shook her head and Tamt settled back into place by the door. The Jao guard showed no effects at all, just like the Jao members of the command deck crew.

Caitlin looked back to Miller, who had released the console and straightened, but still looked a bit green around the gills and showed a few sweat beads on her forehead. She nodded at Caitlin, who had to smile. Miller was always trying to prove herself to the Jao. If they took no notice of the discomfort of a jump, neither would she, as far as she was able.

Over the course of the next minute, the other three battleships reported in, all having jumped safely.

The screen brightened, then just for a second, Caitlin could see the darkness of space punctuated by distant stars. The fiery plasma closed in again. They were enveloped by starfire. That was the part to which she would never become accustomed.

Her heartbeat accelerated again, which she hadn't thought possible. What was out there on the other side of that brightness? Friend? Foe? Or, most likely, more dead worlds?

"Shedding plasma," one of the bridge crew said, a slight Krant male Caitlin had seen on duty before but never picked up his name.

Ten more minutes passed. The sensors detected the other ships of the fleet arriving. Caitlin checked her watch when she thought no Jao were looking. The plasma thinned. The periods when their instruments could see lengthened. Nothing was close to the star. At least no Ekhat seemed to be waiting on them. This was most likely going to be another disappointment.

Then the plasma cleared for the last time. They were out of the photosphere.

"Scanning," one of the Jao said.

Caitlin released the harness and stood to get a better view of the main screen. Techs were checking the system's orbits for habitable planets. Most star systems had one, occasionally even two or three, if you counted marginal worlds where the gravity would be too high or too low, no liquid water existed, or the atmosphere was unsuitable for breathing without assistance.

"Coming about," said the navigator.

Lieutenant Vaughan suddenly spat out a single hard-edged word. "Damn!"

Had he spotted something? Caitlin squinted at the screen, then saw what he had already spotted.

"Oh . . . my," she said.

Miller said something even stronger.

CHAPTER 3

Caitlin leaned over to Vaughan. "Are those what I think they are?" The large vision screen was now set to distance imaging, and the images on the screen were not direct visualizations of whatever objects the ship's detection devices were focusing on. They bore a closer resemblance to old-fashioned radar blips, although they were the product of equipment that was much more sensitive and complex. Still, from past experience—even more, from the obvious tension of the human and Jao crewmen on the command deck—Caitlin was pretty sure she was looking at Ekhat warships.

Quite a few Ekhat warships.

"Yes," Vaughan said grimly. "That's an Ekhat fleet. Six ships, at a minimum."

As if to add emphasis to his words, a loud signal started blaring. That was: *battle stations*—or the Jao equivalent, rather, which more properly translated as *Prepare to fight the enemy.* In this as in all things, the Jao tended to be literalists. When humans might say, *To arms!* the Jao would say *Take up weapons!*

Given a choice between poetry and prose, the Jao would pick prose every time.

Vaughan was looking elsewhere on the detector screen, however, at some sort of largish blobby thing in the corner that Caitlin didn't remember having ever seen before. He pointed at it.

"See that? I'm not a sensor specialist, but that indicates an inhabited planet. Inhabited and technologically very active. Which means that for the first time in my experience—or any human's experience, so far as I know—we've stumbled onto an Ekhat world."

Dannet was suddenly standing next to them. "You are correct. This is not something many Jao have ever seen, either. Or at least, survived to tell about it."

"This just gets better and better," Caitlin muttered. From the corner of her eye, she could see Wrot shifting position to *accepting-reality*. She hadn't intended for anyone to hear that, but Wrot missed very little. She knew he took some pride in that, as well. He twitched his whiskers again. She'd have to find out from him what that particular fillip of body-speech meant.

Wrot didn't say anything, though. He just turned his head to track Fleet Commander Dannet. The big Jao was back to moving around the command deck much like a restless panther.

That was a pretty good analogy, in fact. Caitlin had learned in the battle of Valeron that Dannet was nothing if not a fighter—and was a firm believer in the old human adage that the best defense is a good offense.

Abstractly, Caitlin figured, that was a splendid quality to have in a naval commander. It could get pretty hair-raising, though, when—to use another old human expression—the shit hit the fan.

Sure enough. Caitlin was an expert in reading Jao body language, and was particularly fluent in the Narvo dialect of that complex quasi-tongue. Dannet's posture was one she'd never seen before but was not at all difficult to interpret despite being a tripartite posture. Not knowing the formal designation, Caitlin settled on *eager-but-held-in-check-anticipation-of-triumph.* No doubt the Jao had a more economical way of putting that, but the expression captured the gist of it.

Dannet wasn't even considering the possibility of fleeing from the scene. She wanted a battle, and despite the odds seemed to feel she had a good chance of winning it.

Caitlin had no idea *why* the fleet commander would feel that way. She herself, were she not strictly maintaining a posture of *resolution-in-the-face-of-peril*, would probably be showing the human equivalent of *looking-for-a-way-out*. She thought of trying for a more difficult tripartite position, but she didn't think she could keep her hands still enough to add a convincing *adamant* to what she was already displaying.

"Have the Ekhat detected us?" Dannet asked one of the technical officers. Caitlin didn't know the Jao's name, but from his console's position on the command deck she presumed he was in charge of sensors and detection.

"Almost certainly, Fleet Commander," he replied. "But we won't know for certain until—" He broke off for a moment, looking at something on one of the screens that Caitlin couldn't interpret from a distance—and probably couldn't have interpreted even if she'd been standing right in front of the screen herself.

"That makes it definite, Fleet Commander. The enemy has spotted us and..."

Again, he paused for a moment, studying another screen. "And now they're heading toward us."

What he really meant was "and now they've begun an approach which, presuming various intricate maneuvers in response to this solar system's gravitational constraints and our own actions, will eventually result in their intersecting our course." But Jao had no patience for such pointless crossing of t's and dotting of i's.

Lieutenant Vaughan was pushing control pads on his console and muttering into the microphone he was wearing. Caitlin tried to ignore him, and dropped back into her seat and fastened her harness. Things looked like they were about to get interesting, and she had no desire to emulate a ping-pong ball in the command deck.

Dannet turned away from the tech officer and toward Terra-Captain Uldra. "Reverse course back into the photosphere." Over her shoulder, she said to the com officer: "Order the other battleships to prepare for an ambush. Tactical variant Gamma Bravo is most likely, but variant Delta Delta is also possible. Light attack craft should take Station Gamma Rho and wait for opportunities."

There was a faintly distasteful tinge to her body posture that almost made Caitlin laugh. Those Greek-derived tactical terms were completely human and not something any Jao—much less a Narvo—would have taken to readily. But the expedition's personnel was more than seventy percent human, and even the purely naval personnel were only one-third Jao. So, whether the Jao liked it or not, compromises had been made everywhere, including in tactical doctrine and parlance.

Being fair to Dannet, while she sometimes could not quite restrain her irritation from showing, she did accept the political realities—and sometimes displayed an acute ability to use the resulting hybrids to good effect.

Vaughan pushed more pads and muttered into his microphone some more.

The fleet commander continued giving orders to the com officer. "Instruct the supply ships and personnel ships to remain in the photosphere as long as possible. If any of their shielding begins to look seriously compromised, they have permission to retreat back to the framepoint of origin. But tell them that I would much prefer it if they remained with the fleet."

"Yes, Fleet Commander."

"Tell the *Ban Chao* to prepare for a boarding operation."

Caitlin had to keep her jaw from openly dropping. The *Ban Chao* was the expedition's troop transport. It might be better to say, armored assault ship, since the *Ban Chao* was designed to survive battles within a star's photosphere.

Only Jao—*only damned Jao lunatics*, was the way Gabe Tully had put it—would have designed a ship like the *Ban Chao*. It probably took a Jao to even conceive of such a ship.

The *Ban Chao* had been designed and built to withstand ramming impacts that would have crushed the hulls of even *Lexington*-class battleships. And the ship's crew and the troops held within its massive frame could take positions in complex harnesses which had been designed and built to keep them alive no matter how great the impact, so long as the hull itself wasn't breached. The *Ban Chao*'s engines were the most powerful yet designed and built, and those engines powered shields that were strong enough that *Ban Chao* could keep a shattered Ekhat ship within her own protective bubble after she rammed it. Otherwise the Ekhat ship would simply be consumed in the hellish environment of a solar photosphere.

In short, the *Ban Chao* had been designed for the express purpose of boarding Ekhat warships in mid-battle, even within the plasma of a star, which is where most experts expected it to be used. (Only the most visionary [i.e., wild-eyed optimists] considered a ram could be done in open space, given the speeds available.) And the reason it had been so designed was because humans insisted on something that would not have been conceived by a Jao—to wit, that their military intelligence was sadly lacking in data concerning not only the Ekhat but, most importantly, the many slave species that the Ekhat used for most of the tasks of crewing their ships. They'd already tried to interrogate an Ekhat captured at the battle of Valeron a couple of years ago, with signal lack of success. The lack of intelligence needed to be made up; the only way to do that was to capture some slaves; and the only way anyone could think to do that was in the middle of a battle.

So, the *Ban Chao.* But it would not have occurred to Caitlin until now that the assault ship would be used in a battle where the Jao-human-Lleix forces were so obviously outnumbered. And Tully was over there, because that's where the majority of his troops were, and he had determined that if this very circumstance came about, however low the probabilities might be, he was going to be with the assault group.

Wrot leaned over. "We're in space, so it is the fleet commander's call, as you humans would put it. But if you didn't want an aggressive fleet commander, you probably shouldn't have selected Dannet." He straightened back up with a touch of what Caitlin decided was *smug-repose*.

That should have called for a retort, but there wasn't much she could say to that. Her former mentor Professor Jonathan Kinsey had once commented that, while the analogy had its limits, there were a lot of ways in which the two greatest of the Jao kochan—Pluthrak and Narvo—were analogous to the two greatest city-states of ancient Greece. The Pluthrak being the Athenians, of course, and the Narvo being the Spartans.

The analogy was something of a stretch, especially the one between the Pluthrak and the Athenians. The Spartan analogy, on the other hand . . . was probably much less so. The Narvo were indeed the great warrior kochan of the Jao species, known and respected as such by all the other kochan. They had all the traditional Spartan virtues as well as many of the traditional Spartan limitations.

One of those virtues, Caitlin reminded herself, was that the Narvo won most of their battles.

She smiled herself, then. She wished she could have mentioned that to Gabe Tully. He might find it a bit of a comfort at the moment.

Probably not, though.

"Crazy fucking Jao," muttered Gabe Tully. The mutter was loud enough that several of the Jao assault troops gathered in the small assembly chamber assumed postures of *amusement*, some of them combined with *feigned-indignation*.

The postures were crude, of course. These were rifle carriers from lower-rank kochan, not sophisticated scions of Pluthrak, Narvo, or Hij. Many of them were from Krant kochan, which made them the Jao equivalent of hillbillies. The rest were now part of Terra taif, but had their origins mostly in the lesser kochans affiliated with Narvo or Dano.

Tully ignored them as First Sergeant Luff and a couple of senior Jao turned postures to the troops that squelched the mirth. Even though Luff was not Jao and didn't pretend to know any of what he considered the effete body language of the upper echelon Jao, none of the troops had trouble reading the angles of *his* body. Tully wondered what the Jao equivalent for *make-my-day* was.

He turned to Lt. Vikram Bannerji. His newly assigned intelligence officer was looking alert and raring to go. Tully wasn't surprised. He'd already come to the conclusion that Bannerji was a geek in uniform, and like all geeks he'd ever known, had bizarre enthusiasms. They were the sort of people who looked forward eagerly to playing games that sane and normal people would find either boring or incomprehensible.

In Bannerji's case, the bizarre enthusiasm was for all things Ekhat. Where someone like Tully himself—sane, normal—saw only crazed killers, someone like Bannerji saw fascinating subtleties and complexities. Of course, Gabe had thought to himself, Bannerji was also someone who thought all the cultural ins and outs of Hindu society, including the remnants of the caste system, were logical, coherent, and sensible. Go figure.

Bannerji was an upper-crust Indian, born in Mumbai, educated in Oxford. If it weren't that the lieutenant's voice carried just a touch of the melodious tones of his native land, Tully could have closed his eyes and almost believed he was listening to the poshest of posh Brits.

"So what can you tell me, Lieutenant?" Tully asked. He nodded toward the big screen at the far end of the assembly chamber, which depicted the same images that were coming into the control rooms of the *Lexington* and the *Ban Chao* and every other warship in the fleet. You could say this in favor of the Jao—they weren't given to stupid security fetishes the way human officials so often were. They saw no reason that the soldiers who'd be doing the fighting shouldn't get all the information they might need.

"Which faction are we going to be dealing with? Can you tell yet? And if so, what difference is it likely to make in tactical terms? If any?"

Bannerji got that look on his face that Tully was coming to dread. God forbid a geek should give a simple answer to a simple question.

"Well... Until we get a better look at the ships, I can't tell anything for sure, Colonel. But once I can—"

Gabe cocked a skeptical eyebrow. Bannerji shook his head. "Oh, sure, Colonel, all the factions have their own variations on ship design. Major factions, anyway. Not all of the subfactions and splinter groups do, though."

Gabe rolled his eyes. "Subfactions. Splinter groups. How do you parse the difference with a pack of homicidal maniacs?"

Bannerji grinned, white teeth contrasting sharply

with his dark face. He turned his head and gestured at a Lleix standing a few meters away. "We ought to bring Ramt into this."

The Lleix was rather young, gauging by her height. Ramt glided forward with the sort of ease and grace that Tully had come to recognize as a sign that she was affiliated with one of the long-established *elian*. He was a little surprised. As a rule, the Lleix who'd been willing to join the expedition came from the newer *elian* created by *dochaya* members.

"Ramt's from Ekhatlore," Bannerji explained. He got a wry little smile on his face. "The only one I could sweet-talk into coming along. She's okay, though, for a nob."

Nob was a slang term for those Lleix who belonged to the elite *elian,* as the Lleix themselves ranked these things. Only humans used the expression, though.

Bannerji repeated the question. Thankfully, he didn't do it in Lleix, as he often did. *Trying to improve my command of the language,* he'd say. Never mind that the Lleix were a hundred times better linguists than humans or Jao would ever be. As far as Tully was concerned, for a human to take the time and effort to learn Lleix was just pointless. Well . . . being fair, there was no other way to read Lleix texts.

If you were so inclined. Which Tully certainly was not.

After she heard the question, Ramt turned to face Tully and said: "For our purposes, Colonel, it will make a big difference if you want to capture slaves."

"How so?" Tully asked.

"There are four main factions of the Ekhat: Interdict, Melody, True Harmony, and Complete Harmony, all of which are committed to the purpose of the creation or attainment of something called the Melody. They all believe that the Melody must be, can only be, created by Ekhat."

Ramt held up a digit, in mimicry of human fingers. "The Interdict believes that work cannot even begin on the Melody until the universe has been purified of all other life-forms. They use no slaves of any kind."

She spoke in fluent, unaccented English—with just a slight touch of a drawl. If you were listening to a recording of her voice, about the only way you might be able to guess the speaker wasn't a native born-and-bred Oklahoman or Texan was because the diction was formal rather than colloquial. That wasn't because Lleix couldn't speak idiomatic and slang English; it was because such informality was foreign to their nature.

Another digit was raised. "The Melody faction believes that the work can begin before the purification is complete, but that only the Ekhat can do anything even remotely connected to the work. Very few of the Melody subfactions use slaves, and the ones that do only use borderline sentient species for very specific tasks."

The digit count was now three. "True Harmony faction goes beyond the Melody in believing that slaves can be used for any task for which they are of use, except for anything that involves directly crafting the Melody. They harvest many species in their campaigns."

Ramt raised the fourth and final digit. "The Complete Harmony faction stands at the opposite end of the Ekhat spectrum from the Interdict. They are beyond even the True Harmony in their belief that not only can the Melody be created now, but that even non-Ekhat species can assist in its creation. And Jao records," she said as her aureole elevated, "as well as surviving Lleix records, indicate just how well they can move their slaves to adopt the Ekhat goals and beliefs. The Jao were their product, after all."

Ramt lowered and joined her hands before her. "If we are facing the Interdict or Melody factions—any of their many branches, it makes no difference in this regard—I would recommend that you make no attempt to board one of their craft. The chances of finding slaves are slim. And even though the Melody do use slave species, they kill their slaves so quickly than none of them will know much of anything beyond their own narrow specialization. It would be a lot of risk for no benefit."

"I'll take that under advisement, as I once heard someone say," Tully responded. "Thanks."

Tully headed for the nearest lift to the command deck. He needed to share this with Vanta-Captain Ginta. As for Ramt's advice . . . Tully snorted. He would be delighted to recommend to Fleet Commander Dannet that they forego boarding an Ekhat ship if it turned out to be Interdict or Melody. Fat lot of good it would do him. She pretty much set the standard for crazy fucking Jao, as far as he was concerned.

Caitlin shrank back in her chair. The view in the display changed as the *Lexington* pulled back behind the curtains of plasma, edges starting to fuzz out as the ions swirled around the ship. But it looked as if the blips representing the Ekhat ships were actually growing larger. Six of them, rushing after the *Lexington* into a trap framed by her three sister ships.

She had been along for the ride when Dannet had captained this same ship in a solo action that had ended up destroying five ships from the Melody faction. She wasn't particularly afraid now; the odds, after all, were noticeably better this time around. But it was still battle, and she couldn't help remembering the quote Ed had recited after she tried to describe the events of that first combat: "Battle is an orgy of disorder." He credited it to someone named Patton. One of these days she'd need to read up on him.

He'd told her one other maxim in that same conversation: "No plan of battle survives contact with the enemy. That's why he's called the enemy."

So Caitlin pulled her knees up to her chest in the Jao-sized seat and wrapped her arms around them, closing her teeth on the questions she wanted to ask. Now was not the time to be distracting any of the command center personnel.

She could see Wrot out of the corner of her eye, standing in a relaxed *waiting-for-an-expected-conclusion* posture. Well, that was almost what it was. His whiskers were just a bit too forward in position, adding a hint of *boredom* to the picture.

Caitlin smiled, and relaxed a bit more.

CHAPTER 4

Quarter-Tone-Ascending charged into the command module of her ship, followed closely by her mate Ninth-Flat. Several of the attendant servients were trampled in their rush, their cries of pain and distress and death adding to the urgency of the building harmonies.

"What occurs?" she keened. "What is this discordance in the harmony?"

"Strangers," one of the youngling Ekhats uttered a recitative from his position. "Unknown ships. Not Ekhat."

Quarter-Tone-Ascending slapped the speaker away from his station with her foreclaw, leaving him lying broken on the deck. "See to him," she snapped to Ninth-Flat as she stepped between the servients operating the station. "Show me," she said.

One of the operators fumbled the controls. Quarter-Tone-Ascending snapped his head off, and the nearest servient stepped into his place. "Closer," she shrilled.

"More detail." The sense of impending dissonance increased.

Behind her Quarter-Tone-Ascending could hear the rasp of Ninth-Flat's forehand blade as he completed the broken male.

The display sharpened to reveal a large ship, ovoid in shape. Quarter-Tone-Ascending was so shocked she almost lost her grip on the flow of harmony. "Not Jao," she intoned. "Not Lleix. Not Ekhat. Who? Who brings dissonance?"

"It matters not," another Ekhat voice sang. Quarter-Tone-Ascending spun to face another station, only to behold the visage of Descant-at-the-Fourth staring at her from a communicator. "They have no place!" the senior Harmonist of the system continued. "They break harmony! They pollute! Unharvest!" Descant-at-the-Fourth's voice was true and pure, so much so that Quarter-Tone-Ascending was both admiring and jealous. "Destroy!"

With that final atonal arietta, the communicator signal shut off.

Quarter-Tone-Ascending belled out the only conceivable command—"Attack!"—and led her daughter ships toward the intruder. The six ships of their squadron swarmed forward, almost racing to reach their target, all desiring to add the note of that destruction to the universal melody.

"Still withdrawing," Flue Vaughan muttered into his boom microphone. "Terra-Captain Uldra is conning the *Lexington*. No further commands issued to other battleships. Formation is shaping into a shallow funnel, with *Lexington* at the point at rear. FC Dannet is watching instruments."

How will we ever learn to work with Jao at higher command levels? This was the first time that Vaughan had seen either the Terra-captain or the fleet commander in a true combat situation, and it bore home to him just how alien the Jao were. Their reliance on sensing "the flow" and acting in concert without verbalizations was just eerie to watch. Dannet had issued no further orders after the initial commands, but still the Jao captains of the other ships positioned them in the most advantageous locations for what was coming. Even with the viewer set to distance, Vaughan could see that.

"No further commands," Vaughan spoke into his boom mic again. "Ekhat are pursuing *Lexington.* No detectable formation or stratagem."

There was a low murmur of conversation in the command center among the various human members of the crew and between them and the Jao ranks. But all were keeping an eye on the fleet commander, who stood watching the viewscreen, position *neutral*, eyes black.

"Now," Dannet said.

The viewscreen flashed to short-range display, and the Ekhat ships showed up in more detail, seemingly hurtling through the photosphere to assail the *Lexington.*

"All gun decks, fire as you bear," Terra-Captain Uldra ordered.

Kaln krinnu ava Krant stood on the A gun deck of *Pool Buntyam* as deck commander, her status as a senior tech notwithstanding. Her body was poised in the angles of *readiness-to-wreak-revenge*. It was not a polite posture to take by regular Jao cultural standards. Kaln didn't care. She was of Krant kochan; small, struggling, with no ties or associations to more prosperous kochans, overlooked and looked down on by the more affluent. Looked down on, that is, until Krant associated with Terra taif. Politeness was not a consideration to Kaln; not here, not now. Humans sometimes called her kochan hillbillies, and once she understood the full meaning of the term Kaln had embraced it.

Her eyes glittered green with rage; an emotion shared to its full depth and intensity by all the Krant crew who stood to the guns with her. Ekhat of the Melody faction had destroyed three Krant ships some time back. Kaln had survived, along with Krant-Captain Mallu and some of the crew of the ship that had held together long enough to destroy the Melody ship. She hadn't forgotten. Nor had her fellows.

Today was payback time. Today, after over two years of waiting, they faced Ekhat again. But there was no comparison between their old Krant ship and *Pool Buntyam.* Today they would hammer the Ekhat with their beautiful new ship. And it didn't matter if these ships weren't Melody faction. Today, all Ekhat were the same.

Kaln felt the flow, rode it, waiting, anticipating, until it felt as if green sparks should be shooting from her stiffened whiskers. Just as the flow crested, Krant-Captain Mallu gave the word through the com: "Shoot!"

Twelve 200 millimeter cannon fired as one.

Quarter-Tone-Ascending stood in the center of the command module. There was no time to descend to the dance chamber, no time to prepare a grand performance plan, no time to prepare her mind for the music to come. There was only time to unite with Ninth-Flat and stand and improvise an aria of death and destruction, extinction and eradication, genocide and glory. Their voices twined around each other, soaring, leaping, finding new heights of murderous passion, flowing out over the communicator to overmaster and draw the daughter ships in to follow her lead in the dance.

The Trīkē servients added their piping chorus behind the booming voices of the two great Ekhat.

"Onward!" Quarter-Tone-Ascending sang as their ship entered the outer plasma layer of the sun. "Erase the strangers!"

Echoes of her motif came back through the communicator from the daughter ships.

"Damn, that's cool" Flue Vaughan muttered as he watched the streams of 200-millimeter rounds flaring through the plasma, somewhat like tracer rounds used to do in the old movies. They were depleted-uranium sabot rounds, and the fierce solar plasma sublimated a layer of molecules with each passing second, but their velocity was so great that they didn't lose much before arriving at their targets.

The solar plasma really interfered with the viewer, but Vaughan could make out faint bulges in the visual texture. "Bow waves off the Ekhat ships," he said into his mic as he pressed another pad, capturing a view for later study. "Need to talk to old sub crews. We're operating in a fluid here. Maybe they would have some ideas."

He watched as volley after volley after volley flew out, targeting the lead Ekhat ship.

✧ ✧ ✧

The aria duet continued, echoes from the daughter ships fading as they entered the plasma. Quarter-Tone-Ascending and Ninth-Flat, in synchrony, took a servient from each side of the command module, held it up, and began slashing limbs off with their forehand blades, slowly, in counter-rhythm to each other. The agonized squeals of the dying servients added a most wonderful descant to the aria.

Their ship shuddered. Quarter-Tone-Ascending shrieked in anger, pulling the aria in an unplanned for direction. Ninth-Flat lost synchrony, and she lashed behind her with her own forehand blade, feeling it bite without looking.

The Trīkē servients were ululating in terror, working their controls at furious rates. The young Ekhat were beating the servients, flogging them to higher pitches of frantic labor and shrill terror.

The ship shuddered again, and several bolts of flame flew through the compartment. One passed behind Quarter-Tone-Ascending, and Ninth-Flat fell silent.

Kaln stood watching her gun crews work the weapons, her posture nothing more than pure blunt *satisfaction*. With four Lexingtons in the fray, none of the Ekhat ships had a chance. And the fact that her ship, her *Pool Buntyam*, was one of them only made the emotion that much stronger.

Her crews went about their work smoothly, feeding the rounds and the liquid propellants into the chambers of their cannons with efficiency. If one or two of the crew members had body angles of *foreseen-retribution*, well, she would overlook that.

Kaln did not own a human watch. She didn't think

in terms of seconds. But the volleys crashed out from the guns in synchrony with the flow. And she could feel the completion approaching.

Caitlin watched in awe as, one by one, the torrents of metal that the *Lexington* and her sister ships threw at the Ekhat ships caused them to disappear from the viewscreen. She had been told more than once of the effect of a depleted-uranium sabot crashing through the side wall. The fiery hell that would have been created in each ship before their shields failed and the solar plasma overwhelmed them didn't bear thinking about.

One by one the blips faded from the viewscreen. It seemed to take hours, but after a glance at her watch, Caitlin knew it had only been minutes. Less than half an hour to send an entire Ekhat squadron to oblivion.

Down to one blip now, which seemed to be spinning and swooping randomly, but Caitlin wasn't able to determine if it was due to damage or intent on the part of the Ekhat. Whether by accident or not, that last ship seemed to be evading a lot of the fire from the battleships. She heard Vaughan muttering rapidly into his microphone, and he was playing the push pads on his station like it was a piano or an accordion.

Suddenly the blip took a careening curve and headed directly for the *Vercingetorix.* Caitlin sucked in her breath, and Vaughan's hands stilled on his station's pads.

"All guns cease firing," Terra-Captain Uldra ordered.

"Cease firing immediately," Kaln heard Mallu order. The repeater viewscreens made it clear the order had come to keep them from firing at their sister ship. They watched as the Ekhat approached the *Vercingetorix*.

Quarter-Tone-Ascending's rage was almost as consuming as the fires that raged in the great dance chamber which the command chamber overlooked. Her voice continued to pulse out her aria of death and destruction; solo, now, since her mate lay dead behind her.

She was splashed with ichor and blood; white from Ninth-Flat and several of the youngling Ekhat in the chamber, purple from the many Trīkē who had been slaughtered. Her mind didn't hold the concept of an abattoir, but any sane species would have been horrified.

One by one, Quarter-Tone-Ascending had heard her daughters grow silent. One by one, the echoing voices had dropped from the music, until she alone was left, throwing her defiance and her hate at the strangers.

Locking her legs so that she would not fall, with her only working manipulator claw Quarter-Tone-Ascending grasped the head of the nearest immature male Ekhat and forced his mind into union with hers. Other species would have called it child rape. For her, it was her last tactic.

The young nameless male stepped forward and took the pilot's controls from the Trīkē, shifting the course of their dying vessel by main strength to charge the closest of the stranger/enemy vessels.

Quarter-Tone-Ascending stood behind him, pouring her voice into him, pounding him with the pulses and peaks, urging him on to their mutual immolation.

The command deck of the *Lexington* was almost silent. Humans and Jao alike watched the viewscreen.

Most of the Jao had slipped into angles of *observing-impending-destruction.* Fleet Commander Dannet and Terra-Captain Uldra both stood in impeccable *gratified-respect*, the posture that recognized expected honor. Wrot went beyond that, adopting *honorable-recognition*, as flow deepened and crested simultaneously.

The blips merged.

CHAPTER 5

Quarter-Tone-Ascending shrieked in mingled fury and dismay as the stranger/enemy ship moved at seemingly the last moment—not enough to dodge their charge, but enough that the central mass of her ship would miss the other. Only subordinate structures, struts and trusses, made contact, crumpling against the nose of the stranger/enemy and scraping down its side.

The Ekhat ship was left spinning toward a plasma cell. All controls were dead, although the Trīkē continued to work them frantically, apparently in the belief that their Ekhat masters would produce a miracle.

As her ship was carried downward in the current of the cell, Quarter-Tone-Ascending lost both her aria and her grip on what passed for sanity among the Ekhat. She began shrieking, tunelessly, swinging her forehand blade around her, completing/slaughtering the remaining Ekhat and those Trīkē who couldn't evade her.

Her last vision was of the flood of solar plasma that

suddenly burst into the chamber as the ship's shields failed and the hull materials began to vaporize. The heat of that moment matched the heat of her rage.

And then there was nothing.

Flue Vaughan studied the readouts on his panel, then raised his eyes to the viewer. The solar plasma seriously degraded the accuracy of even the Jao science instruments, but it looked very much like the *Vercingetorix* was still there.

He glanced over at Caitlin, and saw her smiling. She looked up and said something to Wrot, who nodded his head and shifted his position into something Flue couldn't read. The Welshman's command of Jao body language was improving, but still couldn't be considered more than elementary.

A readout on his panel caught his attention. "Fleet Commander," he called out. Dannet turned his way, head tilted and ears lowered, which Flue did recognize as an abbreviated form of *curt-attention*. "*Lexington*'s A and C gun decks report seventy-seven percent combat load remaining, E deck has seventy-five percent."

He watched as Dannet absorbed that information. If the other battleships had similar stock levels, that meant that nearly twenty-five percent of the fleet's gunnery ammunition stocks had been used up in a single engagement. That didn't exactly fill Flue with warm feelings. Dannet's posture went *neutral*, and she returned her attention to the viewscreen without a word.

Flue shrugged, then looked back at his own panel.

Caitlin sat back, limp with relief. They'd done it. Or rather, Fleet Commander Dannet had done it.

Six Ekhat ships destroyed with no losses to her own fleet. She looked up at Wrot, and he bent toward her.

"I'd say that was a good day's work," she murmured.

Wrot's whiskers twitched as he shifted to *cautious-optimism.* "Indeed. The only other instance I can think of where a Jao force won so . . . forcefully was the battle at Valeron."

Which was where Dannet, then Terra-captain of the *Lexington*, had defeated and destroyed five Ekhat ships. Caitlin realized in a new light just how large a gift the Narvo had given Terra taif in the person of Dannet.

"But," Wrot continued with one of his ubiquitous human phrases, "don't count your chickens before they've hatched. If there were this many ships waiting at the sun, who knows what else might be in the system."

"I didn't need to hear that," Caitlin muttered.

"Fleet command: take the ships out. Formation Epsilon Alpha," Dannet ordered, "*Lexington* to take point. And take a full load of plasma."

Flue nodded to himself. Bold moves, but with a certain amount of caution as well. Epsilon Alpha inverted the cone formation, and Dannet had put *Lexington* in the lead. Which, he had to admit, made sense, since it had the most practiced crew.

He muttered more notes into his microphone. After a moment, he looked over at Wrot and caught his attention. The Jao stepped over to stand by his station.

"What is 'the flow' telling you now?"

Wrot considered for a moment, then shrugged—he was one of the best at using human gestures—and said, "Time to move forward."

"So all the other ship-captains will follow *Lexington*?"

Wrot gestured toward the viewscreen. "As you can see."

Flue looked and could see that the other battleships were indeed moving, following Terra-Captain Uldra's lead out of the plasma. And he thought he could see hints that the other ships were following them.

"We have got to get a communicator that works in plasma," he groused. He punched a pad, then said for his notes, "Talk to the sub dudes and the science dudes. Will sonar or something like it work in the solar plasma? Can we use it for pulse codes?"

Descant-at-the-Fourth stepped around the great hall of the ship's pyramid, waiting impatiently, manipulators absentmindedly shredding the corpse of a servient who had dared to squeak while she was singing. Since Quarter-Tone-Ascending's aria had faded into the music of the sun, she had been directing a pavane between the remaining ships in the system, orchestrating them to coalesce in a dance of seven ships around the massive harvester/purifier that she, as one of the signal voices of all the Complete Harmony factions, had at her personal disposal.

Now she waited for the return of Quarter-Tone-Ascending's daughter-group, wanting those tones for the melody. Her mate, Second-Strong-Cadence, maintained the music behind her, riding on top of the chorus of immature Ekhat and servients. Their time of mating would occur soon, the music hinted.

Descant-at-the-Fourth's head tilted suddenly, and her manipulators squeezed what remained of her servient toy into protoplasmic jelly. A thin whistle issued from her mouth as the harmonies in the system tilted; dissonance obtruded. She watched as an ovoid shape, sheathed in plasma, emerged from the sun. Sharp staccato notes crescendoed and accelerated in her fury as it became obvious that the interlopers had defeated Quarter-Tone-Ascending.

A new theme emerged, overwhelming Second-Strong-Cadence. Within moments it was echoed back to Descant-at-the-Fourth from the other ships. The pavane wheeled, and began flowing toward the sun.

"Destroy! Unharvest!" Descant-at-the-Fourth sang as more interlopers began to emerge from the solar plasma. "Purify!"

"Cachu!" Flue muttered in his native Welsh as they cleared the last of the plasma veils and the sensors were finally able to provide clear resolution of what lay in store.

"More Ekhat," he continued, slapping at pads on his console to pull the sensor data into his files. "How ducky."

He stilled as Dannet lifted her head from where she was studying the sensor details over the shoulder of the lead sensor officer.

"Light attack craft to Epsilon Delta, north and south. Support ships remain at the photosphere transition for further orders."

Vaughan pulled that into his files, and tried to make sense of the fleet dispositions. He could see no advantage in placing the lighter ships in the offset formation Dannet had just ordered them to. He ground his teeth. "Bloody flow."

✧ ✧ ✧

Descant-at-the-Fourth's song fought against the dissonance that threatened to overwhelm the system as ship after ship emerged from the sun. She descended to the great dance chamber of her ship, followed by Second-Strong-Cadence and every other Ekhat on the ship not required to make the servients operate the vessel. All the Trīkē servients not actually at controls were also summoned.

Gabe Tully's jaw clenched as the repeater screen in his command deck on the *Ban Chao* finally gave him a clear view of what the Terra taif fleet faced.

Beside him Lieutenant Bannerji whistled. "Eight of them. Wow."

"What's the matter, Lieutenant?" Gabe asked with a grin. "Think Dannet can't take them, after wiping out their sun patrol?"

"Oh, no, sir," Bannerji replied earnestly. "It's just, this will be one of the biggest Jao/Ekhat engagements for the last hundred years or so. And we've got a ringside seat."

"More like we're sitting in the ring," Gabe muttered. He pointed at the sidebars displayed on the viewscreen. "So what can you tell me about this fleet?"

Bannerji pointed his pad at the viewscreen, pulling the data off and matching it into the databanks he had stored. "Hmm, yes, that matches . . ."

"Vikram," Gabe said with a bite. "Give."

"Oh, yes, sir," the lieutenant looked up with a flash of white teeth. "According to the Jao records, the ship types aren't from the Melody faction, probably not Interdict, either. Most likely either Complete Harmony or True Harmony." He ran his fingers over the screen of his pad. "I'd say Complete Harmony."

"Okay, so they're Complete Harmony. What does that tell me that's useful in knowing where to point *Ban Chao*?"

Bannerji pointed his pad back at the viewscreen. Four of the Ekhat ships turned orange. "Those four are smaller than the others. Think of them as cruisers, maybe. Scout ships, small expeditions like the attack on Terra, that's what they're usually used for."

Three more of the ships turned green. "These three are main battle craft, about the size of the Bond's *Harrier*-class ships. Any one of those would be a good target."

The last Ekhat ship turned red. "But this one," Bannerji's Oxonian tones took on an air of excitement, "this one is the prize. It's been at least two generations since a Jao has seen one of these. They call it a World Harvester, and they've only seen them used when the Complete Harmony goes in and literally harvests a planet, taking all life-forms for use in their service in some way."

"Uh-huh," Gabe said, frowning. He looked around at his company commanders and command staff. "Well, gentlemen, I expect that's going to be our target. Let's take that thing away from them."

Wolfish smiles lit up all around the room.

"Give us the tech readouts, Vikram," Gabe ordered, and heads bent over pads as the data flowed.

Caitlin was hugging her knees again, watching as the viewscreen showed the Ekhat ships approaching closer. Or at least, it seemed like the *Lexington* was standing still and the Ekhat were rushing toward them, when the reality was that they were actually all in motion toward each other.

She looked up at Wrot again. "Is that normal?" she asked. "All that moving around? I thought they would just charge right at us again, like the ships in the sun."

Wrot's angles shifted to *willingness-to-tutor*, with a hint of *amused* added at the end. Caitlin resisted the temptation to call him a smartass.

"In some confrontations in the past, they have done this," he said. "Some of the Bond strategy circle almost understand it as a ritual choreography. It has never seemed to help them much, but they still do it." He shrugged. "The Ekhat are not sane."

"Fleet Commander," the head sensor officer called out, "the central ship is a World Harvester."

All noise in the command deck stopped for just a moment. Then Dannet's head twisted toward the communications officer. "Inform *Ban Chao* and Colonel Tully that that is their target."

Caitlin pressed back in her seat as the normal noise resumed in the command deck. She wanted to protest, but knew she couldn't. She had *oudh* over the mission, but not over the combat. For better or ill, that fell into Dannet's hands, and it had already been proven that the fleet commander was superb at her job.

For Tully's sake, Caitlin hoped that would continue to be so.

Such was Descant-at-the-Fourth's control that when she began the new song, within moments Second-Strong-Cadence and the immature Ekhat had locked into it. Their individual urges were sublimated to her song. They followed her steps, they barked and staccatoed and glissandoed with amazing integration, even for Ekhat.

To a human, it would have sounded like the ultimate cacophony. To the Ekhat, it approached divinity—or it would have, if the Ekhat had had a concept of God. But even Descant-at-the-Fourth was impressed with the facility with which the others achieved her design.

Having established the ground, the foundation for her work, Descant-at-the-Fourth waved her manipulators. As the other Ekhat continued in the ground, she and Second-Strong-Cadence began a new theme; and with that Descant-at-the-Fourth's genius was revealed.

A new harmony sprang into being, one that vibrated strongly against the dissonance brought by the invaders. Against the rock-hard ground maintained by the others, she and her mate moved and sang, now mirror imaging each other, now offering thesis and antithesis, every step and every note strengthening the harmony.

The other ships echoed back the song, enriching the harmony and buttressing it against the dissonance.

As it crested, the first of the Ekhat ships flung themselves against the intruders.

The second phase of the battle seemed to last forever. And through it all, Flue Vaughan felt somewhat like a musician trying to play Bach with one hand and Rachmaninoff with the other, all the while singing the classic song "Stairway to Heaven." His fingers flew from one pad to another, sampling data flows, pulling data and status snapshots into his files as he muttered notes into his mic. He glanced up at the viewscreen as often as he could, but mostly he was watching the readouts and bars of his workstation display.

The opening laser attacks had little impact. The *Lexington*-class ships had the strongest defensive screens yet known to the Jao, and they were carrying screens of solar plasma along with them. What little energy penetrated through those barely warmed spots on the hull metal. Flue knew that wouldn't last, though. As the ships drew closer, and as the plasma cooled and attenuated, the Ekhat lasers would have more and more effect on even the Lexingtons, much less the smaller ships.

He kept one eye and one ear focused on the fleet commander. Dannet had issued no commands since the order to *Ban Chao*, but she and Terra-Captain Uldra were discussing something. He noticed Wrot heading in that direction, as well.

"More of that bloody flow," he muttered.

Lim slowly refolded the edge of her robes with care. She was watching her fingers rather than the viewscreen repeater. Caitlin Kralik had authorized a feed of the command deck viewscreen signal to the Ekhatlore *elian* quarters, ostensibly to aid Ramt in collecting data about the Ekhat. Ramt had extended the use of that privilege to the two members of Terra-lore *elian*, so she and Pyr were now seated in Ramt's common room, watching the repeater even though he was on the *Ban Chao*.

Or rather, Pyr was watching it. Lim was avoiding the view. This was her first time to experience what the humans called *combat*—if she could be said to be experiencing anything at all seated on a Lleix-designed bench inside a human-designed room behind the armor and defensive shields of a Jao/human-designed battleship. Ignoring the slight vibrations felt through the decking, the viewscreen repeater could have been a human television in the Terra-lore quarters back in the Lleix refugee settlements in the mountains of Colorado.

But Lim knew that wasn't the case. Intelligent beings were fighting and dying all around her, and it was disturbing to her that there was no sense of the struggle, no sense of the *combat*, no feeling that she was involved. That bothered the young Lleix, bothered her deeply.

Lim was slowly coming to the realization that her understanding of *sensho*, of the Lleix concept of right-living, was beginning to evolve. And she knew that some of the tall elders, such as the Starsifters just down the hall from where she sat, would be shocked that her *sensho* would vary from the way *sensho* had always been. And others would simply frown and whisper, "She is from the *dochaya*. What can be expected from such?"

At the moment, though, she was hoping very hard that Colonel Gabe Tully would survive this battle, this *combat*. She desired more than ever the teaching he had promised her.

Wrot settled into the angles of *query-for-the-purpose-of-commencing-action*, but said nothing. Dannet's posture was a solid *determination-to-prevail*, but she said nothing. Terra-Captain Uldra ran a rapid kaleidoscope of *surprised/uncertain/uncomfortable* before he settled on *neutral*.

"The flow . . . is not," Uldra said.

"Say rather, it is opposed," Wrot replied, shifting to *adamant-purpose*. "We must continue as we've begun."

The other two also shifted to *adamant-purpose*, and began issuing orders.

CHAPTER 6

Vaughan captured Dannet's orders. The battleship formation began to rotate, just as the individual ships rotated on their respective axes. It only took him a couple of seconds to catch on to why: to reduce the impact of the Ekhat lasers on the ships. He felt good about that realization for, maybe, half a second.

He sobered when he caught a message sent by *Vercingetorix*. One of their gun decks was open to space and sealed off, damaged by the collision with the last of the Ekhat ships that had attacked them inside the star. He suppressed a shudder, and hoped the crew had managed to evacuate safely. Another note was made; this time about the fact that between the battle off Valeron and this one, in two collisions two different Lexingtons had lost a gun deck, a full spine. *Make sure that one gets to the design group.*

The Welshman continued to watch and make notes as Dannet stood, hands behind her back, watching the viewscreen, head slightly tilted. He got the feeling she was waiting for something, but he couldn't tell what.

"So," Gabe Tully concluded, looking around at his jinau officers in the assault group, "we only have general guesses as to what the interior of that ship is going to look like. Fortunately, we don't have specific objectives in mind. It's just ram the ship, debark, create as much hell and destruction as we can, capture as many Ekhats and slaves as we can, and get out while the getting is good."

Gabe saw First Sergeant Luff's mouth quiver for just a moment, before he forced it into a straight line.

"Able Company will lead out," Gabe continued, looking at Captain Sato Kobayashi, the Japanese-born company commander. "Sato, terminate every Ekhat you see in that space. They're too dangerous to let get close to us while we're trying to unship. If we can capture some elsewhere and drag them back to the ship, great. But any of them in the entry space needs to be turned into quivering little pieces of Ekhat meat. Anything that's not Ekhat but is carrying a weapon also gets hammered. Got it?"

Kobayashi gave a sharp nod, and entered notes on his pad.

Gabe turned to Captain Torg krinnu ava Terra and First Lieutenant Richard Boatright, commanders of companies Baker and Charlie respectively.

"Once the entry area is under control, you guys will debark. Each company will leave one fire team for entry space and ship security, under the command of Major Liang."

Major Shan Liang, the executive officer of the

assault group, looked up from where he was making notes of his own. "And where will you be, Colonel?"

"Probably with Able Company."

Tully saw identical frowns appear on the faces of both the exec and the first sergeant. He held up a hand in a "stop" signal.

"Don't start, guys. I've seen Ekhat in action; with the exception of Torg, none of you, no matter how experienced you are, can say that. You have no idea—you can't know—just how insane and crazy it will be to face them."

"I heard that from some of the troops who were with you at Valeron," Luff said.

Tully shook his head. "And anything they told you just is nothing compared to the piss-your-pants feeling of seeing a giraffe-sized sort-of-praying mantis with too many arms and legs charging you like a racehorse with the intent desire of turning you into a smorgasbord of cold cuts and a stain on the deck."

"What he said," Captain Torg muttered.

"The best I can do to share the experience is for me to be with Able and First Sergeant Luff to be with Charlie; that's the best I can do," he repeated. The first sergeant's frown disappeared at that. "And Shan," Tully turned to the exec, "that leaves you holding the bag at the ship. If things go well, you'll just be helping corral the specimens. If things go in the crapper, you'll be the last-ditch defense of the *Ban Chao*. Don't let me down."

Major Liang's face set in very determined lines. "You got it, Colonel."

Tully looked at Luff. "What's that old Marine motto you like to trot out, Top?"

"You mean 'Improvise, Adapt, and Overcome,' sir?" Luff grinned.

"That's the one." Tully looked at his officers. "Guys, this isn't going to be a set-piece battle. Watch your sensors, watch the walls, watch your backs. Don't trust anything. Drop communication links every time you change directions. Fall back if you have to. Yell for help if you need to. This is about breaking shit and grabbing prisoners, not about heroic last stands or forlorn hopes. Everybody clear on that?"

"Yes, sir."

"Yes."

"Yes, Colonel."

Tully stood. "Good. Now go prep your troops."

Vaughan didn't catch what it was that the fleet commander saw at that exact moment. He'd have to dig it out of the recordings later. But Dannet shifted to a different posture and said almost matter-of-factly, "All battleships, Fire Plan Alpha 3. All subordinate ships, seal the edges of the zone. No one escapes."

And with those calm orders, the second phase of the battle for the system began.

Fire Plan Alpha 3 called for the battleships to all concentrate their lasers on the same ship. It took a bit of coordination, Vaughan noted. Dannet had to issue some rapid corrections to get the *Arjuna* to target the desired ship, but before long all the lasers from all four battleships were focused on one of the smaller Ekhat ships. Despite the attempts of the target to evade, the Jao/human laser crews kept the heavy beams from the battleships focused on the Ekhat ship as if they had been glued there. And in truth, a multithousand-ton spaceship just doesn't dance around like a third-grader playing dodgeball, so it wasn't that hard.

It only took a few minutes for the heavy lasers to overload the defensive screens of the Ekhat ship, and it was rendered into an expanding cloud of navigational hazards.

A few minutes more saw the second of the lighter Ekhat vessels also destroyed.

Descant-at-the-Fourth staggered as the dissonance brought by the invaders resurged as the second of her ships disappeared in a flash of light. For just a moment, her voice wavered, and Second-Strong-Cadence and the other Ekhat lost their way altogether. In that moment, the harmony disappeared.

Kaln krinnu ava Krant stood by Krant-Captain Mallu, since the lasers were the weapons in use in this phase of the battle. She looked up suddenly, and found her eyes locked with his.

"The flow is free again," she said. The captain nodded.

Kaln's head twisted in an odd direction. She left the command deck without a word. Mallu let her go without comment. Her sense of flow was stronger than anyone else's on the ship, and if she needed to be somewhere else, he trusted her.

Tully watched as his jinau troops, human and Jao alike, stepped into their shock frames. There was no way around the fact that the *Ban Chao* was going to take one monster of a hit when it rammed into its target, and the frames were designed to keep the troops from flying all around the deck when that happened. This was the first time they would be used in combat, though, and he really hoped they worked as well now as they did in the tests he'd seen.

"Hope those things work as advertised, Colonel," First Sergeant Luff said as he stepped up beside him, faceplate to his combat suit standing open.

"You and me, both. But five-to-one Murphy shows up somewhere."

"No takers, here, sir. My momma didn't raise no fools." The sergeant's Jamaican accent got a little stronger. "But we'll deal with that if we have to."

"Feel free to 'Improvise, Adapt and Overcome' as necessary, Top," Tully said with a grin.

"Will do, sir, will do." He looked around. "Looks like we'd best get locked in place ourselves."

"Yep." Tully slapped the sergeant's armored shoulder. "Lead the way. It's Ekhat killing time."

Not a few of the troops drew some comfort of the almost identical evil grins on the faces of the two men.

Vaughan's head snapped up to the main viewscreen. "Yes!" he exulted. For some unknown reason, the remaining Ekhat ships had lost their cohesion and were simply swarming toward the Terran fleet. The World Harvester was bulling its way through its own fleet in what Flue would have called a reckless charge in another situation, leaving the smaller ships to scatter in disarray and attack as best they could.

The two remaining smaller Ekhat ships were pushed out of the way. Dannet, reacting in that matter-of-fact Jao manner, divided the battleships' fire between them, and they were being hammered. One of them disintegrated into another fireball when heavy beams from one of the larger Ekhat craft caught it from the rear. Dannet shifted the fire of the *Lexington* to the fourth smaller craft, and it simply disintegrated, seemingly at the moment those lasers hit its screens.

"Tell Krant-Captain Mallu the World Harvester is his, but he is to coordinate with *Ban Chao*," Dannet ordered after bare moments of studying the plot that now occupied the viewscreen. "Uldra, take the north, *Arjuna*, the south, *Vercingetorix* the one that lags to the east. Subordinate squadrons; make sure the dead ships are really dead. Go."

Caitlin's knees were back under her chin, and her arms were wrapped around them. She was aware of Captain Miller standing behind her and Tamt standing by the door to the command deck; and she was aware of Lieutenant Vaughan doing his frenetic best to capture everything of note about the battle and Fleet Commander Dannet's operation of same. But her focus was on the main viewscreen, which was displaying the same data as Dannet's tactical station. The fleet was moving in obedience to the fleet commander's orders, and that included the *Ban Chao*. *Be safe, Tully,* she thought.

Tully stood motionless, shock frame gripping his suit. He could have moved slightly if he'd wanted to, but with ramming another ship in the plan and his suit closed up, it was safest to just stay put. He kept one eye on the feed from the command deck's tactical display that was piped to his helmet's display, and another on the light bar that ran around the rim of the troop assembly area. The light bar was a reassuring green, so the ram wasn't imminent—yet.

He spared a thought for his suit.

Humans as a race seemed to specialize in *ollnat*. That was the Jao word for it, anyway. Sort of.

What the Jao of most of their worlds thought of when they used the word "*ollnat*" in reference to humans translated as *foolishness*, or *daydreaming*, or *time-wasting*. But to Jao such as the leaders of the Bond, or those who had experienced the conquest of Earth from the "winning" side, or even the newly associated Krant kochan, *ollnat*, more than anything, meant *innovation*. And humans were made for innovation, it seemed like. Much more so than the oh-so-stodgy Jao were, at any rate.

The Jao had brought advanced technology with them when they conquered the Earth, and for the most part had made little effort to control it during the occupation years. But the continuing human low-level resistance to the occupation had made it difficult for Jao-tech-based businesses to get started until recently. In the three or so years since Aille krinnu ava Pluthrak (now Aille krinnu ava Terra) had supplanted Oppuk krinnu ava Narvo as governor of Earth, that had changed. There were now easily two dozen or more prosperous companies whose products were based on innovations from the Jao tech-base, with who knows how many startups right behind them. Half of them had the word *ollnat* as part of their company names.

One of the best was The Ollnat Works. It had started in the Pacific region when a Chinese engineer named Li discovered that the Jao had something they used in their spaceships that made Kevlar look like a paper towel. He teamed up with a couple of friends that he'd met in college in California—a Gujarati business genius named Ghosh from Mumbai, and a marketing savant named MacDonald from Brisbane. The rest was history.

The marketing guy called their product Super-K (over the objections of the engineer) for Super Kevlar. Their first production item was fabric woven from small extruded threads of the compound. It had the weight of heavy canvas, and the bullet stopping power of a centimeter and a half of armor plate.

Tully's experiences in the boarding action during the Valeron expedition had made him very aware that the standard Jao-designed spacesuit was, to put it mildly, not well suited for any kind of close combat. Tully's description was considerably blunter than that. And that lack of suitability had been at the top of his list of things to fix when he got back.

He'd had a full-on rant already worked up and rehearsed and ready to deliver to Ed Kralik as soon as he could report to the general, only to discover that Kralik had anticipated him and that The Ollnat Works had teamed up with the spacesuit manufacturers to begin delivering improved combat suits for the fleet troops literally the day Tully's feet touched down on Earth again.

Tully grinned at the thought. Let the old-school Jao think what they would about humans and *ollnat*. The Jao grunts who filled many of the ranks in the fleet jinau troops had embraced the new suits with the same fervor with which most of them had joined Terra taif.

The light bar suddenly changed from green to yellow.

"Command deck to assault team," a human voice said in Tully's ear-set over the main assault team com channel. "Target has begun deceleration to avoid entering the star. It appears to be focusing its fire on *Pool Buntyam.* Estimate three minutes to ram. Light will go red at minus fifteen seconds. Acknowledge."

"Acknowledge three minutes to ram, red at minus fifteen. Tully out."

Caitlyn waved Wrot over. He moved closer, and she spoke.

"What's happening now?"

Wrot looked over his shoulder at the main viewscreen. "Dannet has ordered the battleships to englobe the World Harvester, and to destroy the remaining lesser Ekhat ships. This will isolate the World Harvester near the sun for *Ban Chao* to make their assault attempt on it."

"So when is Tully going to do that?"

Wrot didn't miss the reference to the man rather than the ship. He looked at the viewscreen again. "I'd say they've already begun."

Tully tried to shake his head, but the shock frame was still holding him. "What a hit," he muttered.

He wasn't sure what he had been expecting from the impact of the ram, but the actual event proved to be beyond that expectation. The kinetic energy of the *Ban Chao*'s reinforced bow penetrating the Ekhat ship's hull had been extreme. None of the designers had been sure how the assault troops would experience it as they were cocooned in their shock frames. Tully decided it was an order of magnitude higher than being in a car wreck, but between the combat suits and the shock frames his troops could deal with it.

The light bar switched to blue, and the human voice from the command deck spoke over the all-unit com channel again as the shock frames released the troops and began to withdraw into the floor and ceiling. "Ram completed. Front assault doors clear to open. Deploy troops immediately. Acknowledge."

"Acknowledged. Tully out."

Tully was positioned right behind the leading elements of Sato's Able Company. He could see most of them were pulling their weapons into position and orienting themselves toward the big blast doors that were sliding apart to open the way into the assault ramp.

"Able Company—report."

"All up, all ready, all go," was the reply in the Japanese captain's slightly accented English.

"Baker Company."

"All ready," came the response from Torg.

"Charlie Company."

"Good to go, Colonel." Lieutenant Boatright sounded a bit nervous—that was okay, because Tully was more than a bit nervous himself. But he also sounded like he was in control.

"Tully to command: open the front assault doors."

"Opening doors now," came the response over the com channel.

Tully felt more than heard the big outer doors opening. "Able Company go!" he heard Sato order.

The leading jinau raced down the ramp into the Ekhat ship. Tully and Sergeant Luff followed. Expecting something like the madhouse of the boarding action in the Valeron campaign, he was surprised to see Able Company faced with very little resistance. No Ekhat were visible, and only a handful of other life-forms, most of which seemed to have been riddled by the shrapnel generated when the *Ban Chao* had burst through the hull of their ship. Their spacesuits had irregular holes in them, anyway, and they were leaking bodily fluids of various colors.

Tully looked around while Baker and Charlie Companies exited the *Ban Chao* and pushed the perimeter out further. They were in a relatively large open space. There was no clue why it was there or what it was used for, other than the existence of a lot of flat panels strewn around the deck. But there were what appeared to be doorways scattered around the perimeter. He started marking them on his heads-up display, and as soon as the last jinau hit the deck he sent the diagram to the rest of the troops and started barking orders.

"Able take the red door, Baker the green, Charlie the yellow. Throw sensor packs through the blue doors as you go by them so that the troops who stay back can get a heads-up if something is heading that way. Stay in contact, and yell if you need help. One hour out and back, but keep an ear open for the XO or me to call it quits early. Go!"

Flue Vaughan's head came up as the communication officer said, "Fleet Commander, *Ban Chao* reports successful ram and penetration of World Harvester hull and entrance of jinau into ship. Minimal damage to ram portion of hull, but remaining hull integrity good."

He checked the data-stream from the *Ban Chao*.

So far, so good. The damned design actually worked! Now, if Colonel Tully and his jinau assault team can just grab a few prisoners and get off again safely.

Vaughan didn't know it, but his thoughts were being echoed by others in the command deck, notably Caitlin Kralik and Caewithe Miller.

The harmony had been replaced by shrieking fear. Descant-at-the-Fourth picked herself up from the heap of servients she had landed upon when the whole ship had lurched and rung like a colossal tone bar, chittering with rage. The surviving servients scuttled for cover, adding to the cacophony as they ran.

Second-Strong-Cadence was floundering nearby, all his left legs broken from being snapped by the torque applied in the whiplash of his body as it was caught between two pillars. Their mental bond was broken. She completed him with her forehand blade as she stalked by. His distracting noise ceased after that moment.

She gathered herself, but before she began to attempt to establish a new harmony, to attempt to win back her system, one of the immature Ekhat sang out, "Intruders on the ship! Lower hall! Moving through the passages!"

Descant-at-the-Fourth sang a tone so high, so sharp, so savage that it could have cut glass.

"Death!" she intoned. "Complete them all! Let them be silent in the face of the Complete Harmony!"

She launched herself at the nearest door, which dilated just barely in time to allow her to pass, followed by the four surviving immature Ekhat and as many of the Trīkē servients as could keep up.

✧ ✧ ✧

By Tully's suit sensors, Able Company had moved almost half a kilometer. Not in a straight line, of course. They had taken several turns, leaving paint markers and communication links every time. As it turned out, the com links were a necessity, because something in the halls kept the com units from passing the walls.

They had yet to see another living being. It was almost eerie, walking through the oddly proportioned doorways that followed swooping lines and intersected at something other than right angles. Twice they had dropped off fire teams to cover major intersections and provide some coverage of the advancing company's back.

"Talk to me, Shan," Tully murmured into his comm.

"Charlie Company has about a half-dozen of some small slave species," the XO replied. "They don't want to come quietly, so it's all the troops can do to keep them controlled even with their limbs tied down."

"Tell Boatright to pull back," Tully ordered. "He can leave sensors behind and leave a fire team back up the hall in case something ugly comes that direction, but he needs to get those prisoners back to the ship ASAP."

The XO passed that order on, then continued his report with, "Baker Company has no prisoners. But Torg reports that they've had several attacks by slaves of more than one type, none of which survived. He said, quote, 'This is starting to remind me of Chicago.'"

That last gave Tully pause. Chicago had been the site of the bitterest battle between Jao and humans during the conquest of Earth. The Jao had learned then to hate humans' inventiveness and improvisational ability with what passed for passion among the stolid folk. If Torg was feeling that kind of vibe...

He looked at his display—forty-nine minutes since they started. "Tell Baker to return to ship. Same orders as Charlie: leave sensors and a fire team in the hall. I'll pass the order for Able to reverse direction as well."

"Understood."

"Oh, and Shan? Keep everyone on their toes. We ain't out of the woods yet."

"Right."

Kaln krinnu ava Krant had walked down the gun line in her gun deck and triggered the load process for each of the guns one at a time. They were now loaded, and she was back at her deck commander station. From there she watched the tactical display on her station as the *Pool Buntyam* engaged the World Harvester. The Krant ship's lasers were proving to be more powerful than the Ekhat's, which meant they were doing more damage than they were receiving. Kaln watched the battle, and at one particular point began using her command station to aim the guns.

Once the guns were aimed, she stood loosely, posture *neutral*, waiting.

There came another point, and she pressed a command button. The twelve guns fired in rapid sequence.

The last gun had no sooner fired than a com signal came through at the station.

"Kaln, what are you doing?" The peremptory demand was from Krant-Captain Mallu, and she had expected it.

"Supporting *Ban Chao*," she replied.

"Are you going to do that again?"

"No."

The captain said nothing in reply.

Kaln leaned toward the tactical display, posture slowly shifting to *anticipation.*

The attack came ten minutes after Able Company had begun to retrace its steps through the almost-maze of corridors back to their entry point. They were in sight of the second fire team they had detached, ready to pick them up and continue rolling down their path, when what seemed like a horde of Ekhat and other creatures burst out of three small doorways and overran the detachment. There was a flurry of yells over the com band and a flurry of shots, but it was over in a few seconds. The fire team didn't sell themselves cheaply, surrounding themselves with dead slaves and even an Ekhat, but they went down. The surviving attackers continued on down the corridor toward the main body.

There was no time for orders. The leading jinau troopers dropped to one knee and began shooting. Servients began to drop, but the Ekhat—all too many of them—continued hurtling toward the troops.

"Grenades!" Captain Kobayashi yelled, anticipating Tully by a split-second. Several flash-bang and fragmentation grenades flew from the jinau in the rear.

Having had at least a couple of seconds' warning, the jinau were braced and prepared when they were hammered by successive waves of concussion. The attackers were not so fortunate. Tully watched several of the servients literally blown asunder by grenades that landed under their feet. One of the smaller Ekhat was picked up and slammed against the passageway ceiling by another grenade, and even the largest of the great aliens was staggered by the blasts.

That gave the jinau a few seconds.

"Fall back!" Tully ordered over the com. As the jinau made an orderly retreat past him, Tully reached out and grabbed one particular trooper.

"You locked and loaded, Corporal Johnson?"

"Betcherass, Colonel!"

"Wait for my signal, then let them have it."

Johnson, who was a very large human, said nothing more; he took his position in the center of the passageway, and waited, weapon in hand, as the last of the jinau trickled by him.

The last of the Ekhat heavy ships ceased firing and broke apart. Lieutenant Vaughan pumped a fist silently, then flushed as Dannet looked over at him. He quickly scanned his readouts, and opened his mouth to bring something to the fleet commander's attention when the communications officer beat him to it.

"*Vercingetorix* reports that they have lost atmosphere on two more of their weapons spines—two of the laser decks."

Flue shaped a silent whistle. Fifty percent of the battleship's offensive capability lost in one battle. He started querying the *Vercingetorix* for more details on their damage.

"*Vercingetorix* should withdraw to the photosphere transition and take station on the support ships," Dannet ordered. "*Lexington* and *Arjuna* shape course to join *Pool Buntyam* in supporting *Ban Chao*. Subordinate squadrons, continue neutralizing the Ekhat debris."

✧  

"Crazy ass Ekhat," Tully muttered. None of the attackers, Ekhat or slaves, carried anything other than hand weapons—blades for the most part. No guns, no lasers. It had been that way in the Valeron boarding action as well. He didn't understand it—*maybe it's against their religion*, he thought—but he was thankful for it. It let him wait an additional few seconds before giving the order.

"Now, Johnson!"

The big human was standing three meters in front of the rest of Able Company. He leveled his weapon at waist height, and pulled the trigger.

Johnson was carrying a new weapon, one only recently cleared for jinau use, and only for use in space or in dealing with Ekhat. It was a recognizable descendant of the flamethrower, but it was nastier—much nastier.

Twin streams of clear liquids jetted from the nozzle of his weapon, flying over and past the attackers. An instant later, holocaust arrived.

There was a massive flare. Billows of flame rolled back down the passageway, stopping short of Johnson and the other jinau, although Tully thought he could feel some heat transferred through the faceplate of his suit.

The twin tanks in Johnson's backpack contained the two components of a hypergolic propellant—aerozine 50 and nitrogen tetroxide—easily storable as liquids at room temperature, yet absolutely guaranteed to explode or flash into flame when combined. Tully had seen them demonstrated in the open. Their effect in the confined space of the passageway was almost indescribable.

Of course, the components were incredibly toxic, and in an onworld situation would undoubtedly create some nasty pollution.

On the other hand, Tully considered, the weapon worked whether in atmosphere or the near-vacuum of space, and the Ekhat had no room to complain about cruel and unusual tactics.

One lone Ekhat came out of the dying cloud, droplets of flame splattering from the joints of its suit. It staggered, but still headed toward the jinau with obvious intent.

Johnson leveled his weapon again, and gave a short burst that landed directly on the Ekhat. When the flash of light cleared, there was only a huddled mass lying on the passageway floor with flames licking up from it.

The big human pointed his weapon nozzle up, and looked back with a large evil grin visible through his faceplate. "Ekhat *flambé*," he pronounced.

Tully gave the flames time to die down, and to make sure that nothing was stirring down the passageway. "Move out, Captain Kobayashi," he finally ordered.

The jinau picked their way through the blackened remains of the attackers with comments like "Crispy critters" and "Hey, Johnson, does flame-broiled Ekhat taste like chicken?" But they dropped the humor when they got to where their fire team had been overwhelmed. Several of the Jao troopers took up the task of carrying the bodies. None of them, Tully included, wanted to leave them there.

Descant-at-the-Fourth hurtled down her chosen passageway, followed closely by a couple of immature Ekhat and a throng of the Trīkē servients.

Jao! The other group had reported Jao among the invaders!

The greatest mistake ever made by the Complete Harmony faction, deny it though the harmony masters might, was the uplifting of the Jao. And now that mistake was challenging her harmony in her system.

There was no further report, but she knew where the invaders were, where they had to be. She began a new statement of her aria, singing with force. The youngling Ekhat with her picked up on it immediately, and she felt the harmony begin to strengthen again.

She halted her mob before it exited the passageway, waiting for the harmony to crest…

Now!

Able Company had exited their passageway, carrying their dead, and were halfway across the open space when the XO shouted, "Behind you!"

Tully spun to see a mob of Ekhat and slaves pouring toward them from one of the side passages.

Twelve depleted-uranium sabot penetrators slammed into the World Harvester ship in quick succession in an extremely tight grouping. The liquefied metal plasma that erupted in the ship's engine room vaporized all Ekhat and slaves present, and destroyed all of the control equipment in the room.

The ship's drive shut down.

So did the artificial gravity.

On the gun deck of the *Pool Buntyam*, Kaln's posture slid to one of *iron-retribution*.

✧ ✧ ✧

Descant-at-the-Fourth screamed as she felt the harmony crumble. She lunged toward the invaders, but found herself floating in midair. No matter how she struggled, she could not put a foot to a surface. Slowly spinning, overcome by her rage, she screamed again and again, atonally, with no thought to harmony.

"Recoilless, take out the Ekhat now!" Tully ordered. "Forget trying to save one for the science guys," he added as an afterthought. "Just nail them."

Three Jao and three humans moved up with the heavy recoilless rifles, while the rest of the jinau cleared the back blast lanes. Tully watched as they quickly and methodically eliminated the floating Ekhat. Even one of those monsters couldn't shrug off the impact of an explosive charge.

Tully saw someone move up beside him from the corner of his eye. His display showed the symbol for First Sergeant Luff. They watched the jinau absorb and overwhelm the remnants of the final charge. Many of the slaves were taken out by the explosions that finished off the Ekhat. But capturing those few that remained in one piece turned out to be a bit of a challenge.

"Looks like we need to schedule some zero-gee drills, Colonel," Luff said finally.

"Yep," Tully responded. "See to it after we get back, Top."

"Yes, sir."

"It's all over but the reports," Tully said to the officers. "Major Liang, get us back on board."

"On it, Colonel."

"*Ban Chao* has separated from the World Harvester, Fleet Commander," reported *Lexington*'s sensor officer.

Caitlyn sat up straight at the news she had been waiting to hear. "What success did they have?" she asked. *And is Gabe alive?* was unspoken for the moment.

"Colonel Tully reports nine Ekhat slaves captured and an estimated thirteen Ekhat and an unknown number of slaves killed in the fighting. Six jinau dead, fifteen injured."

Caitlyn relaxed, and looked up to see a grin on Caewithe Miller's face that looked to be a match for the one she felt stretching across her own visage.

She looked around as Dannet gestured. "Finish it," the fleet commander said.

The three battleships moved in concert like a lion pride, closing on the wounded Ekhat vessel.

CHAPTER 7

The World Harvester was lying naked in space, helpless before the fleet. That didn't stop the lasers of the three battleships from carving it into pieces, helped along by a variety of explosions from within. It wasn't long before a last titanic explosion broke the ship into three unequal pieces that slowly spun away from each other.

"Subordinate ships, guard the remains of the World Harvester," Dannet ordered. "Support ships and *Vercingetorix*, rejoin the fleet."

Caitlin unstrapped from her seat and got to her feet. For a moment, she felt lightheaded, but it passed. "So when will we be ready to leave this system?" she asked Dannet.

The fleet commander turned to face her. "Not yet, Director Kralik. The fleet still has one task remaining."

Caitlin was surprised. She'd figured that since the Ekhat ships were destroyed, they could leave. "And that is?"

Dannet waved a hand at the main viewscreen, where the image of a planet was on display. "To make sure there are no Ekhat left in the system." She turned to the communications officer. "Battleships take formation Gamma Rho again, head for that planet, prepare for bombardment."

Caitlin shook her head for a moment, as if to settle her brain. The thought that there was still fighting to do had definitely caught her off guard. She walked over to stand next to Lieutenant Vaughan's station.

"There are Ekhat on that planet?" she asked quietly.

"Looks like it," the Welshman replied. "Sensors show something that might be either a small city or a midsized military post by our standards."

"Damn," Caitlin muttered.

It took some time for the fleet to close on the planet, but well before they arrived in orbit *Lexington*'s sensors confirmed first of all that the planet was another that had been stripped almost to bedrock by Ekhat sterilizations, and second that there was some kind of Ekhat facility or post under a dome near the shore of a lifeless sea.

Dannet looked over to her aide. "Can *Vercingetorix* launch its bombardment weapons?" The Fleet Commander was not one to indulge in the Terran "humanization" of tools; ships were "it," not "she" to Dannet.

Vaughan touched a pad on his console. "They report no damage to those weapons systems."

Dannet turned to the communications officer. "Orders to *Vercingetorix*: launch all bombardment weapons at the Ekhat base. Orders to *Arjuna*: prepare to launch bombardment weapons; wait for my order."

Caitlin leaned over to Vaughan. "Is the fleet

commander going to order the ships to gather plasma balls from the sun?"

"No," Vaughan hissed back.

"Why not?"

"Because it's a stupid weapon."

Both Wrot and Dannet glanced over at them. Vaughan gave a quick cutting motion with his hand, and returned his full attention to his panel.

Caitlin stepped back by her bodyguards, just that little bit miffed. "If it's so stupid a weapon," she muttered, "why do the Ekhat use it?"

"Because they are unsane," Tamt volunteered. "Everyone knows that."

"But that doesn't mean they're stupid," Caitlin replied. "Why would they use a stupid weapon?"

"Lieutenant Vaughan?" Dannet pronounced.

"Sir?"

"Provide an explanation to Director Kralik, so she will cease fretting."

Caitlin felt her face getting hot as she flushed. Vaughan beckoned to her, so he wouldn't have to leave his console. She stalked over, trailed by Tamt and Captain Miller.

"Sorry to have my stupid question interrupting your work, Lieutenant, but I really would like to understand why the Ekhat would use a stupid weapon."

"It's not a stupid question," Vaughan said, touching a couple of pads on his console before he looked up at her, "and the short answer is nobody knows. Everyone blames it on the Ekhat being crazy, but really, nobody knows for sure."

"So why is it a stupid weapon?"

"It's a terror weapon," the Welshman said, "and

like many terror weapons, it's very inefficient. The plasma ball that landed on China did a lot of damage, granted. But all the post-strike analyses that've been done in the last couple of years indicate that the damned thing almost missed."

"Missed its target?"

"No," Vaughan replied, "missed the Earth."

Caitlin's jaw dropped.

"Really," Vaughan maintained. "Combining our records with what we can collect from the Jao, it looks like the ball was probably taken from as deep in the sun as the Ekhat can extend their shields, probably down to the level where the plasma is near the density of molten iron. Then they pulled out a ball of somewhere around ninety kilometers diameter, and they trundled that off to the planet they wanted to bombard—in this case, Earth.

"Each ball had so much mass, they could barely contain it in their shields, and they could barely move it with their ships. Ekhat ships are not inferior to the ships the Jao had at the time they attacked us. Didn't you wonder why it took so long for the Ekhat ship to arrive at Earth, when the Jao ships could make the trip faster? As it is, one ship overstrained its systems, lost shield containment and was vaporized by its own plasma ball. If we'd had the *Lexington* in service back then, the second ship probably would never have made it close to earth. It was moving slow enough that the kinetic weapons should have punished it to the point where the same thing would have happened to it."

"No one ever pointed that out to me before," Caitlin said. "What else didn't they tell me?"

"It gets crazier," Flue said. "The Ekhat don't have a way to aim a plasma ball."

"What?" Caitlin exclaimed. "That's crazy!"

"What I said," Flue grinned. "They carry the ball along until they're near the planet they're attacking. In our case, they were just inside the stratosphere. Then they drop the shields around the ball and take their ship someplace else, leaving the ball to fall and land wherever. Our damage was bad enough, but if they had waited longer to release the ball, the destruction would have been much greater and more widespread. The plasma lost a lot of energy just spreading out and interacting with the atmosphere before it hit the ground."

"You said they almost missed."

"Yes." Vaughan sobered. "They actually came in at a slight angle, and like I said, they let the ball loose higher than would have been optimum. It was almost an ocean strike because of that, and if it had been even a few more degrees off of vertical, it might well have just roared through the atmosphere and back into space. Either one of those would have really messed up the wind and weather patterns, maybe even more than the land strike actually did, but they wouldn't have done the damage that really happened."

"So it's a stupid weapon because they can barely control it and they can't aim it well," Caitlin said.

"Correct. They could have done as much damage with a handful of hydrogen bombs or a couple of big asteroid bolides, easier and with greater precision."

"So they're crazy."

Flue nodded with another grin.

"So what are we going to use instead?"

The Welshman turned and touched a couple of pads on his console. A display lit up.

"That," he said, pointing to the display.

Caitlin looked at the picture. "A missile?"

"No," Flue said. "That is a super-penetrator. Twenty meters long, two meters in diameter, titanium shell, a mass of depleted uranium at the head of it, followed by a tactical nuclear or sub-nuclear charge, and powered by the smallest of the Jao space drives that we've yet been able to build. It's also got some rudimentary shield capability, but given its designed use, that's not so much of a big thing."

"Wow," Caitlin said, as Caewithe Miller gave a low whistle beside her. "So when did we get those?"

"They've been under development for a long time; since right after the conquest. In secret, of course. That was all wishful thinking, naturally, but even among the techies there were some diehard rebels. But when Aille became governor and the R&D firms got access to the Jao tech-base, the plans got pulled out, dusted off, and updated. There was one test on a sizable asteroid with a subnuclear charge, which created a cloud of fast moving gravel, then it went to production. They had a dozen ready for us right before the fleet began searching." He shrugged. "It was one of those 'just in case' weapons, and although no one, Dannet included, expected to need them, no officer worth his paycheck is ever going to turn down an available weapon."

Flue's head twitched, then he touched a console control and looked up at the main viewscreen. "And now we get to see it in action."

Caitlin focused on the screen, which had split to show two different pictures. "What's this showing me?"

"One is a feed from a camera on the penetrator itself, and the other is from a camera on one of the ships," Flue replied. Both pictures began to change as the penetrator began to move. "It's designed to start out slowly, then kick into high gear when the onboard sensors get a good lock on the defined target and the most direct path to it."

Caitlin let the rest of her questions die. There was no sound in the command deck. Everyone was observing the launch.

The penetrator missile started out slowly, as Flue had said it would. There was a blue glow from the aft end, which seemed to fluctuate a bit as it maneuvered toward the planet. Maybe a quarter hour or so went by silently until the missile seemed to stop in one place and hover for a moment. For some reason Caitlyn was reminded of a hummingbird, which brought a smile to her face.

Suddenly the blue glow brightened almost tenfold, and the missile began moving again. Within seconds it was obviously hurtling along at multiples of its previous speeds. The missile almost disappeared from the external view until the camera adjusted, and the camera on the missile began to show some signs of vibration as it plunged into the atmosphere.

The target dome swelled almost as if it was a ball thrown at Caitlin's face. Within seconds, it filled the entire frame of view of the missile's camera.

The missile's side of the display went dark. Caitlin wrenched her eyes to the external view. She didn't see the missile strike, but she did see the hole made by the missile when it penetrated the dome.

For another couple of seconds nothing happened.

Then the dome seemed to jump. Cracks appeared in the dome material, and pieces of it fell inside. A large dust plume blew out of the holes.

It was surreal to watch the destruction in silence. Caitlin kept expecting to hear an earth-shattering kaboom, or a really long roll of thunder, or something. Nothing. Only destruction and upheaval in deafness. The Jao said nothing. Even the humans in the command deck remained silent.

The viewscreen split into three feeds: one remaining on the dome, and two more providing the same feeds as at first, only with a different missile. The drill was repeated.

This time Caitlin focused on the dome feed, and she was rewarded with a glimpse of the streak of the second missile as it penetrated the dome. As with the first, it punched straight through, followed by a second or two of no visible reaction, and finally the ground jumping under the dome. This time the dome collapsed altogether, and the dust plume was much larger.

Again the viewscreen reset with the three feeds as *Vercingetorix*'s third penetrator was launched. Again Caitlin was rewarded with the glimpse of the missile streaking to the impact. But this time, since the dome was gone, when the nuclear charge blew the watchers could see massive amounts of debris tossed into the sky, and now great holes were seen to be opening up beneath the remains of the Ekhat base. Much of the rubble and remnants of structures were collapsing and sliding into the holes.

After a few minutes, the dust plumes and rubble slides had stopped. The Ekhat base looked like nothing much more than a large gravel heap, with an occasional boulder scattered throughout.

One of the humans on the command deck began clapping. He was quickly joined by others. In a moment, they were all standing and clapping and cheering. Including Caitlin. *Payback for China.* Her mind visualized white Ekhat blood dripping from some of the stones and soaking into the dirt of the planet that the Ekhat had sterilized. That didn't bother her at all.

The Jao, of course, just shook their heads and adopted various postures like *disdain-for-foolishness*, or what might be expressed as *glad-that's-done.* But here and there on the command deck, Caitlin caught glimpses of *joy-at-judgment*, and Wrot was standing with a blatant *sly-enjoyment-at-another's-doom.*

Dannet, of course, was in her usual seemingly effortless *neutral.* The fleet commander had turned and was facing Caitlin, seemingly waiting for Caitlin to notice her. When she caught Caitlin's eyes, she spoke.

"This task is completed, Director Kralik. What are your directives for our next task?"

CHAPTER 8

At that moment, something crystallized in Caitlin's mind; something that she realized had been growing for some time.

"Fleet Commander Dannet . . ."

"Yes, Director Kralik?" Dannet had looked away for a moment, but her head swiveled back to face Caitlin. Her eyes were green, but her posture was very neutral. Not even one of her whiskers twitched.

"The fleet will return to Ares Base as soon as any emergency repairs are completed."

"As you instruct, Director." Caitlin listened, but found no trace of irony or sarcasm in the fleet commander's voice. Her angles were now expressing *dutiful-compliance*; her eyes were fading to black. Caitlin suspected that Dannet might not be happy with the command, but she still respected who had *oudh* in this mission. Even if it was a human.

The *Ban Chao*'s captain had brought the great craft to a halt some distance away from where the remnants of the World Harvester tumbled slowly through space. In his harness, Tully was drenched in sweat. He clutched his weapon even though the battle was over, there was no one left to fight, and they were safe—for the moment. Knowing that, though, and actually feeling it down in his marrow were two separate matters. He wasn't sure his heart rate would ever ease back down to normal.

They had raided a freaking Ekhat Death Star! Or at least, that's what it felt like. As of yet, he couldn't quite wrap his mind around that fact.

"Shit!" he said as he flipped his face-shield open. "I don't want to do that again anytime soon!" The faces of the six he'd lost from his command were burned behind his eyes. He was going to be seeing them in his sleep for months, he was sure.

Tully had been one of the last of the jinau to reboard the ship. Ahead of him he could see the troopers splitting up to head for their quarters, shrugging off their harnesses and starting to peel off parts of their suits. They were good protection, but the suits did get a little hot and gamey after a while.

"Do you know where we're going next, Colonel?" a gangly youth with shaggy black hair and a private's single stripe asked. One of his front teeth was broken. Tully cudgeled his memory for the boy's name.

Willis, he realized, Willis Ciappa, recruited out of one of the last of the rebel enclaves in the Appalachians.

"Not yet, Ciappa," Tully replied. "When I know, you'll know. We'll be leaving as soon as some repairs are done, though."

"What if the Ekhat follow us?" another soldier said,

this one a broad-shouldered sandy-haired female built like a truck.

"Frame travel doesn't work like that," he said, having had the same worries himself and secured an explanation some time ago. "It doesn't leave any kind of trail to follow. We would have had to tell them where we were going."

A nearby sergeant, one of the ones that General Kralik had provided, snorted. "Like that would happen!" Cold Bear, Tully's mind prompted him with the name. Joe Cold Bear, from North Dakota. He'd been one of Ed Kralik's original jinau troops, and the general had passed him on to Tully when he gave him his colonel's eagles.

The *Ban Chao* shuddered. Tully staggered, regained his balance, then tried to think about anything but the amount of damage they'd taken. "I'm going to check on the prisoners."

Ciappa shuddered. "They're a right despicable bunch," he said. "Serving the Ekhat like that. I'd rather be dead."

"They never had a choice," Tully said. "Just like we humans didn't have a choice once the Jao defeated us. They're victims, not collaborators."

"Hard to tell the difference sometimes," Ciappa muttered.

Tully caught the sergeant's eye and jerked his head. Cold Bear pushed the private toward their company quarters. "Private, go clean your weapon, go clean your suit, and for God's sake, go take a shower."

The sergeant led the protesting trooper away. Tully remembered thinking a lot of things himself about the Jao and the conquest when he was growing up in a rebel camp. Many (though not all) of those things turned out not to be true. Ciappa was just going to have to learn through experience. He'd signed up for this adventure; now he was having to live it.

Tully's stomach crawled as he made his way through the narrow hallways toward the Holding Area, which had been specially designed for prisoners. Supposedly it was secure enough to contain even an Ekhat, though Tully knew even if they caught one, it would just kill itself the first chance it got if they didn't drastically restrain it. The one they'd captured in the Valeron boarding action hadn't lasted long, despite all its limbs being burned off by lasers during the action. They'd gotten it back to Earth, but only barely. Tully hadn't gotten a straight story yet on how it had died; only some wildly contradictory and usually gory rumors. The freaking Ekhat were crazy enough that it may have eaten itself, for all he knew.

The *Ban Chao*'s massively armored hull was reportedly compromised in a dozen places, but its highly trained damage control squads were already on it. He heard banging and swearing in external compartments as he moved along. From what he'd heard over the com net, though, the damage was relatively minor, especially considering that they'd rammed a freaking dreadnought!

Six fully armed jinau stood outside the Holding Area. Tully peered into the observation window set into the wall beside the door. The aliens had been stripped of their suits, and now sprawled on the floor, entangled with each other. Their bodies were long and sinuous, and such a glossy deep black that they gleamed with iridescent highlights. They had short stubby arms and sleek narrow skulls. They were four-legged and built low to the ground. At the moment, they weren't moving. He guessed they were still alive, but it was hard to be sure.

"Any trouble here?" he asked the closest guard, a Jao wearing Terra taif's blue harness.

"We have watched them, but they do nothing but cower," the Jao said with a contemptuous flick of his ear. "They are not worth the energy it would take to kill them."

"They are slaves," Tully said. "I don't think they've ever had the chance to be anything better."

"Slaves cannot help us," the Jao said. "Only more and better ships; additional intelligent allies like the Lleix; beings that know how to protect themselves."

"From their close association with the Ekhat, they might have important information vital to our struggle against their former masters," Tully said, somewhat alarmed. "See that nothing happens to compromise their potential usefulness."

Fortunately, though the Jao were baffled by the concept of compassion, they thoroughly understood making oneself of use. It was one of their highest values. The guard's stance shifted into *reluctant-assent*. The others would take his lead, Tully knew.

Inside the Holding Area, the gleaming bodies shifted, slithering over one another in a fashion that reminded Tully all too strongly of snakes. He shuddered.

"They're still alive?" said a human voice from behind his shoulder. "That's a good sign."

He turned and met the gaze of Vikram Bannerji, who had put away his gun and armor and resumed his intelligence work. "At least they didn't pick up that particular meme from their masters," he said. "If they were Ekhat, they'd have all killed themselves by now."

Bannerji spread his hands on the thick observation glass and peered in. "I can't wait to interrogate them." Within, the clustered bodies shifted, as though aware of his interest. They buried their faces against one another's shimmering hide. "The things this lot might be able to tell us!"

Or not, Tully thought sourly. It was entirely possible they might be no more intelligent than a St. Bernard or no more able to communicate than a great ape. "When will you get started?" he said.

"As soon as I can get Ramt over here from the *Lexington*," Bannerji said with a trace of frustration. "She should be able to translate if they speak any of the known Ekhat dialects. If they have their own language, or some other Ekhat dialect, she'll be able to learn it faster than I can."

The young lieutenant looked around at Tully. "I think they belonged to one of the subfactions of the Complete Harmony." His eyes glittered behind his glasses. "They might even be the same subfaction that upraised the Jao into sentience."

The *Ban Chao* shuddered.

"What was that?" Bannerji said, looking back over his shoulder. His face paled.

"Maybe a bit of debris," Tully said.

"Oh." Bannerji turned back to the window. His hands shook a bit; although how he could have any nerves left after what they'd just been through, Tully didn't know. "I thought maybe we were under attack again."

Tully looked at the unresponsive aliens again, then clapped Bannerji on the shoulder. "Keep me posted,

Lieutenant. Anything happens with these things—anything at all—you notify me ASAP."

"Yes sir, Colonel."

Tully's pad rang with a com call just as he was almost out of his suit. One of the enlisted jinau helped him get free of it, and he grabbed the pad.

"Tully here."

"Colonel, you might want to come up to the command deck."

Tully recognized the voice of Shan Liang, his executive officer.

"I'll be up as soon as I scrape the stink off."

"Actually, Gabe, I think you want to get here ASAP if you don't want to miss it."

Shan's use of his first name told Tully that whatever was in the air, it wasn't anything very official or touching on the jinau. Curiosity intrigued, Tully replied, "On my way, then."

Jinau and crewmen made way for Tully. He was, after all, both the senior jinau officer in the fleet and a member of the personal service of Aille krinnu ava Terra. He had to snicker when he remembered just how high he had come, and just how much trouble he had caused Aille in that rise.

When he entered the command deck, Vanta-Captain Ginta krinnu vau Vanta motioned him over to stand with him and Major Liang in front of the *Ban Chao*'s main view display.

"They found an Ekhat base on the fourth planet, Colonel Tully," Ginta said. "Dannet is about to deal with it." The captain's body was angled in a posture Tully didn't recognize. Not officially. But he thought that *hunger-for-revenge* probably expressed it. No Jao alive would not be excited to see large numbers of Ekhat removed from the universe.

Tully understood that attitude very well. Once you got through the frou-frou manners and all the funny body language, most Jao were pretty basic folks, he'd decided. At least in most respects. Like this one. As it happened, he agreed with them; the fewer Ekhat in the universe, the better off the universe would be.

Tully and Liang watched in silence as the penetrator missiles were sent into the dome one at a time. At the end of the exercise, they and the other humans on the command deck celebrated, just as all the human crew in the fleet celebrated.

After the noise died down, Ginta looked at Tully and said, "We will remain in the system long enough to make necessary repairs, then Director Kralik has ordered that we return to Ares Base."

"How long before we jump?" Tully asked.

Ginta gave the shrug adopted from the humans. "When flow is right. Perhaps one or two of your days. Let your jinau clear the decks away."

And interrogate the prisoners, Tully thought, or at least try to. He just hoped it wasn't going to be like having a conversation with a malfunctioning lamp.

Tully supervised the interrogation of their prisoners. Or what passed for an interrogation. It looked like more of a joke to him, something like trying to have a conversation with an earthworm just before you used it to bait the hook.

Vikram Bannerji had directed the guards to separate one of their slithery guests and isolate it in a separate room. The table had been replaced with an ordinary chair for Vaughan and a bench for the Lleix, Ramt, who was to do the translating. Ramt had been observing the aliens' interaction for hours each day, trying to absorb the scant verbalizations they uttered on their own.

She reported that they seemed to use both a basic Ekhat dialect and their own language, which of course made some sense. The Ekhat were not going to pollute their exalted minds with a slave species language, but the slaves would still have their own tongue.

The shimmering black beast rushed about the room, trying to find another of its fellows. Bannerji and Ramt let it run its fear out, hoping evidently that it would eventually calm.

Finally it knocked Bannerji into the wall, but that seemed to frighten it even more and it cowered into a corner.

"Slave creature," Ramt said in an Ekhat dialect, "calm yourself."

Tully and Bannerji both had programmed their pocket coms to translate.

The beast ducked its head and seemed to be trying to fold in upon itself.

"How is your kind designated by the masters?" Ramt said.

It did not answer, just burrowed harder.

"Answer, worthless wretch!" Ramt said. "By what name does the Complete Harmony designate your kind?"

It collapsed to the floor, quivering.

Ramt glanced over at the observation window. "Continue," Tully said. "We can't give up that easily. They will talk to us—eventually."

The interrogation went on for two more hours. The

slave never once made any kind of meaningful vocalization. They finally joined Tully in the observation room.

"I recommend that we put it back with its fellows," Bannerji said, "and observe it then. Perhaps it will at least try to tell them where it's been and what happened to it."

"They are worthless," Ramt said, "just semi-mindless trash the Ekhat use and then throw away."

"They will not be worthless to us," Tully said, crossing his arms. "I will not allow it."

Bannerji glanced at him. "Yes, sir," he said and snapped off a salute. "We'll make these suckers work for us, no matter what it takes."

Tully nodded. If they could make the rebels on Earth turn their hands to work with the Jao, they could make a few beaten down Ekhat slaves see it their way too. It was just a matter of time and persistence... and the right approach, he thought ruefully, rubbing his neck where Yaut used to grab him to throw him where he was supposed to be.

Glimnitz shuddered as the loathsome pink and brown creatures dragged him back to his fellows and shoved him inside the sterile room. His fellow Trīkē swarmed him, pressing their lengths to his in a futile attempt to find comfort. Alas, there was no comfort outside the sphere of the Great Ones. There was no joy if one could not serve until the moment of the next note and then the next. No songs existed in this terrible place. They could look forward to nothing but death.

"What do they want with us?" Solvaya asked, an undersized female. She was faulty, having torn off a leg in the battle and now had trouble walking.

"They ask questions," Glimnitz said as the rest crowded in for comfort. "Questions and questions about the Great Masters!"

She limped back and forth at the edges of the group, unable to draw nearer. "Did you answer?"

"As soon as they have what they want from us, we will be spaced, you can be sure of that," Glimnitz said. "Silence is our best protection. Tell them nothing. Eventually the Great Ones will find this ship and destroy it themselves. Then we will all be at peace, knowing we have done our best."

In the event, it took nearly three days for the fleet to achieve readiness to leave. *Vercingetorix* had by far the worst damage, and was accordingly the last vessel to be ready.

While the fleet waited on the battleship's repairs, Tully spent most of his time with Lieutenant Bannerji and the Lleix Ramt in the interrogations of the Ekhat slaves.

Attempted interrogations, that is.

Down on the lower deck, the squirmy Trīkē were still not talking to anyone but each other. Ramt was making progress translating their vocalizations, but not nearly as much as she would have if they would speak *with* her too. They weren't like real individuals, she thought, as she tracked comments and responses around the room. What one thought, they evidently all thought. They could embellish upon a statement, modify it, expand it, but they seemed utterly unable to contradict an idea once it had been expressed.

Was that an artifact of their slave status? Ramt edged closer to the one-way glass. Had the Ekhat bred the ability to even conceive of opposition out of these pathetic creatures? She made notations on her pad, thinking how to turn this to their advantage.

She keyed the intercom on. "Report on condition!" she barked in Ekhat.

The Trīkē hesitated, clumped in the center of the detention chamber. "Master?" one of them chirped, then they were all abasing themselves, falling to the floor, squirming over and under one another.

"Report!" she said again.

"This is a dreadful place," one, larger than the rest, said. "Take us back to the divine Ekhat! Let us serve the true song again!"

"You shall go nowhere until you report!" Ramt said, trying to evoke the hatefulness of a true Ekhat.

"It is cold here," the Trīkē said, "and oh so very bright! Our eyes burn and there is no work. We are desolate with nothing to do."

They could adjust the temperature and lighting, Ramt thought. Work was another matter. "Your work," she said, suddenly struck by a notion, "your current assignment, is to converse with our new slaves, the Lleix. Teach them how to speak properly and how to work for the Ekhat."

The iridescent black bodies stilled. "Then we will hear the next note?"

"You will hear it as soon as I do," Ramt said, then shut off the intercom. First, she would have conditions altered more to their liking, then she would present herself inside their detention chamber and see if she had at last found a way around their all too natural cautions.

✧ ✧ ✧

Even Caitlin Kralik came over from the *Lexington* to observe the captives. She watched Lieutenant Bannerji and Ramt work with the Trīkē, as they'd learned the sinuous black aliens called themselves.

"They may actually be quite low on the intelligence scale for species," Bannerji said. "They don't seem to be able to conceive of an existence where they are not slaves."

"Then, for now," Caitlin said, "they should consider themselves our slaves. We can worry about liberating them later."

Bannerji stared at her. "That's—" He shook his head. "That's—genius. It just might work."

He nodded at the door. "Ramt and I will try that."

The Lleix joined him as he slipped through door. Inside the detention chamber, the Trīkē rushed to the back wall and cowered in a sinuous pile of sleek, iridescent black bodies.

The wretched creatures were coming after them again! Trīkē 10988, also known as Solvaya, cowered against the wall. Why did they not decently kill their captives? Trīkē had no purpose outside the divine Ekhat. Their magnificent ship was gone. The great note being composed by their masters was left unsung, choked off into nothingness before it could be broadcast. There were no Ekhat here to slaughter them for failing to win the battle as was right and needful. So it was not even left to them to die well and please their masters in that way.

The two aliens who came into the room were different from one another in many respects but alike in their stiffness. They spoke the Divine Language. The masters, Solvaya remembered from the few times he had been granted a glimpse, had been quite stiff too.

"Slaves," the smaller one said in a piping voice, "you will speak to us."

They piled themselves against the wall, diving under and under one another, trying to conceal themselves from the alien wrongness that had invaded their space.

"You were the Ekhat's slaves," the other stiff creature said. "They are dead. Now, you are our slaves and you will speak to us!"

Solvaya was forced out by the bodies of her fellows. For a moment, there was nowhere to hide. She was painfully exposed.

The smaller alien stepped closer. It had coverings of some sort draped over it, a false hide, as though it was molting. Disgusting!

The larger one prowled near. "What are your duties?"

Solvaya could not think; she was so afraid.

"Report!" the stiff ones said. "Report!"

"We run the ship," the Trīkē said. "We service the engines, adjust the controls, but mostly we wait for the next Divine Note."

"Good," the smaller one said. "You are our slaves now."

"Where is our work?" Solvaya replied in a low tone. "Will you sing one of the great notes when victory is achieved?"

"Perhaps," the smaller one said, "if you work hard."

"Where is our work?" Trīkē 31766 said from behind. "What shall we do to please our new masters?"

"Where is our work?" the others babbled together. "Where is our work?"

"Your first work is to talk to us in your native tongue," the smaller one said. "Then we will see."

"Talk?" they echoed.

"Tell us of the Ekhat ship," the creature said. "Tell us of your duties."

So Trīkē 10988 sat on the floor, folded her stubby arms, and began to explain.

CHAPTER 9

Dannet had ordered that all but a skeleton crew be transferred from *Vercingetorix*. If the wounded ship didn't survive the framepoint jump, she wanted as many of the crew to survive as possible. So it was on the third day after the battle that, crew transfers completed, the fleet moved well away from the dead planet and the debris fields of the battles and, one ship at a time, activated their jump procedures and left the nameless system where long ago the Ekhat had raped a world of its life-forms, and where recently the universe had returned the favor.

Dead Ekhat floated in dead ships in space before the dead planet, almost like retributional offerings on an altar before a dead god. On the fourth planet the fragments of dead Ekhat were slowly mummifying from the cold and near-vacuum in the wreckage of their base.

The universe's tutelage on the consequences of hubris was harsh.

CHAPTER 10

A starship appeared in the depths of the sun. Slowly it clawed its way from the plasma, through the corona, out into empty space.

Third-Mordent almost cringed. The dissonance! What had occurred here? Descant-at-the-Fourth had built such strong harmony in this system, and now it was gone, replaced by dissonance that shrieked. What had happened?

Slowly the small Ekhat ship moved away from the sun, slave crew lashed by Third-Mordent's tongue and not infrequently directed by blows. Bit by bit they gathered information: no active ships in the system, large debris fields where none existed before, ship fragments slowly spinning through space.

Third-Mordent almost broke when they found the wreckage of the World Harvester. To know that Descant-at-the-Fourth, one of her own collateral ancestors, was gone . . . it almost put her own song away.

Then they discovered the planet.

Ekhat do not pale, or blanch. But Third-Mordent's tegument lost sheen; so much so that the next-highest Ekhat on the ship sang a query.

Third-Mordent's response was slow in coming. "We return. This account must be taken to our harmony masters."

For once her song was quiet. "Someone has dared to break our harmony. There will be a price for this."

Soon the Ekhat ship left the system.

Dead ships still floated in space. Wisps of rarefied atmosphere touched lightly on rubble on a dead planet.

PART II
Into the Dark

CHAPTER 11

The voyage to the system containing Ares Base would take four jumps. Or rather, it was supposed to take four jumps. However, when the fleet finished arriving in the third target system of the jump series, *Vercingetorix* reported a problem. Caitlin didn't try to follow the technical discussion of the engineer techs any farther than to figure out that it was a problem with the jump technology, it wasn't major, but it would take a while to repair and the battleship wasn't going anywhere until the repair was done.

So the fleet settled into a stable orbit around the planetless sun and waited on the fleet's techs to get the battleship fixed. As soon as that was accomplished, Caitlin summoned Fleet Commander Dannet and the other top officers of the expedition to her ready room.

It was time to admit reality. The expedition had not borne fruit in the fashion hoped for, with the discovery of more technologically able alien allies, so their primary goal was unattained. On the other hand, they had struck a real blow against the Ekhat. Of course, the Ekhat were really going to be pissed now.

Caitlin sighed. Like they hadn't been pissed before. They'd been destroying sentient species across the galaxy for thousands of years just because they were bat-crazy. She didn't think it was possible to make them *worse*.

"How long will it take to make the necessary repairs?" she asked Fleet Commander Dannet.

The big Jao flicked an ear, her jaw angled in *faint-concern*. "They will be done when they are done," Dannet said.

She waved a hand at Lieutenant Vaughan, who added, "Preliminary estimate of three days, Director."

Caitlin let her own angles go to *appreciative-of-effort*. The four Lleix present gazed at her with their black eyes, but said nothing, clearly unable to perceive the under-message of the moment.

"I see," she said carefully. "Do we have any word on the prisoners yet?"

"Not much," Tully said. "Ramt and Lieutenant Bannerji are just now managing to get them to communicate with us. So far, about the only thing they've been able to confirm is that the ships we defeated were under control of a faction of the Complete Harmony. Bannerji thinks that it may even be the same faction that uplifted the Jao to sentience so long ago."

A ripple went through the room at that thought. Jao ears flicked and Jao lines slid into complicated postures.

"I called this meeting because it's time to reassess our plans." Caitlin moved on to the main point of the meeting. "The results of our entire exploration program, culminating in the events in our last exploratory jump, have pretty well established that it's pointless to continue down the Orion Arm of this galaxy toward its center. The fact that we ran into an Ekhat world is just one more indication that there are probably no surviving non-Ekhat species on this side of Jao/human space."

"Certainly not within practical travel distance," Wrot concurred. "And the possibilities of finding anyone helpful outward from us are almost nonexistent."

There was a long moment of silence. Humans nodded or looked down. Jao shifted through a variety of postures, most ending in variations of *waiting-agreement.*

"That's one of the reasons I've ordered the fleet back to Ares Base," Caitlin continued. "Plus we've been on the move for months, and after that series of battles, we need to resupply and rearm, if nothing else. One of the things that will also be done while we're at the base is to determine the fleet's next course of action, but I'd like some feedback and input from you right now on that thought. I realize that you haven't had long to think about it, but give me your thoughts, please."

Caitlin looked around the table. "Any suggestions on a new path forward?" she asked.

Krant-Captain Mallu shifted in his seat, looking *thoughtful*. "We could travel along the Sagittarius Arm instead," he said after a moment.

"That would be difficult to initiate," Fleet Commander Dannet said. "The distance between the two galactic arms is much greater than the distance ships normally jump using the Frame Network."

Caitlin schooled her body to reveal nothing but *anticipation-of-success*. "Solutions?"

Mallu flicked an ear, dropping his gaze to hint at *modesty*. "We can retrace our jump routes back toward Terra until we find a scattering of stars in the gap that will allow us to cross. This method employs a single ship to lead the way by using the Point Locus created by the entire Fleet's FP generators. After that initial ship makes a successful transit, it serves as the anchor point for the rest of the fleet to cross over."

Caitlin frowned. It sounded risky. Subsequent discussion followed that theme. No one disagreed that it was conceivable, even feasible. But more than one of the ship captains indicated that the risk of loss would be higher than in their voyages to date.

Matto, the elder and larger of the Lleix Starsifters *elian* members with the fleet, spoke up. "There are trails of stars between the two arms. Between our records and those of the Jao and Terrans, we can identify the best route. Others will have to make risk decisions after that."

At the end of the discussion, Tully keyed something into his pad, and looked up. "It's either that or go home without achieving our objective," he said.

And Jao did not honor those who tried and failed, Caitlin thought to herself, no matter how great the effort. It was important to all from Terra taif, most especially the humans on this expedition, for Caitlin and the search to do well if they wanted their taif to retain a continuing voice in the leadership of their world.

"All right," Caitlin said, slipping into the angles of *calm-assurance*. "We will meet again on this after we return to Ares Base." She moved to *firm-resolution*. "In the meantime, we will all study this potential course of action and see if we can find problems with it. It's better to deal with those before they happen."

As the others stood and headed for the door, the Lleix blinked at Caitlin with their narrow black eyes. Their necks curved gracefully. Lim of the Terralore *elian* gazed at her. "If we are to function as requested, we need further unrestricted access to ship's databanks," the Lleix said in her fluting voice.

"I thought you already had it," Caitlin said in surprise.

"No." Lim said nothing more, twitching a fold of her colorful robes to make them drape even more perfectly.

"I will look into it," Caitlin said.

The four Lleix left in a single file, trooping solemnly like ducklings headed for a pond, Starsifters *elian* in the lead.

"What was all that about?" Tully said as the rest left.

"I don't know," Caitlin said. "Who would have restricted the Lleix's access?"

"I did," Dannet said, rising to her feet.

Caitlin let her neck bend to a subtle indication of *inquiry?*

"They have been prying further than their needs would seem to require," Dannet said. "They are outsiders after all with a long history of, admittedly rightfully, distrusting the Jao. There is always the possibility at least one or more of the Lleix expedition personnel wish us and our mission harm."

Caitlin gazed steadily at Dannet krinnu ava Terra, once of the famed kochan of Narvo. No one who had lived through mad Oppuk's rule of Earth could ever forget that; to the humans who survived that rule, Narvo's fame was rather infamy.

Dannet gazed back, her body perfectly still, and for once, perfectly neutral.

"Due to events in Earth's past, *I* might have had good reason to wish you harm," Caitlin said carefully, "but you know I do not."

"You are human," Dannet said. "Humans are prey to many logical inconsistencies, but emotional subterfuge is seldom one of your weaknesses. Once you make up your minds, you rarely change them."

That was a compliment of a sort. Caitlin's lips twisted into a wry smile. "Give the Lleix unrestricted access again," she said finally, "but have a digest sent to me every day on what data they mine. I will keep an eye on them myself while the rest of the crew is making themselves of use in more practical ways."

Dannet nodded, then shifted into the tri-partite *compliance-with-command-received.*

Repairs were made; more slowly than Caitlin had hoped, but best to get it right—a mistake could cost big later. It took four days, not three, but in the end everything that could be fixed outside of a dry dock was taken care of.

Caitlin again was on the command deck when the word came that *Vercingetorix* was as ready to travel as she was going to be. Dannet looked to her with an abbreviated form of *inquiry* implied in the tilt of her head and the position of her ears. Caitlin responded with a human nod, which flowed into a simple *approval.* After all, she thought to herself, nothing said that every posture had to be eloquent and elegant. Sometimes simple was good.

Maybe it was just her imagination, but the build-ups to the jumps during the return hadn't seemed as trying as the jump had been into the system where they'd eliminated the Ekhat fleet and outpost. There was probably a reason for that, but she didn't know what it was. One of these days, she decided, she really needed to get at least the high school version of jump science.

The ship was doing some vibrating, true, and the loud hum had built up. Caitlin watched as Captain Uldra stood behind the technology stations on the command deck, head cocked, either listening to the sounds, or waiting for the flow to complete, or both. Whatever he was waiting for, it apparently arrived because he straightened and said, "You may jump, Navigator Annen."

There was that same infinite second that Caitlin always felt, where all her senses seemed to be short-circuited and cross-wired, then they dropped back into space. Since Ares base was connected to the Jao Frame Portal network, they didn't have to emerge from the jump inside a star. That didn't bother Caitlin at all. It always seemed a bit odd to her to feel relieved that she was now sitting inside a stellar blast furnace.

Moments after *Lexington* broke into clear space, the sensor officer announced, "Ares system confirmed. Ares Base thirty-seven degrees port from axis. Challenge received from guard fleet."

"Announce the arrival of the fleet," Dannet ordered, "and request orbit instructions. Let them know we will proceed when the rest of the fleet arrives."

Dannet's ears were flipped back, and there was a hint of *displeasure* about her posture. Caitlin suspected that it had more to do with having to issue specific detailed orders than anything else. But with human and integrated Jao/human crews, Dannet couldn't rely on all crew members having *wrem-fa* muscle memory to know almost instinctively what had to be done.

The fleet commander stood back from the workstations, hands clasped behind her back in a human-influenced *waiting* position, angles otherwise sharp and clean, letting Terra-Captain Uldra do his job without her interference as the other ships appeared from the corona one by one.

Caitlin moved up beside her and adopted a similar position. After a moment, Dannet spoke in a tone barely loud enough to be heard.

"Is this going to be the end of the exploration expedition?"

Caitlin snorted. "No. To paraphrase a Terran English leader from a few generations back, 'This is not the beginning of the end, but the end of the beginning.' We will be going back out."

Dannet said nothing for a long while. When she finally replied, she used only one word.

"Good."

CHAPTER 12

Ares system always looked odd to Tully. The star involved was a smallish red giant, so that was different from Terra's system right away. The system had several planets but no Terra equivalent: There were two small rocky orbs near the sun, and two Jovians and a super-Jovian farther out. The smallest of the Jovians was still larger than Terra system's Jupiter. It orbited just barely outside the liquid water zone of the system. It, of course, was not accessible by humans or Jao. However, it did have a truly impressive suite of moons, including one that was in the Triton class.

Given the name of the system, it was no surprise that the planets were given names that had associations with Ares in Greek mythology. The Triton moon was named Enyo, for the sister of Ares, goddess of war and bloodshed. The planet it circled was named Alala, for the goddess of the war-cry. The super-Jovian got the mouth-twister name of Kydoimos, demon of the din of battle, and the other Jovian was labeled

Polemos, a war spirit who was another brother of Enyo and father of Alala.

The two rocks near the sun received a couple more of the mouth-twisters. The closest to the sun was named Proioxis, or Onrush, and the other was Palioxis, or Backrush.

Tully just muttered whenever he saw the display or a schematic of the system. "Why can't they just give planets regular names? What's wrong with naming a planet 'Fred'?"

"Did you say something, sir?" First Sergeant Luff asked.

"No. Just muttering."

Luff was silent for a few moments, then said, "Pity they can't name these planets something easier to wrap your tongue around."

Tully just chuckled.

Ares Base had been established on Enyo. Tully was surprised to see just how much it had grown since they had last been there. The view out the boarding tube viewports as he debarked the shuttle right behind Caitlin Kralik was nothing short of impressive. But that shouldn't be surprising, he realized. The system was becoming the arsenal of the human/Jao armadas that were on various drawing boards. It was going to have to be big.

He and Luff followed Caitlin and her bodyguards down the boarding tube and through a massive double door that wasn't quite an airlock but definitely would seal the opening off at need. At that moment, Caitlin sprinted down the hallway until she was close enough to leap into her husband's arms.

Ed Kralik—Lieutenant General Ed Kralik, to Tully

and Luff—caught his wife and held her with apparent effortless ease as he proceeded to kiss her very thoroughly. Neither one of them showed any signs of coming up for air any time soon.

Tully chuckled again as he followed the bodyguards past the fervent embrace. "Get a room, Caitlin," he called back over his shoulder. Caewithe Miller laughed, and a couple of the human bodyguards gave snorts and sneezes that sounded suspiciously like choked-off laughs.

Caitlin finally released her kiss and stretched her toes down until they reached the ground. Then she snuggled into Ed's embrace.

"Missed you."

"Missed you," he replied.

She leaned back and looked at her husband. Despite the warm smile on his face, there was also an air of calculation. "So, how long until we can find a bed?"

Ed burst out laughing. It was so infectious that Caitlin finally joined in.

Caewithe Miller arose to full consciousness slowly. After a time of drifting near the boundary of sleep, she finally opened her eyes and stretched. Her lips curled in a smile; it was nice to be off *Lexington*, even if the room they'd given her at Ares base wasn't quite as nice as her room on the ship. Just four walls, a ceiling, and a floor, with a built-in bunk along one wall. But it was a different four walls, ceiling, and floor than she'd been staring at for most of the last year, so she was good with that.

Even better than that, her whole security team had been given three days' leave. Granted, it was on Ares base where there wasn't a whole lot to do yet, but just being able to sleep until she woke up was near-heaven, and not being on immediate call as Director Kralik's chief bodyguard was absolute joy. She loved working for Caitlin, but it still was nice to not feel tied to her, even for as short a time as three days.

Caewithe rolled out of the bunk and padded to the fresher on bare feet. After a quick shower and passing a depilatory wipe over her arms and legs, she picked out the loudest, loosest, and least uniformlike clothes she had and headed out to find some breakfast.

According to her com pad, there was an officer's mess down . . . there it was. Once inside, Caewithe headed for the nearest beverage dispenser and punched for a cup of Irish Breakfast tea. Hanging around with Flue Vaughan had led her to develop a taste for different kinds of tea, and she had really come to like this one. And despite what Flue usually proclaimed, she didn't think the dispenser formulations were all that bad. She sniffed of it. Smelled like tea to her.

"Caewithe!"

Hearing her name, she turned to see Vaughan himself sitting at a table in the farthest corner with a Jao whose dark russet pelt marked him as one of Krant kochan and whose *vai camiti* looked vaguely familiar. He waved her over as the Jao stood and moved past her with a nod. She took her cup over and settled into a chair at Flue's table, propping her feet up on another chair.

"Going native, are you?" Flue grinned.

"As long as they'll let me," Caewithe replied. "If I could, I'd be in a lounge chair out on a beach somewhere soaking up sun and drinking mai-tais one after another."

Flue shuddered. "Barbarian. Fruity drinks with little paper umbrellas. No class at all."

"Nope." Caewithe grinned, then nodded toward the door. "Who was that? He looked familiar."

"Jalta krinnu ava Krant, second in command on *Pool Buntyam*, and one of the best sensor techs in the fleet. We were discussing some differences between their instruments and *Lexington*'s."

Caewithe felt momentarily stupid; she'd been around Jalta several times. She should have remembered him.

She looked at Vaughan. "You're in uniform. Not taking some time off?"

"Can't. The fleet commander has me running like I'm on a cricket pitch, one task after another."

"Too bad." Caewithe gave him a big smile.

Vaughan muttered something.

"What was that?" Caewithe asked.

"Nothing." Obviously searching to change the subject, Vaughan said, "I've been meaning to ask you—what's it like working for Director Kralik?"

"'Sfunny," Caewithe said, "I grew up thinking she was a world-class bitch, because every picture I saw of her and every story I heard or read talked about how she was always in the middle of the Jao."

"Yeah, I saw the same things," Flue said. "But then Aille took down Oppuk."

"I saw her just before that happened, with that Banle guard she had. She didn't look very happy then, and it was pretty obvious that Banle was there more to rein her in than to protect her." Caewithe shook her head. "I started thinking about it then, and decided that maybe she wasn't so far gone as I thought she was. Then I was there at the final showdown..."

"Where Tully executed Oppuk?"

"Yeah."

Flue grinned. "Man, I wish I could have been there! I mean, I've seen the video, but still..."

"I about freaked out when that Narvo elder called Tully out to do it. Yaut didn't have any trouble with it, though. Guess he knew Tully better than the rest of us. They call it 'putting down,' like putting a cat or dog to sleep when they get so bad they can't be helped." Caewithe shivered. "That's what Oppuk did a lot of, especially toward the end. He killed one of Caitlin's two older brothers, and just about killed her. That's what set Yaut off."

"Don't want to mess with Yaut," Flue said.

"Carve that on a moon somewhere, man."

They both laughed.

"Anyway, after that it was pretty clear that she was not what I thought she was, and when word got around that they were forming a guard detachment just for her, I applied for it. Didn't expect to be the commander, but you take what you can get."

"Amen to that," Flue said. "So what's she really like?"

"Just good people, Flue. About as nice as they come."

Vaughan had his mouth open for another question when his com pad pinged at him. "Okay, got to run. My next meeting is clear across the base."

He stood and slid the pad into a pocket. "See you tonight for dinner?"

Caewithe wrinkled her nose at him. "If I don't get a better offer, maybe."

They exchanged grins, and he headed out the door whistling. "Now," Caewithe mused, "I wonder if there's a poker game anywhere that a girl can sit in on?"

She began tapping on her com pad.

CHAPTER 13

Caitlin hadn't expected to have the search strategy meeting right away, but in the event it took over a week before she could gather all the people together she wanted. When she groused to Ed about it, he just laughed.

"Be glad you're getting them that soon," he said. "I've learned more about ships and supplies than I ever wanted to know since I took the base commander's job. I shoulda joined the navy. But the base is only partly functional, so the ships' crews are doing a lot of the loading and unloading of supplies. Even Tully's troops are having to bear a hand for this. And the ships' officers need to be available while that is going on, especially on the ships that need repairs."

"Speaking of repairs," Caitlin began.

"You're going to lose the *Vercingetorix,*" Ed said.

"Crap!"

"She just needs too much work that we can't do here." Ed continued. "In another year or so we'll have a shipyard that could service her, even as banged up as she is. Now, the best thing to do is ship her off to Earth."

"Isn't one of the Jao worlds closer?"

"Yeah," Ed replied. "But that ship is a bastard mix of Jao and Terran designs and technologies. There's no Jao yard that could handle her, even if they would. No, the *Ricky* will head for Earth as soon as they put a little more spit and super tape on her. Hopefully they've got something they can send to replace her."

"Yeah, for once that Jao time sense could come in handy," Caitlin quipped.

When the meeting finally happened, Caitlin decided to follow Jao flow patterns by letting the attendees enter the big conference room before she came in preceded by her primary bodyguards Tamt and Caewithe and her husband.

Only to the humans would it possibly have seemed strange that Ed Kralik was at the table for what was Caitlin's meeting. To the Jao, the fact that he was Caitlin's husband was immaterial. What mattered to them was he was the commander of Ares Base, and not incidentally and perhaps even more importantly, he was in the service of Aille krinnu ava Terra, governor of Terra and first kochan-father of Terra taif. In every way but one the base commander was the political and social equal of his wife. So he sat at the table by right.

The one way in which Ed was subordinate to Caitlin was the same reason she had been the one to call the meeting and why she entered the room last in the Jao manner: she alone had *oudh* over the search effort. Crusade might be a better word for it. But effort or crusade, regardless of what it was called, she alone was the leader, reporting directly to Preceptor Ronz, member of the strategy circle of the Jao Bond of Ebezon, the organization that stood as parent kochan to the cubling Terra taif. In this she perhaps even surpassed her service to Aille.

Caitlin suppressed those thoughts, along with an attendant shiver, as she took her seat between Ed and Wrot. She looked around the room. All the fleet's senior officers were there, including Tully and his executive officer and first sergeant. There were a few additional people in the room from the base staff: a senior Lleix elder named Narso from the Starsifters *elian* sat flanked by Brakan and Matto of the fleet's staff, and another elder named Gram was seated with Ramt of Ekhatlore. Pyr and Lim sat for Terralore, ignored by the Starsifters and somewhat acknowledged by Ekhatlore. Caitlin made a mental note that their plans for the integration of the members of the Lleix *dochaya* ghetto-class into mainstream Lleix society seemed to be lagging behind their integration into human/Jao society. If the Lleix elders weren't careful, they were going to lose them. The liberated *dochaya* members would assimilate into the Terra taif and leave the skeleton of Lleix society behind them.

She set that thought aside, with a note to return to it later, and tapped her finger on the table. The low murmur of side conversations halted, and everyone looked her way.

"In the absence of a directive from the Bond of Ebezon," Caitlin began, "we will continue with the search."

Heads nodded, and postures of *willing assent* were seen all around the room.

"But the efforts of the last two years have almost conclusively proven that we will not fulfill our search here in the Orion Arm."

She looked around the room to drive home her next point.

"I have *oudh* over this. I have decided. We will not continue our search here in the Orion Arm. We will go elsewhere."

Silence. No one spoke, although Jao after Jao adopted *obedience to directives* as their posture.

"In our last meeting, it was proposed that the search move to the Sagittarius Arm." Caitlin turned to the Starsifters. "You said that you would provide information as to possible Frame Jump paths between the two arms." She sat back in her seat and crossed her arms, visibly turning the focus of the meeting to the Lleix.

Narso, the base Starsifter elder, needed no further encouragement. He stood to speak, and his aureole flared to its greatest extent.

"We have gathered all information from Lleix records and Terra taif databases and mapped three possible routes," he began. He gestured to Matto, who ran his fingers across a com pad. A holographic projection flared into view above the table with three different colored lines snaking between bands of stars that were obviously the Orion and Sagittarius Arms, and had labels to validate that assumption.

"They all share one common step," Narso continued as a ring appeared around the point at which the lines diverged. "The first sun outward is what Terrans call a Class M7 star. It is a red giant, which ordinarily would be a good target star for this kind of Framepoint jump, because the photosphere would be somewhat tenuous. However, this particular star is also a variable star of the type humans classify as IS. Unfortunately, there are insufficient astrographical records available from Jao, Lleix, or Terrans to reliably determine its pulsation period or its pulsation extremes. And there is enough interstellar dust between us to interfere with precise observations. In short, we are not certain just how regular or irregular its symmetry becomes."

Caitlin noted that most of the Jao in the room had shifted to angles indicating *concern, unease,* or even in a couple of cases, *alarm.* She shifted her own position to *confidence in adversity.* "I am not an astronomer, Elder Narso," she said. "Explain this in common language I can understand, please."

Narso's aureole fluttered. "That will not be very precise, Director."

"I can live with that," Caitlin said. "Continue."

"If the pathfinder ship emerges when the star is in extreme contraction, they are at substantial risk of emerging in depths of plasma that will overwhelm its shields and destroy it. Similar risks exist if the star's spherical symmetry is distorted and the ship emerges in a portion of the star that is still contracted."

The humans in the room had expressions ranging anywhere from worried to appalled. Caitlin didn't look at Ed; she knew what his concern would be.

"Can you put a quantification on that risk?" Caitlin asked. "Ten percent? Fifty percent? Somewhere in-between?"

Narso looked to Brakan and Matto, then back to Caitlin. "We . . . are uncertain."

Caitlin sat up straighter. The Lleix *elians* seldom

admitted to less than absolute certainty. That followed right behind their insistence on consensus. To have an elder say this in a public forum indicated there were deep divisions within the Starsifters who had been involved in their discussions.

"So give me the range," she said.

Narso's aureole flattened in distress. "We have so little good data," he began.

"Then give me a guess!" Caitlin snapped.

Narso looked to Matto, who fingered his com pad again. A chart appeared in the holographic projection, obscuring part of the star field.

"The most favorable estimate is a ten percent risk," Narso said in a low tone.

"That's not too bad," Caitlin began, only to be interrupted by the Lleix elder.

"The least favorable was in excess of thirty percent."

That almost choked Caitlin. A one-in-three chance of losing each ship? That was a no-go.

"That's too high a risk." She looked to Dannet. "How can we reduce that?"

The Fleet Commander gave her a direct gaze, angles sloping into *accepting responsibility.* "We send a pathfinder ship through. If it survives the trip, it stays in the system for several days making observations, then returns a message ship to the fleet with the observations which allows us to pick the times of least risk to make the jumps."

"And if it doesn't survive?"

Dannet's angles morphed through *gratified-respect* to *aspire-to-be-of-service.* "Then we send another pathfinder through."

That thought caused Caitlin's stomach to churn.

The thought of ordering Jao and humans to such a horrible death was not one she welcomed. But it would work; she admitted that. Sooner or later, a ship would survive and return the needed data.

"Is there another star we can use for the first link in the chain?"

Narso shook his head, something the Lleix had adapted from the humans, much as the Jao had also done.

"No, Director. All other reachable stars lead to routes where the overall risk in the chain of jumps is greater than through this one."

Caitlin looked down at where her hands rested on the table, one bracing her com pad and one loosely holding a stylus, for all the world as if she were not involved in a discussion involving almost certain death for members of her fleet staff. She took a deep breath, held it for a moment, and felt her nostrils flare as she released it.

"Very well. Continue with the presentation."

The discussion that followed took the better part of half an hour. Caitlin followed most of it, but still felt a bit at sea as far as knowing which was best. She kicked herself when she realized that the only ones talking at that point were humans and Lleix. The Jao had been silent for some time, and Dannet's angles were hinting of *impatient irritation*. And that provided both an answer and some relief. She sat up and tapped the table. All voices stopped; all eyes turned to her.

"Fleet Commander Dannet, have you heard enough?"

"Yes," Dannet growled.

"Is the flight possible with our current ships?"

"Yes."

"Have you made your decision as to the path to take?"

"Yes."

"Then this part of the discussion is over. Thank you, Elder Narso."

The Lleix elder continued to stand for a moment, as if not certain what had just happened. Brakan made a slight coughing sound, and the elder inclined his head and resumed his seat.

"Fleet Commander, in the previous meeting Krant-Captain Mallu indicated that a leading ship would have to make the first jump, and it would then serve as an anchor point for the other ships as they made their own jumps." Caitlin's voice was calm. She focused her mind on that calmness, as she schooled her body to present *considering-choices*. It took some effort. "You said a few minutes ago that we would need to send a pathfinder ship. Is that still the preferred approach?"

The ship captains, Jao all, said nothing but looked at Fleet Commander Dannet, whose ears moved to flag resolution as she said, "It is the only approach until the Frame Network can be extended."

"Then who is the pathfinder?" Caitlin asked. "One of the *Lexingtons*? Or do we wait for something else?" Her stomach started churning again, and she drummed her fingers on the table, which startled the Lleix present. They abhorred any form of patterned noise, linking it to the Ekhat and their dreaded songs. Caitlin sighed and stilled her fingers, taking up a posture of *quiet-receptiveness-to-information*.

Some of the Jao in the room looked at her as if she had mouthed nonsense. The rest looked to the fleet commander.

"*Ban Chao*," Dannet said. "The ram ship design was based on a Jao pathfinder design, but was made larger, tougher, and stronger. Ton for ton, *Ban Chao* has the strongest hull and the most powerful shields in the fleet, though it is somewhat more lightly armed than the battleships."

Vanta-Captain Ginta krinnu vau Vanta flicked an ear and then sloped his shoulders in *recognition-of-duty*. His kochan was allied with the great Dano. He would not be seen to shirk a reasonable opportunity to be of use. That would shame both Dano and Vanta. "Yes," he said, "that does make sense. We will only take minimal crew, though. There is no point in risking trained lives unnecessarily. The assault troops we normally carry should off-load to the other ships."

"Not happening," Tully said, his face flushed beneath his tan.

All the Jao at the table glanced sharply at him, their body angles speaking of *disbelief* and *irritation*. Ed Kralik stirred beside Caitlin. She looked over at him as he spoke. "Colonel Tully is right," he said. "We have no idea what the *Ban Chao* will jump into. We have no idea what military technologies you might encounter. You could be attacked as soon as you come out of the jump, and you won't have a way out. That being the case, I'd say you should jump loaded for bear."

Caitlin saw most of the Jao were confused by his metaphor. "You're saying that *Ban Chao* should be loaded with every troop and every weapon that we can possibly load aboard her before she jumps, even the jump into this variable star."

"Damn straight!" Tully replied instantly.

"Correct," Ed said in support. "It will risk the jinau, but better to risk them and not need them than to leave them behind and find out you need them after all. As commander of Ares Base and commander of all Terra taif jinau, it may or may not be within my *oudh* to order it, but if it doesn't happen you will not want to deal with me."

Caitlin looked at her husband. What she saw was Lieutenant General Kralik directing his eagle's gaze at everyone else in the room.

Dannet stirred, angles flowing into something that Caitlin translated as *agreement-with-no-brainer*. She couldn't remember the exact Jao name at the moment, but that was what it meant.

"General Kralik is right," the fleet commander said, "*Ban Chao* will take full crew and troop load and as much extra weapon load as can be squeezed into it."

"All right," Caitlin said. She looked at Tully. "Make sure you have everything you need before you jump. It will be a bit difficult to send back for anything you forget."

"Grandmothers and eggs, Caitlin," Tully responded, tapping notes into his com pad.

Tully's face lit up with glee at the fleet commander's pronouncement. Tully's repressed energy was about to blow a fuse. The man was crazy, Caitlin thought. He liked to be in the vanguard, seeing what was happening. He was infernally curious. That often got him into trouble, but occasionally gave him great successes. "All right," she said, "but you have to promise not to get killed."

Vanta-Captain Ginta looked at her sharply. He was a well-made individual with reddish gold nap and a heavily marked *vai camiti* composed of three stolid thick lines. "Humans can promise such positive outcomes?"

"They can," she said, "and then do their dead level best to make sure they keep their word."

"I won't let them kill me," Tully said, "and if they do, you can dock my pay."

Ginta's ears flattened in blatant *bafflement*. "If you are dead, you will not care about your pay."

"Right," Tully said. He winked. "Are we done here? I've got work to do now."

Caitlin considered for a moment, working around the yawning gulf in the pit of her stomach. This was a decision with much larger repercussions that anything she had faced before. But all things considered, there was no choice. Not to do this would fail their people. She thought of the Ekhat, and her resolve firmed.

"Yes," Caitlin said, "it is decided and directed. The fleet will jump as soon as Fleet Commander Dannet is convinced we are ready. The *Ban Chao* will lead the way." She tapped the table. "Make it happen, people."

With that, she stood and, in keeping with her use of Jao protocol, waited for her bodyguards and her husband to precede her out of the conference room.

As she walked through the door, she heard Tully saying, "All right! Now the fun begins."

On the way back to her quarters, Caewithe Miller walked next to Caitlin.

"I thought Tully told me once that we are in the Sagittarius Arm of the galaxy," the guard captain said. "How can we be moving to the Sagittarius Arm?"

"I thought the same thing, myself," Caitlin responded, "at least for a little while. Bad information from a news program, I'm afraid. We and the Jao are actually in the Orion Arm. We got it straightened out before long, fortunately before we embarrassed ourselves too badly."

A few more steps down the corridor, then, "What

was with Tully just now?" Caewithe asked. "Why was he fighting to be on the *Ban Chao*? He'll just be in the way."

"Tully's got an insatiable urge to be at the leading edge of everything," Caitlin said. "Aille understands. That's why he was off in the mountains with the rebels half the time. He'll make something positive out of this situation, you'll see."

"Bleeding edge will be more like it," the younger woman muttered, and her cheeks were flushed.

Caitlin studied her as they walked. She knew their history as an on-again/off-again couple. "Tully never had a family. He was an orphaned rebel camp brat, surviving as best he could on what he could steal. If he told the truth twice a day, it was an accident. He was spying on the Jao when Aille ran across him, for God's sake, which would have led to a swift execution if anyone else had detected him. If he didn't live his life at this sort of fever pitch, he would have been dead long ago."

"Yeah, I figured that out a while ago," Caewithe said. "That's why I finally broke it off with him. He's fun for a time, but I can't make a life with an adrenaline junkie."

Caitlin gave her surprised guard captain a hug around the shoulders. "I could tell it hadn't worked out," Caitlin said, "but I didn't know why. I really wish it had, though. I like both of you guys, and you would have been a great couple."

Caewithe shrugged. "I really like Tully, too, but living with him would be like living with a hand grenade with the pin pulled. I couldn't do it. So I let him go while we were still friends."

"I'm not what you would call experienced at this

stuff," Caitlin said with a wry grin, "not with my background, but I'd say that was probably a wise decision. No sense in destroying your friendship over something if it never had a chance at success."

"Nope."

They walked in silence for a few moments, taking the next left and then the next right. Caitlin looked at her guard captain out of the corner of her eye. "So, you started looking yet?"

Caewithe gave a snort. "Got right to that point, didn't you?" She laughed as Caitlin started to sputter. "It's okay, it's okay. Actually, if you want to know, Lieutenant Vaughan is starting to look interesting. And I love that Welsh accent."

"Good," Caitlin said as they reached her quarters. Caewithe and Tamt took up their posts by the door. "You just smile at him and use that Alabama drawl of yours."

"Standard southern belle practice," Caewithe said with a grin. "Been using it on Yankees for generations; hasn't failed us yet."

After the door closed, Tamt looked over at Caewithe. "I'll take the post and call up one of the other guards. Lieutenant Vaughan said something about going to the officer's pool."

Caewithe thought about it for a moment. She had a swimsuit . . . yeah, it would work. "Thanks, Tamt. I'll owe you one."

The burly Jao guard just waved her on.

CHAPTER 14

Caitlin's com pad pinged. She looked up, a bit surprised and a bit disgruntled, since she had set the pad to route all calls to one of her assistants except those coming from the top officers in the search fleet or in the base command. So if someone got through to her, it had to be someone pretty important with something they considered serious enough to call her. That didn't bode well for her schedule for the rest of the day.

She tapped her pad, and Gabe Tully's face appeared.

"Sorry to disturb you, Caitlin, but we need to see you."

"We?"

"Yeah, me and Lieutenant Bannerji and Ramt."

It took a moment, but then it clicked for Caitlin that those two people were the ones doing the interrogations of the Ekhat slaves they'd captured. Yeah, she'd consider anything in that area to be serious enough to call her.

"Okay," Caitlin responded, reaching for the pad. "Let me see when I can clear you a meeting time."

"No, you don't understand," Tully said. "I think you need to come to the *Ban Chao*. Real soon now, if you get me."

The picture in Caitlin's com pad began shifting. Tully was obviously turning his around. In another moment, the picture stabilized, and she could see the Ekhat slaves sitting in a row. A couple of them were wagging in the hind end like excited puppies, but it was the fact that they were all sitting neatly and more or less still that caused Caitlin's eyes to open wide.

"I'll be there within an hour," she said.

"Right." Tully broke the connection from his end.

Caitlin tapped her pad to open another call. "Caewithe, I need to go to *Ban Chao* now. Yes, I know it's not scheduled. Get ahold of the command deck and get a shuttle cleared for us, please. Let me know which one, and I'll meet you at the bay." She tapped her pad again to break the call.

Caitlin looked at her work station and tried to decide what she could finish in the next five or ten minutes, closing down the rest of the files. All the while, in the back of her mind was running the thought that if those two Ekhat experts had made a breakthrough of any kind with the slaves, she would kiss them both.

The com pad pinged again just as Caitlin finished sending a note to her assistants telling them where she was going and to not let anyone disturb her for anything less important than an Ekhat attack. Caewithe's message floated there: Shuttle 9 at Shuttle Bay Green 2. She shut down her work station, grabbed the com pad and headed out the door. "Did you get the message?" she asked as she paused by the guards.

"Yes, Director," the Jao guard said, falling into place ahead of her. "Shuttle Bay Green 2. Captain Miller and Tamt will meet us there."

"Let's go, then."

And go they did, moving through the corridors at a brisk pace with a burly human and an even larger Jao leading the way. Everyone else took a cue from the Jao in the corridors and cleared out of the way.

Tamt was standing by the shuttle and waved her through the hatch, following her through. Navy crew shut and locked down the hatch as they made their way to their seats. It was empty except for them and the crew—one of the perks of being The Director, Caitlin supposed. No one questioned her about this kind of thing. If she said she needed to be somewhere, then everyone in range would focus on seeing that she got there. A heady brew of authority, Caitlin thought. Her shoulders twitched, shaking off the allure, as she sat in her seat and fastened her harness.

Tamt took the seat next to Caitlin, and Caewithe Miller took the seat across from her. Caitlin waited until the pilot had maneuvered the shuttle out of the shuttle bay, then looked at her guard captain with a grin.

"So, have you seen Lieutenant Vaughan lately?"

Caewithe didn't say anything, just nodded with a grin of her own.

"They've been spending more time in the water lately than we Jao," Tamt rumbled from beside Caitlin. Caitlin turned her head enough to see flecks of green in Tamt's black eyes, and her ears and whiskers tilted enough to hint at the posture for *blatant humor*, which probably ought to be translated as *ribald humor*. Jao humor, such as it was, tended to be pretty blunt. She looked back at Caewithe and raised her eyebrows.

"I have this one swimsuit, you see," Caewithe said with a wicked grin.

"Cruel, evil woman," Caitlin said, laughing, "to lure the poor boy on like that."

"I'll let him catch me before too long, I think." Caewithe's dimples appeared, then she laughed.

"You're the first humans I've seen who pursue this mating thing properly," Tamt said. "Although the officers' pool is kind of public for a mating ritual."

Caitlin started laughing as Caewithe spluttered. Tamt's delivery of those lines was very matter of fact and dry, which just made it funnier. From the wiggle of Tamt's whiskers, it seemed she agreed.

"Okay, that was funny," Caewithe admitted, "but let's leave my love life—or lack of it—out of the conversation now, unless you want to start talking about yours."

Tamt shrugged. "Is nonexistent. Terra taif has offered potential mates, which is more than Kannu ever did." That was the first time Caitlin could remember Tamt referring to the kochan she had belonged to before being called to Aille's service and subsequently joining Terra taif. "But I won't have cubs right now. A battle-ready fleet doesn't provide the right environment for Jao cubs. They need space to roam and lots of water to play in before they must learn to be of service."

"Do you want cubs?" Caitlin asked, looking at the being who was perhaps her first real female friend.

"Perhaps," Tamt replied. "Before Yaut found me and called me to Aille's service, when Oppuk ruled Terra and none of us knew when we would die from a sniper's bullet, I would have said no. Now, sometimes I think I would."

Caitlin looked at Tamt for a moment longer, then looked away with a quiet resolve that her friend would have that opportunity.

They sat in silence for some little while after that. Caitlin pulled her com pad out to see if any further messages had come through. Just about the time she was through with that, the crew announced that they would be docking with *Ban Chao* shortly.

Tully met them at the shuttle bay, along with Major Liang, his executive officer, and First Sergeant Luff. "Hi, Caitlin," he said. "Glad you were able to make it. I really think you need to see this." He nodded to Tamt and Caewithe, but didn't say anything. Given what Caewithe had told her, that didn't surprise Caitlin. They were both probably a little uncomfortable.

"Okay, I'm here," Caitlin said. "Let's deal with this, gentlemen, shall we? I've got to be back on *Lexington* before too long."

"Right. This way, then." Tully gestured toward a hatch and led the way in approved Jao style.

Caitlin found the corridors in *Ban Chao* to be just as mazelike as the corridors in the *Lexington*, as well as somewhat more congested. But the crew and jinau of *Ban Chao* made way for them just as well as the *Lexington*'s crew did, and before long they were entering a compartment that had a large window in one side of it that looked out over another compartment.

"Hello, Ramt, Lieutenant Bannerji," Caitlin said, greeting those who waited their arrival.

Both responded with a quiet, "Director Kralik."

Caitlin moved to the window. She could see a glistening black mass of slowly moving bodies in one corner of the other compartment. It looked for all the world like a mass of puppies huddled together in sleepy togetherness. Nonetheless, her shoulders still twitched at how alien the Ekhat slaves were. Oh, she knew how weird that sounded in a universe where she had endured Ekhat and lived with Jao and Lleix. But still, the slaves were very different.

"So, what is it you want me to see that I had to come to *Ban Chao* rather than you com me or come to the *Lexington*?" Caitlin asked.

Tully pointed to Bannerji, who flipped a switch on the wall and barked something in what could only be Ekhat. Caitlin hadn't been exposed to much of the language, but it was unmistakable. She did have to suppress a chuckle at the effect Bannerji's British accent had on the alien tongue.

The effect on the slaves was extreme. The pile of black bodies in the corner flew apart as if a grenade had been pitched into it. They rolled and scrambled and scurried and scrabbled until they were standing in the line that Tully had shown her in the com pad call.

Before Caitlin could say anything, Bannerji spoke, and the line shifted to a circle. Again he spoke, and the circle morphed to a line again, only this time on a slant. One final command, and the slaves returned to the original straight line.

Caitlin's mouth quirked. Her first reaction was to make a quip about producing an alien drill team.

But then what she had seen sank in. "You're able to communicate with them, to get them to follow instructions."

"To a limited extent, yes," Bannerji said. He waved a hand at the window. "They are like so many Labrador retrievers—more intelligent than we first thought, and eager to please."

Caitlin laughed. "I thought they looked like a bunch of puppies huddled there in the corner before you said anything."

"They are very gregarious," Ramt said, stepping forward to join the conversation. "More so than any Terran species, even dolphins or whales."

"Are they as much fun to work with as Labradors?"

"Yes and no." Bannerji chuckled. "They are much stronger, and if they run into you they can knock you flying. And given their, ah, conditioning at the hands of the Ekhat, avoiding injury in themselves or others is not a high priority. But once we got them to calm down, then yeah, they're fun."

"We must continue to be careful," Ramt cautioned in her even tones. "They are not dogs. They are not tame animals. And for all that they are sentient beings, they are also hideously 'programmed,' to use a human word, to consider themselves as nothing in relation to the Ekhat. At the right—or wrong—word, they will kill themselves; or they are just as likely to attempt to kill whichever one of us is with them."

Caitlin took a deep breath, then released it. "You're saying they really are slaves, not just prisoners or drafted labor."

"Bred and born to it," Bannerji said soberly. "So much so that I wonder if it will ever be possible to emancipate them without tinkering with their genetic code."

Anger began to rise within Caitlin. The Ekhat could never be forgiven for this. "Okay. No quick fix here, obviously. But this can't be why you asked me to come over. What do you want?"

Ramt and Bannerji looked to where Tully leaned back against a wall with Liang and Luff, arms folded.

"I think we need to keep them with the fleet." Tully straightened and clasped his hands behind his back.

"Why?"

"This is the first time we've managed to get anyone from an Ekhat ship to talk to us, even a little," he said. "Ramt and Vikram here are getting more and more out of them every day. Little bits, granted, but get enough of them and put them together, and who knows what we might find? I want to let them continue to work with the slaves."

Caitlin shrugged. "Makes sense to me. So what's the problem?" She was beginning to see that there must be some kind of issue with Tully's plan.

"The problem is that Gram of the Ekhatlore *elian* wants them left here at Ares base for him and some of his fellow Ekhatlore to study."

"Ah."

"Yeah. Number one, I don't think they'll do any better than these two at working with the slaves." Tully jerked a thumb at where Ramt and Bannerji stood together. "Number two, we won't get any information they might develop in anything like a useful time frame; and last but definitely not least, there's no guarantee they will be able to keep them alive."

Caitlin understood Tully's points, and the last one in

particular was important to her. None of the captives taken from the Ekhat ships during the Valeron battle had lived long. The sole Ekhat they had captured by lasering off its legs had gone into what seemed like a catatonic state not long after being taken aboard the *Lexington*, and had died before it got to Earth. The few slaves that had survived the battle hadn't lasted much longer. They all seemed to just lose the spark of life and fade away, one by one. So the fact that Ramt and Bannerji had managed to not only keep these slaves alive, but get them to actually start interacting with humans and Lleix made them the experts, as far as she was concerned.

"Let me guess—Gram is senior to Ramt in the Ekhatlore *elian.*"

Ramt folded her hands together. "He is. And I have not the stature within the *elian* to stand against his orders."

"Hmmph. Not a problem," Caitlin said. "I have *oudh* over this whole effort. It's my decision that it is necessary for the slaves to remain with the fleet so that we can derive immediate benefit from any intelligence gained from them."

Tully grinned.

"But," Caitlin said, raising a hand, "can we divide the group? Leave some here and take some with us?"

Both Bannerji and Ramt shook their heads. "No," the human said. "We think one of the reasons they've survived is because we have enough of them together to reach a critical threshold to keep a colony of them alive. If we reduce that, even by just one or two, we may drop below that threshold, and then we'd lose all of them."

Caitlin nodded. "Makes sense to me. So," she turned to Tully, "that's my directive, Gabe. We keep all of them."

"Right." Tully's grin flashed again for a moment, then he sobered. "But there is one other thing..."

Caitlin sighed. "Spit it out, Gabe."

He spread his hands at waist level. "I think they need to be on a different ship. If *Ban Chao* is going to be leading the way with these pathfinding jumps, you run a greater risk of losing them."

Caitlin's stomach lurched at the thought of losing the ship and everyone aboard, including Tully. But that discussion had already happened, and she couldn't go there now. It took a moment, but she moved beyond that thought and said, "Okay, point. We'll move them to *Lexington*. And these two as well." She pointed to Bannerji and Ramt.

"Hey, wait a minute," Tully objected. "Vikram's my intelligence officer. I'm going to need him."

"Have Ed assign you another one," Caitlin said. "Right now he's one of the two best Ekhat slave wranglers in the universe, so he's not any more disposable than they are. My orders," she declared, staring Tully in the eye.

Tully stiffened and his jaw set for a moment, then he unbent. "Yes, Director." He looked to Bannerji and Ramt. "Pack your stuff, guys, and get ready to move." Then to Liang and Luff. "They're going to *Lexington*. Make it happen, preferably without breaking either the prisoners or anyone else." Back to Caitlin with a wry grin. "They're all yours."

CHAPTER 15

The morning of the jumpoff for the big voyage, Caitlin gave Ed a long and lingering last kiss at the mouth of the boarding tube to the *Lexington*. At length, she broke away, held her hand to his cheek, and whispered, "You be careful."

His mouth quirked, then he folded her into a massive hug that caused her ribs to creak. "You, too," he said. "You come back to me."

Caitlin nodded as she broke the hug. She placed her hand on his heart, to be pinioned a moment later by one of his. "I will," she said.

She finally turned from him and walked into the boarding tube without looking back. If she hadn't, she might not have gone at all. Tamt and Caewithe followed close behind.

Caitlin proceeded directly to the Command Deck. All her gear was already in her quarters, and she could just as easily follow their progress from there, but today she was too nervous to shut herself up down there. It helped to be in the middle of things.

She was one of the last to arrive. "This is not going to be a single jump for the fleet," Wrot said, meeting her as she entered from the lift. "First, the fleet will retrace our path to one of the former stars we checked out at the edge of the Orion Arm, then the *Ban Chao* will jump to the first star in the path to the Sagittarius Arm."

Caitlin nodded. "And then we wait." In response to Wrot's nod, she asked, "How long?"

Wrot shrugged, and stroked the place on his cheek where his bauta scar had once been. "Oh, we will know within a few hours if the *Ban Chao* survived the jump. If the Frame Network can connect to the ship, then they survived."

That was good news, Caitlin realized. She'd been afraid they'd have to wait for the messenger to return before they'd know if the *Ban Chao* had survived. "And then we wait," she said. "How long for that?"

"The Starsifters *elian* believes it will take about a week of observations by Terran measures before the rest of us can jump."

"A week," Caitlin said. "Joy."

Wrot responded with another shrug.

It wasn't long before the fleet—no longer a flotilla—was ready to move. Fleet Commander Dannet gave the order.

Jumping was familiar now, that gut-twisting feeling of being nowhere and everywhere at the same time. *Lexington* went first. Caitlin closed her eyes as the great ship *leapt*. They were going back to a star already checked out. There should be no surprises, no fleets of Ekhat ships waiting to fire upon them. "Easy-breezy," she murmured as minutes later they emerged in the star's photosphere.

Jao voices read off the readings. Flue Vaughan was at his station, tapping pads and murmuring. No one seemed upset. The smell of overheated wiring came to her faintly, but the repair crew was on it in an instant. Even Dannet was calmly striding about the bridge, not striking anyone who incurred her displeasure. It was oddly anticlimactic.

Within a couple of hours, the rest of the fleet had followed without incident. "Now," Dannet said. "The *Ban Chao* will go on."

"And we sit around here and wait," Caitlin said, "which is in many ways the hardest part." Suddenly, she understood why Tully had insisted upon going.

She should have gone too.

The *Ban Chao* was not a small ship, though smaller than battleships like the *Lexington* and the *Pool Buntyam*. Tully tucked himself in a corner of the Command Deck and watched its crew, mostly Jao, busy themselves for the blind jump. The assault troops were suited up and locked into their shock frames. Everything was ready.

More could go wrong with such a jump than a regular one, even when going to a normal star, much less the variable that was their target today, but the Jao were used to the operation. If they couldn't jump blind, they'd never get anywhere they hadn't already been, limiting to say the least.

Vanta-Captain Ginta gave the order to jump. Tully was a bit startled. He'd expected more of a build-up to the moment, maybe even an inspirational speech; but then again, these were the Jao. They didn't get overly dramatic. They had a job and they did it. Anything else was just emotional histrionics to them.

The awful inside-out feeling crawled over him, sizzled down through his bones, threatened to make his brain boil out through his ears. He felt like the top of his head was going to melt. Was it just his imagination or was this jump actually worse than the others he had been through? He pressed his back to the bulkhead and tucked his hands into his armpits.

Jao voices rose around the command deck and he thought he detected a thread of alarm. The ship shook as though in the grasp of a great hurricane. He was hard pressed to keep his feet. Vanta-Captain Ginta was darting from console to console, checking readings, directing adjustments, his voice stressed.

Finally, with a great heave that knocked Tully sprawling to the deck, the ship arrived—somewhere. The shaking ceased. He pushed up from his stomach. The viewing screen was a blaze of over-bright light. Sweat dripped down the back of his collar.

"We have pulsation!" a voice said.

"Inward or outward?" Vanta-Captain Ginta asked.

The speaker hesitated. "Inward."

"Full power!" Ginta said. "Get us free!"

The bridge crew had only seemed busy before. Now, they were frantic, adjusting this, augmenting that, running about in controlled chaos. And there was nothing Tully could do except stay out of the way. He heaved back onto his feet.

"The inward rushing current is pulling us with it,"

a Jao officer said. "We can slow the process, but we don't have enough power to break away."

The Starsifter elder apparently knew what he was talking about, Tully thought. He craned his head, trying to see what the crew was doing. They had to get out of the photosphere as quickly as possible. The shields wouldn't hold forever. He'd seen back at the battle of Valeron what happened to ships who encountered a star's fire with a naked hull.

"Come port eighty-four degrees and down sixty," Ginta said, peering intently at a screen.

The ship vibrated, caught in the immense forces of the solar tides as the crew tried to follow orders. It shook so hard that Tully lost his balance again and fell heavily to his knees. He felt so damned helpless!

Thank goodness the rest of the fleet had not followed on their heels. The Jao were innately cautious in their practicality. He'd never had more reason to be grateful for that than he did at the moment. And for the moment, he almost regretted on insisting the jinau remain onboard.

"We have to ride it until the pulse reverses," Ginta said. "Then we can use it to push us out of the photosphere."

But could they last that long? The viewscreen now showed a vast canyon of fiery white-hot plasma, laced with flickers of red and blue and yellow, around them. They were sliding along, all but out of control, fighting with every erg of power they could wring from the *Ban Chao*'s engines, trying not to get pulled in too far.

There was an electronic squeal, then something failed. The lights on the command deck went out and the emergency lighting flickered on with a sickly orange tint. Ginta didn't seem to notice. He pulled a tech out of his seat before a monitoring station and manned the controls himself.

Just like Dannet, Tully thought numbly. Hands-on all the way.

The ship bucked and shook and quivered as though trying to escape Ginta's firm hand. Tully wished there were something—anything—he could do to help besides stay out of the way.

"Pulse slowing," a voice said. "Wait, wait."

"Reversal initiated," Ginta said as though discussing if he would take a swim. "Brace for impact."

Tully swore and scooted back against the wall. A second later, they were hit so hard, his teeth clicked together and he bit his tongue. His head collided with the wall and for a few seconds, he was dizzily out of touch with the situation.

He swam back up to full alertness, his mouth tasting of blood.

"—full power!" Ginta was saying, unusually animated. "If we don't free ourselves from the photosphere with this pulse, we may not last long enough to make a second try."

The *Ban Chao* shook and wavered. The command crew was frantic, increasing this and adjusting that. He only hoped they knew what they were doing.

"Increase power!" Ginta said.

"But we are already exceeding all safety parameters," said a female Jao tech.

Ginta knocked her to the floor and took her place. "Safety parameters cannot help us here," he said grimly and pushed the lever down. The ship shook, as though in the grip of an angry giant, then—they were free, moving through increasingly less turbulent plasma, and finally gliding out into blessedly black space. It even seemed cooler, although Tully knew that had to be an illusion.

"We are out," a Jao female said. "Hull surface readings falling, although we still have to shed the plasma we picked up."

Tully regained his feet, soaked in sweat. He was suddenly glad that Caewithe wasn't here. It was hard enough to be brave with no one looking.

He toured the command deck, looking at the monitors and readouts over the shoulders of the techs. He could read a few of them, but those few told him very little.

"Any sign of civilization in this star system?" he asked one of the sensor techs.

"Nothing in the way of technology," she said absently. "At this distance, we might not pick up other signs right away. Not that we expected any, in a system like this one."

"Establish orbit around the star," Vanta-Captain Ginta said.

Tully tried to imagine the *Lexington* or the *Pool Buntyam* leaping into that hell and shuddered. The *Ban Chao*, being somewhat smaller and with correspondingly more powerful engines, was more maneuverable. Could the larger battleships have handled those conditions? He wasn't sure they could, and he was very glad they hadn't had to find out the hard way.

"Orbit established," one of the command deck crew said. Tully looked over his shoulder and read the distance from the sun. He pulled his com pad out of his pocket and converted the Jao number to human measurements. The *Ban Chao* was about twenty light-minutes out, or a bit more than twice the distance from Earth to the Sun. He relaxed a little at that.

He relaxed even more when messages from Major Liang and First Sergeant Luff arrived on his com pad indicating that the assault troops had come through the jump wrapped in their shock cages with nothing more than bruises.

After watching the command crew for a few more minutes, Tully left the Command Deck and went to his quarters where he showered for a good fifteen minutes, letting the cool water sluice through his hair. Try as he might, though, he couldn't wash away the feeling of having been very nearly burnt to a crisp.

CHAPTER 16

The Bond of Ebezon, standing as kochan parent to Terra taif, had constructed several structures on Terra for their own use. All of them were low in build, with the curving lines that pleased the Jao. Most of them were built on coastlines of seas or large lakes. None of them were large; pretention was not part of the Bond's mode of operation. Unlike the actual kochans like Pluthrak or Dano, the Bond's focus was not on planets as such. Planets were not possessions to them; they were merely platforms from which to launch ships, squadrons and fleets.

Preceptor Ronz acknowledged that. Nonetheless, over the last two years he had gravitated to one particular Terran Bond structure as a place to go when he wanted solitude, quiet, and time to think.

It was located on the coast of that large island that the Terrans called Greenland; a misnomer if ever there was one. The Terrans had apparently been concerned about a global temperature warming trend before the

Jao arrived. Glacier melt on Greenland had been one of the things some of them had pointed to as evidence of "global warming." However, various bolide strikes on the planet during the planetary conquest and early years of the occupation by the Jao had thrown enough dust and particulates into the atmosphere that the trend had not only been arrested, it had been reversed. And nowhere was that more evident than on Greenland.

Ronz stood, hands clasped behind his back, posture effortlessly *neutral*, and watched the snow swirl outside. Unlike many of the Jao, he liked cold weather; it was one of the reasons he was drawn to this particular location.

At the moment, he was appreciating the randomness of the snowflakes dancing, yet all the while they eventually submitted to gravity and settled to the ground. A metaphor for something? Perhaps. And perhaps simply a beautiful act by the universe.

One particular swirl swept a cloud of the falling snow upwards. His eyes followed it, and remained gazing upward. Something was changing.

"Caitlin, what are you up to now?" he murmured.

The messenger ship from *Ban Chao* had returned with five days of solar studies on the IS class star during Caitlin's sleep shift. When she awoke that morning, the Starsifters had finished reviewing the data and were ready to report to her and the fleet commander.

"The report indicates that it was good you sent *Ban Chao*," Wrot said without greeting as they met at the door of the conference room. "I don't think any other ship, not even *Lexington* or *Pool Buntyam*, could have survived what they jumped into."

"It was an appropriate use of assets," Dannet said as she entered behind them. Again Caitlin was reminded that Jao were not human. That casual disregard of personal risk of hundreds of crew and jinau just grated on her.

Taking her seat, Caitlin looked to Brakan and Matto. "Well?"

Matto manipulated his com pad, and another hologram sprang into view, a large red globe.

"The target star," Brakan said. "With the extrapolation from the measurements taken from *Ban Chao*, we can tell you that even for an IS class variable it is odd. The good news is its cycle seems to be about sixty days for full expansion and contraction. The almost good news is that it appears the expansion cycle is mostly stable, but does fluctuate slightly."

Matto touched his com pad again, and the hologram began a slow expansion to a point almost half again as large as the original, then began contracting.

"That minimizes the risk?" Caitlin asked after watching a full cycle.

"Yes, Director," Brakan replied.

"How soon can we jump?"

"In approximately twelve Terran hours," Brakan said.

Caitlin looked to Dannet. "What's our status?"

"All ships ready for jump," the fleet commander replied.

"Give the orders, then."

"Yes, Director."

Dannet and Wrot both assumed angles for *committed-to-action*, and the fleet commander and the Lleix rose and exited the conference room. Wrot looked to Caitlin. "A challenging beginning," he said.

Excitement flooded Caitlin, an excitement she hadn't felt since not long after beginning the search for other civilizations. "Maybe so," she said, "but we have to start somewhere."

Twelve hours later, Caitlin was once again on the command deck of the *Lexington*, seated at the station near Lieutenant Vaughan's that had become her customary location. He had taken time to program a couple of data feeds from his station to hers, so that she could have at least a minimal idea of what was occurring without having to ask questions or distract any of the crew.

Tamt was standing by her, and another of the bodyguard detail was beside the door. Captain Miller was supposed to join them shortly.

Caitlin knew she was keyed up. She knew that the *Ban Chao* had survived the jump, so that paved the way for *Lexington* to jump next. She hoped that meant that *Ban Chao* had not suffered damage or casualties, but that wouldn't be clear to them until they arrived themselves.

And if Tully wasn't there to meet them, she'd kill him.

She gripped the chair arms as buildup toward jump began.

"First framepoint generator set," one of the crew announced.

"Second framepoint generator set." That word from another tech came on the heels of the first announcement. Caitlin could feel the vibration in the ship's structure through her feet.

"Third framepoint generator set." Now the vibration

was stronger, and she thought she heard a low hum, almost a growl.

"Fourth framepoint generator set."

"Fifth framepoint generator set."

The last two reports came one right after the other, and the vibration jumped markedly. Caitlin looked down at her hands and noticed that her knuckles were white. She made herself relax, and shifted her posture towards *calm-in-storm.*

Dannet, of course, had been standing watching everything, unmoving except for her head turning, angles all *neutral.*

Terra-Captain Uldra looked at readouts over a tech's shoulder, then straightened.

"Navigator, you may jump."

Tully watched as one after the other, the other ships of the reinforced fleet exited the photosphere of the target star, each seemingly none the worse for the experience. Apparently having the pathfinder ship go ahead really did make a difference in how the other ships could travel. It made Tully all the more appreciative for the Jao's skill in frame travel.

The first four ships to follow *Ban Chao* were the battleships: the veterans *Lexington, Arjuna,* and *Pool Buntyam,* followed by *Sun Tzu,* the replacement for the wounded *Vercingetorix.* Tully heaved a sigh of relief when the last of them cleared the edge of the photosphere and joined the others in clear space. With that much firepower now in place, even if the system had held those who would contest the fleet's passage, the chances of them succeeding were now remote.

There was a span of a few minutes between ships.

When the next one came out of the photosphere and its shape became clear on the main viewscreen, Tully sat up and took notice.

Vanta-Captain Ginta for a moment slumped into formless posture, then assumed the angles of *beholding-pleasant-encounters*. An air of relaxation moved through the room in a wave.

Tully stepped up beside the captain and pointed at the screen. "What's that one?"

"Bond Ship 15467," Ginta replied.

"Uh-huh," Tully said. "You want to tell me what kind of ship that is and why she's with us?"

"That is a framepoint ship," Ginta said. "It will travel with the fleet and lay framepoints after each jump. Without it, it will be a very long and slow voyage home."

Tully considered that for a moment. "Good ship to have with us."

"Indeed." The captain's voice was dry enough to serve as a desiccant.

It took a few hours to bring the fleet through the Locus Point jump and out into clear space in the target star system. The fleet wasn't much larger in terms of combat power than it had been, but Fleet Commander Dannet and Lieutenant General Kralik had agreed that if the fleet was going to go in harm's way so far from their home stars and without quick access to Ares Base or the other systems of the Jao/human alliance, they'd need to take a lot of supplies with them. Under Caitlin's *oudh* Dannet had commandeered every available ship in or near the base system to serve as stores and ammunition ships. Kralik hadn't emptied the warehouses and storage nexuses of the base to fill those ships, but what he had ordered had put a severe dent in the base's supplies.

Caitlin was at dinner when the last ship cleared the corona transition. Her com pad beeped at her, and she tapped the accept control with her fork handle while she swallowed a bite. A recent picture of Ed was replaced by Dannet's face staring out at her.

"Director Kralik," Dannet began in her usual direct mode.

Caitlin choked down the last of the bite in her mouth. "Yes," she husked.

"All fleet ships have arrived and are in orbit. Several are in need of minor repairs, but nothing serious was experienced."

"Good." Relief flooded through Caitlin.

"I have ordered Bond Ship 15467 to begin laying and activating the framepoint."

"How long will that take?" Caitlin asked, turning schedules in her mind.

Dannet gave her the typical Jao "as long as it takes" expression through the com pad.

The com pad chimed again, and a message from Lieutenant Vaughan scrolled across the bottom of the screen: "Estimate thirty-six to forty-eight hours to deploy, activate and test."

"Never mind." Caitlin waved a hand to clear the issue away. "I will call a meeting tomorrow for all senior captains and commanders. Word will go out soon."

"Understood."

And with that the com pad cleared and returned Ed's picture to Caitlin's view.

Tully took a shuttle over to the *Lexington* to join Caitlin's meeting.

Wrot fell in beside him as they entered the conference room. "So, how was the jump?"

"Fine," Tully said blandly, catching a glimpse of Caewithe's trim figure out of the corner of his eye. She smiled at him for a brief second. He flushed and dropped into his seat.

Wrot took the seat next to him and gave him a direct look.

"No harder than usual," Tully said. "There were a few tight moments but the Vanta-captain really knows what he's doing."

Wrot's whiskers moved and his head tilted in one of the Jao postures. Tully guessed at *disbelief*.

"Okay, we almost got burnt to cinders," Tully said in a low voice. "Drop it, will you?" His relationship with Caewithe Miller might be in the past, but still, the last thing he wanted to talk about in front of her or Caitlin was how bloody scared he'd been.

Wrot stroked his cheek, and murmured, "We must compare notes."

"You've been on a pathfinder jump?" Tully asked.

Wrot's form communicated *smug* even without using Jao body language. Tully could read that rather well.

Caitlin cleared her throat, and Tully faced forward.

"I've been giving this a lot of thought since our return to Ares Base," she said. "From what we've seen of the Ekhat presence in the Orion Arm of the galaxy, they appear to have started closer to the center and worked their way out. We have no clue as to whether or not they're in the Sagittarius Arm. Once we arrive there, if we don't see them, we will head inward from that point. I believe that will increase our chances of finding an extant society." She glanced around the table.

"Or increase chances of encountering the Ekhat if they are also in the Sagittarius Arm," Wrot commented.

Caitlin nodded. Tully noted a tightness around her mouth. She wasn't happy about that possibility. "A risk I believe we must run."

Tully also noted that she had not called for discussion. She was growing into this leadership stuff, he thought to himself.

Caitlin looked to Fleet Commander Dannet. "I would like to make the next jump as soon as the framepoint is set and functional. Please plan accordingly."

"We will be ready," the former Narvo said. "Is there anything else?"

Caitlin stood. "No. Keep me informed of progress."

Dannet rose to her feet, her large-even-for-a-Jao body dwarfing all but the Lleix. The rest of the council followed. Tully lingered for a moment, hoping for a quick word with Caewithe. But Caitlin swept out the door ahead of everyone and her bodyguard of course had to go with her.

He started to follow after them, only to see Lim step in front of him.

"Colonel Tully," she began. He nodded in response, and she continued, "We have an agreement that you will teach me to fight. I am ready to begin."

"Whoa, whoa," Tully held up his hands. "I agreed to have you taught to fight. But things are a bit up in the air, right now."

"And in this fleet, when will they not be?" She looked down and folded her robe a little closer to her body.

Tully noted that Lim's command of English idiom

was rather good. But then, he would expect no less from a Lleix.

"Fair point," Tully acknowledged. "Part of the problem is that the man I want to begin your training is on *Ban Chao*, not *Lexington.*"

"That is not a problem," Lim replied. She looked at him, black eyes focused on his. "Pyr and I were joined by Garhet of Terralore a few days ago after it was decided that we need to have at least one of us with each of the senior Terra taif leaders. Pyr and Garhet will remain on *Lexington* to observe and interact with Director Kralik and Wrot. I volunteered to move to *Ban Chao* to observe you and your jinau leaders. If it is acceptable, I can return to the ship with you now."

"Wait a minute," Tully said, holding up his hands again.

"You do not want me?"

"No," Tully said. Lim seemed to stiffen, and he hurried to say, "I don't mean I don't want you on the ship. You just caught me off guard is all." God, now he was getting in trouble with prickly extraterrestrial women! What next? "Look, if you want to come over to *Ban Chao*, I'll approve that. And yeah, it will make it some easier to start your training. But you're going to be surrounded by Jao and humans, with no other Lleix on the ship. You sure you want to take that on?"

Lim stared at him for a moment, black eyes unblinking, aureole doing a slow rise around her head. "How will that be different from my life before now?"

Tully looked at Lim; saw the set of her shoulders, the full extension of her aureole, and the stillness of her hands. "Right. We leave for *Ban Chao* in an hour. Can you be ready by then?"

Lim gave him a human nod, turned and exited the conference room. Tully stared after her. "Women," he muttered. "Can't live with them, can't live without them, and can't leave them behind."

He thumbed the call list on his com pad. A moment later First Sergeant Luff's face was looking at him out of the surface of the pad. "Colonel? Something I can do for you?"

"Yep," Tully said. "Top, I need you to notify whoever is in charge of quarters on *Ban Chao* that we need to find a room for one more. Lim of Terralore *elian* is going to be joining us."

"A Lleix?"

"Yep. And Top?"

"Yes, sir . . ."

"I'd like her in ship officer country if you can manage it, but close to me and to the jinau quarters." He started to thumb off the call, but stopped to say, "Think of her as a new lieutenant, Top—lots of book knowledge but short on experience."

"Joy." The first sergeant's tone was so dry it could have withered a field.

Tully laughed. "She's pretty sharp, Top. I doubt she'll make many of the mistakes a fresh shavetail would make."

"No, she'll make new and unusual ones." Luff's tone shifted to one of resignation.

"See to it, Top."

"Yes, sir."

Aille krinnu ava Terra was preceded into the Earth headquarters of the Bond of Ebezon by Yaut krinnu ava Terra and Nath krinnu ava Terra. They had been requested to attend upon Preceptor Ronz not long after a courier ship had arrived from Ares Base.

The preceptor greeted them as they entered the building. As with most Jao structures, the concept of straight hallways with doors opening off of it never seemed to have occurred to the designers. Ronz watched as they shifted almost unconsciously to a more relaxed carriage of their bodies. He had noted before that Jao who spent a lot of time with humans would often minimalize their body postures. It was curious to him that even these three, members of the top five figures in Terra taif, appeared to be doing it.

He beckoned without words, and they followed around a curving wall into a dimly lit space with cushions and other Jao arrangements scattered around. At a gesture from him, they all settled onto soft dehabia blankets, all the while eyeing him closely, *blatant-curiosity* written into the lines and angles of their bodies.

"It is possible," Ronz began as his Pleniary-superior Tura entered the room quietly and settle to a blanket of her own to one side, "that the human propensity for *ollnat* may have passed into excess."

Aille's angles flowed into *focused-attention*. "In what way?" he asked.

"Caitlin Kralik has reported on the progress of the survey expedition," the preceptor replied.

Ronz said nothing further, looking over the three leading members of the Terra's new *taif*. They were smart and fit, their nap lustrous with frequent swims. Aille had the advantage of being rather openminded for a Jao, able to adapt quickly, a long-time characteristic bred for by Pluthrak, his birth-kochan. Ronz watched angles flow across and through Aille's body so swiftly that even he had trouble following the changes. He appreciated that Aille made no effort to mask or neutralize those movements. It indicated a trust that not many would have been willing to offer, not even to one who stood in the place of a parent kochan.

Aille's body settled into *perceived-boldness*. "She has abandoned the search?"

"Yes and no," Ronz said with a fillip of *admiration-of-perception* in his own angles. "Caitlin has concluded that the Ekhat are so prevalent in this galactic arm, and the possibilities of finding surviving sufficiently civilized races to ally with us are so low, that another approach must be developed."

"And did she propose such an approach?" Nath asked, her angles reading *foretold-certainty*.

"No." Ronz stood and crossed to look out the elliptical window, staring into the moonlight. "She has wielded her *oudh* and decided. Caitlin will lead her fleet across the void to the Sagittarius Arm, and establish her search there."

"Ah," was Aille's only response. He went *neutral* for a moment, then flowed into *wry-amusement*. "*Ollnat* with a vengeance, as Wrot might say."

"Indeed." Ronz turned his back on the window to face them, moonlight pouring around him and turning him into a shadowy figure. "Where a Jao with her charge would systematically examine every possible system, gleaning in a well-harvested field, Caitlin has decided to move to a different field altogether. And can we say that she is wrong?"

Silence.

After a moment, Ronz sighed, and returned to his former position. "Even if I wanted to stop her, by now they are either about to leave Ares Base, or they have already begun the voyage."

Yaut broke his silence. "And what does Wrôt have to say about this? He will have reported as well, I'm sure."

"Wrot," Ronz began, his angles pure *neutral*, "is deeply concerned. He does not question Caitlin's *oudh* as such, where another might, but he questions whether the risk that she is undertaking lies within that *oudh*."

"He would not say that much without making a recommendation," Yaut growled out, leaving unsaid the *so tell us already* to let his angles of *impatience* speak instead.

"Wrot made no recommendations, but he did suggest that the Bond get directly involved in the expedition."

"Would that be wise?" Aille said, his golden-brown body abandoning *curiosity* for *concern*. "The Bond does not take sides in kochan affairs."

"No, it would not. There are reasons I would rather not go into at this point," Ronz said, "but the Bond has been by no means unanimous in its support of the policy I have followed here on Terra. If I officially involve the Bond in this matter, I will possibly raise up conflict within the Bond which would be much better avoided, not to mention stirring the currents of politics among and between the kochans."

The room was silent again as the others contemplated what had been said.

"What ship?"

The voice was almost atonal, the pitch and placement was so sloppy. Third-Mordent was instantly infuriated even before the hologram field flickered and filled with the face of a lesser Ekhat.

"Put me through to a harmony master," she fluted in response in descending quarter-tones, her anger adding an edge to the notes.

"What ship?"

Third-Mordent's fury flashed, and she spun to put her face close to the hologram pickup. "You disgrace to the Harmony! You dare to intrude! I bring word for the harmony masters, and only them! Once they find that you have delayed me, you spawn of a servient and a defective male, they will give you to me."

She could feel her vision narrowing in the predator's stare; feel her foreshoulders pulling into attack position. Her right forehand blade rose into the field of the hologram pickup.

"I will eat your progeny! I will geld your mate! I will rend you like a servient! I will kill your progenitors, and theirs! I will purify your line from the Harmony, you stain on the fabric of the Melody!"

The hologram field blanked as she swung her forehand blade at it. Third-Mordent sat back on her haunches, panting. In a moment, the field swirled before presenting a different visage to her.

Third-Mordent's rage evaporated instantly. She recognized this Ekhat. The tegument faded to the shade of old ivory; the age grooves around the mandibles; the scar that creased the tegument around the left eye; all established that this was the oldest living harmony master in this quadrant, Ninth-Minor-Sustained.

"You bring dissonance to this system," the harmony master sang in cold bell tones, ringing in full step ascending. "Justify yourself or be purified."

"Harmony has been broken," Third-Mordent keened, her dirge echoed by the Ekhat behind her.

Ninth-Minor-Sustained stiffened. "Explain!" Her voice glissandoed down into almost a subsonic tone. It throbbed even through the communication link into the hologram projector.

"Descant-at-the-Fourth will add no more notes to the Melody," Third-Mordent sang again in descending whole tones, each sharp-edged, each precise. "Her system is filled with dissonance. All voices are dead. Her harvester and its dancing daughter-ships are broken, stumbling in aimless orbits."

The harmony master's eyes widened and her head moved forward just slightly. She became essence of predator, and despite herself, Third-Mordent shrank back.

"Come to me here!" Ninth-Minor-Sustained intoned. A light flared on a panel in Third-Mordent's ship, a tone pinged.

The hologram emptied.

CHAPTER 17

Ronz felt the moment shift. The others in the room were immobile for the space of a long breath. Then Aille moved, his head turning to look up at an angle. His companions echoed him.

Terniary-superior Tura looked rather to Ronz. "Something has changed," she said. "What, though?"

Ronz tilted his head as his angles moved to *perseverance-in-darkness*. "Undoubtedly the universe will reveal it to us before long."

He stopped for a moment to consider. That moment; that jar to the Jao time sense, had flipped a counter in his mind. He considered it for a moment, then shifted his angles to a simple *resolution.*

"I believe it will be best if Aille leads a task force to join up with Caitlin's expedition." He looked directly at the younger Jao. "You have perception that even Wrot lacks. And, if it were to come down to it, you have the authority to supersede Caitlin if you think it proper and necessary. I strongly doubt you will need to do so, though. And it is true that she most likely could benefit from your guidance."

"And it might give Wrot something new to consider, as well," Aille mused. Yaut's ears flicked in humor.

Aille's eyes flickered green with excitement. Ronz was amused. He knew how much the governor of Earth had hated being left behind when the expedition to Valeron to find the Lleix had been planned, and then again, when Caitlin was sent out to find more sentient allies against the Ekhat. Aille was still young and in his prime. He craved activity, not unlike the humans who assimilated into Terra taif.

And things were fairly quiet here on Earth, Ronz reflected. Aille could be spared for the moment. Reconnaissance patrols had found no evidence of Ekhat in nearby quadrants. The new taif could proceed without him for a while and the experience would temper him, make him an even better leader.

Lim stepped through the hatch of the gig and into one of the boarding bays of the *Ban Chao.* Colonel Tully turned from where he was speaking to a large man wearing jinau blue and beckoned to her. "Lim, this is First Sergeant Adrian Luff."

"Nice to meet you, ma'am," the large man said in a melodious voice. He nodded at her.

She tilted her head and considered Luff. Taller than Tully, bulkier, shaved head, skin a dark brown. From the lines seaming his face, also older than Tully.

"Where are you from, First Sergeant Luff?" she asked.

"Jamaica, ma'am," he replied with a large smile that showed many white teeth.

Lim nodded. That explained why his voice and accent sounded different from Tully's. The sheer variety of local accents just in North America, much less all of Earth, had been confusing to the Lleix when they had first arrived at their sanctuary. Now, those of Terralore *elian* accepted them as if they were part of the natural order. And on Earth, of course, they were. Another manifestation of *ollnat*, perhaps.

"I've asked Sergeant Luff to show you to your quarters and give you a tour," Tully said.

Lim inclined her head, and looked toward the sergeant.

"Right this way, ma'am," he said with another of those shining smiles. He extended his hand toward the nearest hatch.

Aille, Yaut, and Nath went back to Aille's office and scanned the ready list of ships available. He decided to take the two newest battleships, and a group of support craft, always necessary. One other ship, a rather special one, made the list. Aille placed a call to Rafe Aguilera.

"Rafe," Aille said when he contacted Aguilera. "We'll be taking the *Trident* with us." The engineer had already been notified by Yaut of Aille's mission along with those of Aille's direct service who were still on Earth.

"Not without me, you don't!" the engineer said. "She's my baby!"

This was not meant as a literal statement, of course, though humans often referred to inanimate objects as progeny in an attempt to express their great fondness for them. Jao, though, were not nearly so sentimental about their own children, so statements like that only baffled them until they became familiar with the humans. Then they just ignored them.

The *Trident* was an experimental craft for which Rafe Aguilera had been part of the design team and the technical manager during its construction project. The Ollnat Works had proposed it after combining some old Jao technology with interesting concepts floated by some naval types who seemed to have the ability to think farther outside the box than most humans.

Of course, all Jao technology was old. Aille was becoming increasingly aware of that fact as the humans of Terra taif obtained more and more access to Jao databanks and used their own systems to perform intensive research queries. "A bad case of cultural paralysis," he'd heard one human tech mutter to a group of his fellows one day. Aille would, from time to time, marvel that the Jao had managed to survive against the Ekhat when their rate of improvements had been so low. That might be simply because the Ekhat were at least as conservative as the Jao when it came to innovation.

Trident had been designed for one thing, and one thing only: to blockade a star against the entry of hostile ships. Nothing could prevent Ekhat ships from arriving in Terra's sun, but it would be the mission of *Trident* and others of her class to see to it that those ships never made it out of the photosphere.

The Ollnat Works and their naval advisors had taken a page from human history and another from the concept behind the design of *Ban Chao*. *Trident* was a ram ship, pure and simple. Her main weapon was her hull. More than one human had laughed at the thought of a naval concept that had been old with the Roman Empire becoming the latest innovation in interstellar navies.

The nose of the *Trident* was a mass of asteroidal iron that had been refined outside the orbit of Mars with solar-pumped lasers, then moved to the orbit of Terra where it was mated with a hull that was loosely based on *Ban Chao*'s design but with some significant differences. It had been massively strengthened, with longitudinal support beams running the length of the hull to the ring of steel that circled the aft hull just before the mouths of the engine nozzles.

And what engines *Trident* had been given! They were the latest design from the engineering groups, larger and significantly more powerful than the engines powering *Ban Chao*, much less those driving the *Lexington*-class ships. They occupied not only what would have been the engine room of a *Ban Chao* assault-class ship, but a goodly portion of what would have been the large spaces allocated to the assault troops the assault ship would have carried. The engines not only powered the ship for ramming operations, but they also powered the heaviest radiation screens yet developed for Jao/human ships. Those, combined with the massive heat sinks that occupied the rest of the troop space, meant that a *Trident*-class ship would be able to remain on station within a star for a long time.

Of course, humans being humans, they were arguing about what to call the ship. Not the name of the ship itself—almost everyone was happy to use *Trident* for both the ship and class names, particularly since it carried happy resonances for a very successful ship type of the United States of America, Terra's dominant political unit prior to the Jao conquest. No, what they were arguing about, of all things, was how to describe the classification of the ship. Rafe Aguilera was partial to calling it a "subchromine." Others were using "solar submarine." Aille himself saw nothing wrong with calling it a ram ship; that was its designed function, after all. And a few of the humans were beginning to follow that logic. It was a matter of *ollnat*, he supposed, that after having designed and built what promised to be a breathtaking warcraft, they were wasting time and energy arguing about what to call it.

Aille felt he was beginning to understand Wrot's penchant for human gestures and proverbs. Sometimes shaking his head seemed to be the only appropriate reaction to the Terran natives.

"All right," he said, knowing that he startled Aguilera with his easy acquiescence. In truth, he'd planned all along to use Aguilera's talents and experience. Aguilera could be a bit crusty, but he knew what he was doing.

"Do what you need to get *Trident* ready," Aille said.

"When do we leave?" Rafe asked on the way out the door.

"Soon. When time is right."

Rafe stuck his head back around the doorframe. "That—doesn't seem like enough time." His tone was doubtful.

"It will be just enough time and no longer," Aille said. The rightness of it pulsed through him. Jao always knew how long something would take. He knew Rafe understood that too. He'd worked with the Jao long enough at this point not to question their time sense.

"Then we'll be ready," Aguilera said.

Aille knew they would.

Yaut found that he had little to do in preparation for the expedition except arrange for others to take over their responsibilities on Terra while they were gone.

In terms of the taif, that was not difficult. Nath krinnu ava Terra, formerly Nath krinnu Tashnat vau Nimmat, but now first kochan parent of Terra taif along with Aille, would remain behind. Given how gravid she was at the moment, that bordered on an absolute necessity. She would be supported by Hami krinnu ava Terra, last of the three Terra taif elders. With Wrot already away with the exploration flotilla and Yaut about to leave with Aille, there was no question that Hami also had to remain behind. Yaut considered her a canny old female. Her birth kochan of Nullu, subordinate of Dree kochan, had lost a real asset when she chose to leave and join Terra taif.

In terms of local government, there were always questions. Humans were prickly if you misunderstood their rank. Often, they misunderstood it themselves, thinking they were more important than they really were. Or sometimes they engaged in outright lying about their status, something a Jao really couldn't do. Body-speech always betrayed the truthfulness, or lack of it, at any particular moment. Even Oppuk the unsane had never been able to disguise his feelings for long. Only senior Bond officers and members of the kochan elite like Aille or Fleet Commander Dannet could even hold the angles of a simple *neutral* for very long.

It was fortunate that Caitlin's father was still serving as President of North America, Yaut mused. Of all the human leaders in place worldwide, he had the best understanding of the Jao. He also had the most stature among the human leaders, so that he exerted more leadership and control over them than anyone else could muster. Not that that meant they bowed to his every wish. Yaut had, more than once, heard him muttering phrases about herding cats. But despite their bickering, they trusted him and would follow his lead on important things.

The window on Yaut's com pad cleared to reveal the face of President Stockwell staring at him. "Vaish," the president began, the *I-see-you* Jao greeting of a subordinate to a superior. Strictly speaking, the president did not report to Yaut. But as Aille's *fraghta*, Yaut was the fourth most important person on the planet right now, which effectively made him even higher in practical rank than the President of North America. Hence, President Stockwell being politic.

"Vaist," Yaut replied, the usual Jao *you-see-me* response to Stockwell's greeting.

"What can I do for you?" the president asked.

Yaut appreciated that the president didn't waste any time on "chit-chat" or "pleasantries." He had an almost Jao directness about him. Of course, between his surviving many years directly under the claws of Oppuk and his daughter Caitlin's subsequent proximity to Aille as one of his service, he had probably as much practical understanding of the Jao as anyone except his daughter and Professor Jonathan Kinsey, the most public human expert on Jao, who also happened to be one of Stockwell's chief advisors.

"Aille will be off-planet for some time." Yaut came directly to the point. "I will be with him. If you require support or direction, contact Nath."

Stockwell nodded. "When will you leave?"

"Soon," Yaut responded.

The president's mouth twisted. "A day? A month? Give me something a human can understand."

Yaut shrugged. The human expression had become ubiquitous among the Terra taif Jao. "More than a day, less than a week. I think."

Stockwell nodded. "How long will you be gone?"

Yaut just looked at him.

Stockwell grimaced again. "Right. As long as you must. Do you have a guess?"

"No."

"Short or long?"

Yaut considered. The flow changed from moment to moment, but right now it was saying, "Long."

It was obvious that Stockwell was not pleased at that news. "Okay, while Aille is out puttering around the planets and asteroids, we'll keep things flowing here on Earth."

Yaut's head tilted to one side as he took the angles of *correcting-inadvertent-error.* "You misunderstand, President Stockwell. We will not be in Terra system at all."

Stockwell's eyes widened. "Aille's going to Ares Base?" That, of course, was the most logical destination for Terra taif's most prominent member.

"To begin with," Yaut said.

"And?"

"He intends to take reinforcements out and join your daughter in her search."

"Oh." Yaut could see understanding unfold in the human's mind by watching his face and posture. Stockwell sat back in his chair and ran one hand through his hair. "So he really will be gone a long time."

"I believe I said that."

"And if I have things that I really need Aille's input on . . ."

"Don't wait to call him."

"Right." Stockwell sat forward again. "Do you need anything else from me, Yaut?"

"No. This call was for your benefit."

"Right." Even Yaut could hear the tone of Stockwell's voice reflecting his tension over receiving this information. "I believe I'll wait until after he's left to announce this trip."

Yaut shrugged. "As you will, but everyone around Aille either knows now or will know by tomorrow."

Stockwell shook his head.

The permissions and orders advanced to Third-Mordent from Ninth-Minor-Sustained brought her ship directly to the harmony master's docking stage. She left her ship in the care of the younger Ekhat and entered into the station. Of all the tones she heard when she passed through the entryway, one immediately locked into her mind and drew her forward. She didn't know the path she followed, but several lengths of hall and several corner turns later she stood before two Ekhat on the edge of entering predator mode, crouched, heads beginning to lower, red-rimmed eyes focused on her as she approached. She came to a stop before them, restraining her own predator instincts with moderate difficulty.

"You are Third-Mordent," one of them sang in jagged tones.

She said nothing; just let her forehand blades ease out enough to show their gleaming white edges. After a moment, the other sang, "Enter."

The doors opened before Third-Mordent. She passed between the two guards and entered the great hall, where she was greeted by a towering wave of sound. Choirs of many different types of servients, many of which had been uplifted by the Complete Harmony, were clustered around the periphery of the room, each cluster producing different leitmotivs and harmonies. Any combination of clusters would seem dissonant, yet the complexity of the whole was an aural structure that was nothing less than a buttress of harmony for the Melody. The staccato chants, the screams, the yammers, the soaring glissandos into aria figures; Third-Mordent would have called it all divine if she had had a concept of God.

In the center of the great room, turning slowly from left to right, stood Ninth-Minor-Sustained. For the barest moment, Third-Mordent considered her. The harmony master had wide repute among the Complete Harmony faction; among all Ekhat of any knowledge, for that matter. And she was old; with her own eyes, Third-Mordent saw that the harmony master's tegument was even darker than it had appeared in the hologram projector of her ship, having moved from white past old ivory and approaching weathered bone. That and the harmony master's size made her easily the oldest Ekhat Third-Mordent had ever seen.

Third-Mordent remained still as the doors closed behind her. She saw the harmony master's head tilt suddenly. In the next moment, Ninth-Minor-Sustained had spun and was suddenly confronting her, head looming high. Third-Mordent remained still, every muscle tense under her tegument, the barest edge of forehand blades showing.

They made a tableau filled with menace as the music sounded all around them. Third-Mordent could sense predator aggression tensioned in the great legs of Ninth-Minor-Sustained, could see the left forehand blade start to ease out of its sheath. For her part, the full edge of both forehand blades was exposed, and she could feel her vision beginning to narrow to the form of the harmony master.

Third-Mordent had no idea why she was here. Ninth-Minor-Sustained had ordered her presence without explanation. She had no illusions that she could defeat Ninth-Minor-Sustained if the harmony master's purpose was to exact a price for being the messenger of dissonant disaster. Ninth-Minor-Sustained was renowned for being a formidable fighter, and her scars and her survival to reach her current size proved that beyond a doubt.

Only the slim thought that there might be another reason for her own presence kept Third-Mordent from springing into an all-out assault on the harmony master, suicidal though it would have been. But she was poised for it, muscles tensed, leaning forward slightly, when suddenly Ninth-Minor-Sustained stepped back once, twice, and again.

Third-Mordent almost fell over as the object of her focus removed herself. Disoriented for a moment, she heard Ninth-Minor-Sustained sing for her ears alone, "So you are not a fool to waste yourself to no purpose. Well."

The harmony master turned a quarter-turn and passed a manipulator in a motion to draw focus to the choir clusters. "What would you add to this?"

Third-Mordent forced her muscles to relax, and

stood straight. Her forehand blades folded away; her manipulators were carried high, poised to be of use. She turned her mind to the music again, this time listening to it with all of her attention.

Ninth-Minor-Sustained did not rush Third-Mordent. She was allowed to listen to a lengthy portion of the performance.

It dawned on Third-Mordent that the music was a great canon when she finally heard one of the clusters return to themes they had uttered when she entered the room. She looked around, counting the clusters. If they each had their own theme, this was the largest canon she had ever heard of.

There! Another cluster began its theme again. So many themes; none were familiar. She listened again for a full iteration of the canon, auditory sensors at their most sensitive, hearing as each cluster sooner or later restarted its theme.

Ninth-Minor-Sustained remained silent.

Now Third-Mordent had the whole form in her mind. She saw the structure as she heard it, and there were moments . . . there!

Third-Mordent had an inspiration for a theme—a motif, really—and the moment for it to begin was fast approaching. She gathered herself as tensely as if she were going into predator mode, focused on one thing alone. She even felt her vision beginning to narrow down.

The moment came. Tone erupted from Third-Mordent; high and piercing, it keened and wailed, soaring above the other themes, held by her breath support until it descended in fractal tones to a quavering that morphed into a hard pulse. She broke the pulse at just the right moment, then launched again into her motif. This time it was harder, sharper, containing an edge of rage that she could not suppress, still touched as she was by the disaster she had seen the wreckage of in Descant-at-the-Fourth's system.

When Third-Mordent broke after the pulse the second time, Ninth-Minor-Sustained raised a manipulator to prevent her launching a third iteration of the motif.

"Interesting," the harmony master said for Third-Mordent's hearing only. "It has the virtue of simplicity, but it carries all before it. A worthy addition, I think it."

Third-Mordent watched, almost appalled, as Ninth-Minor-Sustained stalked over to the largest cluster and divided it in two. At a sign, one continued with its original theme. The other waited until the harmony master, judging the passage of the work, cued them. The new cluster reproduced Third-Mordent's motif. To perfection, she noted in the haze of surprise that was in her mind.

It came to Third-Mordent that the performance was of Ninth-Minor-Sustained's work, and that the harmony master had considered her improvisation of sufficient merit to be included in the structure of the canon. Shock followed upon shock.

Ninth-Minor-Sustained turned to Third-Mordent. "Come." Nothing more than that, but the younger Ekhat followed the harmony master as if she were being towed by a cable.

CHAPTER 18

Lim accompanied Tully to the command deck of the *Ban Chao* for the second pathfinder jump.

"They've installed jump seats along the back wall," Tully murmured as he led her through the door. "The first pathfinder jump was a little rugged, so they've beefed up the seats and restraints all over the bridge." He touched a dark spot on his face and winced. "Vanta-Captain Ginta says they've learned the tricks now, and this jump will be smoother." He sat down and fastened a harness across his torso. "I'm still going to belt in."

Lim took the seat next to the human's, carefully arranged her robes, and fastened a restraint across her lap.

"Have you observed a jump before?" Tully asked.

"Not from a command deck," Lim responded. "Will it be much different from what I have seen?"

"I doubt it," Tully said. "Especially since this crew is mostly Jao. They all act like it's just another day at work, even when it's as risky as sliding down a mountain slope on one ski with no poles."

Lim turned her head to look at Tully. Having spent most of her time on Earth in the North American region called Colorado, she understood his metaphor. It seemed apt. But it surprised her to see him grinning at her.

"Lighten up, Lim," Tully said. "Man, don't you guys ever laugh at anything? Crack a joke? Something?"

"Your propensity for 'humor' is one of the things we study in Terralore *elian*," Lim said. "There are theories that it is somehow connected to your ability to do *ollnat*."

Tully snorted. "Just about everything we do is connected to *ollnat*, Lim. It's how we humans have survived for thousands of years."

"From the research Terralore *elian* has done, *ollnat* has almost destroyed you as well."

Tully shrugged. "We're still here, aren't we?"

And against that argument, Lim had no counter.

"Whoops, here we go," Tully said facing forward.

"Set Framepoint One," Vanta-Captain Ginta ordered.

The door opened and Yaut preceded Aille onto the command deck of the *Footloose*. Aille had named the ship himself, and then named the sister ship the *Fancy Free*. He understood that humans might have preferred something weightier with more gravitas, but he thought they took this whole naming matter far too seriously, and was not above making some sly fun at their expense. Preceptor Ronz got the joke. Yaut didn't.

Privately, though, he had to admit that names actually made it easier to keep track of the ships once they were deployed and knowing which one you were referring to at any given moment. Two figures, both Jao, turned to meet them.

"Governor Aille," said the larger of the two, Terra-Captain Sanzh krinnu ava Terra, displaying a firm *ready-to-be-of-service*. Before joining Terra taif, he had been Sanzh krinnu Kasem vau Aris, a secondary kochan associated with midtier kochan Aris, from the far side of Jao space. His pelt was plush, slightly longer than most Jao's coats, of a most unusual blond shade. Aille had heard one of the humans call it a "palomino" tint. His coat was so light in color that his white *vai camiti* was almost indiscernible against it, which many Jao found unfortunate.

"Terra-Captain Sanzh," Aille replied. "Is all ready?"

"Waiting word from *Trident*," the Terra-captain said. "They signaled a last minute, ah, *glitch*."

Aille let his angles flow to a tripartite *humored-reception-of-awkward-news*. "Rafe said the ship would be ready. It will be. Prepare for jump, Terra-Captain."

The Terra-captain said nothing, simply turned and began issuing directions to the nearby bridge crew. Aille turned to the other Jao who had been waiting his attention.

"Governor Aille," she murmured, angles set in a perfect *neutral*.

"Pleniary-superior Tura," Aille said in turn.

He recalled his last meeting with Ronz. The preceptor had come to him at the Pascagoula base which had become the center for ship designs and refits. It had surprised him greatly when the preceptor was announced. Before he could do more than rise from his seat, Ronz had entered the room, followed, as he usually was, by Tura.

"Preceptor," Aille had said, speaking first as his was the lower rank.

"Aille," Ronz had replied. And then, in Jao fashion, had continued directly with, "I have added one more to your party. Tura will go with you."

Aille's head had tilted, ears moving forward as his angles slipped into *consideration.* "You believe she will be needed to restrain Caitlin's *ollnat*?"

"No." Ronz had showed no angles at all, in his typical manner. He was perhaps the hardest Jao alive to read if he didn't want to be read.

"You anticipate a need for the presence of the Bond?"

"Say rather, I anticipate a need for the authority of the Bond."

Aille had heard what Ronz said; and just as importantly, what he hadn't said. He then looked beyond the preceptor to where Tura had stood, angles all *neutral.* Her eyes were black; there was no sign of tension in her stance. There had been nothing to be read there.

That same calm stature, that same set of *neutral* angles faced Aille now on the command deck of the *Footloose.* There was no doubt in Aille's mind that the pleniary-superior was on this deck for a reason. But he did doubt that he would be able to determine what that reason was just now. Ronz was the premier strategist of the Bond of Ebezon. His assessments were far-seeing; his strategies indirect and subtle—witness Aille's supplanting of Oppuk as governor of Terra.

Did Tura even know why she was there? Aille considered it well within Ronz's methods to have given her direction to go without giving her a reason as to why. It would be in keeping with the preceptor's approach to strategy, after all; no one knew that better than Aille. He decided not to ask her; not now.

At that moment, the main viewscreen flashed and Rafe Aguilera's visage came into view.

"*Trident* to *Footloose.* We're ready to jump at any time."

Aille turned from Tura to Terra-Captain Sanzh. "Order the jump, Captain."

Lim noted that everyone on the command deck, Jao and humans alike, seemed to relax a bit as the *Ban Chao* cleared the corona transition. Tully in particular seemed to almost go limp as he sat back in his seat and sighed. "Glad that's over."

She turned and considered him. "Do you not like frame travel, then?"

"Ah, that would be a big 'No.'" Tully ran a hand through his short hair. "But when Aille says 'Go,' and Ed Kralik says 'Go,' I go."

"Would it be easier to travel if you weren't on the command deck?" Lim was curious. To those of her people who came out of the Lleix *dochaya*, Tully was second only to Caitlin Kralik in terms of being revered; more so than any of the current Lleix leaders, she had to admit. This was a side of Tully she hadn't seen before, and she was curious.

"Not a chance," Tully said with emphasis. "If something goes wrong when we jump into a sun and I end up being little flakes of carbon floating around in the solar plasma, I at least want to see it coming so I can kiss my ass goodbye."

He grinned at her, at which point Lim gathered that the last statement was another manifestation of human humor.

"Come on," Tully continued as he released his

harness. "Now that we're here, it's going to take another couple of days at least before anything else interesting happens out there. I've got someone I want you to meet."

Lim freed herself from her restraint and stood to follow Tully's lead out of the command deck. They took a lift down a couple of decks, then Tully led her down a long passageway and around several bends before they walked into a surprisingly spacious exercise deck filled with jinau, humans and Jao alike.

She had seen human-style exercise machines before, so the sight of them being utilized by many humans was not a surprise. A few of them had serious expressions on their faces as they handled what were obvious great weights. Several of the others, though, were joking with each other as they went through their repetitions. Human humor was almost ubiquitous in Terra taif, Lim noted. Unsurprising, that was.

On the other side of the room from the machines a number of exercise mats were laid on the floor. It was there that the Jao were clustered. She looked back to make sure; yes, there were no Jao on the exercise machines.

"The Jao do not use the machines?"

Tully shook his head. "No. Their muscles are harder and stronger than human muscles to begin with, and then with the amount of swimming they do almost every day, they're in constant trim. It's almost like they were genetically optimized to be in superb condition all the time."

"But they were," Lim murmured.

Tully stopped and turned to stare at her. "What?"

"You did not know?"

The human shook his head.

"It was part of what the Ekhat did when they uplifted them to sentience."

"And you know this how?"

Lim moved a hand in the Lleix gesture of displaying the obvious. "We have lost much of the Lleix knowledge over the ages as we were hunted and hid, but some pieces we retained. This was part of what we knew about the Jao, and was one of the reasons why we feared them so much."

Tully stared at her, then shook his head sharply. "Just when I think I understand you people, one of you says something like that, and I realize that I really don't know that much about you. You really were hiding for centuries, weren't you?"

Lim nodded, using the human gesture. "Longer. The Jao were hunting us for the Ekhat before your Roman Empire was born."

Tully said nothing; just shook his head again and turned to watch the troops. Lim stood beside him and observed.

The Jao and the human jinau on the mats were all involved in unarmed combat practice. After a while, Lim became aware of one group of humans standing around a mat where a human not dressed like the jinau was apparently working with the troops. One after another the jinau assaulted him; one after another he defeated them with smooth movements.

"Who is that man?" Lim asked Tully, indicating the human she had been observing.

"That's who I want you to meet," Tully responded. "His name is Zhao Jiguang, and he is perhaps the deadliest human I've ever met."

"Is there a reason he isn't dressed like the rest of the jinau?"

"That would be because he isn't a jinau," Tully said with a smile.

Lim stared at him, and she felt her aureole rising. "Is this an example of your humor? How can he be on this ship and not be one of the jinau?"

Tully sobered and held his hands up in front of his shoulders. "He's a master of a martial art called Tai Chi. He came to Lieutenant General Kralik after the plasma disaster in China. He won't join the jinau, but he did offer to train our troops and the general took him up on it. We're lucky to have him on the ship."

Lim looking again at the non-jinau human. He had stopped the exercise, and was talking to those surrounding him. To her eye, this Zhao person seemed not very impressive. He was not even as tall as Tully, much less one of the elders of the Lleix. He was not large. He was soft-spoken. Yet the humans around him were all focused on his words. As she watched, Zhao stopped speaking and placed his hands together before him. It was surprising to her that they all bowed to him; a bow which he returned. She knew that many of the so-called Oriental cultures used bows in formal manners, but it had never occurred to her to see it in a place like this, filled with sweating, grunting humans and Jao striving with each other.

Tully touched her on the shoulder. "Come on."

Lim followed him over to the mat. Zhao looked toward them as they approached.

"Gabe!" Zhao's face was split by a wide grin.

"Hey, Joe," Tully said with an answering smile. They grabbed each other's hands in a strong handshake, then Tully placed his hand on Zhao's shoulder and turned to beckon her forward. "Joe, this is Lim, of the Lleix Terralore *elian.*"

Zhao's grin slipped away, and he turned to face Lim. "I've wanted to meet one of your people for some time," he said, putting his hands together and giving a slight bow. "It's an honor to finally get the chance."

Lim noted that his English was quite good, although with a very slight accent. "Are you from Beijing?" she asked in Mandarin.

Zhao's eyes widened in delight, and he clapped his hands. "You speak Mandarin!" he exclaimed. "That is so cool!" He laughed for a moment. "Actually, my family is from Nanjing, although I was raised in San Diego." He beamed at her.

Tully cleared his throat from behind him. "She wants to learn to fight, Joe."

Zhao's expression changed as sharply as if a switch had been flipped. He directed a piercing glance at her. Lim stared back at him. They stood thus for a long moment. At last Zhao broke the silence.

"Do you like tea?" he asked in Mandarin.

Of all the questions he could have asked, that was not among what Lim expected. She tilted her head slightly, considering him. "Except for Assam, yes."

Zhao's eyes crinkled a bit as he gave a small smile. "Good. You will visit me in my quarters, tomorrow morning, perhaps in midmorning?"

Lim considered him again, tilting her head slightly the other direction. "Yes," she said after a moment.

Zhao bowed again to her, looked to Tully long enough to say, "Gabe," and turned and left them there.

"You know, it's rude to talk as if other people aren't there," Tully remarked as Zhao left the exercise space.

Lim deduced he was indulging in humor from the small smile that kept slipping around his mouth. "If Zhao Jiguang had wanted you to be a part of the conversation, he would have spoken to you in English."

Tully laughed. "Fair answer, Lim. You're learning how to deal with us. Now, let's go find some lunch. If we're lucky, Joe made some of it."

Lim stopped. "Zhao Jiguang is a cook? I thought he was a fighter."

Tully took Lim's arm and urged her along. "Joe's not a cook. He is many things; one of which is a Tai Chi master, another of which is a master chef. Now come on, let's go check it out."

"Emergence in Ares system confirmed," the lead sensor officer called out. "Ares Base 118 degrees off port axis."

Aille looked around as Yaut stirred. "Too much talk," the fraghta muttered.

Aille let his angles slip to simple *humor.* "Humans talk, Yaut. Better that they talk about their work than not." Yaut's angles morphed to *irritation.* Aille's blended a component of *sly* to his.

"Guard ships query received. Sending our response." That from the communications tech, a short Jao.

"*Trident* emerged behind us," came from the sensor officer again.

Terra-Captain Sanzh looked to Aille. He nodded. "Navigator, direct us to Ares Base," the captain ordered.

"Kralik will not be happy to see you," Yaut predicted.

Aille said nothing, but his body flowed into the angles for *reluctant-agreement.*

CHAPTER 19

Ninth-Minor-Sustained spun to face Third-Mordent after they entered the room. Third-Mordent had no idea where they were, but her reflexes dropped her into predator mode in reaction to the harmony master's sudden movement. The thought was still in her mind that, despite the harmony master's approval of her motif, she still might exact a price from Third-Mordent for bringing word of what she had seen.

"Descant-at-the-Fourth was the longest surviving of my descendants," Ninth-Minor-Sustained fluted. "Fourth generation removed." She flicked open a forehand blade and carved a line in her own tegument.

Third-Mordent's body had tensed and her vision had narrowed when the harmony master had opened the sheath of the forehand blade. The sight of the white ichor oozing from the gash Ninth-Minor-Sustained had opened sent a quiver through her body. Only the sight of the open forehand blade kept her from assaulting the harmony master.

They stood thus in a tableau for what seemed an endless period of time to Third-Mordent. Gradually she became aware that Ninth-Minor-Sustained was staring at her, steady gaze over the intervening forehand blade. It took great effort, great self-control, to put away the predator's mind and ease the tension in her own pose, raise her manipulators, and return the harmony master's gaze.

"I had hopes for Descant-at-the-Fourth and her line," Ninth-Minor-Sustained dirged. "Was her system truly dissonant?"

"Six ships missing altogether," Third-Mordent keened softly, "yet unusual traces in the solar corona indicated where they died. Seven ships dead in fragments dancing aimlessly around the star with the shattered corpse of Descant-at-the-Fourth's World Harvester. Nothing but ruin and broken rubble at the planetary post." She stopped for a moment, then sang in descending quarter-tones, "All trace of the Melody in the system gone. Gone as if it had never been."

Ninth-Minor-Sustained lowered her head, still staring at Third-Mordent. "Then she is gone, and all her surviving direct progeny."

To that Third-Mordent could only assent.

The harmony master folded her forehand blade back into its sheath. She turned and walked over to face what Third-Mordent first assumed was a viewscreen displaying a field of stars. It was a moment before the younger Ekhat realized that it was really a transparent window. That surprised her, as very few Ekhat liked to be reminded of the near presence of the emptiness of space.

"You are of the line of Descant-at-the-Fourth." The

harmony master was not asking a question with that bit of melody.

"Yes," Third-Mordent responded with a glissando.

"Not of the most direct line," Ninth-Minor-Sustained intoned.

"Yet still of her progeny," Third-Mordent responded in kind, "fifth generation removed in a collateral line."

Ninth-Minor-Sustained stood silently, still, gazing out the window. Third-Mordent said nothing; she knew nothing to say that hadn't been said. Whatever the harmony master's purpose, it was opaque to the younger Ekhat, who was just now coming to grips with the thought that she herself was in the line of Ninth-Minor-Sustained. She had not known. Few Ekhat could trace their lineage very far back. Mortality among young Ekhat was very high, between the fratricide among their peers and the casual violence of their elders. The odds of one's direct progenitors surviving long enough to communicate with sapient offspring were very low.

Yet Third-Mordent could now count her line back ten generations to no less than Ninth-Minor-Sustained, preeminent harmony master, one of the leaders of the Complete Harmony faction, wickedly adept at combat, survivor of the longest odds. Her mind could just barely begin to grapple with the implications of that knowledge.

All thoughts fled Third-Mordent's mind as Ninth-Minor-Sustained spun and leapt on her, smashing her to the floor and pinning her under the harmony master's great weight. One forehand blade hung poised before her eyes, and she felt the edge of the other kiss her throat ever so slightly.

Third-Mordent clamped down on her instincts, hard. She knew that even the slightest movement on her part would bring her death. The struggle she fought in her own mind was every bit as fierce as the struggle she would have attempted against the harmony master; every bit as desperate; every bit as ruthless. And almost as fruitless; but not quite.

Not. Quite.

Every muscle tensed, and her tegument rippled. But Third-Mordent, by the barest of margins, did not struggle. She could sense the great head of Ninth-Minor-Sustained lowering above her, mandibles and maw approaching the back of her neck. Her tegument rippled again, but still she did not move.

The exhaled breath of the harmony master touched the tegument just behind her head. It took the last bit of control Third-Mordent had to remain still.

"You cannot defeat me," Ninth-Minor-Sustained . . . crooned. "You can never defeat me."

Third-Mordent made no response; she focused on controlling herself. A long moment passed.

The forehand blade at her neck was removed so deftly Third-Mordent was not aware of its absence for long moments. She felt the pressure of the harmony master's weight shift the barest of instances before massive pain in three different locations sheeted through her system, paralyzing her for what seemed almost an eternity.

The pains faded; the one at the base of the skull lingered longest.

"Get up," Ninth-Minor-Sustained fluted in a monotone. She said nothing else, but Third-Mordent understood what was not said, and struggled to her feet.

The younger Ekhat stood facing her very distant ancestor, manipulators raised as high as she could raise them in the lingering pain, forehand blades still sheathed but trembling.

"Control," the harmony master uttered in a whisper of an aria. "You think you have it. You are wrong. But I will teach it to you."

Third-Mordent shivered at the solid, austere harmony in Ninth-Minor-Sustained's voice.

Lim stood before the door of Zhao Jiguang's quarters, and raised her hand to the signal plate. The door opened just before her finger touched. Zhao stood before her, dressed much as he was the previous day in loose trousers and long loose tunic of a light gray color.

"Ah, Lim. Please come in," Zhao said in Mandarin.

He gave a slight bow, which Lim returned before she stepped through the doorway.

Zhao pointed to the small seating area in his quarters. "Please, choose a place to sit. I will return with the tea momentarily."

Lim examined the three low chairs—barely more than stools—that were grouped around an equally low rectangular table. After a moment of observation, she chose a seat on one of the long sides of the table, facing another chair across the table, with the third chair to her left. She was still not certain why she had come. This human did not look to her to be as dangerous as Gabe Tully had insisted he was.

She refolded her robes, then locked her hands together in her lap and looked around the room. It was small, as most spaces were in the ship. Indeed,

Lim's own quarters was barely larger in total than the room in which she sat.

Her eye was caught by a low box lying on the table opposite the third chair at the open end of the table. It was black, perhaps five of the human centimeters high, and it contained fine white sand. The sand had been brushed into patterns by some sort of tool, and there were three small stones placed within the patterns; one smooth and shining black, one smooth and gleaming white, and one coarse and dull red.

She was still looking at the box when Zhao arrived with the tea. He set a black wooden tray before the third seat. On the tray was a black teapot, low and round, rough surfaced, with golden highlights limning the outlines of a long beast.

Flanking the teapot were two round handleless cups of a matching finish and pattern, each sitting upon saucers shaped like Terran leaves, with gold traces outlining the veins of the leaves.

Zhao lifted the teapot and poured steaming tea into each of the cups. Setting the teapot down, he placed a saucer and cup before Lim and the seat opposite her, which he then settled neatly into.

"It is good of you to come, Lim," Zhao said with a slight forward bow, still speaking Mandarin.

"It was good of you to invite me, Master Zhao," Lim replied in the same language.

Zhao cupped his hands before him, then spread them to the sides in a smooth gesture. "Please, call me Joe. I am not so pretentious as to require being addressed as 'Master,' especially not by one of your people."

Lim repeated the gesture. "Then call me Lim, for I am no master, either among my people or yours."

Zhao smiled, bringing his hands together around the cup before him. "Then we are two friends of a common friend, Gabe Tully, who are met to become friends of each other over shared tea." He lifted the cup and smelled of the vapor arising from it.

Lim followed suit. She found the cup surprisingly heavy for its size, but lifted it to sniff of it. "It smells excellent," she exclaimed in surprise.

"I have family in Nanjing," Zhao said, "who sent me quite a bit of premium Oolong tea just before I shipped out." He smiled. "For some reason, many of the Chinese and Japanese among the jinau wish to be my friends."

Zhao took a sip of the tea, then returned his cup to its saucer. Lim did likewise, finding the flavor of the tea matching the excellence of its scent. She set it cup down, unfortunately not as gently as Zhao had. It made a noticeable "clunk" as it encountered the saucer. She tilted her head and looked at Zhao, her aureole rising.

He smiled again. "Cast iron," he said. "All of it; pot, cups, saucers. Japanese make, but very nice. I inherited them from my mother when she died."

"Is this part of the tea ceremony, then?" Lim asked aureole now extended fully.

"No, not part of the ritual." Zhao shook his head. "I'm actually not very good at the ceremony," he said with a note of chagrin. "My mother used to tell me I wasn't patient enough. I did not bring the utensils with me. But," a gleaming smile appeared, "when we return to Earth, I will invite you to our home and my sister will welcome you with the full ceremony."

They drank their tea slowly and quietly. When

Lim had emptied her cup, she held it up at eye-level to examine the creature molded into the side of it. "Dragon?" She looked at Zhao. He nodded with another smile, and lifted the pot to refill their cups.

Aille followed Yaut into the workspace of Lieutenant General Ed Kralik. His flotilla's jump to Ares system had been uneventful. He suspected the next few moments might provide sufficient storminess to balance that out.

"Governor," Kralik said from where he stood before his desk. "I was surprised to hear that you had traveled all the way out here."

"Ed Kralik," Aille replied. "One is of use wherever one is needed."

"So what use is the governor of Terra going to be put to in Ares Base?"

The general sounded a little skeptical, Aille thought. That was probably to be expected; Kralik had a lot of experience with Jao. "Business of Terra taif," he responded.

Kralik's eyes narrowed. "The only business the taif has out here is Ares Base or . . . Caitlin!" The human clasped his hands behind his back. "If it was something to do with the base, I'd have already heard about it. So what is it about Caitlin that has you abandoning your post and jumping to the middle of nowhere? Are you demoting her?"

Aille's angles slipped into *calmness-in-turbulence* in the face of Kralik's human version of pure unalloyed *stubbornness* that even a Jao could recognize. "No," he said. "She will retain *oudh*."

Kralik's human face took on an expression that

could only be called a glower. Aille was one of the best Jao around at reading human postures, but that one wasn't hard to understand.

"Have you seen something? Is she—the fleet—in danger?"

Aille shrugged, using the human gesture to attempt to calm the general. "No, nothing is foreseen."

"Then you'd better have your navigators talk to the Starsifters here." Kralik's mouth quirked. "That first step into the long dark is a doozy, from the word the fleet sent back."

That led to a short discussion as to what a "doozy" was, followed by a short discussion about the nature of the "doozy" in this context, which in turn led to Yaut stepping to one side to send orders via his com pad.

Kralik looked back to Aille. "You still haven't told me why you are personally leading this trip."

"Ronz believes that Caitlin might find my presence of benefit," Aille said. "And the ships I bring, of course."

Kralik's face went to an expression that could have passed for *neutral*. He said nothing for a long moment, then licked his lips and said, "The Preceptor ordered this?"

"Preceptor Ronz suggested that I could be of great use if I joined Caitlin in the search for allies," Aille responded.

"And you're not just joining her, are you? You're taking reinforcements to her." The glower returned to Kralik's face as he crossed his arms across his chest. "So he suspects something, doesn't he?"

"I have told you what he told me," Aille said.

Yaut returned to Aille's side, which drew Kralik's eye. Aille knew that the fraghta, despite his years of association with humans, was still somewhat more brusque and fond of *wrem-fa* methods than was perhaps of maximum use in dealing with them. He turned and looked at Yaut, the tilt of his head and the angle of his ears giving what Caitlin might have called a shorthand version of *my-responsibility*. Yaut's whiskers twitched back and forth in irritation, but he said nothing.

Aille returned his attention to the human. Kralik was staring him in the eye, which, tall though he was for a Terran, still required him to look up at the governor.

"I'm going with you," Kralik said, once he realized he had Aille's focus again.

"You will stay at Ares Base," Aille said. "You are not required for this."

Kralik's face paled. "I really don't care if I am *required*," he bit the words out. "You've sent my wife in harm's way, such that you're giving her the strongest combat fleet in this region of our alliance. The Bond is sending you to join her. I will not sit here on my butt and wait for God knows what."

Aille tilted his head. He said nothing, waiting on the human to conclude.

Kralik's nostrils flared. He turned to his desk and took from its stand the bau that Aille had awarded him for exemplary service early in their relationship. The carvings on that rod of shell began with the siege and destruction of Salem during the last days of the governorship of Oppuk, but they had been added to and augmented in the years since then. The service it denoted would have made any Jao proud.

"You gave me this," the human said, looking to where his hands almost cradled the bau. "You took me into your service, and you gave me this. I've taken your orders, I've done your work, I've been 'of service' wherever you sent me, including sitting here at Ares Base when Caitlin was out jumping from star to star not knowing what she was going to find."

Kralik looked back up and locked eyes with Aille again. "And now you are going to join her, crossing the void to the Sagittarius Arm, going where no Jao or human has gone before, and Ronz is concerned enough about it to send you to join her. Caitlin is out there," he pointed above his head with the bau, "Wrot is out there, Tully is out there, and now you, and Yaut, and even Rafe Aguilera for God's sake, are going out to join her. Whatever it is that has Ronz so concerned ought to 'require' that you have your A team with you. All the rest of your service will be out there with you, and you're going to leave me behind? I don't think so."

The bau lowered and Kralik said quietly, "You need your service with you, and I'm part of that service. I have military and jinau expertise that no one else in that fleet has. Whatever the Bond thinks you're going to encounter, you need me." He held the bau up between them, in front of Aille's eyes. "You still don't understand humans as well as you think you do. If you leave me here, you will have told the universe that you don't value or trust me. You will have broken everything this represents between us."

Aille reached out and took the bau from Kralik. The human released it readily. Aille turned it over and over in his hands, feeling the carvings with his fingers.

Kralik argued well, Aille decided. It was true that he was expert; far more so than Gabe Tully. That alone was perhaps not sufficient to bring him. But his other point was also valid, and perhaps was even the stronger one in this era of Jao/human relations.

Aille handed the bau back to the human and felt the flow of time sense. "You have until we finish onloading supplies to give your orders. If you are not on board when we seal the hatches, you will be left behind."

He turned without another word and headed for the door, Yaut preceding him. As the door closed behind him he heard Kralik speak to a com pad, "Get me Mrat krinnu ava Terra."

"Impudent human," Yaut muttered as they walked down the hall, angles stiff with *offended-sensibilities.*

"What would you have done in his place, Yaut?" Aille asked.

The fraghta snorted. "I would have ordered myself aboard your ship, and made sure that you didn't see or hear of me until after the ship jumped."

"Not so very different, then," Aille murmured.

Yaut said nothing as he continued to stalk ahead of him.

CHAPTER 20

Zhao leaned forward and poured more tea into Lim's cup, followed by his own. The last few drops fell slowly from the spout of the dragon pot into his cup. "Last of the pot," he said with a smile. "We must savor it."

Cradling his cup in both hands, Zhao looked at Lim. "Tully said you want to learn to fight. Can you explain?"

Lim went still, holding her own cup before her and looking down into it. The tea seemed to be an ebon fluid as it sat within the black enameled iron cup, and she caught a glimpse of her own face reflected within the dark mirror.

"I . . . The Ekhat have driven us and harried us for so long. We have lost so much. We . . ." she looked up at Zhao, to see him sitting very still, "we Lleix are not a warrior people. We have no *elian* like the jinau, or your human armies. I told Tully, I no longer wish to be helpless."

"Ah," Zhao said, a small smile crossing his face.

"That is a worthwhile goal. And it is one in which I may be of some small help."

He drained the last of the tea from his cup, and set it down on its leaf saucer with a click. "To begin with, we must ask and answer the question, 'Who is Lim?'"

Lim followed suit in drinking her tea and setting her empty cup down. Her hands moved to rearrange the folds of her robe, without thought or volition on her part, almost as if they were separate discrete beings. "I am Lim, of the Lleix," she replied after a long moment of silence.

Zhao shook his head gently. "No, that is your source, what you are out of. It is not who you are."

"I am Lim of Terralore *elian*," she tried again.

"That is what you do, not who you are." Zhao's voice was calm and soft.

A very long moment passed with no sound but the whisper of her fingers adjusting the brocade of her robes. At length, she forced them to still and looked back at Zhao. "I am Lim of the *dochaya*." She felt empty as she said that, expecting him to accept it and refuse her.

"That is what shaped you," Zhao said. "And from what Tully has told me, it was a hard shaping, one that wounded and scarred you." He stopped for a moment, and Lim felt the depths of the wounds and the strictures of the scars as she had not since right after she had been rejected at the Festival of Choosing years ago. She looked down, not surprised to see her fingers grasping her robes, crumpling the fabric. It took another effort to force them to relax and smooth out the brocade.

"But..."

Lim's head jerked up as Zhao continued.

"...that is still not who you are."

Lim tilted her head as she studied the faintly smiling human, who sat across the table from her, motionless with his hands resting lightly on his thighs. She considered him; then tilted her head the other direction as she considered his responses to her statements.

"I..." she hesitated, "am Lim." She said nothing more.

After a moment, Zhao's smile grew broader, and somehow brighter as his eyes narrowed and the skin crinkled at the outside corners. "Precisely so," he said. "Exactly so. You are Lim. You are a person of worth. That is the foundation of your life, and upon that foundation we lay the first stone—you are now my student."

"Electromagnetic signals detected."

Flue Vaughan's head snapped up at that announcement from the human sensor tech, and he hit five separate control pads on his workstation with two motions of his hands.

Terra-Captain Uldra faced the tech. "Artificial or natural?"

"Very regular," the tech responded. "Analysis indicates data content. Artificial."

Vaughan hit more controls.

"Source?"

"Out-system." The tech tapped controls of her own. "Weak signals that aren't aligned with any significant bodies in the system. Not much out that direction except gravel and dust until you hit the system's edge."

Terra-Captain Uldra looked to Vaughan, who touched another control on his workstation.

"What is it?" he heard growled into his earpiece a few seconds later.

"Sorry to disturb your rest cycle, Fleet Commander," Flue said, "but I think you'd best come to the bridge."

"Why?"

"Signals."

There was a click in his earpiece. Vaughan looked back to where Uldra was still looking at him. "She's on her way."

Uldra nodded, and returned his focus to the tech.

Third-Mordent felt Ninth-Minor-Sustained's forehand blade slice across the tegument of her left foreleg as she spun away in panic from the harmony master's attack. She leapt to her right, trying to get far enough away that she could turn and resume her defense.

"Stop." Ninth-Minor-Sustained's voice fluted down an arpeggio, cold as steel that had been in space in the shadow of a planet.

Third-Mordent froze in place. That had been the first lesson that her ancestress had taught her. It had been painful to learn, but learn it she had. When Ninth-Minor-Sustained said halt, she meant it.

Third-Mordent waited in position, trembling with both fear and bloodlust, as Ninth-Minor-Sustained walked softly around her to face her, looking her eye to eye. "You do not anticipate well," the harmony master intoned. "You should have blocked that last cut, as well as the two before it. Your jump was ill-advised at best, and most likely would have resulted in your death if you had faced an opponent of any skill and experience. You will study the files I send you tonight, and we will begin again tomorrow."

The harmony master turned and walked away down the performance hall, leaving Third-Mordent still frozen. As she neared a door, she looked back and sang, "Release."

Third-Mordent almost fell when the tension released from her limbs. She straightened slowly, folding her forehand blades away and raising her manipulators. They trembled a little; her mind was trembling, as well.

The door opened at Ninth-Minor-Sustained's approach. There was a squeal as she made a sudden lunge through the doorway, then the door closed again as she turned back with an Anj servient in her manipulators. The creature squirmed in the harmony master's grasp, its piping squeals echoing from the walls of the hall.

"Control," Ninth-Minor-Sustained whisper-sang, "begins with control of yourself. Do not move."

Third-Mordent froze again. The harmony master walked up to where she stood, holding the Anj right before her. The squeals of the servient were beginning to affect her; her vision began to narrow.

Ninth-Minor-Sustained exposed the edge of one forehand blade, and barely kissed the Anj with it. Dark blood began to ooze from the resulting slice, and the servient's cries grew louder.

The harmony master took one manipulator, dipped the tip of one of the dactyls in the servient's blood, and then dabbed it around one of Third-Mordent's olfactory sensors. The scent of the fresh blood impelled Third-Mordent toward predator mode; vision further narrowing, manipulators dropping and forehand blades rising.

Ninth-Minor-Sustained's manipulators twisted suddenly and snapped the spine of the Anj. The servient shrilled in agony, then subsided to moans as the harmony master dropped it to the floor in front of Third-Mordent.

She lost sight of the harmony master's great form as she focused in on the wounded servient, dragging itself across the floor, leaving a dark smear of blood behind it. Low chirps and moans accompanied its struggles, further inciting the young Ekhat to go into predator mode.

"Control," Ninth-Minor-Sustained sounded a whisper-aria behind her. "Do. Not. Move."

Third-Mordent managed, somehow, to continue her freeze. Inside her skull, her predator senses raged, seeking to leap onto the Anj and rend it into gobbets. Something, though . . . something kept her still. Some facility of her mind, dimly awakened as yet, still exerted iron constraint over her and locked her body down. Nothing twitched. No shivers or trembles. Nothing.

Ninth-Minor-Sustained gave a whisper of satisfaction.

The moans of the Anj began to shape a motif in Third-Mordent's mind. A chaconne, it would be, she thought. The blood on the floor took on a luster to match the music beginning to form in her thoughts.

Zhao Jiguang picked up a cup of tea and sipped on it as he contemplated the medical images.

"Hmm. More proof that God has a sense of humor. Ball and socket joints for the shoulders and hips I understand, but for the elbows and knees? Wow." He set the cup down and grasped his chin between his thumb and forefinger. "Well, at least she'll be flexible."

"Hmm. Center of mass is lower than on a human. Female thing? Human similarity?" Zhao flipped over to another file and compared two images side by side. "No, same propensity in the males. Hip structure is massive. Wonder if they developed on a heavy-gravity world?" He made a note. "Ground and center will be affected."

Zhao flipped back to the first image file. "Okay, flat feet. Very flat. Wonder if they can move up on their toes at all?" He made more notes.

After a few more minutes of study and thinking, Zhao was raising the tea cup to his mouth again when he flipped to the circulatory system mapping, at which point he blew tea all over the workstation's viewscreen.

Zhao didn't curse as he wiped off the workstation surfaces. That was not due to lack of incentive, but rather to lack of sufficiently inspired invective. *Two* hearts? *Two* parallel circulatory systems? How was *chi* supposed to flow through a system like that?

It was about that moment that Zhao realized the depth of the challenge he had accepted when he agreed to teach Tai Chi to Lim. It was also about that moment when he decided that Gabe Tully, while not precisely evil, perhaps had more than a bit too much yin in his system, and apparently not enough yang. He would have to meditate on how that was possible, given that Tully was otherwise the poster child for yangness.

He turned back to Lim's med file, and continued his research.

Caitlin was roused from a dream featuring her husband by a com pad tone. It took a few moments to come to full consciousness—she really didn't want to leave even a dream about Ed. She finally opened her eyes. "What?"

"Sorry to disturb you, Director," came the voice of Lieutenant Vaughan. "Fleet Commander Dannet requests your presence on the bridge. We've got signals, ma'am."

"On my way!"

She threw the covers back and bounced out of the bed. Two steps into the bath cabinet, where she shucked off her sleep suit, used the toilet and grabbed a cleaning towelette to wipe face and body in place of the shower she really wanted. She stepped back into the other room, pulled on fresh clothes from the drawers under her bed, ran her fingers through her hair, and grabbed her com pad as she headed toward the door. It irised open just before her nose hit it.

"Bridge," she said to the bodyguards who snapped to as she plunged past them. She heard them following as she trotted down the corridor towards a lift.

The lift door opened. Caitlin strode out onto the command deck, followed by her bodyguards, and headed for where Fleet Commander Dannet stood with Uldra. Behind her, the lift door hissed again as it irised open. She looked behind her, and saw Wrot enter and follow in her steps. A moment later, the four of them were standing together.

"Talk to me," Caitlin said. "What have we got? Intelligent signals?"

"Yes, Director," the fleet commander replied.

"Signals with structure, at any rate. The assumption is intelligence-generated."

"Can we . . . no," Caitlin corrected herself, "of course we can't read them yet."

The lift door hissed yet again. Dannet nodded toward the Lleix who entered the command deck. "They will begin the effort to decipher and translate. But we need not understand the content to locate the source."

Chulan and Helot headed for the sensor techs. Pyr and Garhet split off and stood near the command group. Caitlin nodded to them, and returned her attention to Dannet.

"So, do we know where they are coming from yet?"

Dannet's frame assumed the angles of *awaiting-assured-information*. "Several of the flotilla ships are spreading out now. It will take some time, but we should be able to establish sufficient parallax to be able to determine the source star."

CHAPTER 21

Aille stared at the image of the great red sun in the main viewscreen. Solar flares from the IS class variable were evident as it neared the end of its contraction cycle. He looked to Terra-Captain Sanzh as he completed giving orders to the navigator.

"Caitlin's fleet made an assault jump through that star?"

"Yes, Governor."

Aille's angles shifted to *gratified-respect*, echoed a moment later by Yaut. "Let us be thankful that General Kralik had the wisdom to find a Frame -oint ship, and that Director Kralik had the wisdom to take it with her fleet."

He looked out of the corner of his eye to where Ed Kralik stood. The human's posture was not Jao, but every line of his face and body was so still that it appeared to be the human equivalent of the *neutral* that Pleniary-superior Tura was displaying on his other side. Aille suspected that Kralik was getting a much deeper appreciation of just what Caitlin had been doing for the last year or more. It also looked like the general didn't much care for that knowledge.

Aille turned his focus back to Terra-Captain Sanzh. "Has your navigator located the next Frame Point?"

"She has."

"Pass orders to the other ships. When she is ready, begin the jumps."

Lim looked at Zhao across the mat.

"You want me to what?"

"Put off your robes, please." The human was calm. "You are not human. I am sure I can teach you, but before I can begin I must see how your body moves. I can only tell so much from video images."

They were standing on a mat in a corner of the gymnasium compartment. Human and Jao jinau were working at every machine and every mat in sight. All seemed to be ignoring them.

Lim considered Zhao's request. Looked at from his perspective as a teacher, she decided it was reasonable. She began to open her robes, preparing to remove them as Zhao had asked. His eyes widened and he held up a hand. "You can go in the dressing room to change."

Lim stopped and looked at the human, tilting her head slightly as she considered him. "Lleix have no nudity taboo," she said after a moment.

Zhao's eyes crinkled as he grinned. "But humans do, and even more, we are curious. If you strip down here, we'll be surrounded by the curious and neither we nor they will accomplish anything this afternoon."

Lim restored her robes to their normal hang. "You

don't want me in my robes, and you don't want me in my skin. Just how is it you expect to accomplish your goal?"

Zhao's grin grew even wider as he held up a bag. "Inside this is a set of workout clothes that I think will fit you. You should be able to figure out how to put them on; you've seen humans in similar clothes for years now." He handed it to her and pointed toward a door. "You will find cubicles in there where you can store your robes and put these on."

Lim took the bag, and did as she was asked. Once in a cubicle, as Zhao called it, she carefully hung her robes—first outer, then inner—from hooks in the wall. And he was correct; she had very little trouble with donning the loose trousers and the sweatshirt that were in the bag. It did help a little that he had attached labels that said "front" to one side of each.

She looked at herself in a mirror that hung on the back of the cubicle door. A very strange reflection stared back at her, a Lleix head popping out of human clothing. If only Jihan could see her now, she mused. Even the head of Terralore *elian*, Jihan, herself considered radical by many of the Lleix who had reluctantly followed her lead, might be taken aback by what Lim was doing. She raised her hand to shoulder level. The sight of a Lleix hand coming out of a human sleeve gave her a moment of insight into human humor.

She reached for the door handle, and left to join Zhao on the mat.

Third-Mordent spun out of the reach of the Ekhat facing her in the dance hall. A male, he was bigger than she, and made it clear he would put her down if he could. He had sung nothing in her hearing; had simply rushed her as soon as Ninth-Minor-Sustained had admitted him into the room.

She recalled her ancestor's instructions given moments before the male was admitted. "Control. You will control the fight. You may strike lightly with your forehand blades, but no biting. Dominate him by your skill, not your rage."

Despite his size, the male was not as fast as Third-Mordent, and so their dance took an inevitable pattern, with the male making short rushes and turning in the center of the room as Third-Mordent danced around him, forehand blades flicking out, creating patterns of cuts on his white tegument. White ichor oozed out until the male looked as if he had been rolling in it.

The pattern spoke to Third-Mordent, called to her, until an aria took shape in her mind. As she evaded one strong rush, she began to sing the aria, high, strong and cutting, fractal-toned. Her steps began to follow the melody patterns; swooping, jumping, sliding. The male was confused, and as she sang, he more and more would respond to the melody, steps and cuts falling into the pattern of Third-Mordent's music.

She began to shape the music, using it to drive him back, back, back; cutting off his attempts to reach her flanks. The music grew—in length, in volume, in complexity, in power—and the male continued to retreat before her, eyes rolling wildly, forehand blades flailing almost at random as she danced in to make more touches with her own blades.

The aria crested in a blast of rapidly down-pouring fractal notes that drove the male to huddle on the floor. Third-Mordent brought the aria to a conclusion with a single attenuating tone that died away slowly until even she wasn't quite sure when it ended.

Ninth-Minor-Sustained entered the room from another door and advanced until she stood before Third-Mordent. "Not what I anticipated," she sang. "Effective, though." She turned to look at the unstirring male. "Complete him."

Third-Mordent turned her head to look at her ancestor, saying nothing but raising a question just the same.

Ninth-Minor-Sustained spun and stared down at her progeny. Third-Mordent held still.

"If he cannot resist even a youngling like you better than that, he is not strong enough to be bred. Complete him. Now."

Third-Mordent lifted a forehand blade and did as she was commanded.

Caitlin's com pad pinged, and she tapped it with her finger. Lieutenant Vaughan's face appeared. "Yes?"

Vaughan grinned at her. "We have sufficient data that the Starsifters have identified the probable source of the signals. It's a G5V class star much like our sun, lying near the edge of the Sagittarius Arm proper. We'll be out of the interarm void when we land there."

"Good!" Caitlin's face spread in a grin of her own. "I'm ready to be in new territory, and it's great that we have a possibility this fast. When does Dannet think we can begin the shift?"

"We're waiting on the Bond ship to finish tuning the new Frame Point, then we'll be ready to leave. All ships report ready now."

"Do we have a read on planets?" Caitlin asked.

Vaughan looked down then back up. "Enough to know there are some."

"Notify me when the Bond ship reports."

"Will do, Director."

Vaughan's face winked out of the com pad. Caitlin sat back, laughing. It was all she could do to not rub her hands together. They had survived the jumps, and now... now it appeared she was going to be proven right. A prospective civilization with at least some level of industrial technology was in their sights.

Caitlin gave up restraint and clapped her hands together, laughing louder. It was going to work. After all this time, Preceptor Ronz's vision was going to be proved out. If the old strategist was here, she'd have thrown her arms around him in a big hug. She wrapped her arms around herself instead.

"It's going to work," she whispered.

"Hey, Joe," Zhao heard from behind him as he walked down the corridor. "Wait up." He turned to see Gabe Tully—Colonel Tully, actually, since he was in uniform and wearing his rank emblems—walking toward him. He walked backward slowly, waiting on Gabe to draw even to him, at which point he resumed normal progress. "Were you looking for me?" he asked.

"Actually, yeah," Gabe replied. "First off, that Szechuan beef with artichokes and quinoa pasta was awesome the other night. That needs to go into the regular meal rotation."

"Yeah, the head cook's already hit me up for the recipe. I suspect you'll see it again before too long."

"Great!" Tully grinned, which made him look even

younger than he was. And that reminded Zhao that Tully, for all his rank, was not exactly a graybeard yet.

"And since that was first, there must be a second. Hmm?" Zhao arched his eyebrows.

Tully looked around, then dropped his voice. "How is Lim doing? I mean, don't violate any master/student stuff, but I'd like to know if she's doing okay."

"No great secrets, Gabe." Zhao spread his hands. "We're actually moving kind of slowly, because I have to rethink everything from how it works with a human body to how it will work with a Lleix body. I mean, one body, one head, two arms, two hands, two legs, two feet, yeah—but it all works differently, if you see what I mean." He grinned.

"Yeah," Gabe grinned back. "I kind of figured it might. But she's doing okay?"

"Better than okay. I have to slow her down, make her do other stuff. She's pretty focused."

Gabe snorted. "Oh, yeah. Lim could teach focus to a laser drill."

Zhao laughed, but he could see the point.

Gabe looked around. "Okay, gotta split off here and go be the colonel. Thanks for the chat, Joe."

And with a wave of his hand, Gabe was gone down a cross-corridor.

Zhao chuckled. Gabe talking about Lim being super-focused was a bit of the pot and the kettle, he thought.

Caitlin strode into the command deck, followed by Tamt, Captain Miller, and a couple of the rank and file bodyguards. She stopped three steps inside to take stock of the crew. Caitlin could always get a feel for how serious things were just by watching the command deck staff. Even the mostly stolid Jao would develop stiffness in their angles if things got dicey. The humans, of course, could be read like a book; more than that—after working with and reading Jao postures, reading humans was like reading a primer. Her mouth quirked at that thought. Somehow she didn't think most humans, including her father, would appreciate being compared to "See Dick run," when someone like Aille would be like reading James Joyce's *Ulysses*.

The crew was serious, on task, excited, but still relaxed. So, no one expected trouble with this jump. Good.

She stepped up beside Fleet Commander Dannet.

The big Jao looked her way. "Director. The fleet is ready to proceed."

Caitlin let her angles flow into *accepting-information*, then on to *accepting-responsibility*. "Very good. Begin."

She walked over and sat down at her customary station. She was actually learning to read some of the readouts that Lieutenant Vaughan routed her way.

Dannet turned to the communications officer. "Orders to *Ban Chao*. Jump when you are ready."

Caitlin sat back in her seat, excitement building. This was it! A chance to meet a new species who perhaps knew nothing of the Ekhat. An opportunity long desired, now at hand.

She leaned forward in her seat, waiting for *Lexington* to follow the pathfinder.

PART III
On Strange Shores

CHAPTER 22

Tully let his breath out after *Ban Chao* stabilized in the target sun. He could see Lim looking at him from where she sat on one of the jump-seats, and held up a hand. "Don't say it."

She closed her mouth and looked at him. He could see the thought behind her eyes. *If you don't like to Frame Point jump, why are you here?* But since it was unspoken Tully ignored it.

Vanta-Captain Ginta krinnu vau Vanta stood in the center of the command deck, listening to every conversation and comment, reading the sensor reports from the bottom of the main viewscreen while he watched the currents of the sun around them. Tully relaxed a bit more when Ginta ordered, "Take the ship out of the corona. Show me damage control reports."

The sensor report bar shrank in size and the damage control report bar popped into place on the viewscreen. Since it was a Terran-built ship, the displays usually used human colors as defaults for readouts and reports, so

Tully had no trouble translating the mostly green bar with a couple of specks of orange as "Came through with flying colors, maybe scraped the paint a little bit."

He pulled his com pad out and checked on the jinau. As they had been doing this whole voyage, they rode out the jump in armor standing in their shock frames. All green there as well . . . wait, there was an orange blip. Tully touched it and it expanded to show detail. He snorted. Apparently Private Ciappa managed to get crossways in his shock frame and got his arm severely bruised in one of the jolts the ship had suffered when it first dropped into the sun.

Tully shook his head as he put the com pad away. You had to wonder about the private. A good kid; honest, hard-working, wanted to do well. Just not the sharpest knife in the drawer. Ah, well, Sergeant Cold Bear would see to him, and probably give him an earful about just how stupid he'd been this time around.

Ban Chao crossed the transition from solar corona region to clear space. "Take us to ecliptic north. Widesweep sensors!" Ginta ordered.

Tully stood and moved to stand beside the Vantacaptain. "So, we're good?" Ginta nodded. "When do we know if we're in the right system?"

The sensor readouts on the main viewscreen changed. A plot of the system rapidly took shape, showing three, four, no, seven planets. Ginta pointed to one quadrant of the screen, and said, "About . . . now."

Human numbers and Jao characters jumbled together in that quadrant, and sorted themselves out. One of the human command crew whistled.

"What?" Tully asked, restraining himself from grabbing Ginta by the shoulder.

The Vanta-captain shifted to a posture that Tully sort-of recognized as expressing good humor or cheerfulness. He looked over to Tully and jerked his head at the screen. "That, Colonel, indicates there is more electromagnetic energy emanating in this system than Terra produces even now. It looks like . . ." he paused as the numbers changed, then continued, "at least three separate planetary sources, plus at least two lunar sources from moons of one of the outer planets, plus a few moving sources in the system."

"So, lots of radio and TV," Tully said, "and moving . . . you mean they have spaceships?"

Ginta gave the human shrug. "We won't know for sure until we get close, but probably."

"Caitlin's going to *squeee* over this," Tully muttered.

Flue Vaughan whistled when the readouts began feeding him real-time information after *Lexington* crossed the corona transition line of the target star into open space. Seven planets. Reading from the star out, first there were two rocky types near the star, only one of which was in the liquid water zone—barely. There was a third rock ball much farther out, definitely outside the liquid water zone. Beyond that were two Jovians and a Neptune cousin. The count was completed by something that was closer to a planetoid than a planet wandering in the outer edges of the system.

Caitlin Kralik got out of her seat and came to look over his shoulder. "Okay, what do we have? Did we get the right system?"

"Oh, yeah," Vaughan said. "This is the jackpot. We have technology here, here, and here." He highlighted first the two inner planets on his workstation main screen, then the third planet, and finally the more distant fourth planet. "Very strong electromagnetic activity that is regular and patterned, so almost certainly artificial. And," he paused for a moment, "it doesn't match any known Ekhat patterns." He looked at her and grinned. "We found it, Director. This is what you've been searching for all along—a technological civilization to reach out to."

Caitlin felt her facial muscles stretch in the biggest grin of her life. Vaughan's expression matched hers. When she looked around, so did Caewithe Miller's.

Another civilization! One unknown to Jao, to humans, and please, God, to the Ekhat as well. Another people to recruit to the resistance against the Ekhat.

And this was only the beginning! Where there was one, there would be others. She was as certain of that as she could be.

She wanted to laugh; she wanted to dance. In the end, she did neither, restraining her glee to a single fist pump.

Third-Mordent stood at Ninth-Minor-Sustained's side watching various Ekhat moving through the harmony master's great hall, listening to the servient choirs.

"Watch," Ninth-Minor-Sustained whispered in an arietta pitched for Third-Mordent's hearing only. "Watch for control, and learn."

One of the Ekhat, a female, was slightly smaller than Third-Mordent, which made her the youngest in the hall. Third-Mordent didn't know who she was. She wasn't in any of the faction lists that Third-Mordent had been studying at Ninth-Minor-Sustained's directions.

The young female moved stiffly, her head constantly moving to increase angles of vision around her. It seemed to Third-Mordent that the female was on the verge of dropping into predator mode. This thought was reinforced when her red-tinted eyes became visible.

None of the other Ekhat in the hall seemed to be aware of the young female. Ekhat of various factions stepped carefully around one another, with an occasional glimpse of a forehand blade but no other indication of the mutual antipathy that existed. This was perhaps due to the fact that they were in Ninth-Minor-Sustained's hall, and none wanted to do anything that would provoke the harmony master. She had a reputation for completing arguments or conflicts begun by others in a very final manner. Third-Mordent, having been personally schooled by the harmony master, thought that such restraint on the part of those milling around in the hall represented the height of Ekhat wisdom.

That all changed in an instant. A larger, and therefore older, Ekhat male from a small splinter faction backed away from an even larger female of a more predominant faction at the same time that the young female was stepping back in a similar situation. Their hindquarters touched.

The young female jumped as if she had been kicked, then spun, forehand blades fully extended, slashing indiscriminately at every being near her.

Three Anj servients in one of the choirs were eviscerated. Their blood splashed across the rest of the choir, who trembled and moaned, but remained in their place and before long resumed their chanting.

The male whose touch had stimulated the young female's frenzy screamed as both rear legs were slashed open. His wailing formed a counter motif to the Anj cries as his legs failed and his hindquarters hit the floor in a growing puddle of white ichor.

One other reacted too slowly to avoid damage and received a deep slash along one flank.

Third-Mordent watched as forehand blades snapped open all around the hall. The servient choirs all scurried back against the walls and huddled on the floor as their Ekhat masters rampaged; shouting/screaming/keening/shrieking. At first, it seemed as if Dissonance had invaded the hall, but after a moment harmony began to emerge as half-tones/quarter-tones/fractal-tones splattered across the Ekhat sonic spectrum and merged into a towering colossus of aggressive harmony that had an almost physical presence in the hall.

The cries of trampled servients and wounded masters in counterpoint began to tease at Third-Mordent's senses, almost alluring her to add her blades, her voice, and perhaps her ichor, to the frenzy. Ninth-Minor-Sustained still loomed at her side; that presence served to leach away the siren call of blood and blade dances.

Third-Mordent noticed that Ninth-Minor-Sustained was looking in one particular direction in the hall. She followed the harmony master's gaze and focused on one Ekhat in particular; a female who, although not as large as Ninth-Minor-Sustained, was still imposing. To Third-Mordent's eyes, the other female was still, which she found odd. There was no movement to the female; not even her tegument twitched; yet she seemed to exude threat, as all those near her to took pains to stay a distance away.

"That one," Ninth-Minor-Sustained sang quietly,

barely audible over the harmony mélange that pressed upon them, "that one has control."

It was as if the harmony master had judged everyone else in the hall, and dismissed all but this female. Third-Mordent focused her attention on the female. She chirped an interrogative.

"Seventh-Flat," the harmony master responded.

That registered with Third-Mordent. The large female was a very important member of a Complete Harmony faction that mostly opposed Ninth-Minor-Sustained. Now she had Third-Mordent's undivided attention.

Several of the other Ekhat were down, either dead or dying. Most of the rest were wounded to one degree or another; white ichor streaked almost every white form in the room.

The young female who had provoked the confrontational performance had managed to avoid serious damage. She was currently backed into a corner, waving her forehand blades at any Ekhat who drew near. Until this moment, the members of the factions had focused on others who were nearer and more dangerous. That was no longer the case.

Two Ekhat, one female and one male, moved towards the young female from opposite sides. It was not a coordinated attack: the two were from different factions. From their movements, however, they were among the most adept of those in the hall.

The youngling was trapped in her error of having placed herself in the corner. She now found her movements restricted, and was unable to avoid/evade/elude the blade dancers who approached her. There was a whirlwind of flying flashing forehand blades, and then the young female was lying on the floor, broken. The two attackers immediately turned on one another.

Seventh-Flat's forehand blades flicked out. Third-Mordent watched as she danced through the hall, leaving a trail of smashed and maimed Ekhat behind her, until she confronted the two blade dancers. They had a bare moment of warning before she intruded in their dance, changing it to a deadly *pas des trois*. As good as they were, their dance was graceful, exhilarating, and foredoomed.

Third-Mordent watched Seventh-Flat's skill with some admiration. The blade dancers were beset from the onset, forced to the defensive from the first stroke. Seventh-Flat kept them reeling back and back and back, using her size, strength, and speed to force them down the hall.

In the end, Seventh-Flat simply outdanced them, and in a final flourish of her blades left first one and then the other staring at the hall with blind eyes as their final breaths left their bodies and ichor oozed from rent flesh.

"Formidable," Ninth-Minor-Sustained whisper-sang.

The nature of the harmony in the hall had changed. The choirs were huddling, with many of the servient members damaged. Many of the Ekhat were either dead or wounded so severely they could not contribute tones to the work. And even those who were still mobile and still able to sing began to fall silent as Seventh-Flat picked her way back up the hall to where the young female Ekhat lay whose reactions were the catalyst for what had happened.

Third-Mordent was surprised to see the young female attempt to raise her head when Seventh-Flat loomed over her. Third-Mordent heard the beginning of a keening tone from the youngling, before Seventh-Flat completed her with a sudden quick stab of a forehand blade.

Seventh-Flat looked to where Ninth-Minor-Sustained stood. She made no song, no tone, no sound at all; simply stared at the harmony master. At length, she flicked her forehand blades, snapping the ichor that coated them into straight lines on the floor. The blades folded back into their sheaths, and Seventh-Flat turned and left the room; still atypically silent.

"That one," Ninth-Minor-Sustained intoned softly after the door closed behind Seventh-Flat, "that one is dangerous. She will lead her faction before long."

Third-Mordent absorbed that prediction.

CHAPTER 23

It had been six days since the fleet had emerged in the system from their last jump. Dannet had congregated the fleet well to the galactic north of the star, above the system's ecliptic. There they had waited while the Lleix, especially the Terralore *elian*, finished learning the language of the natives—or languages, rather. According to Lim, there was evidence of at least five different languages in use. One of them seemed to be dominant, however. The majority of the transmissions from the two inner planets were in that tongue, as well as all the transmissions from the outer reaches.

It was a situation much like Terra before the conquest, Caitlin mused. Many more than five languages then, true, but even then English had been the dominant tongue, despite the arguments of the French and the Chinese to the contrary. The conquest and occupation had simply sealed that position, as the Jao only learned one human language, and refused to speak to anyone who wasn't conversational in it. Hopefully they would avoid that position of hubris here, but they had to start with something, so language number one it was.

Caitlin looked at where the three Lleix sat together in her conference room. "Okay, tell me what you've got." She sat back and let the Lleix take over the command meeting.

"We have detected at least five different primary languages in the broadcasts from the home planet we have listened to," Pyr began, "as well as several dialects of at least two of them. Only one of those languages is in use in the other system locations, so we have focused on interpreting that one. All the names we will use are from the primary language." He looked Caitlin's direction.

"Understood," she said, and waved a hand.

"The system primary is called Khûr," Pyr continued.

His pronunciation of the word had a very nasal timbre. "Khûr," Caitlin said, trying to reproduce it. "Okay, I'm going to have to practice that one. Go on."

"The name means Holy Light in the primary language," Garhet picked up the thread, "and that colors almost everything else we have been able to learn about the people."

Lim spoke next. "It's not clear if they consider their star to be a god, or if they only consider it to be a monumental sign of divine favor. There hasn't been that much background available in the broadcasts. But they call themselves the Khûrûsh, which translates to People of the Holy Light."

The nasal sound hit twice in that word. "Khûrûsh," Caitlin whispered to herself, trying to push the sound through her nose to get the proper nasal tone to the u's. Such an interesting sounding name, for the first independently contacted extraterrestrial race in human history.

"The home planet is Khûr-shi, which translates to Khûr's home." The sensor reports had established that the planet was a bit smaller than Earth, but occupied a similar location in its system as Earth did in the human solar system, albeit it was the second planet out instead of the third because the system didn't have a Mercury analog. Multiple continents, blue water oceans, ice-caps, slight axial tilt; not an exact duplicate of Earth, but very similar. The fleet techs didn't have an exact read on the atmosphere yet, but what they could determine was also a close match to Earth's. Jao, Lleix, and humans could probably walk around without needing air masks.

"The major moon is named Khûr-liyo, which means Khûr's little sister. The minor moon or planetoid is named Khûr-io, which we think means something like Khûr's dog or Khûr's wolf. It is definitely a reference to an aggressive animal of some kind, but we haven't seen a picture yet of what it could be like." From the sensor reports they knew that Khûr-liyo was approximately 2600 kilometers in diameter, which made it not quite three-fourths of the diameter of Earth's Luna. This meant it was less than half the volume of Luna, and presumably less than half the mass. Khûr-shi would have noticeable tides, the science guys had reported, but not as strong as those of Earth. Khûr-io, on the other hand, was too small and too far out to have much of an effect on the surface of Khûr-shi.

Caitlin reminded herself that the Lleix were speaking from only six days of listening to old-fashioned radio and television broadcasts, and they'd only deciphered the video output three days ago. It was a miracle they had come up with what they had. "So what are the people like?"

"Scientifically and technologically, they appear to be somewhat beyond preconquest Terra," Garhet said, "but we see nothing that indicates that they have any form of interstellar travel yet."

Tully stirred in his seat down the table from Caitlin. "Are all their signals in the clear?" When Garhet looked to him and raised his aureole, Tully expanded, "Do they encode any of their signals, or is everything open for everyone to listen to and read?"

"Some three percent of what we have listened to in the last six days has been coded. Multiple systems have been used." Garhet spread his hands. "Some we have deciphered. They appeared to be used by commercial interests. Others still resist our efforts, and those we suspect belong to governmental organizations."

"Or military," Fleet Commander Dannet added. Garhet nodded in acquiescence to the statement, but said nothing further. The point had been made that this civilization was not an elysium. With that dark thought in her mind, Caitlin motioned for the briefing to continue.

Pyr touched a control on his com pad, and a hologram sprang into being above the table, slowly rotating to give everyone a chance to view the figure. "This is a representative member of the species."

"It's a damn fox," Caitlin heard Tully mutter. She had to admit that the face was definitely vulpine, and the russet colored fur and mane just reinforced the perception of a vertical fox; with one slight change from the Terran model—it had six limbs. The hologram blinked to another image, this one of a different

Khûrûsh, caught as if in the act of running on all six limbs.

"What they look like doesn't matter," Caitlin said. "What is their society like?"

Lim took over. "Very structured, very controlled."

Caitlin raised her eyebrows when nothing more was said. "Can you give me more than that?"

The Lleix were silent for a moment, then Lim said with what appeared to be reluctance, "They are much more authoritarian than Jao, or even Lleix." Caitlin pursed her lips and almost whistled, stopping when she remembered the Lleix phobia. "Out of human history, there are strong parallels with pre-Meiji Japan."

Caitlin sat back, absorbing that.

"Jeez," Tully muttered. "Shogun, and all that? That could be a pain."

"Not necessarily," Caitlin responded. "One great advantage to a hierarchy is if you make solid contact with the top rank, you're in all the way."

"Yeah, and if the top rank doesn't want to have anything to do with you, what happens then?" Tully said with a grimace. "We really don't want to set off an interstellar World War II here."

A few of the Jao's angles slipped to versions of *bewildered*, but most of them understood the reference. The Terralore *elian* Lleix knew recent human history better than the humans did, of course, so they understood both the reference and the thrust of the comment. They said nothing.

Caitlin thought for a moment, considering everything that had been said, then tapped the table and said, "Okay, here's how we're going to do it . . ."

✧ ✧ ✧

A day later the *Lexington*'s command deck was operating like a well-oiled machine. Jao and humans alike knew their jobs, and did them well. Caitlin looked around as she joined Wrot and Fleet Commander Dannet in the open space in front of Lieutenant Vaughan's console.

"Sensors report that they are still lashing us with radar, Fleet Commander," Lieutenant Vaughan reported from his workstation. The one that Caitlin usually sat at had been given to Pyr the Lleix, with Garhet standing beside him. Lim had returned to *Ban Chao.*

The natives had not taken long to notice the arrival of the fleet seven days earlier. By the time the last of the *Lexington*-class ships had emerged from the photosphere of Khûr, the first radar signals had begun to reach them, emitted from Khûr-liyo and various spacecraft scattered around the system. It had never let up. There had been no attempt to contact them; no spacecraft sent their way; simply the radar.

Dannet made no comment, and gave no useless orders such as "Keep me posted," or "Let me know if anything changes." Being Jao, she took it for granted that such would be the case. And with the *Lexington*'s crew trained to the high level it occupied, it would be the case. So the fleet commander looked to Caitlin, and said, "All is ready, Director."

Caitlin took a deep breath, and replied, "Very well. Begin."

Dannet turned to the command deck. "Orders to the fleet: execute. Terra-Captain Uldra, begin."

With that, the approach to the Khûrûsh began. Caitlin watched the main viewscreen to see the fleet split. All of the support ships, most of the lighter warcraft, and *Sun Tzu* remained in their galactic north position. The rest of the heavy ships, being *Lexington*, *Arjuna*, *Ban Chao* and *Pool Buntyam*, shaped course for the second planet from the sun.

Lexington began broadcasting a high-powered announcement crafted by the Lleix asking for peaceful contact in each of the five languages aimed directly at the home planet on all the Khûrûsh major communication frequencies.

Zhao Jiguang watched, arms folded, as Lim neared completion of the Sixty-Four Forms. She really was quite good, he admitted to himself. Even with the time it had taken him to adapt the forms to the movement ranges of the Lleix body, she had still learned the essential forms as fast as anyone he had ever taught. He was seeing her two hours every day, and he was sure that she was spending much of her off time working the forms as well. It showed. Her focus and intensity was almost scary.

Zhao had had talented—even very talented—human students before, who had learned at very fast paces, but even the best had been somewhat slower than this person who was not even of Earth. He had indeed been forced more than once to instruct her to take a slower pace; to even take time off. And he had to wonder if this was unique to her, or if all Lleix would perform this way.

Ah, Lim was coming out of Grasp the Bird's Tail and moving to Gather Heaven to Earth, the final form. Zhao straightened as her arms went through the reaching up motion. As her arms descended to rest by her side, he took a staff from a nearby rack.

Lim completed the form with a slow exhalation of breath; Zhao moved to stand before her.

He wasn't surprised to see that her eyes were closed. He knew more than one Tai Chi practitioner who would practice with their eyes shut. "Well done," he said.

Lim's eyes flew open, and she put her hands together and gave a slight bow to him. "Thank you, *sifu.*" She had found the honorific for a Tai Chi instructor in the Terralore database, and he had been unable to convince her it wasn't necessary to use it with him. For all that, she had determined to wear a karate gi, rather than human sweats or the loose Chinese style clothing that Zhao himself wore. He had no problem with that, actually. He was not that much of a purist, to the despair of some of the other Tai Chi masters in southern California.

Zhao set one end of the staff on the deck and clasped his hands around it together about shoulder height. He looked at Lim, staring deep into her eyes. She gazed back steadily. A long moment passed. When Lim did not look away, Zhao smiled. "Here," he said, holding out the staff, "take this."

Lim looked at it, but did not reach out to take it. "What is that? A weapon?"

Zhao snorted. "It's a piece of wood. Take it."

Lim slowly reached out both hands and took the staff, holding it in front of her with one end on the deck. "It is made of wood," she said, "but that is not what it is."

Zhao chuckled. "You grow subtle, my student. You are correct, it is made of wood, but that is not what it is. You will take this with you, and keep it with you at all times. When you believe you know what it is, tell me."

So far there had been no response from the Khûrûsh other than even more intensive radar signals. "The cooks could put a cow out on the hull and it would be well-done in an hour from the radiation," Flue Vaughan muttered.

The sensor techs had already reported the increased radar signals, so Vaughan just noted it in his logs, and continued watching Fleet Commander Dannet; who, at that moment, was approaching Caitlin Kralik.

"We are drawing near to the limit you set, Director." Dannet's voice was brusque, which was unusual neither for Jao in general nor for her in particular. "Do you still insist on your directive?" Her angles were all *accepting-of-direction*, though, from what Vaughan could tell. His interpretation of Jao body-speech was continuing to improve.

Caitlin took a deep breath. Flue watched her out of the corner of his eye. Yes, she had *oudh* over the search effort, but the fleet commander seemed to press her at times. Flue wasn't sure if Dannet was expressing a certain distaste for the director, or if it was legitimate under her position as fleet commander to ensure that certain orders were confirmed. Either way, it looked like Caitlin was getting a bit tired of it.

"Yes, Fleet Commander," the director said in stern tones, body angles portraying *absolute-command-to-subordinate* in what even Vaughan recognized was a flawless posture. "All the other ships will halt one million kilometers out from the planet outward from Khûr-liyo's L4 libration point, while *Lexington* moves to the L1 point. We are *not* going to come in like an invading fleet."

Lexington was headed for an orbit between the planet and the moon, while the rest of the flotilla waited almost three times the distance from Earth to its moon. Vaughan had heard Caitlin's explanation in the command meeting. She did not want the Khûrûsh to feel as if the Jao/human fleet was looming over them or "taking the high ground," as Tully had put it. So *Lexington* would go in alone, and the rest of the flotilla would park far enough away that hopefully they wouldn't be an adverse psychological component in the attempt to establish communications and a relationship, but still be close enough that if for some reason things dropped in the crapper they could come running.

The sensor techs had already confirmed that *Lexington* was bigger than any craft the Khûrûsh had in space at the moment. It was also pretty obvious to Vaughan that the drive systems the Khûrûsh were using with their ships weren't anything in comparison to the Jao drives. *Lex* ought to be imposing enough, Vaughan thought, that the Khûrûsh would respond to the messages that were being broadcast.

Nothing. Even after the rest of the flotilla halted and *Lexington* continued on her own, no response from Khûr-shi. Only the incessant radar signals, which, as unbelievable as it seemed, were only increasing in strength and intensity.

"I can't believe we're not getting a response," Caitlin said as they neared Khûr-liyo. "When the Jao came to Earth, we humans were addressing them as soon as it was clear they were intentional travelers from outside the solar system. Why are these folks not talking to us?"

She looked at Vaughan. He shrugged. "No answer, Director. No responses. Just more radar."

Tully slapped the mat in surrender, and Sergeant Luff quit trying to insert his foot into his ear. Tully rolled over onto his back and accepted a hand up from the sergeant. He was breathing hard, and nursing a mat burn on his elbow. "You know, Top, I'm getting tired of you polishing the mat with my face."

Luff gave a slight smile. "You're improving, Colonel. You've started making me sweat a little, anyway." His white teeth flashed in his coffee-colored face.

"Nobody likes a smartass, Top."

The sergeant said nothing, just laughed with that deep resonant Jamaican voice.

Tully wiped his forehead off. Whether or not the sergeant was sweating, he definitely was. He looked over to the mat where Zhao and Lim were working together. "You think she's getting it?" he asked.

Luff spread his hands. "Wrong guy to ask, Colonel. I know Tae Kwon Do and Jiu-Jitsu. I know enough about Tai Chi to recognize it, but that's it. But from the outside, I'd say she's making definite progress. Joe's done a great job of adapting it to fit the Lleix conformity. Watching him has got me thinking about how to adapt Tae Kwon Do for the Lleix. I don't know that any of them will ever want to learn it, but the mental exercise is good; and who knows, maybe I'll come up with something new and unique."

A raucous klaxon burst sounded three times, then a Jao voice came over the announcement systems. "All crew to battle stations. All jinau to assault stations. This is not a drill."

Everyone in the gym surged toward the exit. Tully darted forward, yelling, "Make a hole, people! Make a hole!"

The troops opened a pathway through the throng, and he plunged through it with Luff on his heels.

CHAPTER 24

Third-Mordent stood in the center of Ninth-Minor-Sustained's great hall, listening to the antiphonal servient choirs render her latest work, a ricercare inspired by the actions of Seventh-Flat during the blade-dance that had left so many Ekhat completed. Unlike Ninth-Minor-Sustained's usual practice, she had segregated the choirs by species: Anj, Trīkē, and even hard to locate and preserve Huilek, not common in the quadrants controlled by the harmony master's faction. Two small choirs of each servient species provided strong voicing of the characteristic timbres of each species, which Third-Mordent had used in building the piercing harmonies of the ricercare.

A flicker of motion caught out of the corner of her eye resolved into the presence of Ninth-Minor-Sustained. Third-Mordent immediately went still.

Ninth-Minor-Sustained listened to the ricercare with what appeared to be pleasure, judging from the manner in which her forehand blades exposed their edges at certain moments in the work. The shrill descant of the Anj brought an edge of agony to the work as it was laid atop the staccato chanting of the Huilek. The fundamental structure of the work was declared and determined by the resonant point and counterpoint of the Trīkē singers. There was an invidious, inexorable, even implacable motion imparted to the music by the cycling of the fundamental theme by the Trīkē that elevated the work well above a level that an Ekhat of Third-Mordent's attainments should have reached.

As the work began its third iteration, Ninth-Minor-Sustained intervened with a fluted "Cease." There was immediate quiet. The choirs were frozen in place, panting. "Disperse," the harmony master intoned. Within moments, the two Ekhat were alone in the room as the last of the Trīkē hurtled through a doorway, all six limbs scrabbling to make the turn in the corridor as the door irised shut behind it.

Third-Mordent remained still. Her control was excellent by this point. There was no pressure from instincts or hungers; only alertness and focus as Ninth-Minor-Sustained stalked around her.

The harmony master moved to face Third-Mordent. "Excellent," she trilled. "You have learned the first lesson of control: do nothing without intent." That took the form of a semi-toned downward scale.

Ninth-Minor-Sustained looked away from her descendant. "This was interesting," she sang in a soft soliloquy. "I will remember the choirs." There was a moment of silence, before the harmony master sang in multitoned voicing that verged on Dissonance, "Destroy the music."

That almost made Third-Mordent lose her posture. Perhaps an eye twitched, or a manipulator quivered for a moment. Ninth-Minor-Sustained whirled and shrieked, "Still!"

The tonal blast affected Third-Mordent's central nerves, causing jets of pain all along her central nerve trunk. Her vision whited out instantly, and for long moments even her physical sensations were loosened. Gradually all sensations returned to normal, and her eyes cleared. It surprised her that she was still standing in the same position. It would not have astonished her if she had been sprawling on the floor when her perceptions resumed.

Ninth-Minor-Sustained was very close to her, edges of forehand blades exposed. The harmony master's gaze was very sharp. Third-Mordent returned the gaze in kind.

After a moment Ninth-Minor-Sustained's blades retreated into their sheaths, and she moved back one step. "Good," she returned to the soliloquy mode.

Third-Mordent remained silent. At length, the harmony master turned and walked over to the window in the corner, the one that gave a viewpoint into space.

"It is time for you to learn the second lesson of control," Ninth-Minor-Sustained sang in a pure tone, its simplicity underscoring the import of the lesson. "Never give anything away." The harmony master looked to Third-Mordent. "Release."

The younger Ekhat retained her posture for a long moment after Ninth-Minor-Sustained's command. The harmony master was staring out the window, but Third-Mordent could see her ancestress's eyes reflected in the window surface, so she knew that she was still under observation herself. Only when there was no doubt in her mind that she would betray no weakness did she move, taking deliberate steps until she stood just to the left of the harmony master. She remained silent, and waited. A long moment passed. Ninth-Minor-Sustained at length made a gesture of approval.

Third-Mordent broke her silence. "Why?"

Nine-Minor-Sustained was, predictably, indirect. "First, never reveal all your skill to anyone. Not in harmony; not in blade-dancing; not in melody. Never."

Third-Mordent dipped a manipulator in a gesture of understanding.

The harmony master continued with, "Second, never praise anyone not of your faction, your lineage, or under your control. Never." With another whisper-aria, Ninth-Minor-Sustained sang, "The ricercare was well done indeed, but if I could see Seventh-Flat limned in its harmonies, so could others."

Third-Mordent again fluted, "Why?"

This time Ninth-Minor-Sustained was more direct, responding in dirge mode, "The youngling that began the blade-dancing," and there was no question who was being referred to, "the one that Seventh-Flat completed, was the latest and last of her personal progeny, newly come from the contests of the creche."

Third-Mordent absorbed that and considered all the implications before responding, "Can Seventh-Flat touch you?"

Ninth-Minor-Sustained's response was, "Not yet." She turned from the window and left without another note.

The Khûrûsh response came as the *Lexington* crossed the orbit of Khûr-liyo. Unfortunately, it was not a response that Caitlin wanted to hear.

"Spacecraft launches detected!" a Jao sensor tech

called out. "Coming from three locations on the moon. Three, no, more, ten, sixteen, eighteen craft detected."

"Twelve more detected launching from two bases on the planet," a human tech called out.

"What propulsion system are they using?" Dannet snapped out.

"Wait, wait," the Jao tech said. Numbers and characters flashed up on the main viewscreen. "Nothing like Jao or Ekhat systems."

"It's an atomic rocket engine," the human tech called out. "High thrust, hydrogen fuel, speed and duration of maneuvering limited only by amount of reaction mass."

Vaughan's fingers were flying, pulling in the sensor reports and at the same time calling up the human files he had a vague recollection of reading while he was in the naval academy. He looked at the readouts. The Khûrûsh craft were already building up a surprising velocity. But the shielding on those things was criminally thin. Granted that the atomic piles in those rocket engines couldn't be very large, but the radiation being emitted would be lethal in very short order to anyone not behind shields of some kind. They weren't even as effective as the NERVA designs the humans had never put into use.

"Uldra, take evasive action!" Dannet ordered. "*Pool Buntyam*, *Ban Chao*, join on *Lexington* from north, *Arjuna* from south."

"What are you doing?" Caitlin demanded.

Vaughan suppressed a snort. "Bloody obviously buying time," he muttered as he continued to make notes of what was going on.

The fleet commander turned to Director Kralik.

"That," she said, pointing a finger at the main viewscreen, "is a hostile launch. Those are warcraft, closing on an attack heading. We are getting some maneuvering room until we can see what their plans are, and calling in reinforcements so they can be of use when we need them."

"You don't know they're going to attack," Caitlin responded.

"Missile launch!" the human tech shouted. Dannet looked sternly at the director, and her body flowed through a sequence of angles Vaughan couldn't follow. Then she turned away.

Everyone on the command deck turned their eyes to the main viewscreen, where small slivers of light had detached from the leading group of the ships launched from the moon and were racing ahead toward the *Lexington*. "Laser decks, fire on the missiles!" Terra-Captain Uldra's voice snapped that order out immediately.

Caitlin turned to Pyr. "Shut off the automatic broadcast, and for God's sake start telling them to back off before they get destroyed! Tell them we want to talk, not fight, but we will defend ourselves. Get that out now!"

Tully was stripping off his workout top as he hurtled into the bay where his combat suit was waiting. His orderly, Corporal Enrico Toro, handed him the communication bud, and he shoved it into his ear while the orderly took his boots off.

"Tully here," he almost shouted. "Talk to me!"

"Colonel, the aliens are attacking the *Lexington*," a command deck tech relayed.

"Which aliens? Ekhat?" His mind immediately jumped to the worst-case scenario.

"No, Colonel," the tech responded. "This system's aliens, the . . . Khûrûsh."

"Give me Vanta-Captain Ginta," Tully ordered as he started pulling on the combat suit.

"Ginta," came through the communication bud.

"What's the situation?"

"A number of small spacecraft have taken off from the moon and the planet and are shaping fast-path assault vectors on *Lexington*. Dannet ordered *Arjuna*, *Pool Buntyam* and *Ban Chao* to move forward."

"Any overt hostilities yet?" Tully's mind was racing. This was why Ed Kralik had put him here, dammit, and he was on the wrong ship!

"Not yet," Ginta said. "Ah, wait . . ." Tully froze with one arm in the suit and the other waiting to plunge into the sleeve Swift was holding. "Missile launches. *Lexington* is deploying lasers in antimissile mode."

"Okay, Ginta, I'll get out of your fur so you can fight your ship. I'll only break in if I see something critical." Ginta dropped out of the loop without another word, and Tully finished his motion. "Tech?"

"Yes, Colonel?"

"What's your name?"

"Eanne."

A Jao name, so a Jao tech. Tully pulled his helmet on and checked the com connection while Corporal Toro checked to make sure the join and seals were good. "Give me a captain's feed on my suit," he ordered. A moment later the heads-up display flickered and he got a small size view of Ginta's main viewscreen display. "Thanks. Keep me linked in to that, and keep an ear open for me to shout in if I need to."

"As you direct, Colonel."

Tully watched the feed while Swift helped him fit his gloves. Once they were on and sealed to the corporal's satisfaction, Tully made alternate fists and pounded them into other palm just to make sure he was set. He gave a thumbs-up to Swift, and headed out into the main assault bay.

Quite a few troops were already fitted out and grouping in the main bay, with more arriving every few seconds from the smaller bays scattered around the edges. Tully kept one eye on the feed while he looked around.

"Top? XO?"

"Sir," the sergeant responded.

"Colonel," from Major Liang.

"On me. Now."

He toggled the ID control under his left armpit so it would appear on their screens. Within a few seconds he could see two combat suits going against the flow as they headed in his direction. They had their face-shields open, and he followed suit as they arrived in front of him.

"Okay, not much data available yet. *Lexington* is being attacked by a flotilla of small ships, a bit smaller than our shuttles. Dannet has ordered *Arjuna*, *Ban Chao* and *Pool Buntyam* forward to support *Lexington*. I don't know if there will be any call for us, but we will stand ready. From the size of these ships, there won't be any all-out assault opportunities like with the Ekhat ship. They don't even look big enough to need a company assault. Major, get with the company commanders and dust off the plans for platoon and fire-team assaults. I can't tell you what to expect, because I don't know myself, but if Dannet does call on us, I want something available right then, not after an hour of discussion."

"Got it, Colonel." Liang turned away, calling the company officers.

Tully looked at the first sergeant. "Keep an eye on things, Top. I've got to pay attention to the situation."

"Yes, sir."

Tully closed his face-plate again and focused on the heads-up display. It looked like life was getting interesting for *Lexington* and her laser crews.

Lim stood against the back wall of the main assault bay, holding the staff with one hand. The mob of jinau troopers, both Jao and human, held her eyes while she listened in on an all-frequencies com bud that Gabe Tully had given her. It was fascinating to her to see the jinau sorting themselves out and forming up in their groups as she simultaneously heard Major Liang and the company officers discussing ways and means of committing mayhem in unknown ships, with muttered comments from Tully overlaying it all.

These humans . . . these Jao . . . they were prepared to fight—to wreak violence on other intelligent beings—for a purpose. Lim was straining to understand why, in the hopes that if she could fathom that, she would be able to better understand her own self, which was growing increasingly un-Lleix, she was afraid.

"Do not attack those ships!" Caitlin ordered. She could hear Pyr speaking passionately into a microphone, putting her message out.

Dannet stiffened and turned to face her, but before she could speak one of the sensor techs spoke up.

"More ships coming around from the opposite face of the planet. Looks like . . . at least another twelve ships."

"Orders to *Arjuna*," the fleet commander snapped, not looking away from Caitlin. "Move to intercept and interdict those ships. Orders to *Pool Buntyam* and *Ban Chao*: maneuver to the flank of the ships from the moon, and prepare to fire."

"Do not attack those ships!" Caitlin said again firmly, her body positioned in the angles of *adamant-purpose*.

Dannet's body shifted to *ultimate-responsibility*. "They are enemy. They are attacking us. We must defeat them to be safe."

Caitlin let her body's posture shift to pure *adamant*. "They are not Ekhat, Fleet Commander. They are no threat to us. Their missiles are too small to be anything much more than smart rockets, and they are too slow to be mass-heavy projectiles that could punch through us. Your lasers will take care of them, and if anything slips through, that's why the ship designers put armor on these ships."

Dannet's angles slipped for a moment, and Caitlin laughed in reply; laughed with an edge, but laughed. "I read the reports, Fleet Commander. I know something of what we're facing here. They're not that much farther ahead of Earth than you think."

Caitlin let her angles move to *command-from-superior*. "I have *oudh* over this search, and I say you will not destroy the only chance we've had to find new allies because of a lack of restraint. You will not repeat the mistake that was made with the Lleix!" She stared at Dannet, daring her to cross that line.

Vaughan flinched at that last statement from the director. He watched the confrontation from the corner of his eye as he continued to monitor his readouts and mutter an occasional note into his recorders.

Slowly—very slowly—Dannet's angles morphed to *acceptance-of-instruction*. At the last, she said, "As you direct."

The fleet commander turned away from Director Kralik. "Orders to all ships: defensive fire only."

CHAPTER 25

Tully was watching the feed of the combat on his helmet display when Vanta-Captain Ginta came back into the circuit to him. "Director Kralik has ordered only defense against the missiles. We are not to fire on the Khûrûshil craft themselves."

Tully snorted. "No-brainer, man. It's hard to make allies of anyone after you've wasted a bunch of their people."

"Indeed."

Tully thought he detected a tone of dry irony in the one-word response from the captain. "Any word from the fleet commander about taking over any of the ships?"

"No." And with that, Ginta was gone again.

Damn.

Caitlin looked to Pyr and Garhet. "Any response from any of the Khûrûsh ships?"

"No, Director," from Garhet, as Pyr continued sending out the message.

"The planet?"

"No, Director."

Caitlin turned and stalked over to where her bodyguards were standing. There were four, including Caewithe and Tamt. She crossed her arms and frowned at the deck.

"What's wrong?" Caewithe asked.

"The stupid Khûrûsh won't talk," Caitlin snapped. "I don't know if they're isolationists or xenophobic, or what, but they won't talk. We're smashing everything their ridiculous excuse for a space navy can throw at us, and *they won't talk!*"

She fumed in silence for a moment before Tamt said something that was covered by one of the techs calling something out behind her. "What did you say?"

"I said," Tamt spoke louder, "you have an assault ship filled with jinau. Capture one of the Khûrûshil ships and 'invite' the crew to come speak with you."

"An excellent idea," Caitlin heard from behind her. She looked over her shoulder to see Wrot giving a Jao smile to Tamt. "An idea worthy of the one whose service you are in." Aille, in other words. He shifted his focus to Caitlin. "From the mouths of babes, Caitlin. If they won't listen to you, then bring them in and make them face you." He shrugged. "Not very subtle or elegant, perhaps, but we're Terra taif, not Pluthrak kochan, or even Narvo. We're just one step above the hillbillies." His muzzle wrinkled in a Jao smile. "Direct and blunt is good, in this case."

Caitlin turned the thought over in her mind. It went against her grain, but even she could see that the big ships couldn't keep playing keep-away from the Khûrûsh craft forever. She turned and faced back across the command deck.

"Fleet Commander Dannet!"

"Yes, Director?"

"Order *Ban Chao* to capture one of the Khûrûshil ships, take the crew captive, and bring them aboard *Lexington*."

Dannet's angles almost snapped into *ready-compliance.* That was an order she was obviously gratified to receive.

As Dannet gave the order, Caitlin muttered, "Come on, Tully, make this work."

"Colonel Tully," came the tech's voice in his ear.

"Yes, Eanne."

"Fleet Commander has ordered *Ban Chao* to capture a Khûrûsh ship. Vanta-Captain Ginta directs that you be prepared to board whatever target is chosen and take the crew into custody."

"On it."

Tully triggered the company com link. "XO, Top, company COs, link to me now."

He waited for the pips to light up on his heads-up display to show they had linked to him on the company command frequency. "Okay, here's the skinny. *Ban Chao* is to take one of these little ships and remove the crew. I assume they will eventually end up on *Lexington*, but that's not our decision. So, have you guys worked out a plan for boarding one of these things?"

"Yes, sir," Major Liang responded. "Lieutenant Vaughan on the *Lex* gave us a readout on their general size and estimated configuration, based on the *Lex*'s sensor feeds."

Tully's display flickered as the imagery fed into his helmet display. "Damn," he said, "that's nice work. Remind me to do something nice for Vaughan when we get a chance." He did a quick study of the ship. "Okay, call it fifteen meters in diameter, and roughly one hundred meters long. That's not even a rowboat in comparison to *Lexington* or *Ban Chao*. What do we know about the inside?"

Colored outlines were superimposed over the ship outlines. "Red appears to be a nuclear reactor"—that was close to half of the ship—"yellow appears to be storage for liquid hydrogen fuel"—that took up over half the rest of the ship—"and green appears to be the crew compartment."

Tully studied that. "Any clue at all on how many crew?"

"Best guess is between four and six, eight at the most," the XO said. "That's not much volume, and if they allow any radiation shielding at all between the crew and that nuclear engine, that's going to take away some of that space."

"Hmm. So who's got the shortest fire team?" There was a moment of silence, with the ghost of a chuckle from First Sergeant Luff. "Come on guys, surely you thought of that. From what the Lleix pulled out of the broadcasts, the typical Khûrûsh-an is shorter than we are by a bunch. The interior of that ship is not going to be scaled to us, and I can't see sending someone the size of Corporal Johnson or Sergeant Luff over there. So who's got the shortest fire team? Top?"

Luff's voice had a hint of a laugh. "That would be Charlie Company, First Platoon, Able team, Colonel—Sergeant Boyes and his mob."

"Perfect." Tully grinned. Boyes was short and slight, but was as hard as a carborundum drill bit. Anybody who served on his team had to be just as tough, because Boyes would have run them off if they weren't. And coincidentally—or not—none of them were much taller than their sergeant.

"Okay," Tully said. "Boatright, it's your team, you brief them on what we know about the ship. Make sure they understand the plan is to capture the crew, not ventilate them. Top, you get with the armory and make sure that they're loaded with close-quarter weapons, including some nonlethals."

"Yes, sir!" from the lieutenant.

"On it, Colonel," the first sergeant assured him.

"XO, have the rest of the troops stand by. Who knows what other fun this picnic might provide?"

In the event, it proved to be extremely frustrating. For a few moments, here and there, Tully almost chuckled. The elephantine *Ban Chao* was trying to corral and capture something on the order of a Jack Russell terrier, and every time it looked like it was going to happen, the Khûrûshil ship would skitter to one side and evade the much larger Terran ship.

After a couple of hours and several failed attempts, Tully took steps.

"Eanne."

"Yes, Colonel?"

"Can you patch me through to Director Kralik?"

There was no response from the tech, but in a moment a pip of light showed up on his helmet display, and Caitlin's voice was in his ear. "Yes?"

"Caitlin, I know you don't want to trash the Khûrûshil ships, but you're going to have to order one of them disabled by *Pool Buntyam*, or we're never going to get this done."

There was a moment of silence, then an "All right," which sounded as if it had been dragged out of Caitlin.

The light pip went out, and Tully grinned for a moment. Then he sobered up, and hit the command frequency again. "Heads up, Boatright. *Pool Buntyam* is going to disable one of the ships. Have your team ready."

Caitlin ended the com call from Tully. Her first reaction was to get angry at Tully for interfering. That didn't last long, though, as she remembered something Ed had told her when the searching expedition was about to voyage out for the first time.

"I'm giving you Tully for your overall jinau commander," Ed had said. "Not because he's a member of Aille's service, and not because he's become a good friend, although the first would be an acceptable reason and the second would be understandable. I'm giving you Tully because he's good at what he does, because he's got a good reputation among the troops, and because he'll shoot straight with you. I'm especially giving you Tully because he'll tell you what he thinks is right, even when you don't want to hear it. If he tells you anything, *especially* if it has anything to do with combat, *listen to him.* Got it?"

"Got it, Ed," Caitlin whispered in the here-and-now. She slipped the com pad back into a pocket, and looked around the command deck. "Fleet Commander," she called out.

Dannet faced her direction with her angles sliding into *attention-to-oudh.* "Yes, Director?"

"Please have *Pool Buntyam*'s laser crews disable one—and only one—of the Khûrûshil ships in front of *Ban Chao*. They are to make every effort to avoid damage to the crew compartment."

Dannet's angles moved to *gratified-compliance*. She looked to Terra-Captain Uldra. "As the director has ordered. Advise *Pool Buntyam* and *Ban Chao*."

Caitlin crossed her arms and leaned against Lieutenant Vaughan's workstation as Uldra issued orders to her weapons officer. She looked over at Tamt. "That was a great idea. I guess I'll keep you around a while longer."

Caewithe snickered.

Krant-Captain Mallu krinnu ava Krant heard the orders from Fleet Commander Dannet. He looked across the command deck of *Pool Buntyam* to his officers.

"Kaln, give the target selection to weapons."

As the senior tech moved to a console, Mallu's pool-sib Jalta, who was also his Terniary-Commander on *Pool Buntyam*, moved closer and said quietly, his angles all *neutral*, "Why Kaln? Why not the weapons officer?"

Mallu knew Jalta very well, and knew that for his pool-sib to go to the trouble of mustering a formal posture, especially *neutral*, meant he had concerns about something. He moved his own angles to a definite *confidence-in-orders*, and said, "Kaln rides the time-sense better than anyone else we have. You remember what she did in the last battle. I will use anything that gives us an edge. If you ever take command of this or any other ship, you will too."

They looked at each other, still for a moment. Then Mallu stepped past Jalta to stand behind Kaln as she leaned forward, put a finger on the workstation screen, and said, "That one. Put a high-level blast here," she tapped the screen, "and a medium level shot here." The tech straightened and turned to stare Mallu in the eyes. "That will disable the craft."

Mallu looked at his weapons officer.

"Do it."

Tully saw the laser strike happen. He was watching his helmet display. *Pool Buntyam*'s lasers didn't emit light in the visible spectrum, of course, so his first clue that they'd been fired was when he started seeing pieces of the hull of one of the closest ships begin spalling and spinning away from the ship. It took him a moment to understand what he was seeing.

"Boatright!" he snapped.

"Sir!"

"Get ready. I think we'll have our target right where we want it any moment now."

Pool Buntyam's lasers continued to savage the Khûrûshil ship. Its thrust suddenly shut off, and Tully's jaw started to drop as he saw the lasers literally cut through the body of the ship, so that the aft portion began spinning rapidly away.

The forward portion, with the crew compartment and the remnants of what was presumed to be the hydrogen fuel tank began a slow forward tumble.

Tully was really glad he wasn't taking a ride on that ship. His stomach lurched in sympathy.

Lim watched as the jinau troops sorted themselves out, most standing to one side or another of the assault bay. A small group of human jinau—actually small jinau, as well, being dwarfed by most of the Jao and even some of the other humans—moved toward the other end of the bay, grouping behind one of their leaders.

A large jinau moved toward her, opening his helmet faceplate to reveal First Sergeant Luff's smiling face. "You'll need to leave the bay, ma'am," he said. "We're going to evacuate the atmosphere from it." He pointed to a nearby opening. "You can go through that hatch, then up the stairs to the control room right there"—now he pointed to a window in the wall above her head—"if you want to see what happens. I doubt there will be much to see from here. All the excitement will happen outside the hull."

Lim moved through the hatch, handling her staff with care, and heard the sergeant shut the hatch behind her. She found the stairs to the control room, in which she found one Jao and two human crewmen sitting at consoles. They glanced at Lim, but said nothing. She could stand behind them, though, and watch over their heads at the jinau in their places.

Why do they do it? Lim wondered, still mystified.

CHAPTER 26

Mallu watched over the shoulder of the weapons officer as the Khûrûshil ship broke into two pieces. Kaln's angles went to *satisfaction-at-distress-of-foes.* The weapons officer began to set up the orders for the next attack.

"Wait," Kaln said as the workstation viewscreen showed the broken ship still launching missiles from the manned portion of the ship. She studied the diagram of the ship for a moment, then touched the screen again. "Two short medium strikes, here and here to close the missile ports." She moved her finger on the screen. "Then a longer medium strike here to open the main storage tank and bleed out the hydrogen."

Kaln stood tall again, angles shifting to *satisfaction-at-task-well-done.* "That will prevent them from blowing anything up when *Ban Chao* approaches. The only weapons they will have will be what hand weapons they carried aboard."

Mallu's own posture shifted to a fairly clean form of *gratified-respect*. It was perhaps a bit more than was warranted, he thought, but he had been hanging around with a bunch of upper-class Jao the last year or so. Maybe some of their affectations were beginning to "rub off on him," as Wrot might say with one of his interminable human quotations.

His whiskers quirked in humor when he realized that Jalta had assumed the same posture.

The weapons officer ordered the next strikes, and they landed precisely where Kaln had said they should. That portion of the ship ceased spitting missiles, and began rolling even more than before.

"Weaponless," Kaln said in a smug tone.

Mallu could only nod to her.

Caitlin grew furious as she watched the attack on the Khûrûshil ship. "I said disable the ship, dammit, not destroy it!"

Flue Vaughan looked up from his workstation. "That is exactly what they did, Director. For all its smallness when compared to *Lexington* or even *Ban Chao*, that was in essence a spacegoing nuclear bomb. And a weapons-grade x-ray laser is not exactly a surgeon's scalpel. To be certain to nullify the threat, they had to take out the nuclear rocket." He touched a pad on his workstation and checked a readout. "Actually, I'm surprised they did it with as little damage as they did. That ship isn't much more than a cockleshell by our standards, and enough energy to quickly take out the rocket section could very easily have shattered the entire ship. Someone's got a good hand and a good eye over on *Pool Buntyam*."

"Probably Kaln krinnu ava Krant, if I know Krant-Captain Mallu," Wrot said as he moved up beside Caitlin. "A most resourceful Jao. And Director," he added, stressing Caitlin's title, "Lieutenant Vaughan is absolutely correct. You must remember that, for whatever reason, these people attacked us. We may have our reasons for avoiding their destruction, but we can only carry that so far. If it comes down to them or us, there is no choice."

That was a thought that Caitlin had been avoiding, but now that Wrot had brought it to the forefront of her mind, there was no question where her responsibility lay. She could not throw away the lives of her friends, crews, or troops simply because she was reluctant to order weapons live. She at last accepted that.

"Very well." Caitlin sighed. But there was something else she could do. She moved to stand beside Fleet Commander Dannet; Wrot following behind her. "Once *Ban Chao* reports that they have the crew of the Khûrûshil ship secured, order the ships to return to the one-million-kilometer point. We will remove the temptation for the Khûrûsh to attack while we interrogate our guests."

Dannet's angles were *neutral.* Her sole response was, "As you direct, Director."

"Colonel Tully," Vanta-Captain Ginta's voice sounded in his ear.

"Here, Captain." Tully linked in his officers and First Sergeant Luff.

"I assume you have been receiving the signal feed of the disabling of the target craft."

"We have."

"The last strike opened the fuel tank to space. The venting of the hydrogen has imparted spin to the portion of the ship you will be boarding."

Tully looked at the feed. Yep, no question that the remnant of the broken ship was moving faster than before. "That's not good," he said. He could see Luff's head nodding vigorously in agreement.

"The fleet commander is adamant that this operation be concluded as quickly as possible," Ginta said. "Therefore we will move *Ban Chao* into place to intercept the spin of the craft with the armored ram portion of the hull."

"Ouch!" Tully heard one of the officers mutter.

"Order your people to their shock frames, Colonel. This will be not very different from the impact of ramming the Ekhat ship. Wait."

Ginta's signal cut off.

"Top, you heard the captain, get the men moving," Tully ordered. "Charlie Company first, then Able, then Baker."

"Tully." Ginta was back on.

"Yes?"

"I see no way to identify hatches to break through, and given the beating that hull will have taken by the time we bring it under control, I doubt they would open anyway. Take that into account in your plans."

Tully looked to where Lieutenant Boatright was holding a thumb up. "I believe we have that under control, Captain."

"Good."

There was a moment of silence, then Eanne's voice was heard, "Yellow light at estimated one minute to impact, red light at estimated fifteen seconds, tether crews move at blue light, assault teams move at green light."

"Yellow at one minute, red at fifteen, tether crews at blue, assault at green." Tully looked to his helmet display, where he had acknowledgment lights from the officers and Sergeant Luff. He switched to the general troop frequency, and heard the announcement going out from Major Liang. He switched back to the command frequency. "Got it."

"Good hunting, Colonel," Tully was surprised to hear from the tech.

"Thanks."

There was silence in Tully's ear.

One of the humans, the one in jinau uniform, looked around at Lim. "Ma'am, you either need to strap in or return to your quarters." She pointed at an empty seat next to her workstation. "It's fixing to get pretty rough in a few minutes, and you could get hurt if you don't strap in somewhere."

Lim considered the young woman's request, then nodded her head and took the directed seat. The last occupant of the seat had obviously been a human, and not a large one at that. It took Lim a few moments to get the straps resized and fastened across her torso correctly, especially since she did not lay the staff on the floor.

Task accomplished, holding the staff vertically in one hand, she looked to the human and said, "I am Lim. Can you tell me what is about to occur?"

The human smiled and said, "I'm Sergeant Lacey Marasco. All I know is Director Kralik told Fleet Commander Dannet that *Pool Buntyam* should take down one of the ships that are attacking us, and *Ban Chao* should capture the crew and bring them to *Lexington* for discussions and, if need be, interrogations."

"Thank you."

The human—Sergeant Marasco—smiled again and returned her attention to her workstation and the view out the window before her. Lim sat back in the seat, and thought.

She knew that Caitlin Kralik had *oudh* over the search effort to find other sentient civilizations. She knew that both Jao and human organizations tended to be very hierarchical; not that the Lleix weren't, but the Lleix cultural need to have consensus for every decision was far outside the Jao/human/Terra taif norm.

Lim had seen Caitlin in operation; how the director would seek information, would seek opinions, would upon occasion—much to the contrary of Lleix methods—seek recommendations from those who were younger or lesser in rank. Yet in the end, the final decision would be made by Caitlin—whether it aligned with the lesser ranks' offerings or stood against them—and by her alone.

So in a very real way, by acting upon her orders, the jinau would be the hands of Caitlin Kralik. They would carry out her order at her direction, without being consulted as to whether it was the right thing to do, without establishing consensus. She ordered; they acted.

It was at that moment that Lim gained an insight that had been eluding her ever since she joined the exploration task force—all members of the task force, even Fleet Commander Dannet, were in the task force for the purpose of being Caitlin Kralik's hands. Or to put it another way, they existed to extend her reach.

That thought intrigued her.

Tully started toward the front of the shock-frames, only to find his way blocked by two large figures. His display told him it was Major Liang and First Sergeant Luff. The major held up three fingers, and Tully switched to the alternate command frequency.

"Colonel, where are you going?" Liang asked.

"I'm going to lock in behind the boarding team."

"Uh-huh," Liang replied, as Sergeant Luff crossed his arms. "You're planning on following the boarding team, aren't you?"

"The thought had crossed my mind. You have a problem with that, *Major*?" Tully stressed the rank to underline his own.

"Actually, Colonel, I do. I know you're a damn good leader, and I know that most of the men would follow you to hell and back. But I also know you jumped a bunch of grades in a short period of time."

Tully couldn't believe his ears. He'd always thought Liang liked him, or at least found him acceptable as a commander. "Yes, I did. And you also know I didn't ask for that. General Kralik put me here. You got a problem with *that*?"

"Only when the lack of the experience you missed in those rank jumps means you're about to do something, ah, ill-advised."

Tully was willing to bet that the final word in that sentence was a last split-second substitution for "stupid."

"Colonel, you're almost a brigade commander, for God's sake," Liang continued. "At that rank, you just don't lead from the front anymore. You can't. You're too damned important to the operation, any operation, to be in the front rank and get picked off by a lucky hit. You especially don't lead a simple fire-team-level evolution. That's what you have sergeants and lieutenants, and yes, even captains for."

"I don't ask my men to do anything I won't do!" Tully bit the words off. One corner of his mind was surprised at the fury he was feeling.

"The men know that, sir," Luff finally said something. "Everyone knows that you will do whatever has to be done. And that's important, both for them and for their opinion of you. But at the same time, if you start taking risks like this for no critical reason, they'll start wondering if you've lost it. You're smart, and you're lucky. So they want you to be smart and not push your luck."

Tully snorted, but before he could say anything else, the major spoke again.

"Colonel, if nothing else, remember why you're in this position. I'm sure that General Kralik gave you the same speech about there being a lack of field-grade officers that he gave me. Well, that's true enough, but for this assignment he'd have found somebody, even if it was only me. There are enough competent field-grades in the ranks that he would have been able to put someone good in your position. But it's obvious to anyone who stops to think about it for a minute, the general needed something more than a jinau officer for this job. He needed someone who could move in the highest circles, and someone that Director Kralik would listen to. Other than the general himself, that description fits you more than any other jinau officer. You have an obligation to Director Kralik, to the general, and to your troops to not take stupid chances." This time the major didn't seem to have any trouble using the s-word.

Now Major Liang crossed his arms, standing side by side with the sergeant. Tully looked at the two large men, and from the feeling in his gut he ought to have steam blowing out of a pressure relief valve at the top of his suit. But he also knew, coldly, objectively, that they were right. Oh, he didn't want to admit that. His jaws clenched so hard he felt the pressure behind his eyes. It absolutely went against his grain to have to admit that his safety had that kind of priority on it that he couldn't share all the risks of his men in the regular course of operations.

It took a long moment, but finally Tully's jaw relaxed. "You're a couple of bastards, the two of you. You know that, don't you?"

Luff chuckled in his deep voice. "Colonel, that's part of our job descriptions. Didn't you read the fine print?"

"Fine," Tully said, waving a hand. "I'll just stay back here in the back rank. Is that far enough away from trouble to suit you?" He knew his voice sounded surly. At the moment, he didn't really care. It was enough that he was doing the right thing.

"Thank you, sir," the major said. "If you're staying with Baker Company, I'll post with Able." Tully waved a hand again, and Liang headed toward the front of the shock-frame assembly.

Tully felt a change in his environment. It took him a moment to realize that the atmosphere was being pumped out of the assault bay.

He looked at Luff, who hadn't moved. "You baby-sitting me, Top?" There was an edge to his voice, and again, he didn't care.

"No, sir," Luff replied. "The company officers suggested I slot in back here, and Major Liang agreed."

"I'll just bet he did," Tully muttered. The pumps quit. "Well, let's get locked in, Top. Things are about to get interesting."

Sergeant Boyes heard a ping and saw First Sergeant Luff had tapped him via the unofficial sergeants' frequency. "Tell me you have good news for me, Top," he responded.

"The colonel is slotting in with Baker Company, Boyes."

A flood of relief washed through Boyes. He'd been very nervous that the colonel might try to ride shotgun on his team, and that was the very last thing in the world he wanted right then.

"Thanks, Top. Good to know. I owe you one."

"Too right you do. First three rounds are on you next liberty," Luff replied.

Boyes grinned in response to the humor in the first sergeant's voice. "You got it." The yellow light flashed on. "Gotta go."

Luff's light went dark. Boyes switched to the team frequency. "Heads up, boys and girls. It's show time."

CHAPTER 27

"Atmosphere evacuated," the Jao crewman in the assault bay control room said.

At that moment, yellow lights flashed on in the bay and on the control room workstations. "Brace yourselves," Sergeant Marasco said. "This is liable to rattle our teeth."

Lim pushed back against the seat, and made sure that the bottom end of the staff rested on the deck between her feet and was held firmly between her knees in addition to being gripped by her hands.

The lights flashed to red.

"Here we go!" Marasco yelled.

Whangggggg!

The red light went off after the vibrations of the contact had damped down, and the blue light flashed on. None of the jinau moved because the shock frames hadn't released, but Tully knew that ship crewmen were now moving to attach tethers to the broken Khûrûshil ship for the purpose of tying it to *Ban Chao*. With the atmosphere evacuated, he couldn't hear anything from his external audio pickups, but he could feel vibrations through his feet that told him the armored ram was being opened to allow the assault team to exit. He watched his helmet display, seeing the icons of maintenance craft exiting to attach lines to the very slowly twisting target. They stayed in the shadow of the craft as much as possible, as the other Khûrûshil ships were still firing missiles in the direction of *Pool Buntyam* and *Ban Chao*. The bigger ships' lasers were picking them off, but there was still debris flying around.

The cables got attached in what seemed relatively short order, and winches in *Ban Chao* began pulling them in. It didn't take long until the wrecked craft was floating in front of *Ban Chao*, with most of its movement damped.

The light flashed green, the shock frames released, and Charlie Company moved forward. Tully wanted a better view of the operation than his helmet display would give, so he moved to a wall panel.

"Eanne, give me a split feed of the operation display on panel..." he peered at it through his helmet screen, "AB9A."

The tech said nothing, but in a couple of seconds the screen flickered to life showing four views in its quadrants. Tully watched as a couple of human jinau fired a canister round of sensors at the target. There was a brief sparkle of lights as the sensors, each tipped with something called Space Glue by the humans, stuck and adhered to their various locations, flashed a light and sent a signal back to their control unit to lock in their feedback.

Nothing was visible in the next step, but Tully knew that each of the sensors was sending out sonar pings across a wide frequency range. All of them collected the results, fed the data back to their control unit, and the result was . . . Bingo, a map of the interior of the Khûrûshil ship. *Ollnat* again, combining off-the-shelf technology from the petroleum seismic industry and the medical scan companies.

"Colonel Tully, do you see the map?" That was Lieutenant Boatright.

"Yes, Lieutenant. I see it. And I see that you have one large open space relatively forward in the hull. Is that your target?"

"Yes, sir."

"Go for it."

"Will do, sir."

Caitlin was getting the same feed as Tully by way of Lieutenant Vaughan's workstation. "I thought they were going to bring it into one of *Ban Chao*'s shuttle bays, or the assault bay. What's left of the ship is not all that big."

Vaughan shook his head. "Not while there's a risk that there still might be something on that ship that could go boom. None of the ships could take that chance, not even *Ban Chao*."

"Oh. Right. Got it." Caitlin thought about that for a moment. "Now I see why Tully's had the jinau drilling in zero gravity."

"Boarding through the assault bay ramp only works when the target ship is big enough for the ram to penetrate," Caewithe Miller offered from her bodyguard position behind Caitlin. "Otherwise, you swim through space."

"Hmm," Caitlin mused. "So Tully's been thinking about this kind of thing already."

"That's why General Kralik made him the colonel," Miller replied, "or at least one reason. Gabe's got more out of atmosphere and out of ship experience than any other officer."

"Any other human officer," Tamt inserted into the conversation. "There are many Jao officers with more experience."

"But how many of them are in Terra taif?" Miller asked.

Tamt gave a human shrug, but didn't say anything.

Wrot picked up the conversation. "None, that I know of. Most officers with that kind of experience either died in the conquest phase or left after Oppuk became governor. That should have been a warning to the Naukra . . ." the Jao council of kochans, ". . . of what was to come, but none would see it then, not even Pluthrak. And so," he circled back to the original topic, "we have Colonel Tully being of use at the moment. He is good, you know, for a youngling. If he survives long enough to learn subtlety, he could be . . . formidable."

Caitlin started to laugh at the idea of Tully being subtle. Then she had second thoughts, and even third ones, especially considering whose opinion she was hearing. Wrot was not the least subtle of Jao; for all that he cultivated a rough and brusque manner. His service to Preceptor Ronz of the Bond of Ebezon was evidence of that. "Gabe Tully being subtle," she said, "could be a scary thought."

It didn't surprise her at all to see Caewithe Miller nod in response, with a sober expression on her face.

✧ ✧ ✧

"Boyes," came through Sergeant Boyes' ear bud. "Carter here. Come on over."

"Roger that," Boyes replied to the boarding team sergeant. He switched to the team frequency. "Okay, you apes. Our turn. Head for the shack."

One by one his fire-team jumped for the Khûrûshil ship, himself last; and one by one they made landings of one degree or another on the broken hull. The sergeant was the first to make it to the boarding shack, a plastic tent where the walls were filled with air and made rigid by applying electrical charges. The bases of said walls were bonded to the hull with more Space Glue and electrical charges. A much weaker version of the technology allowed the jinau teams' feet to stick to the hull.

Boyes stood by the door, naming his troops as they entered. "Nolan, McClanahan, Singh, Gomez, Kemal, and me," as he stepped into the airlock and moved through into the main chamber.

"That all of you?" came from the figure with the Carter name patch on his suit standing opposite the inner airlock door.

"Yep," Boyes said as another jinau followed him in and closed the inner airlock door behind them.

The shack was roughly four meters wide and seven meters long, and tall enough that even First Sergeant Luff could have stood unbowed within it. There was plenty of headroom for Boyes and his team.

"Okay, three of you on one side and three on the other," Carter said. "Laroche, there, is going to lay out a door for you. Stay out of her way and don't step on it."

The other jinau began applying long lines of sticky

cord to the hull metal, laying it out with care and making sure that one particular side of it always was in contact with the hull. After outlining a rectangle maybe one and a half meters by three meters, she inserted a short rod and stepped back. Carter checked a gauge on his wrist.

"Okay, boys and girls, we have the equivalent of about three thousand meters altitude atmosphere in here now, which is about as good as it's going to get. Laroche just laid a shaped charge. Stand well back, and when I tell you to, face the walls. That should blow a hole through the hull and open the door for you. If it doesn't, then we'll apply the handy dandy door openers." Here Carter held up a device that was obviously a distant descendant of what used to be called the Jaws of Life. "I've seen your plan, but tell it to me again."

"After the door opens . . ." Boyes began.

"We throw the flash-bangs and step back," Nolan and Kemal said in unison.

"We take entry lead," said Singh and Gomez.

"Mac and I follow," Boyes said.

"We take the rear and guard their six," Nolan and Kemal finished.

"Weapons?" Carter asked.

"Super-Tazers." Singh and Gomez held them up.

"Net guns." Boyes lifted his, echoed by McClanahan.

"Shotguns with rubber slugs," Nolan said. Kemal just grinned.

"Backups?" Carter asked.

Boyes and the rest of his team all slapped the holsters where they each carried a high-capacity 10 mm pistol, sized for the combat suits. Those were weapons of last resort on this mission, but no one, from Colonel Tully on down, denied that last resorts could be exercised. Boyes also reached up and touched the knife that was sheathed hilt-down to the left of his sternum.

"The rest of my team is in the airlock, and as soon as you finish entry they'll come in and be backup," Carter concluded.

"Outstanding," Boyes said. He was pumped on adrenaline. "Let's do this thing."

"Right," Carter said. "Face the walls."

CHAPTER 28

Thoomp!

As designed, the shaped charge had directed almost all of its energy downward against the hull. Boyes felt the equivalent of a hard push against his back from the spillover. He spun in place, to see Clark and Laroche placing their door-openers in the cracks formed by the charge and triggering their operation. A few seconds later they discarded the metal plate and stepped back.

Nolan and Kemal already had the flash-bang grenades in motion through the opening, one-two-three-four.

As soon as the grenades had exploded, Singh and Gomez pulled themselves through the opening, back to back, Super-Tazers leading the way. "Damn!" Boyes heard one of them call out as he pulled himself through on their heels. His external audio sensor began picking up sounds of conflict. As his helmet rose above the interior edge of the opening, he could see Singh and Gomez both facing to his left, firing their weapons as quickly as they could.

Boyes looked to his left. "Crap! Clark, I see six, seven, eight hostiles. Two down, four with what looks like clubs or pipes, and two hanging back." As soon as he moved clear of the opening he brought his net gun to bear on the closest Khûrûsh-an and fired.

"Shit!" Tully heard Sergeant Boyes exclaim. The video feed from the sergeant's helmet was really bobbing around. "They're faster than snakes, and tell the video folks they're not that much smaller than we are."

Tully could see the Khûrûsh crewmen dodging and bouncing from wall to wall, swinging lengths of whatever they were holding in each hand. One of them looked for all the world like a four-armed Bruce Lee, his arms were moving so fast. Only the fact that he was having to duck net shots kept him from really laying out one of the boarding team.

Damn, but he should have ignored Liang and Luff. He belonged in that fight!

Just as Tully was about to call out an order, he saw one of the Khûrûsh-an fold up around his midsection, and he realized that the shotgunners had now entered the fray. Even a low-charge rubber bullet could take a man down if it hit right. Looks like the same was true of the Khûrûsh as well.

"Yeah!" Boyes heard one of his team yell as the Khûrûsh began to go down before the rubber slugs fired by Nolan and Kemal. He and McClanahan made sure they stayed down by firing nets at them to keep them tangled up and stuck to the deck for now.

"Lieutenant Boatright," he said over the company frequency as the action started slowing a little.

"Boatright. Go."

"Their suits are tougher than ours. The Tazer darts

are just bouncing off. You have to hit them with the rubber slugs to slow them down enough to net them."

"Understood."

The last of the four club-armed Khûrûsh, the one whose arms were moving like radial saw blades, went down after being hit three times by the rubber slugs. Just as McClanahan fired a net over him, Boyes saw the larger of the two remaining Khûrûsh-an raise what looked like a pistol. His shout of "Gun!" coincided with the weapon firing. There was a bit of a flash, and he heard Kemal grunt. He looked to see the young Turk's left forearm floating in front of him, cleanly severed just below the elbow, with blood spurting from his arm.

Things seemed to go into slow motion at that point. Boyes felt himself release his net gun and move for his pistol. His hand seemed to almost be moving in water, it felt so slow. He could see the Khûrûsh-an moving his weapon to target on Nolan. He was pulling the 10 mm from his holster, but it still seemed so slow—too slow. It came up, up, up, and he squeezed the trigger.

Just as the pistol fired, the Khûrûsh-an moved slightly, and what was supposed to be a shot to the shoulder hit him in the throat instead. Everyone, human and Khûrûsh-an, froze for a moment.

"Ah, Lieutenant Boatright?"

"Talk to me, Sergeant."

"Their suits aren't tougher than a ten mil, sir."

"Damn."

"Eanne!" Tully shouted.

"Colonel?"

"Get me connected with the Lleix on *Lexington* who are talking to the Khûrûsh!"

Eanne said nothing, but in a few seconds Tully heard, "This is Pyr," in his ear bud.

"Pyr, this is Gabe Tully. What is the Khûrûsh command to surrender?"

Pyr didn't ask any questions. "*Noh-rah-zhoh.*"

"Great! Stay connected." Tully connected to the Charlie Company frequency. "Sergeant Boyes, you're about to hear the Khûrûsh command to surrender. Pyr, say again."

"*Noh-rah-zhoh.*"

There were now four 10 mm pistols aimed at the last Khûrûsh-an standing, who was holding one of the gunlike weapons. Boyes flipped his external audio on and shouted "*Noh-rah-zhoh*! *Noh-rah-zhoh*!"

He jabbed at the Khûrûsh-an with his pistol, and forcefully pointed to the deck with his other hand. After a moment, the last Khûrûsh-an bent and placed his weapon on the deck, then stood and held all four arms straight out.

Nobody took their attention off of the Khûrûsh-an, but Boyes' tension ratcheted down a little. "Carter?"

"Go." That was Carter's voice, but Boyes knew the lieutenant was listening.

"We're ready for the backup and the intelligence team to board. Need a bunch of restraints. These dudes have four arms, remember. Looks like we may need a couple of litters or backboards for their wounded." He looked to where Gomez was dealing with Kemal's wound. "Add a medic and a litter for Kemal." He paused for a moment. "And a body bag, I guess, unless command wants to leave the dead one here."

CHAPTER 29

"*Ban Chao* reports that the target crew has been taken aboard, as well as whatever intelligence information could be readily retrieved," *Lexington*'s communication officer announced. "Hulk has been abandoned, they are withdrawing to the million-kilometer rally point."

"Order a withdrawal by all ships to the rally point at cruising speed," Fleet Commander Dannet ordered. "Cover *Ban Chao*'s withdrawal."

Caitlin moved to Lieutenant Vaughan's work station. "Well?"

He held up a hand. "Initial reports coming in. The Khûrûshil ship had a crew of eight. Two were seriously injured by the disabling attack or the forced entry, unclear yet which it was. They have been retrieved. The commander was killed during the boarding action."

"What?" Caitlin was aghast. "They were supposed to take them alive!"

"According to the preliminary reports," Vaughan repeated, "he was firing a deadly weapon at the boarding team in the constrained space of their command deck, and had already seriously wounded one of the boarding team. The team lead was trying for a disabling shot, but the Khûrûsh commander zigged when he should have zagged." He looked up with a quirk to his mouth. "That's a direct quote from Colonel Tully, by the way. He also said, 'No blame for Sergeant Boyes. I'd have done the same thing.'" Vaughan concluded with, "Boyes is the team lead."

Caitlin took a deep breath, but before she could let it out, Wrot moved into her field of vision. His eyes locked with hers, and she remembered their earlier conversation. She let the breath out in a rush, and said, "Fine. I guess we should be glad the price wasn't any higher than that. Keep me posted, please, and let me know when they're ready to send the crew to *Lexington.*"

"That's it?" Tully asked. "That dinky little thing took off Kemal's arm?"

There are only so many basic configurations a portable hand-carried weapon can assume once a culture rises above the axe-and-sword and pike-and-bow levels. The weapon that Sergeant Boyes was dandling in a clear plastic bag wasn't too much different in size and shape than a Beretta pistol.

"That's it," Boyes said.

"And it's not some kind of laser?"

"No, sir. One shot, one brief flash, and Kemal's arm was floating in the air and he was bleeding like a, pardon the expression, stuck pig."

"So there was no cauterization effect?"

"Nope. His arm looked more like it had met up

with a meat saw and lost. No burns, no blisters, no hint of heat at all."

"At least the docs got his arm reattached." Tully shook his head. "And we got two of these things?"

"Yes, sir. The guy I shot and the guy who surrendered both had one. I still don't know why he surrendered. All the others went down fighting."

Tully shrugged. "Not important at the moment. Lim and the Lleix will get it out of them if anybody can. XO," he said, turning to Major Liang. "Send one of these to *Lexington* for the science types over there, and keep one of them here and turn it over to the armorers. Suggest strongly to *Lexington* that they proceed with great caution. Give our guys orders to be very careful in how they inspect it. I have a hunch these folks may have things to teach us about batteries and capacitors."

Tully's com pad pinged. He touched a control. "Yes?"

"Colonel Tully, I need Sergeant Boyes to join me in the interrogation room, please."

"What's up, Lim?"

"The surviving officer will not speak to me. I wish to see if he will speak to the one who conquered him."

"Conquered? What does she mean, conquered?" Boyes muttered. Tully waved a hand at him, and he shut up.

"Officer?" Tully queried. "You've identified their ranks?"

"Colonel," Lim sounded annoyed, if that was possible for a Lleix, "we can read their script, we've been watching their videos for days now, and they love to talk about their space service. Yes, I know their ranks. Now please have Sergeant Boyes join me."

"On our way."

Tully stood up. "Top, Boyes, you're with me. XO," he turned to the executive officer, "I want an inventory and initial assessment of everything that was pulled off that wreck chop-chop. Boatright," he looked to the Charlie Company commander, "I need an after-action report ASAP to forward to Director Kralik. The rest of you," with a glance at the other commanders, "clean up and start the next drill cycle."

For the next several cycles, as she dealt with tasks Ninth-Minor-Sustained had given her, Third-Mordent considered the implications—all the implications—of what her ancestress had said, and perhaps even more importantly, what she had not said. Her understanding of "Never give anything away" was now advanced.

Lim turned from the one-way mirror in mingled frustration and relief as Colonel Tully entered the viewing room, followed by First Sergeant Luff and Sergeant Boyes. "I only needed him," she said with a nod at Boyes.

"Maybe so," Tully responded, moving to the mirror to view the interrogation room, "but I need to be in on this. Boyes, come look at this."

Lim stepped to one side to allow Boyes room to step up to the glass. Luff moved up and stood behind the shorter sergeant, well able to see over the top of his head.

For several moments, they all watched as the Khûrûsh-an paced back and forth, mostly walking on the middle and hind limbs, but twice raising up to walk on hind limbs only for a few steps.

"I wouldn't swear to it," Boyes finally said, "but I think that's the one who surrendered."

"It is," Lim responded.

Boyes winced. "Jeez, that's not going to make me his favorite person, is it?"

Lim shrugged, frustration resurfacing. "He won't talk to me. Let us see if he will talk to you."

She led the way to a door next to the viewing window, and placed her hand on the door handle. Boyes looked to Colonel Tully, who nodded. Boyes squared his shoulders, and said, "Let's get it over with, then."

Lim nodded, opened the door, and motioned Boyes through with her staff. She followed, closing the door behind them.

The Khûrûsh-an spun at the sound of the door closing, and his fur bristled up to the point he seemed almost twice as large. He backed into a corner and rose up on his hind legs. Boyes realized he was almost looking the creature in the eye.

Unlike when they faced each other across the command deck of the wrecked spacecraft, the Khûrûsh-an was not holding all four arms stretched out with spread-out hands. No, here the arms were curved forward, with the hands curled like claws—which they might well be, Boyes realized after a look at the fingers.

The Khûrûsh-an hissed at him, if something that sounded like a baritone steam-kettle could be called a hiss. Boyes reached out and grabbed Lim with his left hand and pulled her behind him as he drew his sidearm with the other.

"*Noh-rah-zhoh*!" Boyes shouted the surrender command, and jabbed his left hand down at the deck just as he had done when he had faced this same Khûrûsh-an just hours before.

Sergeant Luff put his hand on the doorknob, ready to intervene in what was happening in the interrogation room.

"Wait," Tully said. "Let's see how our boy does. But stay ready."

"They did what?" Caitlin decided that she couldn't be shocked any more. Even this latest weirdness didn't rattle her.

"The Khûrûsh destroyed the disabled craft after *Ban Chao* and *Pool Buntyam* left it behind," Vaughan replied. "Both parts of it."

"Destroyed it how? Lasers, self-destruct mechanism, took it apart with wrenches?" Okay, she was still capable of sarcasm and frustration.

"They launched four missiles at it, and blew it into scrap."

"But they had no idea if any of their people were still on board!" That idea did bother Caitlin. "Why would they do that?"

"That might be why they call them aliens," Vaughan said with that quirky smile he'd been flashing at Caewithe for some time.

Caewithe laughed at that.

"Funny man," Caitlin turned away. Behind her, she heard Caewithe giggle again.

"I said, *Noh-rah-zhoh*, you SOB!" Boyes snarled at the Khûrûsh-an again, aiming the pistol directly between his eyes while again jabbing at the floor forcefully.

There was a very tense moment, before the steel seemed to evaporate out of the alien. His outstretched arms drooped first, then he settled to first four limbs on the deck, then all six. Finally he lay prostrate, and began chanting something in a soft voice with his nose pointed at the floor.

Boyes kept his pistol aimed at the alien's head, dropping his aim as he moved. But after a minute or more of the chanting, he stepped back a step and said to Lim, "What's he saying?"

Lim lifted a hand, but didn't respond for another minute or more. Finally she said, "It's a lament, in what passes for a classical form. The officer you shot was his father."

"Ho, boy," Boyes muttered, focusing his attention back on the Khûrûsh-an again. "Why isn't he jumping all over me?"

Lim continued as if he hadn't said anything. "In addition, his father was his clan-lord. His chief, if you will. He was second in command under his father."

After another long moment, Boyes said, "So what else is he saying?"

"He's lamenting the death of his father, and the ending of his clan. His surrender has ended his clan line, as he has no living brothers or sisters, and his mother is also dead. He surrendered because with the clan-lord dead that was the only way he could spare the lives of their retainers on the ship."

"You mean the crew were..."

"Literally servants of his father in his position as clan-lord, yes." Lim paused and listened for a moment more. "Now he's asking forgiveness of his ancestors for having been taken alive by the monsters from the dark. He's very confused as to how we could have come out of the sun when we are clearly monsters. But he's promising to watch over the retainers as best he can, and to maintain what honor he can until he comes to them—which he hopes will happen soon, but it's up to the monsters."

The alien ceased his muttering, then looked up at Boyes and rattled something off quickly.

"He says his name is Kamozh ar Mnûresh, and he is your slave."

Third-Mordent summoned her chosen choirs to return to the hall. She would see to their completion herself. Her understanding of "Never reveal all your skill to anyone" was now crystal clear.

CHAPTER 30

"Director," Fleet Command Dannet said, "you may want to look at the main viewscreen."

When Caitlin did, she saw the familiar schematic of the Khûr system. It took a moment for her to see the additional clouds of symbols spreading out from the various planets and headed toward the elements of her fleet.

"Is that what I think it is?"

"If you think those are fleets of ships launched by the natives of the system and heading toward us, then yes." Dannet's angles were at *dealing-with-the-moment.* "And some of those launched from the outer planets are of respectable size."

Caitlin turned to Pyr. "Have we had any response at all to our messages?"

Pyr folded his hands together. "No," he said with a trace of sadness.

Caitlin looked back at the viewscreen. "How many?"

"Fifty-nine total from the homeworld," Lieutenant

Vaughan said, "all heading toward us. Sixty-five from the inner world, all headed for our main fleet. Seventy-five from the third planet, and one hundred and nine from the gas giant, all headed inward but no definite target yet."

Caitlin snorted. "We know who the target is."

"Well," Vaughan acknowledged, "it's too early to tell if they're aiming for our little group or our main fleet or both."

"They have ships the size of Harriers," Dannet added to the conversation.

"They won't be as good as Harriers," Caitlin countered.

"But they won't be as easy to kill as those small ships we just encountered, either."

"You assume we're going to be fighting them," Caitlin said with a frown.

Dannet said nothing, simply moved to a *neutral* posture, which for her at this moment was almost provocatory.

Caitlin thought for a moment, then looked to Vaughan. "Get me a line to Gabe Tully, please."

Vaughan touched a series of controls on his workstation.

"Tully here," came the response over his speakers in a few seconds.

"Gabe," Caitlin said, "have you got anything at all out of your guests yet?"

"Nope. We just got the surviving officer to start talking to us. Haven't got past the name, rank, and serial number stage yet."

"Damn," Caitlin responded. "Okay, number one thing we need to know is if we leave the system, how far will they pursue us? Number two thing we need to know is we know they have much bigger ships than we've seen, but do they have heavier weapons?"

"You got it," Tully said. "Tully out."

Caitlin crossed her arms and stared at the floor. *We can't make friends if they won't talk to us. And even if we continue here and just keep blowing their missiles up, sooner or later something's going to go wrong and we're going to be even worse off in trying to make connections. I don't really want to do this, but I don't think we have any choice. Time to get out of Dodge before we burn a bridge we'll really want later on.*

She looked up. "Fleet Commander, all ships to return to main fleet as soon as possible, then head for galactic north at best speed until we pass the boundary of the system. We will defend if attacked, but not return fire unless I order it."

Dannet shifted to *compliance-to-oudh*. "As you direct." She turned to issue orders to the fleet.

Wrot stepped up beside Caitlin. "Remove the possibility of confrontation until we understand this system. A good idea."

"No," Caitlin muttered. "Not a good idea. It's just the least-bad idea at the moment."

Boyes looked at Lim, the Khûrûsh-an momentarily forgotten. "He's my what?"

The alien—Kamozh—chattered again. Lim listened, then held a hand up and turned to Boyes. "He says that he is your slave by right of conquest and surrender." She shrugged. "Or at least that's as close as I can come to it. There are additional strands of meaning that do not work well in English."

Boyes looked at Kamozh still lying on the floor, and holstered his pistol. He gave a wild-eyed look for a moment at the mirror that was the observation window.

The sergeant walked over to the small table that had been pushed to one side of the room and sat down on it. He gestured at a chair for Lim. She took a seat, holding her staff in one hand. "Honestly? A slave? I thought only the Ekhat went in for that stuff."

Lim shook her head. "There are no exact parallels between the Khûrûsh and you humans, but if you think of Shogunate Japan blended with equal measures of Homeric Greece and the British Raj, you're approaching a concept. Except that their emperors are very smart, and very perceptive, and very capable. Also not given to allowing second chances for failure."

"But I can't keep a slave! I mean, even if Colonel Tully let me, what would I do with him?"

"Leave that for the colonel and Director Kralik," Lim said.

Boyes took a deep breath. "Okay, try talking back to him. Tell him I said he's got to talk to you to talk to me, and I will take it very badly if he gives you any problems. And tell him to sit up."

"I have changed your directive slightly, Director." Dannet approached Caitlin.

Caitlin just looked at the big Jao, and crossed her arms, not going to a Jao posture.

"I have ordered the main fleet to head for the system limits now rather than wait for the return of our group. We will join them on a converging course."

Caitlin looked at the main viewscreen, where the Khûrûsh fleets were moving toward them. It wasn't hard to understand the fleet commander's reasoning. The sooner they were out of the way, the sooner there would be no risk of contact.

"Very well."

The fleet commander turned away, and Caitlin looked back at Wrot. "Does anything about this whole experience seem fishy to you?"

"In what way?" Wrot asked.

"Everything that's happened since we came into this system." She walked away a few steps, then turned and walked back. "I mean, nothing has seemed right since we got here. This is a high-technology civilization. Not as high as the Jao, but definitely at least a little ahead of where Earth was when you Jao first arrived.

"When your first fleet moved in, as soon as we understood you were from the stars, even as you made your assault landings, we started sending you all kinds of communications, trying to get some kind of understanding of who you were and what you wanted."

Caitlin repeated the walk away and return steps. "Here, nothing. Nada. Zilch. We know they know we're here, because of the radar. But they never offered anything."

Walk away, return. "I could almost accept that as a manifestation of extreme caution. Or pathological isolationism. Maybe even cowardice. Except that once we began the approach, once we initiated a communication contact using their frequencies and their language, the only response we got was an attack. No warning, no cautions, no waveoffs; just a full-bore attack."

She stood by Vaughan's workstation. She knew he was listening, as well as Wrot and the Lleix at the next workstation.

"We've been reacting," she said, "not analyzing. My fault. I wanted the contact to work so badly that I didn't consider that these folks are not us, and their universe view is apparently very different from ours. But it's not too late to think about that."

Caitlin looked around at those close by: Wrot, Vaughan, Lim and Garhet, Caewithe and Tamt.

"Maybe they're crazy. Maybe they're insane, like the Ekhat. But I have trouble believing that that could be a successful survival strategy for more than one race. And I refuse to believe that there are only three sane races in this corner of the universe."

Human, Jao, and Lleix heads all nodded. They were tracking with her so far.

"So why would a whole race and civilization respond this way? Why would their reaction be 'Destroy the invader,' at first contact, without even a single attempt to talk?"

There was a long moment of silence, broken by Pyr. "There has to have been a resounding traumatic event in their history that changed their cultural outlook."

Caitlin considered that thought, then nodded. "I can buy that. So what would have caused this kind of mindset?"

"Paranoia," Vaughan said quietly. Caitlin turned to him, realization dawning in her own mind. "We're not..."

"...the first alien race they've met," Caitlin completed the thought. "Damn, but that makes sense. That would explain everything that's happened." She thought some more, then said, "Open that channel to Tully back up, please."

After a few moments, she heard, "Tully here. What's up, Caitlin?"

"Colonel Tully, we're coming to the conclusion over here that the Khûrûsh have had at least one bad experience with another alien race, maybe more than one."

There was a whistle, then, "Yeah, I can see that. We're starting to get more conversation going, over here. I'll make sure that gets added to the questions."

"And one more thing, Gabe," Caitlin said.

"Yeah?"

"I really want to know if they have ever seen or heard of the Ekhat. Show them pictures of Ekhat and Ekhat ships. If they've been traumatized, well, who do we know is the most likely candidate to do the traumatizing?"

"Got it. Will do."

"Thanks."

Third-Mordent was again blade dancing; again with a male who was larger and stronger and perhaps faster. He was also smarter than her last opponent. He did not rush her, simply strode forward, forehand blades at the ready, head down and red eyes glaring at her.

She danced aside from his first blow, diverted his second to the side, and spun inside the reach of his blades, blocked both the grasping claw and the small manipulator with a movement of one of her own forehand blades while she reached up and carved a crescent around one of his eyes with the other.

The male recoiled with a hiss of pain, and Third-Mordent danced away, untouched.

White ichor was flowing down over the male's eye, half-blinding him. He repeatedly shook his head, slinging the ichor in spatters around him, but the gash was wide and the flow profuse. His manipulators would not reach that high.

At that moment, Third-Mordent knew that she could complete the male. It might take her more than a few passages in the dance, but she could do it. Ninth-Minor-Sustained had not cautioned her against it, so it would be permitted. She cocked her head to one side, viewing the male from the perspective that displayed the fresh wound to its best advantage. Would completing this one be wasteful, she considered. Fewer males survived the creches than females, and there had been generations that had been blighted by a lack of viable males.

Third-Mordent formed a leitmotif in her mind, then sang it. The male turned his head so that his clear eye focused on Third-Mordent. She danced around him in a controlled slow pavane; he turned to follow her.

She sounded the leitmotif again; his body started trembling. At first it seemed to be the predator urge—but no, his head was lifting. Still, he was poised with forehand blades ready, tensed, poised, intent. It surprised her that, as intensely as he appeared to desire to spring on her, he was restraining himself. She darted a glance at Ninth-Minor-Sustained, who stood at one end, a looming monolith, unmoving.

Third-Mordent focused her gaze back to the male, sounding the leitmotif a third time. He edged away from her, raising his forehand blades. She flowed to one side; the male turned, but stepped back a pace. She stepped the other direction. He backed away from her.

Step by step, slow move by slow move, she danced and he retreated.

He ended in a corner, hemmed in, unable to dance away. Third-Mordent paused in front of him, poised, one forehand blade still and one drawing a slow line in the air. The one clear eye moved between the moving blade and her face. The blade stopped, and so did the eye.

The pose held for a long moment.

"Enough." Ninth-Minor-Sustained broke her silence and her pose. Third-Mordent stepped away and relaxed, lifting her own head and folding forehand blades away.

The male didn't move as Ninth-Minor-Sustained approached him, singing a soliloquy. Her manipulator lifted a cauterizer to treat the male's wound, and Third-Mordent smelled the odor of burned flesh. Ninth-Minor-Sustained stepped back and waved a manipulator at the male, who folded his own forehand blades away and moved to the nearest door, slipping through it when it irised open.

Third-Mordent stood still, head high and manipulators lifted, as Ninth-Minor-Sustained turned to face her.

"And now you see the third lesson of control—controlling others. We begin—now."

Third-Mordent felt a frisson of fear at how Ninth-Minor-Sustained's voice did a rapid glissando into her lowest register. The fundamental pitch she attained resonated with overtones that pierced Third-Mordent's mind in ominous ways.

Lim turned away from the hologram that was floating in front of the entranced Kamozh. "He says they have never seen anything like that ship."

"Okay, show him the Ekhat next," Tully said, watching over Boyes' shoulder. The Khûrûsh-an had reacted in surprise when Tully had entered the room, but had quickly settled down when Tully had simply merged into the Boyes/Lim group.

Lim touched a control on her com pad, and the hologram flickered and changed to the floating form of an Ekhat adult.

Kamozh recoiled with another baritone hiss. He chattered away at Lim, pointing an emerged claw at the hologram.

"He says that that is a monster indeed, nastier than anything they have ever seen."

"So they have never seen the Ekhat before?"

Lim spoke to Kamozh. He chattered back at her. She turned back to Tully. "Never to his knowledge."

Caitlin pointed to Vaughan. "Put it on public, please."

After a moment, Tully's voice was heard in the command deck.

"Caitlin, here's what we have at the moment. First of all, the larger ships use more missiles, some of the same type as we've seen, but some also with nuclear warheads."

Dannet turned at that note and began issuing quiet orders to the communication technician.

"Second," Tully continued, "according to the one guest who is talking, once we get beyond the orbit of the outermost planet, the Khûrûshil ships should break off. Definitely if we move on past the outer cometary ring.

"And last, they have apparently never seen the Ekhat."

"Okay, thanks. Keep us posted if you get more information out of them."

"Will do."

Some hours had passed, and the Terran fleet was moving well beyond the shell of the fifth planet's orbit, continuing to head for the frontiers of the Khûrûsh system. Caitlin's flotilla had rejoined the fleet without more combat, although the Khûrûshil ships from the inmost planet had launched a few missiles at their closest approach, a couple of which *Pool Buntyam* had blown out of existence just to be safe. The Jao propulsion technology was definitely superior to the natives', and once the Terran ships were clear of the possibility of direct interception, their lead kept increasing.

Once the fleet was clear, Caitlin returned to her quarters.

She had not intended to go to sleep, just to rest for a few moments, but she awoke to her com pad pinging at her. Rolling out of the bunk, she tapped a control. "Yes?"

"Director, you'd better get back to the command deck." That was a Jao voice she didn't place. "We have ships jumping into the sun."

"Who . . . never mind. On my way."

Caitlin didn't say anything to her guards as she flew by them. They managed to catch up to her by the time she reached the lift to the command deck. "Come on, come on, come on," she urged the lift.

When the doors opened, Caitlin burst out into the command deck. "What's happening?" she demanded.

"Two ships in the sun, one emerging from the

photosphere," Terra-Captain Uldra responded as the lift door irised open and a dripping wet fleet commander entered the deck. Dannet had obviously been in the pool when the notice reached her. "More about to arrive." The lift door irised open again, this time admitting Lieutenant Vaughan who slid into his workstation and started tapping control pads like a drummer.

"Are they Ekhat?" Caitlin's heart was in her throat.

Before Uldra responded, one of the communications techs called out, "Contact made, asking for Director Kralik."

"Put it on the screen," she ordered, pointing to the main viewscreen. The system template display snowed out, then cleared to reveal a very familiar face.

"Hello, Caitlin," said Aille.

PART IV
On the Frontier

CHAPTER 31

"It appears that you found your goal," Aille continued from the main display.

"We did and we didn't." Caitlin ran one hand through her hair. "Yes, they are a developed spacefaring culture. But," this time she ran both hands through her hair, resisting the urge to pull it out, "they appear to be xenophobic to an almost insane degree."

Aille's position shifted, but she couldn't tell quite what angles he was assuming. "Like the Ekhat?"

"No," Caitlin replied. "Or at least, not quite that bad. But they will not talk, and they attacked us as soon as we approached a planet. Now, less than a day later, they've launched a massive attack from all their planets. We're headed out of the system to keep from having to destroy them in self-defense. You need to do likewise. Get your ships out past the cometary ring, and we'll join up then."

Aille nodded. "Agreed. We will talk."

The viewscreen blanked, then reset to the display of the system schematic with the various Khûrûshil ships noted with past and projected trajectories all shaping toward the Terra taif fleet components.

Caitlin looked over to Wrot. "Okay, what is Aille doing here? Not that I'm not glad to see him, or anything, but having him pop up here is just really odd."

Wrot's posture changed, moving through several until it settled into the angles of *reluctant-convergence.* "My doing, I suspect. I sent word to Preceptor Ronz of your plans."

"You *what*?" Caitlin stared at him in disbelief.

"When we arrived at Ares Base, I sent a report to Ronz describing your decision to move the search to the Sagittarian Arm."

Caitlin crossed her arms. She was pleased with herself that her response was in a moderate tone. "Okay. Was there any particular reason why you felt a need to do that?"

Wrot shrugged. "You made a significant change in the direction of the effort. I reported that to him."

"Without telling me." That wasn't a question.

"It wasn't necessary for you to know. It would have changed nothing you did."

Caitlin felt her teeth grinding together. She turned away and clasped her hands behind her back to keep from assuming the simple angles for pure *outrage.*

He's not human, Caitlin reminded herself. *He's not backstabbing you.* She knew Wrot well enough to know that he would have no problem being blunt to her face. A snort escaped her at that thought.

She felt her jaw relax and turned back to face the old Jao.

"Do I have *oudh* over this search and this fleet, or not?"

"Director, you do." Wrot had shifted to *neutral* angles, but his whiskers kept shifting to something hinting of *concern*. He did not drop his eyes from Caitlin's however.

"Then why? Why go behind my back with this?"

"Not behind your back," Wrot said. "Parallel lines. You have *oudh*," he continued with a wrinkle to his muzzle, "but the preceptor is the sponsor of the search. I am under your *oudh* for the tasks of the search, but I remain under his when he asks for opinions and reports."

"But why would he want that? Does he not trust me after all?" She fought to keep the whine from her voice.

Wrot's ears flipped out and his whiskers tilted in the abbreviated posture for *wry-humor*. "The preceptor trusts you as much as he trusts Aille," he said. That caused Caitlin to blink in surprise. "But he is also the preeminent Bond strategist."

"So?" Caitlin asked after a long moment of silence.

Wrot's angles moved from *wry* to *sly*. "Caitlin, Preceptor Ronz understood all the truth and dependent corollaries about the saying 'Don't put all your eggs in one basket' long before he ever heard it."

"So you're a reality check on me?"

Wrot huffed in irritation. "No, nor am I a spy, or anything else like that. Stop thinking like a human."

"Then what?"

"Mmm, you might think of me as a parallax view."

That thought stopped Caitlin's thoughts. "So what did you tell him? No," she said immediately after, "I don't want to know."

She turned away again and took a slow walk around Lieutenant Vaughan's station, breathing slowly and deeply. Her anger had not totally faded, and neither had her concern.

"Did you think I had some reason, some motive, to try to keep my decision to relocate the search a secret?" she said over her shoulder. "That would have been pretty stupid, after pulling into Ares Base and stocking up on everything there was to get."

Wrot shrugged. "You're not stupid," he replied. "You might recall that neither am I."

Caitlin took several steps away, and stood watching the main viewscreen, squeezing her hands tightly where she gripped them behind her back. She felt the eyes of the group clustered near Vaughan's workstation staring at her.

At length, Caitlin turned and paced back to face Wrot. "Do I have *oudh* over this search?" she softly repeated her question, looking up into his eyes.

"Director, you do." Wrot said nothing more, moved nothing, simply stood in *neutral*.

"Good." Caitlin nodded at the confirmation. "We're done with this, then. Except—" she released her hands and assumed angles for *absolute-command-to-subordinate* "—you will not communicate outside this fleet in any way without my express approval. Understood?"

The old Jao said nothing, but his angles shifted to *obedience-to-lawful-commands*.

Caitlin looked at the others, including Vaughan. "Not a word," she said. "Not. One. Word."

Her tone was much the same as it always was. Nonetheless, everyone obviously felt discretion was the better part of valor at that moment. No one spoke.

Aille took position beside Terra-Captain Sanzh and watched the main viewscreen in *Footloose*'s command deck, waiting for the rest of his flotilla to arrive. Three of his seven ships were now clear of the photosphere, one was still rising in the plasma currents, and the sensor tech had reported that the rest should emerge from their jumps very soon.

"Directions, Governor?" Sanzh asked quietly as the fourth ship crossed the transition of the photosphere.

"Have your navigator shape a course that takes us directly away from those fleets," Aille said, with a nod toward the viewscreen, "but in such a manner that we can before long bend to galactic north and join with Director Kralik's fleet."

The Terra-captain gave a brief version of a simple *compliance* posture, then moved toward the navigation workstation.

Aille waited for time to complete. It didn't feel that it should be long.

He spent the time considering both the tactical and the strategic situation found with these new aliens. It did not surprise him that Caitlin had found another intelligent race with a high technological civilization. It did, however, surprise him how quickly she had done so. He mulled that while he watched the main viewscreen display, with the changing fleet dispositions. *Ollnat*, he at length decided. Always *ollnat* with these humans. Caitlin's decision to move to the Sagittarius Arm was such a perfect example of why the Jao needed Terra taif.

At that moment the last of the flotilla's ships emerged into clear space. Terra-captain Sanzh looked to Aille, angles flowing into *awaiting-direction*. Aille considered the viewscreen's presentation of the system and the ships within it. The time flow crested.

A thought occurred to Aille at that same moment. "Contact Rafe Aguilera on *Trident*," he ordered.

The viewscreen cleared, then showed Rafe's face. "Sir?"

"Rafe, here is your field test for *Trident*. Go back into this sun, and cruise the northern quadrant until you're either down to a week's supplies or you are ordered out."

Rafe's eyes narrowed and he peered into the pickup as if he was trying to read postures. "You reading something into this, sir?"

"No," Aille responded. "But if something does happen, I think I want you there, not out among the comets and dust clouds."

"Gotcha," Rafe said. "Cruise the north quadrant until you tell us to come out. Do you want reports?"

Aille thought about that. He had discovered some time ago that humans had almost a fetish about reports. They would invent reasons to create and demand reports. The Jao disliked this.

On the other hand, Aguilera was good at his job. "Yes, on whatever schedule you like."

"Will do, sir. Anything else?"

"No."

The viewscreen blanked, and after a moment *Trident* turned and moved back toward the sun. It wasn't long before the big ship was lost behind the curtains of plasma. Aille then turned to Terra-captain Sanzh. "Go."

Pleniary-superior Tura appeared at Aille's side as the captain passed the word to his navigator, who in turn passed the word to the other ships of the flotilla. "Why did you leave *Trident* behind unsupported?"

"So it would be of use. That is what the ship is designed for, after all."

Tura accepted that with no visible reaction. She said nothing more, and after a time moved over to watch the navigation workstation.

"Honored *Rhan*, please permit us to make an ending."

It startled Kamozh to hear himself addressed as clanlord. For just a moment, he expected to hear his father's voice respond to the address. But then bitter memory of what had happened a few hours ago resurged to the forefront of his mind.

The young Khûrûsh-an leader turned from where he was watching a display of the seemingly receding system primary. Khûr had been the primary god of his people for ages. In the last few generations, however, as the knowledge of the Khûrûsh increased, and as they attained spaceflight and moved out to other planets in their system, more and more of the people began to think that whoever and whatever might be considered to be the creator of the Khûrûsh themselves, the star was not it. Kamozh considered himself to be an enlightened and educated individual, but even so, at a very basic, very elemental level of his being, seeing the star dwindling in size in the viewer awakened an almost atavistic sense of panic that the young officer was having a bit of trouble squelching. Perhaps even more than a bit.

He was not surprised to find all five of the surviving crewmen of the clanship *Lo-Khûr-sohm* abased before him in the "embracing dirt" position. In addition to the old clan leader, they had also lost Penzheti, their chief engineer, wounded when their ship had been shattered around them by the monsters in their great ships. The survivors were flat on their bellies, heads curved to the right, limbs outstretched except for the right forehand curved around to cover their eyes. All except one, that is, and his lips wrinkled a bit in sad humor to see his father's most trusted servant, Weapons Master Shekanre, head raised enough to stare at his new clan leader and ask for death.

"We have failed the Khûr-melkh," Shekanre said, "and we have failed your father and you. Please permit us to make an ending, that we might expiate our failures."

"How will you do it?" Kamozh asked, out of a sense of morbid curiosity. "We have no weapons."

"I will end each of the others," Shekanre replied, "then I will tear out my own throat."

The old weapons master could probably do that, Kamozh mused. The main artery to the head was located just under the skin at the front of the throat, and it could be ripped open with their own claws, although it was not exactly easy to accomplish, especially on oneself. It was not, however, the customary way to commit suicide among the Khûrûsh. But of all the Khûrûsh Kamozh knew, Shekanre was at the top of the list for having both the strength and the self-discipline to execute himself in that manner.

The fur on the back of Kamozh's neck bristled at the thought. He closed his eyes for a moment. When he opened them again, Shekanre was fully abased and no longer looking at him. It took a moment for Kamozh to find his voice.

"Get up, all of you." Kamozh clapped forehands and midhands together sharply. "No one is going to die. And besides, you look silly."

There was a flurry of motion as all of the retainers pushed up and settled on their haunches, midhands on the floor and forehands at their sides. Kamozh looked at them all with a lifted lip, exposing eyeteeth as a mark of sharp emphasis.

"Which one of you had the brilliant idea that you should just waste your lives and leave me by myself among these monsters?" The tone of his voice was somewhat humorous. The growl that followed was not.

Most of the others looked at the youngest of the retainers, who had the grace to look abashed and turned his head away from Kamozh. "Ah, Neferakh," Kamozh said drily, "you have read one too many of the old tales. This is the real world, not the realm of heroes and sorcerers and night warriors."

There were chirrups and chuckles from the others, until Shekanre said, "Your father, *Rhan* Mezhen, would have allowed it, *Rhan*, for the honor of the clan."

"Perhaps he would," Kamozh replied, "but I am not my father."

They all fell silent at that, for it had been only hours since their clan leader, Kamozh's father, had been killed by the monsters before their very eyes.

At length, Kamozh continued with, "My father was honorable, and did his duty and fulfilled his responsibilities to his death. And it is just as well, probably, that he has passed into Khûr's presence, as he would find no honor in being a slave of the monsters."

There was another moment of silence.

"For myself," Kamozh said, "I believe that honor is larger than the stories make it. I believe that honor is deeper than the lines that lead to the throne of the Khûr-melkh." There was a sharp inhalation from several of the retainers. "I believe that honor is wider than the dance of Khûr-shi and her sisters around the

Holy Light. And I believe that we will have honor here, if no other way than to each other."

"Here—here among the monsters?" Shekanre asked. "Among the enemies of Khûr?" The retainers were all wide-eyed, even the weapons master.

"Even so," Kamozh said. "I don't know if it is Khûr who has placed us here, or the Trickster. But we will have honor."

The retainers were silent, but one by one slipped back into the "embracing dirt" position as they placed themselves in submission to his leadership. Even Shekanre did so, saying nothing.

Kamozh looked at them, and sighed. "Get up," he said quietly. "All of you, get up. We will meet the future on our feet, not our bellies."

CHAPTER 32

The door to the command deck irised open as Yaut drew near. Aille followed his fraghta through the opening, flanked by Pleniary-superior Tura on one side and Ed Kralik on the other. He noted Caitlin Kralik's eyes widened slightly—he suspected in surprise—at the sight of the Bond of Ebezon officer, last seen at the side of Preceptor Ronz. This was followed by immediate delight at the sight of her husband.

Of course, Caitlin wasn't the only one who evidenced surprise. Even Wrot's whiskers twitched a bit. Interestingly enough, it was Fleet Commander Dannet whose stance never wavered from as pure an example of *neutral* as Aille could remember seeing.

It had taken more time by the human clock to join the newly arrived flotilla to the exploration fleet than the humans had expected, Aille thought. To the Jao, time was accomplished when it was accomplished, but even for them the span from arrival to joining hovered for longer than desired before moving to completion.

But what had been to the Jao a bubble of waiting time, had been long dragging hours to the so-linear humans, he knew.

As he stepped onto the command deck, Aille saw that for all her skill and knowledge in Jao-ness, Caitlin remained human in moments of crux. Instead of having all her subordinates displayed before her in the Jao manner, she stood to the fore, with Wrot and Dannet to her left, three Lleix to her right, and Captain Miller and Tamt directly behind her.

"Vaish," Caitlin began, moving her arms into the angles for *recognition-of-authority.*

"Vaist," Aille replied, his own angles showing a simple *pleasure*. He advanced to face her. "Well done, Director." He took her hand to shake it in the human manner. "Well done, Caitlin. Well done to find another spacegoing culture in so short a time."

He saw the young woman's mouth twist a bit. Human-style *regret,* perhaps, or even *dissatisfaction.*

"It took longer than I wanted," she said shortly, "and we haven't found an ally. At least, not yet."

"But you found someone else without destroying them," Aille said. "And that is something we Jao have not excelled at. So again, well done, all of you." He swept his gaze around the command deck. Here and there Jao angles fleetingly morphed to and through *pleasure-at-proper-commendation*, while human crew exhibited smiles ranging from small quirks of the mouth to large grins.

"And now," Aille concluded, "show us what you have found."

"This way to the conference room," Caitlin said, with a nod to Tamt. The burly guard's lines went to *attending-to-duty*, with a hint of *righteous-pride* creeping in. She led the way to a separate door leading from the command deck, which irised open as the approached.

Third-Mordent looked through the view glass down onto the floor of Ninth-Minor-Sustained's large workroom. She heard the door hiss open behind her. The faint reflectivity of the glass gave her an image of who it was, so she did not turn as her ancestress joined her.

As was often her wont, Ninth-Minor-Sustained said nothing. Third-Mordent had yet to develop enough to respond to that powerful silence with the like, so she at length intoned, "Thirty-seven Ekhat," in a soliloquy tone, soft, yet not infirm.

That was the count of the beings in the workroom. Thirty-seven Ekhat, of varying sizes, demeanors, and dispositions. Even through the glass she could faintly hear the dissonance produced as they confronted each other, singing savage attacks, competing with fractal tones and harsh stops and glissandos. Forehand blades were flicking in and out of sheaths around the workroom.

There was a brief clash between two of the Ekhat and another, swift and furious, lasting but a moment before they broke apart and rushed in different directions in the room. Third-Mordent continued to observe.

"Attend," the barest whisper of song from Ninth-Minor-Sustained. Third-Mordent shifted her gaze and focus to her ancestress, who now had assumed what could only be called a mentorship over her. The concept was not unknown among Ekhat, but it was rare that two unmated mature individuals could retain a relationship long enough beyond the passage of simple knowledge or skills to arrive at this level. All too often, the weaker of such a pair simply became dead meat when the stronger tired of her.

Third-Mordent remained wary, but did not dispute with her ancestress. At this moment, she said nothing.

"Go create order," Ninth-Minor-Sustained fluted. Third-Mordent waited for Ninth-Minor-Sustained to expand upon the instruction. Silence was all that was delivered.

Third-Mordent turned again to the view window, watching the flow of the individual bodies in the workroom; the shifting combinations of momentary allies that invariably dissolved into foes again; judging the dissonance that continued to incrementally rise, pulse by pulse by pulse.

She felt the moment arrive, that moment when a bell-tone sounded in her mind. Turning without a word, she left Ninth-Minor-Sustained standing at the view glass and moved to the lift that would take her to the great workroom.

Lim stepped onto the mat. She was tired—almost weary, if the truth were known—but that was not unfamiliar to one from the *dochaya*. She stood straight in her blue gi that she had adopted, and grounded the staff at her side.

The master was sitting at the other end of the mat in what he had told her was a lotus position, hands resting on his knees, eyes closed. It made Lim's legs ache just to look at him, for her legs would not bend in those directions without either breaking bones or tearing flesh. Yet she knew it was not the limberness of his body but rather the limberness of his mind that made him what he was, and while she could not attain some of his physical capabilities, she could aspire to his mind. So she settled, legs slightly apart, and let her center drop low in her body, taking slow deep breaths as she did so, grasping the staff with both hands and letting some of her weight rest upon it.

She didn't know how long she waited. It was odd how time sometimes seemed to stretch when she was near the master. But long or short, the moment came when his eyes popped open and he took a deep breath.

"Ha!" Master Zhao said with a smile. He arose to his feet in a single supple movement that Lim could not even describe, much less hope to emulate. "And are you ready to resume, my student, after the recent excitement?" he asked in Mandarin.

"Yes, *sifu*," Lim replied, inclining her head in the only respect he would allow her to present.

The master stepped closer, looking up to her with the warm brown eyes that were so different from her own black. "And have you thought on your staff, student Lim?"

"Yes, *sifu*."

"And your conclusions?"

Lim moved the staff in front of her. "It is a piece of wood."

Zhao's smile broadened.

She leaned on it. "It can support."

Zhao nodded, still smiling.

Lim took the staff in both hands and held it horizontally before her. "It can be a weapon."

"Indeed," the master replied. "All of those are

true statements, especially the last one. But is that its purpose?"

Lim shook her head in the almost universal human posture for negatives. "No, *sifu.*"

"Then what . . ." Master Zhao stopped as Lim took the staff in one hand and raised it up. His eyes tracked the staff as it slowly was lowered until the end of it barely rested atop his black hair.

"It extends my reach, *sifu.*"

Master Zhao laughed with joy and took the staff from her. "You have learned the lesson of the staff, my student." He stepped to one side to place it back in the rack he had pulled it from some time ago. Lim felt a warmth inside her as his simple praise was absorbed.

Turning back to her, Master Zhao said, "We will find more ways to extend your reach." He gave a slight bow, which Lim returned.

"*Sifu*, I would continue to carry the staff," Lim said.

"And why would that be?" Master Zhao said.

"I do not think I have learned everything that can be learned from it."

Master Zhao raised his eyebrows. "I see." He simply looked at her for a long moment, then continued, "All right. It is true that there is more than one lesson to be learned from the staff. You may continue to carry it." He raised his hands. "And now, come, let us push hands and see what we can see."

Lim raised her own, and moved forward to be tested and taught.

The door from the lift to the workroom irised open, and the raw sound being generated by the

Ekhat in the room washed over Third-Mordent. She stood still; not-moving, listening/feeling/tasting the dissonance. There was a faint sense of order in it, the very faintest of harmonies, almost imperceptible. Indeed, she realized that if not for the tutelage of Ninth-Minor-Sustained she would not have had the skill/sense/perception to hear it, that the raw sound would have been like raw sewage to her.

Third-Mordent focused on that hint of order and harmony. It took some moments, but before too long a theme formed in her mind; an aria, appropriately enough. With that, she stepped through the open doorway and let it iris shut behind her.

She eyed the milling crowd, direct vision unimpeded by the glass. In a moment Third-Mordent realized she was the smallest Ekhat in the room. Even the smallest of the crowd topped her by an increment.

None of the others had noticed her yet where she stood still near the door. She raised her head to its highest extension, and began to intone the aria. Her pitch was high; the timbre soft; the volume low. The sound carried, but was perhaps felt more than heard.

Third-Mordent was near the end of the third iteration of the theme when a few of the crowd began to fall silent and drift away from the throng in the middle of the room. Some of these noticed her and slowly moved in her direction. One by one they drifted near.

When the fifth iteration of the aria began, the two or three Ekhat nearest her began to sing it along with her. By the third motif, all of the drifters had aligned themselves on her, and were singing. Even as Third-Mordent watched, three more turned from the contention in the center of the workroom and established themselves on the edge of the group surrounding her. They joined the melody almost immediately.

By now close to a third of the original group had joined Third-Mordent's melody, were singing according to her harmony. The aria had become the strongest force in the workroom, and the remaining unaligned Ekhat had all turned to face her.

Third-Mordent stepped forward with deliberation, continuing to hold her head high despite the urge to slip into predator mode. She could feel the tegument around her neck hardening, trying to contract and pull her head lower and forward. She overrode the instinct, and began to sing even louder.

She focused her attention on the three largest of the remaining Ekhat, seeing from their posture and stances that they were strongly resisting her building harmony, her attempt to assimilate them into her structure.

Pitching her voice to batter now, rather than entice, Third-Mordent elevated both volume and tone, leading her structure to assault the remainder. She was rewarded by several of them shaking their heads.

Suddenly there was a rush of Ekhat in Third-Mordent's direction. She stood her ground, prepared to blade dance, but the flow divided and went to each side of her, swelling both the composition of her structure and the volume of her aria.

Two-thirds of the Ekhat in the room now stood beside or behind Third-Mordent, and most of the rest were drifting away from the center. Only the three largest, the three resisters, were still opposing her theme, her aria, creating only dissonance as they tried to combat the harmony that almost dominated the workroom.

At last, the three made common cause and adopted a common theme that they could sing. They made a strong presentation of it, but it was too little, too late. The towering wave of Third-Mordent's structure almost crushed their song even as it began.

Third-Mordent advanced again, approaching the center of the workroom to directly confront the triad of resisters. She felt the others beginning to curl around the edges of the room, advancing to assimilate all who stood in their paths.

The largest of the resisters, head down, eyes red, gave a piercing shriek that just for a moment interrupted the harmony. In that moment, the three snapped open their forehand blades and attacked.

Third-Mordent stood her ground, her own forehand blades ready, still singing. As the resisters neared, she suddenly shifted to a descant theme above the melody of her aria, which she projected directly at the central attacker. Just before the resister entered Third-Mordent's scope, she stumbled.

That opening was all that Third-Mordent required. The blade dance that followed was short but intense. The dissonant squalls of the resister tore at Third-Mordent's descant, just as her larger forehand blades tore at Third-Mordent's body. Yet the stumble had opened a gap, and before the resister could recover Third-Mordent was inside her guard.

It ended with the resister keening on the deck of the workroom, one forehand blade cut off entirely, the other broken, all legs on one side cut in various places so that they would not serve their functions.

The resister still tried to stand; still tried to attack, mouth gaping open to exude mindless screeching. But all she could do was push her stricken body around on the deck, small manipulators reaching out to grasp her foe.

Third-Mordent stepped back, flicked her blades to clear them, and folded them away. The descant strengthened as she turned to see the other two resisters mobbed by the other Ekhat in the room. Their completed bodies lay in widening pools of ichor. They had not gone down alone; there were three others completed and several more with serious gashes in their teguments.

Third-Mordent took the aria and descant to a cadence, where she paused. The room fell silent. The other Ekhat stood spaced around her, gazing at her, some with heads held high, others on the verge of predator mode with heads lowered and reddened eyes.

A low rumble filled the room. Third-Mordent spun to see Ninth-Minor-Sustained standing in the open lift door, intoning a pitch so low that Third-Mordent didn't think she could emit it herself. Even as she listened, secondary tones were added, imparting a resonance to all who stood in the room.

When Ninth-Minor-Sustained added a difficult tertiary tone, Third-Mordent felt her mind recoiling, sliding away from what she was hearing. Yet the others in the workroom stood straighter, looked around as if uncertain where they were, and began leaving through the outside doors, by ones and twos and threes.

Ninth-Minor-Sustained's voice fell silent afterward. Third-Mordent stood still, head high, manipulators raised, as her ancestress approached. Ninth-Minor-Sustained looked around at the completed Ekhat, ending with a long stare at the panting crippled red-eyed hulk that had once been a dominant female. Her eyes finally lifted to Third-Mordent, and her head twisted in an effect of inquiry.

"I failed," the younger Ekhat replied in a dirge. "I did not bring harmony to all."

There was a long silence.

"Hear me," Ninth-Minor-Sustained whisper-sang. "It was no failure. It was not total success, no, but it was no failure. You built harmony, you included others, and you held against dissonance and attack. It was no failure."

Ninth-Minor-Sustained moved to loom over the wrecked resister, who had mindlessly pushed with her legs until the hulk of her body had wedged against a wall. "All were older than you, all were from fecund lines. This one, and these others"—a manipulator waved at the other two completed resisters—"were all from your ancestress's progeny: this one from a direct line from Descant-at-the-Fourth, the others from collateral lines."

Third-Mordent approached. "Why?"

"Your most dangerous enemies will always be those first of your own lineage, and second of your own factions."

There was a long moment filled only by the panting of the resister while Third-Mordent began considering the thought that she was most at risk from those with whom she had the most in common. A door seemed to open in her mind, enlarging her perspective. It almost drove her to predator mode.

Again she asked, "Why?" in different tones and with a glottal stop.

"To see what you would do," her ancestress replied

as she turned away from the ruined hulk of a still breathing, still bleeding Ekhat.

"And?" Third-Mordent's pitch was high and ascending, a demanding query.

Ninth-Minor-Sustained seemed to take no notice of her descendant's importuning. "It was a lesson that your lesser ancestress never learned."

That brought Third-Mordent up short, as if a cable had been thrown around her neck to throttle her. She had been wary of Descant-at-the-Fourth. That Ekhat had been truly formidable, and dangerous to all around her. Yet she had envied her as well, and had taken satisfaction at being descended from her fierceness, even in a collateral lineage, even now that she had met Ninth-Minor-Sustained. It disconcerted her to hear her elder ancestress's words.

"Within all factions of the Ekhat," Ninth-Minor-Sustained returned to a whisper-song, "control of others is more often attained by subversion. You can force alignment for a short time, but is that control? You can destroy one by strength and assault, but is destruction control?" She looked back at the one who had been near destroyed by Third-Mordent. "To turn one to your purposes, whether in knowledge or not, is more skillful. If such ones as these must be completed—and if you survive, complete them you will—let them be completed for your purposes."

Ninth-Minor-Sustained turned back to the wrecked resister. "This one is from your lineage, from my lineage. She is from your creche, from two cycles ahead of you. You may have seen her there, before she survived the final tests and was released." There was a moment of stillness. "Complete her. Now."

Third-Mordent bared a forehand blade, and approached. The resister stirred enough to raise her head again and screech thinly at her, all tone gone, all melody gone, only dissonance left. She tried to lunge at Third-Mordent, but her head fell to the deck as her muscles gave out. Third-Mordent's forehand blade pierced the nearest eye, transfixed the brain, and severed the major neural ganglions at the top of the spine. Completed at last, the final breath poured from the resister as a moan, her desperately wounded body sagging into the spreading pool of her own ichor.

"Have your wounds tended," Ninth-Minor-Sustained intoned. "The one near your eye is dangerous."

Third-Mordent summoned servients to clear the room and tend her wounds, with her ancestress's last whisper-song still ringing in her mind: "Control."

CHAPTER 33

"Well done," Aille said again at the end of the sharing of knowledge about the Khûr system and its inhabitants. Caitlin shook her head, but said nothing. The three Jao newcomers looked at the hologram of one of the captured Khûrûsh-an which was slowly rotating above the conference table. "They could be a formidable people," Aille continued as his angles shifted to a simple *introspection*. "It's unfortunate that they seem to be so . . ."

"Paranoid is the best word, we've decided," Caitlin completed the sentence.

"As you say." Aille kept his gaze fixed on the hologram for another long moment, then he turned his head to face Caitlin, angles shifting to *curious inquiry*. "You have *oudh*, Director Kralik. What do you plan to do next?"

"Me?" Caitlin said in surprise. "I thought you . . ."

"No," Aille interrupted. "This is not my responsibility, not under my control. I do not have authority. Yours were the hands into which Preceptor Ronz gave the *oudh,* and he did not send me out here to replace you. The search is still yours to direct."

Aille saw the rest of the Jao in the conference room shift their angles to various permutations of *agreement.* Even Fleet Commander Dannet did so.

Caitlin turned to Pleniary-superior Tura. "Then you haven't come to replace me?"

Tura's angles immediately returned to a seemingly effortless *neutral.* "No, Director. The Preceptor did not dispatch us to supplant you. You will remain."

Ed Kralik nodded. Aille saw Caitlin's observation of that action, and likewise saw her sit up straighter and her shoulders shift back, all human forms of displaying *resolution.*

"Then why are you here?" Caitlin asked. Her tone contained a certain sharpness, Aille decided. Understandable, perhaps, at least to and for a human.

"Preceptor Ronz sent us," Aille replied. "He did not share his reasons."

"The Preceptor is a Bond strategist," Yaut said. "He holds secrets until they expire of age."

Caitlin's mouth curved in a reluctant smile. "Okay. So the decision is still mine. What do you advise?"

"Decisions do not need to be made now," Aille said. "Give your Lleix and jinau officers some time with these new guests of yours. Let them see what they can develop." He stood. "Meanwhile, spend some time with your husband."

Caitlin's smile took on a different character.

"Terra."

"Te-hra," Kamozh tried to duplicate the sound that Lim, the voice of his master Boyes, pronounced.

"Terra."

"Ter-rrah." Kamozh tried again.

"That is close," Lim said. "Sergeant Boyes wants you to learn the Terran language if you can. You will probably find it easier than Jao or Lleix, and all on this expedition speak it."

"Boyesh," Kamozh attempted the name of his master.

"Boyes."

"Boyeshsss." Kamozh wrinkled his muzzle. "The 'sss' sound is hard for us."

"I understand," Lim replied, "but it is a very common sound in Terran."

"I—we—will learn it," Kamozh said, looking around at his retainers. They all indicated understanding of the implied command.

Kamozh looked back to Lim. "Is it permitted to ask questions?"

Lim folded her hands in front of her. "Within reason," she replied. "I will inform you if I am not allowed to answer or if I do not know the answer."

"Why do you carry the long rod." Kamozh gestured toward the staff.

"The staff." Lim used a Terran word that was new to Kamozh. Of course, since they had just begun to learn the language, almost all Terran words were new to them.

"Shtaff . . . no, ssstaff."

"Correct."

"Was it a mark of office? A tool?"

"It could be considered a tool," Lim said, "in some places by some people. In others, it could be considered a weapon."

"A weapon," Kamozh said, with a look to his retainers.

Shekanre in particular looked interested. "Are you then a warrior?"

Lim made a motion with her hands that mimicked a Khûrûshil gesture denoting humor. Kamozh was again surprised at how well she and her fellows knew his culture, at how much they had assimilated. If he closed his eyes while she spoke, she sounded almost like a resident of the southern continent. He thought he caught hints of the capital city in her speech.

"No," Lim said. "Sergeant Boyes and his fellows and officers in the jinau are the warriors. I serve the same masters they serve, but I am not jinau. I am studying with a master teacher who is also a fighter, though, and he has me carrying the staff for a time to learn a lesson."

Kamozh heard a muffled sound behind him, and looked around to see Shekanre's muzzle wrinkled. That caused a certain memory to surface in his own mind. He turned back to Lim and made the humor gesture himself. "I believe I understand. I once was directed to carry a heavy hammer for days to properly learn a lesson my father's weapons master had set me."

"I would like to meet this master teacher," Shekanre said in a low voice.

"I will enquire if that can be done. If not immediately, perhaps soon." Lim rearranged the folds of her robe. "But now, back to Terran."

Kamozh sighed. Learning the monsters' language was harder than he'd thought it would be.

He'd rather carry a hammer.

Caitlin's com pad pinged. Faced with setting down her wine glass or disengaging her hand from Ed's, she gulped the wine and set the glass down, then touched her pad. Lieutenant Vaughan's face appeared in it.

"Yes?"

"The communications survey has been reestablished, ma'am."

"Thanks for the word, Flue."

The picture blanked out with no further comments, and Caitlin turned back to where her husband was running his thumb across the back of her hand, which sensation was sending a tingle up her arm.

"You're monitoring the Khûrûshil communications?"

"Of course we are," Caitlin replied. "But this was about something else. I gave Dannet an order after the meeting to get our people listening outward again."

"You're looking for another civilization?" Ed sounded surprised.

"Yes. Regardless of whether or not we can somehow connect with the Khûrûsh, we can't stop here."

"Hmm. I guess I can see that," Ed said. Then a leer crossed his face. "But meanwhile, where were we?"

Gabe Tully looked at both Second Lieutenant Vikram Bannerji and his replacement as Gabe's intelligence officer, First Lieutenant Joe Buckley. Gabe had tapped Buckley from the jinau company serving on the *Lexington* when Bannerji had transferred to work with Ramt in dealing with the Ekhat slaves. Like most of the officers in the jinau in the exploration fleet, he was doing work that in the old pre-Jao days would have been done by someone probably a couple of ranks higher than his current rank. But between the loss of military troops during the Jao conquest, the Jao emphasis on "being of service," and the Jao's elimination of separate military arms and their resulting waste of duplicated functions, a lot of younger officers were filling what used to be called staff positions when they weren't in combat suits.

"So that's it, Colonel," Buckley concluded his briefing. "According to Pyr and Garhet, the Khûrûshil civilization is definitely only slightly ahead of the pre-Jao Terran culture in terms of actual technology, but because their culture is more homogenous, they actually made better progress in getting out into space than we did."

"Anybody got a read yet on why they're so paranoid?" Tully asked.

"Not that I've heard," Buckley answered. "We're all waiting to hear if Lim and Sergeant Boyes manage to dig some explanations out of your guests."

"Well, they've gotten past the introduction stages. Maybe Lim will get some data out of them soon. Have the tech geeks on *Lex* managed to get the computers we yanked out of that ship running yet?"

"Yes and no," Buckley said. "They think they've got them running, but what they've been able to find is so heavily encrypted by a culture that they have no Rosetta Stone for, that at the moment they're just muttering about it. It may take a breakthrough from over here to get them in."

"Right." Tully looked over to First Sergeant Luff, only to see him making a note on his com pad. "We'll pass the word to Lim and Boyes to see what they can do about it."

Tully looked at his own com pad for a moment, then said, "Bannerji, what are you getting from the Ekhat slaves? Anything that will affect us?"

"Hard to say, Colonel," the young Hindu replied.

"Every day we learn a little bit more about the slaves. They're called the Trīkē, for example. And they definitely came off of a Complete Harmony ship. In fact, that whole squadron was Complete Harmony."

"Does that tell us anything we didn't already know?"

Bannerji shook his head. "Nothing new. Just confirmation of some of our lower-level theories and suppositions. Fleet Commander Dannet and the senior captains were not surprised. The four factions don't seem to relate very well to each other. In human terms, it's almost like they're four religious denominations that to an outsider look to be almost identical, with very minor differences that to themselves are unconquerable divides. The Interdict in particular has been known to occasionally communicate with the Jao with an aim to discommode one or more of the other factions."

Tully remembered his first trip inside a star, and felt a chill run down his spine. "You mean like they did with Aille right before the attack on Earth."

Bannerji's face took on a very grim and hard cast at the reminder of the cataclysm that had engulfed part of southern China and almost lapped over into his homeland. "Yes, sir," was all he said.

Tully shrugged. "If Ekhat want to see other Ekhat die, I'm okay with contributing to that cause. Anything else?"

"The Jao are a little stirred up."

"How so?"

"They really don't like the Complete Harmony. They're the ones who uplifted the Jao, after all."

"That going to affect anything that Caitlin has in the works?"

Bannerji shrugged. "They're Jao."

"Right." Jao, Tully thought, who even now still mostly deserved the modifiers *crazy fucking* in front of their species name. "Keep me posted."

"Yes, Colonel."

CHAPTER 34

"Ship 15467 reports that the framepoint has been placed and tested and is now working properly. They confirm that they have activated the firewall so that no Ekhat can access it."

Lieutenant Vaughan delivered the report to Fleet Commander Dannet as soon as she entered the command deck. He had to suppress a chuckle, though. "Firewall" was one of the human words that had become almost ubiquitous among the Jao in the fleet, for some reason. The Jao had a perfectly good equivalent term for the security concept, but it was four syllables long, and for some reason the fleet techs had latched onto the human word instead, to the amusement of the humans in the crews.

Dannet, pelt still damp from a good hard swim, spoke to the communications tech on duty. "Tell all ships to add it to their files."

Flue leaned back in his workstation seat. The last five days since they had crossed the cometary ring and moved into the deepest space outside the Khûr system had been good for the fleet, he thought. Everyone had been so tensed up from the long jumps, and then the combative situation they had jumped into here, that they had all been super keyed up. Even most of the Jao, who could have served as dictionary definitions of 'phlegmatic,' had been jumpy.

Getting out of the combat zone and letting the crews stand down had been a good start, he thought. Taking the time to transfer some crew and supplies from the newly arrived ships to the rest of the fleet had also helped lower the stress levels a bit. And just several days of regular activity had been good.

All in all, he decided, things were calmer now than they had been for some time. He almost wished something would happen.

An alert went up on the main viewscreen, echoed on Flue's workstation panel. *I was kidding!* he almost yelled as he jerked straight and sent his hands dancing across his control pads. *I was kidding!*

"Targeted by a laser!" one of the human techs yelled.

"Gamma-ray frequencies," a Jao tech elaborated.

"Very narrow dispersion," the first tech continued in a calmer voice, "low amplitude."

Communications laser, Flue thought.

"Source?" Terra-Captain Uldra snapped.

There was a momentary silence as the techs queried their instruments. "Five degrees above ecliptic," the human tech responded at last. "Uh . . . and it's hitting our shields at a location and angle that places the source outside our orbit."

"Fleet to alert status," Dannet ordered. She looked to Flue. "Inform Director Kralik."

Before Flue could do so, the Jao tech spoke loudly over the increased noise of the command deck, "Signal is modulated."

Oh, boy.

Third-Mordent responded to a summons from Ninth-Minor-Sustained, finding her ancestress in the harmony master's main performance hall, where Third-Mordent had first met her. There were no choirs today; no performances; no dance. There was, however, a male standing near the harmony master. She froze after two steps past the entry, forehand blades beginning to emerge.

"Stand," Ninth-Minor-Sustained fluted. There was no command in the tone, no imperative. Only calm certainty.

Third-Mordent eased her forehand blades back into their sheaths and stepped carefully farther out into the hall, all the while examining the male. He looked familiar. His posture was tense, but he was not in or near predator mode—his head was held up and his manipulators were held high, digits folded away.

Just as Third-Mordent recognized the male as the last one with which she had blade-danced, he began to croon, stepping away from Ninth-Minor-Sustained. It was a simple sound, almost an arietta, though not quite, high-pitched, slow-moving, resonating within her.

Third-Mordent fell into synchrony with the male, dancing with him slowly. She unsheathed her forehand blades.

The male did not respond in kind, instead dancing in a circle around Third-Mordent, still crooning. Third-Mordent felt herself responding to the dance and the song, mirroring his steps while moving her forehand blades between them, beginning to echo his song. It disturbed her that she was responding rather than rejecting. It further disturbed her that Ninth-Minor-Sustained was not intervening.

The male extended a manipulator as he danced, pointing it at Third-Mordent. The digits unfolded, revealing one of them to be unnaturally long, with a bulbous bioluminescent tip literally glowing a sharp green color. Her eyes locked to that light instantly, and her voice strengthened as it sang the male's song.

They danced together now, step matching step, note matching note, circling around a common center, narrowing the span with each completed orbit. Third-Mordent found that she could not unsynchronize with the male now. As he stepped, she stepped. If he dipped his head, her head dipped. She could feel his mind close to hers, his thoughts . . .

Suddenly the male stood directly before Third-Mordent, green-glowing digit raised before her eyes, his song flowing through the channels of her mind. Her steps slowed to a bare movement. Her forehand blades drooped as the glowing digit approached her. Her head raised to full extension, and her contribution to the song ceased as her mouth dropped open and the physiognomy of the interior of her mouth shifted. Cartilaginous flaps moved, sealing off both the primary trachea and the esophageal channel. She could feel them move, feel the changes happening in her body as a previously closed channel was opened.

The digit with its green bulb entered her mouth. Third-Mordent could feel it pass her outer teeth. It moved deeper, and suddenly she gave a violent twitch as her secondary masticators snapped shut and severed the digit behind the green glow.

The male whipped his manipulator out of her mouth. Third-Mordent's primary teeth grazed the manipulator's tegument as they reflexively closed.

Her entire body locked in place as she felt the severed digit with its packet of genetic codes being moved by the musculature of her mouth toward the newly opened channel. Slowly it moved, until it tipped over the edge and was moved down the channel by peristalsis until it arrived in the fertilization chamber.

The flaps moved back to their normal positions, sealing off the fertilization channel and opening back up the primary trachea and esophageal channel. Third-Mordent felt her head release and drop. Her forehand blades returned to their sheaths. She noted that the male's manipulator had retreated close to his body, digits all folded away.

Ninth-Minor-Sustained stepped closer, halting when the male's song took on a warning note and he stepped between them.

"You are now mated to Fourth-Tone-Quaver," Ninth-Minor-Sustained sang to Third-Mordent in a panegyric form. "He is the best of your generation. Your progeny will be strong."

The door to the command deck irised open. Caitlin restrained herself—with difficulty—from pushing ahead of everyone else in the car, and let the others exit ahead of her in proper Jao fashion. Tamt and the night-shift guards led the way, followed by her husband, which at last allowed her to move.

The guards peeled off to either side of the door,

which irised shut behind Caitlin. She reached out and grabbed Ed by the arm, making him drop back beside her. Tamt had moved to stand by Lieutenant Vaughan's workstation. Caitlin towed Ed in that direction.

"You say we've got another contact?" Caitlin asked.

"Yes, Director Kralik," Vaughan answered, eyes on his readouts and fingers moving like spiders on amphetamines.

"Where from? The inner system?"

"No, Director."

Caitlin turned to look at the main viewer. "From . . . outside the system?" Vaughan said nothing, but an orbit schematic flashed up on the viewer, with a line tagged to the Terra taif fleet moving out toward the dark between the stars. "So where are they? Do we know which star?"

Vaughan looked up. "It's not a general pickup, like we did when we found the Khûrûsh. They found us. It's a focused com laser."

Caitlin heard Ed inhale sharply. She felt as if she had just taken a good jolt to the head. "What did you say?"

"I said they found us."

"You mean . . ."

Vaughan nodded, his hands stilled for a moment. "Yes, Director. There is at least one other ship out here, and it appears they want to talk with us."

"Ohmigod." That slipped out of Caitlin's mouth.

"I agree," Ed said. "Do we have actual communication with them yet? Can we tell anything about them?"

"No communication with them yet, General," Vaughan looked back down at his readouts, and his fingers started moving again. "But they do appear to be using Khûrûsh protocols with much higher com technology than the system has displayed before now. Ah, it looks like we have finally linked up to it."

The main viewer flashed a couple of times, then a picture of a Khûrûsh-an materialized on it. The alien said about three short sentences, the picture froze for a moment, then it seemed to repeat.

"That's a recording," Vaughan said at the same time as one of the human techs on the command deck.

Dannet looked over at Vaughan. "Summon Pyr and Garhet to the command deck."

CHAPTER 35

Caitlin turned as Ed stirred while Vaughan tapped controls and spoke into his mic. "Lleix?" he muttered.

"Yeah, they're the only ones who speak Khûrûsh," Caitlin said quietly.

"Oh, yeah," Ed said. "I forgot about the prisoners."

Vaughan finished talking, and Caitlin looked at him. "Are Aille and Tura still on *Lexington*?"

Vaughan tapped pads on his workstation. "No, Director. They appear to be back on *Footloose*."

Before Caitlin could respond to that, the door irised open and Pyr emerged. "Garhet will be here soon," he said as soon as he stepped onto the deck. "He was asleep when the directive reached us."

Dannet waved at the cycling message on the main viewscreen. "What is that saying?"

Pyr listened to three iterations of the message. "The message is three short statements," he said after that. "We know you have Khûrûsh prisoners. We want to talk. Respond on a reciprocal bearing."

"Do we have any idea where they are?" Caitlin asked in a tone that was much calmer that she felt.

Dannet waved to Terra-Captain Uldra.

"No, Director. And there is no guarantee that we would locate them by following the signal path. There are too many ways to redirect a signal."

"But," Dannet added, "they cannot be very far away. They do know that we took prisoners from that Khûrûshil ship. Light-speed signals of the event and any Khûrûshil communications about it will limit how far out they can be and still be able to contact us with a laser."

"We have no idea who they are, where they are, or how many of them there are." Caitlin's statement was not a question.

"Correct, Director." From Terra-Captain Uldra.

Caitlin looked at Vaughan. "Send a request to *Footloose* advising Aille and Tura that something new has come up and requesting them to join us on the *Lex*. Send an order to *Ban Chao*. I want Colonel Tully, Lim, the Khûrûsh officer and the sergeant that captured him on this deck ten minutes ago."

"Yes, Director."

Vaughan started tapping pads as Caitlin turned away. After a moment, she looked back over her shoulder. "And have somebody locate Wrot and wake up Captain Miller. I want them up here as well."

Vaughan almost slammed his meal tray down on the table next to Caewithe's. "Sorry," he said, "but I've got to eat and run."

Caewithe's mouth twisted. "I thought you were supposed to be going off shift. What about a swim and some fun?"

"Sorry," Vaughan mumbled through a mouthful of sandwich. "We just got a new contact, and Dannet wants me back on the command deck in ten."

"A new contact?" Caewithe sat up straight. "Does Caitlin know about this yet?"

"Oh, yeah." Crumbs shot out of Vaughan's mouth as he tried to speak. He swallowed manfully. It almost hurt to watch the mouthful go down. "Yeah, she's on the command deck, with Tamt and some of the bodyguards."

"Figures." Caewithe grabbed her fork and started shoveling food in her mouth. "I'll come with you," she said. "If I can't see you off-shift, I'll have to settle for on."

The two inhaled their dinners, and stood to carry their trays to disposal. Before Vaughan could get his hands on his tray, Caewithe grabbed the front of his shirt and planted a hard kiss on his mouth. "Not that I'm complaining," he said when they came up for air, "but what was that for?"

"A promise to each other," Caewithe said with a grin. "Next chance we get, we're going swimming. I've got another new swimsuit."

Vaughan groaned as he gathered his tray. "You're killing me, woman. Where do you find new swimsuits in the middle of alien space light-years from any human store?"

"I have my ways," she said smugly, leading the way to the tray disposal chute.

Tully grabbed his go-bag from the hands of his orderly, Corporal Toro, and turned back to Major Liang and First Sergeant Luff. "No, I don't know what's going on. I just got orders to get Lim, Boyes, Kamozh, and myself over to the *Lex* sometime yesterday."

"Something's up," Liang said.

"Ya think?" Tully gave a short bark of a laugh. "Whatever it is has apparently got Caitlin really up in the air, or she wouldn't have ordered it that way. So, being the sneaky, underhanded, pessimistic sort that I am, put the troops on first stage alert. I have no idea what's going on, but let's get prepped for it anyway. I want them ready for action at fifteen minutes notice."

"Got it, Colonel," the XO said, buttressed by a firm nod from the first sergeant.

"See to it," Tully said, and headed out the compartment door. "Sergeant Boyes, where are you?" he said through his communications bud.

"Just handed off to my assistant squad leader, Colonel," came the reply. "Running for the shuttle bay now."

"Right. I'd better not beat you there." Tully paused a beat, then said, "Command."

"Yes, Colonel Tully?" was the response from a command deck com tech.

"Where are Lim and the Khûrûsh prisoner?"

"Waiting at the shuttle bay, with guards."

"Right. Tully out."

A few minutes later, after going around three corners and down one deck, Tully arrived at the door to the shuttle bay. Lim and Kamozh were indeed waiting for him, as were Sergeant Boyes and two jinau serving as guards.

"Lead the way, Lim." Tully waved a hand in the direction of the waiting shuttle.

The Lleix looked down at the Khûrûsh-an at her

side, and said something in the language. He made a movement with his left middle hand, and they stepped off through the door.

Tully looked at the two guards, both Jao. "We'll take it from here, guys."

"Are you sure, Colonel?" one of them replied. "If that one goes Oppuk on you, he's equipped with a lot of natural blades to make your life 'interesting,' as you humans say."

"Positive," Tully said. "Get back to your squads. Life in general may be about to get 'interesting' again."

The two guards both gave a brief rendition of *obedience-to-orders*, and headed back up the corridor.

Tully shook his head. "'Goes Oppuk,' huh? I haven't heard that one before." The meaning was obvious, though, and he started to grin.

"Oh, yeah, Colonel," Boyes said with a matching grin. "That's been making the rounds for a while. Came out of Terra taif, of course. It's got human written all over it."

Tully laughed. "Too right, Boyes, too right. Only a human would think of something like that." He laughed again, then said, "Come on, Sergeant. Let's go see what kind of trouble we can get into on the *Lex*."

Caitlin turned as the command deck door to the main lifts irised open again. The last time it had been Vaughan returning from grabbing a fast meal, accompanied by Caewithe Miller. That had saved Caitlin from having to summon her bodyguard captain, who was on her off-shift but would have wanted to be here for this.

This time the door opened to admit Gabe Tully,

Lim, a jinau whom she assumed was Sergeant Boyes, and a Khûrûsh-an who could only be the captive officer Kamozh. Gabe started toward her, but her eyes were drawn to the sight of Kamozh seeing the main viewscreen. He froze, eyes narrowed and fixed on the recording. After watching a few loops of it, he raised up on his hind feet, turned to Lim and spoke loudly and rapidly, all four hands moving in the air. He stopped, waited a long moment, then something in a low tone as he dropped down to his mid-hands and settled his hindquarters on the deck.

"So what did he say?" Caitlin asked. "He looked pretty excited."

"*Rhan* Kamozh says that the viewscreen is lying to you."

"Oooo-kay," Caitlin responded. "How does he get that out of that little bit of picture and that message?"

"First, the . . . person . . . in the recording is wearing the robes and crest of a clan that died out close to two hundred Terran years ago, with the markings of the clan-heir at that. Second, the person is female, and very, very few of them are allowed off-planet farther than the orbit of Khûr-liyo."

Lim's voice almost sounded dry at that point. Caitlyn thought for a moment that there was a disapproving note in her voice. Lim went on, and Caitlyn dropped that train of thought.

"Third, the very fact that she is calling you is treason, for the Khûr-melkh Sheshahng—think of him as an emperor—decreed long generations ago that there was to be no contact between our people and the devils from the outer dark. It is treason, and an affront to *re-heshyt*," here Lim used a Khûrûshil word that she didn't bother to translate right then. "Such would be unthinkable to any right-living Khûrûsh-an. So therefore, he says, it is obvious that the viewscreen is lying to you."

The door had irised open in the middle of Lim's translation. Yaut and Wrot had entered the command deck, followed by Aille and Pleniary-superior Tura. The four Jao had stood to listen to the rest of the translation.

When Lim finished, she placed both hands on the staff she had entered with. Caitlin decided she would ask about that later. Kamozh folded his upper arms and leaned back a bit.

Caitlin looked at where Fleet Commander Dannet had joined the group around Aille. Tura and Dannet both had flawless *neutral* angles that nonetheless were distinctive to each. Wrot and Yaut were displaying something on the order of *simple-curiosity*, although Yaut's had a definite flavor of *impatient* from the tilt of his head.

Aille, on the other hand, was displaying a posture that was so rare Caitlin had only seen it recorded, never in action: *concession-to-oudh.* Her mouth twisted. Aille was making it very clear without a single word that the decision to be made was hers alone.

Caitlin didn't look at Ed. She felt him stir just a bit, though, and turn to face her at a slight angle. He said nothing—he didn't have to. She knew he would support her in anything she decided, as would Gabe Tully. She drew a great deal of comfort and strength from that, as she faced what might be the most important decision ever made by Jao or humans alike.

She took a deep breath, and held it for just a

moment. Caitlin could feel the eyes of everyone on the command deck resting on her—humans, Jao, Lleix, and Khûrûsh alike—waiting to see what she would do.

"Fleet Commander Dannet," she finally said, "Return a signal, please."

"As you direct, Director Kralik," Dannet replied. "And the message?"

Caitlin considered that for a moment, then gave another wry grin and said, "We hear you. What do you want?"

Dannet's angles flowed from *neutral* into *obedience-to-instructions.* But then, without a pause, they flowed into *gratified-respect*, which was more than Caitlin had ever thought she would ever receive from the fleet commander.

As Dannet turned away to give orders and Pyr, Lim and Kamozh moved to a nearby workstation, Caitlin looked over at the rest of what she thought of as her command group. Tully was grinning the biggest grin she had ever seen on his face. Ed had moved to stand behind her. She couldn't see his face, but she could feel the bedrock of his presence. Aille and the others, even Tura, all slipped into an echo of *gratified-respect*, which just for a moment caused her vision to blur.

"Well done, Caitlin," Aille said. "Well done."

PART V
Watch in the Night

CHAPTER 36

Back in their quarters later that day, Ed Kralik looked at his wife. Caitlin looked as if she had been wrung out and hung out to dry. He brought her a glass of wine where she sat curled up in the corner of the settee, then took the armchair that was across from it.

"Interesting day," Ed began. "Things always this exciting?"

"What was that definition of war you told me? The one about boredom?"

Ed smiled. "You mean 'utter boredom for many months, interspersed with moments of acute terror'?"

"Yeah, that's the one." Caitlin took a healthy sip of her wine. "That pretty much defines how I feel about it. Only lately the 'many months' have been compressed to a few days. First that battle in the Ekhat system, then the jump through the M-class star, then more jumps down the star chain as quickly as we could make them, then the arrival here, only to be attacked by the very people we want to make friends with." She looked down at the glass. "I've been on edge so long, I'm not sure I know how to relax any more. And now we've got someone else contacting us, instead of the other way around." She shook her head.

"Aille's right, you know," Ed said. "You've done very well, given what you've encountered. I'm proud of you."

Caitlin looked up at him with a bit of a shy smile. "Thanks."

That reminded Ed that growing to maturity under the thumb of Governor Oppuk, Caitlin probably hadn't received a lot of praise. Which thought led to the memory of how the ex-governor had died in both agony and ignominy, which in turn generated a certain amount of pleasure in Ed's mind. "So now we wait," he said.

"Yeah," Caitlin replied, sliding down on the seat and resting her head against the top of the cushion. "Now we wait. And I can do waiting, but I really hate it."

The news about the possibility of new contact with even more unknown spacefaring races swept through the exploration fleet. Director Kralik didn't even make an attempt to control the spread of information. Even if she had attempted to order the information restricted to the command deck personnel on duty at the time, it wouldn't have worked. As it turned out, the only thing faster than the human hallway rumor mill was the Jao version of same.

The Lleix met together at Ramt's request. She was still the only member of the Ekhatlore *elian* with the fleet. In light of the fact that the fleet was headed into the Sagittarian Arm, the Starsifters *elian* had replaced Brakan and Matto with two members who were more knowledgeable about that area of the galaxy. From Lim's point of view, this had a pleasant side-effect as Chulan and Helat were both younger and less rigid than their predecessors. They treated the Terralore *elian* members from the *dochaya* with something that approached courtesy, anyway.

"So were the images of the Khûrûsh-an in the message actual or computer generated?" Ramt asked.

"Khûrûsh-en," Lim corrected. "A noble-born female uses a different form of the case, or so Kamozh tells me. Obscure, he says, but proper." There was a pause while the others absorbed that bit of information.

"According to Lieutenant Vaughan, the com techs couldn't tell for sure. Even with enhancement, the signal had degraded enough by the time it arrived here that it could be either," Pyr finally answered the question.

"That means we do not know for sure if the signal is from Khûrûsh who have escaped or migrated from their government's control, or if it is from someone else." Chulan relayered his robes.

"But who else could it be?" Garhet said. "We have received no signals from other systems. There should be no one else close to Khûr."

"I do not know," Chulan replied. "And that is what frightens me."

"Indeed," Helat said, his aureole rising and lowering in slow cycles. "First the Ekhat, then the Jao, and finally the humans. All strange, all frightening, all blowing us around the stars. Now the Khûrûsh, who seem almost as unsane as the Ekhat. The thought of someone not Khûrûsh pretending to be Khûrûsh..." He left the sentence unfinished.

"What do you think, Lim?" Garhet turned to her.

She sat silent for a long moment, hands together, not moving. "We are here being of use, whether invited by the Jao and Terrans or directed by our *elian* heads. What will happen, will happen."

All five of the other Lleix lifted a hand in the sign for agreement.

"It does not matter whether the Khûrûsh-en in the message is real or not. What matters is someone else wants to talk with us, and we should make every effort to meet them, to know them. Every ally we can gain brings us that much closer to extinguishing the Ekhat, as they have done to so many others and so nearly did to us. I will do anything to see that happen."

Lim knew that her voice was stronger than was customary for inter-*elian* discussions. She knew that anger had tinged her tones and words. She didn't care.

There was another moment of silence.

"Even for one of Terralore *elian*," Helat ventured, "that is strong language."

Something crystallized in Lim's mind at that moment; something that she realized had been growing in a quiet back corner of her mind for a while.

"That may be true," she said. "But I will be leaving Terralore."

All of the others looked at her with surprise and shock in their postures and the fluttering of their aureoles. Her own slowly extended and stood firmly across the crest of her head, a most decisive presentation.

"Leave Terralore?" Pyr said. "But... what will you do? Where will you go?"

For a moment, Lim almost grieved at the blow she had dealt to one of her oldest and closest friends. For a moment, her aureole started to droop. But then her mind strengthened and her aureole straightened.

"I will become a Wordthreader," she declared.

The others looked at each other.

"A Wordthreader?" Ramt said. "There have been no Wordthreaders for ages. The last one was killed..." She paused, then turned toward a work console.

"When we were driven from Thrase," Lim said, referring to a planet they had been forced off of long before their last home on Valeron. "Almost fifteen hundred Terran years ago."

"How will you join an *elian* that was extinguished so long ago?" Ramt asked. "It cannot be done."

"Then I will refound it," Lim replied. "They were the ones who spoke for the Lleix to other peoples. We need that *elian* again." She looked down at her robe and refolded the pleats. "I will begin it."

The others looked at each other. In all the flurry of establishing new or reestablishing faded *elians* after the Lleix removed to Terra, this was one that had never been discussed. After some length of silence, Pyr murmured, "May the *Boh* smile upon you."

Vikram Bannerji sat on the floor, surrounded by the glistening black bodies of the Trīkē captives. Over the last few weeks, he and Ramt had been able to get them to calm down—somewhat. He was still at risk of being knocked around by the muscular hexapods, and there had been more than one day where he had gone to bed nursing bruises.

"Solvaya," he said in Ekhat, speaking to the one

with the damaged leg. She pushed her way through the milling crowd of her fellows and plopped her hind end down on the deck in front of Vikram, looking up at him with large eyes that were so black they seemed to have no pupil.

"Yes, Vi-ka-rum," the Trīkē said, all hands and feet on the floor and fidgeting like a Terran puppy. "How can I be of use?"

Vikram had to remind himself that even though that phrase sounded Jao, it was actually Ekhat, who probably meant something different by it than the Jao did.

"Tell me again what you do on the great ship."

"I serve the great masters," was the unsurprising response. Every attempt to question the Trīkē either individually or collectively elicited that as the initial response. Getting them to move past that point had taken some work. Today Vikram was going to try a different approach.

"Who are the great masters on the great ship?" Ramt had made the observation that talking about the Ekhat in the past tense made the Trīkē nervous, so they used present tense only, implying that their masters were still alive.

Even so, Solvaya crouched down and began to shiver a little. She turned her head away from him.

"Solvaya, you must answer," Vikram said quietly.

The other Trīkē pulled away slightly, all crouching. Solvaya lowered her head to the floor.

"Solvaya," Vikram said once more.

"We do not say their names," she finally responded.

Vikram's eyebrows rose in surprise. "Why not?"

"Because they hear us. They always hear us, but saying their names makes them listen. Then they pay attention." The little captive shrank down as low as she could, closing her eyes and folding her forehands across her mouth.

It was pretty clear that she wasn't going to say anything further. The rest of the captives were starting to get skittish, so Vikram decided to end the session.

"All right, Solvaya. You've been good. You will all get some treats at dinner."

Vikram stood slowly to avoid jostling the surrounding Trīkē, and made his way with care to the door. Once he left the room, he moved to the monitors to see what the video pickups showed. One by one, the other captives moved to Solvaya and nuzzled her. Once she finally looked up, they all piled together in what Vikram and other humans who had seen it called "the puppy pile," the formation from which they seemed to draw a lot of comfort. He watched for quite a while, but they didn't stir out of the pile for a long time; not even when he triggered the delivery of their meal and the promised treats.

When Ramt returned from her meeting, he played back the recording for her. "What do you make of that?" he asked after it completed.

Ramt listened to Solvaya's words a couple of more times before she responded. "Doubtless they were monitored on their ship, just as they are here. And knowing the Ekhat, can you doubt that their response to any possible slight or disrespect would be severe and brutal?"

"Um, I don't know," Vikram said.

"They are slaves," Ramt said, "not children. They served on highly sophisticated and technologically advanced spaceships, which meant they had training accordingly. They are not stupid. They know we are observing them. You've seen them identify and look at the video pickups just like I have. The fact that they do not make a big deal out of it means that they are accustomed to being observed at all times. So what else can Solvaya be talking about?"

Vikram shivered a bit at the thought of being under constant monitoring by anyone, much less the Ekhat.

CHAPTER 37

"We will come to you."

Caitlin looked on with a set expression as Garhet translated the response to her message. As before, it was a recorded message, presented by what appeared to be the same Khûrûsh-en that had presented the first message. She waited a moment, and the recording looped back to the beginning.

"That's it?" she said. "That's all we got?"

"Affirmative," said a human com tech.

Caitlin looked at Fleet Commander Dannet and Terra-Captain Uldra. "Do we know any more about them at this point? Anything at all?"

Dannet looked over at Lieutenant Vaughan's work station, and Caitlin followed his gaze. "Lieutenant? Can you put it in human terms for me?" she said.

"We received the second message about twenty-seven hours after we sent out your response, ma'am," he said, looking down at his readouts. "If they responded as soon as they received it, that means they were about thirteen and a half light-hours from us at that point in time. It might be less, depending on how long it took them to decide on their response and get it recorded, but it can't be any more than that."

"So they were potentially two and a half times as far from us as Pluto is from the Sun at its aphelion, but maybe not, and we don't have any idea as to how fast they can travel." Caitlin's last statement was not a question.

"No, Director. If they have better technology than ours, they could be here in thirty minutes, or it might take them two weeks. We'll know how good they are when they get here."

"And we have no idea how many there are." Another statement, to which Vaughan made no reply.

Caitlin looked over at Dannet. "Fleet Commander, I assume you have some thoughts on how we should prepare ourselves to receive our unknown visitors."

Dannet's angles slipped from *neutral* to a rock-solid *willingness-to-be-of-use* combined with *ready-to-act*. "Yes, Director."

Caitlin took a deep breath. "Notify Aille, Pleniary-superior Tura, and all ship captains of the response. Implement your plans. Defense only at this time."

Dannet's angles shifted to a fierce *compliance-with-oudh*. She turned and began issuing orders to Uldra. The command deck crew became very busy.

Caitlin took another deep breath. "God help us all."

"Amen to that," Vaughan muttered behind her.

In the event, it took somewhat longer than Lieutenant Vaughan's minimum estimate of thirty minutes.

Dannet's orders dispersed the fleet in an arrangement

that was somewhat opposite of what most human tacticians would have arranged. Vaughan made lots of notes about it. The six *Lexington*-class craft were keeping formation between the outer dark and the system, with the supply and maintenance ships grouped near a couple of large cometary bodies and the lighter combatants standing out-system from them behind the perimeter set by the battleships. A very few fast ships were moved about a half light-hour out in several directions because the fleet commander insisted on a heightened sensor and com tech watch by all ships in as close to a 360-degree pattern as possible. She had no desire to be caught unaware by anyone, even someone who might prove to be friendly.

After the first day, Dannet allowed the ship crews to stand down from their alert status. This left many of the crew with a certain amount of off-duty time, which explained why Flue Vaughan was waiting by the side of one of the pools. He was looking at his com pad, when he heard someone say, "I thought I told you to turn that thing off."

He looked up to see Caewithe Miller approaching. She bent over him, took the com pad out of his hands, and gave him a lingering kiss. "Mmm," he said when she pulled away. "Where've you been all my life?"

"Looking for Mr. Right," Caewithe replied with a grin as she stuffed the pad into her bag, which then landed on a nearby bench. "Haven't found the bastard yet, so I guess I'll make do with you until he finally shows up."

"Is that so?" Flue clambered to his feet. "Well, I guess I'd better take advantage of the situation while I can."

"What's that supposed to mean?" Caewithe asked.

"This," Flue answered, and he pushed her into the pool.

After a moment, Caewithe came back to the surface, spluttering. Flue was still laughing when she fixed him with a dark glower and muttered, "Bastard."

"I thought that was Mr. Right?" he said as his laughter faded away into a big grin.

"Him, too." After a moment, she moved closer to where Flue was now sitting on the edge of the pool with his feet in the water. He looked down to where she was treading water. He wasn't sure yet if this was a girl he wanted to take home to meet his mother, but he had to admit that there was some definite attraction. Smart, tough, competent; Caewithe was all of that. The fact that she was physically attractive was an added plus. All in all, he felt an increasing draw to her as days passed and they managed to find a few hours here and there in their noncongruent schedules to spend together. Like today.

"Flue?"

"Um-hmm."

"What do you think they're like?"

"Who?" Flue said, almost absent-mindedly as he continued to study her face. The pointed look she focused on him brought him back to the present moment. "Oh, you mean the new aliens?"

"No, I mean the King of England and the royal family. Of course, the aliens. Bastard," she muttered at the end.

He chuckled. "Actually," he said, "your guess is probably as good as mine. They are apparently rather more advanced than the Khûrûsh, but until we meet them we don't know how much more advanced. We don't know if they're native to the Khûr system, or if they come from out there somewhere."

Flue stopped for a moment, then continued with, "We really only have two fairly solid observations about them."

"Which are?"

"They seem to know at least something about Khûrûshil culture; and they appear to have pretty sophisticated sensor and communication technology, since they were able to pinpoint us with a gamma-ray laser from what may be a ridiculous number of AUs away. Outside of that, we really don't know anything at all."

"What do you think they'll be like? I mean, should we expect them to be like the Jao, or the Lleix, or..."

Flue shrugged. "To be civilized enough to master space flight, maybe even interstellar flight, we have to hope that they have enough in common with us to be able to truly communicate."

"But the Ekhat..."

"The Ekhat are an aberration," Flue interrupted. "They are the exception that proves the rule. The only reason they still survive, I think, is because they reached space first in our region of the galaxy. Their genocidal posture and what little we know of their culture is not geared to be a long-term survival strategy once they lose their qualitative and quantitative edge, which they will do in the future if they don't manage to overwhelm us first. The fairly near future at that, I think."

Flue slid into the water and leaned back on his elbows on the edge of the pool. "Even the Khûrûsh are understandable," he said. "Outside of their xenophobia, they're roughly analogous to humans. And I'll wager once we know the reason for their xenophobia that will be understandable as well. So, yes, even in a universe that contains the Ekhat, I expect these new folk will be someone we can talk to without necessarily opening the conversation with lasers or missiles."

Caewithe swam nearer. "You're sure about that?"

"Yes."

"Good." She moved closer and laid a hand on his chest. "I'll take your word for it."

Caewithe swarmed up Flue's body until her elbows were resting on his shoulders and she was looking down at him. "Enough serious stuff. Let's play."

With barely a ripple or gurgle of displaced water, Tamt rose out of the water next to them. "The mating pool is on the deck below this one," she said, whiskers twitching back and forth.

"Will you stop that?" Caewithe demanded as Flue laughed raucously.

Lim walked into the gym, followed by all the Khûrûsh prisoners, who were in turned followed by a couple of jinau armed with Super-Tazers and net guns. She was not happy that they were tagging along, but the conversation with Colonel Tully had left no room for disagreement.

"I'm taking a big enough chance just letting them loose from their spaces at all," he had said. "They can't be totally disarmed without amputation, and we don't have enough of a track record to know if we can fully trust that surrender or not. You will take the guards, each and every time they leave their quarters, until I or Director Kralik say differently. Understood?"

There was no other response than "Understood" when the colonel spoke in that voice. That didn't mean that Lim liked the situation, and she had left a look with the colonel that should have made that clear.

However, that was then, as Wrot sometimes quoted, and this was now. She brought the prisoners to the side of the mat where she drilled with Master Zhao. "You may stand or sit here," she said to all of them, "but do not leave this immediate area. There are those who will be nearby who might misinterpret your actions."

"They will obey," Kamozh said. "It is my honor that they handle." His left mid-hand shaped a symbol to the side. **<Act in honor>**, Lim read from it.

All the Khûrûsh crewmen dropped their hind ends on the floor and went still, leaving their mid-limbs to support their elevated torsos. Kamozh and Shekanre, his weapons master, remained standing on their hind feet, folding both mid-limbs and upper arms across their torsos. The guards stood some distance behind them.

Master Zhao entered from the hall door. "Lim," he said in Mandarin as he approached, "do we have friends or observers here?" He waved at the Khûrûsh.

"Observers, yes," Lim replied as she placed her staff in its rack, then stepped onto the mat to face the master. "Not friends, yet. But perhaps friends to be. That remains to be seen."

"Good," Zhao said with a smile. "To convert a foe to a friend is an accomplishment to be greatly desired and valued. You must introduce me after we are through."

"Yes, *sifu*," Lim replied. She bowed; Master Zhao returned the bow; they began to push hands.

The meld of Third-Mordent/Fourth-Tone-Quaver moved down the hallway in synchrony, female a half-body length ahead of the male. Feet moved and touched down in unison. Heads turned to face the same direction at the same instant. If Third-Mordent bared the edge of a forehand blade at an immature Ekhat who wasn't scurrying out of the way fast enough, Fourth-Tone-Quaver's blade also peeked out from its sheath.

Within her own mind, Third-Mordent wondered at her new existence. She was still solely Third-Mordent, still herself alone. Yet she was connected at some very basic level to Fourth-Tone-Quaver. She did not hear his thoughts, but if he moved or stepped before she did, her body echoed his; just as his echoed hers if she led.

As the female, Third-Mordent was the dominant, but Fourth-Tone-Quaver was no slave submissive. She was aware of his strength, aware of just how fierce he would be if predator mode overtook him.

Everyone moved out from before them in the corridors of the base, even senior mated pairs who were many cycles older than they; pairs that had reputations for rage or skill. The servients disappeared into service corridors in waves. No one—not even the oldest/largest/strongest, whether pairs or solitaires—lowered their heads or exposed even a bit of a forehand blade.

It was Third-Mordent's first hint at just how

formidable she might be; or rather, just how formidable Ninth-Minor-Sustained had shaped her to be with Fourth-Tone-Quaver dancing at her side.

Four more days passed in the Terra taif fleet. Vaughan was on duty, gathering data and observing his readout.

"Crap!" exclaimed one of the human techs on duty. "Where did that come from?"

CHAPTER 38

Vaughan's hands froze. According to his readouts, there was a ship outward from *Lexington*—a pretty good-sized ship, if his instruments were to be believed—which had not been there ten seconds ago. And it wasn't all that far away. Radar returns indicated a million kilometers or so—call it three light-seconds.

"Captain to the command deck! Fleet Commander to the command deck! Director Kralik to the command deck!" Those orders rapped out from the officer commanding the deck watch, and Vaughan noted com techs putting the word out to those individuals.

The gravity/mass detector indicated the ship was real. It massed less than a *Lex*-class. In fact, it massed less than one of the Bond's *Harrier*-class ships, although not much less. That was a pretty respectable-sized ship out there, Vaughan thought. Which made the question about how it had managed to sneak up on the Terra taif fleet without warning one of great importance. He imagined that the question about whether or not a starship could be stealthed had just moved from the *idle speculation* category into the *how the hell did they do that?* category. Somebody back in the Terra system was liable to make some money, Vaughan decided. Nothing served as incentive more than knowing that something could actually be done after the fleet apparently got caught with its pants down.

The main door to the command deck opened, and Fleet Commander Dannet and Terra-Captain Uldra charged through. They were both dripping wet, obviously having been in one of the pools when they got the word. Everyone ignored that, even the humans.

"Nobody let them get that close," one of the human sensor techs replied brusquely to questions from the two senior officers. "There was nothing . . . not by radar, not by lidar, not even a twitch from the gravity/mass detector. Nothing, and then all of a sudden it was there and every alarm on our boards was going off. Here, watch the sensor playbacks if you don't believe us."

Uldra did exactly that, while Dannet passed orders to the fleet adjusting the ship stations a bit, and asking for confirmation from other ships as to what they saw. Detail radar scans were coming back now, and they were painting an interesting portrait of sorts of the hull of the stranger. Longer and leaner in proportion than the configuration of a *Lexington*-class, the hull seemed to be fairly smooth. There was the odd bump here and there, but nothing that broke the long lines of the vessel. To Vaughan, that implied a ship that would enter atmosphere.

"Com laser targeting us, same as before," one of the com techs reported.

"Main viewer," Dannet ordered. She looked to the

workstation manned by the Terralore *elian* since the first messages had come in. Pyr was sitting there, eyes fixed on the viewer. The fleet commander's gaze moved to Vaughan, who nodded to her that he was ready. Dannet said nothing, but returned her own focus to the viewer.

The main door irised open again and Caitlin Kralik stepped through, followed by her husband and guards. The door shutting might have been a signal, for the system schematic displayed on the viewer blinked off at that moment, to be replaced by what appeared to be the same Khûrûsh-en that had delivered the earlier messages. Vaughan noted that she was wearing a different robe than she had in the earlier messages. She spoke a short phrase.

"Eleusherar Path Ship *Starcloud* speaking to the unknown fleet," Pyr said in translation. "Do you understand us?"

Pyr looked at Caitlin, who nodded and said, "Respond."

"Terra taif ship *Lexington*," Pyr said in Khûrûsh. "We understand you. What do you want?"

There was a few seconds lag time, a bit more than that between Terra and Luna, then the Khûrûsh-en spoke a couple of phrases, and the picture in the display blinked off. "Contact lost," a com tech announced rather unnecessarily.

Caitlin looked to Pyr. "What did she say?"

"They will open a channel again in a twelfth of the planet Khûr-shi's rotation. At that time they request to speak to the fleet's leaders."

Caitlin absorbed that. "Right. Inform Aille and Pleniary-superior Tura that their presence is necessary on the *Lexington* as soon as they can get here. Order Colonel Tully to get himself, Lim, and all the Khûrûsh guests here within the next hour. And ask Krant-Captain Mallu to join us as well."

"There is some latitude in your bonding," Ninth-Minor-Sustained intoned. Third-Mordent listened intensely. She felt . . . something . . . that told her that Fourth-Tone-Quaver did likewise. "You have been locked in to the simplest mode of expression, that of unison. It is possible to reflect rather than echo. That is the second stage. The third stage is to harmonize."

They were standing in the center of the harmony master's performance hall. Ninth-Minor-Sustained stepped around the meld of Third-Mordent and her mate. "Stand," she fluted as they started to adjust to her movement. Third-Mordent almost felt the shadow of the harmony master as a weight when it passed across her tegument or that of her mate.

"Today, you will begin with echo, and move to reflect," Ninth-Minor-Sustained sang as she drew in front of them again. "Use this theme."

The harmony master paused for a moment to allow the vibrations in the room to damp. After full silence arrived, she sang a theme that Third-Mordent, after a moment, recognized as the theme she had added to the harmony master's canon on the day that she had first come to the attention of Ninth-Minor-Sustained. The theme impressed itself into Third-Mordent's mind even stronger than the day she had created it.

Ninth-Minor-Sustained stepped out of their collective field of vision. "Begin," she intoned.

Third-Mordent began to sing the theme at the same

moment as Fourth-Tone-Quaver. As the first iteration neared its conclusion, Ninth-Minor-Sustained sang, "Dance!" to them.

Third-Mordent's forehand blades snapped open and she stepped into a blade dance, one that Ninth-Minor-Sustained had imprinted on her not long ago. She felt/heard Fourth-Tone-Quaver moving with her, step by step, blade movement by blade movement, tone by tone. It was a true echo, she realized, understanding what the harmony master had told her. But how to do a reflect? Every attempt she made to change her steps or movements was echoed by her mate. Frustration began to mount in her, and her movements became sharper, faster, more lethal in intent.

"Stand," Ninth-Minor-Sustained sang as the fourth iteration approached its completion. Third-Mordent and her mate completed their movements and stood in silence. "Release until I return," the harmony master intoned. Third-Mordent looked around to see her ancestress leave the hall.

"If we survive, we will be great," came a whisper song from Fourth-Tone-Quaver. Third-Mordent froze in place. She wanted to spin to view her mate, but the synchrony... She focused her mind, locked it on the thought of facing Fourth-Tone-Quaver. After a moment, something changed/moved/adjusted. She wasn't sure what it was, but it was there. Slowly, a fraction of a step at a time, she moved her body, edging it around until she could see her mate fully with one eye, rather than only through her peripheral vision. He had not moved.

"What do you mean?" she lilted back.

"The harmony master," the male began an aria. "It is known to the males that she will sometimes gather in one who catches her attention, and mold her. Many of them break. Many. And are completed. But the few who survive, they rise, they breed, they become important. And a very few, they shape the Melody."

Third-Mordent's mind spun around the thought that the males knew this, when she and her sister creche-mates did not.

"We knew when you appeared, when the harmony master called you forward, that you could be such. You are the first in a long time, a most long time, that she has called. If you survive, your progeny will be among the most valued, highly desired. We all wanted to mate with you, to know that our lineage had been chosen to meld with yours and be among the greatest."

Now Fourth-Tone-Quaver moved himself, edging to his right. Third-Mordent felt the synchrony trying to make her adjust her position to match, but she forced control on her body and held it motionless. The male moved as if exhausted or weighted down, but before long he had moved around until they were face on toward each other.

"We fought for you," he resumed the aria. "We are not supposed to. The harmony masters decree against it, and their discipline is harsh. But to have a chance, to mate with one like you who could one day be a harmony master . . . there were fights. Many of the lesser males were completed."

"How many?" Third-Mordent whisper-sang.

"I completed four," her mate sang back. "There were others. But after you completed one of us—one of our best—most drew back."

"But you did not?"

"I would have my progeny among the great," Fourth-Tone-Quaver sang fiercely.

Third-Mordent looked at the scar on the tegument of the male's face. "Yet you blade-danced with me. I came very close to completing you."

"When the harmony master calls, one answers," Fourth-Tone-Quaver sang in an elegiac form. "None can withstand her. I would either survive or I wouldn't, but either way, I would have danced with the best." He waited a beat. "I would have my progeny among the great," he repeated. "I may not survive to see it, but I would not give that up, and so I am now mated to you."

Ninth-Minor-Sustained chose that moment to walk back into the great hall. Fourth-Tone-Quaver ceased his song. But as the harmony master approached them, Third-Mordent heard in her mind, *If we survive, we will be great.* She could not be absolutely certain, but she didn't think it was a memory.

CHAPTER 39

Precisely at the scheduled time the signal from the stranger ship was received. Dannet ordered it displayed on the main viewer. When the picture came up, it was the same Khûrûsh-en that had provided all the previous communications.

Unlike those earlier communications, this time she did not begin speaking as soon as the picture cleared. Rather, after a few seconds of the time lag, she appeared to be examining the group that stood within the range of the command deck's main video pickup.

Flue Vaughan tried to imagine just what her impressions might be: The mixture of Jao, humans, and Lleix, seen for the first time, had to be somewhat at least intriguing. What a motley collection they had to seem at first.

The Jao had been compared to ambulatory seals by the humans when they first conquered Terra. Flue had to admit that when you considered wild feral seals and not trained performers from zoos or aqua-parks, particularly prime predator specimens like the leopard seal, that was probably an apt comparison. Oh, their heads were more otter-shaped than seal-like, but the size and musculature of their bodies, and their grace in the water, all matched well with the big seals. The smallest Jao in the room was Tamt, and she was 1.9 meters tall and every bit of 180 kilograms, maybe more. And their shiny pelts and vivid *vai camiti* markings enhanced their impressiveness.

Then there were the Lleix; tall, silver-skinned, a couple of them topping even the tallest of the Jao, aureole crests rising and falling. A striking contrast to the Jao, but just as physically impressive in their own way.

By contrast, the humans were wildly variegated in size and build; unimpressive anthropoids, skinny, slight—scrawny, it might be said. Even Colonel Tully and General Kralik, who as humans went were pretty large, weren't so much when compared to their allies.

The Khûrûsh-en's head and eyes had been tracking back and forth across the beings standing on the command deck. She finally spoke.

"My name is Shemnarai. I speak for the Eleusherar Path and this ship, the *Starcloud*," Pyr said in translation of her opening sentences. "I see that you are indeed from beyond the Khûr system—indeed, from beyond any system of which we know. May we know who you are, and who leads you?" Pyr ended his translation, and looked to Caitlin.

"We are the Terra taif exploration fleet," she began, and paused while Pyr translated for her. Vaughan saw her glance sideways at Aille, who said nothing but adopted angles for simple *encouragement*. "I am

Caitlin Kralik, Director over the exploration program." She waved her hands to each side of her. "These are my associates and officers." Another pause for Pyr to translate. "We do come in peace, although I realize it may not seem that way from what happened in the Khûr system when we tried to open communications with Khûr-shi, as you undoubtedly witnessed."

After a few seconds time lag, the Khûrûsh-en emitted a sound that sounded almost like a bark, then spoke. "Yes, we did observe your attempts to reach out to my cousins. Unfortunately, there was no way that we could warn you."

Pyr finished the translation, then said, "That odd sound was something akin to a human laugh."

"I would like to discuss with you how and why you might have warned us," Caitlin said dryly, "but first, can you explain who and what the Eleusherar Path is, and its relationship to the government of Khûr and the Khûrûsh."

Shemnarai talked for a few sentences. Pyr began to show signs of surprise, which progressed to shock. His aureole stiffened to full extension, and his hand could only be described as fluttering. When she paused, he rapidly spat out several sentences of his own without providing a translation.

The Khûrûsh-en appeared to listen with a tilted head, then began to speak again, this time for the better part of five minutes. When she paused again, the screen blanked.

Pyr sat for a moment, aureole starting to waver, hands wandering across the front of his robes.

"Well?" Caitlin demanded. "What did she say? Why did she cut off the connection?"

"Pardon me, Director," Pyr said in almost a mumble, "but it is just such a surprise."

"Then share the surprise," Aille said, stepping closer.

"She is . . . they are . . ." Pyr began. He stopped, took a deep breath, then began again. "The Eleusherar Path represents a body of federated star systems in the Sagittarian Arm. A . . . large body."

"How large?" Caitlin said in the still moment that followed Pyr's statement.

Pyr lifted his hands to touch fingertips together. "Somewhere close to four thousand systems. She said she hadn't seen a current census in a while, so it might be more."

Flue felt shocked now, and from the expressions and angles on the rest of the leadership group there on the command deck, he wasn't the only one. Even Dannet had slipped into *disbelief*. Four thousand? He wasn't sure how many worlds the Jao hegemony occupied, but it certainly wasn't four thousand. This was stunning.

The goal for the entire exploration effort was to find another civilization like the humans—high technology, reasonably civilized, able to become willing partners and effective allies in facing the Ekhat. But this . . . the hairs on the back of Flue's neck stood up. This was entirely another order of discovery. This reordered the universe.

"Wow," Gabe Tully muttered.

"What he said," Caitlin added. "Are you sure about that number?" She asked Pyr.

"Yes," he replied aureole starting to settle down and hands coming together across his chest. "That's why I asked her immediately to confirm and explain.

Her response was to repeat the number, and to say that they would discuss this and more when they are allowed to meet us face to face. She said that Khûrûsh level atmosphere will be adequate if we invite them to come aboard our ships. She said to discuss these issues among ourselves and send them a signal when we are ready to open discussions."

"Director," Aille said, angles falling to *deliberate-questioning*, "you have *oudh* over the search itself. I think, perhaps, that we must now consider whether what we have found falls within that *oudh*."

Pleniary-superior Tura said nothing, but her *neutral* angles seemed to Flue to have an edge to them.

By the end of their time with Ninth-Minor-Sustained, Third-Mordent and Fourth-Tone-Quaver had adapted to their new condition to the harmony master's satisfaction—mostly. "You will improve," she intoned to them. It was both a promise and an order.

"Return tomorrow at the same signal," Ninth-Minor-Sustained sang in staccato notes. "You will work with servients then, dividing yourselves to direct them."

The harmony master left again. Third-Mordent looked at her mate. "Reflection mode," she intoned, and launched into an aria that soared, layering half-tones and quarter-tones that built and built and built until it at length descended in a glissando to the deepest tones she could generate. Not so strong as Ninth-Minor-Sustained's deep tones; but then, she was not of an age as her ancestress, and her smaller body just could not match the harmony master's at the extreme edges of performance.

The dance she accompanied the aria with was harsh; aggressive; even assaultive. Less subtle than her norm, certainly. Her forehand blades wove through the air so fast that the sibilance of their passing enhanced the aria.

Fourth-Tone-Quaver faced her across the room. He did not sing; his male voice was limited and could not reach the extremes that Third-Mordent was pressing. But his dance steps were as certain as hers as he mirrored her dance, his blade skills were every bit as forceful as hers. Third-Mordent could tell that he was pushing himself beyond his own limitations, attaining a new level of intensity that she almost called female in its power. That in turn challenged her to excel, and her voice took on a new edge as she danced.

The aria drew to a close. Third-Mordent folded her forehand blades into their sheaths. There was a slight tremor in her manipulators as she held them up. She was weary, and in serious need of sustenance.

She looked over at her mate. Fourth-Tone-Quaver's forehand blades were slow to sheathe themselves, and his manipulators trembled visibly. He was even more drained than she was; not surprising in a male, even one as robust as Fourth-Tone-Quaver.

Fourth-Tone-Quaver lifted his manipulators and spread their digits. "I see the mating probe has begun to regenerate," Third-Mordent whisper-sang.

The male held the truncated manipulator up. The stub of that digit had healed quickly, and was longer now amid the other digits than it had been even the previous cycle.

He said nothing, but *If we survive, we will be great*

entered her mind again. Fourth-Tone-Quaver held her gaze, and moved one manipulator in agreement.

Ninth-Minor-Sustained watched her descendant and her new mate from the observation window high up in the end wall. She forced her optimism down, and ruthlessly suppressed her jubilation. This one—this progeny at such remove—had so far surpassed all other progeny except Descant-at-the-Fourth. That one had shown such great promise, but had not passed the final test. This one—this one could surpass that mark. This one could become the harmony master that the Complete Harmony needed; needed more than any other member of the faction except herself knew.

So many had failed; broken. So many had been left bleeding from a foe's blade dance. So many had been completed by Ninth-Minor-Sustained herself, because they were not adequate. And none—not one of the few who had attained the level of Third-Mordent's control, skill, and lethality—had passed the greatest test. Not even Descant-at-the-Fourth.

Ninth-Minor-Sustained began to keen softly at the thought of another possible failure.

CHAPTER 40

Caitlin took her seat at the conference table, waving everyone to be seated. She still was in shock at the revelation they had just received.

She looked around the table. The humans all had a poleaxed "deer in the headlights" look. The Jao, other than Aille and Tura, were all struggling to achieve angles like *attention-to-responsibilities* or *neutral.* Even Yaut and Wrot and Dannet were having trouble evidencing enough composure to achieve even those simplest of angle sets. The Lleix were sitting still, seemingly composed, until you noticed their aureoles rising and falling like slow fans.

"Four thousand systems," Caitlin said softly. "Four. Thousand." There was silence for a long moment. "Pyr, are you sure that's what she said?"

Pyr looked at Lim and Garhet. "Yes, Director," Lim replied. "We all heard it. There is no doubt that she said four thousand, especially since she said it twice."

Caitlin looked over at Tura. "Pleniary-superior Tura,

how many star systems do the Jao occupy? I've never seen a published figure, just statements like 'Lots.'"

"The Bond of Ebezon does not maintain an official inventory or census," Tura replied. Her angles, at any rate, were still in a seemingly effortless *neutral*. The thought crossed Caitlin's mind that the Bond training, reputed to be fierce, must be exactly that to hold in the face of this.

"Does the Naukra know?"

Yaut chuffed. Wrot spoke from beside him. "The Naukra can barely keep track of how many kochan there are, and where the official residence for each is located. Knowing how many planets some of the high kochans occupy or control would be considered interference in kochan business by most."

"So how many kochan . . . no, forget that," Caitlin said. "It doesn't matter how many kochan there are. But it does matter how many planets are under Jao control. Before I decide whether or not to relinquish *oudh* over this situation, I have to have some idea of whether or not we—all of us; Jao, human, and Lleix—approach any kind of parity with this Eleusherar Path. And I refuse to believe that the Bond doesn't have a reasonably accurate idea of how many planets their own people control. I've been around Ronz, you might recall."

Ronz was scary smart, Caitlin remembered, and probably the most subtle person she'd ever met. He would not have accepted ignorance on something this important.

Aille looked across the table at Tura. "I agree. Give her what she asks for. We do need to know this." His angles shifted from *neutral* to *reasoned-declaring* as he spoke.

Tura looked around the table before she spoke.

"The Bond does not consider this to be especially critical information," she began after a moment. "Yet we have our reasons for not disclosing this to the rest of our societies, or to the humans in particular. It is not that we do not trust the humans, as such. It is, rather, that we wish to contain and observe the humans' *ollnat* for a few more years before we open the doors wide, so to speak. Therefore, what I am about to say must be considered privileged, not to be shared beyond this group. This is subject to Bond discipline."

That last sentence froze everyone in the room for just a moment. Caitlin swallowed. Bond discipline went beyond merely rigorous. Jao had sometimes died undergoing that discipline.

She saw Gabe Tully swallow as well. Perversely, that made her feel a little better.

"I think everyone understands your position, Pleniary-superior," Caitlin said. "So what can you tell us?"

"Our estimate," Tura replied, "is that the Jao occupy or otherwise control approximately five hundred systems. I can't be more definite than that, because certain of the great kochan, as Wrot stated a few moments ago, do not disclose information about much of their affairs." She looked at Aille. "For example, Pluthrak openly acknowledges occupying four systems. We suspect they may have another three. Narvo," Tura looked at Dannet, "claims five, and we suspect at least another two." She looked back to Caitlin. "The number of actual worlds occupied would be slightly higher. There are a few systems with two inhabitable planets."

"Five hundred will do for discussion," Caitlin said. "Five hundred versus four thousand."

"That is a significant difference of scale," Aille said.

"But four thousand of what?" Ed Kralik leaned forward. "Four thousand systems like this one, occupied by a system-limited race of paranoids? Or four thousand systems with full-blown interstellar capability and weapons tech to match? Or something in between?"

"Good point," Caitlin said. "Quantity isn't the only measurement to consider."

"I, for one," Lim said, "would like to know why their speaker is a Khûrûsh-en. Is this a federation of Khûrûsh, and we've stumbled over a colony of mental defectives? Is she a computer-generated image facing us for something else much different, or disturbing? And for that matter, are these people responsible for the condition of this system's civilization?"

"Yeah," Gabe Tully supported Lim, "what she said. We all think there must have been some kind of initial contact that went bad. If these folks were responsible for screwing the Khûrûsh up this badly, I'm not too awful sure I want us getting buddy-buddy with them. Who knows when they might try the same thing with us?"

Everyone else in the room looked a little appalled—or at least a little discomfited—at his statement. Tully snorted. "Y'all haven't read enough science fiction," he said, "or at least not the right kind. You've overlooked one big possibility."

"What's that?" Caitlin asked.

"They might be lying."

Kamozh looked up as the speaker in the door emitted the tone that indicated someone wanted to enter the quarters given to the Khûrûsh prisoners. He waved a hand, and Neferakh moved to open the door. In stepped Lim the translator, Colonel Tully, and Sergeant Boyes, the human to whom he had surrendered himself and his retainers in order to preserve their lives.

"We apologize that you have not yet had a chance to meet with our leaders," Lim said. Kamozh had actually figured out pretty quickly that Sergeant Boyes was not an upper-rank leader among the monsters. But he had thought until they were relocated to this new ship that perhaps Colonel Tully had been the great leader. That, it now appeared, was not the case.

"We are your slaves," Kamozh replied. "We will do as you command."

Lim translated that to the humans, both of which adopted facial expressions that Kamozh tentatively labeled as sour.

Colonel Tully spoke several sentences, which Lim then translated. "We do not consider you to be slaves."

"Nonsense!" Shekanre interrupted without apparent thought. Everyone looked at him.

He had a stubborn expression on his face, although he said nothing more until Kamozh gestured with his left forehand. **<Permission to speak.>**

"We were conquered. Defeated. Beaten. To save our lives, *Rhan* Kamozh surrendered. That means we are your slaves. Pure and simple." Shekanre sat back on his haunches and crossed all four arms.

"While he is a superb weapons master," Kamozh said drily, in a tone that caused Shekanre's ears to droop a little, "Shekanre is not perhaps the most tactful of speakers. He has, however, summarized our position rather well, I think. There is no place for such as we now in cultured society."

"Colonel Tully has different thoughts about this," Lim replied, "which I will now continue to explain—if there will be no further interruptions." She paused for a moment.

Shekanre's ears drooped further, and he dropped his mid-hands to the floor and settled himself to listen. Kamozh repeated the gesture to speak to Lim.

"Colonel Tully says that neither his race nor the Jao practice slavery now, not even of defeated enemies. We Lleix have never done so." She paused for a moment, then said slowly, "At least, not as you mean it."

There was a moment of silence, until Lim took a deep breath, and said, "No, the Lleix did not practice slavery in the sense of battle captives or those bought and sold. But we did have, until recently, the *dochaya*."

Kamozh listened as she explained the purpose of the *dochaya*—to receive the members of each generation of Lleix who were not sufficiently comely, brilliant, or suave to find a future and be accepted into an *elian*. She described as well the role of the Jao and humans—particularly then-Major Gabe Tully—in seeing to it that the *dochaya* came to an end. "And such was I," she concluded, "released, freed, and given new worth and purpose as a member of Terralore *elian* and entrusted with responsibilities in this great fleet."

Kamozh made a complex gesture, **<Respectful question>**. Lim paused and gave the speak gesture to him. She was really learning the hand language well, Kamozh noted. "You say that the humans and the Jao do not practice slavery now. Does that mean that the humans and Jao have practiced slavery in the past?"

Lim gave a slow nod along with the gesture for assent. "Yes, both cultures have had periods in their history where slavery occurred. They have not done so in many years, however. In both races, such practices are now considered to be, ah, uncultured."

Shekanre started to rise and bristle, only to subside at a swift gesture from Kamozh. The young leader looked to Lim, and said, "Uncultured, is it? Do you understand just how much weight is carried by that term in our language?"

"I believe so," Lim replied. "I have read *The Pillow Book of Keki-Sheri*. There was a copy salvaged from your ship."

Shekanre's eyes narrowed and he started to rise again. Kamozh allowed it this time, for he was astounded as well. He was also surprised at the spike of anger he felt because they had found his father's well-studied copy of the book and dared to appropriate it. But, he reminded himself, he had lost the right to that anger when he surrendered.

He took a deep breath and held it for a moment, then released it and turned back to the conversation.

For an alien monster to claim to have read the writings of the greatest courtesan of Khûr-melkh Anibal the Great, a courtesan who even now, generations later, was considered to be the very namesake and image of grace and culture, was astounding. But to have that same alien levy by implication the charge of "uncultured" against his race based on having read those writings; ah, now that was hard.

"If you believe in courtesy or kindness to those who cannot resist you," Kamozh said slowly, "I would ask of you that you be very careful how you use that term. Used carelessly, it has caused the death of entire clans." Lim gave the bow and gesture of assent again.

"Let us accept your argument—for the moment—that we are not slaves. What, then, is our status?"

"At the moment, according to Colonel Tully, you are in essence involuntary guests, whom we have with—perhaps unfortunate—intent pressed into our service to meet an immediate need."

"That would imply that once this service is completed, our status may become something other."

"Indeed," Lim replied, making the gesture for humor. "That is why we now wish to take you to the leaders of the fleet, to explore those possibilities."

Kamozh considered that. After a moment, he rose to his full height, gesturing to the others to do so as well.

"Then direct us, most worthy Lim, to that meeting."

CHAPTER 41

The doors opened before Third-Mordent, and she entered the strange hall with Fourth-Tone-Quaver following to her right. This was not their usual meeting place, and she wondered why the harmony master had directed them to meet her here.

The door closed behind them. Third-Mordent looked around. This hall was unusual; she'd never seen one like it before. It was almost rectangular, but not quite elliptical, either. There was a row of pillars that marched at what might have passed as a diagonal in another space. And the lighting was both indirect and uneven.

They moved into the center of the room. Ninth-Minor-Sustained was not present, and Third-Mordent wondered at that. Her perceptions elevated, her head began to lower, and her forehand blades started to ease out of their sheaths. She sensed Fourth-Tone-Quaver making the same movements.

Six doors snapped open around the perimeter of the room. Through each door charged an adult Ekhat, females all, in full predator-mode. Their tuneless shrieks assailed their ears even before their charging figures reached the mated pair.

Third-Mordent felt the predator mode rising in her own mind to match that of the hunters before them, but she suppressed it almost without thought. "Reflective Harmony!" she intoned. Fourth-Tone-Quaver moved around behind her, their forehand blades snapped open in unison, and the blade dancing began.

Third-Mordent leapt closer to the row of pillars. Fourth-Tone-Quaver did likewise. They trusted the pillars to impede the paths of the hunters coming from the starboard and basso doors for just a few moments, giving them those invaluable moments to focus on the three coming from the larboard and treble doors.

Leaving Fourth-Tone-Quaver to face the treble door hunter, Third-Mordent wounded the foremost of the larboard hunters with a series of lightning blade strokes that ultimately half-severed the arm mounting the left forehand blade and ruptured the right eye of the hunter, leaving it weeping ichor. She took wounds of her own, of course. There was no time to be subtle and extended; not facing these foes. There was only the direct path, and the costs it exacted. She accepted those. She might not have been able to prevent the wounds, but she could take them in places that were not immediately crippling.

Even as her forehand blade lanced the eye of her first foe, she spun within her own length and impaled the second foe through the neck with the second blade.

This was not fatal, of course—or at least, not immediately. Third-Mordent took the risk of not withdrawing the blade, because it left her inside the reach of the other's blades. She gave three slashes with her free blade, disabling the nearest forehand blade and severing several of the large muscles of the nearest leg. The manipulators and claws scrabbled at her, inflicting superficial cuts to her tegument, which she ignored.

She felt Fourth-Tone-Quaver attack the other side of the hunter, and immediately withdrew her blade from the body of the foe, who was now sagging due to both front legs being unable to sustain her weight.

Third-Mordent spun again, catching a glimpse of Fourth-Tone-Quaver's first target lying still in a spreading pool of white ichor. A flash of pride in her mate went through her mind, even as she sprang forward, that he, being male, took down a full mature female in predator mode.

Her mate matched her step for step as they raced by her first foe, one on each side. They each swung at her as they went by. Third-Mordent's blow was blocked. Fourth-Tone-Quaver's was not, and she heard the foe collapse behind them.

The largest of the hunters was still struggling to get through the pillars. Without pause or direction, the two of them threw themselves at the two hunters who had bypassed the pillars. Their momentum became a weapon, as they blocked the hunters' initial blows, delivered slicing cuts on their outward legs. Third-Mordent managed to hamstring the rearmost leg on her foe. She left that weaker foe to Fourth-Tone-Quaver, and directly assaulted the other hunter.

Even in predator mode, that one had enough perception to try and defend against her, waiting for one or the other of the remaining hunters to join her to pull Third-Mordent down together. Third-Mordent did not give her that opportunity, pressing her back and back until she was pinned against the pillars directly in front of the final hunter who was caught as she emerged from the pillars. That one squalled, and slashed at the hindquarters of Third-Mordent's current foe, which distracted her enough for Third-Mordent to break through her guard and thrust through an eye to sever the ganglia.

Third-Mordent took the moment to turn and find Fourth-Tone-Quaver being closely pressed by the fifth hunter, despite the crippling of her leg. Third-Mordent hamstrung her other hind leg, giving her mate the advantage as she spun again to confront the final hunter.

A burning slash on her own haunch told her that she had left it almost too long. She came around with forehand blades waving in rapid strokes that wove a defense before her for the moments necessary to center her balance and take in the stance of her foe.

This was the largest Ekhat Third-Mordent had ever faced, other than Ninth-Minor-Sustained herself. She was almost of a size to compare to Seventh-Flat. She was strong, and moved in such a way that she was obviously experienced. This one Third-Mordent could not take unaware, or feint out of position, or overpower. This one she would have to simply outdance. Unfortunately, this hunter was fresh and on her guard, while Third-Mordent was beginning to tire.

They dueled back and forth, forehand blades moving so fast as to almost disappear from view, trackable only by the sound of their passing through the air. The multiple hissings almost formed a motif in Third-Mordent's mind.

That moment of perception cost Third-Mordent

dearly. The hunter found a flaw in her defensive web and broke through with slashes that Third-Mordant managed to take on the thicker tegument of her shoulders instead of her less-protected blade arms. Even worse, as Third-Mordent danced back to disengage and put more space between them, her left-rear foot slipped in one of the pools of ichor collecting around the bodies of their already defeated and fallen foes. That threw her off-balance just enough that the hunter pressed the advantage so strongly as to deliver slash after slash, thrust after thrust, winning through Third-Mordent's defenses often and increasingly, inflicting wound after wound, each nearer to being critical or disabling.

Unable to center or balance, lurching, battling back with desperation, Third-Mordent could sense the nearness of death—and of defeat, which was worse than death. But just before that moment was delivered to her by the hunter's blades, Fourth-Tone-Quaver arrived and attacked the hunter and drove her back a step by surprise and sheer ferocity. The hunter recovered quickly, and if all she had faced was the male, he would have been completed in short order. But by then Third-Mordent had recovered her balance and center, and had slotted in at the flank of her mate.

It did not take long, after that. The hunter was good—dangerously good. But the united, coordinated, synchronized attacks of the mated pair were more than a single Ekhat, even a large female in the abandon of predator mode, could withstand.

The struggle ended as the mates struck down the hunter's forehand blades in synchrony, and in the same moment slashed and severed the main vessels in the neck. They constrained the forehand blades of the hunter as the ichor gushed down her front and pooled at her feet. Her gaze grew vacant; she wavered, and all in a moment sagged to the floor.

Third-Mordent and her mate, weary as they were, spun and looked back across the floor. Behind them was one dead Ekhat. Both of the Ekhat that Fourth-Tone-Quaver had faced alone were dead.

Of the three that Third-Mordent had faced alone, the most recent, the one in whom she had severed the nerve ganglia with the cranial stab, was also dead. But the first two were still alive.

She approached the hunter that she had half-disarmed and half-blinded. It was but the work of moments to complete her.

At the same moment, Fourth-Tone-Quaver completed the hunter whose forelegs had been lamed.

The two mates drew together in the center of the room. For a moment, they wearily faced each other, observing the splashes of ichor from their foes and the dripping of ichor from their own wounds.

Together they snapped their forehand blades to sling the ichor off of them, then folded them back into their sheaths.

Third-Mordent could feel Fourth-Tone-Quaver's weariness. If anything, it exceeded her own. The male had been tested perhaps more than she.

In unison, they whisper-sang, "If we survive, we will be great."

After a moment, the basso door opened, and Ninth-Minor-Sustained entered, followed by several servients.

"Withdraw," the harmony master intoned. "Let these of my servients close your wounds. Say nothing to anyone about this."

Not a word, not a motif, about having passed yet another test. Third-Mordent looked to her mate. *If we survive, we will be great.*

They surrendered to the ministrations of the servients, and wearily left the room.

Ninth-Minor-Sustained stood alone amidst the carnage, surveying ichor and death and destruction no matter where she looked. *Tremble,* she sang with fierceness in her mind. *Tremble, those who thought that the destruction of Descant-at-the-Fourth meant the end of my line; for this, too, is my progeny. Tremble, those who would stand against us, for she is swift and deadly and fell. Feel her wrath, those who skirt my shadow and swallow my excrement.*

Tremble.

She summoned servients from the general service pool, and waited. When they arrived, she sang her orders in a complacent little aria. "Clear this away, and dispose of these failures."

With that, she exited the room, knowing that her orders would be obeyed. And knowing that the rumors would spread.

CHAPTER 42

Kamozh was ushered into a large room in which were several of the different types of monsters the Khûrûsh prisoners—no, he was to think of himself as a guest now—that he and his fellow guests had seen so far. There were only the three types, Lim had confirmed for him after he asked in one of their conversations. The intimidating Jao, who if one looked at them with squinted eyes, could almost be the mountain ogres from the ancient tales and legends. Other than the little details, like missing a pair of arms. But they were large, they were fast, and the "guests" had seen some Jao wrestling in the gymnasium and seen them absorbing and shaking off blows that would have killed any Khûrûsh-an, returning to the fray with apparent zeal.

The Lleix, who approached the height of the tallest of the Jao, reminded him of nothing like ogres. Them he compared to outsized *fancha* beasts, who spent their lives moving slowly through tree-tops, slowly eating leaves, and slowly blinking at anything that intruded into their realm. He tilted his head; that perhaps wasn't the most apt comparison, for Lim was not slow—not dilatory. But there was still something about Lim that reminded him of the *fancha*.

And the humans, who, divided in size and shape, reminded him of nothing so much as the *huriku*, another race of tree-dweller, scavengers for the most part, yet nonetheless dangerous at times when a madness would set in and cause a pack of them to run wild, attacking anything and everything they encountered. They were small, but in the right circumstances vicious.

Kamozh knew it was foolish for those thoughts to be in his mind, for of a certainty the monsters that he was facing were not the familiar legends and animals of his people and world. These were strangers, from beyond the light of divine Khûr, unhallowed—indeed, unholy—whose purpose in coming to Khûr was unfathomed by the Khûrûsh but could only be unsanctioned and pernicious.

So he had been taught. He looked around at his retainers; it was apparent from their postures and from the bristle and set of their hair, particular the neck ruffs, that they had similar memories. This had been their belief, their tradition, their doctrine, for more generations than he had fingers and toes with which to count them.

He knew he should hate the monsters. It was because of them that the clanship had been destroyed; that his father and their engineer retainer had been killed; that they, the survivors, were now slaves of the dark and, even if they truly were guests, would never be allowed to return home.

He'd never again see the house that had been

clanhome for most of the history of the clan. He'd never again swim in the chill waters of the lake whose shores the clanhome had been set beside. He'd never again see the edge of Khûr appearing over the shoulder of Mount Teshi.

And perhaps most importantly, he'd never hold a child in his hands and know that it was his heir, heir to the high seat of Clan Hoshep, and that through that child the clan would endure. Clan Hoshep began dying when his father was killed, their clanship was destroyed, and he had surrendered. It would die the real death when he drew his last breath. They were revenants of a dead clan. Nothing less. Nothing more.

He knew he should hate them; the monsters who were here, who had done these things. But he had spoken with Lim, and with Boyes, and with Tully. He had seen how they had tried to treat him and his retainers with at least rudimentary consideration and courtesy; surprising from monsters. And he had seen the pictures of even greater monsters than these; monsters which these were at best watching for and at worst fearful of.

It seemed there might be more to the universe than the priests and storytellers and historians would admit, or perhaps could conceive. He shrugged his shoulders and flexed his hands. Let it not be said that the last of Clan Hoshep would not face the outer dark.

Kamozh looked up from his momentary distraction. It must not have been a long moment, for Lim was still looking at him with a slight sidewise tilt of her head, waiting for his attention to come to her. Once she saw she had it, she turned toward the monsters.

✧ ✧ ✧

"This," Lim announced, "is Kamozh. He was the executive officer aboard the ship that was intercepted and boarded. It was the clanship *Lo-Khûr-shohm*, which means that it was manned totally by either direct clan members or retainers of the clan. His father, Mezhen, was both the commanding officer of the ship and the *Rhan*, or head, of Clan Hoshep."

"This is starting to smack of the Scottish Highlands," Lieutenant General Kralik muttered from where he sat at one side of the U-shaped table.

"Or Hatfields and McCoys," Colonel Tully muttered from the other side.

"Not bad comparisons, perhaps," Lim responded. "But the best comparison might be Tokugawa Shogunate Nippon, only in this case the emperor has kept his imperial thumb on top of everything and is fiercer than any of the shoguns that might have arisen along the way."

"So he's what, minor nobility?" Caitlin asked.

"As a head of clan, *Rhan* Mezhen would have been both a regional governor and an economic and military bulwark in the society." Lim paused for a moment to trace down a thought. She wanted to make sure she stated the next part correctly. "Less than a duke," she finally said, "but more than a baron. An earl, perhaps."

Wrot stirred from where he sat beside Tully. "Perhaps the kochanau of a mid-tier kochan, associated with Hij or Jak."

Lim nodded. That was a good Jao equivalent.

"So," Caitlin mused, "he's not a member of the ruling family, whatever they call it, but he's high enough up in the hierarchy they would probably know who he is. Any chance he could get them to talk to us?"

"No, Director," Lim said.

"Why not? Isn't he the new clan head since his father died?"

Lim shook her head. "No. In both the minds of the society and the minds of he and his men, surrendering to us made them nonpersons. They are slaves of demons of the dark, and are no longer people, much less members of an honorable clan."

Caitlin took a deep breath, then let it out slowly. "I'm really beginning to dislike this culture. Okay, we've been rude to them long enough. Introduce us, please."

Lim turned back to Kamozh and the others. He had gathered from the smattering of words that he had understood that he and his retainers had been the topic of discussion, which didn't surprise him. The discourtesy, implied or overt, did rankle his fur a bit; but he reminded himself again, he gave up the right to that anger when he surrendered to the monsters. So now he just looked up at Lim, and waited.

"Kamozh, before you are the leaders of this exploration fleet." Lim indicated the end of the table, where a human sat between two of the large Jao at the table that formed the base of the U. "From left to right, you see Aille, the governor of Earth, which is the base for the fleet; Caitlin Kralik, the director of the exploration fleet; and Pleniary-superior Tura, a high officer from the Bond of Ebezon, an important command group of the Jao society."

"Ah," Kamozh said. "Is one of higher rank than the others?"

"Director Kralik has lower social rank than Aille and Tura, but she has been given *oudh* over the search effort, which means she has absolute command and authority over the fleet."

"Ah," Kamozh said again. He faced directly at Caitlin and made the complex hand gesture **<greeting to great authority>**.

The human said something. Kamozh was getting a little distracted and more than a little tired of having to wait on the translation. He looked at the human, but made no attempt to listen to her, treating her voice as background noise to what he resolved was a conversation with Lim.

Lim began with, "They welcome you to the battleship *Lexington*, and offer regrets for the manner in which you were captured."

Kamozh heard some of his retainers stir, and he made a hand sign with the right mid-hand, **<Still>**. The movements ceased.

"Although we would have preferred to be destroyed outright rather than taken as slaves, we cannot step in that stream again." Kamozh used both forehands to sign **<Khûr's fate>**. "We would rather be occupied and of some use, but we would also rather not be involved in combat against our people. We would take death over that." This was followed with the simple sign for **<absolute truth>**.

Lim spoke to the human, who rattled something back at her.

"Director Kralik guarantees that this will not be asked of or ordered to you." Lim repeated the **<absolute truth>** sign. Kamozh wasn't sure if he believed that or not, but he had no way of validating it, so he hackled his neck ruff and waited.

The human spoke again. After a moment, Lim said,

"We have more video recordings of the Khûrûsh-en who spoke for the other group of outsiders."

"The one who was lying to you?" Kamozh interjected.

"Yes. We want you to watch them and see if there is anything you can tell us about her or them."

<Assent> was his response.

Lim pointed to a panel on a nearby wall. It lit up.

There were two recordings; the first rather short, the second somewhat longer. When they were over, Kamozh and all the retainers were on their hind feet, Shekanre at his side and the others ranked behind them.

Kamozh glanced behind, gathering a quick glance of the others with faces turned away from the panel and all four hands shouting **<Lie!>**

To his right he could hear Shekanre's breath rattling in his throat, presage to an outburst; he could see all of the weapons master's hands flexing.

Kamozh returned his gaze to the panel, where the frozen figure of the Khûrûsh-en was still displayed, and contemplated it, trying to understand what its very presence meant, trying to set aside the horror of its words for just a moment. But after that moment, he raised his forehands and shaped the sign for **<Khûr Avert>** at the same moment he said the words aloud, followed by an emphatic cough.

Holding the sign before his face for a long moment, Kamozh then dropped his hands with a deep sigh and turned his back on Lim and the monsters. He looked at his retainers, all of them consumed with fear, even Shekanre. "Stand down," he ordered quietly.

After a moment, the others began to relax. Their eyes were still narrowed, and their neck ruffs distended, however, and Shekanre was still emitting moments of growl, so they hadn't settled much.

"Be still," Kamozh said, while his left mid-hand shaped **<Honor of the clan>**. It took a long moment—one that seemed almost timeless—but when Kamozh turned back to face Lim they had all dropped their midhands to the floor and their ruffs were settling. He badly wanted to heave a deep sigh, but that would not have presented the aura of control he needed to keep in front of both his retainers and the monsters.

Now that the moment of shock was past, anger began to burn; great anger. Righteous anger. Wrath. And he didn't care if he was entitled to it or not as a slave or guest of the monsters.

All of the monsters were showing more tension than had been evident even moments before, and two of the Jao sitting at the sides of the table had risen, though they were seemingly restrained by the lifted hand of the monster Director Kralik. Lim had stepped back from him. The atmosphere seemed charged.

Kamozh directly faced Lim. "Do you have any idea what you have done?" he demanded.

"No," she replied. "Instruct me."

Kamozh shaped **<No>** with emphatic force. "Send us back to our quarters. I must calm my retainers—and I must calm myself—before I can speak to your masters. Tomorrow. Now please allow us to leave."

Lim turned to the Jao guards, and apparently issued orders. They looked at Kamozh and pointed at the door. He gathered himself and led the way, the rest falling into line behind him, guards bringing up the rear. He could hear the rising conversation levels as the door irised shut behind them.

CHAPTER 43

"What the hell just happened?" Ed Kralik demanded. Caitlin held her peace, waiting for both Yaut and Dannet to resume their seats before she lowered her hand.

Caitlin looked to Lim. "What did Kamozh say? What was going on?"

Lim settled into a seat. "I do not know. He said they needed to go back to their quarters and calm themselves, and he would meet with us tomorrow."

"Calm themselves? What for?" That from Yaut.

"Obviously something in the videos distressed or angered them," Wrot said.

"Distress first, anger second," Aille said. "But anger appeared to be predominant by the end, at least in the leader's body."

Trust a Jao to read body language, Caitlin thought. "The question is why? What did they see or hear that triggered this?"

Tully set his com pad down on the table with a loud

clack. "How did we react when she announced they had four thousand systems?" He gave them a moment for that to sink in, then continued with, "Remember, our theory is that they were traumatized by an early contact with outsiders. Their whole society is paranoid toward outsiders, to the extent that their predominant religion is that the Khûr system is the next thing to heaven, the Khûrûsh are but a little lower than the angels, and anyone and everyone else are demons from the outer dark."

"Yikes," Caitlin said after a moment. "We just told them that they are outnumbered at least four thousand to one."

"Yep," Tully said. "And remember what they said about captives and slavery. It must look to them as if there are Khûrûsh slaves serving those demons. Or there might be demons who look like Khûrûsh."

"Or worse," Caitlin said slowly, "there might be Khûrûsh who have become demons."

The Third-Mordent/Fourth-Tone-Quaver meld entered the main performance hall of Ninth-Minor-Sustained. The harmony master was standing in the corner of the room as she had done so many other times in Third-Mordent's experience, gazing out the window at the outer dark.

Third-Mordent came to a halt. She wasn't consciously aware of why; perhaps some hint of tension under the tegument of Ninth-Minor-Sustained's shoulders or back. Perhaps the tilt of her head as she gazed out the window. Perhaps the angle a leg formed on the floor of the room. But something within her urged caution more strongly than it had ever done since the early days of being under the harmony master's control.

Fourth-Tone-Quaver had instantly stopped when she had. Third-Mordent could sense the tension in his body but retained her focus on the harmony master. Her own tension was so strong that Fourth-Tone-Quaver could not have overridden it even if he had desired to, and she could not allow the distraction of attending to his ignorance. In this, he had no choice but to remain locked in with her.

"Regrets," Ninth-Minor-Sustained whisper-sang in another elegy. "The universe looks so beautifully sterile from here; so clean; so ready to embrace the Melody." She paused for a long moment. "Yet it is such a lie. The universe is so fecund; so spoiled; so rotten with aberrant life that even we of the Ekhat, even we of the Complete Harmony, can be tainted with it."

Third-Mordent made no response; simply observed the harmony master with focus and care.

For a long moment, there was no movement; no sound.

With no warning, no indications of any kind, Ninth-Minor-Sustained suddenly leapt from her stance and landed in front of the meld, forehand blades already open and coming to rest on the necks of Third-Mordent and her mate.

It was like the very first days of being with the harmony master. *Fight/flee* flooded Third-Mordent's mind, but she locked down her body, forcing her control almost to the cellular level, to prevent a reaction to the presence of Ninth-Minor-Sustained within her instinctive reaction area. A single movement could/would prove fatal.

"Control," Ninth-Minor-Sustained intoned. "What are the precepts?"

"Control yourself," Third-Mordent returned in an aria, "never give anything away, control others."

There was a moment of silence.

"Stand," Ninth-Minor-Sustained fluted. Without moving the forehand blades, she reached out a manipulator and rested it on Third-Mordent's head. Third-Mordent clamped down even harder on her body, stopping even the tegument twitch that started with the touch of another on her.

"You will spawn soon," the harmony master sang, withdrawing her appendage. "Be ready."

Ninth-Minor-Sustained made small swift movements with her forehand blades, then stepped back from the meld. Third-Mordent felt ichor ooze from small cuts that the harmony master had made on the tegument of her neck and upper back, and knew that identical cuts had been placed on Fourth-Tone-Quaver.

Ninth-Minor-Sustained flicked her blades to clear them, then folded them back into their sheaths. "There is another control," she returned to the intoning mode. "Control of information."

Third-Mordent relaxed to a small degree. "Is that the same as the second precept?" she fluted.

"No. There are times you will want others to know something, or part of something, or the edge of something, or nothing. This you must learn." The harmony master paused, then concluded with, "And the price you will pay to do it."

Kamozh looked up as the door signal rang. All the others looked to him. He made a gesture with his right mid-hand, and continued to cradle a cup with his forehands while Neferakh went to open the door. As Kamozh expected, Lim stepped into their quarters, followed by Colonel Tully and Sergeant Boyes.

It was near the middle of the great ship's day cycle, Kamozh thought. The monsters had given him the time he had asked for. He was a bit surprised that Lim had not come for him much earlier.

She nodded to him. "*Rhan* Kamozh," she said, "Director Kralik and the others would like to meet with you again, if you are prepared."

Kamozh considered her for a moment. "I am not *Rhan*," he replied. "How can I be, when all Khûrûsh who live in *re-heshyt*, right life, would undoubtedly consider me dead at best, and a slave of demons at worst? Khûr-melkh Shmenkhat has undoubtedly pronounced Clan Hoshep dead and given our clanhome and assets and responsibilities to others."

"The director has ordered that you be treated with the respect and honor you deserve as *Rhan*. You live; you exist; you have your clansmen and retainers. Your Khûr-melkh cannot make you disappear by a wave of his hand."

"Can he not?" Kamozh murmured. But then, Lim had said nothing that he hadn't considered on his own, the last few days.

Colonel Tully said something, with that curve to his mouth that Kamozh had learned meant a human found something humorous. He was struck again by the motility of their expressions, how much more emotive they could be than the face of a Khûrûsh-an. Other than lifting a lip to expose teeth, there was little he could do to emulate a human. On the other hand, the human use of hand gestures was very crude and primitive.

"Colonel Tully reminded me of an old Terran story," Lim said. "One about a king named Canute—something like your Khûr-melkh—who was wise enough to know his limits, and proved it to his attendants by one day standing on the shore and ordering the tide to not come in. He says to think about it."

Lim fell silent. Kamozh considered the story. It resonated with him, for some reason. But now was not the time to consider such stories.

Kamozh set his cup down, and rose to stand on his hind legs. "I am ready. Let us not keep the director waiting." He turned to the others. "Shekanre, with me." His left forehand shaped **<attention to duty>**. "The rest of you, practice your English."

It didn't take long to retrace their steps to the meeting room. The monsters were arranged in much the same way as yesterday, with the human Director Kralik facing him directly, flanked on each side by what appeared to be the same Jao. The facial markings seemed to be the same, at any rate.

Director Kralik spoke as soon as Kamozh and Shekanre had come to a stop beside Lim in front of their table. "Accept our apologies, please," Lim translated. "It was not our intent yesterday to cause you sorrow, grief, or distress. But we desperately need information that we believe only you can provide. Please tell us why your people are so . . . I don't know your word for this, Kamozh."

"Describe it," he said.

"The characteristic of hating outsiders, those who are not Khûrûsh. You don't talk to them; you attempt to destroy them; you seem to fear them."

"The word you want is 'xenophobic,'" Kamozh said quietly. "And we have good reason to be that way. We have the very best of reasons to hate and fear non-Khûrûsh. They nearly destroyed us."

Kamozh listened as Lim translated. There were reactions around the room from what she said, but he spoke again on the heels of her words.

"Hear, then, of the Time of Troubles, when Khûr Himself seemed to turn his back on his people."

CHAPTER 44

"By rights," Kamozh said, "I should have one of our poets singing this. We have sagas and elegies and laments from this time; hero-tales and final stands; massacres and martyrs. I cannot do it justice."

He paused for a moment, then set his mid-hands on the floor and settled himself. Shekanre did likewise, beside him.

"Four hundred years ago," Kamozh began, sitting back on his haunches and using his left forehand and right mid-hand to make the twinned signs **<averrance of truth>**, "we were a different people. Our poets have called it a golden age, a time of peace and harmony, where no one was hungry and no one raised a hand against another. Myself, I have read enough history to know that it was no such thing. But we were a more open people, then.

"We had begun to venture away from Khûr-shi, our planet. There was a scientific outpost on Khûr-liyo, the large moon, and we had visited Khûr-io, the smaller moon. We thought we were so wise, so knowledgeable, so smart. We found out otherwise.

"In the third year of Khûr-melkh Khatzhetnor, son of Khûr-melkh Anibal the Great, who had united the planet under a single ruler, the demons came from the outer dark.

"We had made the transition generations earlier away from the thought that Khûr was the only sun in the universe. But only the most radical of us had seriously considered the idea that we might not be the only intelligence in the universe. So it was a great wonder when their ship entered the system; a wonder and a shock, even to the radicals. It is no small thing to find that your wildest ideas are indeed truth."

Kamozh stopped for a moment while Lim caught up with his words. This was the first time he had attempted to recount this history, and it was unsettling. He folded his mid-hands together, and contemplated them for a long moment, well past the point where Lim finished her translating.

"They made no secret of their coming;" he eventually resumed, "at least, not then. It was a largish ship; smaller than your *Lexington*, I believe, but perhaps not by much. They did much as you did, sending radio signals out on our most commonly used frequency bands, with effusive compliments. And we welcomed them; oh, how we welcomed them.

"We were awed when they landed a tender by our then-capital city, Azhnaton. Those who exited were tall; almost as tall as you Jao and Lleix. They moved like supreme predators, smoothly and with grace, yet were soft-spoken. We took them on tours to visit all our cultural sites, our business centers. They were especially complimentary to our scientific research centers.

"Twelve days later, they struck. Shuttles erupted from the ship in orbit, and more came from behind the nearest planet. They landed everywhere, seizing control of all major centers. They launched devastating bombardments on our major military centers, which we had *not* shown them. They shot anyone who got in their way. They took captives and tried to use them as hostages—their first miscalculation."

Kamozh rose to his hind feet, and started pacing. The monsters—human, Jao, Lleix—all sat motionless, saying nothing. His voice grew harsher.

"The last known message from Khûr-melkh Khatzhet-nor was a single word: 'Resist.' And we obeyed. Our people rose up, led by the clan leaders and the remnants of our military. We still had people alive to lead us who had fought in the consolidation wars. And we were not afraid. We spent our lives like pouring out water."

Kamozh stopped, holding his forehands out before him, making the sign of **<grief>**. "Our records of that time are of course fragmentary. But the most educated estimates are that we lost close to a quarter million people within five hands of days. But that was only the beginning of the tale."

He began pacing again. "Their every attempt to take hostages ended in death—theirs and ours—for we would not allow them to hold hostages. We would attack, and attack, and attack until the hostages were either freed or dead. More often than not, the hostages would themselves rise up against their captors and fight them until they forced the monsters to slay them." He held out a forehand before the monsters, and flexed the digits, baring the claws. "Khûr equipped us with natural weapons, you see. We could not be disarmed. And they learned to be wary of us, even when weary, or hurt, or seemingly abandoned. Even the young would strike at them when they got close enough. Before much time had passed, they had learned that lesson, and simply killed anyone and everyone who got close to them. And as none of us wanted to be slaves of the monsters, we accepted that."

Kamozh stopped again. This time he held all four hands before him, making a fourfold sign of **<crushing grief>**.

"The struggle continued for many hands of days. And gradually they began pulling back from the greatest of our cities, the ones that were more cultural centers than anything. We thought we were defeating them. We thought they were perhaps going to retreat, maybe even back to their ships." His voice strained, rasping, words becoming choppy. "We were such fools!"

Kamozh stopped. His throat had closed up. He stood silently before the monsters, unable to speak for a long moment. They waited, saying nothing, while he closed his eyes and mastered himself, forcing the grief back down his throat. "There came a day," he resumed at length, "when they struck back. Within moments of each other, what we later determined to be were aimed asteroids fell from the sky at almost perpendicular angles over the three cities."

That got a reaction from the monsters, Kamozh noted, particularly from the humans, who looked at the Jao for some reason.

"The cities were destroyed. Their center districts were vaporized, and the damage from the air blasts, the fireballs, and the seismic shocks extended to great distances."

Kamozh stopped again. This was proving more difficult than he had thought it would be. Trying to describe to monsters the damage done by other monsters made him want to scream. How could they appreciate the horror, the very blasphemy of what had happened to Khûr-shi—Khûr's Home—the cradle of his people? But they were still sitting, still waiting, still apparently wanting his final word.

"The shock to our people was great. Almost—almost enough it was to make us surrender. We fell silent as a people for days, trying to understand what had happened. The monsters took advantage of this, of course, pushing their troops in and taking control of areas that had been resisting.

"Some of us recovered before others, and took up the struggle again. From what records have survived, it was a very grim time, between the death and destruction caused by the troops and the death and destruction caused by the asteroids. Poetry of those days refers to suicide with longing."

Kamozh stopped again, settling to his haunches again. Lim took advantage of the moment to ask, "How did you win?"

"We didn't win," Kamozh said, "at least not totally on our own." Lim looked at him without saying anything. "The monsters were occupying more and more territory. That we probably could have dealt with, eventually. But their great ship was overhead all the time, and they could rain fire and destruction down on any place they chose. And we knew that if it looked like they were losing again, there would be more asteroids.

"The devout among us say that Khûr Himself aided us. Others try to find a more natural explanation. But all the accounts are in agreement that as we were nearing the end of our strength, our ability to resist, there came a night when there were two great explosions in the sky. Brilliant flares of light. The great ship in orbit was the first. It seemed to shatter into many pieces, most of which subsequently impacted on Khûr-shi.

"The second occurred in our asteroid belt. We theorize it was another ship, and indeed, we found traces of worked metal and alloys consistent with the ship that had been in orbit when we finally ventured that far in our own system."

Kamozh gave a quick **<Khûr's Blessing>** with his left mid-hand. "We do not know what caused the explosions, but that was the beginning of the end for the monsters and their troops. The survivors on the planet held out for many, many days, but knowing that the ship was gone emboldened our fighters, and we eventually swarmed them down."

The young Khûrûsh-an stopped again, to allow Lim to finish translating without distraction from him. When she had completed, he continued. "There came a day when Khûr-shi was ours again. It had taken almost a year, but no monster's foot trod our planet's ground.

"You wonder why we are xenophobic?" Kamozh rose to his hind feet again. "Over a fourth of our people *died* in this action. Our planet, our system, was polluted by their presence. Entire clans were destroyed. Our culture was savaged, our economy wrecked, our planet was given scars which can never be erased.

"It took the blood of an entire generation to remove the monsters. It took three generations to recover. It took five to take to space again and begin to fortify the other planets, to make outposts. We will not be taken that way again.

"We have museums devoted to nothing but reminding us of this past, showing us the artifacts of the time, showing us the twisted steel beams from bridges and buildings destroyed by the airbursts from the asteroids, showing us the ashes of those who were incinerated in the fireballs, showing us the rows of grave after grave after grave of those who died in the resistance. And it was Khûr-melkh Sheshahng, the youngest and only surviving son of Khûr-melkh Khatzhetnor, standing on the rim of the crater that had been the heart of Azhnaton, who gave the command that no Khûrûsh-an is to ever have any contact or relationship with monsters from the outer dark. It is the ultimate treason. And it is my shame that I have done so to save the lives of my retainers."

He stopped again to let Lim translate. When she was finished, he said, "We are xenophobic, yes. Do not blame us for that. We have been shaped by the violence and cruelty of others. All we have to offer the outer dark is this."

Kamozh raised his right forehand, claws bared.

CHAPTER 45

There was no immediate response once Lim finished her translation. After a long moment, Kamozh set his mid-hands on the floor, and sagged a little. By the Shining Lord, he was weary. Telling that story, as short as it was, had been so intense that he felt as if he had spent all day at strenuous labor.

The human, Director Kralik, finally spoke. She did not speak for long. Lim began translation as soon as she was through.

"You will have trouble believing this, *Rhan* Kamozh, but we sorrow that your people endured this. There are times of trial and disaster and, yes, horror in the history of every race I know of. Even we," Lim waved her hand at the other occupants of the room, "have histories of such, and some not that long ago. So having endured similar events, we understand your grief, and anger, and hatred, at least in part.

"And yes, the temptation to hate is strong. Yes, we understand xenophobia, for our peoples have known it as well. Yet the persistence of hate can poison a people, Kamozh. It can warp a society. And at some point, a people must relinquish that hate, or they risk becoming what they hate."

Kamozh absorbed that thought. He heard Shekanre inhale sharply beside him.

The director continued. "I am not saying you can or should forgive those who brutalized your people. But are we—those of us in this fleet—those people? Should we be blamed for the crimes of others, which we did not commit and from which we drew no benefit? Is that justice, when we have done no harm to anyone other than the crew of your ship, and that only because we could not get anyone to talk to us otherwise? Would your Lord Khûr consider that part of *re-heshyt*?"

Lim left Kamozh no opportunity to respond, as she continued with the translation. "Yet let us lay that aside for now. You have told us that none of your people associate from those who are not Khûrûsh. Yet you have seen yourself evidence that there is at least one Khûrûsh-en associating with un-Khûrûsh. Just as we have done as little harm as we could in treating with your people, so we do not desire to allow others to harm the people of Khûr if we can prevent it. Will you work with us in at least this much—that we together can gain an understanding on how your people can be in an interstellar ship when your people have been banned from that type of contact? To see what may be directed at your people even as we speak?"

Now that, Kamozh thought, was something that had not occurred to him. He had been so fixated on the "how" of the presence of the female in the messages that he had not thought beyond that to wonder *why* she was there. And that, he admitted as both curiosity and anger began to build in him, was a question to which he really wanted an answer.

"Director Kralik," he responded, "in that much we can indeed find common ground. I and mine will willingly serve you in this search for understanding and truth. Even though they will not accept us any longer, we will still endeavor to shield the people of Khûr."

The corners of that so-flexible mouth of Director Kralik bent up, which he was coming to understand was an indication of pleasure.

"We will work together toward that goal, *Rhan* Kamozh," she said.

Caitlin looked around at the others after the two Khûrûsh were escorted back to their quarters. "Wow," she said.

"Yeah," Tully responded. He looked to Aille. "Caitlin's right, you know."

Aille turned his head. "In what way?"

"The part about some of us knowing what they feel like."

Ed Kralik picked up the thread of the conversation. "If you hadn't removed Oppuk when you did, you might have seen an uprising like that on Earth. Maybe not that absolutely focused, as we appear to be much more diverse than the Khûrûsh, but a bloodletting approaching that magnitude was moving from possibility toward probability."

"Ah." Aille slipped into *neutral* angles. "I can see that. Yet there would have been one significant difference between here and Terra."

"And that is?" Caitlin asked.

Aille looked to Tura, who said, "Terra had no other aliens in the system willing to destroy our ships."

"You caught that, did you?" Ed said.

Tura did not respond, but Krant-Captain Mallu spoke up. "What do you mean, General Kralik?"

Ed sat back in his chair. "There are several questions about this account. I don't dispute Kamozh's information. At a remove of four hundred of their years, the facts have probably been nailed down pretty hard. But that account was from the Khûrûsh point of view. Looked at from the opposing force point of view, there are at least three things that should jump out at us."

"Why so few?" Dannet said.

"That's the first one," Ed agreed. "An interstellar invasion fleet consisting of two ships, no matter how large, doesn't make any sense. Maybe they were launched by a resource-poor system, or maybe they were refugees or survivors from a disaster or conflict in another system and that was all that managed to get here. But that's a big unknown that is making me nervous."

"Where's the rest of them?" Tully said, holding up two fingers.

"Right," Ed said. "Especially with what might have been an advance force, I would really expect a second and even a third wave. But four hundred years? Looks like they're not coming. Still makes me nervous."

"And the third one is who or what took out the invasion ships?" Caitlin said. "I get that. But why is that an issue?"

"For the two explosions to have happened in that close a synchrony," Ed explained, "that argues intelligent coherent planned attacks. But if that's the case, why did the relief stop with that? Why didn't they aid the struggle on the planet? Were they that indifferent to the suffering of the Khûrûsh?"

"What he said," Tully interjected. "And if the folks we're talking to were responsible, why haven't they contacted the Khûrûsh since then?"

Caitlin looked around at the others, gathering return looks but no additional words. "So, we have questions, but no answers."

"Yet," Tura said.

"Right. So, does anyone believe we shouldn't contact the aliens?"

All the Jao in the room adopted either *neutral* or *submission to oudh* angles. The humans all shook their heads. And Lim and Pyr followed the human suit.

"Okay," Caitlin said with a sigh. "I agree." She looked at Lim. "Get us a connection with the *Starcloud*, please."

It took several minutes for the connection to be made, but before too long the face of the spokesman for the alien ship appeared on the display panel.

"Since you are making contact," the Khûrûsh-en said, "should I assume you are ready to meet with us?"

Caitlin waited for the translation to complete, then replied, "Greetings, Shemnarai. I am Director Kralik, leader of this fleet. We are willing to meet with you in seven Khûrûsh days."

"That is acceptable. We will call again shortly to discuss the details of how to achieve the meeting."

The connection closed. They all looked at each other.

"Ready or not, here we go," Ed murmured.

"I'm ready to name this ice ball we're hiding behind," Caitlin said.

"To what?" Tully asked.

"Rubicon."

PART VI
A Greater Tide

CHAPTER 46

Caitlin stood in Shuttle Bay Green 1 of the *Lexington*, waiting for their guests to arrive.

In the end, it had only taken five Khûrûsh days to arrange for the meeting—three to negotiate how it would proceed, one to decide to agree, and one to set up the logistics of it.

The aliens had first taken a craft of their own from the *Starcloud* to one of the Bond's Harrier ships which had been moved into position roughly midway between *Starcloud* and *Lexington*. There the representatives of the Eleusherar Path disembarked, and their craft returned to *Starcloud*. Then they had boarded a Terran shuttle, which was in the process of conveying them to their destination.

Caitlin wiped sweaty hands on her slacks. This was stupid, she thought. She had been meeting and working among aliens almost her entire life. Why was she so nervous? She should be excited.

She took a deep breath, and released it. She was

excited. But she was also nervous. What was happening now should have been way above her pay grade—meeting with the representatives of an honest-to-God interstellar federation—talk about something right out of science fiction! Her dad should have been here, handling that, not her. But both Governor Aille and Pleniary-superior Tura insisted that she had *oudh*, and must take the lead. Everyone had agreed that it would be best if she would handle all conversations unless she asked for input or responses from one of the others.

The shuttle slowly nosed into the bay. Caitlin took a look around one last time. Ed, Aille, Tura, and Tully beside her: check. Krant-Captain Mallu, Fleet Commander Dannet, Yaut, and Wrot before them: check. Captain Miller, Tamt, and elements of her bodyguard detail before them: check. And to one side, *Rhan* Kamozh and his weapons master: check. The representatives of the aliens had insisted on at least some presence of the captured Khûrûsh. She wasn't sure why it was such a big deal to them, but it did add to the enigma of the aliens. One more question added to the list, she thought. *Wonder how long it will take to get answers we can trust?*

The shuttle settled to the deck. The propulsion unit cycled down and out. The hum of the unit faded away. After a minute or so, the hatch began to open.

Right, Caitlin thought. Time to pull up her big girl panties and be about it.

The host beast was large, Third-Mordent thought. Not as large as an adult Ekhat, not by any means. But larger than any of the servient breeds that she knew of; larger by far. Even the Anj in attendance on the creche masters seemed almost diminutive in comparison.

Third-Mordent knew the theory; having grown up in a creche, she could not have avoided it. The host beasts were not quite sentient, but provided an admirable balance between the mass of the body and the size of the neural ganglia in the body. Both were necessary for development of prime progeny. And compared to some of her memories from the creche, this unit could be the largest host beast she had ever seen. That promised a good start for the progeny of her meld.

She looked at Fourth-Tone-Quaver, and found he was looking at her. *If we survive, we will be great.* That thought was in both minds.

Ninth-Minor-Sustained turned away from a conversation with the creche masters. She approached Third-Mordent with care, moving slowly and with indirect motions that couldn't be mistaken for attacks. An Ekhat about to spawn was the very definition of agitated and irritable. Fourth-Tone-Quaver already bore three open slashes from where she had punished him for approaching her too closely.

The harmony master observed her eyes, her posture, the positioning of her manipulators and forehand blades. At length, she touched a manipulator to her neck, slowly and gently. She withdrew it in the same manner. "You are ready," she whisper-sang, making a gesture to the creche masters.

Spawn! Third-Mordent could feel changes happening in her body, much like when she had mated. The muscles running along her spine thinned down.

From her perspective it seemed to take forever, but she knew from her time in the creche that it was only a short time.

She heard the creak as her skeletal members began shifting, opening a channel that ran along the top of the spine.

The changes were coming faster. Third-Mordent was inspiring and expiring great gulps of air, fueling the furnace that her body was becoming.

There was a ripping sound, being emitted as the tegument over her spine began to tear, beginning at the base of her neck where it joined her shoulders. Her mind was so inflamed that she felt no pain as the tegument separated all along the length of her spine. She could feel ichor rising up to ooze over the edges of the open channel.

There was motion in her back. Something began to pop free from the channel in the spine. Bit by bit, column segment by column segment it tore loose, rising into the air until it arched overhead. It was slim and limber. It was dripping white ichor. There was a wickedly pointed terebra at the tip, which seemed to quest this way and that.

The creche masters urged the herd-beast closer to Third-Mordent. The ovipositor waved in that direction, then paused, hesitating. *I want my progeny to be great!* sprang into her mind. There was no-thought; the ovipositor swerved and struck, lancing the terebra into Fourth-Tone-Quaver's shoulders just below the neck, driving its way in and down until it pierced the major nerve ganglia found there, whereupon it pumped paralyzing toxins into the ganglia that controlled all voluntary movement.

The effect was instantaneous: Fourth-Tone-Quaver's legs gave way, and he collapsed on the floor.

The ovipositor withdrew and struck, and struck, and struck again and again. With each strike Third-Mordent pumped a capsule into Fourth-Tone-Quaver that her body had prepared, each containing a nymph generated by the union of spermatophores from Fourth-Tone-Quaver with her own receptors. They were quite small at the moment, and each was surrounded by a hard but thin shell of the same material as her forehand blades. Now that they were out of Third-Mordent's spermatotheca and buried in a host, the shells would dissolve, and they would begin to feed.

Third-Mordent managed to keep her spermatotheca from emptying itself, rising out of the spawning frenzy enough after six strikes to close the outlet valve of the chamber before all the fertilized receptors were gone. The ovipositor, its reason for emergence fulfilled and no further capsules available, slowly withdrew from its final strike into Fourth-Tone-Quaver's body. It wavered in the air for a long moment, as if seeking another target, but then began contracting. Segment by segment, it laid itself down in the spinal channel, until it was totally hidden. The skeletal creaking resumed as the spinal segments resumed their normal positioning. The edges of the split in the tegument began to bond together.

She looked down at Fourth-Tone-Quaver as the spawning frenzy continued to drain out of her mind. She could see him still conscious, still focusing his eyes on her. But the unity she had felt was gone. Still, *If we survive, we will be great* resonated in her, along with *I want my progeny to be great*. The first would be fulfilled in her; the second would be begun by him.

Ninth-Minor-Sustained's voice intruded on her consciousness, singing what was almost an imprecation. "You will tend the male carefully. You will preserve and protect him to the highest degree. You will keep him conscious for as long as possible, that the nymphs may consume the most active and alive ganglia." She paused for a moment. "Do not fail me," she intoned in a downward-sliding cold glissando. "Or even more critical, do not fail her." She pointed a manipulator at her descendant. "Her wrath would be worse than mine."

Third-Mordent straightened, lowered her head slightly, and let the edges of her forehand blades show.

"Come," Ninth-Minor-Sustained sang in a triumphal aria. "You have done well. We will continue as you have begun."

CHAPTER 47

The first person through the hatch was a human jinau who stepped down the ramp and stood to one side. She was followed by Garhet, who had gone to the Harrier to provide translation services. But then the representatives/envoys appeared in the hatchway, and Caitlin's gaze was riveted by them.

There were two of them. One appeared to be Shemnarai, the Khûrûsh-en who had so far been the main spokesman for the Eleusherar Path. She was walking on her hind legs, and dressed in flowing robes in which crimson seemed to be the predominant color. Caitlin caught a stir among Kamozh's people from the corner of her eye. Then her eyes were caught by the second representative.

"Oooo-kay," she heard Tully mutter. "Is that a walking walrus?"

The alien in question was a head taller than Tully, and almost as broad as Tamt. He—Caitlin assumed it was male—was of a quadruped design analogous to the human/Jao/Lleix model: two legs and two arms, one head with bilateral arrangement of various sensory organs. But the immediate impression on the humans was "Teeth!" As in large tusks or fangs hanging out of the mouth.

"Try a smilodon," Ed said as the alien walked into a patch of stronger light. "Think saber-toothed tiger."

"Cool," Tully said.

Caitlin's brain shifted from walrus to cat, and she saw what Ed was getting at. It was a very felinoid face that was looking back at her. A walking, intelligent saber-toothed tiger, she thought. Just how remarkable was that?

The envoys stopped, and both of them made some complicated, almost convoluted, hand gestures that for Shemnarai involved all four hands. Then the felinoid spoke—in Khûrûsh.

"Our greetings and thanks to you for receiving us in peace. May your paths be peaceful and your days full of light." He waited for Lim to finish translating, then spread his open hands in an obvious social gesture of courtesy, and perhaps of respect.

His—Caitlin assumed the felinoid was a "he," even though she knew that might be a human-centric assumption—voice was an incredibly deep and resonant bass, so low that it bordered on passing into inaudible ranges for humans. It was also very musical, and just for a moment she lusted to hear him in some of her favorite operas and shows.

Caitlin gave herself a mental shake, and returned a similar gesture. "Our greetings and thanks to you for coming in peace." She figured it couldn't hurt to parallel the greeting. "May your paths lead to your goals." She had to bite the inside of her cheek for a moment to stifle a giggle as she suppressed the desire to complete the greeting with the old Irish saying, "And may you be in heaven a half hour before the devil knows you're dead." She didn't think they were ready for discussions of either humor or religion just at that moment.

"If you will come with us," Caitlin continued, "we will get out of the way of the support crews and go someplace a bit quieter where we can talk without having to shout." As usual, the shuttle bay was a bit on the noisy side as the maintenance crews began to move around the craft, checking externals and connecting fuel and evacuation hoses.

That deep voice rumbled. "Agreed," Lim translated.

"This way, then," Caitlin said. She stood still for a moment to allow most of the others to lead the way, then turned in company with Aille and her husband, gesturing to the envoys to follow.

One of the reasons for the days-long delay in receiving the envoys was a discussion about how to receive them. The humans wanted to use Caitlin's large conference room with its expansive table. The Jao were perfectly willing to meet in the shuttle bay. The Lleix were ambivalent.

In the end, they had been guided by Kamozh.

"Since these monsters seem to know something about we Khûrûsh, greet them as we would. Set a large open room, with fabric draping the walls, softer yellower lighting than your conference room, with seats of different sizes, styles and heights. It will put both me and their Khûrûsh-en at a disadvantage if we have to sit on the floor because your seats do not allow Khûrûsh to sit comfortably, and you have no guarantee that anyone else they send will fit in your chairs either."

Caitlin admitted to the wisdom of that advice immediately, and so it had been done. The large table and most of the human and Jao-sized chairs were removed, and several large benches and even two or three small low platforms had been brought in. It turned out there weren't large quantities of attractive cloth on the ship, but they found enough to drape at least one panel on three of the four walls, and they supplemented them with colored lights. With the overhead lights tuned to a yellowish frequency, she had to admit it was a more restful atmosphere than its usual configuration. The thought lurked in the back of her mind that she might consider leaving it that way.

The conference room door irised shut behind the aliens. The guards who had trailed the pack remained in the corridor. Tamt was with Caitlin, but Caewithe Miller had elected to remain in the corridor where she could both monitor the conference from concealed audio/video pickups and coordinate any response that might be called for. While Caitlin could appreciate her bodyguard captain's professional paranoia, she really hoped such responses wouldn't be necessary.

Caitlin turned to the envoys and took the opening step. "My name is Caitlin Kralik," she said, standing tall and placing her hand on her chest for a moment, "and I am the director of this fleet."

"Director," came back the translated response from the felinoid. "Is that a military rank?"

"No," Caitlin said. "This is not a military expedition, but rather a nonmilitary exploration mission."

"Your vessels are armed, are they not?" Shemnarai said.

"We are explorers," Caitlin said with a smile. "We are not fools, however. The nature of successful exploration is to be prepared for as many eventualities as one can think of." She shrugged. "Which explains why we survived our initial contact with the Khûrûsh with no damage to speak of."

"Indeed," responded the felinoid. There was a moment of silence, then he continued with, "You are not from this region, are you?"

Caitlin caught a flash of a grin on Tully's face, and almost choked. It was an almost telepathic moment, as she could see him thinking of one of his hillbilly associates in a similar situation saying something like, "Y'all ain't from around here, are ya?" It appeared that some things were almost universal.

It took her a moment to get back on track. "That would be 'No.'"

Third-Mordent looked up from the carcass of her meal, having swallowed the last gobbets she had torn from the food beast. It had been one of the higher-order creatures—bordering on true sentience—that the station maintained for moments such as this, when one of the higher-ranking Ekhat was in need of the richest of sustenance.

This one knew it was in trouble when the two great Ekhat had stalked into the room and Third-Mordent's forehand blades had swept out. It had gobbled in panic, then leapt into motion with all six limbs churning as it attempted to elude the predator.

Third-Mordent now admitted that the spawning

session had taken more out of her than she had expected. It had taken her an almost unconscionable amount of time to spike and complete the food creature. She had been almost lethargic. But the first few bites of hot meat reeking of adrenal enzymes and pheromones of fear brought her focus back.

Her manipulators wiped at the trails of ichor that dripped from her face. She looked to where Ninth-Minor-Sustained waited by the entry with no external signs showing of anger, dissatisfaction, or contempt.

"Are there repercussions to be suffered for wasting the male?" Third-Mordent fluted. "I know that you had planned on our mating."

There seemed to be an emptiness in her self-image, as if part of her had disappeared. But in a way, it had; Fourth-Tone-Quaver had been locked so tightly to her being, had been such an extension of her will, that to know he was no longer there was as if half her body had been disabled.

"None," Ninth-Minor-Sustained intoned. "You have passed the greatest test I could set, one that even Descant-at-the-Fourth had failed."

Test? Third-Mordent considered everything that had been a part of the recent past. Everything had been a test, it seemed. To what could her great ancestress be referring? Except . . .

"The spawning?" Third-Mordent whisper-sang.

"The spawning, yes, the spawning," Ninth-Minor-Sustained uttered in a triumphal arioso motif. "A male is undoubtedly one of the finest hosts that can be provided for nymphs. His muscle and neural tissues and his fear and adrenal enzymes stimulate the nymphs in ways that no other creature can."

The harmony master came to a full stop for a long moment, then continued in a dirge form, "But few of us can rise above the bonds of the mating and make that choice. And it must happen in the first spawning, when the mating bonds are still somewhat flexible. If it doesn't happen then, only death can break the mating bonds, and then it is too late. We cannot recover where we were."

"So what will become of me?" Third-Mordent responded in the same dirge form. "Am I beyond use now? Am I fulfilled, to be sent back out in the ships?"

"No!" the harmony master returned to the triumphal motif. "No, you are not fulfilled, you are freed. Now I admit to you that I had dared to hope that you might rise to harmony master. And now, having passed this test, I sing to you that it has moved from hope to probability. Survive, my progeny; survive what is coming and you will dominate the great and stalk among the greatest."

If we survive, we will be great. A faint echo of Fourth-Tone-Quaver still seemed to resonate in Third-Mordent's mind.

CHAPTER 48

"Before we continue," Caitlin said, "allow me to introduce the other members of mission who will be involved in our discussion." She ran down the list of those who had stood with her in the shuttle bay, spacing them in groups to facilitate Lim's translations: Mallu, Dannet, Yaut, and Wrot first; followed by Ed, Gabe, Aille, and Tura; and concluding with Kamozh and Shekanre.

The felinoid and Shemnarai both stood as the introductions were made, either nodding or making small hand gestures as names and ranks were announced. However, when Kamozh and Shekanre were announced, both envoys faced the two Khûrûsh and made very elaborate and complicated hand gestures, which seemed to startle Kamozh before he made gestures back.

When that was completed, the envoys faced back to Caitlin. The felinoid spoke for a few moments, then paused for Lim's translation. "We ask your pardon, Director Caitlin Kralik, but we must give honor to those you have in your custody. They are our reason for being here in the first place."

"And may we know who you are?" Caitlin said with a bit of an edge in her voice.

"Ah, please pardon us again," came the response. "We are thoughtless guests, I am afraid. You know Shemnarai already, first communication officer for the Eleusherar Path Ship *Starcloud*. And I am D'mishri ap Vashirhi, co-captain and protocol officer of that same ship. You may call me D'mishri as a short form. Please accept the welcome of the Eleusherar Path to our region of space."

"Thank you," Caitlin said, mind racing as she considered the implications of their titles. "Please, be seated again so we can continue our discussion in comfort."

Caitlin continued to think rapidly as everyone settled into their seats again. Once the rustling stopped, she said, "I'm sure that you are as curious about us as we are about you. Since you have a position of protocol officer, do you have a preferred method for this type of first contact?"

The felinoid—D'mishri ap Vashirhi, Caitlin reminded herself—sat back and folded his hands across his chest. "Really, for this initial discussion, nothing ever seems to work as well as simply exchanging questions and answers for a period of time. Establishing a social connection has proven to be the greatest benefit in opening relationships with each new species we meet." His deep voice rumbled wordlessly for a few moments in what Caitlin guessed might be a chuckle-equivalent. "The only rule is that you do not lie. If you do not wish to answer a question, either at the moment or forever, simply say so."

Caitlin could feel the eyes of everyone in the room on her. She took a deep breath. "Agreed."

The felinoid seemed to relax a bit. "You are the hosts and the newcomers—you take the first question."

Caitlin licked her lips. "Shemnarai stated in an earlier transmission that your civilization spans some four thousand star systems. What is the Eleusherar Path, and what is its role?"

There was a bit of a rumble after Lim finished translating the question. "A good first question," the response finally came. "Simply put, the Eleusherar Path is a multispecies, multicultural, multidisciplinary organization that serves as a metagovernment for the Eleusherar Array, the four thousand stars that are grouped in this region of this arm of the galaxy. Our role is to be facilitators in the passing of data, information, designs, and people between the various systems in the Array."

He paused to allow Lim to complete the translation, then said, "I see what appear to be forms of three different species in this room. Do you represent a single organization, and are you representative of all the cultures in your region?"

"Yes." Caitlin saw D'mishri absorb the short answer with a blink of his eyes. "How many species and cultures are there in the Eleusherar Array?"

D'mishri blinked his eyes again. "The latest information I have is that there are approximately 1,950 species and 2,493 cultures in the Array."

Caitlin was taken aback by that information. Sentient species in the thousands, and a plurality of cultures among them? *What have we run into?* She began to feel even more out of her depth, and looked to Aille and Tura. Aille's angles were *gratified-respect*, and Tura flashed a quick morph from her customary *neutral* to *encouragement* for a short moment before she returned to *neutral*. Great. They were leaving it in her hands still. She glared at Aille for a moment, then turned back to D'mishri as he asked his next question.

"Do you represent a single government?"

"Yes and no," Caitlin said. "We are mostly from a single government, but we are pursuing our exploration mission on behalf of both that government and our metagovernment." The Bond of Ebezon could be considered a metagovernment, she decided. Close enough, anyway. "Next question," she said. "What is the most important function of the Eleusherar Path?"

"We preserve planets," was D'mishri's simple response.

"It has begun," Ninth-Minor-Sustained intoned. She waved a manipulator at the repeater display of the system from the central controllers display on the command deck. Seven ship symbols had appeared at the edge of the system, four flashing Complete Harmony glyphs, and one each flashing Interdict, Melody, and True Harmony glyphs.

Third-Mordent watched as after a moment, they all began to move in-system, headed for the station in which she stood. As she watched, additional symbols and glyphs began to appear at almost random places and times.

"What occurs?" Third-Mordent sang as a motif.

"A nexus in the Melody approaches, nears, portends," Ninth-Minor-Sustained sang in a syncopated arietta. "The harmony masters can feel it, and move to address it. Because they move, others will as well."

"They come here?" Third-Mordent whisper-sang.

"We are the nearest foundation to where it portends," the harmony master responded. "If it were elsewise, we would be among those who are aship."

"Why?" Third-Mordent returned to her motif.

"A convocation forms whenever a nexus looms," Ninth-Minor-Sustained intoned. "All who feel it are drawn to the nexus. There will be . . . discussions among all who attend. Dances will be danced; many will be completed; decisions will be reached by those who remain. Leaders may be . . . challenged. This will shape the responses and actions of the factions and subfactions to the nexus."

"And what is the cusp of the nexus?"

"The preservation and fulfillment of the Melody. Always and only that." Ninth-Minor-Sustained's voice plunged down a glissando to a cold low pitch, resonating within their space until Third-Mordent's being seemed to vibrate in tune with it.

CHAPTER 49

"What . . ." Caitlin stopped, frustrated, as it was the envoy's turn for a question.

D'mishri waited for a moment, then said, "What is the most important function of your metagovernment?"

"To lead the struggle against the Ekhat." There, Caitlin thought. Let him chew on that for a cryptic answer. Turnabout, tit for tat, and all that. "What do you mean by 'preserve planets'? Please answer in some detail."

D'mishri rumbled again, and Caitlin got a definite feeling of humor from it. "Well asked, Director. But to answer the question I will have to give you perhaps more detail than you expect.

"To begin with, there are many governments in the Eleusherar Array. Most are single system based; a few are single planet based within a system, and a very few include multiple systems. We of the Eleusherar Path coordinate and facilitate—interface, if you will—with all systems and governments. We do not dictate what kind of government each planet or system or culture will have: oligarchy, totalitarian, popular vote, aristocracy, monarchy, even anarchy. Systems are free to communicate with each other, free to attempt to establish relationships and even to trade with each other. Systems are free to attempt to colonize fallow systems. Systems are free to attempt even to wage war with other systems and conquer them, without the Eleusherar Path being involved or intervening—with one exception."

The envoy's voice grew darker, and he seemed to become more solemn.

"That one exception is the utilization of weapons that risk the serious wounding or the full destruction of a planet itself. Then the Eleusherar Path will intervene to stop such attacks, and will use any means necessary, up to and including the destruction of the attackers' homeworld to bring them to an end."

There was a long pause after Lim finished the translation. D'mishri at length repeated, "Excessive use of nuclear weapons, excessive use of hyperkinetic weapons, any use of asteroidal bolides, any use of panspecies toxins—all of these will bring a response from us. Any means necessary." That last phrase was repeated slower and quieter than those that preceded it; Lim repeated that effect in the translation.

Caitlin looked around the room. The humans looked stunned; the Jao were all struggling with various angle sets, most sliding toward *alarm* or *incredulity*. Aille and Tura, of course, were maintaining seemingly effortless displays of *neutral*. But Wrot was attempting the more rare tripartite *wary-respect-for-seemingly-ultimate-authority*.

Before D'mishri set out his next question, Kamozh

stirred. All eyes shifted to him as he stepped off his bench and rose to his full height, forehand and midhands clasped before him. He took the steps necessary to bring himself directly in front of the envoy, perhaps six human feet from him.

After a moment, D'mishri made a gesture with one hand, one that Caitlin thought looked familiar from some of the interactions between Kamozh and Lim during the meetings the fleet leaders had had with the young Khûrûsh-an.

Kamozh suddenly thrust all four hands forward in signs, and snarled a word. Caitlin looked to Lim, who simply said, "You lie."

Kamozh stood with all four hands holding the **<negation>** sign, lip curled slightly after having snarled his challenge to the new monster. He didn't look away even when the monster's Khûrûsh-en began to rise.

The monster made the sign for **<restraint>**, and the female settled back down. Making a creditable version of **<denial>** with his left hand, the monster said, "In what manner, *Rhan* Kamozh?"

Kamozh heard the Lim monster translating to the old monsters, but paid attention only to this new monster, this D'mishri ap Vashirhi. After a moment, he released the repeated sign and lowered his hands. His lip was still curled, however, and he was sure the monster had taken note of it.

"If your Eleusherar Path 'preserves planets,' where were you when Khûr was invaded by monsters from the outer dark four hundred years ago? Where were you when millions of our people died? Where were you when the monsters slammed not one, not two, but three asteroids into Khûr? Where was your vaunted protection when we were nearly ended as a people?"

His indictment rang strong, echoing faintly in the room. Shemnarai stirred again, and again the monster signed **<restraint>** and she settled.

Lim finished translating behind him, and the room fell silent.

"That is your history," D'mishri ap Vashirhi. "You may not credit it to us, but we grieve that it happened. However, your history is incomplete."

"In what manner?" Kamozh snarled, claws flexing on his hands.

"It lacks the accounts of those things that occurred where the Khûrûsh had no eyes, had no way to see things that nonetheless occurred."

Shemnarai raised her forequarters, and signed **<truth>** with both forehands. She held the posture for several moments, then resumed her former position. Kamozh considered her for yet another moment. She was calm; waiting.

"And what would these unknown accounts add to our tragedy?" Kamozh at length asked.

D'mishri-monster sighed deeply. "Four hundred Khûrûsh years ago, the Eleusherar Array did not extend this far. We were not far away, as interstellar distances go, but our knowledge, our observations, our coverage did not reach Khûr—yet.

"The people who attacked you were the Veldt. They had arisen in a system approximately five light-years inward toward the core from here. Their root species, as with yours, was a carnivorous predator. And they were worthy branches from that root.

"They had recently made contact with the Array, but had not yet joined. They decided that they wanted to be a multisystem polity, and they picked your system to provide that expansion. They had detected your early radio signals, you see."

"So we attracted them?" Kamozh asked, almost unwillingly. "It was nothing more than that? We didn't know to hide, and they followed our radio signals like a beacon fire on a dark night?"

"Exactly so," D'mishri said. "That simple, that tragic. And almost they succeeded. It was a far closer battle than you can imagine now." Kamozh bristled, and the envoy signed **<restraint>** to him this time. "You see, we of the Path found out about their plan after they launched the three ships that assaulted Khûr."

"Three?" Kamozh said. "We thought two."

"Three," D'mishri said firmly. "The assault cruiser in orbit around your world, and two support ships back in the asteroid belt where the bolides were prepared. Since we had no major post in this region at that time, all we could do was send a small flotilla behind them to observe . . . or so we thought.

"Our ships were smaller, and faster, and apparently the Veldt advance force didn't think anyone could or would follow them, for our ships gained on them and were only a few weeks behind the advance ships when they arrived—just in time to witness the orbital bombardment of your planet.

"We had three small ships, with minimal armaments. Our people made a decision to expend all to take down the advance ships, trusting that when the regional base received their laser com bursts that they would take care of the rest."

"Expend all?" Kamozh said, not liking the sound of that.

"Yes. I said our ships were minimally armed. Each of them had some defensive armaments, but only one ship-killer missile apiece. To insure that the missiles would have their best chance, the three ships each carried the missiles to the shortest possible launch ranges, such that when the atomic warhead exploded to power the x-ray lasers, two of them were destroyed by being too proximal to the blasts, and the third was heavily damaged. They were essentially suicide missions made on behalf of the people of Khûr, even though you were not members of the Array."

"None survived?" Kamozh asked after a moment.

"None," the envoy replied softly. "The crew of the third ship were unable to make sufficient repairs to their craft. It drifted through the system. We found it in orbit around the outermost planet when we were finally able to get another mission to Khûr."

"Why did you not contact us then?" Kamozh demanded.

"*Rhan*, it had been twenty of your years. Your people had withdrawn behind a shell. You would not have received us then, just as you will not receive us now. The very few times we've allowed one of your patrols to glimpse one of our ships, they've been attacked. Every time. With no attempt to communicate. Just as the ships of Director Caitlin Kralik were attacked. So tell me, what should we have done?"

Kamozh had no answer for that question. He could tell, however, that the envoy had more to say, little though he wanted to hear it, so he signed **<speak>**.

"It took us twenty years, because every time we

thought to send someone your way, we had to deal with the Veldt first. We lost two fleets in dealing with their followup expeditions, and another in gaining access to their inner system. We were, in the end, forced to treat them as they had treated you, only more so. A large asteroid from their outer cometary shell was converted to a bolide, and launched on their planet. The descent was devastating. The entire culture was destroyed. We were unable to locate survivors, although we continued to observe for generations."

Kamozh was horrified. The monsters could bring themselves to murder a species, to murder a planet? How could they stand in the light of day after doing so? How could they claim to be cultured?

"We came as soon as we could," D'mishri concluded, "but it takes a long time to move from star to star, you see. We have maintained an overwatch here since then."

Kamozh said nothing. His mind was whirling.

Shemnarai again raised up and signed **<truth>**. "I have traveled to the Veldt system," she said. "I have seen the planet. It is as the captain has said."

". . . it takes a long time to move from star to star, you see," Lim translated. Caitlin heard the words, but only understood their import after a beat. "Wait!" she hissed as Lim started to carry on. "Say that again!"

"We came as soon as we could, but it takes a long time to move from star to star, you see," Lim repeated.

Caitlin looked around in a hurry. Ed and Gabe were as wide-eyed as she felt, and the Jao were mostly showing angles for variations of *shock*. Even Aille and Tura's *neutral* angles were slipping a bit.

"Not a word!" she hissed. "Not one freaking word until we're alone."

She looked back at Kamozh and the envoys. The Khûrûsh-an seemed to be drooping. She could imagine the shock he was undergoing.

"D'mishri, Shemnarai," she said, "may we suggest that you be given an opportunity to visit the quarters you have been assigned to freshen up, and to give *Rhan* Kamozh an opportunity to assimilate the information you have given him."

The protocol officer rumbled and made a sign. "We are late in our day cycle, Director Caitlin Kralik. Might I suggest we resume in nine Khûrûsh hours, so that we might attain some rest?"

"Agreed," Caitlin said. She tapped a signal on her com pad, and Caewithe Miller opened the door. "Captain Miller, please see to it that all our guests are shown to their quarters, please."

It took a few moments to get sufficient Lleix aligned with the groups to make sure that communications could be had, but before long the door irised shut behind them all.

Caitlin immediately said, "Did everyone catch that last bit?" She looked around the room.

No one responded, until Ed spoke up. "You say it."

Caitlin took a deep breath.

"They don't have an FTL drive."

CHAPTER 50

Ninth-Minor-Sustained beckoned to Third-Mordent. She stepped up beside the harmony master, and gazed out through the observation point.

The great room below had been formed by collapsing walls and decks between various rooms, creating a much larger open space than Third-Mordent had believed was available in the station. She was impressed by the flexibility of the design and construction that permitted such an action, and she sang as much in a short motif.

"This is one of the six largest stations the Complete Harmony maintains," Ninth-Minor-Sustained intoned. "And I believe that none of the other three major factions possess one as large, although it would be difficult to verify that with the Interdict. Very insular, they are."

"Yet there are Interdict below, are there not?" Third-Mordent intoned.

"Sufficient so that I have had to clear the servients

from the space and the adjacent corridors," the harmony master responded. "They have already completed thirty-six of the Trīkē."

Third-Mordent was surprised the count was that low. The Interdict's ban on servients of any type was known to be absolute.

"How many?" she returned to her motif.

"Seventy-two . . . no, seventy-seven ships," Ninth-Minor-Sustained intoned, consulting a readout panel on the adjacent wall. "Four hundred sixty-nine harmony masters, assistants, attendants, progeny, and ship captains from all four major factions and at least eleven subfactions. The ichor should start flowing soon."

It was as if it had been choreographed in a great dance. At that moment, Third-Mordent could see two females in the great room unsheathe their forehand blades and slash away at each other. One was obviously better than the other, and completed her foe in a span of heartbeats.

"I expected better than that from a member of True Harmony," Ninth-Minor-Sustained whisper-sang in dirge mode. "Yet if her skills were no better than that, better that she be completed so that she would not pass her heritage on to descendants. The race is improved."

"How can they not have FTL?" Gabe Tully demanded. "The Jao have it. The Ekhat have it. They've been in space for thousands of years. Why don't they?"

"The framepoint drive is dependent upon the proper understanding of what even humans find to be one very abstruse equation of gravitics," Pleniary-superior Tura said quietly. "If they have not developed gravitics theory and technology, or if they have not formulated that equation, then that would explain it.

"The Jao inherited it from the Ekhat. No one knows if they developed it themselves or took it from predecessors. The number of faster-than-light civilizations we have encountered otherwise can be numbered on the digits of one paw." She held up a hand accordingly. "And of those, only the Lleix have survived contact with the Jao, if barely and only through the agency of Terra taif. The mathematical odds of a species developing FTL technologies and prospering because of it do not seem favorable."

There was a moment of silence. Most of the Jao had adopted angles reflecting a theme of *shocked-disbelief*. The humans all had a stunned "deer in headlights" look—including, Caitlin was sure, herself.

"That's just hard to believe," Ed said. "How can they control four thousand inhabited stars with only slower-than-light transport and communications?"

"They don't," Aille said. "Remember what the envoy said: this Eleusherar Path is a metagovernment. They are facilitators. They specialize in spreading information, ideas, and designs, and occasionally people; not hardware or cargo."

Ed nodded. "For a mail run, they wouldn't even necessarily have to slow down. If they're hitting .6c or so, it would be wasteful to decelerate. But if a system could compress their data hard enough, they could squirt data packages to an oncoming ship with a laser, and could receive new data the same way."

"Indeed," Wrot said. "They would have enough time to send redundant copies, to make sure that nothing was lost in the transmission or reception. Both ways."

"Pony Express to the stars," Caitlin heard Gabe mutter, which made her laugh.

"So they're basically mailmen, with one big rule and a big hammer to enforce it," Ed continued. "How big is this Eleusherar Array? Any guesses?"

"I don't know," Caitlin said, "but I know who probably does." She touched her com pad. "Chulan? Helot? We need you in my main conference room immediately."

D'mishri looked to Shemnarai after the door to their quarters irised shut behind them. "Well," he said, "that wasn't what I expected."

"Why?" the Khûrûsh-en replied. "I knew as soon as I saw some of their Khûrûsh guests among the welcoming party that these questions would arise. I will admit, however, that I am a bit surprised at how quickly they came up."

"We were making progress before that interruption, though," the captain said. "I really want to know who or what the Ekhat are, if the primary purpose of their metagovernment is to combat them."

"I really want to know," Shemnarai said, running her forehands through the fur on her head, "why they all reacted strongly to something you said in your response to *Rhan* Kamozh."

"All of them?"

"All but two of those huge Jao, the ones called Aille and Tura, I think. They all jerked and looked at each other, and Director Caitlin Kralik said something fast that their translator didn't translate. And right after that is when she suggested we take a rest break."

D'mishri thought back to the last few minutes of the discussion. "Hmm. You're right. I didn't pick up on it then because I was focused on the *Rhan*, but they definitely did react. And it was late in the conversation, too. Do you think it was the description of the bolide strike on Veldayar?"

"Maybe," Shemnarai said. "The only other thing you mentioned was how long it took to get our mission here accomplished. But that's so mundane. The speed of light is the speed of light, after all. Why would they be reacting to that?"

Kamozh stalked into the common room of his quarters, trailed by Shekanre. The others took one look at him—fur bristling, eyes narrowed, lips curled and claws extended—and scrambled to their feet, looking behind him and all around for danger.

"Out!" Kamozh snarled. "I need to think, and I don't need you distracting me. Find another place to be—now! And that goes for you as well," he looked back over his shoulder at Shekanre.

The weapons master made an **<at your command>** gesture, but said nothing as he walked past and gathered the other retainers. They exited into the short corridor on the other side of the room, leaving Kamozh as alone as he desired.

Kamozh looked around, picked up a pillow, and began systematically dismantling it.

The retainers gathered in the room where four of them slept. It was the next largest space in their quarters.

"What happened?" Murerhukha asked in an almost-whisper. "Why is the *Rhan* so angry? He's not mad at us, is he?"

"No," Shekanre replied. "He's just like his father, *Rhan* Mezhen, when he's faced with a challenge. He's heard some things today that are really hard to understand. He needs to make sense out of them, and quickly. But whatever he does with them, it's going to change how he sees our world forever. I think he sees that already, and I don't think he likes it."

• • •

The conference room door irised open, and Chulan and Helot, the two members of the Starsifters *elian* entered. Conversation ceased immediately, and the two Lleix seemingly stepped into a pool of silence. Neither seemed to react; but Caitlin saw Chulan's fingers tense for a moment on the folds of his robe, so she would have bet that they were sensitive to that unusual silence.

"Glad you could join us so quickly," Caitlin said. "We have a question for you in your role as Starsifters."

The two Lleix bowed slightly. "One hopes that we can answer your question as easily as you ask it," Chulan said.

"The envoys that we are hosting said that they represent an organization of approximately four thousand systems. How large a volume would that be?"

"We do not have firm data for this," Helot said. "Any answer we give would be only an estimate."

"Understood," Caitlin said. "Do your best."

Helot pulled out his com pad, fingered the controls, and showed the results to Chulan, who nodded. Helot looked back toward Caitlin. "Using a baseline assumption that approximately three percent of stars have planets that are potentially habitable by oxygen breathing life, that would require a volume of approximately 1.5 million light-years."

"Woof," Gabe said. "That's a pretty big space."

Chulan looked to him. "How large that space would be would depend on its configuration. At a minimum, it would have to be . . ." Helot handed him the com pad, and he glanced at it ". . . a cube 114 light-years long and wide and high, or a sphere with a diameter of approximately 142 light-years."

"Or it could be in the shape of a fried egg, not very tall but way spread out," Caitlin said.

"Or an angry octopus," Gabe said with a grin, "with arms going every which way."

"Exactly," Caitlin said. She turned to Tura. "How large a volume does the Jao controlled region make up?"

"I'm not sure that the Bond has considered that," the Bond officer replied.

"Guess."

Tura tilted her head slightly, letting the *neutral* angles soften for a moment. She appeared to be considering something. At length, she said, "As you say, a guess. Perhaps 400,000 cubic light-years."

Tully had his com pad out now. "Five hundred systems in 400,000 versus four thousand systems in 1.5 million. Our density is much less than theirs. How come?"

"The Ekhat," Aille said, "and the Frame Network."

Gabe frowned, then said, "Right. The Ekhat have 'purified' so many worlds that the options and the seed stock available to us are considerably reduced. But the FTL drive? How does that figure?"

"Because we can jump from peak to peak," Wrot said, "instead of having to slog through the valley step by step. We can spread farther faster, bypassing the destroyed systems."

Caitlin saw Gabe chewing on that thought. "Okay," she said, "until we get more data, like a star map, we're not going to know just how widespread this Eleusherar Array really is. But for now, I think we'd better assume that the volume is pretty spread out."

"Agreed," Aille said. Tura nodded in confirmation.

"So," Caitlin steeled herself to face the most important question, "do we tell them about the Frame-Point Network?"

CHAPTER 51

"The moment nears completion," Ninth-Minor-Sustained sang. "Two thousand seven hundred and fifty-seven Ekhat convocate. Seven hundred and thirteen ships from the four major factions and twenty-three subfactions. This is the largest convocation since that in which the True Harmony separated from the Complete Harmony."

Third-Mordent looked through the observation window. The great room had been expanded further, but the crush of bodies that could be viewed was still great and intense. It seemed like every few moments forehand blades were being bared, and more often than not, the tegument of those in sight from the window had crusted ichor marking slashes.

"Is there a place for us in all this?" she sang to the harmony master. "Is there a target for our aim, our blades?"

"Soon we will descend," Ninth-Minor-Sustained fluted. "Soon we will begin the work to purify the stars of those who removed Descant-at-the-Fourth and her daughters from the Melody."

At that moment, the panel on the wall rang a tone. The harmony master raised a manipulator, touched a pad, and read the glyphs that scrolled across the screen.

"We will descend now," Ninth-Minor-Sustained sang in staccato ascending tones. "Information control I promised to show you; information control you shall witness."

She led the way toward the outer door. "Stay with me," she intoned. "Watch those around us with care, especially those from Complete Harmony factions. They will have most to gain in the short run if we are disadvantaged." They swept through the opened outer door, into the corridor, and down to the bank of lifts at the end. "Leave confrontations to me. Do not show your blades unless they attack you directly."

Third-Mordent moved at the side of her ancestress. She uttered no sound; her mind was split at the moment: focused on the matters at hand for the most part, while a theme was teasing her, a theme that promised complexity and scope.

The lift door irised open, and the cacophony filling the great room bludgeoned its way into the lift. There was precious little harmony in it, and little that resembled melody. The tumultuous vociferations bordered on pure dissonance, and Third-Mordent wondered how Ninth-Minor-Sustained could proceed into it with evident dispassionate advertence.

"Control," Ninth-Minor-Sustained whisper-sang before she moved. Third-Mordent schooled herself before she stirred a foot to follow the harmony master.

A bubble of space and not-noise seemed to move with Ninth-Minor-Sustained, Third-Mordent observed.

Almost immediately she started hearing whisper-songs from all around; some from far enough out in the milling bodies that they were hard to detect; some from close enough that they were very clear.

"...great harmony master...best Complete Harmony has had for a hundred generations...stay out...way..."

"...do not challenge her or any of hers. No one has survived for generations..."

"...who is that with her..."

"...do not know, but moves just like her...deadly..."

That last was a bit louder than the rest. Third-Mordent bent her gaze in that direction for a moment, and changed the angle of her outside forehand blade sheath for just that moment.

"...see..." came the barest whisper of a song.

Third-Mordent returned her gaze forward and drew herself into the most controlled mind, feeling it settle in all her ganglionic centers, feeling the edge it gave her; the predator movement without descending into predator mode. Those around her moved away, not scrambling, but pressing against the crowd to make space for the death on six legs that they saw, almost as if it were an aura; more than even the harmony master gave, if she had only known it.

Third-Mordent uttered nothing as time passed. She moved at the side of Ninth-Minor-Sustained, listening as harmony masters and captains approached her ancestress one by one and exchanged melodies with her. Always she was sensitive to those around them, and although she never even gave the barest glimpse of a forehand blade edge, if it seemed that others would press too close on one side or another, she would slip to that side. She never faced any Ekhat down, but the sight of the essence of predator standing to their fore—unfrenzied, totally aware, yet all the more deadly because of that—caused every proximal Ekhat to discover the virtue of restraint and the wisdom to avoid confrontation.

Seventh-Flat was the first to approach directly, large enough that she could be seen stalking through the mass. There were yelps and screams in her wake, as those who were pushed aside encountered others who would make no way for them. More ichor flowed, yet the mass parted before her and none would raise a blade to her.

Third-Mordent thought she understood why Seventh-Flat approached. As a major subfaction leader in the Complete Harmony faction, she knew and was known by Ninth-Minor-Sustained. They were not allies; not at all. Yet the younger leader might consider common cause in this most unusual of circumstances. As Ninth-Minor-Sustained had noted, it had been long generations since a convocation of this magnitude had taken place. It occurred to Third-Mordent that none might be alive who had been there. So both might be somewhat disquieted at what might occur, and both might consider common cause; it would likely serve neither well for the Complete Harmony to lose standing or prominence.

"Jao?" Seventh-Flat intoned when she at last stood before Ninth-Minor-Sustained.

The harmony master did not reply for a moment. Seventh-Flat lowered her head a bit. Third-Mordent moved a shoulder, bringing the sheath of a forehand blade to a different angle. Seventh-Flat shifted her direct gaze to Third-Mordent.

"It might be rewarding to know," Ninth-Minor-Sustained sang soliloquy form, "what losses the Melody has suffered in their *Ghemeilien* sector coreward."

Seventh-Flat went still. Ninth-Minor-Sustained sang nothing more; simply stalked past the lesser leader. Third-Mordent made no sound of her own as she glided past Seventh-Flat, but she made certain that her balance was perfect, and she listened with care to everything that occurred behind her.

The pattern continued. To a captain, Ninth-Minor-Sustained intoned, "Consider that Complete Harmony lost two squadrons, a World Harvester, and a planetary base in *Aleif* sector spinward." To an Interdict leader she sang, "The Jao threaten the attainment of the Melody more than all other corruptions combined." To a Melody faction master Ninth-Minor-Sustained did an arietta, "The Interdict will threaten you more than the Jao." To a True Harmony faction master, she used an arioso mode, "The Jao have a new resource. What is it?" And to another Complete Harmony faction leader, she whisper-sang, "Have you viewed a map lately?"

There were others. Third-Mordent observed as the harmony master progressed through the great space, never staying long in once place, seemingly never retracing a path, and always—always—giving information to whoever approached her, but never the same piece of information, and never the same emphasis.

The change happened slowly, almost subtly. Third-Mordent watched it happen, almost without recognizing what she was seeing.

CHAPTER 52

The fleet representatives for the discussions with the envoys had been trimmed by directorial fiat. Dannet and Mallu returned to their fleet duties. Caitlin kept Gabe Tully and Ed for the humans, Aille, Tura, Wrot, and Yaut for the Jao, and added Ramt from Ekhatlore *elian*. Pyr and Lim would join her as representatives for the Lleix.

"Before we get started," Caitlin began, "Ramt, it was decided yesterday that we're not going to voluntarily reveal the existence of the Frame-Point Network and faster-than-light travel, so please be careful how you phrase any statements or answers to questions you make."

"You are lying to them?" Ramt asked, concern evident in her posture and the lifting of her aureole.

"No," Caitlin said, "we'll play fair. If they ask, we will tell the truth. We're simply not going to make it easy for them."

"Ah." Ramt tilted her head as she considered that.

She said nothing more, but the lowering of her aureole indicated she accepted that position.

"Anyone have any second thoughts about our FTL decision yesterday? Last chance," Caitlin said. No one said anything, although Gabe frowned. He apparently was still of the opinion that the allies needed to keep the existence of FTL travel from the envoys, but had nothing more to say about it than he had yesterday.

"Right," Caitlin said.

Kamozh heard a slight whisper of sound, and looked up to see Shekanre standing in the door to the rear corridor. The weapons master said nothing; simply looked at his commander and clan head, who sighed and displayed **<enter>** with his left forehand.

Shekanre stepped forward and allowed the door to close behind him. He looked around, at the shreds of cloth and stuffing and furniture scattered around the room. "Like father, like son," he murmured.

"What?" Kamozh said, not certain he had heard correctly.

"The clan gardeners at the clanhome despaired when your father was faced with major decisions and challenges. He would wander through the gardens while pondering, and you could trace his path by the shredded vegetation and trees. There was one year where he had three problems in two months. He managed to kill a mature maomem tree by the end of his consideration of the third."

"Is that what happened?" Kamozh said, drawn out of his state of mind. "I was rather young. I do remember when the tree was replaced almost overnight, but I don't remember anyone telling me why."

Shekanre chuckled. "That was because *Rhan* Mezhen had gouged the trunk of the tree so deeply during his deliberations that at the end the gardeners had despaired of the tree even surviving, much less being presentable in the garden again. I'm not sure a couple of the senior gardeners ever forgave him for that." He chuckled again. "It was a beautiful tree."

Looking around the room again, Shekanre added, "Compared to that, you are restraint personified." He looked back at Kamozh. "So, do you know what you are going to do?"

"Perhaps," Kamozh sighed. "What we were told fits well with what we know of the culminating events of those times. And their explanation is very plausible. But..."

"But there is the question of why a Khûrûsh-en—an unknown Khûrûsh-en—sits beside a monster of the outer dark as if they are well known to each other, and why she wears the crest of Clan Isha, which died out two hundred years ago."

"Yes," Kamozh said, brows lowering and lip curling, "there is that."

The door signal sounded.

Kamozh and his weapons master companion had barely settled into their places next to Lim when the door to the conference room irised open and Pyr ushered the envoys through to the seats they had occupied in the earlier session. He then took his position beside Lim.

D'mishri and Shemnarai both gave what amounted to formal nods before they settled themselves. The felinoid opened the conversation, beating Caitlin to the punch by literally a split second. "Good morning to you, Director Caitlin Kralik and your associates," Lim translated. "We are pleased to be able to resume our enlightening conversations with you."

Gabe coughed into his fist, obviously making a nonverbal comment on the apparent gladhanding of the envoys.

"And good morning to you, D'mishri and Shem-narai," Caitlin responded. "And please, if you will, just call me Caitlin. Using my title and full name is a bit cumbersome for you, and to be honest, a bit wearying for me."

"As you direct, Caitlin," D'mishri said with another nod.

"Picking up where we left off yesterday," Caitlin began, "I believe it was your turn with a question."

"Ah, yes," D'mishri said. "Let us go back to the answer you gave yesterday, that the primary purpose of your metagovernment is to lead the struggle against the Ekhat. Who or what is the Ekhat? Please provide sufficient detail for us to gain a reasonably full understanding."

"Anticipating your question," Caitlin said with a grin, "I have asked Ramt, our leading expert on the Ekhat, to respond."

"This," Ramt said as she fingered a control on her com pad, "is an Ekhat." A holographic projection of an adult Ekhat appeared in the center of the room. It began to rotate slowly to give everyone a view of all sides of the creature. "They are highly intelligent, and possess technology which is among the most advanced of which we are aware. They are also, by our standards, not so much insane as unsane. They cannot even be mapped into our understandings of sanity and mental makeup and capacity."

Ramt tapped her com pad, and a hologram of a human joined the projection to provide perspective and scale. Both the felinoid and all three Khûrûsh reacted to that. After a moment, during which he looked at Gabe and Ed, then back to the hologram, D'mishri said, "Large."

"Very," Ramt added. "By our standards: vicious, violent, depraved, destructive. Their stated racial goal, supported by every member of their race, is the elimination of all non-Ekhat life from the universe. We know they have formed factions due to differing opinions on how that may be accomplished, which has led to some apparent rivalry, which in turn is probably why their destruction has not been absolute in our region. They are guilty of genetic and chattel slavery, genocide of sapient species, and systematic elimination of planetary biome, both lithic and aquatic, across a huge swath of our home region. The available records are admittedly incomplete, but we can trace their assaults back over thousands of years and can identify over seven hundred systems that have been sterilized at a planetary level. How many have been so treated in regions beyond ours is unknown, and almost unthinkable."

"Our three races," Caitlin said, "Jao, Lleix, and humans, have banded together for self-protection and self-defense against the Ekhat. And yes, to you Khûrûsh, this is a race that is unfortunately worthy of being called monsters."

"Hard to believe," D'mishri said.

Ramt tapped her com pad again, and the hologram

was replaced with an image of a destroyed world. "In this fleet's explorations," she said, "we located over sixty worlds that had been rendered lifeless; like this one, scoured to bare rock."

Caitlin watched as the envoys and Kamozh and Shekanre observed the presentation. They obviously grappled with this information. The envoys seemed to struggle with it more, perhaps because of their charge to protect worlds. The two native Khûrûsh, because of their history, were more inclined to think the worst of everyone and everything beyond the limits of their own planet.

At length, D'mishri said, "If what you say is true, then there is a sentient species that is truly evil in the universe."

CHAPTER 53

Third-Mordent became aware of small knots of Ekhat forming in the throng, coalescing frequently around one or more of those who had approached Ninth-Minor-Sustained. She attempted to keep them under observation, but the harmony master continued to wend her way through the great room, which meant that these groups would fade from her vision as masses of other Ekhat occluded them. But then, other such groups would come into view as they progressed.

Some of the knots only lasted for moments, dispersing as the members pointed in different directions and moved away. Others maintained their existence, drifting with some unmeasured tide, with bodies leaving and joining.

Those who lasted more than a few moments became nexuses of a sort. Third-Mordent wished that she was back up at the observation point, where she could have an overhead view of the tides and currents among the mass of Ekhat in the great room. But even where she was, she could see patterns emerging: smaller nexuses absorbing and spinning off bodies representing the ganglia, sending messages throughout the room; while larger nexuses represented bodies and limbs, poised to take action as their masses increased.

"The Jao!"

"The Jao!"

"The Jao!"

"The Jao!"

That refrain began to increase from around the great room. But it was no echo, no reverberation. It was the sound of many Ekhat voices intoning, some quietly at first, but increasingly louder and louder. There was no unison to it; rather, a constant susurrus, not unlike the scream of a plasma ball entering atmosphere.

"The Complete Harmony sabotaged the attainment of the Melody by uplifting the Jao!"

That was shrieked by, ironically enough, a leader of the Melody faction. She was ranting in imprecatory style to anyone who would listen to her. Here and there in the room, Third-Mordent could hear that theme being taken up. Yet Ninth-Minor-Sustained seemingly ignored it. Third-Mordent tried to grasp why, but that motif was eluding her.

The cacophony in the room splintered, as various themes began to emerge. The harmony thus engendered danced the blade's edge of discordant without—quite—falling.

"The Jao are nothing!" This time it was an Interdict master who used an aria form to sing out over the top of every voice near her. "We need only track them to their lairs like the subsentients they are!"

And another: "It is the Interdict who risks the success of the Melody!" This was a True Harmony voice.

Third-Mordent was unable to track all the accusations and attacks. She abandoned listening and watched instead.

"We find little to choose between you," Kamozh said, both midhands signing **<foreboding>**. "But I will grant you that even those who assailed us so long ago did not seem to be such demons of destruction."

Kamozh turned to Caitlin. "I wish to ask a question of your other guests, Director Kralik."

She nodded to him. "Go ahead, *Rhan* Kamozh."

He faced back to the envoys. "If you have been in the Khûr system for as long as you say you have, and if you know our history as well as you indicate you do, I presume you are aware of the decree of Khûr-melkh Sheshahng who banned all contact between the Khûrûsh and any who come from outside our system." He didn't phrase it as a question, but D'mishri gave an understandable version of **<assent>** with his left hand. "Then I suspect you will understand why my question is: how is it that Shemnarai, who appears to be a Khûrûsh-en of some beauty, sits before us as an envoy of your Eleusherar Path, while wearing the crest of a clan that died out over two hundred years ago? Feel free to drown me in detail. I await your answer with an appetite."

Kamozh settled back on his haunches, waiting for he wasn't sure what, other than it was certain to be quite a story. He felt Shekanre beside him almost quivering with curiosity.

D'mishri looked to Shemnarai and said nothing; simply gave her **<speak>**.

Everyone appeared to be gazing at Shemnarai. Kamozh certainly was, with a certain amount of intensity and hunger. There was a long moment of silence, after which she descended from her seat and rose to stand on her hind feet.

Before she spoke, Shemnarai gave a very complex bow to Kamozh, one he had only seen in formal court settings. She finished with all four hands signing **<honor to the clan lord>**.

"Let me first set your mind at rest, *Rhan* Kamozh: I am as much a Khûrûsh as you." She gave him **<utter truth>** with all four hands. "Cut me, and I will bleed Khûrûsh red. Wound me, and my tears will be as Khûrûsh salt. I am as good a daughter to Khûr as you are a son. I am not a demon of the outer dark in Khûrûsh guise. Nor am I a slave of the Eleusherar Path, but rather a willing member and supporter."

Shemnarai began to pace back and forth between Kamozh and D'mishri. "We always knew we would have to give an accounting of ourselves to the homeworld one day, and we have looked forward to it since the beginning. But this isn't exactly how I thought it would happen." She waved a forehand at the surroundings.

"The short answer to your question, *Rhan* Kamozh, is that ships of the Eleusherar Path have been in our system for almost four hundred years. And in that time, one of the things they have done until relatively recently, is when a Khûrûsh spacecraft experienced difficulties, they would gather round and, if no other recourse was available, they would rescue the crew from that ship before they died.

"The first time they did that was when the clanship *Il'Shan Tuo* disappeared almost three hundred years ago. The eldest son and *Rhan's* heir of Clan Isha was the captain. The crew was on a mission to found the first base within the major asteroid belt. Unfortunately, they experienced an engine malfunction that veered them off course, and before they could shut it down and regain their original heading, the ship grazed a moderate-sized asteroid, which damaged it severely and sent them spiraling even farther off course."

Kamozh watched as Shemnarai stopped and used all four hands to make the complex **<honor to the worthy>**. "The damage to *Il'Shan Tuo* was severe. The surviving crew were unable to make repairs to either propulsion or communications before they were so low on air that they were about to die. It was at that moment that a large ship appeared and took the wreckage of the clanship aboard."

Shemnarai's hands signed **<unlooked-for fortune>**. "It took some doing on the part of the Eleusherar Path crew, but they finally convinced Captain Nefreptah to open the wreckage up and allow the crew survivors to emerge."

Her hands shifted smoothly to **<unlooked-for survival>**. "The Path attempted to return the survivors to Khûr. They contacted the space force headquarters. The only reply they received was, 'There are no survivors of the disaster that overtook clanship *Il'Shan Tuo*.' And when an Eleusherar Path ship attempted to approach a Khûrûsh ship, it was fired upon until it left the area."

<Duty beyond death> was the sigil Shemnarai's hands now crafted. "The Path was willing to attempt to sneak the survivors onto the surface of Khûr. It would have been an almost suicidal mission, because even if they managed to penetrate the orbits and atmosphere to land safely, they would have almost certainly been detected when they attempted to leave. Captain Nefreptah would not allow that. By then the survivors had heard the story you were told yesterday, and more, they had seen some of the evidence that the Eleusherar Path could present. Captain Nefreptah said the following."

Shemnarai raised both forehands, and with one digit touched a control on a wristband on the other arm. A voice was heard in the conference room, deep and resonant for all that it was coming from a tiny speaker.

"We will not allow brave people to sacrifice themselves for no just cause. You have given us sanctuary, at a time where our Khûr-melkh has cast us out. We will not see you trade your lives for what would be at best a few days of our walking the surface of Khûr and breathing its air. We would be found out, and under the declaration you have already heard we would be executed. No, our new friends, no. You have declared that you ride the outer reaches to provide some measure of protection to our people. Let us ride with you. Let us mount the ramparts alongside you, for although our world calls us dead, we will be faithful to our duty even so. Though they know it not, their estranged sons and daughters will defend them from beyond the grave."

The recording came to an end; the voice fell silent. A moment later, so did Lim's quiet translation. The silence extended for a space. At length, Kamozh stirred. He took to the floor and raised to his hind feet, matching Shemnarai's posture, and his four hands returned to her **<honor to the worthy>**, with an emphatic cough. Beside him he felt more than heard Shekanre come to the same posture. They held it for a slow twelve count, then released it.

Kamozh pointed to the Clan Isha crest around Shemnarai's neck. "Captain Nefreptah?"

"My ancestor."

He gave to her the full honor of the *Rhan's Greeting*, given only from *Rhan* to *Rhan*.

CHAPTER 54

There was a large flat display on one wall of the great room. Third-Mordent had noted it when she had followed Ninth-Minor-Sustained out of the lift. It showed two different colored patterns which overlaid and interlaced each other. It took her a moment to recognize that the larger pattern in pure white was a notional map of the Ekhat Frame Network. With that clue, she arrived at the assumption that the smaller pattern in the ugly harmony-shattering flat yellow lights must be a similar map of the Jao network. For a moment, she was surprised—it seemed larger than she remembered from her last view of such a presentation.

As she turned away from that observation, Third-Mordent noticed that more and more of the mass were looking toward the display. She turned her attention back to those around them, still sensitive to movements toward Ninth-Minor-Sustained, but also looking at where they were focused.

At that moment, Ninth-Minor-Sustained stepped

close beside her and whisper-sang for her ears alone, "It begins. Observe."

Two more yellow lights appeared in the map at that moment, making a long narrow protrusion well past the rim of the white lights. There was a pause in the great room, as if everyone present had inhaled at the same time.

The voices erupted again, even more frenzied than before, and this time their motifs were edged. Aria strove with arioso strove with stretto strove with fugata. Harmonies towered in one moment, to slide and collapse the next. Marcato struggled against staccato against martellato. The transition of themes as Third-Mordent turned her head bordered on vertigo.

"Jao . . ." "Jao . . ." "Jao . . ." "Jao . . ."

Third-Mordent began to hear that name again, from all directions, intoned, whisper-sung, pushed, restrained, more and more voices at every moment. Every time she moved, the web of sound and song shifted, as if it were draped around her, constantly moving. She began to feel sensations of contact with her tegument, yet when she looked, all near her were pressing against each other to avoid her.

"Ah," Ninth-Minor-Sustained breathed in a single tone. Third-Mordent immediately focused her perceptions in the direction the harmony master was facing. One of the main doors to the great space had been opened, and there were swirls and eddies in the mass before it.

"Some are leaving," Third-Mordent whisper-sang. "Do I need to halt them?"

"Observe," the harmony master breathed again.

The movements among the mass were larger, and

the swirls were beginning to merge into a tide. And again, agitated Ekhat were not accepting of others. Forehand blades began to flash again. Fresh sprays of ichor began to decorate nearby walls, the floor, and the hides of any who passed in close range of the impromptu blade dances.

Another main door was opened, and within three notes a major portion of the mass began to flow that direction as well.

A third door opened, with similar results.

It wasn't much longer before there were only some few of the Complete Harmony Ekhat still in the great room. Well, not counting several completed Ekhat lying in puddles of ichor here and there.

One of the remaining Ekhat approached Ninth-Minor-Sustained. Third-Mordent said nothing, made no overt moves, but returned to the hypervigilance that had been her mode since she had left the lift.

Seventh-Flat paused some distance away from Ninth-Minor-Sustained. To Third-Mordent's perceptions, Seventh-Flat was tensed, controlled, but there was a hint of red in her eyes and her head kept lowering just a bit. Third-Mordent did not take her eyes off of the faction leader.

The harmony master sang nothing. Her posture was composed. Seventh-Flat confronted her, yet Ninth-Minor-Sustained did not accept the confrontation. Third-Mordent could tell that Seventh-Flat, despite her tension and her hints at predator mode, was also increasingly uncertain.

The silence was finally broken. "Why?" Seventh-Flat intoned in almost staccato whole tones rapidly ascending. "Why now?"

Ninth-Minor-Sustained made no response; simply stood before the younger faction leader. After a moment, Seventh-Flat bared the merest edge of one forehand blade, then spun and hurtled through the nearest door.

"What just occurred?" Third-Mordent finally asked her mentor.

"Just a few moments ago, everyone here learned that the Jao have become much more dangerous to us. They have found a path to the next galactic arm."

Third-Mordent's mind spun, and she looked over her shoulder at the display panel that was still showing the Frame Network maps. Of course, that was what that extension of yellow meant. If her focus had not been on the Ekhat around her, she would have realized it herself. "And?"

Ninth-Minor-Sustained shifted to arioso mode, a descending motif, "This will stir all the factions. And some . . . many . . . will seek them out. Either they will succeed, in which case the Jao will return to their previous prey status; or the Jao will complete them, which will tell us something about the Jao, and reduce the number of those who contest with us." The harmony master flashed her forehand blades open for a moment, then returned them to their sheaths.

"And Seventh-Flat?" Third-Mordent intoned.

Ninth-Minor-Sustained turned and led the way to the lift. "Several cycles ago, her subfaction sent a fleet of eight cruisers to a new system that the Jao had invested. None returned. It was all but one of the ships her faction possessed. They requested reinforcement from the harmony masters in order to make a fresh, larger assault. The resources of the major subfactions were fully committed at that time, and the harmony masters denied the request."

Third-Mordent almost stopped at that revelation. In the mildest of arias, Ninth-Minor-Sustained had revealed to her why Seventh-Flat had antipathy toward Ninth-Minor-Sustained. Indeed, she was surprised that the younger leader had not bared her blades and attacked just now.

When she sang that to Ninth-Minor-Sustained, the harmony master sang a negation, then continued with, "She has more control than that. You would do well to study her, both to learn and to prepare. As the Melody grows and extends, it may well bring you to face her."

They entered the lift, and the door irised shut. Ninth-Minor-Sustained tapped a control with a manipulator, and the lift began to rise. She looked to Third-Mordent. "I tell you again," she intoned, "that she is very good at control. She may well be the most dangerous of the Ekhat of her generation and aboard this station."

"Why does she not confront you, then?" Third-Mordent sang.

"She knows me too well," was the return. Third-Mordent waited, knowing there had to be more to it than that. As the lift doors irised open, Ninth-Minor-Sustained whisper-sang, "Seventh-Flat is my progeny, of Descant-at-the-Fourth's generation, but of a different line. Controlled, dangerous, sometimes subtle. What were my instructions to you earlier?"

Third-Mordent recalled them, and intoned, "To watch especially those of the Complete Harmony."

"Why?"

"Because they would have the most to gain."

They walked out of the lift, and Ninth-Minor-Sustained went to the window placed on the outside wall, where she could see the dark that surrounded the station.

"This is a cusp of the Melody," the harmony master whisper-sang. "We are at equal danger from without and within."

"The Jao . . ." Third-Mordent began.

"And Seventh-Flat, more than any others." Third-Mordent could see Ninth-Minor-Sustained regarding her in the reflection of the outer window. "Be prepared for both."

PART VII
Upon the Ramparts

CHAPTER 55

It was now day five of the conversations with the Eleusherar Path, and progress had been made. Caitlin had pled the case that she and her associates could not devote all day every day to these discussions, and the envoys had agreed to meet only in the mornings for four Khûrûsh hours. That gave them time to consider the results each afternoon, and they did stay in fairly frequent contact with their ship *Starcloud.*

Caitlin was still tap-dancing around the issue of the FTL drive, but the envoys had mostly been asking questions about societies, laws, interspecies relationships, etc. They hadn't opened the technology can of worms yet, although Caitlin was expecting it at any time.

Kamozh had been very quiet since Shemnarai's story, contributing nothing on his own initiative and only responding to questions.

"Good morning, Caitlin," D'mishri said in very stilted English, which startled her. He nodded and settled onto his seat.

"Good morning to you, D'mishri and Shemnarai," she responded. "I am surprised that you have already begun learning my language, and I apologize that I cannot return the compliment—yet."

D'mishri waved a hand in a relaxed gesture. "We are—specialists, you might say," returning to Khûrûsh. "She is a communications officer, and I am a protocol officer as well as a captain, so it is the kind of thing we do. Your Lleix are already picking up on the fundamentals of the Eleusherar Path language, and it won't be long before they will provide that to you as well."

"Nonetheless, it was gracious on your part," Caitlin said.

Losing Ramt for the past few days had put a kink in the program that she and Vikram Bannerji had laid out for working with the Trīkē captives. But he had carried on with the oh-so-eager to please beings, whom he couldn't help but like. They reminded him a lot of six-legged Labrador retrievers—or maybe more of ambulatory dolphins, given their intelligence level. He now agreed with Ramt; their captives were very intelligent. And it grieved him, in a way, to see them so . . . so . . . so *submissive*. What the Ekhat had done to them went beyond a crime, went beyond a crime against humanity (broadening the definition of the term a bit). It was an affront to God, Who- and Whatever he might be considered to be. It gave Vikram an insight to the parents and grandparents of some of his American friends that he had never possessed.

"Solvaya," he called out in Ekhat. She eeled her way out of the crowd and limped over to the ramp that led up to what Vikram thought of as "The Speaker's Box," a small platform that put the low-slung Trīkē at something closer to eye level for conversations.

"Hi, Vi-ka-rum," Solvaya said, all six feet dancing on the platform and her skin shifting around. "How can I be of use?"

"Solvaya, do you remember the other day when you told me that the masters always heard you."

All movement stopped and she ducked her head. "Yes," was the quiet answer.

"Can they hear you now?" Vikram had been wanting to ask that question since the day after that earlier conversation, but Ramt had discouraged it. She was afraid it would stir up the Trīkē again. But, Ramt wasn't here right now, and he really wanted an answer.

Solvaya's head raised up again, and she stared at him, black eyes glistening just as much as her hide did. "I do not know. I will find out."

Before Vikram could stop her, she barked a phrase at her fellows in their native tongue, which Vikram was not at all versed in. All the rest looked at her, and most responded with one or two syllables, then returned to what they had been doing. Vikram snorted at that. Didn't look like the question was going to be very disruptive.

One of them answered back for several seconds, the equivalent of three or four human sentences, Vikram thought. Once he was done, Vikram looked back to Solvaya.

"No."

"Do you mean no, they cannot hear you, or no, they can hear you but they cannot find you?" Vikram was pleased with that question.

"They cannot hear us," Solvaya said, looking down for a moment. But then she raised her head. "But they can find us. They can find you."

Vikram froze. His brain raced, and it took a conscious effort to begin breathing again. "What . . . what do you mean, they can find us?"

"Cortanz worked with the Jump network engine. He says that the masters can track the Jao nodes."

"They can . . . see . . . where the Jao make new Frame Points?"

"Yes."

"Oh, shit." In the back of his mind, Vikram's education railed that at such a moment of crisis, his only expostulation was so plebeian. But the rest of him ignored that as he scrambled for his com pad.

"Come on, come on," he urged the pad as it tried to connect with Caitlin Kralik's com pad. "Crocodile shit!" was his reaction when he got an *Unavailable* message.

He hit the speed dial for Colonel Tully, and started hyperventilating as he waited for a connection there. *Unavailable* came up on the screen. "Elephant shit!" he screamed, startling the Trīkē.

Vikram pulled on his hair . . . or at least he tried to, forgetting that it had been cut really short to stay out of his way when he was in a combat suit. Who could he call? The educated part of his mind was suggesting new and unusual expletives. The rest of him was still ignoring that part of his mind.

He stabbed at another number, and let out his breath in a whoosh as it connected.

"Lieutenant Buckley? Vikram Bannerji here. Listen, don't talk. I've got to get through to Colonel Tully. I got something out of the Trīkē that he and the brass need to hear ASAP, and I mean like yesterday."

"Bad karma, huh?" Buckley's voice came through on the com pad.

"So far beyond bad karma that it makes the apocalypse look like a wedding feast. Really. I lost my override key when he moved me to the prisoner interrogation detail, but since you got my old job that means you got the override key. Time to use it, old chap. Override the privacy controls and get me through to the colonel."

Buckley was silent for a moment, then said, "Okay, but if he rips me a new one over this, I'll pass it along with interest."

"Just do it!"

"Uh-oh."

Rafe Aguilera instantly appeared at the elbow of the head sensor tech on the command deck of *Trident*. Terra-Captain Domt krinnu ava Terra, formerly of Dano kochan, stood at the other elbow a split-second later.

"What do you mean, uh-oh?" Rafe said. "I don't like hearing that word on my new ship."

The sensor tech pointed at his screen and the associated readouts. "Uh-oh," Rafe echoed. He looked over at Domt. "Captain, get ready to fight your ship." He looked over at the nearest com tech. "Punch me a signal to *Lexington*, now!"

CHAPTER 56

"Ah, this isn't a question," Ed offered. "But I would like to say that your stealth technology is pretty damn sharp. That may be trade material once we get relations regularized." Pyr did the translation honors, as Lim had not arrived yet.

"We will pass your compliments on to our engineers," D'mishri replied.

"Your own stealth technology is also rather effective," Shemnarai added.

Stealth technology? What was the envoy talking about? Before Caitlin could continue that thought, Shemnarai continued.

"To have flown your fleet through our screen without any hint of its passage . . . well, let us say that it left our sensor techs feeling very low, after various officers made known their opinions of that event. In fact, the fact that you unmasked near Khûr caused several tactical officers to nearly explode."

Ed grinned. "It's good for a tac officer to have his perceptions challenged."

"Indeed," D'mishri agreed. "Reducing their complacency, whatever the cause, cannot be considered unfortunate. But as you say, before long we hope to be comparing notes about our technologies, and that will be at the top of our list."

Oh, crap. Caitlin realized what had just happened. The envoys had observed the fleet's arrival in the system, but had attributed it to masking or stealth technology in operation rather than an FTL drive. But that had caused their respective ears to perk up, and now they were going to be asking questions about it. So, ready or not, she would be revealing the existence of the Frame-Point Network before long.

Gabe frowned and pulled his com pad out of a pocket. He tapped a control, and after a couple of seconds his eyes opened wide. "Caitlin!"

"What?"

"Trouble. Big trouble." He jumped out of his chair and in three steps was handing her his com pad. "Here."

She took it and scanned the short message. Her eyes opened wide in horror, and the hair on her neck prickled.

> *Trīkē say that Ekhat can track formation of Jao Frame-Point nodes. Tell Director Kralik.*
>
> *V Bannerji*

She looked up to find all eyes in the room on her. She opened her mouth to say something, only to find herself preempted. An alarm klaxon began sounding, and the ship-wide annunciator began blaring, "All crew to battle stations. All crew to battle stations. This is not a drill."

The message repeated three times. The klaxon continued sounding, and after a moment, there was another announcement, "Director Kralik to the command deck. Director Kralik to the command deck."

Caitlin thrust the com pad back in Gabe's hands, and stood. "Right. Meeting adjourned. We're heading for the command deck, including you two." She pointed at the envoys. "I'll explain when we get there." She headed for the door, and it irised open just as she got there. "Move it, people."

The door from the lift irised open, and Caitlin led the exodus out of the lift compartment. She didn't have time for the Jao reverse status thing. A quick glance showed Lieutenant Vaughan at his workstation, hands and fingers flying like a concert pianist in the fast movement of Rachmaninoff's Third Piano Concerto. Fleet Commander Dannet and Terra-Captain Uldra were present, standing behind the sensor techs and listening to their reports.

Dannet looked up at their entrance, and stepped toward Caitlin. "What do we know, Fleet Commander?"

Dannet looked at Vaughan, and pointed at the main viewscreen which was showing a system schematic. The lower left quadrant of the screen blanked, and then was replaced with the face of Rafe Aguilera. The picture quality wasn't the best, and the tonal quality was a little uneven, but Caitlin ignored that.

"*Trident* to *Lexington*. I hope you get this right the first time, because we ain't got time to go over it again. Sensor readings now show . . . how many . . .

at least eight inbound Ekhat craft. Looks like they've found us, sure as hell. I don't know if you have any plans for that, but if you don't, I suggest you make some PDQ. We'll take out as many as we can, but this baby's untested and this testing ground is a long way from home. We'll do our best, but there's only one of us, and the odds aren't great. We'll keep updating you on the sensor reads. Aguilera out."

The message winked out and the system schematic was restored to full coverage of the screen.

"That came in by gamma ray laser from *Trident* just before we sounded the alarm," Dannet said, displaying angles for *neutral*. "What are your orders, Director?"

Caitlin looked to where Aille and Tura were standing behind Yaut and Wrot. "Governor, Pleniary-superior, do I have *oudh*?"

"You do," Aille said.

"Agreed," Tura confirmed.

Caitlin turned back to the fleet commander. "Send all ships capable of combatting the Ekhat back into the system. Focus on defending the settled planets first. Make it happen."

Dannet said nothing, but her angles flashed to *gratified-respect* before she turned and began issuing orders.

Caitlin turned to the Jao. "Lieutenant Bannerji sent Gabe a message that the Trīkē believe that the Ekhat can trace the Jao Frame-Point Network and see new nodes being added. Looks like they're right. We led them here; we can't let them destroy the Khûrûsh."

"Agreed," Aille said. Tura said nothing.

"Next," Caitlin said, turning to the envoys and Kamozh and beckoning them closer. She looked at

D'mishri. "It's not a stealth technology—it's a faster-than-light space drive, and yes, it really works. The Jao and the Lleix have been using it for a long time. Unfortunately, the Ekhat also have it, and apparently they also have something else that we didn't know about—they can identify where the Jao have set up something called 'nodes.' We'll talk about the technology and how it works later, but what you need to know is that they have apparently followed us here. Before too long, Ekhat ships are going to start boiling out of Khûr the sun, with the sole purpose of destroying every living thing in the system."

Caitlin pointed to D'mishri. "You need to call your people. If they want a chance to fight planet killers, this will be the fight of a lifetime. I hope your weapons technology is as good as your stealth technology, because we're going to need it. And I hope there's a whole lot more of you than *Starcloud*." She pointed to Pyr. "You're with him. Get him a communication link to wherever he wants."

Next Caitlin used both hands to point at Shemnarai and Kamozh. "You two need to spread the alarm in-system. Alert the Khûrûsh authorities that the worst monsters in the universe are about to come flying out of the sun. Keep telling them. Show them pictures of Ekhat ships and Ekhat monsters. Tell them they are the ultimate planet killers, that they make the Veldt look like amateurs in comparison."

Caitlin stopped for a moment. The fur around the necks of all three Khûrûsh—Kamozh, Shemnarai, and Shekanre—was bristling, their eyes were narrowed, and all twelve hands had claws extended. "Look, I'm sorry that this is happening. I know it's hard to take, especially after being victimized once already. But your civilians have got to be warned to take shelter, and your military and ships have got to be mobilized. I don't have a lot of hope that the ships can help much, but you can never tell. And try to get across to them that we're not the enemy, and neither are the Eleusherar Path. If they still want to be xenophobic and attack us after this is done, fine. We'll deal with that later. But if we don't get the Ekhat stopped, there won't be a later."

CHAPTER 57

Caitlin pointed to Garhet, and said, "You're with the Khûrûsh. Get them communication links, and start getting the word out."

Caitlin pointed at Lim and Ramt. "Lim, you're with me. Ramt, get back to Lieutenant Bannerji and see what else you can dig out of the Trīkē. Move."

After a moment, bodies stopped moving, and Caitlin looked around. Gabe Tully stepped up. "This is a fleet action. You don't need me here. I'm getting back over to *Ban Chao* with my troops before the fun begins."

Caitlin wanted to protest, but she knew he was right—that was where he needed to be—and if he didn't get there now, he wouldn't get there at all. "Okay, Gabe. But be careful."

Even as she said it, Caitlin knew how stupid that sounded. Gabe just laughed, and said, "I'm just going to be a spectator on this one, Caitlin. It's the ship drivers that need to be careful, if they can." He nodded to her and Ed, and headed toward the lift.

D'mishri came back over to her. Pyr translated, "I have passed the alert to *Starcloud*. They have already begun to spread it to all available ships."

"Good," Caitlin said, almost absent-mindedly. A thought occurred to her, and she turned to face the envoy. "I should get you a shuttle and get you back to your ship. Hang on." She reached for her com pad.

"Wait," came the word back from Pym. "I would remain here, if you will. I can give you some understanding of our ships and tactics, and you can give me some understanding of what we face."

"Good idea," Caitlin said. "Pleniary-superior," she called out to Tura and beckoned to her. When she arrived, Caitlin said, "Please give Captain D'mishri a crash course on Ekhat capabilities and tactics." Tura nodded, beckoned to Pym and D'mishri, and headed for the empty work station next to Lieutenant Vaughan's.

"And remember . . ." Rafe Aguilera began.

Terra-Captain Domt changed posture and raised a hand. Rafe didn't recognize the angle set, but he suspected it would translate to something like *time-for-the-yard-ape-to-shut-up-and-let-the-captain-take-over.*

"We know the functions, Engineer. It is my command now. Please make yourself of use by adding yourself to the engineering and damage control team." With that, Domt turned and began issuing orders to the navigator and maneuvering control crew.

She's right, Rafe thought. *You're an old tanker, not a swabbie. Let the pros handle this*. He pivoted and went to stand beside the ship's engineer, who did happen to be an ex-swabbie named Leonard Hollar.

Former Commander Hollar had been a nuclear propulsion engineer on a boomer for the US Navy in the pre-Jao days, and had proven a fast study in getting up to speed on the Jao propulsion technology.

"Rafe," that worthy said when Rafe settled in beside him.

"Lennie."

"So, we really going to get to try out *Trident* for what she was designed for?"

Rafe shrugged. "We have Ekhat incoming, so yeah, I'd say so. Unless we want to let them have a free rein in this system and destroy the people who live here."

"Not on my watch," Hollar growled.

"Yeah," Rafe said. "Mine neither."

"First vessel appearing now!" came the call from the sensor techs.

"Right," Hollar said. "Here we go. You watch the heat sink and heat transfer systems, and I'll watch propulsion and shields."

"Got it," Rafe said. "And it's show time, boys and girls," as Terra-Captain Domt began barking maneuvering orders.

Gabe Tully literally jumped through the hatch of his shuttle. The Jao crewman standing in the airlock immediately punched the controls to get the hatch closed without Tully saying anything, so he headed for the nearest seat. When one of the pilots appeared in the compartment, Tully called out, "I'm it for this trip. Get us back to *Ban Chao* now!"

The human replied, "You got it, Colonel. We'll be moving in twenty seconds."

The copilot disappeared, and that hatch closed

as well. Tully pulled out his com pad and hit one of the speed dial buttons. It took a second for the signal to get routed through *Lexington*'s and *Ban Chao*'s networks, but in a moment it pinged and showed connected.

"Shan!" Tully said.

"Yes, Colonel?" the executive officer replied.

"Troop status?"

"Buttoned down in quarters at the moment due to the battle stations announcement."

"Okay, but in case you haven't heard," Tully said, "we've got Ekhat ships incoming, at least eight, maybe more. Director Kralik has ordered the combat-effective ships back into the system to try and protect the natives. The Ekhat'll be coming in assault-style into the sun, so *Trident* will get first crack at them, but any that get by them will be up to the rest of us.

"I'm on my way back. Set up an order for the troops to gear up, but don't put a timestamp on it until after you get an estimate from the command deck as to how long it will take to get back in-system. Don't try to guess based on the time out—I suspect we'll be going back a lot faster than we came out."

The shuttle had been moving for the last thirty seconds of their conversation. Tully was about to query the pilots when his com pad pinged with a message: ETA BAN CHAO 12 MIN.

"Shuttle crew tells me I'll be back on board in less than fifteen minutes, Shan. I want at least a list of options waiting for me when I get there. Like everything else the last few months, I don't know what's coming up, but I want to be ready to respond if we get an opportunity."

"Will do, Colonel."

"Tully, out."

"*Trident* reports first Ekhat ship emerging . . . now!" announced the lead com tech on the *Lexington*'s command deck.

CHAPTER 58

Terra-Captain Domt had positioned *Trident* well, Rafe decided, as the first Ekhat ship completed materializing in the sun. She'd obviously guessed well as to the vector the ship would possess when it came through, for it was barely a half-kilometer away and moving toward them.

"Full power now," Domt ordered.

"Full power, aye," one of the human propulsion techs answered as he slid a hand up a control. Rafe snorted. *Another swabbie.*

Rafe felt—or maybe sensed was a better word—a change in the background hum of the ship. He knew the only reason that he could possibly do that was because he had been in on every step of the design and construction of *Trident*. The pre-Jao US Navy used to call the first crew of a new ship "plank owners." Navy or not, Rafe was the lead plank owner for *Trident*. He knew her better than anyone, even Lennie Hollar. So when the main engines kicked their thrust up to maximum in response to the tech's touch on the controls, he did feel it. And he had to restrain his desire to lean forward to offset the g-forces his mind knew were being exerted, even though Jao gravitics technology counterbalanced the acceleration being poured out from the mouths of the great engines.

Trident had larger and heavier engines than had ever been put on a craft built by Jao or their allies. Ever. Seriously big-ass engines, such that Rafe could see the increasing of velocity on the readouts within three seconds of the command being given, even with the sheer mass of the ram ship. *Run or die, sucker. Run or die.*

The main viewscreen had been divided into two presentations: one being the equivalent of a plot of the interior of the sun, showing the positions of both *Trident* and the Ekhat ship; and the other being a computer realization of what could be considered a camera's view of their approach toward their target.

Rafe watched, spellbound, as the image of the Ekhat grew larger and larger in the viewscreen. His hands were fisted at his sides and his jaw ached from his teeth being so clenched. It grew, and grew, and grew, until it filled the virtual camera feed completely.

The plot presentation changed suddenly, as the Ekhat seemed to suddenly understand the danger they were in and tried to veer away. But their post-jump velocity was so low they could not evade *Trident*'s final approach. Too little, too late.

The moment of impact, when it arrived, was felt—and heard—by everyone. Even given the great mass of *Trident*'s built-up forward structure, the Ekhat ship was massive enough that when *Trident* plowed into and through it, the impact resonated throughout the hull.

The Ekhat ship was not flimsy, by any stretch of the imagination. Flimsy ships wouldn't survive framepoint jumps. But compared to the mass of the purpose-built ram ship that was *Trident*, it collapsed without resistance. Rafe could hear pieces of it as they scraped down the side of the ram. The hull conducted that kind of vibration rather well.

The last of the remnants of the Ekhat ship spun away to vanish in moments in the massive heat of the star's interior. Rafe watched over the shoulder of the engineering techs as they ran through the system checks. He and Lennie Hollar exchanged evil grins, and Lennie licked a finger and drew a short vertical line in the air.

"One down."

The first of many, Rafe hoped. Terra taif had quite a score to level with the Ekhat, and they were a long way from being even.

D'mishri tilted his head to one side. "It sounds as if these Ekhat are nothing but anarchists." He waited for Pym to translate.

"Do not try to map them to anything you understand as sanity," the Jao—Tura, he thought her name was—replied through the translator. "There must be some underlying structure to their beliefs and behavior, because they have been the most dominant culture, if that word can truly be applied to them, in our part of the galaxy. But experts from more than one civilization have tried to model their behavior, and have all uniformly given up. Expect anything and everything from them."

"So your weapons load has been lasers powered from

ship power plants, and some recent experimentation and moderate success with kinetic weapons?"

"Essentially," Tura said.

D'mishri sat back, and clapped his hands together. "Then we will prove to be a surprise: a pleasant one to you and your allies, and a most unpleasant one to your foes. Let me have that communication link again."

From the small office they had commandeered with Director Kralik's authority, Shemnarai and Kamozh had sent all the data they could present quickly: warnings, pictures of Ekhat ships, pictures of Ekhat, pictures of destroyed worlds. Shemnarai had all but pleaded with the authorities. Now it was Kamozh's turn.

He faced the video pickup. Shemnarai had insisted that he present a personal message to the Khûrûsh authorities and people, as there were still those among both who would remember him.

"This message is for those who will listen to the truth. Some of you will recognize me. I am Kamozh ar Mnûresh, and until very recently I was clan heir and second in command of the clanship *Lo-Khûr-shohm*. During the recent incursion of those we call monsters, the clanship was destroyed, and with the death of my father I became *Rhan* of Clan Hoshep. I speak to you now because those who destroyed the clanship rescued the survivors. And now you will turn away, because I am to be considered as dead, by edict of Khûr-melkh Sheshahng and by tradition. But if you will not hear me alive, then for the sake of Khûr and the sake of the Khûrûsh, hear me as a voice from beyond the grave, from beyond the wall between life and death.

"The universe is wider than we have attempted to understand for almost untold generations, and it contains more than we have allowed ourselves to even dream about. Some of what it contains is wonderful, and beautiful, equaling the best of Khûr-shi. But there are also those things that are darker and more evil than anything the Khûrûsh have experienced, even during the Time of Troubles.

"It is of the last I must warn. A time of harrowing is rapidly approaching, one that could test the Khûrûsh more severely than even the Time of Troubles. Hear me, oh my fathers, oh my brothers. Send the people now to take what shelter they can find. Do not refuse, do not delay, do not ignore."

Kamozh paused for a moment, to let those words settle and perhaps sink in.

"And those of you who defend our system, arise and take flight, and face the light of Khûr, for soon from the depths of our sun, our holy light, will come a greater incursion, and one this time not bent on peaceful contact. No, this time comes the greatest of conceivable evils, a race so evil as to make our previous foes look like spoiled children; a race so evil that they would use the very holy light of Khûr itself to scour the faces of the planets until they are but sterile rock. Remember them—remember the Ekhat."

Another pause, just long enough to delineate a boundary, over which Kamozh now stepped.

"Arise, oh my fathers," the young clan-lord said, voice deepening and growing louder. "Arise, oh my brothers." Louder yet, all four hands seeming to rise palms up of their own volition. "Arise, and fly." Voice crescendoing, driving to a peak. "Mount up, oh my fathers, my brothers. Mount up and face what comes, that Khûr and the Khûrûsh, our god and our people, will know that even at this late generation there is no lack in our breed of those who will stand between the people of Khûr and the ravening darkness."

A long moment of utter silence, then Kamozh took a deep breath, and resumed in a quieter tone.

"You have but hours. Do as you will. But if you fly, know that help unlooked for may come. Do not despise it if it does. And recall what Keti-Sheri said: 'There is no truer test of an ally than if they will stand beside you in the face of your greatest foe.'

"Kamozh, *Rhan* of Clan Hoshep, out."

The light beside the video pickup winked out, indicating that it was no longer active. Kamozh dropped his hands, slumping a little, as the tension in his body released.

He started to turn, only to stop transfixed at the sight of Shekanre lying in the position of abasement, flat, limbs outspread, head curved to the right and right forehand covering the eyes.

"What are you doing, old friend," Kamozh asked quietly. "Get up. There is no reason for this display."

"I doubted you, my *Rhan*, doubted that you were sufficient to your inheritance."

"So did I, Shekanre. I still do. You are forgiven your doubt. Now get up."

"No, my *Rhan*. You are worthy."

"He is right, you know." Kamozh's head turned to see Shemnarai stepping away from the side wall of the small room they were in. "You are worthy of being followed, and your call will bring them out. The ships will fly, because of your words, and it may just chance that our people will face the outer dark with something besides fear in their hearts. And if they do, it will be because of you."

Kamozh watched, almost stupefied, as Shemnarai, heir to an even more prestigious clan than his own, slowly and gracefully lowered herself to the floor, positioned her head to the right, and covered her eyes, giving to him ultimate respect and submission.

CHAPTER 59

"Finally!" Fifth-Cadence sang out in an exalted aria as her ship dropped back into space in the target star. "Escalate us as quickly as possible," she intoned to the younger Ekhat monitoring the Anj servients at the controls. "I want to begin hunting Jao as soon as we clear the photosphere."

She turned her back on the viewer, rehearsing the theme she planned to use to unify her crew and spur them on in the hunt. If she had remained facing the viewer, she might have been able to interpret the excessively roiling currents of plasma off to a forequarter. The lesser Ekhat on the command deck lacked the experience to see what was coming. And they would never gain that experience.

Fifth-Cadence's first clue that something was about to go very wrong was when the deck under her feet lurched upward, just before the hull was crushed open to admit solar plasma at temperatures well above the melting point of carbon. Her mind had just begun to recognize that when the plasma washed over her, ending her awareness of everything.

Leonard Hollar made another score mark in the air as *Trident* left another Ekhat ship vaporizing in her wake. "Two down."

Rafe was watching the control readouts, but he held up a hand for a fist bump. "Now for the hat trick."

"Ten bucks says thirty minutes to do it," Hollar said.

Rafe looked at the system plot and the sensor readings about incoming ships. "I got twenty bucks on twenty minutes."

"You're on."

"*Trident* reports two Ekhat destroyed, but scans showing nine more on the way."

"*Trident*?" D'mishri turned to Ed Kralik as Caitlin was deep in conversation with Aille and Tura.

"An experimental vessel that we designed to cruise within a star to blockade it against just such attacks. She's the first of her class and on her shakedown cruise, so this is field-testing with a vengeance. If it proves out, we'll build a lot of these to cruise within the stars of our homeworlds."

The envoy's voice inflections changed as he spoke to Pym. The translation became, "It cruises deep within the star for extended periods of time?"

"Yes, sir," Ed replied. "I'm a ground troop commander by training and experience, but I've had to pick up some knowledge about ships because I was in command of a big logistics base before I joined the fleet recently. So I can tell you that our regular ships, like *Lexington*, here, can be in shallow to moderate solar depths for a few hours, and *Trident* and her planned sisters are designed to be in a star for days or weeks at a time, but I can't tell you *how* they do it."

D'mishri made a sound that almost sounded like a big cat purring. Ed almost laughed, but stifled it. The envoy's next response translated to, "I don't find it unusual for a ground commander to not be up to date on the details of ship construction. But it does sound as if you may have things to teach us about shields technologies. Something else for the list."

"List?"

"The one that begins with 'Faster-than-Light Drive.'" The envoy made an expression that Pym didn't have to translate. Ed could read *evil grin* in the felinoid face just fine.

"Ah. That list." All of a sudden, Ed started thinking of a way to change the topic of discussion. This conversation was headed for areas way above even his pay grade.

Tully finished putting on his combat suit, taking the gloves and helmet from Corporal Toro and putting them on the bench beside him. "Ginta waited just long enough for you to get on board, Colonel, and then he really kicked this thing in the tail," Major Liang said.

"Yeah, looking at the numbers," Tully replied as he tapped on his com pad, "I'd say he skipped right by 'screaming fast' and 'overdrive' and went directly to the 'bat out of hell' throttle stop. Which is basically what Caitlin—Director Kralik, that is—ordered. But I still don't have a read on how long this will take. Do you, Shan?"

"According to Ginta," Major Liang replied, "because

we won't be tied down with the logistics ships and the framepoint ship, all the big combat units will be maxing their drives out. He says *Ban Chao* should be approaching the home planet's orbit in a little over three hours, and the rest will be not too far behind us."

Tully whistled. "Damn, that's fast. And no, Top," he said, holding up a hand as Sergeant Luff opened his mouth, "I don't want or need to know just how many kilometers per hour that is." Luff closed his mouth and chuckled.

"All right," Tully got serious. "I don't know if the jinau will be called on for operations during this action, but if we are, I suspect there won't be much time to act. I want everyone suited up, carrying a combat load, and ready to hit the shock frames no later than a half hour before we hit that orbit line, so set a countdown timer. Top, you get a feed from the command deck, and if our ETA changes, or if they think we're going to have Ekhat in range before that, change the timer and let all leaders know, down to squad level."

"On it, Colonel."

Tully stood to walk out into the assembly area, then turned back. "And Top?"

"Yes, sir?"

"Hard loads for everyone. If we have to insert anywhere, we won't be looking for prisoners. The Rule of Engagement will be if it's on an Ekhat ship, terminate with extreme prejudice regardless of what it looks like. Load the troops up for bear, alligator, sasquatch, and anything else you can think of."

"We're seeing movement in the Khûrûshil ships," one of the sensor techs called out on *Lexington*'s command deck. Caitlin lined up with Aille, Dannet, and Tura to view the system plot on the main viewer. "More ships lifting off from everywhere, and most of them moving inward, positioning themselves between the primary and the planets."

"A good plan," Aille said, "if their ships were more than lifeboats armed with rock throwers." His angles showed a rare *dissatisfaction-with-imminence*. "I . . ." he hesitated, "would rather they survive."

"Yet if Ekhat break past *Trident* soon," the fleet commander said, "anything they do to distract or impede the Ekhat advance, anything at all, no matter how small, no matter the cost, will be worth it." She turned to face Kamozh and Shekanre who had come to stand behind the command group and eavesdrop through Lim's translations. "This, you understand, is the price of your people's paranoia and xenophobia. You could have been raised to a more effective tech level by those around you, but you would not." Her angles had shifted to *unpleasant-viewing*.

Dannet turned back to the system plot. Caitlin looked to the Khûrûsh. "She's right, you know," she said quietly.

Kamozh's translated response came back in a moment. "We know. We even agree. But being right is cold comfort at this moment."

Caitlin knew that feeling, but before she could say anything, one of the com techs announced, "Message from *Trident*: prepare to deal with leakers. Three Ekhat look to show up at very near the same time. They will try to take them all, but three to one odds are pretty good to get at least one of them out of the star."

"Crap," she heard Ed mutter, while her heart sank.

CHAPTER 60

"Uh-oh," Hollar muttered as three Ekhat ships materialized in the sun within seconds of each other. "This could be trouble."

"Nah," Rafe said after watching the plot for a few seconds. "Their vectors all go in different directions. Even if they knew we were here and wanted to cooperate in ganging up on us, they're going the wrong directions. So we'll only have to take on one at a time." After a few seconds, he added, "But it looks like at least two of them are going to get by us, because there's only one of us, and their vectors are so different that we won't be able to get more than one before the others exit the photosphere. Damn. I hope the fleet's in place, because otherwise it's going to be Hell's Kitchen come calling for the natives."

Rafe proved to be a prophet as far as dealing with this trio of Ekhat ships. Two of them did escape the photosphere to open space, but the third one was nailed by *Trident* overhauling it from behind and smashing through the rear quarter of the ship. He looked at the clock, grinned, and stuck his hand out toward Hollar. "You owe me a Jackson."

"Bastard," Hollar muttered as he pulled out his wallet and took out a twenty dollar bill. Holding it up before him, he said, "Double or nothing?"

Rafe snatched the bill and wadded it into a front pocket. "Not a chance."

"Bastard."

Rafe chuckled, then fell silent as they turned back to the viewscreen.

"Mother of..." Hollar said quietly. "Do I see thirteen incoming tracks?"

"That's what I count," Rafe replied just as softly. "Want to bet on whether or not we survive?"

"Shut up."

Silence reigned on the command deck of the *Pool Buntyam* after *Trident*'s latest report. "Three destroyed," Krant-Captain Mallu finally said, "two breaking out, and thirteen yet to arrive? What are we facing?"

Kaln squared her angles into *facing-the-depths*, and said, "It is a raid like we haven't seen in generations." She looked at the captain and at his pool-sib Jalta. "When we get close, man the gun spines as well as the laser spines."

"Why?" Jalta asked.

Kaln didn't respond directly, saying only, "If we don't, you will regret it." She turned and headed for one of the sensor tech positions. Jalta started after her, *irritation* in his angles, only to be restrained by Mallu's hand on his shoulder.

"Remember the last battle we were in," the captain said.

Jalta did remember the day the fleet took on thirteen ships, one of them a World Harvester, and what Kaln had done then. His angles slumped to *confused.* "I don't understand. How can she know?"

"She rides the time," Mallu said. "I don't understand, either, but there is no harm to what she suggests, and after last time I can see that it might do some good. So see to it." Jalta's angles assumed *compliance-with-orders*, and he headed for a workstation to put Mallu's orders into action.

"*Trident* reports third ship destroyed, two definitely escaping, thirteen more appearing soon."

Caitlin looked to the Eleusherar Path envoys. "We're still too far out. Will your people be able to take a hand yet?"

Pyr did the translations to and from D'mishri. "It's possible, but the probability is not high. Our ships were scattered around the outer system in stealth operation; not as far out as you, but distant. And it took a while for the word to be passed. It will simply depend on who was where in comparison to which way these ships go."

"Damn!" Caitlin said. She looked to Fleet Commander Dannet. "Can't we get there any faster?"

"I have ordered maximum drive settings for all ships, Director Kralik." The big Jao's fur was starting to clump, a sign that she needed to take a swim.

"Don't you have an operating reserve, or a setting that can be used in emergencies?" Caitlin was starting to feel a little desperate. She really didn't want to see what she suspected was going to happen.

Dannet stared at her. "If we push our engines beyond their rated maximums, we run the risk of engines failing, or worse, destroying themselves and their ships."

"If we don't get there faster," Caitlin said, "we're liable to see planets destroyed. Tell your captains to push it to the wall, or whatever the right figure of speech is. These people stand to lose all; we will risk all to defend them."

Dannet continued to stare at Caitlin for a moment longer, then her angles morphed from *eager-to-combat* to *gratified-respect.* "At your command, Director Kralik." She snapped an order to Terra-Captain Uldra, and another to the head com tech before completing her conversation with Caitlin. "Perhaps there is a time for wild abandon. Let us hope we are both still available to count the cost when the end is attained."

"You know, Top, it's amazing what a little time can do," Tully said.

"How so, Colonel?"

"Not quite five years ago, I was a fat, dumb, and happy PFC just like Private Ciappa, and I thought I knew more than any sergeant or officer who ever lived. Now look at me, wearing colonel's eagles, and wishing to God I had listened more and goofed off less back then."

"For a mustang who came up through the ranks a little quicker than usual, you've done pretty well." Luff gave one of his deep chuckles. "And, begging the Colonel's pardon, I seriously doubt you were ever fat, and you were smarter than Ciappa when you were coming out of your mama's womb. Maybe you were happier back then, but I doubt it."

"Maybe you're right, Top," Tully laughed as he reached for his helmet. "Maybe you're right."

"Command deck to Colonel Tully and all jinau leaders." It was a human voice.

"Tully here. Who's this?" Tully had his helmet on by now, and his readout showed that all the officers and First Sergeant Luff were on the command frequency, so he didn't have to signal anyone.

"Lieutenant Oberlin, sir." Tully remembered meeting her in one of the officers' mess compartments.

"Go ahead."

"Fleet Commander Dannet has ordered that all vessels take thrust to absolute maximum."

"I thought we were already at maximum," Tully said.

"We were at maximum rated power," Oberlin said. "Based on designs and tests, the maximum rated level has a safety component. Dannet has just ordered us to ignore the warnings and increase thrust to actual maximum output. Think of it as maximum military drive."

"How much does this increase *Ban Chao*'s speed, and how much does it increase our risk?"

"It has increased our speed by a factor of 1.2, perhaps as much as 1.3."

"You've already done it?" Tully asked carefully.

"Captain Ginta has obeyed the Fleet Commander's orders."

Tully sensed that that topic was closed to further discussion. "And the risk?"

"No one knows for sure. Definitely more wear and tear on the engines. While failures of Jao-designed engines are rare, they do happen. If one fails, we just lose that much thrust. But if one goes 'Boom,' all bets are off and we'd best have our insurance paid up."

"Gotcha," Tully said. "Unknown but probably slight increase in risk, but if an engine decides to pack it in we become a short-lived glowing cloud of debris."

"Pretty much," Oberlin agreed.

"Nothing we can do about that," Tully shrugged. "More important question: how much does this advance our arrival?"

Tully heard a chuckle from Oberlin. "That's why you've got me on the line, to give you a real time estimate. The Jao up here just went from 'soon' to 'more soon.' I figured you'd want something a bit more quantifiable."

"You figured right," Tully replied. "Now give."

"We will arrive at the orbit demarcation in fifty-five minutes from . . . now," Oberlin said.

"Right. Keep us posted if anything else changes."

"You got it, sir."

"Tully out."

The sound changed slightly as Oberlin dropped off of the command frequency. "You heard Lieutenant Oberlin," Tully told the rest of the group. "Get everyone vertical, zipped up, packed up, and ready to rock and roll. Baker Company takes the lead this time, followed by Charlie and Able. Top, XO, on me."

"Yes, sir," came the chorused responses.

Tully stood up and watched as the assault bay suddenly became the site of more or less controlled chaos. Leaning perhaps more to the less. The armored figure of Major Liang pushed through the throng until he joined First Sergeant Luff before him.

"This is not open for discussion," Tully said after he switched to a private com band. "Top, you and I will be slotting in with Charlie Company. Shan, you will be slotting in with Able Company."

"Yes, sir," from Sergeant Luff.

"No arguments from me, Colonel," the executive officer said.

"Good." Tully made brushing motions with his hands. "Then let's find our places."

"Hoo, boy," Rafe muttered, watching the sensors of the approaching Ekhat. "Looks like we're going to get five one right after another."

Hollar sucked air in through his teeth. "Doesn't look like we'll be able to take them all."

"No," Rafe said. "Especially since it looks like some of them may be coming in to the south quadrant of the sun. We don't have a prayer of getting down there in time to tag any of them."

Hollar nodded. "We'll have enough to do up here."

"Aaaaaaand, here we go," Rafe said as the first ship materialized from its Frame Point jump. Terra-Captain Domt issued her orders, and the two engineers watched as *Trident* was aligned on the Ekhat vessel and the engines were punched up to full speed.

Trident made her run, but just before impact the unexpected and very unlooked-for happened.

"Second emergence!" one of the techs shouted. "Right above the target!"

Rafe watched the plot, horrified, as the new Ekhat emergence created a fratricidal collision with the first ship. It wasn't a total immolation—at least, not at first. Spires and buttresses touched and interlocked between the two craft, and then *Trident* smashed into her target.

The lower of the two Ekhat ships immediately began to break up and vaporize, but the greater mass of it lasted long enough to exert leverage and torque on the second ship to create a slow-motion whipsaw effect on it and bring it crashing down on the top of *Trident*'s hull.

"Oh, shit!" Rafe muttered, as red lights lit up all over the engineering board.

CHAPTER 61

Rafe spun. "Captain Domt! That impacted directly on the heat sink. It's carrying close to a full load, and the bleed-off mechanism just got shafted in a big way. We need out of the sun, like NOW!"

"Due north," Domt ordered the maneuvering officer. She pointed at Hollar. "Full power, no reserve, no red lines. Do it!"

"Aye-aye, Captain!" Hollar said as he reached over the shoulder of one of the engineering techs and shot a slide to the limit of its run.

Hollar stepped back. "All we can do," Rafe said.

"Yeah, just about," Hollar replied. "Except I wish I had my childhood rosary with me."

"Yeah," Rafe said with a snort. "Me, too."

"*Trident* reports two more ships destroyed, but three will escape the sun and be in open space shortly."

"Damn," Caitlin said again as the com tech kept announcing news she didn't want to hear.

"*Trident* reports that they have sustained significant damage to their heat sink and bleedoff systems as a result of the last engagement, and they must exit the sun now."

"Damn." This time Ed said it for her.

"Heat sink?" Caitlin asked Aille.

"New *ollnat* technology," Aille responded. "Something Rafe Aguilera found in some of your journals. It allows the ship to absorb and store much of the solar heat energy while they are in the photosphere, and discharge it either after exiting the sun or when they trail a special radiator within the sun."

"Discharge heat within a sun?" Caitlin asked. That was one of the crazier things she'd ever heard.

"I did say it was *ollnat* technology," Aille said with a flip of his whiskers that toyed with the angles for *sly-humor.*

"*Trident* clear of the photosphere," the com tech announced.

"Send them a vector to the support fleet out-system and order maximum speed," Dannet ordered. "With their damage and no offensive weapons, they need to clear the way."

Now if Rafe was only okay, Caitlin thought, she'd take some small happiness that at least someone was getting out of this mess alive.

"Five more Ekhat ships exiting the photosphere."

"Damn!" Caitlin and Ed said in unison.

Rafe was watching the engineering boards like a hawk and listening to the damage repair parties with a com bud in one ear as he listened to the command deck with the other. Hollar had left him on the command deck while he took charge of the repair efforts. It was easier to inspect the damage now that they were out of the solar mass.

"Rafe, you got your ears on?"

"Talk to me, Lennie."

"That motherless Ekhat screwed us good. The radiator exit tube is crushed."

"Can we cut the top of it away and let it trail away that way?" Rafe asked. "We wouldn't be able to retrieve it without someone doing some EVA, but that could wait for later."

"Won't work. Crushed means crumpled and crinkled like a balled-up piece of tinfoil. We'd have to cut away a major portion of the secondary hull just to get to the exit hatch, and then we'd probably have to cut that away as well to get the radiator out."

"Not good."

"Nope. And to top it off, the primary hull over the heat sink is dented."

Rafe whistled. "Mother of..."

"Yeah. That Ekhat must have been built just a bit sturdier than the ones we've seen before."

The battle armor of a *Lexington* was about the toughest alloy that Jao and humans had been able to develop after they started working together. The battle armor of *Trident*'s primary hull was more of the same, only about half again as thick. There wasn't supposed to be anything that could dent that stuff short of an atomic weapon or a head-on collision with a planet. That would have to go back to the design boys... if they managed to survive the next little while.

Rafe took another look at the engineering panel

readouts over the shoulders of the techs. He shook his head. "Lennie . . ."

"Yeah?"

"You got anybody outside yet?"

"Just getting ready to."

"Forget it. The numbers are getting worse. We're going to have to blow the heat sink."

There was a moment of silence.

"You sure?"

Rafe looked at the numbers one more time. "Yeah. It's not far from the point where it will start melting down, and once that happens, we'll lose the engines. You need to get everybody north of frame 73's blast doors now."

"Crap."

"Yeah."

"Well, I left you there to call the plays. If that's the way you see it, we're moving now."

"Gimme a signal when you're clear."

"Will do. Hollar out."

Rafe looked at the board one last time, then turned to locate Terra-Captain Domt. He limped over—his stump was getting tired—and stood to attention in front of the captain.

Domt apparently had some experience with human body-speech, as she cocked her head to one side, and said, "You wish, Aguilera?"

"Captain, we have a problem . . ."

"Where are they?" Octave-plus-a-Fourth intoned shrilly. An Interdict ship, her craft was manned only by lesser and immature Ekhat. No hideously corrupted servients for them. But it did mean that she had to restrain herself a bit. She couldn't be wasting her crew just because she was anxious to kill something . . . like a filthy Jao. She hated the Jao more than anything, except maybe the Melody faction, those who had first created the idea of using lesser species as servients. A dirge-filled day for Ekhatkind, that was.

"Ships at octave seven, treble, staccato," one of the lesser Ekhat—a female; Octave-plus-a-Fourth didn't allow males on her ships; too easily distracted—sang out.

"Who are they?" Octave-plus-a-Fourth demanded through a recitative style. She paused a moment afterward to admire her facility with forms and themes. If only she could show that to her harmony master. Maybe crushing Jao would give her that entrance, that moment of solo.

"Unknown," the lesser female replied in like form.

"Filthy Jao," Octave-plus-a-Fourth whisper-sang.

She paused for a moment, then belled out, "Attack!"

"Crossing the orbit now," Vanta-Captain Ginta himself announced to the jinau command team. "There are seven Ekhat ships free in the system, and *Trident*'s final reports indicate an unknown number still to arrive."

"So what are your orders?" Tully asked.

"Since *Ban Chao* is first in and is faster than the others, Fleet Commander Dannet has ordered us to screen the second planet, Khûr-mar. Our vector has been modified, and we have delayed our deceleration until we are closer to the planet. Fortunately for Khûr-mar's inhabitants, they are relatively close to the homeworld at this season, so we will not be much longer in arriving. Unfortunately for them, two, maybe three of the Ekhat are vectoring for them now, and their share of the Khûrûsh fleet is small."

"How long?"

"Soon."

Tully took a deep breath. He knew better than to ask a Jao about time measurement, but he still forgot from time to time.

"Should the jinau enter the shock frames now?"

There was a moment of silence. "Yes, now," Ginta finally said.

CHAPTER 62

Caitlin watched the system plot on the main viewer. They weren't going to make it. Two more Ekhat ships rose out of the sun, one to north and one to south, and immediately began accelerating to follow the earlier ships toward the nearest of the Khûrûsh planets, Khûr-mar and Khûr-shi. There were multiple ships streaming toward the planets. All that faced them were what could only be considered forlorn hopes of Khûrûsh ship squadrons. The Ekhat ships were nearly as large as the *Lexingtons* of Terra taif's fleet. The Khûrûsh ships looked like canoes in comparison. They would be just about as effective as canoes.

It was much like when *Lexington* had approached Khûr-shi days earlier. Every Khûrûsh ship in the system seemed to have sortied. Apparently Kamozh and Shemnarai's appeals had struck a chord, elicited a response. Unfortunately, the Ekhat had managed to break through *Trident*'s blockade just that little bit too soon, and now they were free to maraud almost unhindered until the Terrans and the Eleusherar Path managed to make their appearance. The outsiders might be able to mostly preserve the planets, but the Khûrûsh squadrons were going to be little more than sacrificial lambs to the Ekhat ships. Nine were in the system now. No, ten, as another blob of plasma emerged out of the solar mass.

Caitlin could see *Ban Chao*'s icon on the viewscreen, approaching the second planet, but still just that little bit too far away to intervene in what was about to happen.

"*Pool Buntyam*, *Sun Tzu*, and first echelon of Harrier Squadron Alpha to support *Ban Chao*. Krant-Captain Mallu to take local command," Fleet Commander Dannet ordered. "*Lexington*, *Arjuna*, and *Fancy Free* to shape course for Khûr-shi along with Harrier squadron Delta. *Footloose* and second echelon Harrier Squadron Alpha to locus coordinates 27.344.69. Eliminate the Ekhat."

Caitlin twisted her hands, knowing that this was going to be a fateful day. Perhaps in more than one way.

Octave-plus-a-Fourth shrieked in triumph as the first ship died, performing staccato downward step-tones until her voice was resonating throughout the command deck. "They die so easily, these Jao."

"These are not Jao," her Conductor said. "They have no shields. They have no lasers. The ships are no danger. They are not Jao. They must be a local fallow species."

"As long as they die," Octave-plus-a-Fourth sang, "I care not who they are."

She shrieked again as the second ship literally flew

to pieces after a full-power laser impacted directly on the nose compartment.

Tully once again had a feed from the command deck displayed on his helmet display. The detail was small, but he could see enough to get a good idea of what was happening—which was massacre.

The dinky little Khûrûsh ships were being swatted like flies—no, like mosquitoes. They were agile, no doubt about it, and they might momentarily evade the two Ekhats that were closing on the planet for a few minutes while they were firing their missiles as fast as they could. But small or not, agile or not, they were definitely fragile, and it only took one impact from an Ekhat laser to turn them into clouds of loosely associated scrap metal with a few organic compounds adulterating the mix.

In just the space of time it had taken to have those thoughts, over half the Khûrûsh ships were gone. Tully watched as they continued to dwindle, one by one by one, until the last vanished from the display.

"Shit," Tully muttered. He knew that this end was inevitable, but there had been that tiny bit of hope in the corner of his mind; hope that somehow, someway, the Khûrûsh could take at least one of the Ekhat down with them to mutual immolation. He shook his head.

"Come on, Ginta," Tully whispered. "Time for some paybacks, man, for us and for them. Get us to the dance."

Kamozh stood watching *Lexington*'s main viewscreen beside Shemnarai and D'mishri. Shekanre stood to his other side. His soul burned as he watched the

Khûrûsh ships before Khûr-mar fading away one by one, each missing icon representing eight to twelve people that he probably knew, fellow warriors, fellow space venturers, fellow defenders—so they thought—of their system. To have their noses rubbed in the hollow nature of their defense was both so redolent of irony as to almost choke him and so painful as to almost paralyze his breathing.

"Brave," D'mishri said softly. "Very brave."

The envoy lifted his hands to sign **<honor to the dead>**.

Shemnarai responded wordlessly by rendering a four-handed **<honor to the brave>**.

The thought that the bravery was wasted, that the adamant purpose had been needless, if only his people had not turned their backs on the rest of the universe, caused anger to rise up within Kamozh, enough that he did choke for a moment.

No flowery sentiments for Kamozh. No noble paeans of praise. Only a four-handed presentation of **<grief>** under-laid by a low rumbling growl that quietly filled the command deck.

Shekanre emulated him after a few breaths. Before long Shemnarai and D'mishri had taken it up as well. The envoy could muster a most respectable growl. The reinforcement simply fanned the flames of Kamozh's anger. As he raised his hands higher and turned them to face outward, pushing his grief toward Khûr the god, Kamozh's mid-hands shifted. The left now displayed **<vengeance>**; the right signed **<implacable>**.

The young clan lord was calling down imprecation upon the Ekhat. He had invoked his god against the greatest evil he knew.

The others drew back slightly as they saw what he had done. Regardless of one's beliefs in a so-called modern era, there was still enough of the old clan heritage in them to make themselves uncomfortable at the thought of deliberately inviting the attention of their god. The clans told stories about those kinds of encounters.

Kamozh continued to stand firm, growl rumbling in his throat.

"New ship at octave five, tenor, marcato," another of the lesser Ekhat sang out.

"Attack!" Octave-plus-a-Fourth intoned. "Purge the Jao from this system."

"Not Jao," the Conductor sang in a soliloquy form. "Unknown. Large. Fast. Dangerous?"

"We have triumphed," Octave-plus-a-Fourth shifted to an aria form. "Let them come, we will cleanse them all and advance the Melody." And her harmony master might take note of her.

"Attack!"

CHAPTER 63

"Colonel Tully," came over his com bud. His helmet display tagged the signal as coming from Lieutenant Buckley.

"Go ahead, Buckley." Tully continued to watch the command deck feed as *Ban Chao* closed on the Ekhat ships vectoring toward Khûr-mar.

"Sir, according to the Lleix and Jao databases, these appear to be older ships, of types that are most often used by the Interdict."

"Tell me why I need to know that."

"By the most modern standards, they're second rate ships, operated by the smallest of the four major factions."

"Okay," Tully said, toggling his display to a closer view of the Ekhat craft. "But again, why do I care?"

"Colonel, one of them is small, not much bigger than a Jao dispatch ship. But the other one's pretty good-sized."

Tully's attention now focused solely on Buckley.

"Big enough to be a ramming target?"

"Could be, sir. I can't get enough detail out of the scans yet to be able to tell you if it's a slow boat freighter or if it's a fast path command ship, but it's big enough that if *Ban Chao* pokes it, it won't fall apart. At least, not immediately."

"Good job, Buckley," Tully patted his intelligence officer on the figurative back. "Get ahold of Lieutenant Oberlin and get her to connect you with a senior sensor tech so you can get the best sensor feeds. Keep us posted on anything else you find."

"Will do, sir."

"All clear, Rafe," came the word from Leonard Hollar. *"Everyone's clear of the area and behind the blast doors either at frame 73 or frame 107."*

So everyone was north of the damaged area or holed up in the engine control room. Rafe pointed to one of the engineering techs on the command deck.

"Video monitors on and tracking, sir. We've got line of sight covering at least eighty percent of the area over the heat sink."

Rafe shook his head. Another note for the design team: need more redundancy on the external observation points. He turned and said, "Captain?"

Domt gave a series of maneuvering orders which shut down the main drive, then maneuvered to position *Trident* moving broadside along her movement vector with the top of the hull pointed back toward the sun. The captain then looked at Rafe and simply said, "Do it."

Rafe keyed his microphone. "Lennie?"

"Yeah?"

"Hold on to your ass. Pushing the button in five, four, three, two, one, now," and Rafe personally touched a control that he had programmed minutes before. He switched his focus to a video display above the engineering workstations.

The first round was a series of shaped charges that cut through the primary hull and thrust the excised portion of the hull away from the rest of *Trident*. Rafe felt a slight tremble under his feet as the charges blew. The hull segment slowly drifted away, twisting as if it were a leaf in the wind as it assumed a different vector. This cleared the way for the next phase.

Ten seconds later, the second round of charges blew. This severed the mountings under the base and surrounding the whole heat sink compartment, as well as all the leads and busses leading to it, just before an array of low-powered thrusters lit off under the bottom of the compartment. They only fired for a few seconds, but that impetus was sufficient for the compartment to move out of the well it had occupied in *Trident*'s hull as the ship continued to drift outsystem at a high rate of speed.

Rafe held his breath. This was one system that they had modeled to the nth degree while designing the ship, and they had certainly tested all the pieces of the module evacuation system, but it was one of those things that until you actually did it for real, you just weren't sure it would work.

He counted seconds, and watched the video display as the compartment floated clear of *Trident*'s hull. "Whew," he finally muttered.

Terra-Captain Domt started issuing maneuvering orders a lot sooner than Rafe would have. But then, he wasn't the captain, and he wasn't skippering a ship with a badly wounded hull and no guns of any kind, so he could see that Domt might actually have a more highly refined sense of survival than he did.

Maneuvering thrusters twisted *Trident* around until her long axis was aligned with her flight vector, and then the main engines came back on-line.

"Rafe."

"Yeah, Lennie?"

"You done?"

"Yep," Rafe replied with a big grin that his friend couldn't see but could probably hear. "It worked without a hitch, which is not something I would have put money on."

"Oh, ye of little faith," Hollar replied.

"Whatever. Anyway, your teams can get back to work now, and EVA should be okay with normal precautions. Just remind everyone working inside, including the guys back in the engine control room, that they'll need to use the B and C spinal corridors to move fore and aft until further notice. The A corridor isn't there anymore."

"Got it. We'll be careful. Don't want anyone trying to breathe vacuum." There was a moment of hiss in the circuit, then Hollar came back on. *"Oh, and Rafe?"*

"Yeah?"

"Good job, man. And give the techs up there an attaboy."

"Thanks. Will do."

"That makes twenty-four Ekhat ships that we know of," one of the sensor techs reported after a brief interval with no ships exiting the sun, "plus the five that *Trident* destroyed in the photosphere before she had to run."

Caitlin said nothing. This was beyond any capability of invective to discharge emotions. They were facing almost twice the number of ships they'd fought in their last battle.

She looked over at Ramt, who had been summoned to the command deck to give whatever insight Ekhatlore *elian* might be able to contribute in what was looking like it would shape up as an apocalypse. Ramt straightened from where she had been studying the sensor reports on the ship arrivals.

"This is obviously an assault, not just a raid. The records I've been able to access don't show an Ekhat gathering this large since the Jao revolted. But judging from the vectors of the ships as they exit the sun, and from what few ship details are visible from this distance, I think these are ships from at least three of the four major factions. And I've never heard of that happening."

"And what are the implications of that?" Aille asked from where he stood next to Tura, both with angles in their usual *neutral*.

"Something has to have stirred them up," Ramt began.

"Ya think?" Caitlin muttered.

"But who knows what it could have been? However, being Ekhat—being who and what they are—there is no cooperation, no coordination of their arrivals and tactics," the Lleix expert continued.

"You mean they're swarming at random, like a bunch of bees from a hive?" asked Ed.

"More like bees from four hives," Ramt replied.

One of the things that Caitlin liked about the Lleix was how quickly they had absorbed English idioms. A thought occurred to her, and she threw it out for consideration.

"From *Trident*'s reports we know that two Ekhat ships collided in the sun. I would say that might prove Ramt's analysis. And I wonder how many more ships may have been self-killed?"

"Oh, now there's a cold thought," Ed said. "But every ship that died in the sun is one less that has to be faced out here. And it wouldn't have bothered me if a few of these had managed to tangle with each other before they got out of the plasma."

Caitlin considered that. "Yeah, me, too."

"The last seven ships out of the sun aren't shedding their plasma," Ginta said to Tully.

"Oh, shit." After that heartfelt comment, Tully continued, "Any of them headed this way?"

"Too soon to tell," Ginta replied.

CHAPTER 64

Caitlin stared at the viewscreen. The random movements of the Ekhat ships as they came out of the sun had to some extent been sorted out as the ship commanders had gathered real-time data about the system into which they had blindly jumped. The various attackers had coalesced into four ragged groups with no attempt at formations. "All the finesse of a barbarian horde," she muttered.

"Less, actually," Ed replied from where he was looking over Lieutenant Vaughan's shoulder. "Much less than even, say, a wolf pack. Reminds me more of an army ant swarm than anything else on Terra."

"There are others who have made such comparisons," Ramt said. "But be careful about doing so. The Ekhat are not like anything else we know, and trying to understand them by analogy can lead to error."

One of the smaller mobs, with two ships in front-runner positions, were vectoring for Khûr-mar. The others, including seven ships lagging behind that appeared to be hauling plasma balls in their shields, seemed to be on a course to confront the Khûrûsh squadrons attempting to shield Khûr-shi. Unfortunately, *Lexington*'s flotilla was not going to be able to intercept them before they got in range of the Khûrûsh ships. Kamozh's people would take their lumps in this action, just as they did in the action before Khûr-mar. But there were more of them, so maybe some would survive long enough to be rescued by the Terra taif ships. Caitlin hoped so, anyway.

"*Trident* has cleared fourth planet orbit," Vaughan said quietly.

"Good," Caitlin replied. "Any casualties?"

"Some injuries reported among the crew. No deaths," Vaughan said. "And Mr. Aguilera is not listed in the reports," he continued with a smile.

"*Ban Chao* entering range," one of the com techs reported. Vaughan started working his workstation again, and Caitlin fixed her eyes on the viewscreen again. *Ban Chao*'s icon seemed to be almost touching the Ekhat icons.

Octave-plus-a-Fourth was confronted by the conductor. "Minor-Sixth instructs you to fall back and let her larger ship take the lead against this foe."

"No! We will attack! We have prevailed! Let Minor-Sixth follow our lead!"

Octave-plus-a-Fourth spun to face her crew. "Attack! All systems ahead!"

Vanta-Captain Ginta watched over his weapons officer's shoulder as the two Ekhat vessels approached. "Target the larger ship," he ordered. The Jao officer said nothing in reply as he adjusted controls and muttered orders to weapons crews.

Ban Chao, although nearly as large as the *Lexington*, was not as heavily armed: no cannon firing the big depleted uranium slugs for up close and in-star combat, and not as many of the big lasers. But the lasers she did have were latest generation designs, and even more heavily powered than the *Lex*'s. She wasn't designed to fight the battles that *Lex* had been designed for, but if she got into one, she could "punch her weight," as one of Wrot's maxims would put it.

"What . . ." one of the sensor techs said.

Ginta's mind started racing as the smaller Ekhat ship changed position by pulling ahead and interposing itself between the larger ship and *Ban Chao*. "Shift targeting to the smaller ship," he ordered. "Hold fire until I order it.

"McAdams!" Ginta barked without turning.

"Captain," a human tech straightened.

"Prepare for ram."

"Sir!" The human bent back over his workstation.

"Tully."

There was a moment's delay, then Colonel Tully's voice came over the nearest speaker. "Captain Ginta. Orders for the assault force?"

"Yes. We will be in a position to ram the larger ship soon. Be prepared."

"We're prepared now," the colonel responded. "Just give us the signals. Tully out."

The oncoming monsters had begun firing at the Khûrûsh flotilla. Kamozh knew they were called Ekhat, but that word meant nothing in any of the Khûrûsh languages, and using it didn't express the hatred he felt nearly as well as "monsters" did.

Only the lead Ekhat ships were firing, as they were blocking the shots of the trailing ships. The Khûrûsh ships were filling the space between them with missiles, but even from the viewscreen Kamozh could tell they were having no effect. The missiles were too slow, and the monsters were either ignoring them as they sailed by or using short laser blasts to destroy them. The irony of the monsters using the same techniques that Director Kralik's ships had used to disable *Lo-Khûr-shohm* and capture him and the clan's retainers was not lost on him.

"In range," *Lexington*'s weapons officer reported. "We won't do a lot of damage yet, but we can at least tickle their screens and distract them."

Fleet Commander Dannet said nothing, simply stood near the workstation of Lieutenant Vaughan and observed the lieutenant's monitors and readouts. Kamozh watched as Terra-Captain Uldra walked over to stand behind the human weapons officer. He wanted to scream that they should fire now with everything they had, anything that might make a bit of difference for his former fellows out there in what he now knew were spaceships that weren't much more than toys . . . dangerous toys, risky toys, granted, but compared to the *Lexington*, that's what they were.

"Open fire with the lasers that bear," Uldra finally ordered. "Gun decks to stand by, but wait for orders."

"Lasers, fire as you bear," the weapons officer repeated into his microphone. "Gun decks, stand by."

Kamozh could see the effects of the Terra taif

weapons almost immediately. The monsters' ships began spreading a little farther apart as they reacted to the unexpected fire; and the remnants of the Khûrûsh flotilla were no longer disappearing with regularity.

He scarcely felt Shemnarai come stand beside him and reach over to take one of his hands in hers.

Tully was getting antsy, waiting for the call. "Lieutenant Oberlin," he said.

"Yes, Colonel?" came the lieutenant's voice.

"Can you get a tech to give a feed of the command plot to my helmet?"

"Can do, sir. It might take a bit," she said.

"Thanks. Tully out."

There was a pause, then the feed appeared in his helmet display. Tully relaxed a bit. Being able to watch what Ginta was doing allowed him to feel the flow of the combat better, and anticipate what he might be called on to do.

The thought that this might be analogous to the Jao's time sense never occurred to him. The universe does provide a bit of irony from time to time.

Ginta was watching the weapons officer's plot rather than *Ban Chao*'s main viewscreen. Actually, he was waiting for the time flow to feel right more than watching the plot.

The moment arrived. "Shoot," he ordered.

Ban Chao's lasers began firing as quickly as they could cycle.

The Ekhat ship's shields failed almost immediately, and the heavy laser shots began blowing hull metal off of the small ship. Octave-plus-a-Fourth continued to shriek "Attack!" at the top of her considerable range and power, barely applying any type of motif to it at all. To the conductor, she was almost toneless, which was perhaps the worst condemnation that could have been uttered.

Just as the conductor started to turn away from the rest of the command deck, one of the laser shots broke through the last of the intervening hull and enveloped the form of Octave-plus-a-Fourth. There was enough energy left in the beam that within a moment, her stridence vanished into motes of carbon.

The conductor's dying thought was that at least the race was improved by Octave-plus-a-Fourth not being allowed to breed.

Ginta looked to his maneuvering officer. "Begin the maneuvers to bring us around and parallel the vector of the second target."

Ban Chao, while almost of *Lexington* size and of greater mass, was also somewhat more nimble, at least in part due to the sheer size and output of her multiple engines. This allowed the maneuvering officer to boost the output of one engine while reducing the power of the others and bring her around to the new heading in what seemed to be a short amount of time. One of the humans at her test trials had called the maneuver "going up on two wheels." Most of the Jao never got the joke. The maneuvering officer, a survivor of the early Earth conquest who had become addicted to old videos about Hazzard County, did.

"Give me enough velocity to overtake the target," Ginta ordered after the turn. "We will make the ram insertion in the port side afterquarter. McAdams," he called out.

"Sir," the human straightened again.

"You will direct the ram."

"Ram, aye, sir. From what I've been able to find out about this class of ship, we'll need a velocity differential of nearly 800 kilometers an hour to have enough energy to punch through that hull."

"Maneuvering," was all Ginta said.

The maneuvering officer's ears flicked in a shorthand *order-acknowledged* angle.

"Command deck to assault team." The ram officer's voice almost startled Tully when it came through his com bud on the all-troops frequency. "Assault in approximately two minutes. Yellow light at minus forty-five seconds, red light at minus fifteen seconds, blue light at shock frame release for assault."

"Yellow at minus forty-five, red at minus fifteen, blue to go. Got it. Tully out."

Tully switched to the all troops frequency. "Okay, boys and girls, it's show time. Get ready to rock and roll. And Private Ciappa, stand still."

CHAPTER 65

Krant-Captain Mallu stared at *Pool Buntyam*'s main viewscreen in which he could see Vanta-Captain Ginta's face against a backdrop of *Ban Chao*'s command deck. "I want you to join with the rest of the ships. You refuse. Explain."

After a very short delay, Ginta replied, "*Ban Chao* is too close to the Ekhat before us. Combat is inevitable. I will ram the ship and release the jinau assault force inside it. If the trailing ships pass us by, I will break free and fire on them from behind as you fire from before. If they congregate to assault *Ban Chao*, they will not be focused on your approach, and your opening salvos will be unexpected and unopposed. Either way, you will gain the offensive advantage, especially if they pass us by, as they will have to defend from two directions, increasing the likelihood of overloading their shields."

"You abandon the jinau?"

"No," Ginta replied. "*Ban Chao* will retrieve them

once the ship action is completed. In the event that *Ban Chao* does not survive, you now know of the plan and will see to their recovery."

Mallu thought of Ginta's plan. It was not what he himself had intended, but there were advantages to it. It didn't take long for him to decide.

"Do it, and report when you assault and when you extract."

Ginta stood behind the maneuvering workstation. "Ram officer?" he asked.

"Ready," McDonald responded.

"Proceed."

The maneuvering officer pushed the engine controls to the level for the optimum ramming speed.

The ram officer looked at his workstation readouts. The systems which serviced the ram head and the assault gate had long since been powered up. He was waiting for the moment of impact. This was only the second ram assault *Ban Chao* had executed—neither of which had been executed in the interior of a star, the operational environment the ship was designed for—and he was not necessarily nervous about it... wary might have been a better word. After all, assault by boarding action had not been common in Terra's navies for at least a couple of hundred years, and who was to say that they had all the kinks worked out of the process yet, especially with all this new hardware.

The surviving Ekhat ship had been trying to fire on *Ban Chao*, but between her own shields and the cloud of debris from the destruction of the first Ekhat ship, those lasers weren't having much effect on the Terra taif ship.

Even though he was sitting in a well-designed chair and strapped into it, McDonald braced his hands against the edge of the workstation. Impact was in less than a minute.

"Colonel Tully!"

"Buckley, this had better be good," Tully snapped.

"I finally got some good detail out of the sensors. Good news, it's not a raider or a cruiser. Bad news, it's not a freighter. It's an older model Interdict exterminator."

"Which means?"

"I'm forwarding a map to all officers and squad leaders. No guarantees that it's accurate, but it's based on one of these that the Jao captured years ago, so it might be a guideline. Otherwise, it's anybody's guess as to crew, other than if it really is an Interdict ship, there will only be Ekhat on it."

"Which is the really bad news," Tully muttered. At that moment the bay lights went yellow. "Crap! Forty-five seconds." He toggled the sergeants' frequency in with the officers. "All of you, check your inputs. Buckley just sent you a file that might hint at the layout of this ship. Give it a fast glance before you pass through the gate." The light went red. Fifteen seconds. "Interdict ship. Ekhat only. No slaves. If it moves, kill it!"

Whangggggg!

"*Ban Chao* has destroyed the leading Ekhat ship, and is maneuvering to ram and assault the second."

That announcement made Caitlin's blood run cold. *Gabe!* She bit her lip to keep from saying anything, then noticed that Caewithe Miller had moved up beside her, eyes on the system plot, doing the same thing to her lip. A nudge to Caewithe's arm brought the bodyguard's eyes to meet hers. Caitlin shrugged, and held out a hand. After a moment, Caewithe took it long enough to give it a hard squeeze, then dropped it and resumed her bodyguard stance, eyes off the screen and on the room around them.

Kamozh saw Lim looking in the direction of Director Kralik, and looked that way himself. That was how he saw the wordless exchange where the two women clasped hands for a moment. He looked back to Lim and signed **<question>** as he pointed to Director Kralik with his chin.

Lim bent down a little so that she could speak quietly. "Colonel Tully is not only the leading jinau officer in the fleet, he is also the direct commanding officer of the assault force aboard *Ban Chao.* And he happens to be a very good friend of both the director and of Captain Miller, her bodyguard commander. So they are concerned."

Kamozh dropped his midhands to the floor as he considered what the translator had told him. Objectively, he had known that the "monsters" of the Terra taif fleet were people, and that they had relationships. Director Kralik's spouse was in the fleet, after all. But until this moment, that had not sunk in to be subjective knowledge. And if Director Kralik could be worried about the welfare of her friends as they moved into combat, just as he worried about his, in what other ways were they alike, the "monsters" of Terra taif and the Khûrûsh?

"Not so very different after all," he muttered to himself.

Shemnarai said from beside him, "No, they are not," in a very quiet tone. He looked down to see that her hand had gathered his and was clasping it. He tilted his head to see it, then looked up to her face. "Not so very different," she repeated as she settled to her midhands beside him. "We will talk after this."

The bay lights flashed to blue and the shock frames released and pulled up out of the way. Tully could see that Torg had marshaled Baker Company not far behind the opening assault doors. Once the doors had opened fully, Torg's squads flowed through the opening. Tully waited impatiently as Lieutenant Boatright's company moved forward, stopping behind the gate of the open assault doors, waiting on the first report.

"Nothing here but a couple of smeared Ekhat, Colonel," Torg's voice finally came through Tully's com bud. "Ready for the next movement."

CHAPTER 66

"Boatright, stand by," Tully ordered. He stepped through the open ram doors to view their field with his own eyes, shadowed by Sergeant Luff.

There wasn't a lot to see. The ram had penetrated the hull and shredded a number of interior walls, but the space was not as large as Tully had expected. Ekhat were rather large, after all. He had trouble thinking of them in corridors as small at the one he saw to his left, but since this was an Ekhat ship, apparently they could.

Right. No mass of Ekhat, other than the two corpses lying almost under the boarding ramp. No slaves charging their guns, since this was supposed to be an Interdict ship, and they didn't do the slave thing. And smeared was a good description. The deck underfoot was coated with white fluids for meters around them. Ekhat must hold a lot of blood.

"Colonel, I think we're about here," Torg said, and a copy of Buckley's map ghosted onto Tully's helmet display, with a small space colored green.

Tully looked at it, then looked at the space around him.

Before he could say anything, Luff spoke up, "Could be, but it could also be here or here," and two more spaces filled in, one blue, one red. They were evenly spaced around what passed for an equator on this ship. "They're pretty similar."

Tully looked around again, especially noting doors and hatches, then looked at the map again, expanding and shrinking each of the three spaces. "This one, I think," he said, leaving the blue space expanded. "Torg, move your people to the left of the ramp, and cluster around those two doors over there. Boatright, move out." Tully started filling in possible routes for each company.

"Charlie Company, go." Tully could hear Boatright's orders and the repeats from the company's sergeants. Charlie Company began flowing by him—or at least, flowing as well as a group of very large beings in rather large combat suits could flow. He grinned at that thought.

"Kobayashi, move up and be ready to join us. Boatright, cluster your people around that large double door to the right." After a moment, Tully said, "Okay, Kobayashi, down the ramp and cluster by the three hatches that are directly in front of the ramp."

Once all the jinau were down and grouped by company, Tully said, "Heads-up, troops. Take a fast look at your maps. Able, you've got green; Baker, you're red; Charlie, you're blue. This is like an urban warfare scenario, guys. I know plenty of you, both Jao and humans, have some experience at this, but some of you don't, so I'll keep it simple. Open every door you go by, even if you have to kick it in, and be prepared to shoot. Throw a grenade down every cross corridor you encounter.

"This is supposed to be an Interdict ship, so there probably won't be any slaves to be seen. If you see some that you can capture without risk, give it a try. We can always use more interrogation subjects. That is definitely a third priority, however, behind killing Ekhat and behind keeping yourselves and your fellow fire team members alive. Otherwise, anything that moves—anything that looks like it might move—shoot on sight. You've got some of the new armor piercing ammo, which is supposed to penetrate even the Ekhat suits. This is the field test. If it works, great. If it doesn't, use the flame guns to toast them and then shoot them after their suits burn off."

"Colonel Tully." That was Ginta's voice, which was unexpected. Tully held up his hand to flag everyone else he was taking another com signal. "Captain Ginta? I'm in the middle of an operation."

"I am exiting *Ban Chao.*"

It took Tully a moment to figure out what the Jao meant. "You mean you're pulling *Ban Chao* out of the target?"

"Yes?"

"You can't do that!"

"I must, to support *Pool Buntyam* and the other ships as they combat the remaining Ekhat on this vector."

"Shit!"

"We will come back for you."

"You'd damn well better," Tully snarled.

"If we don't, you can dock my pay," Ginta replied.

That response was so unexpected that Tully was

taken aback. A Jao with a sense of humor as skewed as his own? Who would have thought it?

"You have five of your minutes," Ginta said, and the com channel went dead.

"Move out," Tully ordered the jinau as he dropped his hand. "Now. Get through the doors, and try to get past something that seals ASAP. *Ban Chao*'s pulling out. The rest of the fleet needs her for the fleet action for this planet. That means we're on our own until she comes back. Watch your backs, people. Don't do anything stupid. I will personally crucify anyone who buys the farm because they were stupid. Go."

He watched as the jinau began filing through their assigned doorways. After a moment, he missed the presence of the first sergeant. He looked around, only to spot the sergeant back in the mouth of the ram gate, backing down the ramp as he pulled a load out of the ship. "Three troops . . . each company . . . to me . . . now." The big man was panting from exertion.

Luff straightened as the load cleared the end of the ramp and the jinau dashed up. He started slamming packs into the arms of each of them. "One extra load each of ammo, of grenades, and of juice for the flame guns. Make them last."

With that, the carriers turned and headed for their doors again, moving as fast as they could under the extra loads. Tully watched as the Able and Baker jinau cleared their doors, then he and Luff grabbed the arms of the last Charlie jinau, the one carrying the fluids for the flame guns, and hustled him through the double doors, which other jinau stood to slam them shut on their heels.

"Tully to Ginta. We're clear."

"Good hunting, Colonel."

"You, too."

A massive vibration began in the fabric of the ship, rattling their bones from feet up, visually distorting the walls around them. It grew stronger and stronger, peaked, then began dying away, until a few seconds later, it was only a memory as the residual harmonics dampened to the point where they couldn't even be felt in the decks.

"Colonel . . ."

That was Boatright. Tully held up one finger, and the lieutenant fell silent. Tully switched to a private channel and pinged the first sergeant.

"Yes, sir."

"And what was that about?"

"Colonel, we're going to lose enough troops on this mission. Even more since we won't be able to retreat to *Ban Chao* to resupply. Those few extra loads just might keep a few more of the boys and girls alive."

There was no joy in the sergeant's voice, no warmth, no burble of a chuckle lurking under the surface. There was only the steady hard tone of someone who had done what needed to be done, and be damned to the consequences.

Tully sighed. "Okay, Top. Good thinking. And I hope that you're right about this keeping more of our troops off the butcher's bill. Remind me to have a word with the ship drivers when we get back, though. This isn't happening again. Now, let's let the lieutenant get his show on the road." He flipped back to the company frequency. "I'm back, Boatright."

"Right, Colonel. If you'd take center post, I'll take forward behind the leading scouts."

Tully studied Boatright's diagram. "Good, but I recommend you let Top post back with the rearguard."

A moment later, a pip for the first sergeant appeared toward the bottom of the diagram.

Boatright looked to Tully as if he was expecting the colonel to say something. Tully just nodded. "Move out," Boatright ordered.

As Charlie Company began its advance down the corridor, Tully muttered to himself, "Yea, though I walk through the valley of the shadow of death, I will fear no evil, 'cause I'm the meanest son of a bitch in the valley."

He heard a snort. A glance at his display revealed that he hadn't disconnected from Sergeant Luff.

"You eavesdropping, Top?"

"You caught me, Colonel. But I thought that was my line."

"Tell you what, Top—we'll talk about it after this little walk in the dark is done."

CHAPTER 67

Caitlin looked at the system plot again. "What am I seeing, Lieutenant? The icons are so close together I'm not making sense of it."

"Come look over my shoulder, Director," Vaughan said. She did so, with Ed at her side.

Vaughan pointed to a smaller screen in his workstation, then started tapping controls. "Okay, we have twenty-four Ekhat ships that have survived *Trident* and exited the sun—so far."

"No more, please," Caitlin said. She noticed that Caewithe was to her left, and Lim and Kamozh and his companions to Ed's right.

Vaughan shrugged. "Not up to me, sorry. Anyway, of the twenty-four," one group of icons was suddenly outlined in yellow, "seven have peeled off on a vector for Khûr-mar, the inner planet. Ramt's assessment is they are probably Interdict ships, which would make some sense of why they would avoid the others. Of those, these two," two icons changed to solid yellow, "were intercepted by *Ban Chao.* One of them, Ekhat One, was destroyed. The second, Ekhat Two, was taken out of the fight after *Ban Chao* rammed it and offloaded the entire assault team." Caitlin clenched her fists at that statement, but continued to try to pay attention to the Lieutenant's presentation.

"*Ban Chao* has now left Ekhat Two," Vaughan continued, tapping more controls, "and moved to rendezvous with the fleet detachment commanded by Krant-Captain Mallu." Those icons were now outlined in blue.

"So that gives Mallu, what..." Ed said, "*Pool Buntyam* and *Sun Tzu* for heavy ships, *Ban Chao* as a limited application heavy, and three lighter ships from one of the Harrier squadrons."

"Harriers aren't exactly lightweight," Vaughan looked up.

"No, but they aren't in the same class as a *Lex* or even *Ban Chao.*" Ed grabbed his chin between a thumb and forefinger. "So we've got basically two battleships, three heavy cruisers, and what might be called a pocket battleship, against five ships of unknown capability, right?"

"Yes. Ekhats Three, Four, Five, Six, and Seven," Vaughan said. "We can't tell much about them except their size, but they're all at or near the mass of a Harrier, which would indicate they're pretty nasty customers."

"But outside of the jinau troops being trapped inside of Ekhat Two, that's going to be pretty close to an even match." Small comfort to Gabe and his troops, Caitlin thought grimly.

"Right. Unlike what's coming our way," Vaughan

said. Caitlin got dizzy for a moment as the workstation display spun through a fast recalibration phase, then settled into a display oriented on Khûr-shi. "Three groups of ships," Vaughan began, "here, here, and here." They were outlined in red, purple, and teal.

"Four large ships in the lead, Ekhat Eight, Nine, Ten, and Eleven, outlined in red. They each mass more than a Harrier, if not quite as much as a *Lex*. Ramt is pretty certain that they are not dedicated combat ships, but rather a class of heavily armed multipurpose ships that is a common design mostly used by the Melody faction, according to the Jao files."

"Light cruiser equivalents?" Ed asked.

"Mmm, medium to heavy, depending on when they were built and who built them. Some of this class have come close to Harrier strength."

"Ouch," Ed said.

There was a moment of silence, then Caitlin forced herself to ask, "What's the next group?"

"Ekhats Twelve through Seventeen are in purple. They're a mixed bag of what looks like someone just scraped up whatever hulls they could get quickly and kicked them our way. Thirteen and Sixteen," two icons pulsed, "are pretty heavy, more than the Melody ships, but still no larger than Harriers. Twelve and Seventeen are smaller, but their profile fits some of the True Harmony's raiders, according to Ramt, so we're tagging this group to that faction. And the last two are not much more than scout ships, and really don't have any business being here."

"And the last group?" Ed asked.

"Unknown, because they're all carrying plasma balls in their shields. Ekhats Eighteen through Twenty-four.

They've got to be pretty good-sized to be able to do that, but we have no idea as to how big, how they're armed, or even what faction they are from, because the plasma screens our sensors."

Caitlin shuddered. "Those have to be stopped at all costs," she said. "No matter what, those have to be stopped."

"That is Fleet Commander Dannet's intention," Vaughan said.

"So let me make sure I've got this right," Ed said. "Six heavy cruisers, two lighter ships, maybe light cruisers, and two scout ships. Plus seven ships from Hell. Against them Dannet has three *Lexingtons* and six Harriers."

"Yes, General. Plus the Eleusherar Path ship *Starcloud* when it finally catches up to us. It will be of limited use, due to the lack of integrated communication, but they could still do some good if the envoys can pass information back and forth. But even not counting them, if it wasn't for the plasma balls, the odds would probably be slightly in our favor. As it is, well..."

"Dannet has *Footloose* and three Harriers posted well away from and behind our station here. Reserve? They could make a difference if things get dicey here."

"She hasn't confided in me," Vaughan said not quite sardonically, with a touch to his lieutenant's insignia. "But I'm starting to learn how she thinks. I'd say that's more to keep an eye out for an end run around our ships or a sudden diversion to attack the outer worlds. Either way, she can call them running if she decides we need them here."

There was another moment of quiet, which ended

when Dannet straightened, assumed what Caitlin interpreted as angles for *adamant-purpose*, and began issuing orders.

"Right," Vaughan said. "'Scuse me, but life just got interesting."

Kamozh followed the discussion between Director Kralik, General Kralik, and Lieutenant Vaughan fairly well through Lim's translations. Director Kralik's emotion needed little translation, and it continued to impress upon him that there were apparently "monsters," and then there were "monsters."

After the action began, Lim did her best to translate for them, but inevitably for the next few hours Kamozh and the envoys were mostly spectators at a show they didn't understand. They understood enough, though—enough to finish that change of attitude.

CHAPTER 68

Third-Mordent paused in the midst of her choreography of a new blade dance variation. Her head lifted and she looked up and over her left shoulder. After a moment, she straightened and folded her forehand blades away as she turned to face that direction.

"What do you . . . ah," Ninth-Minor-Sustained intoned. "You hear it, do you?"

"Yes," Third-Mordent whisper-sang in reply. "What is it?"

"That, oh my progeny," Ninth-Minor-Sustained sang in aria form, "that was your final test. You can indeed hear the Melody when it calls."

"But why?" Third-Mordent adopted a soliloquy form. "Or rather, why now?"

"The would-be tunesmiths of the race have gone out in search of the nexus," the harmony master sang, "and they are closing in on it. The Melody responds to their movements, to their passions, to their very lives and deaths. They are fuel to the Melody's conflagration."

"Will they succeed?" Third-Mordent returned to whisper-song.

"They must," Ninth-Minor-Sustained intoned. "If they do not, the balance will tip against us, to be restored only by a great pouring out of lives and blood and resources."

There was a long moment of silence, then Third-Mordent moved to look out the observation window at the empty space surrounding the station. Ninth-Minor-Sustained came to stand a couple of paces behind her, and Third-Mordent could see her reflection in the window pane before her.

The harmony master finally broke the quiet. "The Jao are not stupid," she whisper-sang herself, making a soft eerie melody. "They have their limits, but they are not stupid. We, the Complete Harmony, know that better than anyone, having made the mistake of uplifting them and continually trying to improve them until we gave them too much. The Interdict is right in that much—it was our harmony masters, our songs, that crafted the Jao."

Ninth-Minor-Sustained fell silent again. After another long moment of silence, she continued the whisper-song, even softer, "Perhaps we tried too hard to get them to hear the Melody. Perhaps we should have accepted them as they were, and not tried to make them more like us. But, oh, they had such potential. They could have been such a tool; such a help; if only they could have learned to hear."

"So now they stand against us," Third-Mordent sang in dirge form. "Now they would make it as if the Melody had never existed."

"Once they broke with us," Ninth-Minor-Sustained

echoed the dirge, "what choice had they? Once the harmony master Full-Caesura pushed them beyond their limits, pushed them out of our harmony, it was never sung—never dreamt—that they would find it within themselves to oppose us, to become the anti-Melody." The harmony master stepped up beside Third-Mordent and directed her own gaze out the window. "Full-Caesura did not survive that initial event," she intoned in a recitative. "Which is just as well for her sake. Her name is not part of the history files, and her bloodlines to the tenth collateral degree were purged. If I had known what she would do, I would have completed her myself beforehand."

Third-Mordent froze. "You . . . you knew this harmony master . . ." she stuttered in recitative mode.

"A member of my parent's creche generation," Ninth-Minor-Sustained remained in dirge mode. "And as it proved out, one who should have been removed from the breeding lists much earlier. The Complete Harmony has been dealing with the coda of her song ever since."

"And now?" Third-Mordent returned her focus to the darkness of space.

"Now the Jao have risen to challenge the entire race, not just our faction," the harmony master whisper-sang. "Now the nexus approaches. And on the thinnest of forehand blades balances the future of the Complete Harmony, the Ekhat, and the Melody."

Third-Mordent stared out the window. "So thin . . ." she finally whisper-sang in a tone almost as thin as the metaphorical blade.

CHAPTER 69

Tully scanned his helmet display after another round of Ekhat slaughter, and bit down hard on the urge to curse. Eleven jinau dead, and eight more wounded to one degree or another. Versus an unknown number of Ekhat shot down, blown up by grenades, or immolated by the flame guns. And it had been all Ekhat. No slaves of any type had been seen so far, which given Ekhat propensities, made Tully certain there weren't any to be had on the ship. This pretty well proved Buckley's assessment that this was an Interdict ship, since they were the only Ekhat faction that outright banned slaves. Not that that made the Interdict any more acceptable to the Jao-human-Lleix alliance than any of the other Ekhat factions. Tully wanted to spit, but that was contraindicated in a helmet.

The fighting had been worse than even he had expected. It had all the negatives of urban warfare, combined with being limited in their ability to move laterally. They could only go so far before they ran into hull, and when that happened they were in a position to be pinned and swamped by waves of Ekhat. Baker Company had lost five jinau that way, before they placed their two flame gunners at the front of their breakout attempt. They had burned their way out of the encirclement, but it had used a worryingly large amount of their fuel. That did not bode well for an extended battle.

Without the *Ban Chao* behind them, retreating had the same issue. Their best hope was to keep moving onward and outward, until they cleared the ship. Which was what they were supposed to be doing. Tully hated the price for it, though.

"XO," Tully said.

"Colonel," Major Liang's voice responded through Tully's com bud.

"Are you mapping all of our progress?"

"Yes, sir."

"I make it that we've covered maybe a third of the volume of this bitch," Tully growled. He was not happy at the moment.

"Concur. About that, maybe a bit more," the major replied.

"Get with Buckley and see if you can determine where the engine room on this thing is. I want to blow that out ASAP. As I recall, the Ekhat don't do well in null-G, so that would be a big help."

"On it now, sir."

"Top," Tully called out next.

"Sir."

"Make a note for the action report. I really want to have a conversation with the manufacturers of the combat suits about how they don't seem to do very well in blocking penetration by those obscene organic short-swords the Ekhat come equipped with."

"Yes, sir. Can I sell tickets?" Luff sounded serious. He hadn't been any happier about some of the casualties than Tully was.

"No, but I may let you tag team with me."

"Outstanding! Promise?"

"Speaking of swords, we need to take one or two back for testing." Tully's suspicion was confirmed by Luff's response.

"Not a problem, sir. The boys will see to that."

The thought of Ekhat body-parts showing up on the Internet auction sites tickled Tully's sense of humor. His response was lost as two more Ekhat appeared from around a bend in the corridor, heads down, jaws agape, and those damned sword things pointed forward as if they were lances. Suddenly it wasn't so funny.

"Spin the ship," Caitlin heard Terra-Captain Uldra order. That order she understood. Spinning *Lexington* around her longitudinal axis would also spin her shields, which meant that the lasers of the front-running Ekhat ships, which had found their range, would not be able to concentrate on a single limited area of the shield to overload it. Something the humans had mentioned, she knew.

And oh yeah, had the Ekhat found the range. *Arjuna* and *Fancy Free* were taking even more hits than the *Lex* was.

"*Arjuna* reports loss of atmosphere in Laser spine B. Two laser mounts nonfunctional, seven crew dead. Remaining crew continuing to fight in their suits."

That was Vaughan's quiet voice reporting to Fleet

Commander Dannet. Something had broken through *Arjuna*'s shields long enough and hard enough to penetrate the armor of one of the weapons spines and almost cripple it.

There was a stifled cheer from one of the human sensor techs as one of the Ekhat ships disappeared from the plot. "Ekhat Ten gone!" came the report.

"*Lexington* move to advance Alpha position," Dannet instructed Terra-Captain Uldra. "Orders to *Arjuna*—withdraw to trailing Gamma position. Execute now."

Krant-Captain Mallu observed the plot in *Pool Buntyam*'s command deck main viewer. After a moment, he made up his mind. "Harrier element, remain on planar level, withdraw slowly before the Ekhat, take every available shot. *Pool Buntyam* will take north of the plane, *Sun Tzu* will take south of the plane, and *Ban Chao* attack from their rear." Mallu looked to where Kaln was standing in a surprisingly elegant *neutral* posture, so unlike her usual angles. But she said nothing, so he said, "Open fire when flow is right."

He watched the plot as the formation opened out, the two heavy ships moving north and south of the solar plane in something resembling a pincers operation, and the three Harriers assuming something like a line-abreast formation in order to maximize their firepower.

The Ekhat opened fire. There was, of course, no visible light from their lasers, but the energy discharges registered on the Jao sensors, as did the few light contacts with their shields. They were severely out of their effective range; but try telling that to the Ekhat.

Once they had their formation in place, Mallu watched the plot, his eyes focused on the icon for

Ban Chao. It was closing rapidly, and Mallu could feel time approaching. He spared a glance for Kaln, who nodded to him. One more look at *Ban Chao*, which had visibly closed the distance in just that short moment.

"Fire."

The Harriers fired a bare fraction of an instant before *Pool Buntyam* and *Sun Tzu.* The Ekhat made the sad discovery that their personal technology in those ships was not state-of-the-art—at least, not state-of-the-art as practiced by the Jao and Terra taif. The power of the lasers of the *Lex*-class ships was more than they had prepared for; had been designed for, for that matter. Ekhat Six immediately lost all power as several shots from *Sun Tzu* crashed through its shields and apparently destroyed its engine room. Its companion ships pulled away from it, and the rest of the Jao ships ignored it for the moment.

A long moment after that, *Ban Chao* opened fire. The remaining Ekhat ships all took hits in their after quadrants. *Ban Chao*'s lasers were even heavier than a *Lexington*'s, so the unprepared Ekhat ships Five and Seven joined their companion Six in drifting.

By this time even the commanders of Ekhats Three and Four seemed to realize that something was seriously wrong. Mallu watched as they appeared to react in stereotypical Ekhat fashion, boosting their acceleration to the highest degree and lunging for the Harriers.

The remainder of the action was very short. Surprisingly, the two Ekhat seemed to cooperate to the extent that they fired on one Harrier together. The Harrier's shields held for a long moment, then went down just before the combined fire of Mallu's heavy ships overwhelmed the Ekhat and shattered their own shields and hulls.

It was almost anticlimactic. Mallu had never commanded a battle that went so well. He remembered the last fight he commanded, against ships of the Melody faction, the fight that had ultimately led to the rediscovery of the remnant of the Lleix. He had destroyed the two ships that had found him, but he'd lost two irreplaceable Krant ships and crew and half the crew of the sole surviving ship that had limped to a barely reachable port world just before it ceased functioning altogether. That was where the Bond had found him.

Kaln moved toward him, interrupting his thoughts. "We need to move. Leave the others, but we and *Sun Tzu* need to move."

"And go where?" Jalta demanded, his angles an aggressive *judgment-of-foolishness.*

Kaln touched a control on her com pad. "Here," she said.

A point appeared on the system plot, parallel to the path the Ekhat were following to Khûr-shi, but out of effective laser weapons range. Mallu looked at it, and looked at the ships in the trailing segments of the assault.

"*Ban Chao* to retrieve the jinau and neutralize that target. Harriers to eliminate the remaining Ekhat vessels here." Mallu looked at Jalta, and assumed angles for *demanding-ultimate-obedience*. "*Pool Buntyam* and *Sun Tzu* to move to the designated point. Maximum speed."

Jalta stood for a moment, then his angles slowly morphed to *obedience.*

CHAPTER 70

The casualty count was now fifteen jinau dead and thirteen wounded. Tully's jaws ached from his teeth being clenched. He made a decision.

"All units, pull back ten meters and break. Watch around your perimeter, but take fifteen to breathe. Sergeants, check loads and share around if needed. Officers, on me in five."

Tully called up his map of the ship and studied it. From what he could tell, they had penetrated to and through over fifty percent of the ship, but they still hadn't found either the engineering space or the control deck. On the other hand, they had killed a boatload of Ekhat—at not negligible cost to the assault battalion. His jaws started aching again.

Ping!

Tully checked his display. The last of the officers had tagged into the commanders frequency, along with First Sergeant Luff.

"XO," Tully began, "what's the report on where the engineering space is on this bucket?"

"Buckley's been working on that, Colonel," Major Liang said. "Show him, Lieutenant."

A new map flared to life in Tully's helmet display. "Near as I can tell, Colonel," Buckley said, "It ought to be here." A yellow blob pulsed. "Able, Baker, and Charlie Companies are here, here, and here." Red, green, and blue blobs pulsed at the appropriate moments.

Tully studied the map. After a couple of minutes, he said, "Top, who's lightest on loads?"

"Baker Company, sir, in both ammo and fire juice. Also has the fewest working bodies."

"Congratulations, Torg. You're the reserve. Plus you get to watch everyone's back for them, as well."

Torg made no audible reply, but Tully grinned for a moment at the thought of what the Jao's angles might be displaying at the moment. "Okay, heads-up. Able, you'll go this angle." A red arrow arced out of the red blob toward one side of the presumed engineering space. "And Charlie, here's yours." A blue arrow arced out of Charlie's blob to match the red one on the other side. "Baker, as the others move, slide this way and fill the gap as much as you can. You've got our backs." A short green arrow materialized. "Objective is to penetrate the engineering space and destroy the controls with an eye to putting the ship on zero gee. Any questions?"

"Suggestion," Captain Torg spoke up.

"Go."

"Take Horzat and Eolle from my company. They're Jao that have boarded Ekhat ships before, and may be able to recognize what needs to be blown once you get in."

"Great!" Tully responded. "Send them to Charlie

Company, and have them bring whatever you have in the way of breaching charges. I suspect we're going to need it all before we're done."

He looked at the map one more time. "Right. Able, kick off in five minutes. Charlie, kick off three minutes after the two troops from Baker join up. Baker, kick off thirty seconds after Charlie moves. Let's go, people. Make it happen."

"Bond Harrier 65463 destroyed," came the report from a sensor tech confirming what the plot told them. Caitlin watched Ed shake his head. She was too numb to move by this point. That was the fourth of Harrier Squadron Delta's ships that had been destroyed. That only left two still functioning, and one of them had sustained damage.

On the other hand, Ekhats Eight, Twelve, and Fourteen had been destroyed, and Ekhat Fifteen had taken enough damage that it had fallen out of the assault.

"*Fancy Free* reports D laser spine has lost all power. Crew has been evacuated to main hull." Vaughan's report to Dannet was also audible to Caitlin, and she was not too numb to stiffen at that report. With the damage to *Arjuna*, that was almost a third of the battleships' laser armament damaged. Only *Lexington* herself was still able to fire full volleys at the Ekhat from all decks. The other two had to restrict their movements in order to make sure that at least one of their two functioning laser decks would bear on the Ekhat.

"B spine and F spine both report breaches in their hull," an engineering tech reported to Terra-Captain Uldra. "B reports damage to four laser mounts and heavy casualties, F reports no damage and only two casualties. Both decks continuing to fire when they bear."

Caitlin felt Caewithe and Tamt move closer to her. She looked over to see a full complement of her guards standing at the door from the command deck to the hall. "Director," Caewithe began formally, "you need to think about moving to a safer space."

"No." Caitlin wrapped her arms around herself.

"Caitlin," Ed began.

"No, dammit!" She looked up into her husband's eyes. "I brought them here. Every one of them. All those ships, all those crew, and all your jinau. *They followed me here, and I will not cower in a closet while they fight and die in the battle I ordered!*" She hammered her fist into his chest once. "If our positions were reversed, would you do that?" Ed said nothing, but he sighed. "I didn't think so." Caitlin turned back toward the main viewscreen where the system plot was updating. "Forget it, both of you. I'll be here on the command deck until this is settled, one way or another."

"Bond Harrier 99727 destroyed," a sensor tech reported. Caitlin inhaled sharply, but said nothing. There was nothing left to say.

"They die like heroes," Kamozh whispered.

CHAPTER 71

Lieutenant Joe Buckley was following the lead fire team of Able Company down what they thought was the last corridor before they reached what he'd suggested as the engineering space. They hadn't seen Ekhat since they separated from the other companies and started this movement, but that didn't mean they were safe. He kept his eyes peeled and his weapon at the ready. That still wasn't enough.

Buckley barely caught the flicker of movement as the wall just behind his right shoulder flew upward. *There was no sign of a door there!* he thought in mingled indignation and panic.

Even as Buckley started to turn toward the opening, the first Ekhat through hit him with a shoulder and flung him across the corridor to slam against the opposite wall. Buckley managed to stay on his feet and take the impact of the wall on his back, but it still hammered him and paralyzed his breathing for a split second.

The first Ekhat was the largest Buckley had yet seen on this ship, but it ignored him and turned down the corridor in the direction the company had come from and plunged into the midst of the jinau. Shouts and gunfire erupted.

The second Ekhat through the opening was just as large, and it also ignored Buckley as it turned the other direction in the corridor and assaulted the leading troops, which created a stereo effect of shouts and gunfire from that direction.

Then the third Ekhat leapt through the opening. It was even larger that the first two, and it did not ignore Buckley. It angled toward him. He struggled to bring his weapon up to bear on the Ekhat, and managed to fire a few shots into the body of the creature, but it was too little, too late.

Buckley's last sight was the open maw of the beast as it descended on his head. His last thought was *Oh, sh—*, terminated by the *crunch* of his helmet and the skull inside being crushed by the jaws of the giant Ekhat, even as it was being riddled by the fire of the jinau around them.

Charlie Company had made it to the designated corridor that surrounded what Buckley had said was the engineering space without seeing a single Ekhat. Tully stepped back away from the wall to let First Sergeant Luff and some of Charlie's best try to figure out where to plant the breaching charges to get through the corridor walls around the space. They'd already decided to avoid the hatch that they could see a few meters down the corridor. Tully had been prepared to utter some wise comment about not knocking on the front door, but Boatright and his sergeants had already figured that angle out.

"Able Company, status," Tully murmured into his helmet mic.

There was a surprisingly long silence. Just as Tully was about to repeat his query, a voice responded.

"Sorry, Colonel, but we've been busy for the last moment or so."

Tully's jaw started aching again. He could tell from his helmet display that it was Sergeant Cold Bear responding. If Captain Kobayashi wasn't available, that was probably not a good sign. Tully had to work to open his jaws. "How busy?"

"Ekhat busy, sir. They had a concealed door or something on this corridor, and after about a third of the company had passed by it opened up and three of the biggest Ekhat I've seen came charging out. We've been putting them down for the last couple of minutes. Just finished. Captain's doing damage assessment and trying to reorganize what's left."

Getting his mouth open for the next question was even harder. "How bad, Sarge?"

"Three obviously dead," Cold Bear replied, "including Lieutenant Buckley. My display says four more pretty seriously injured. There might be more."

"Shit."

"Yep. Here's the captain."

There was a click in his com bud, and Kobayashi's accented baritone came through. "Colonel?"

"Cold Bear's given me the bad news, Sato. How soon can you start moving again, and when do you think you'll reach the objective?"

Tully heard the captain take a deep breath. "I think

we're within five minutes of the objective, sir, but in order to finish tending to the wounded, I'd say maybe ten minutes before we can pick up and move."

"Understood estimate of fifteen minutes to reach the objective. Keep me posted. And Sato?"

"Yes, sir?"

"Bad shit happens. In this case, about the baddest shit that could happen. Good job to you and your troops in dealing with it, and you can tell them I said so."

"Thank you, Colonel."

"Tully out."

He could see the first sergeant look his direction. "You catch all that, Top?"

"Yes, sir."

"Able's hurting. Tell Boatright and his team leaders to keep an eye out for them, and to be prepared to take up more of the perimeter."

"I'll take care of it, sir."

Tully looked up and down the corridor, watching Charlie's jinau prepping. *Okay, Buckley, I really needed you to stay alive at least a little bit longer. What's on the other side of that wall? And perhaps more importantly, who's on the other side of that wall?*

That consideration forced him to make his decision. "Torg? XO?"

"Colonel?"

"Colonel?"

The two of them spoke almost in unison.

"Torg, start moving this way. Take a path between the two approaches I lined out for Able and Charlie. Soonest, because Able just took some major casualties, and I want you near before we do anything else."

"On the way, Colonel."

"XO, one of the troops Able lost was Buckley."

"Damn," came the response from Major Liang.

"Agreed," Tully said. "Take a look at what Buckley had, and see if you can squeeze any more info out of it. Bring Top into it if you need to."

"On it, Colonel."

"Tully out."

And now it was just down to getting the jinau lined up and the charges laid. *What have I missed?*

Caitlin was cold.

The last Harrier of Delta Squadron was gone. *Arjuna* had lost her entire F spine, and *Sun Tzu* had taken major damage to her B spine. Between the two of them, they had only about as many lasers as one of them had manned when the fight began. It was too bad they couldn't use their cannon decks, but even after what *Pool Buntyam* had done in the last battle against an Ekhat squadron, everyone said that those guns had no role in a battle in open space. Too bad, she repeated the thought. There was just something satisfying about knowing you were pounding your enemy with physical shells.

Unlike her sister ships, *Lexington* had not suffered additional damage, but Caitlin knew that would not last. As her sisters became less effective, more of the Ekhat fire was coming toward the *Lex*.

Against all that, they could only say that it appeared that Ekhat Seventeen had apparently suffered some damage.

Dannet had ordered *Footloose* and her three companion Harriers back to the main squadron to bolster their firepower. The losses hadn't left any choice. But they hadn't arrived yet.

Caitlin had held such hopes, that the Terra taif fleet would defeat the Ekhat and preserve the Khûr system. They all had. But . . .

Bad enough that the Ekhat had managed to find a way to follow them. How? But to send so many ships . . . it was beyond her comprehension. According to Ramt, there were no records of a fleet that large in the databases and records of either the Jao or the Lleix.

Of course, from the things that Vaughan was muttering, the Ekhat hadn't fought a very smart battle so far. But then again, it was becoming apparent that if you had enough ships, and they were big enough and nasty enough, you didn't necessarily have to fight smart to win.

Caitlin looked at the screen. And the seven plasma ships were still there, trundling their way toward Khûr-shi. They hadn't been touched at all.

She grew colder.

CHAPTER 72

In the end, they outlined the hatch with a breaching charge, and blew it first. As it blew inward, three volleys of mixed grenades were fired through the opening. Tully didn't have much hope that the fragmentation grenades would take down many of the Ekhat he was almost certain were in the space, since the unsane beasts seemed to be in perpetual berserker mode to the point where they almost had to be dismembered to be taken down. The flash/bangs should prove at least somewhat disorienting, though, and he really hoped the white phosphorus rounds would splash on at least a few of the Ekhat. After seeing so many of his troops die—especially after seeing how Buckley had died—Tully didn't at all mind the thought of the Ekhat getting a little personal taste of the hell they had been handing out to weaker races for unknown eras.

No sooner had the hatch components stopped bouncing on the deck inside the area than Ekhat began trying to charge through the space. That was the signal for the four flame gunners standing near the hatch to let fly. Three seconds of that ultra-hot treatment was enough to reduce three good-sized Ekhat to smoldering hulks jammed in the opening where the hatch used to be.

"I'm dry," one of the gunners said as he dropped his backpack and flame gun to the deck and unslung his rifle.

"Me, too," said another as he did the same thing.

Tully could tell from their patches that they were the gunners from Baker Company, who had used so much of their supplies in leading the breakout when Baker had been pinned against the hull. That had been taken into account, and they headed for their next assigned positions.

Tully could see other forms moving around behind the mounds of the immolated Ekhat, but the flames that were still roaring around them were apparently keeping the others from attempting to charge through.

That wouldn't last much longer, though, Tully decided. "Go round two," he ordered.

Two more sets of breaching charges blew a couple of seconds later. This time the four remaining flame gunners stepped into the breaches, two into each. As soon as they cleared the openings, jinau began following them through. In just a few moments, Tully was standing in a near-empty corridor near the group of seriously wounded jinau and a couple of walking wounded who were watching over them. Even Major Liang and First Sergeant Luff had gone in with the entry teams, they were getting so low in able bodies.

"This is main drive engineering," came a report that his helmet display indicated was from Horzat.

"Great!" Tully responded. "Let's get the space cleared out, and we'll shut down the gravity. That will let us clean house."

Tully's helmet display gave him some indication of what was happening in the engineering space. The jinau had, as he had hoped, found enough space to be able to spread out and more or less surround the surviving Ekhat, pinning them in their turn against the corridor bulkhead. He had to assume that the Ekhat were being taken down, as orders were going back and forth on the com frequencies and the jinau circle was continuing to slowly contract.

Shouts rose to a crescendo over the network as suddenly the circle was distorted to one side.

"Watch out!"

"Ciappa, drop!"

"They're breaking out..."

Then came one clear message: "Heads up, Colonel!"

Tully had that one bare moment's warning before a large Ekhat bulled its way through the smoldering mounds in the hatchway opening. The flames had died down, and nobody—including Tully—had thought to have one of the flame gunners refresh them.

The white hide of this Ekhat was visibly lacerated and shot up, with white fluid streaking it in contrast to smudges of soot and angry looking burns and blisters. It had no sooner cleared the opening than it spun and headed toward the wounded and their guards.

"Oh, *hell*, no!"

Tully had already pulled his 10 mm sidearm, and now he stepped between the wounded and the charging Ekhat. The sights lined up on the Ekhat's large head and he began pulling the trigger as quickly as he could.

The pistol had a fifteen-round magazine, and Tully was making hits. He even took out one of the creature's eyes. But most of them were just bouncing off of the Ekhat's skull; nothing was stopping it. Tully had extra magazines, of course, but he could tell he wouldn't have time to reload. The Ekhat was too close.

Tully didn't even think about it. He dropped his left hand to his vest as his right hand triggered the last three rounds, pulled a grenade and popped the pin, then shoved it into the mouth of the beast.

"Eat shit and d-*aaargh!*" Tully screamed as the Ekhat's jaws slammed shut on his forearm, followed an instant later by the explosion of the grenade where he still held it in his hand.

Then the mass of the Ekhat slammed him into the deck and everything went black.

CHAPTER 73

Caitlin took stock after the latest flurry of action.

Footloose had shown a noticeably higher acceleration than the Harriers, leaving them behind. She made it back to the main squadron in time to help beat back a concerted attack that left *Arjuna* little more than a floating hulk. In exchange, Ekhat Fifteen, last of the scout-class ships, already seriously wounded, was now just floating debris. But that still left six significant Ekhat combat vessels able to attack plus the trailing group of seven that still were holding plasma in their shields.

Against that they could muster one "fully operational" *Lex*-class in *Footloose* and two damaged sisters in *Fancy Free* and *Lexington* herself. The remaining Harriers would be fed into the fight as soon as they arrived, but Caitlin was afraid that would be too little, too late.

Caitlin looked over at D'mishri. He'd promised the Eleusherar Path had ships that would help. Where were they? Even *Starcloud* hadn't caught up with them yet. Were they really that slow, or were they dragging their feet?

She looked back at the viewscreen. Ekhats Nine, Ten, and Eleven were beginning to press forward again, with Thirteen and Sixteen on their heels.

"Where are your ships?" Kamozh demanded of D'mishri. "These people are dying at the gates trying to hold back this tide. Their other ships defeated the attack on Khûr-mar, but they won't be able to get here in time to prevent the breakthrough. They're going to die in vain, just like our toy ships did, if your ships don't get here soon."

"I know," D'mishri rumbled. He looked down at the communicator resting on the workstation in front of him. Kamozh was starting to be able to read emotions from the envoy's body. The big fangs had made it hard to read D'mishri's face—still did for that matter. But the body, that was another matter. The slumped posture spoke of weariness more than anything else.

"I had some idea as to where some of our ships might have been when *Starcloud* started its patrol," D'mishri added, "but I have no idea where they really were, especially once these Terrans and Jao and Lleix came bursting out of the sun. And travel time and making plans have to be accounted for. I don't know where they are, but I wish by everything I hold dear before the Immanence that they would get here."

The communicator chose that moment to chirp. Five pairs of eyes—D'mishri's, three Khûrûshil, and Lim the Lleix's—locked onto that communicator with varying emotions: surprise, hope, frustration, dread.

D'mishri snatched it up and spoke a short hard

word into it that Kamozh didn't understand. Must have been from his own language, or whatever the usual Eleusherar Path chosen language in this system was.

The envoy listened intently, interspersing his listening with what from his tone were short sharp questions. Kamozh watched as D'mishri straightened, threw back his shoulders, and ran his free hand through his head fur.

The conversation ended with two sharp sentences from D'mishri to whoever was on the other end. The envoy slammed the communicator down and thrust himself to his feet. His shoulders were bunched, and there was a light in his eye that hadn't been there before. Kamozh was on his feet to match him, almost dancing with impatience and pent-up energy.

D'mishri pointed a long finger from which a claw had emerged at Lim. "You need to get me the fleet commander's attention—now!"

"Fleet Commander!" Both Dannet and Caitlin's heads snapped around at the almost shout from Lim. "You must order our ships to withdraw!"

"Why?" demanded Dannet. The demand was echoed in Caitlin's mind.

"Because the Eleusherar Path ships are near, and they are going to attack in less than a tenth of a Khûrûsh hour."

The darkness in Caitlin's mind began to crack at that announcement.

"They're here?" Dannet looked at the viewscreen. There were no additional icons on display.

"Stealth systems, remember," Aille said. He had appeared at Caitlin's side just before he spoke.

"Yeah," Ed muttered. "Top of *our* list."

"Indeed," Aille replied.

D'mishri spoke a quick spill of Khûrûsh. Lim translated, "They're here. Let them carry the fight for a time. At least you can pull back and regroup and try to get major repairs done."

Dannet looked at the envoy, then looked at Caitlin. She said nothing, but the fleet commander seemed to get the message anyway.

"Orders to *Fancy Free*: withdraw in company with *Lexington* to rendezvous point at outer libration point of Khûr-shi's major moon. *Footloose* to cover the withdrawal. Harrier elements to withdraw as well. All execute now."

Caitlin looked at the system plot. She could see the Terra taif ships moving in response to the fleet commander's order, and she could see the beginning movements of the Ekhat ships. It took her a moment to recognize what she wasn't seeing.

"Where's *Starcloud*?" she asked Vaughan.

"Disappeared a few minutes ago," he said, not looking up from his readouts. "Probably under cloak or whatever they call their stealth system so the Ekhat won't see them. I expect they're sprinting forward now that their other ships are apparently in position. And speak of the devil!"

There were suddenly twelve new icons in the system plot, six pairs of them, scattered and curving around the front of the Ekhat formation.

"They don't look very big," Caitlin said as she peered at the system plot.

Vaughan was checking his readouts. "That would be because they're not. They're not a whole lot bigger than some of the Khûrûsh ships that the Ekhat swatted down. I sincerely hope they're a whole lot nastier, because I don't want to watch another massacre."

Lim had been translating for Kamozh and the envoys as Vaughan spoke. When she was done, D'mishri uttered a sound like a gate with rusty hinges being forced open. Caitlin thought that was his equivalent of a chuckle. He began speaking, and Lim translated.

"They are indeed much nastier, Lieutenant. They may be small, but they are fast and carry a very nasty sting."

"Mmm, I'll give you fast," Vaughan muttered as two pairs each moved toward the Ekhat. It quickly became apparent that one pair was vectoring on Ekhat Nine and the other on Ekhat Eleven. "But as close as they're getting it had better be one helluva sting, because the Ekhat are . . . yes, they're firing lasers at the E-Path ships."

"E-Path?" Caitlin queried.

"Eleusherar Path is just too long," Vaughan said with a quirk of his lips. "Hence, E-Path. And what did they just do?" His voice shifted to loud and almost accusatory with that last question, because the little ships had each launched a powered missile of some kind toward their targets, then jinked away at even faster speed.

"The Ekhat will swat those out of—"

There were sudden flares of light in the system plot at the leading points of the missile plots, and streaks of light from those points to the icons of Ekhats Nine and Eleven—which slowly faded from the system plot.

"What the hell was that?" Ed demanded.

"What he said," Vaughan muttered as he pulled data into his workstations. "And . . . aha, back-spill of some very hard radiation. Got it. That, General Kralik," Vaughan said as he tapped pads on his workstations, "had to be nuclear bomb-pumped X-ray lasers. Maybe even hydrogen bomb-pumped. Much more powerful than our continuous power lasers, although obviously with a much shorter firing duration."

"We know about those?" Aille beat Ed to the question.

"They've been a staple in our science fiction for a couple of generations now," Vaughan said, "and we've known they were scientifically feasible for nearly that long. We just didn't have the power and gravitics tech to build them before now."

"More *ollnat*," Aille said, angles moving to a simple *humor.* "I should not be surprised. That is why we partnered with you humans, after all." He looked over at the envoys. "One wonders just how much *ollnat* a culture can express in over four thousand years." That was a thought that hadn't occurred to Caitlin yet. A very sobering thought, at that.

Vaughan changed the atmosphere of the moment when he looked up at Caitlin. "Momma, I know what I want for Christmas."

Caitlin laughed, her mood lightening for the moment.

Vaughan turned to face the envoys. "Why didn't you tell us you had those?"

"You didn't ask," D'mishri responded through Lim.

Caitlin thought she detected some humor in the envoy's tone of voice. She smiled herself in both appreciation of the comment and in renewed hope. "He's right; we hadn't asked that question yet."

Vaughan switched his gaze back to his workstation. "Ekhat moving again, more E-Path ships moving."

CHAPTER 74

"How many crew in one of those ships?" Ed asked, looking toward the envoys.

"Three," the translated answer came back. "Pilot, second pilot, and weapons officer doubling as engineer."

"Oh, my God," Ed said. "The ex-Navy jocks are going to be all over that. That's almost a fighter equivalent there."

Ed turned back to the viewscreen as he stepped up beside Aille. "Governor," Caitlin heard her husband say quietly, his choice of words making it clear which of Aille's various roles he was speaking to, "If they've got that kind of weapons technology, getting that stealth technology just got even more important."

"I agree," Aille said, his angles back in a *neutral* posture. After a moment, he added, "Caitlin, you will continue to have *oudh* over the exploration and search effort. But after this battle is over, Pleniary-superior Tura and I will assume the *oudh* for further discussions and negotiations with the Eleusherar Path. This is somewhat beyond the level of contacts we expected you to make."

Left unspoken was the assumption that they would all survive the battle. Caitlin was not at all sure that that was a safe assumption to make. Nonetheless, she felt a large weight lift from her shoulders. "Thank you," she said.

"Ha!" The exclamation from Vaughan drew their attention back to the viewscreen where the icons for Ekhats Ten, Thirteen, and Sixteen were fading from view after receiving concerted attacks by three pair of E-Path ships. "Damn, that's fun to watch!"

Kamozh looked to Shemnarai. "Are those the weapons that were used to remove the monsters from our skies in the Time of Troubles?"

"A much later version, yes. Even today, four hundred years later, they are very large weapons, to the extent that these attack ships can only carry two of them."

"Ah," Kamozh replied. "Then we Khûrûsh could not build these?"

"No," Shemnarai said. "Not without a significant technology upgrade. You heard the human Vaughan say that they did not have the technology to do it, and they are more advanced than the Khûrûsh."

Kamozh settled back to consider that, until his attention was caught by something on the viewscreen—or rather, something that wasn't there.

The E-path ships vectored back to positions close to where they started. The icons had cleared away, all of them except for Ekhats Eighteen through Twenty-four, the trailing group who still carried a plasma load.

Kamozh chattered something to Lim, his baritone voice carrying a sense of urgency even through the Khûrûshil language.

"Kamozh says the screen has lost an icon. There were four, the E-path attacked three, there should still be one."

Vaughan tapped pads and called up an earlier time-stamp of the system plot. "Crap. He's right. We're missing Seventeen. Dannet, Uldra!" Those two looked sharply in Vaughan's direction. "There's another Ekhat out there that's somehow dropped off our sensors!"

Uldra turned and started snapping orders to his sensor techs. But it was a bit late for that.

"Oh, shit," Vaughan heard Ed Kralik say as an icon flickered into life in front of where the last group of Ekhat had been destroyed.

"He was hiding behind the debris clouds of the destroyed ships," Vaughan said bitterly, slamming his workstation pads to capture the data while he spoke into his mic. With a last triple tap on his pads, he sent copies of all his data from the engagement to *Pool Buntyam*, who at this point looked like it was far more likely to survive what was coming than *Lexington* was. Terra and the Bond needed to get those files.

"Seventeen was one of the True Harmony raiders," Vaughan said. "The Jao files say those suckers are fast. Looks like they're right." The Ekhat icon was moving appreciably toward *Lexington* in the plot. "He's gotten too close for our lasers to bear on him, and the other ships aren't aligned to sight on him. Damn, this is going to hurt. Prepare to be rammed."

CHAPTER 75

Sixth-Mode-Disjunct slapped a Huilek servient out of her way. "All power to the drives," she intoned. Her feet inscribed the beginnings of a blade dance on the deck behind the younger Ekhat who had taken over steering from a Huilek.

Her ship was damaged, Sixth-Mode-Disjunct realized. Severely damaged. That angered her, as she had done great work in the service of True Harmony with this ship. There was no hope for it, though. The alarms shrieking their discordance, the deaths among both the Ekhat and the servients who served the ship, all said this was their last voyage.

"The Jao have found something new," her ship's conductor sang. "This must be discovered. This must be determined and sent back to the harmony masters."

"Shut-shut-shut down the lasers," Sixth-Mode-Disjunct commanded in a stretto form. Ululating Huileks leapt to obey.

Sixth-Mode-Disjunct looked around. Her vision

kept narrowing as she slipped more and more into predator mode, but all beings in sight were in their suits. Good.

She looked to the view of the Jao ship they were aiming for. "There!" she shrieked and increased the magnification. "There!" she sang. "That hole in the armor. Aim for that! We will board the ship, learn their secrets, and purge all the Jao of that ship!"

The view of the Jao's flank continued to expand as they approached. Sixth-Mode-Disjunct began to sing a victory aria.

Ekhat Seventeen was smaller than *Lexington*, but it was traveling at a significant velocity when contact was made. There wasn't an audible sound in *Lexington*'s control deck, but even with her mass there was a sense of a sub-sonic pulse or wave, which left everyone who wasn't fastened into a workstation seat either sprawled on the floor or piled against the back wall of the command deck.

The impact was almost directly on the opening that had been torn in the outer hull of laser spine B. Fragments of the alloyed battle steel that formed that outer hull were spalled off and sent scything through the gun deck. Very few of the gun crews were able to regain their feet when two hatches in the Ekhat hull opened and a small flood of suited Ekhat and their slaves poured out into the gun deck. The crew who had survived the ramming impact didn't last much longer.

The Ekhat gathered their slaves at the hatch into the main ship. One slave was held up to examine the controls. After a moment, that slave touched one of the controls, and the door slid open. As the atmosphere from the corridor began flooding out through the rents in the laser deck hull, the Ekhat led their slaves into the primary hull of *Lexington*.

Sixth-Mode-Disjunct turned to the conductor. "You and these," she delivered in aria mode, waving at the two least of the remaining Ekhat, "will remain here to protect our return to the ship and to capture any Jao who become available."

"What of others?" the conductor sang.

"Capture if convenient, else purify them." Sixth-Mode-Disjunct turned to the two remaining Ekhat, the largest and fiercest available to her from the depleted crew. "Forward! Complete! Purify."

The Ekhat and the slaves repeated her theme, and followed her in a wave down the designated corridor.

"Ekhat in the ship! Entering from B spine! Jinau to corridor B! All crew prepare to defend your stations!"

Flue Vaughan was muttering Welsh curses under his breath as he unstrapped from his workstation and stood up to rip open a drawer under his workstation and pull out his combat vest. Unlike the jinau, he hadn't loaded his vest down with anything other than magazines for his pistol, but he did have more than a couple of those. He figured if he needed more than that on board ship, they were well and truly screwed. Well, there were the knives: one hanging hilt down on the right side of his chest on top of the magazine slots; one fastened to the back right above the waist, hilt to the right; and two fastened to the back just below the neck opening where a hilt could be grabbed with either hand. But Vaughan really hoped that he wouldn't have to be in knife-fighting range with one or more Ekhat. That could really ruin his day.

Vaughan shrugged into the vest and fastened the closures down the front of it. He reached up to the shoulder holster and pulled out his pistol. It was heavier than a standard 10 mm pistol, but there was a reason for that, and the weight was comforting in his hand. Vaughan pulled the slide and chambered a round, then released the magazine and pulled out the single cartridge he always stashed in a side pocket, loaded it into the magazine and inserted it back into the pistol.

The lieutenant hefted the weight of the now fully loaded pistol, then slid it back into the holster. He shrugged his shoulders to settle the weight, reached up and touched all the knife hilts, then reached down to set his workstation to auto-record. He didn't want to miss anything if he suddenly got busy.

Vaughan looked up as Caewithe Miller went by him, headed for where Caitlin and Ed stood in the middle of the open space talking to Aille and Yaut. Tura was standing nearby in conversation with Wrot. Caitlin was noticeably smaller and weaker in comparison to the four big Jao, and Vaughan suspected that Caewithe, as bodyguard commander, was going to try again to get the director to move. Good luck with that, he thought.

Lim took off her robe, revealing her dark blue gi. She folded her robes carefully and draped them over the back of an unoccupied workstation, then picked up her staff.

Kamozh tilted his head as he studied Lim. He recognized the preparation of one who expected to be facing combat. The young clan leader looked to both Shekanre and Shemnarai. "Prepare," was all he said.

The main door irised open, and Hell entered the command deck. Three Ekhat forms scrabbled through what was to them a low doorway one after another, with a gaggle of smaller slaves pouring around their feet. They flooded over the bodyguards posted there, leaving them crumpled in their wake.

The humans all froze for just an instant. Not so the Jao. To a being, they threw themselves at the Ekhat, trampling the slaves in their haste.

Vaughan had his pistol in his hand, looking for an opportunity. It wasn't long in coming.

Caewithe had Caitlin by the arm and was pulling her toward the corner behind Vaughan's workstation. Ed was pushing at them, looking back over his shoulder, trying to get them clear of the mayhem. One of the Ekhat apparently caught sight of their motion. It spun and leapt after them.

Damn, those things are fast!

Ed stiffened, and Vaughan was shocked to see what appeared to be an ivory blade emerge, streaked with blood, from the front of the general's chest.

"*Ed!*" Caitlin shrieked as she tried to reach back for him. She stumbled and fell, taking Caewithe with her.

"Stay down!" Vaughan shouted as the two women struggled to get to their feet. "Stay down!"

The 10 mm pistol was in firing position, and as the Ekhat paused for a moment to flick the general's body off its sword-thing, Vaughan laid the sights on its head.

Crack!

Crack!

Crack!

Ten-millimeter bullets traveling in excess of 600 meters per second carry a lot of kinetic energy, so even the skull of an adult Ekhat in predator mode reacted to the impact of three of them. The fact that they were armor-piercing rounds meant that instead of glancing off the heavy skull, they punched three holes through it and proceeded to blaze three paths of pureed cranial tissue within the skull.

Vaughan was not unsurprised that the Ekhat didn't drop immediately. "Fine," he muttered. "We'll do it the hard way." The impacts of the earlier bullets had caused its head to raise up somewhat, so Vaughan walked a series of shots down its neck.

Crack!

Crack!

Crack!

Crack!

Crack-Crack!

The first four shots caused the neck to displace some and the head to jerk, but the last double tap at the base of the neck caused the beast to just fold up like a rag doll.

"That's good to know," Vaughan said. He decided to chance a tactical reload and released the partially empty magazine from the pistol and slammed in a fully loaded one from a vest pocket with the same hand that caught the ejected one. Two seconds and the pistol was presented toward the chaos happening before him.

The other two Ekhat seemed to be pretty occupied

with the Jao, and the odd team of the three Khûrûsh, Envoy D'mishri, and of all beings, Lim with a staff, were reaping a harvest of the lesser slaves that had followed their Ekhat masters. Since nothing was headed for him at that exact split-second, Vaughan reached down with his left hand and hauled Caewithe to her feet. "What the hell are you shooting?" Caewithe gasped as she came up. Vaughan ignored that as he reached back down and grabbed a sobbing Caitlin by her collar, then threw her sliding across the deck on her butt toward the corner. "Keep her down," he snapped at Caewithe.

With that, he focused ahead, put his pistol back into firing position, and started edging toward where the other Ekhat were.

One of the Ekhat was down, mobbed by what seemed to be a whole pack of Jao, although the number of Jao bodies lying around indicated it had exacted a price for its death.

The other was poised, facing Aille, Tura, and Dannet over the bodies of more Jao. That decided his next target.

Crack-Crack!

That double-tap had the desired effect of blowing the shoulder joint of the left front leg into splinters and shredded meat. The Ekhat rebalanced immediately without more than a dip of its body, which it used to lead into a spin to face Vaughan, correctly associating the sound of the pistol firing with the pain and destruction it had just suffered.

The scream that it uttered as it spun was very painful to hear. Vaughan managed to ignore it as his sights settled onto the base of the throat again.

Crack-Crack-Crack!

An extra shot for insurance, but since the Ekhat collapsed immediately, it probably hadn't been necessary.

The Jao pack was starting to unpile from their dead Ekhat. Vaughan didn't relax his attention as he continued to move slowly toward the middle of the deck. The Ekhat were all down and seemed to be nonfunctional, but he wasn't ignoring the slaves. There weren't many of them left, though, and the last few were being taken down by the Khûrûsh as he watched.

"So who's down on our side, besides General Kralik?" Vaughan asked when he gained Dannet's side.

"Yaut is dead, as is Terra-Captain Uldra," Dannet responded. "Wrot is very injured, but may survive if the medical team can get here quickly. The others..." she said nothing more.

"Looks like you need some attention, too," Vaughan said, looking at some lacerations and missing skin on the fleet commander. Aille and Tura didn't look much better.

"Nothing," Dannet said. Aille and the pleniary-superior didn't even dignify Vaughan's comment with a change of angles, much less a word.

"When this is over, I'm going to figure out how they found us," Vaughan said grimly. He didn't say anything else, but the Jao he was with seemed to understand the unspoken part of his message.

At that moment the main door irised open again.

CHAPTER 76

Vaughan wasn't aware of moving, but his pistol was trained on the doorway before he even consciously registered that the door had opened. He raised it when Tamt stormed into the command deck, followed by a mixture of bodyguards, jinau, and medics. Pointing at Tamt with his left hand to get her attention, he then pointed across his body to the corner where Caewithe was trying to get Caitlin to sit up. The bodyguards followed her as she stomped over there.

The lieutenant did another tactical reload before he slid the pistol back in the shoulder holster, then reached out and grabbed the last two medics that walked in. "You," he turned one of them to face the corner, "that's Director Kralik over there. Go make sure she's okay, and if she needs something to cope, give it to her. She just got a hell of a shock."

Vaughan pushed that medic in that direction. "You," he dragged the second medic over to where the general's body lay, "this is Lieutenant General Kralik. Give me a status on him."

The medic looked at the body lying in a very large pool of blood, then looked at Vaughan. The lieutenant bent down a little bit, and spoke quietly next to the medic's ear, "Look, Doc, you know he's dead, and I know he's dead, but the director just saw her husband gutted in front of her, and she doesn't have both feet on the ground at the moment. So you're going to go through the motions of checking to see if the general is alive, and then you're going to give me that slow shake of the head that doctors do so well, so that she can have a memory that we gave him respect. You got that?"

The medic winced. "Gotcha, Lieutenant. Now let go of me so I can get this done and move on to someone I might be able to help."

Once released, the medic knelt by the general and turned him onto his back. He rested medical sensors on his forehead, on his chest, and on the side of his neck. The sensor readout light stayed yellow, instead of turning green as it should with a living body.

The medic held the sensor unit up to Vaughan, and he could see that the readouts were all flat-lined. Sliding the unit back into his case, the medic reached out and slowly closed the eyelids over the general's vacant eyes. That helped Vaughan more than he'd thought it would. Being around General Kralik had been something like being around, oh, a dynamo. There was something about the man's face and eyes that just energized you if you spent much time with him. It was some kind of obscenity that those eyes were empty now, and closing the lids at least hid that much of the waste.

Vaughan looked over at the corner, to find that Caitlin had been moved to a workstation seat. She was staring at Ed's body with eyes that were so dark as to almost be holes in her pale face. Her tears had not totally ceased, but they trickled down her face now rather than poured.

The trio of Khûrûsh clustered together near the workstation that Lieutenant Vaughan normally operated. They were all splashed with bodily fluids from several different species of Ekhat slaves, most of which smelled unpleasant—especially in combination with others—and all of which were growing increasingly sticky. It was impossible to groom each other, for their claws were coated with the same combinations, as well as having bits and pieces of various pieces of tissue and organs caught under them.

"Where's a lake when you need one?" Kamozh grumbled as he attempted to at least get the worst of the vile stuff off of his forehands.

"I will have to spend at least an hour under the *Lexington*'s showers before I will feel clean again," Shemnarai declared.

"You children," Shekanre said with the rumbling chuckle. "A fine fight it was, for all that it was a sneak attack. A pity that our adversaries were not more of a challenge."

"I understand your sentiment, Weapons Master," D'mishri said from behind them, "but consider the havoc wreaked by the Ekhat, and consider that we non-Jao non-Terrans may have gotten off lightly."

They all looked toward where the surviving Jao were separating the corpses of those who died fighting the Ekhat from those who were seriously injured but still alive.

✧ ✧ ✧

Vaughan finished thumbing the cartridges he'd taken from one of his partially empty magazines into the other partially empty magazine, restoring it to a fully loaded status, and returned them to their pockets in his vest. That gave him a bit of satisfaction, knowing that if it became necessary to shoot again, most of his magazines were at full strength.

The lieutenant looked up as Aille approached out of the bustle of the medics carting wounded Jao off. Other than General Kralik, none of the humans had been wounded, mostly because the Jao in the room had made a frontal assault on the Ekhat and forestalled two of them from wreaking any other havoc. This had given Vaughan time to take down the other two.

Vaughan straightened from where he had been leaning against one of the workstations.

"Lieutenant Vaughan," Aille said.

"Sir."

"Not all of the intruders have been eliminated from the aft end of the B spinal corridor. Accompany me to go review the situation and see it resolved."

Vaughan squared his shoulders. "Yes, sir."

Aille looked behind Vaughan. "Captain Miller."

"Sir?" came Caewithe's response.

"Director Kralik is in good hands. Accompany me."

"But . . ."

Vaughan looked around to see Director Kralik with a hand on her bodyguard captain's shoulder and murmuring in her ear. She released Caewithe, who said nothing more but headed toward Aille. Vaughan flicked a sketch of a salute toward the director, who responded with a bit of a wan smile and a brief lifting of a hand.

Aille said nothing more; simply turned and headed toward the corridor. The two humans scrambled to flank him. Vaughan tried to move in front of him in the approved Jao order, but Aille said, "Forget precedence. Stay by my side." Vaughan tried to look over to Caewithe, but Aille's bulk was in the way.

They had crossed a couple of cross-corridors when Aille spoke. "Your shooting was excellent, Lieutenant Vaughan."

Vaughan shrugged. "Right place at the right time with the right weapon, sir."

"Remind me later that we need to talk about that weapon, Lieutenant."

"Yes, sir."

"Governor?" Caewithe said. Aille turned his head and looked down at her, but said nothing. She continued with, "Have we heard reports on how the *Ban Chao* assault team did?"

"Not yet," Aille responded.

"Oh."

Vaughan kept his eyes moving. He'd already had one very unpleasant surprise this morning. He didn't really want to have a second.

They passed several more cross-corridors before they saw anyone else alive. Several bodies were encountered, both Jao and human, none alive; all either savagely torn with blood splashed on deck and walls or simply lying broken. At that point, Vaughan decided that preparedness was the better part of valor, and he pulled his pistol from the shoulder holster. Caewithe already had hers out. Vaughan really, really wished that Caewithe had been left on the command deck, but when Aille gave orders, everybody jumped. And in the end, that was the job she had chosen. That didn't stop him from resolving to do everything he could to keep her from harm's way.

The first living beings they saw were a couple of medics pushing a gurney with a human jinau on it toward them. The medics and gurney made a turn into a cross-corridor that led to one of the medic stations in the ship before it drew even with the trio, but their appearance and an increasing level of noise from before them told Vaughan that they were drawing closer to the area Aille had received reports from. Aille looked at him, and slowed his pace a bit. Vaughan took the hint and stepped into the lead, stepping carefully, senses alert.

Vaughan's recollection was they were approaching a large open area that was created by the intersection of two major corridors outside one of the main doors into the B spine. As they drew near, he flattened against the right hand corridor wall. Vaughan saw Caewithe adopt a similar posture on the opposite wall.

The lieutenant came to a complete halt and listened carefully for a moment. The sounds that he was hearing were very much like what he'd heard in the command deck. He peered around the corner to see two Ekhat, smaller than the ones that had rampaged in the command deck. One was occupied with plucking the limbs from a—thankfully—dead human jinau, while the other was darting toward and away from three Jao in jinau blue.

There was another Ekhat, apparently a corpse, lying close to the closed hatch to B spine, surrounded by several dead jinau, mostly Jao. There were several other jinau bodies, Jao and human, scattered around the space, but Vaughan couldn't tell if they were all corpses or if some were still alive. There were also numerous dead Ekhat slaves within the space, most still wearing space suits.

"Put them down, Lieutenant," Aille said from behind them.

Vaughan took a deep breath, raised his pistol and focused on the sights, and flowed around the corner. The Ekhat feinting with the Jao was taken first.

Crack!

Crack!

Crack!

Before the Ekhat could react, Vaughan had put a single shot into the shoulder joints of the three legs in his view. Then he swiveled to target the second Ekhat, which had dropped its bloody toy and was turning to face him. The hollow at the base of the neck wasn't in view, so he shifted targets.

Crack!

Crack!

Crack!

Vaughan put three measured shots into the skull. This time, since they entered laterally rather than longitudinally, at least one of them retained enough velocity and energy to blow out the other side of the head. Vaughan saw a spray of white fluid, anyway.

That didn't put the Ekhat down, but it did bring it to a stop. Vaughan took a moment to look at the first Ekhat. Two of its left legs had folded underneath it, and it was unable to support its body with the unwounded legs. It was shrieking and thrashing its legs and arms and the sword things. It was no danger at this point.

"Finish them, Lieutenant Vaughan," Aille said as he stepped out into the open area.

Vaughan didn't say anything, just led with the pistol and stepped carefully until he could see the front of the second Ekhat. He aimed at the base of the throat.

Crack-Crack-Crack!

That Ekhat dropped. Vaughan then shuffled sideways a couple of steps and repeated the process with the crippled Ekhat.

Crack-Crack-Crack!

The Ekhat collapsed, white fluids oozing out from the various wounds.

Aille turned to the three Jao who had been the objects of that Ekhat's attention; all of whom looked somewhat the worse for wear. "Report."

"That's the last of the Ekhat here," the center of the trio said. "Three went up that corridor." She pointed to the corridor Aille and Vaughan and Caewithe had come down.

"Slaves?"

"Unknown. Many followed the three Ekhat."

"Those are eliminated," Aille said.

"Then there may be a few wandering around, lost, but we took care of everything we found here." The jinau Jao looked around, and added, "We and these guys did," with a wave of her hand.

The three Jao adopted angles for *task-completed.* Aille responded with *gratified-respect*, which Vaughan first thought was a bit over the top. After a second look around the space, maybe it wasn't. He took the moment to eject the current magazine from his pistol and replace it with a full one.

CHAPTER 77

Vaughan didn't holster his pistol until Aille had led them back to the command deck. Once another jinau officer had arrived at the area, followed by additional jinau troops and medics, the governor had turned and retraced his steps. There was now a heavy detachment of jinau outside the command deck, including one of the flame gunners. A bit like slamming the barn door shut after the horse has run off, Vaughan thought a bit sourly. His innate sense of fairness made him admit a moment later that he hadn't expected an Ekhat boarding action on *Lexington*, either. Lesson learned in the most expensive way possible, with the lives of crew and troops as the currency, but he was sure that no one who had survived this day would ever forget either the day or the lesson.

His first glance as he walked through the door was at the system plot. The E-Path attack ships were still there, as were all the surviving Terra taif ships. *Starcloud* was apparently still in her stealth mode. That was all good news.

The bad news was that Ekhats Eighteen through Twenty-four—the ships carrying large loads of solar plasma—were also still out there. "Damn," Vaughan muttered. "I really hoped that someone had taken a piece out of them by now."

Vaughan walked toward his workstation. The Jao and human bodies had all been removed, including General Kralik's, but he had to walk through some of the slave corpses, which was distasteful. One of the Ekhat carcasses caused a significant detour from the straightest path.

The lieutenant wondered if there were chainsaws on *Lexington*. He suspected that it was going to require cutting up the looming Ekhat carcasses to haul them away for disposal. Whatever it took, he hoped some of the crew showed up with it soon. Dead Ekhat was starting to hang kind of heavy in the air.

Vaughan sat at his workstation. He wasn't ready to put his pistol away just yet, so the combat vest stayed on his body, and the comforting weight of the big pistol remained in its holster under his shoulder and arm. After a moment, he reached out, turned off the auto-recording, and started reviewing what had happened since the excitement started.

Externally, the answer was "Not much." The plasma ships were still moving slowly toward Khûr-shi, still loosely grouped together but with quite a distance between the lead ship and the two that trailed the pack.

Unfortunately, it appeared that they would be near enough to the planet to make their attack prior to the possible arrival of the Terra taif ships that had been sent to Khûr-mar. They had to be faced with the remnants of the ships that *Lexington* had led into battle, plus the Eleusherar Path. Right now, that did not give Vaughan a lot of comfort.

"How do you feel?" Caewithe asked as she rejoined the group around Caitlin.

"Like my guts have been carved out of me," Caitlin replied in a low-pitched hoarse tone.

Caewithe grimaced. "Sorry. Stupid question."

"Not a stupid question," Caitlin replied with a headshake. "Stupid answer, maybe." She wiped the tears from her face for what seemed like the umpteenth time. It was interesting, in a distant sort of way, that they seemed to be drying up. An eternity ago—Caitlin looked at her watch to see that it had been less than an hour—she had felt as if her universe had ended, and she had wanted to end with it. Now? Now she knew life and the universe would go on.

"This isn't the first time I've dealt with death, you know," Caitlin said. "There aren't very many families on Earth who didn't lose somebody in the conquest and occupation. Many of them lost multiple somebodies." She looked toward the space where Ed had died. "I lost two brothers. Ryan was killed in the conquest, not long after I was born, so I never really knew him. But Brent..." She had to stop for a moment. "Brent was special. He was almost ten years older than me, and I worshipped him. When he turned sixteen and I was a little over six, Oppuk demanded that he become part of the governor's establishment. Three months later, he was dead, crushed by Oppuk's own hands, because he wasn't learning fast enough."

Caitlin stopped again, looking back up at Caewithe. "So, yeah, I've lost someone incredibly important before, someone who filled the center of my life with light and joy. I know this hurt. We're old companions. And I know that the pain does eventually go away, and that life goes on whether we want it to or not. But just right now, I don't much care."

"Should you be here?" Caewithe asked.

"Yes," Caitlin hissed. "I told you earlier I'm not leaving the command deck because I owe it to the people I brought on this voyage to stand here and take it with them. I'm damned sure not leaving now until I see every last Ekhat that followed us here die! So deal with it, all of you," she looked around at her bodyguards. "I'm here until this is over, one way or the other."

Most of the humans had resigned expressions on their faces, but none of them spoke. The Jao mostly had angles that expressed some variation of *approval*. Tamt, on the other hand, was showing *gratified-respect*. "I would expect nothing less," she said, placing her hand on Caitlin's shoulder. "Nothing less."

D'mishri lowered the communication handset. "These attack craft were ships out on a patrol. They can carry a maximum of two of the ship-killer missiles, but only four of them had the full load, so they had a patrol load of ten missiles, of which six have been expended. The four loaded ships will begin their next attack run in a few moments."

Lim translated for the command deck personnel. "So even if they get kills with all four missiles," Dannet said, between giving orders to the fleet and giving orders to the ship crew, "that is still going to leave three ships to be handled." Until they could get Uldra's successor officer to the command deck, she was having to handle both fleet command and ship command.

"Yes," D'mishri responded. "We have more missiles, of course, but they are at our base, which is out-system. There are also other attack ships, but they were too far away to make it here in time to assist. This is all we have in hand. So the remaining craft, plus the craft who expend their second missiles, will stage themselves to perform immolation attacks."

Vaughan was lost for a moment. Immolation attacks? What was Lim trying to translate? Then it crashed in on him. "You mean suicide attacks." That wasn't a question.

"Yes."

CHAPTER 78

"Wait a minute," Caitlin said, getting to her feet and moving toward the others, "you mean your pilots and crew are planning on ramming those Ekhat ships that they can't shoot up?"

"Correct," D'mishri said through Lim.

"That's not happening," Caitlin said. "Nobody throws their lives away like that. Not in my fleet, not on my watch."

D'mishri made a hand gesture that caused Kamozh to stiffen, then said, "But we are not part of your fleet, are we, Director? We are not under your command. We are not allies. We are at this moment simply chance-met strangers come to the aid of a third stranger in a time of trouble."

"It's not right," Caitlin said, crossing her arms.

The envoy was silent for a moment after Lim finished her translation. "Director, in your homeworld, I am certain there are times when there are disasters of one type or another that cause buildings to become dangerous; perhaps a fire, or a seismic event. Do you not have rescuers who enter those buildings knowing they might die, seeking to save someone who cannot leave on their own?"

"Yes," Caitlin said with a frown. She could see where this was going.

"And do not some of those rescuers in fact lose their lives in such efforts?"

"Yes." She bit that response out.

"Then," D'mishri concluded, "you have seen this action before. The crew of those ships will do whatever they have to do to preserve the people of Khûr-shi. They will indeed do whatever they must to prevent a conflagration from literally beginning on that planet. It is our responsibility as part of the Eleusherar Path, and they embrace it. To do less is to fail themselves, and fail the Immanence."

D'mishri looked at the system plot. "In any event, they have begun, and I cannot change their orders."

Caitlin turned her head to see the icons of the attack ships moving. Her shoulders slumped a little. "It's not fair," she muttered.

"Perhaps not," D'mishri replied through Lim. "That does not, however, make it wrong."

Kamozh and Shemnarai looked at each other. The medics has provided some cleansing wipes to them and Shekanre, so that their hands and coats were not as fouled as they had been, although Kamozh's nose still tended to wrinkle from the astringent odor the wipes had left behind. That had allowed them to stay on the command deck rather than retreat for the showers. They had been listening to all the conversations.

"Your people will do this?" Kamozh finally asked.

"Yes," Shemnarai replied. "Why are you so surprised? It's not as though we don't have similar stories in our own histories."

"That's the point," Kamozh said. "Everything I see and hear about the people around us, whether the Terrans or the Eleusherar Path, tell me that they are exactly that: people, not monsters. They are not slavering, soul-sucking abominations bent on the destruction of all that is good. They look different from us, they think different from us in a lot of ways, but at the end of the story, they make the same choices we would make; they make them for the same reasons we would make them; they die the same deaths."

"I could have told you that."

"Of course you could," Kamozh said bitterly. "You've been out here all your life. You know it in your bones. It's a fundamental axiom of life for all of you Khûrûsh who have lived in exile for generations. But for me and mine, it's only been a few hands-full of days, and for the people on Khûr-shi it's been less than that. It's one thing to talk to these outlanders; it's one thing to see them in all their fabulous ships, refraining from destroying us, looking at us as the odd curiosity. It's absolutely a different thing to see them now."

Shemnarai started to speak, but Kamozh flashed a **<Quiet!>** at her with a forehand, and she settled. Kamozh could feel Shekanre's eyes on his back, but he turned his own gaze on the system plot. "They go forward like champions, these Eleusherar Path ships." He turned back to Shemnarai. "I can almost understand *them.* You told me their history, how it intertwines with our own. There is a relationship there, of an odd sort, so I can almost understand them. But the Terrans? Who can explain them? Who can explain these great Jao, these cunning humans, these so-wise Lleix? Who can explain them standing in the gap, dying like heroes to defend our people, who tried to destroy them? Who can explain Director Kralik losing her mate before her very eyes, yet still standing here and arguing for a certain restraint?”

“Crap,” Vaughan muttered as a chorus of mutters arose in the command deck. The first E-Path attack craft had launched its missile. A few seconds later, the missile had fired. The plot tracked the beam, and it appeared to intersect the icon for Ekhat Twenty-one. Nothing happened. The icon continued to glow, and to move incrementally on the viewscreen.

“What happened?” Dannet demanded.

“The laser impacted the Ekhat's screens,” the leading sensor tech reported. “It appears to have at least opened a short gap in the screen, because there was some release of plasma. But it shut down quickly, and there is no evidence of any damage to the ship.”

“Fleet Commander,” Vaughan called out. Dannet turned her head his direction. “This is a new weapon untried for this use. It is possible that the solar plasma provided some type of interference that affected the laser beam. It does for our lasers, after all. Or, it's possible that their targeting was off and the beam did not shoot through the exact center of the shielded ball to hit the ship. That plasma ball is kilometers across, after all. The ship isn't visible, so it would be easy to miss it.”

Dannet looked to D'mishri, but he had already

raised the communication handset, because Lim had been translating in parallel with Vaughan's statements.

The next attack did not occur for several minutes. Apparently the crews of the remaining attack ships were making their own observations as well, and trying to optimize results, as they had not started moving before the envoy's message covered the distance to them. That probably gave them a little additional food for thought.

Three shots left, Vaughan thought. A minimum of four survivors to be dealt with. Things were not looking good for his side.

The atmosphere in the command deck was thick with more than the reek of dead Ekhat. Everywhere Vaughan looked, shoulders were hunched, even among the Jao.

The next attack ship began its approach to the Ekhat ships. It had apparently chosen Ekhat Nineteen as its target. The room was silent except for the massed breathing of its occupants and Vaughan's fingers tapping pads on his workstation.

They could tell when the attack ship made its launch as the ship curved away. It was only a few seconds later when the missile reached its detonation point and the bomb exploded. The system plot showed the laser beam generated as a result, and it seemed to squarely impact its target's shields. The room grew deathly quiet for a few seconds, then a cheer erupted from the human command staff as the icon for Ekhat Nineteen began to fade from the plot.

Good. But unless they figure out a way to kill more than one bird with one missile, we're still going to need the kamikazes.

The third attack went like clockwork, and Ekhat Eighteen faded from view.

A moment later two of the attack craft faded from the plot. Voices were raised again.

"No weapons were fired," the sensor tech spoke. "In fact, they were flying near the destroyed ships. There were no weapons that would bear on them."

Vaughan had a thought, hit a couple of pads, and swallowed. "They ran into the released plasma," he called out.

Dannet turned and D'mishri both turned to face him. "They were burned up?" the fleet commander asked.

"No, sir," Vaughan said, reading his panel. "The plasma expanded once the shields released it, and it would have cooled in direct relationship with the expansion rate. But that just meant that it became floating clouds of gas. Those ships hit large clouds of gas at very high rates of speed. It would be just like ramming directly into the upper reaches of the atmosphere. They would have broken apart."

D'mishri bowed his head for a moment.

Suddenly all the remaining attack ship icons were moving. Vaughan couldn't figure out what was happening. Oh, it was pretty clear that the fourth missile attack was underway. But at the same time the other three attack ships—the two without the second round of missiles and the first attacker which had failed to kill Ekhat Twenty-one—started moving forward as well.

After a few moments, he got it, and tapped controls to throw up projected flight paths on the system plot. It didn't take very long for others to see what he saw: the trio of unloaded ships were pulling ahead of the last armed ship, and their courses were beginning to converge with his. It was obvious they were beginning their suicide attacks.

"Call them off!" Caitlin said to D'mishri.

The envoy spread both hands in an obvious gesture of futility. "Even if I could," Lim translated, "they are too far away for the message to reach them in time."

"Missile launch!" one of the sensor techs called out, and everyone watched its track being added to the plot as its launcher veered away. It was close, oh so close, and for a moment it looked as if everything would work out. But then the suicide ships appeared to make a jog inward just as the missile bomb blew. The pumped laser beam appeared on the screen.

The trio of icons flared and disappeared.

To complete the disaster, the beam was disrupted by the doomed attack ships, and very little of it survived to contact Ekhat Twenty-one's shields, which showed no effect of that contact at all.

Silence fell in the command deck.

"Oh, hell," Caitlin finally said.

CHAPTER 79

No one had any trouble reading D'mishri's body language. Discouraged, depressed, devastated—all those applied.

"What happened?" Caitlin asked.

"Blue on blue," Vaughan said, "friendly fire, whatever you want to call it, the last ship-killer shot took out three of the E-Path attack ships."

"But why?" Caitlin still wanted answers, Vaughan could tell.

Kamozh said something, then poked Lim when she didn't translate right away. She jumped, gave Kamozh a rather un-Lleix glare, then said, "Garrison troops."

"Ah," Aille said, with a brief flow of *understanding* showing in his angles before his usual presentation of *neutral* resumed. He turned to face the envoys. "How long has it been since your forces actually fought in combat? How many generations?"

The response was slow in coming after Lim's translation ceased. After the span of three deep breaths,

D'mishri replied through Lim. "Our young Khûrûsh-an officer has placed his digit upon it, and Governor Aille is correct in his thrust. It has been over two hundred Khûrûshil years, over five generations, since we last experienced space combat in the vicinity of Khûr."

"So all of your people are very adept in your ship drills," Aille said, "but have little experience in larger unit activities, and have no experience at dealing with what the humans call 'the fog of war,' do they? And because of the long travel times, you can't bring in fresh combat experience, because even experienced officers will grow stale if it takes twenty years or more to reach a destination. So things like this happen."

"Correct," the senior envoy said, rising to his feet. "You have found the weakness of our combat systems. It is not the technology; it is the horrible lack of experience out at the end of our voyages that is the problem. And it is the price we pay every time something like this happens. Always we pay in blood to learn the lessons over again after generations." His face turned to the system plot. "And always it is the ones in the small ships who most often pay that price."

Everyone followed D'mishri's gaze. The plot showed the last attack ship had modified its swing away from the Ekhat ships. It had come full circle, and was now headed back toward Ekhat Twenty-one on a reciprocal course. Its engines must have been redlined, because it was moving appreciably across the viewscreen display.

It was another silent moment, watching the icons move. It seemed to take hours, but Vaughan looked at his readouts, and knew that it was only a matter of seconds.

The attack ship icon edged forward and seemed

to touch the Ekhat icon. After a moment, they both faded from view.

The E-Path ships had removed three of the Ekhat plasma ships. That left four: Twenty and Twenty-two separated by some distance, and then lagging behind Twenty-three and Twenty-four in close company. Their icons were still on the system plot, edging toward Khûr-shi. Not a good day for the good guys, Vaughan thought.

"Orders to *Footloose*," Dannet spoke, having resumed her Fleet Commander hat since another deck officer named Balton had arrived to assume the captain's role. Her voice sounded harsh in the silence. "Take up position at coordinate 26.92.214. Orders to *Fancy Free*: take up position one radian 2 to starboard of *Footloose*. Balton," Dannet turned to Uldra's replacement, "*Lexington* to one radian 2 to port of *Footloose*. All ships, execute."

Kamozh watched as the Terran ships relocated to positions to directly oppose the remaining ships of the monstrous Ekhat. Four ships of unknown capability, except that they had enough strength to carry great amounts of Khûr's fire with them with the intent of dumping it on his homeworld, against three of the great *Lexingtons*, two of which were horribly damaged. There was no certainty to the outcome of this contest, but it didn't look good for the Terrans.

The young clan-lord's anger, never far below the surface this day, began to rise again. *It isn't right*, he thought. *It isn't right that these others must defend us. It isn't right that we, so many, many years ago, turned our backs on the universe like children afraid of a nurse's tales. It isn't right that we hid our heads under the covers or crawled under the beds to not see what was truly out here. And now we are still children. Now, when we could have stood in our own courage in our own ships and fought as equals beside these heroes, we must stand behind them like children or arrant cowards. Never again.*

"Never again," Kamozh murmured. "Never again."

Shemnarai turned toward him, and he gestured toward the viewscreen.

Lexington's command deck was quiet, but not silent. The techs were speaking to each other in low tones. Balton and Dannet had things to say to each other, and Dannet had occasion to issue an addition order to *Footloose*. Certainly Vaughan himself was making some noise as he muttered notes into his microphone about what was occurring. He even noted the three Khûrûsh speaking to each other and to D'mishri. But the overall effect was one of quiet as everyone watched the Ekhat icons draw closer to the Terran icons on the system plot.

At length, readouts on Vaughan's workstation began to change. "*Footloose* has opened fire on Ekhat Twenty with her lasers," he reported.

After thirty seconds, the head sensor tech said, "No evident effect so far."

"All ships, fire on Ekhat Twenty," Dannet ordered.

After another thirty seconds, the sensor tech reported, "No evident effect."

Vaughan noted that as well.

The icons continued to move.

"No evident effect," the sensor tech said.

An old icon brightened back to life again. "*Arjuna* back under power," Vaughan announced. But why had she done so at this moment. Ekhat Twenty had passed her some time ago, and Ekhat Twenty-two had just passed her almost close enough to touch, it seemed. Ekhats Twenty-three and Twenty-four, however, were still approaching. *Arjuna* should have remained dark. They would probably have gone right by her.

Then *Arjuna*'s vector became apparent. "Oh, no," Vaughan whispered.

The crippled *Arjuna*'s progress was visibly erratic. Her icon seemed to be moving in little pops. But bit by bit it had aligned itself behind Ekhat Twenty-two, and it was now moving somewhat faster, climbing toward the tail of the plasma bubble, intent obvious to everyone on the command deck.

For the second time today, the command deck got to watch a ship plow to its death in order to take out one of the Ekhat plasma ships. Only this time it wasn't the Eleusherar Path that did it; it was one of their own. *Arjuna*'s icon seemed to overlap the edge of Ekhat Twenty-two's. For a long moment, nothing happened, then they both slowly faded.

There was a scattering of small icons on the plot. "Well, at least she got some of her lifeboats off," Vaughan said in a low tone. "Not very many, though, and no shuttles."

Kamozh stood on his hind legs and rendered a four-handed **<honor to the brave>**. The growl that issued from his throat rumbled such as to fill the command deck.

Beside him, Shemnarai and Shekanre echoed both his signs and his growls.

✧ ✧ ✧

Three Ekhat plasma ball ships left, Vaughan took note. The same three Terra taif ships to block them from the planet. Still not good odds, but slightly better than they were. He updated his files, and downloaded copies to *Pool Buntyam* again.

Dannet turned to Balton. "Give the order."

A moment later, the ship's speakers came to life: "All hands except crew Alpha Prime, prepare to abandon ship. Remain at your stations for now. You will have five minutes from the moment the alarm sounds to reach your lifeboat. Check your lifeboat assignments now. Some have changed due to damage. This is not a drill."

Caitlin spun and advanced on Dannet, anger so strong in every line of her body that even the Jao could have read it. She stopped in front of the fleet commander, placed her hands on her hips, and snarled, "Just what do you think you're doing?"

"There are not enough of us to destroy these plasma ships by weapons fire before they reach Khûr-shi," Dannet replied. "We will not allow them to attack the planet. Therefore, we will take them out in the same manner as *Arjuna.*"

"I forbid it!" Caitlin snapped.

Vaughan couldn't see Caitlin's full face, but he could see her profile, and the shock that crossed it when Aille stepped up to her and said, "Caitlin, you do not have *oudh* for this. Now go prepare to find your lifeboat."

"But . . ."

"No." Aille's voice was firm, and Vaughan read his angles as *adamant-purpose.* He knew Caitlin could read them better than he could, and it didn't surprise him when her shoulders slumped.

"Director Kralik," Dannet said. Caitlin faced the fleet commander. "This is not an imitation of what the Eleusherar Path has done here today. If you had read more of our Jao historical combat reports, you would have seen that this has been done many times by our people."

"And more than a few times by you humans. Both sides of your World War II saw it happen," Aille said, "although more from one than the other."

Caitlin moved slowly toward to the workstation she had occupied so long today. "But the *Lexington*," she murmured, "she's special."

"Director," Vaughan called out softly. She looked his direction, and he beckoned to her with one hand while tapping pads with the other.

"Yes, Lieutenant?" she said when she arrived at his workstation.

"Director, the *Lex* is special. But she's also a tool, and tools are meant to be used. Most of what makes her special is her crew. If the bulk of the crew survives, then what makes the *Lex* special will also survive."

He watched out of the corner of his eye as she considered that. From the way she brightened, she seemed to accept that.

"I'll take that," she finally said. "I still don't like it, though."

"Oh, none of us will like it," Vaughan said, taking his eyes off the readouts long enough to stare her in the eyes. "But we'll make the Ekhat pay, with plenty of interest."

"Oh, they're going to pay," Caitlin said grimly. "I expect it to cost them everything."

CHAPTER 80

"Orders to *Fancy Free*," Dannet stated calmly. "Signal Abandon Ship."

Vaughan watched as the tiny icons of lifeboats began appearing in little glimmers around the larger icon of *Fancy Free*. "That's almost pretty," Caitlin said. She was still standing by his workstation. After several minutes, she added, "that doesn't look like very many, either."

"It's not," Vaughan said. "I suspect their crew losses have been almost as heavy as *Arjuna*'s or ours."

"Damn." Caitlin crossed her arms. "I guess I should be happy that that many will be saved."

"Right," Vaughan said. "*Pool Buntyam*'s flotilla will pick up the survivors."

A few more minutes passed. Vaughan continued tapping his controls and murmuring comments into his mic. He did notice when Tamt and Caewithe moved up beside Caitlin.

"Order to *Fancy Free*: begin attack run." Dannet, still very calm.

At that moment, a new icon appeared in the system plot, directly in front of the Terra taif ships. "*Starcloud* has arrived," Vaughan announced loudly.

A moment later, Envoy D'mishri spoke urgently to Lim, who called out, "Fleet Commander Dannet, call off the attack. *Starcloud* has a different weapons package, and may be able to take out the ships."

At that moment, a flickering line began moving out from *Starcloud* toward Ekhat Twenty. Vaughan frowned. "What the hell is that?"

He didn't expect an answer, but he heard Lim murmuring to the envoys, and D'mishri replying. "An electrically accelerated small mass driver," Lim stated.

Vaughan had to think that one through. The light dawned. "A railgun? Seriously? How big? What's the acceleration?"

Lim murmured with the envoy, then came back with, "A mass similar to depleted uranium, in amounts of a bit over a Terran kilogram, leaving the muzzle with a velocity of somewhat more than six kilometers per second."

Vaughan's hands froze, and his head swiveled toward the envoy. "And just how much energy does it take to launch one of those?"

The conversation between Lim and D'mishri was much longer this time. Vaughan waited with little patience. This was serious stuff.

"If I understand Envoy D'mishri correctly—and he stresses that he is not an engineer—then it takes approximately thirty million joules for a single launch."

Vaughan whistled. That was some serious power. "Okay, is *Starcloud* built around a single gun, then?"

Short back and forth this time. "No. *Starcloud*

has twelve ten-meter railguns on the bow armament, twelve on the stern armament, and forty-eight scattered around the hull."

That brought Vaughan to his feet. "I don't care how efficient their power systems are, they can't be feeding all those guns at once. Are they using some kind of capacitors?"

The conversation this time was longer, with Lim and D'mishri calling things up on her com pad and pointing at various items. She turned back to Vaughan. "The envoy says, yes, they use high-storage fast-recharge fast-discharge capacitors to store the launching charge." Before Vaughan could ask the next question, she added, "Again, if I understand the envoy correctly, they store a thousand joules in a cubic centimeter, so by the time they put a containment shell around a capacitor and put the attachment connections on it, the capacitor is approximately half a meter long, or about a quarter of a cubic meter in total volume."

"Woof," Vaughan said softly. "What are they using for a dielectric in those things? Magic powder? That's at least two orders of magnitude better than anything we have on *Lexington*." He waved a hand as Lim started to speak. "Never mind, I'm not an engineer either. Even if he could tell me and you could translate it, I probably wouldn't understand." Vaughan tapped some pads.

"Never mind the gun," he muttered. "Put power systems technology at the top of the shopping list. Sheesh."

Vaughan looked at the system plot, where the railgun stream was still evident. "What's the rate of fire?"

More conversation with the envoy. "Eight seconds to fully recharge the capacitors, but you can fire with a lesser charge if desired. He says nobody does that, but the design allows for it."

Vaughan froze again. "So with twelve rails, they can put out a full-charge round every two-thirds of a second? Either on a single target or on multiple targets?"

Mutter mutter. "Yes."

"Ho . . . ly . . . ." The syllables were said almost reverentially. "We might just survive this after all."

Vaughan looked up at Caitlin. "I have something else for my Christmas list, Mom."

Caitlin managed a smile. "We make it through this, and I'll see about it."

"Well, there is that," Vaughan muttered, turning back to his readouts.

At that moment, Ekhat Twenty's icon began to fade from the system plot, and a frenzied cheer arose from the humans on the command deck, including Caitlin.

"Too bad they have to operate on the shotgun principle because of those plasma balls," Vaughan muttered. "It would sure be a lot easier if they could pinpoint target the ships."

Everyone was watching the system plot now with what, for the humans, would be called bated breath.

"Retargeting," Lim said on behalf of D'mishri.

Before long the flickering line appeared on the plot, this time headed toward Ekhat Twenty-three. Nothing happened for the longest time. "Longer transit time," Vaughan said quietly.

"Still, we should have seen something by now, shouldn't we?" Caitlin asked.

Vaughan shrugged. "I'd hope so, but it's still a matter of putting the golden BB in exactly the right place."

"*Footloose* still firing lasers. No effect." The command deck sensor tech made his report.

Vaughan shook his head. "Must be big high-powered ships. Between the strength of their shields and the plasma they're holding, regular lasers just can't punch through."

Caitlin looked at the plot, where *Starcloud* was still firing at Ekhat Twenty-three. "They're not getting through, are they?"

"Nope," Vaughan said. "I'm starting to think the first one was a fluke." A quick glance at D'mishri showed the envoy's body language had lost its confidence and started slumping again. "They're throwing a lot of high-energy-potential slugs into that cloud, but the slugs are pretty small, so they just may not be making it through the plasma to the ship with enough mass left to do any serious damage."

"Very likely, Lieutenant Vaughan," someone else said. He and Caitlin looked up to see Dannet standing nearby. She looked from them to the master plot, where the two Ekhat plasma ships were growing closer to the orbit of Khûr-shi. "And we have run out of time. Envoy D'mishri, please instruct your ship to cease operations. Balton," she turned to the replacement captain of *Lexington*, "give the order. Communications officer, order *Fancy Free* to resume the attack."

"Can't we wait a little longer?" Caitlin asked, voice shaking.

"No, Director, we cannot," Aille said, appearing at her side.

"All hands except crew Alpha Prime, abandon ship. All hands except crew Alpha Prime, abandon ship. This is not a drill." The announcement rang in the command deck. It cut off for a moment, then was replaced by, "All fleet command crew to Shuttle Bay Green 1. All fleet command crew to Shuttle Bay Green 1."

"Now, Lieutenant Vaughan," Dannet said as she passed, heading for the main door. "We will relocate to *Footloose*."

"Yes, Fleet Commander," Vaughan said. He slapped three separate pads: one to send another download to *Pool Buntyam*; one to set his console to continue to record; and one to activate a program to send a final download when *Lexington* was five seconds away from impacting her target.

Vaughan stood up, touched his shoulder holster to make sure his pistol was ready, and looked to where Caitlin and Caewithe stood with Tamt and the two other bodyguards who had survived the Ekhat incursion and had made their way to the command deck. "Shall we go, Director?"

Caitlin looked around the command deck, a look of despair on her face. She said nothing, though, and when Aille beckoned her from the door, she began moving toward him.

Vaughan fell in beside Caewithe. "You okay?" he asked quietly.

"Just ducky," she muttered back. "Most of my command is dead, lots of my shipmates are dead, and my ship is about to go kamikaze. Life's great."

Vaughan snorted. "Your principal is still alive. You're still alive. I'm still alive."

"Only because you have the hand cannon from Hell

over there." Caewithe's voice was a little brighter, and a small smile flickered at the corners of her mouth.

"On the contrary; St. George's best, at your service," Vaughan proclaimed, one hand on his chest. "Dragons slain and maidens rescued our specialty."

This time it was Caewithe who snorted. "I ain't no maiden."

"I won't tell if you won't," Vaughan said in an earnest tone. "But you've got to admit that a full-grown Ekhat makes a good stand-in for a dragon." He smiled as that one got Caewithe to actually laugh a bit.

Caitlin walked behind Aille, staring at the fur covering his back. In one small corner of her mind she was disturbed at how dry his pelt looked, and how disarrayed, with clumps here and there formed around recognizable blobs of blood, or in some cases of other less recognizable and therefore more disturbing elements.

Another corner of her mind was disturbed at the conversation she heard behind her between Caewithe and Flue Vaughan. Didn't they realize what had happened? How could they joke when so many people were dead . . . when Ed . . .

But most of her mind was dealing with another issue, and resolved it just as they arrived at the entry port of the shuttle reserved for the command crew. She watched as the Lleix boarded, followed by the envoys and the Khûrûsh guests. Dannet and most of the command deck crew boarded, with Pleniary-superior Tura on their heels. That left Aille and the people behind her.

"Governor," Caitlin said. Aille paused before putting

foot on the ramp. Caitlin waved everyone behind her to board, which they did without a word, although Caewithe and Flue looked back over their shoulders. Good. That would save explanation.

Once they were off the deck and it was just Caitlin and Aille, she looked up at him and quietly, "I'm not going." Aille studied her intently for a moment. At least he didn't order her to board, she thought.

"Why?" Aille said at length.

"I said I was not going to lead this fleet into battle without standing with them," Caitlin said, feeling a bit of her previous fire return to her voice. "I will not leave this ship until the Ekhat are defeated. And," her voice broke a little, "Ed's here. I'm not leaving him. Not now. Not like this."

Caitlin faced up at the first Jao she had ever admired; the one who had managed to save her world; the one who had given meaning to her life for the last few years; and she mustered up the strength to adopt the angles for *adamant-purpose*. She figured that her execution of it was probably sloppy right now. But at the moment, Caitlin suspected Aille would cut her some slack.

"I could order you to board," Aille said, his own angles shifting from *neutral* to *holding-oudh*.

"I would refuse," Caitlin said, firming her own posture and bringing the lines of her hands and fingers into purest alignment.

"I could force you to board," Aille said.

"I beg you not to do so," Caitlin said, her voice growing even stronger. "I have served you well, these years. My family has served the Jao well all my life. We have paid price after price after price for that service. This once—just this once—let me have something for us.

Not because of service or of being of use, but because this is all I want from you. It costs you nothing."

Aille considered her for a long moment. "You are wrong," he finally said, "it will cost me dearly. This day has cost me Yaut, who has guided my steps since I was small. It may have cost me Wrot. It has cost me Ed Kralik, the first human I learned to trust. You are not the only one who misses him. And now, it will cost me you, out of all my service . . . which is perhaps the highest price of all, Caitlin Kralik. But let it be as you have said."

Caitlin was almost dumbfounded for a long moment of her own. "Why?"

"I have learned from you humans that service cannot always be one way. Service must upon occasion flow the other direction, to keep a proper balance. That is, I believe, a lesson that the Jao as a whole must learn. Service must sometimes be returned," Aille said. His angles returned to *neutral*. "Do as you must, Caitlin Kralik. You are your own person now."

Caitlin stared up at Aille, then shook the angles out of her posture and stood before him as a human in every perspective. "Goodbye, Aille," she said, "and thank you." She turned, and began to retrace her steps to the command deck.

Aille watched Caitlin until she turned a corner and was out of his sight. He then boarded the shuttle. "Seal the ship," he ordered the crewman standing by the hatch, "and tell the pilots to take us out."

He heard the hatch close behind him and the crewman mutter into a com bud as he made his way toward the seats reserved for him and his service.

"Where's Caitlin?" Caewithe said, raising up and craning her head around.

"She is not coming," Aille said.

"What?" Caewithe's voice belled out over the conversations in the entire compartment. Silence fell as she began to struggle with her straps. "What do you mean, she's not coming? She has to!"

"Stay seated, Captain Miller," Aille ordered. "She asked to remain. I agreed."

"What?" That expostulation was even louder. "You should have ordered her to board!"

"She is no longer in my service, Captain," Aille said. "Be seated. She is not your concern now. She asked to stay. I allowed it."

Caewithe said nothing more, just went still and dropped her hands to her lap. But her eyes burned into Aille.

CHAPTER 81

Caitlin made her way back to the command deck. The corridors were empty, and seemed to echo. She didn't see anyone; but then, she didn't expect to.

Once Caitlin arrived at the command deck, she picked her way around the hulking Ekhat corpses and through the rows and piles of the smaller slave bodies until she arrived at Lieutenant Vaughan's workstation. She was careful not to touch any of the controls as she took her seat and strapped in.

Time passed. Caitlin wasn't sure how much; she decided she didn't really want to know, so she didn't look at her com pad.

Caitlin didn't know how many people were part of the Alpha crew, so she wasn't surprised one way or another to see three Jao and one human—a woman—on the deck. Thinking about it, she supposed there were a few in the engine room as well.

That, however, brought a horrifying thought to mind. She brought out her com unit, tapped up a dial code, and waited impatiently for it to connect.

"Hello?"

"Lieutenant Bannerji," Caitlin said, "did the Trīkē prisoners get evacuated from *Lexington*?"

"Yes, ma'am, Director Kralik," the lieutenant seemed a little flustered. "They're starting to get used to being moved around, and the quarters we got for them on *Footloose* are almost identical to what they had on *Lex*. We're starting to dock, so they should be in their new space pretty quickly."

"Good," Caitlin said. "I just wanted to make sure they didn't get left behind."

"No, ma'am. They were on the third shuttle, right after all the patients and staff from the medical units got taken off."

Patients! She'd forgotten about them, too. "Thank you, Lieutenant. That's good to hear. Take care of them, now."

"Yes, ma'am."

She could hear a tone creeping into his voice, like he was wondering why she was having that conversation with him. He'd probably figure it out after the word got out of what she had done.

Balton, the replacement captain, looked over at her. When Caitlin had seen that the crew was mostly Jao, she had expected that they would for the most part ignore her. So far, they had. Since she was sitting down and strapped in, she flashed her angles to an abbreviated version of *gratified-respect*. Balton returned it to her, then turned her head back to the control panels.

"All shuttles have departed," the human tech reported. Caitlin was glad that there was at least one other human on the *Lexington*'s final ride. Given the history of the name in Earth military affairs, that was appropriate. "All occupied lifeboats have detached. Ready for action, Captain."

"*Fancy Free* will begin the attack. We will follow," Balton announced.

Caitlin sat back, locked her hands together in her lap, and attempted to swallow the lump that was suddenly in her throat.

The door to *Footloose*'s command deck irised open. For a change, Vaughan was glad the Jao had such screwy ideas about precedence, as it let him charge through the door and head for a workstation well ahead of Fleet Commander Dannet.

Footloose's command deck was laid out almost identically to *Lexington*'s. Vaughan had called ahead and determined that the equivalent workstation to the one he occupied on *Lex* was unoccupied, and he made a beeline for it and threw himself into the seat, ignoring the straps for the moment. A stray thought crossed his mind as he did so; at least they wouldn't have to clean up all the Ekhat corpses in the *Lex*. He pushed that one out of his head as he started slapping pads to bring the workstation system up and started loading his protocols and macros from his com pad. It wouldn't be too long before he would be back in operation, and from the looks of the system plot on the main viewscreen, that would be a good thing.

Vaughan could see both Caewithe and Tamt out of the corner of his eye. They had followed him and were standing near his workstation, staring at the main viewscreen.

He tapped the last couple of pads. Good, everything

was up and running. Data was starting to flow. He looked up at the viewscreen just in time to see the icons starting to move.

"*Fancy Free* is tracking Ekhat Twenty-three," one of the Jao techs said.

"Then we will track Ekhat Twenty-four," Balton ordered. "Maneuvering, align us on that path."

Caitlin watched as the icons on the system plot began to move. The icon for *Fancy Free* was soon in line to fly up the tail of the Ekhat icon in front of it. The display shifted, so that the other Ekhat icon was centered on the display. For a moment Caitlin wondered where the *Lexington*'s icon was. Then she remembered this was a real-life ship, not a video game. Of course she wouldn't see an icon for her own ship. That stirred a dry chuckle out of her.

"Seal your suits," Balton ordered. He looked in Caitlin's direction. "That includes you, Director Kralik."

"Why?" she asked. "If this is a suicide run, why does it matter?"

"Because however so slight the odds, one or more of us might survive," Balton replied, "and I'd rather not have to explain to Tamt that you died of anoxia before she arrived."

Balton's angles showed the odd mixture of *implacable-humor*. Caitlin didn't think she'd ever seen that combination before. But she could tell he wasn't going to relent on this, so she closed all the seals on her suit, pulled on the gloves and sealed them, and finished by pulling the hood and face cover up. She didn't seal the face cover, but Balton turned away, apparently satisfied that she was only a second or so away from being enclosed.

"There goes *Fancy Free*," the Jao tech said. Caitlin watched as that icon began to crawl across the system plot at an increasing rate.

"They must have maxed their engines out to get that velocity," the human tech said.

"We will not do so." Balton said. "All fleet engines were stressed by the run in from the outer orbits. Set our acceleration to ninety percent of the rated maximum. We will still overtake the target with sufficient time to take it out." There was a moment of silence. "Begin," Balton ordered, and the Jao at the maneuvering controls slid four controls most of the way up the control panel.

Caitlin swallowed again. Moment of truth. "Sorry I didn't make it back home, Dad," she whispered.

Kamozh looked at the viewscreen. "That one's moving," he said, pointing to one of the Jao/human icons.

"That is the *Fancy Free*," Lim responded. "She will be chasing the Ekhat ship that is closest to the planet."

"So *Lexington* will target the other one." Kamozh made that a statement. Given the resolve of the Jao commanders, there was nothing to question.

"Yes." Lim's reply was short.

There was nothing left to say, Kamozh thought. It was one thing to watch warriors die in the heat of battle. It was one thing to see them broken in their striving; to see them meeting their foes face to face, and even hand to hand as they had done in *Lexington*. At least then there was always the possibility of survival, of simply beating or outlasting your foe. But this? This intentional embracing of death in order to also obliterate your foe? Despite some of the old sagas, he'd always had his doubts as to whether that kind of thing really happened.

Now he was confronted with it. It was going to play out before his very eyes. Living breathing beings, not even of his own people, were going to immolate themselves in a never-dreamed-of holocaust against the most evil foe Kamozh could never have conceived of on his own in defense of his planet—in defense of Khûr-shi. The sole consolation was that if they succeeded, then Khûr-shi would be safe.

Regardless of whether or not the attacks would be successful, Kamozh had to wonder in the pit of his soul: were his people worthy of such a sacrifice? Was he?

CHAPTER 82

Caitlin felt cold. She sat in the workstation seat, strapped in, hands in her lap, and felt almost icy. When she turned her back on the shuttle and started back to the command deck, she had thought she was angry, enraged, wrathful. She had thought that those impassioned emotions would drive her and fuel her to the end. But in fact—in the moment of executing the act—the heat and the passions had drained away, and she was just cold.

She watched the icons on the system plot on the main viewer. *Fancy Free* seemed to be making good speed in gaining on her target. *Lexington*'s target didn't seem to be growing as much; but Caitlin reminded herself that they had started out closer to their target. They should be making their final run within moments of when *Fancy Free* did so.

The icons moved within the plot. Each incremental change of position seemed to be a slow tick of a clock, counting down to zero.

Caitlin felt cold.

Vaughan stood to go stand behind Caewithe, placing his hands on her shoulders. The tension in her shoulders felt strong enough to break iron bars. Recognizing that this was not the time to speak, he remained silent.

There was little sound in the command deck of *Footloose*; the occasional mutter of a communications tech speaking into a microphone, a quiet question from Terra-Captain Sanzh to one of the sensor techs; one of the humans tapping his fingers on a workstation surface until one of his fellow techs reached over and pressed his hand down, forcing him to stop.

The four icons continued to move, inching across the plot; Ekhat ships inexorably aiming for Khûr-shi, and Terra taif ships just as inexorably aiming to remove them from the system. Vaughan's stomach started to churn. It was one thing to think about a sacrifice being made in the heat of battle. Even human war histories had story after story of men throwing themselves on top of grenades to shield their brothers in arms, or flying planes into other planes or into warships in the heat of battle. But this . . . this calculated pursuit, this was something outside his thought processes. Although the Nipponese fliers of World War II might have understood it.

Caewithe was starting to tremble, and her breath was hissing between her teeth. Vaughan considered trying to wrap his arms around her in support, but from the few words he understood of what she was saying under that breath, somehow he doubted that would be welcome.

"*Fancy Free* making final run," the sensor officer said. A moment later, "*Lexington* making final run."

✧ ✧ ✧

"Now," Balton said, and the maneuvering tech slid the engine controls to the top of their paths.

Caitlin watched as the icon of the Ekhat ship seemed to almost mushroom out as *Lexington* charged forward. One of what she expected to be her final thoughts was that she didn't care what Flue Vaughan said, *Lexington* was special.

There was a huge lurch felt through the fabric of the ship. Before she could call out, the human tech said, "Breaching the shields now. Stand by."

There was a sense of movement, as if something had just shoved the command deck sideways. "They've got currents moving inside the plasma," the human tech said in amazement. "How the hell can they do that?"

"I don't know," Balton said, "but that does explain some things. Can we fight it to the target?"

"Not sure," the human said. "I wouldn't count on it."

Balton was quiet for a moment, then said, "Maneuvering, take your lead from sensors. Steer along the perimeter of the target's shields. If we can't get to the ship, then let's try to break their shields."

"It may blow our shields instead, Captain."

"We're going to die anyway," Balton said. "But if we can bleed off enough of the plasma, then we will have accomplished our strategy, even if the target ship lives."

Caitlin wasn't cold any longer. Watching the skeleton crew wrestle with directing the great mass of *Lexington* back to where her shields intersected with the Ekhat's shields, then forcing the *Lex* to drive along them in the path of the current much like an automobile would scrape along a wall, was heart-wrenching to Caitlin. The thought that they might not succeed in stopping the plasma attack was almost more than she could bear, and the only reason she didn't burst out in weeping or wailing was because she refused to risk distracting the crew.

"Shields overloading," the human tech warned. "Shields past max. Shields arcing, shields . . ."

The deck went dark.

CHAPTER 83

Fancy Free's icon merged with that of Ekhat Twenty-three. There was no sound on the command deck of *Footloose* as they watched and waited for the result. But the result, when it came, was not what they expected. *Fancy Free*'s icon faded away, while that of Ekhat Twenty-three continued to shine as it progressed toward Khûr-shi.

Vaughan spun back towards his workstation as antiphonal curses in multiple languages rang out in the command deck.

"Lieutenant?" Dannet asked, cutting through the noise, which dropped dramatically as everyone realized the fleet commander was speaking.

"I . . ." Vaughan began, fingers flying across the pads, scanning the readouts and displays on his workstation. ". . . can't tell," he finished. "Maybe the sensor techs can dig something out of the detail logs later. It does look," he tapped a couple of pads and looked at another display, "like whatever happened, the Ekhat lost a lot of the plasma; a fourth, maybe as much as a third. The energy readout on what's behind their shields is significantly lower. But there's no sign of *Fancy Free.*"

All eyes turned back to the system plot in time to see *Lexington*'s icon merge with Ekhat Twenty-four's. Again no sound was heard for a long moment, then groans became audible as the Ekhat icon continued to shine, and continued to move toward Khûr-shi just as Ekhat Twenty-three was doing.

Vaughan tapped pads, read readouts, and stiffened. "Wait!" he called out. "The Ekhat is still there, yeah, but it's lost its plasma load!"

Dannet pushed through the crowd. "Say that again."

"The Ekhat ship is still powered and moving, but the plasma ball has been released. Somehow the *Lex* shut down the Ekhat's containment screens."

There was a brief cheer from the humans, cut short by a curt gesture from Dannet as Kamozh and Lim pushed to the fore, followed by D'mishri and the other Khûrûsh. Kamozh spoke. Lim translated, "What of my world? What of Khûr-shi?"

"We cannot stop the final ship," Dannet said. "We have done all that we can do."

Kamozh bowed his head for a moment, then stood tall and raised all four hands in a sign that Vaughan could almost recognize.

"It is enough," Lim translated. "You have done more than any sane individual could have asked. It is fitting that we pay a price for our lack of wisdom all these generations. It will hurt, but we cannot complain about it, for our own choices brought us here." Kamozh executed an elaborate movement of all four hands combined with a bow. "Thank you for what you have done for those who tried to kill you and would have spit upon you."

"The Ekhat still carries plasma, although not as much, and it will release it in the atmosphere of your planet. If your people did not listen to you and take shelter, the loss of life will be great," Dannet warned.

"It will be as Khûr wills," Kamozh responded through Lim.

Dannet turned back to the system plot. "They will both pass around behind the planet and come out on a hyperbolic orbit headed for the outer reaches, trying to find space to make a jump. We will be waiting. Sanzh, order this bearing..."

Caewithe turned up at Vaughan's elbow. "Flue, what is that object there behind the Ekhat that *Lexington* rammed?"

Vaughan had to pull his mind away from Dannet's orders that were spitting out one after another. "What?"

"There's an icon of some kind there trailing behind the Ekhat that lost all its plasma. What is it?"

Vaughan looked at the plot, and yes, there was a small dark icon there. He tapped on some pads. "That," he said with surprise, "is the *Lex*. Or what's left of her," he added darkly.

Caewithe leaned toward him. "Is there any chance that someone may still be alive on her?" The urgency in her voice made it throb.

Vaughan tapped more pads. "No shields. No engine power. Very little intrinsic velocity." He looked up. "Probably not, but then, I wouldn't have bet on her surviving the ram anyway. It's possible."

He winced as Caewithe grabbed his arm in a furious clutch. "You get me a shuttle ordered out. I don't care how you do it, but you get me a shuttle ordered out so Tamt and I can go check."

"I . . ."

"Don't tell me you can't do it, Lieutenant Fflewdwr Vaughan!" Her eyes were intent on his. "You just tap those pads and get me my ride."

A presence loomed up behind Caewithe, and they both looked up to see Aille behind them.

"Do it, Lieutenant, and take a search and rescue team with you, on my orders."

Vaughan took in the *neutral* angles of the governor. "Yes, sir."

He tapped pads for almost a minute, then stood and grabbed Caewithe and Tamt by the arms. "Let's go."

Kamozh watched to the very end, hand grasped in that of Shemnarai, Shekanre standing at his other shoulder, retainers behind him. It seemed to take forever; it seemed to take but a moment; but it took all the iron in his soul to stand there and watch hell delivered on his people.

When the sensor officer said, "They have entered the atmosphere," Kamozh took a gulp of air but said nothing. A few minutes later, the sensor officer said, "They have emerged from atmosphere. Their shields are clear of plasma."

Kamozh released Shemnarai's hand. He raised his hands high, making four signs: **<vendetta> <to the last> <no mercy> <no grace>**. He forced down the howl that wanted to burst forth and shriek his rage and his grief to his god. But the growl that he did emit was perhaps even more chilling.

✧ ✧ ✧

Vaughan watched on his com pad as the plasma ball was released. He heaved a deep sigh when it was over, blanked his com pad off and stowed it away in his suit.

"It's over?" Tamt asked.

"All except for cleaning up those last two Ekhat ships now that they've lost their plasma shields. *Footloose* is making for the point where they'll emerge from behind the planet, and *Pool Buntyam* and *Sun Tzu* are coming up from Khûr-mar. Between them, they'll put paid to those Ekhat, now that they don't have the plasma providing extra shielding."

"Good." Tamt's angles all shrieked of *retribution*. Vaughan was rather glad that they were on the same side at the moment.

Lights blinked on in the darkness. Emergency lights, Caitlin realized. One of them bobbed toward her.

"Are you still with us, Director Kralik?" That was the human tech.

"I . . . I think so," Caitlin managed to get out. She reached up to check, and yes, her suit face covering was sealed, although she didn't remember doing it. "I'm not sure I'm still your director, though, since Aille released me from his service to take this little ride."

"You'll always be 'The Director' after today," the tech said as she helped Caitlin unstrap.

"And you are?" Caitlin asked, suddenly wanting a human connection after having survived what should have been her death.

"Laura Runkle, ma'am, shields tech."

"Well, Tech Runkle, I'm very glad to meet you. What are our chances?"

"Our chances of survival, Director Kralik," came

Balton's voice, "are acceptable, if we can get to the outer hull so we can signal someone in the fleet."

"Why can't we . . . oh," Caitlin said as it dawned on her that if the power to the command deck lighting was down, that probably meant that all other power was probably down. And their suit coms wouldn't penetrate the outer hull.

"I suspect that the engine room is gone," Balton said. "The engines had been stressed today anyway, and then what we did to try and break the Ekhat's shields probably blew one of them. No more than that, though, or the ship would be in shards. The energy backlash would probably have fed back through the engine room. There's no answer from the two techs that were down there, at any rate."

Caitlin swallowed. "Did you succeed in your plan?"

Balton came into the pool of light shed by Runkle's light. "We don't know. But something obviously happened, so we can at least consider the possibility that we did."

Balton turned to the others. "This way. Let's get to the nearest emergency access hatch. Watch your step walking through the trash."

Caitlin heard Runkle give a snort as she helped the director across the room through the maze of bodies. Another Jao with a sense of humor? After the miracles the day had already provided, Caitlin counted this as just one more.

Kamozh turned to Lim. "Ask if they can tell us where the plasma ball landed."

Lim turned to the sensor officer and translated the query. He turned to his techs. After a few minutes, he turned back to Lim and said something. "He says that the passage of the plasma through the atmosphere has so disturbed the weather patterns that they cannot show you in real time the location. Too much dust, too many clouds. But they think it landed here." She turned and nodded to the sensor officer, who said something to one of the sensor techs.

The system plot shrank down to a very small square in the bottom left corner of the main viewscreen, to be replaced by an aerial photograph.

"No," Kamozh whispered, signing **<avert>** with all four hands. A bit of a whine leaked from his throat before he clamped down on it.

"It is what?" Lim asked.

"The three most sacred sites on Khûr-shi—in our entire system—are the sites where the . . . the Veldt," Kamozh struggled to get the name out without cursing, "struck us with their asteroid missiles: Memzhin in the north; Ramezhen in the south; and . . . and there," he lifted a bared claw to point at the viewscreen, "Azhnaton near the center of the world. Azhnaton, the Khûr-melkh's seat, capital city of Khûr-shi, of our culture, before the asteroids fell. They all became memorials to the dead of The Time of Troubles, but Azhnaton was chiefest memorial and shrine, just as it had been chiefest of cities in its life. See the holy lake there in the center? That was the impact site. It was the work of a generation to re-route a river to fill that crater, and make it a place of beauty and contemplation. And now . . ."

Kamozh stopped. Lim looked at him with her aureole fully extended. "Perhaps it will not suffer much damage."

He looked back at her. "As Khûr wills."

✧ ✧ ✧

"We have received signals from *Lexington*," one of the shuttle flight crew announced to the rescue group. "There are four survivors at this point in time, of the six that were known to be on board."

There was a moment of silence. "Come on, come on," Caewithe muttered.

"Director Kralik is one of the survivors."

Caewithe whooped loud enough that Vaughan winced. He couldn't help laughing, though, as she bounced out of her seat and tried to dance a jig with Tamt.

By the time Caewithe had calmed down, the shuttle had taken station off the battleship's forequarter, and launched a line to the survivors who were all standing on the hull around an open emergency hatch.

Caitlin was the first person through the personnel hatch after the airlock was closed. Caewithe grabbed her in an enormous bear hug. Neither of them said anything for the duration of that hug. Caewithe finally broke it so she could place her hands on Caitlin's shoulders and said, "Don't you ever do that again! If you're going to commit suicide, you just take me right along with you."

Caitlin shook her head. "I don't think I'll be doing that again." There was an extra glint of light in her eye, as if moisture had pooled there. She held out her hand to Tamt, who took it in her own out-sized Jao hand and held it with gentleness for a long moment, then released it. But Vaughan saw Tamt's angles release from *retribution* and move to *willingness-to-be-of-service*. In Jao-speak, that was probably a pretty close analog to gladness.

Then Caitlin was holding out her hand to him. "My goodness, Lieutenant Vaughan, I didn't think you could be separated from your command deck workstation."

Vaughan took her hand with a grin. "Well, Director, you know how it is. When this wild woman demanded that I whistle her up a taxi, and then Governor Aille insisted I go along as chaperone," he gave a broad stage shrug, "I didn't have much choice in the matter."

A ghost of a smile played around Caitlin's mouth, fading in and out of the exhaustion that otherwise dominated her expression. There was a bit of a light still in her eyes when she asked, "Did we get it done? Is Khûr-shi safe?"

"You on *Lexington* managed to somehow rip the shields of your target enough that the plasma released. The ship flew on, but it didn't have the plasma ball anymore."

Caitlin actually clapped her hands at that, echoed by the human tech who had boarded behind her. But then she stilled and directed a sharp glance at Vaughan. "*Fancy Free*?"

Vaughan shook his head slowly. "We don't know what happened. She punched through her target's shields all right, and some of the plasma released, but then the shields sealed up again. The target ship itself apparently did not receive much damage, for they continued on and released what was left of their plasma on the planet. We have no idea what happened to *Fancy Free*."

The brightness in Caitlin's eyes increased, and glistened. "Oh, no," she whispered. "After all that..." The brightness overflowed her eyes and began to trickle down her cheeks.

PART VIII
In the Light of Day

CHAPTER 84

"Director Kralik said that the plasma balls are stupid weapons, and we should ask you to explain," Kamozh said. He waited for Lim to finish the translation, and placed all four hands on his hips.

Flue Vaughan smiled a bit. "I must remember to thank Director Kralik, but I'm glad she remembered our discussion." He tapped on a couple of his workstation pads, then turned to face Kamozh, who had the envoys beside him and most of his retainers gathered around. "Here's the short version . . ."

When Vaughan had finished, Kamozh said, "So it's a stupid weapon because it's hard to contain, hard to control, hard to direct, and usually not as efficient at destruction as other available weapons."

"Right," Vaughan replied through Lim. "Although if the Ekhat ever figure out how to open a small window in their shield where they can allow a thin stream of the plasma to come out, that would be a different story. Thank God they haven't stumbled onto that, yet."

"I wish we could see the strike site," Shemnarai said.

"It's been three days," Vaughan turned back to his work station. "Actually, I think the weather has cleared up enough that maybe . . ." He tapped several pads, then pointed to the main viewscreen. "Take a look."

It was an aerial view, of course. It took a moment or two for the orientation and scale of the picture to sink in to all of them, then Kamozh and the native Khûrûsh all stiffened and made signs with their hands. Several of the retainers whined.

"Azhnaton," Vaughan said quietly. "The ground zero for the plasma ball appears to have been the lake." The empty lake bed looked like a raw wound to him; he could only imagine how it looked to the Khûrûsh.

The area of the shrine around the lake had been leveled. The point of view seemed to drop closer. Visible mounds of destruction and debris became visible radiating out from the lake.

"Do we know the death toll?" Kamozh asked, eyes tracing the damage to the holy shrine.

"From the broadcasts we have intercepted today, it seems to be very low," Lim said. "Only a few hundred."

"Yeah, this was once that your people's paranoia paid off," Vaughan said. "The area is not as heavily populated as some of your other cities, and almost everyone took the warning seriously and headed for the underground shelters you have everywhere."

Vaughan tapped another pad, and a different picture came up on the viewscreen. "This was where they attacked our world a few years ago." The devastation was noticeably greater. "We lost over a million people to just one plasma ball."

"We," Lim said after she finished translating for Vaughan, "the Lleix, that is, have lost entire worlds."

Vaughan tapped a pad and put the view of Azhnaton back on the screen. "This is actually less destruction than we expected. Our science boffins aren't sure if that's because they lost some of their plasma due to the attack by *Fancy Free* or if the presence of so much water in the lake had some kind of weird effect on the plasma. Either way, I expect your scientists, and hopefully ours as well, will be studying this for some time to come."

Kamozh looked at the viewscreen again. "It is less than we deserve," he said quietly. "What was destroyed can be rebuilt, as a memorial twice over. What matters is what we do next."

He rose up to consciousness slowly, arriving and floating at that stage where he was sort of aware of what was around him, but still flirting with sleep, fading in and out. At length, his eyes opened and he peered at the softly lit room.

Readout panels to the left; check. A box on a pole with wires and tubes running to and from it; check. Hard bed; check. Rails on the sides of the bed; check. Okay, he was in a medical unit. But why?

Nothing came to mind at first. A lot of memories floated by: Aille, Yaut, Caitlin, jinau, *Lexington* . . . Then a memory seared across his mind like a bolt of lightning: Ekhat. *Ekhat!*

He lunged to sit up, and fell back with a strangled cry as pain shot through his chest. He started to try again, only to feel hands on his shoulder holding him back.

"Gabe, lie still!" He looked up into Caitlin's face. "Lie still, Gabe. You've been wounded, and you're in the medical bay on *Footloose.*"

"The Ekhat?" Tully forced out.

"Destroyed. All of them."

Tully relaxed then, slowly, until Caitlin's hands were not restraining him any longer, were simply resting on his shoulders.

Just as she straightened up, a tall skinny man in a white coat bustled up on the other side of the bed. "Ah, I see the hero has finally awakened." Very white teeth gleamed in a very black face. "I am Dr. Motlana, Colonel Tully, chief surgeon on the *Footloose*, but you can call me Doc or Nelson, whichever you prefer." Another melodious voice, Tully noted, with a bit of a British accent. Not Caribbean, however, so probably African.

"Hi, Doc," Tully said slowly. "Call me Gabe. Why am I here?"

"The short answer, Gabe, is that you are here because you were seriously wounded in the recent battle. The slightly longer answer is that *Ban Chao* had more jinau casualties than their medical bay could treat effectively, so many of the serious cases were transferred to *Footloose* for treatment."

"Serious?"

The doctor's teeth flashed again. "Oh, not so serious that you were at death's door. But serious in that you were a medical mess, oh my, yes. And that is why you are in my medical bay, and in my care. Tell me, what do you remember of the fight you were in?"

Tully rolled his head a little and tried to recall what had occurred. He remembered being in his combat suit, he remembered being in some corridors surrounded by his jinau troops; but he was drawing a blank otherwise. "Nothing much, really. So what happened?" Tully's nose itched and he reached to scratch it with his left hand. His arm felt funny, but it wasn't until he could see it that he understood why. It stopped about ten centimeters below the elbow.

Memory now cascaded back into his mind. The assault on the engine room space in the Ekhat ship. The lone Ekhat breaking out of the containment. His bullets bouncing off its skull. Arming the grenade and shoving it down the Ekhat's throat. And the pain. Oh, yes, he remembered the pain.

"Doc . . ." Tully's voice trembled a little.

"The good news is, you survived and the Ekhat didn't," Doctor Motlana said in all seriousness. "According to the reports, you proved that inserting a fragmentation grenade intracranially into an Ekhat will indeed eliminate the creature. However, according to your executive officer, Major Liang, it is discommended to make said insertion with your hand." The doctor's grin appeared again.

"No shit," Tully muttered, still staring at the place where his left hand used to be.

Doctor Motlana took the stump of his arm in gentle hands, and guided it back down to the bedside. "Your hand would have been lost, no matter what. The combat suit is good protection, but not that good. Actually, it did a good job of protecting your arm above the wrist. It was the Ekhat that took that. Crushed and lacerated the combat suit, crushed the bones, and almost pureed the tissue. By the time you were retrieved from the Ekhat ship, it was too late to salvage it. *Ban Chao*'s medical staff kept everything intact until you made it to my operating theatre. Clean amputation, nice stump. And the new prosthetics are super. You're not feeling it, by the way, because I've got a nerve block administered that will be good for about another twelve hours or so."

Tully took a deep breath, and winced at the more-than-a-twinge of pain in his chest. The doctor observed that. "You are feeling your other wound, though, Gabe."

Tully looked down, but couldn't see much below the sheet that covered him to his armpits. He looked back up to the doctor. "So what happened, Doc?"

"From all accounts," Doctor Motlana replied, "after you blew the head off the Ekhat you faced, what was left of it ran over you and collapsed on top of you. That blunt impact trauma gave you an almost textbook-perfect rib flail injury. Half your ribs are loosened from their moorings either from cracks and breaks in the bones or from tears in the cartilage. That was the main reason why you were sent here from *Ban Chao,* because I am the most experienced thoracic surgeon we have left. And that's the main reason why you've been kept unconscious for three days, to give you some chance for the healing to begin."

The doctor pulled a stethoscope out of his pocket. "I've answered your most pressing questions. Let me listen to your chest, then I'll leave you with Director Kralik while I go tend to your troops."

Doctor Motlana listened to his heart and his lungs, then left with an "I'll be back to check on you soon," flipped over his shoulder.

Tully looked at Caitlin. "Three days?"

She nodded.

"We won, or I wouldn't be here," he said.

"Yes." Caitlin wasn't saying much, which wasn't like her. Even floating in a haze of painkillers, that worried Tully.

"How bad was it?"

Caitlin took a deep breath. "Pretty bad."

"My troops?"

"Thirty-seven dead, twelve seriously injured, including you."

Tully closed his eyes. Faces danced in front of his vision. "The fleet?"

"The ships sent to join *Ban Chao* lost a Harrier, but otherwise took little damage. The ships that stayed with *Lexington* . . ." Caitlin hesitated.

"Bad?"

"We lost all six Harriers of Delta Squadron. We lost *Arjuna* and *Fancy Free*, and *Lexington* is so badly beat up, she may be scrapped. We had to shift fleet command to *Footloose*."

Tully could tell she wasn't giving him everything. "And?"

"The Ekhat . . . crashed a raider ship into a damaged sector of *Lexington*. Six Ekhat and a mob of their slaves boarded the ship, and killed a lot of people."

"Who?"

"Yaut is dead. They're still not sure if Wrot will make it." Caitlin sniffled.

That still wasn't all of it. "Who else? Aille?"

"No, Aille is fine," Caitlin said. After a long moment, she said, "Ed."

Tully reached his hand out toward her, and she took it in both of hers. "I'm sorry."

"Me, too," Caitlin replied. A tear trickled down her cheek.

Major Liang appeared around the corner of the hatch into the room. "Colonel . . ." He stopped. "Sorry, sir, didn't realize you had a visitor."

"Come on in, Major," Caitlin said, releasing Tully's hand and wiping at her face hurriedly. "I need to move on, anyway. Gabe, I'll be back to check on you later."

"Okay." He watched as Caitlin left the room and picked up the bodyguards that had been standing outside that he hadn't even noticed. Man, he hated being on drugs.

Tully beckoned to the major. "C'mere, Shan. How are the troops?"

"Outstanding, Colonel. Except for the wounded, everyone's in good shape and ready to go kick some more Ekhat ass."

"Thirty-seven dead, I heard." Tully was still down about that number.

"Sir, we took out twenty-nine Ekhat in that ship. You can't fight Ekhat in close quarters and not lose troops. Governor Aille said that we did well to lose so little. Ramt said we should be glad the ship was apparently under-crewed."

The major shrugged. "After you went down, we shut down the power systems on that hulk, then re-organized and went Ekhat hunting. By the time *Ban Chao* returned to pick us up, we had cleaned out every single Ekhat. Even Private Ciappa got in on a kill."

Tally's chuckle turned into a cough. "Ow! Damn, that hurts." He pressed his hand gently on his chest. "Maybe there's hope for Ciappa after all. So, morale is good?"

"Morale is great, Colonel. Your reputation as the baddest badass killer of Ekhat is not only intact, it has grown. We have requests for transfers from all over the fleet, even for crew positions on *Ban Chao*."

"So we're back up to strength?"

"Getting there," the major said. "Not much of a jinau force left in the fleet, actually. You heard about *Arjuna*?"

"Yep." Tully said. He tried a nod, and gave it up as *not ready for that yet*.

"A few of her jinau made it out of the ship on lifeboats, so *Ban Chao* picked them up, and we just folded them into our companies. *Fancy Free*'s surviving jinau transferred to us as well. So there aren't many openings left, and there is competition for every slot. Every jinau wants to serve under Colonel Tully."

"Colonel Tully who gets over a third of his force killed in one boarding action," Tully muttered.

"Risk of war," the major shrugged. "On the high side, those jinau who were out in that corridor with you will never have to buy another drink in a jinau bar in their lives."

"How so?" Tully couldn't figure out where this was going.

"Seriously, Colonel. As soon as they start 'No shit, there I was, about to become Ekhat chow when Colonel Tully stepped in . . .' every jinau in the place will buy their drinks for the rest of the night just to hear the story."

"Ha-*Ow!*" Tully pressed his hand to his chest again. "You bastard, don't make me laugh!"

CHAPTER 85

This time they were properly prepared, in a properly equipped conference room that not only had good equipment, but also had good techs to run it. And this time, Kamozh was not dressed in ill-fitting clothing hastily put out by *Lexington*'s quartermaster, meant only to serve until something better could be produced. This time the quartermaster's tailors on *Footloose* had produced some outstanding reproductions of the robes and accouterments that Kamozh would have worn as *Rhan* of the clan. Oh, the robes didn't feel like those his father had worn. They were softer, and lighter, and even a bit shinier, but they looked the part, and that was what was important.

Shemnarai adjusted the drape of the robe, and stepped back between Shekanre and Lim. She tilted her head to one side as she considered his stance and presentation. "Perfect," she said at length. "Do you agree, Weapons Master?"

"Flawless," Shekanre agreed.

Shemnarai straightened and signed **<go forth>** with one forehand and **<conquer>** with the other. She hesitated for a moment, then said, "Are you sure you want to do this? There may be risks to you."

Kamozh barked his baritone chuckle. "What risks can arise that even approach what I have already endured? No, the only risk I must confront is what myself would be like if I do not do this. I suspect I would not like myself very much."

The clan lord turned a bit stiffly, due to the robes, and stepped to the position the techs had told him to occupy. "Ready," he said to Lim.

The Lleix, still leaning on her staff, spoke to the techs. They replied, and she passed the comment on to Kamozh. "You should move to your right just a bit." He did so. "Perfect," came the comment.

"Bright lights," Lim said, as they came on and shone on Kamozh's figure. His eyes blinked rapidly a few times, then settled. "Signal begins three-two-one-now."

Kamozh took a deep breath. This broadcast was going out on all major communication frequencies, strong enough that it would override most local sources. The Terrans were giving him this chance to make his case to his people.

"People of Khûr-shi, and people of the Khûrûsh everywhere. As some of you know, I am Kamozh ar Mnûresh, *Rhan* of Clan Hoshep. I come to you now to bring you great news: we are not alone in the universe.

"As I spoke several days ago when I begged you to let the ships fly to protect our worlds, I have been among the out-worlders for some days now. I watched as the ones called Jao and Terrans came in peace.

I watched as they did their best to turn aside our meaningless and pitiful attacks, destroying only our clanship *Lo-Khûr-shohm*, and that only so they could find someone to talk to. I watched as they left our system because we would not face them.

"I watched as they encountered the out-worlders called the Eleusherar Path, who have served as guardians of our people unbeknownst since the endings of the Time of Troubles.

"I watched as they met each other peacefully, these two great peoples. I watched as they began to speak, and to explore each other's civilization in a very *cultured* manner; one fully as cultured as anything ever done in our history.

"I watched as they recognized the great evil that had come upon us, the onslaught of the Ekhat, before whom our former assailants were but tyros in the art and craft of destruction; the Ekhat before whom our entire civilization would have become naught but dust; the Ekhat who would have rendered our entire system, the creation of Khûr Himself, to be nothing more than scoured airless rocks orbiting Khûr the sun in the basest mockery of the dance of life.

"And I watched as they came to our aid, to our defense, and poured out the wealth of their civilizations and the blood of their peoples to protect us as if we were naught but children.

"They did not have to do that, neither the Jao and Terrans nor the Eleusherar Path. They could have observed from the outside, and then gone their lawful ways. They could have collected the gleanings after the Ekhat were through harvesting the life of our worlds. They could even have joined the attack."

Kamozh raised his forehands in **<absolute truth>**. "They did none of those things. I said they defended us as children, and children we are. Four hundred years ago, after the brutal assault of those I now know were called the Veldt, we had the opportunity to meet the Eleusherar Path. We could have come to know those who are responsible for the fall of the Veldt. There is more to their story than the bit we saw. We could have grown, we could have become adults, able to tend to ourselves and care for our own."

He stopped, and shifted his sign to **<unfortunate>**. "Instead, we turned our back on them, and as children we attempted to hide ourselves away, and pretended that if we did not see the universe, the universe would not see us."

Kamozh stopped and let a moment of silence extend. Finally, he resumed. "But the universe did not reciprocate. And when the Ekhat began to pour out of our sun, our little fleet, our child's toys of ships, were broken and swept away.

"They did not die in vain, those crewmen, those warriors, those Khûrûsh who heeded my call. They died, yes, and they died all too quickly and to too little effect. But they provided an impediment, those toys of ships; an impediment that made the Ekhat hesitate just enough—just that bare moment of enough—that the Jao and Terran ships were able to throw their shield before first Khûr-ma and then Khûr-shi.

"These people, who owe us nothing, these *people*," Kamozh paused a moment for emphasis, "stood against the true monsters of the Ekhat, and they fought as heroes. Would that I were a poet, for their stand deserves an epic like the verses of *The Kelturiad* or

The Song of Kharcharmesh. They stood their ground, oh my fathers, my brothers. They stood their ground, and they fought, and they bled, and they died. They died hard, oh my fathers, my brothers, and they did not die alone. But they died. And in the end, even the arrival of some few of the far-flung ships of the Eleusherar Path was not enough to sustain their sacrifice and preserve Khûr-shi. One Ekhat ship broke through their defenses and poured the fires of the Light of Khûr out upon our home; poured them out upon Azhnaton of the many graves.

"Do not think that the Jao, and the humans, and the Lleix, and the Eleusherar Path failed us. I tell you that if they had not fought, and bled, and *died*, oh my fathers, my brothers, there would have been not one sunfire blossoming on the earth of Khûr-shi, but seven; each greater than what we received."

Kamozh threw out all four hands; the forehands in **<grief>**, the midhands in **<honor to the brave>**. "Our dead keep good company, my fathers, my brothers. And now, it is time for we the living to make the sacrifices meaningful; the sacrifices of the Jao and Terrans in this battle, the sacrifices of the Eleusherar Path over generations, and the sacrifices of those of our own who rose and flew in the face of the Ekhat but days ago."

Kamozh's hands shifted to a fourfold **<arise>**, and his voice gained in strength and depth.

"It is time for we the living Khûrûsh to awaken from our troubled sleep and see the universe for what it is. It is time for we the living Khûrûsh to face the universe and acknowledge it as both beautiful and dangerous. It is time for we the living Khûrûsh to put away childish thoughts, and beliefs, and attitudes, and yes, to put away childish toys."

The signs changed again. The left hands shifted to **<glory>** and the right hands became **<challenge>**. Kamozh's voice became even deeper and stronger, with a rasp of a growl in its timbre. He felt as if his frame had somehow expanded; as if he were a head taller and his shoulders a span wider. He was tingling all over.

"It is time, oh my fathers, my brothers, to take our places on the ramparts among the stars. It is time, oh my fathers, my brothers, to take on the work of adults and warriors, to be numbered among the strong and mighty. It is time, oh my fathers, my brothers, to have the courage to face the universe that Khûr designed in the manner in which Khûr intended for us to do so: on our feet, facing the perils, and glorying in the beauty."

Kamozh stood there for a long moment, the light of challenge in his eyes, holding those signs before those who were viewing him. Then he took a deep breath, and lowered his arms. When he spoke again, his voice was quiet.

"There comes a time in the life of a child when he or she must rise up and take up the tools of life. I have come to believe that this is true also of a people. And that moment is now. Will you, my people, will you come out to us? Will you have the courage to come see what Khûr has wrought? I tell you that we have brothers and sisters who wait upon us." He beckoned to Shemnarai and she moved to stand beside him. "Will you come to meet them? And beyond that all, will you join me? I have called vendetta against the Ekhat, oh my fathers, my brothers, for what they have done. I have called vendetta against the Ekhat, for the honor of the Khûrûsh, and for the honor of those who died defending us. Will you come? Will you stand beside me? Will you bring the wrath of the Khûrûsh, the wrath of Khûr Himself home to the Ekhat?"

Kamozh's voice crested in that moment. He paused for the barest of moments, then said in a quieter tone, "Or will you once again turn your backs to it all, to the everlasting grief of Khûr?"

One last moment of silence.

"For myself," Kamozh said softly, "I would hope that you will come. Kamozh, out."

A moment later the lights winked out, and a moment after that the techs said something to Lim, who translated, "Good signal, good broadcast, good job. They recorded it as well."

Kamozh was drained. Every erg of energy in his body seemed to have flowed out of him when the lights turned off. The young clan-lord fumbled with his fingers at the robe. Shekanre brushed his hands aside and began to divest his lord with both skill and speed, so that it was just moments later that he was standing in just his everyday harness.

Shemnarai came to him, and groomed his head with her forehands. "You were magnificent," she hummed, almost singing. "If they do not come, they do not deserve you."

"It's not about me," Kamozh protested.

"You have made it about you," Shemnarai replied with a throaty chuckle of her own.

CHAPTER 86

Tully was pushing a fork around on his plate. "Damn, this is pathetic," he said. "We can fly starships across the galaxy, but the medics are still serving up cardboard covered in paste. These guys need to get a real chef over here."

"Who would you recommend?"

Tully looked up to see Aille standing in the door to his room. "Well," he said, "I think the average fourth-grader could do better than this."

Aille stepped into the room. "I believe we left all the fourth-graders back on Terra in school."

"Okay, then at least get one of the assistant cooks from *Ban Chao* over here," Tully said with a grin. "Or maybe get Master Zhao Jiguang to come teach these guys how to cook. He can make almost anything taste good, which this," he dropped the fork on the plate, "does not."

"I have wondered upon occasion if it is the excess of *ollnat* among you humans which has raised food preparation to an art form." Aille flowed through a variety of angles that Tully guessed all expressed some degree of humor. "Your obsession with presentation and taste is almost perverted. As long as food is nutritious, does not create illness, and does not fight too hard to avoid being eaten," Aille flicked his whiskers in a move that Tully knew was almost a Jao laugh, "nothing else is of concern."

"Man, it must really suck to be a Jao," Tully said, his grin getting wider. "Your ancestors must have really pissed God off, because it's like you're the fall guys for a really bad practical joke here. You literally don't know what you're missing. Just the Italian food alone: lasagna, risotto, veal parmigiana, chicken alfredo, and spumoni." He swallowed, and pushed the plate farther away. "Now I really don't want that swill."

"Gabe?"

Tully looked up to see Caewithe Miller and Flue Vaughan looking in through the doorway.

"Caewithe, come in!"

She looked at Aille and said, "We can come back later, if you're busy."

"No, Captain," Aille said. "Please come in. As it happens, I remember that I need to talk to Lieutenant Vaughan about something."

"So they have you in a chair today, I see," Caewithe said as she came over to give Tully a quick hug.

"Yep. I think they were hoping I'd be so excited about it that I'd overlook what they were trying to feed me." A dark look crossed his face. "Fat chance."

Caewithe looked at Tully's plate, and an expression of distaste came and went. "I see what you mean. I'll sneak you a cheeseburger from the officer's mess."

"Please!" Tully looked to Vaughan and held out his hand. "Hey, Flue. Hear you did some good shooting the other day."

"Good to see you up and around, Colonel. We need you back, since the general's gone." Expressions went solemn and morose for a moment.

"Call me Gabe. I'll be back as soon as the docs let me out of here." Tully pointed to where Vaughan's shoulder holster was riding. "You still carrying?"

Vaughan gave a sour chuckle. "Gabe, after what *Lex*'s survivors have been through, I doubt that any of us will not be packing twenty-four/seven for a long, long time."

Tully nodded. "I can see that. But you're a flier, a spaceboy. Where'd you learn to shoot like that?"

Flue shrugged. "My Da was SBS, and he trained me up even after the Jao shut down the country armed forces."

"So that's why you swim so well," Caewithe said. "You cheat!"

Everyone got a chuckle out of that.

Tully pointed back at the shoulder holster. "So what is it that you're packing? Word is it's not standard issue."

"Well," Vaughan said as he pulled the pistol out. "It's half a custom design, and half a prototype." He ejected the magazine onto the bed while he was talking, then worked the slide and caught the ejected cartridge in the air. "It started life as a direct lineal descendant of STI International's Perfect 10 ten-millimeter model. I commissioned them to first of all space rate it, lubes and all, so it would function in vacuum without any danger of vacuum welds. Same process as the standard-issue ten-millimeter pistols go through, only more so, them being STI."

Vaughan handed the pistol to Tully hilt first. Tully took it, hefting it.

"Big gun. Heavy."

"It's a very long-slide design," Vaughan said, "partly because the barrel is longer than any of their other Perfect 10 designs: about 165 millimeters, I believe."

Tully laid the pistol on the table. "Grip looks longer, too."

Vaughan flashed a grin. "That's because the magazine has to handle these." He handed the loose cartridge to Tully.

Tully rolled it around until he could get it straight, then held it up between his thumb and forefinger. He whistled. "Just what is that?"

"That," Vaughan said, "is the standard cartridge for this gun. It's a 10 mm, yes, but it's about 42 millimeters long, which is about 17 millimeters longer than a standard 10 mm cartridge. And almost all of that extra length is propellant, not bullet. They did some work on new propellants as well, and the loads they gave me are pretty hot. The test loads they fired measured out at over 610 meters per second."

Tully raised his eyebrows. "Nice." He looked at the cartridge for a moment longer, then tossed it back to Vaughan. "Is that why your slugs didn't bounce off the Ekhat like ours did?"

Vaughan face took on a sober expression. "Partly. The other reason is that I played a hunch, and had STI order up my initial ammo load with armor-piercing. Turns out that was a smart move on my part."

"Why is that?" Now Tully was really getting interested.

"I didn't know it until after the firefight on *Lex*,"

Vaughan said. "Afterward, I dug up the autopsy reports done back on Terra on the Ekhat that they brought back from Valeron after it died. It turns out that both their bones and their hides, which are thick to begin with, are also laced with an organic analog to that same stuff that The Ollnat Works says is the basis of Super-K."

"What?" That sounded from three throats simultaneously, including Aille's.

"Yep. Short little fibers of the stuff scattered thickly through both the compounds of their bones—which are not osseous calcium, by the way—and through the various layers of their skins. The autopsy says it is almost reminiscent of nanotech assemblage, and that the tough fibers make it very difficult to break or crack the bones or tear the hide."

"Shit." Tully stared down at the gun and worked his mouth. "Our armor piercing loads weren't nearly as effective as we'd hoped they would be. But your high-powered armor piercing loads, built on a hunch, worked against them."

"Yeah." Vaughan was very sober now. "That hunch is what kept most of us on *Lexington*'s command deck alive."

Tully turned his gaze to Aille. "So if we'd had this gun issued, most of my jinau would still be alive, and I'd still have my left hand."

Aille reached over and picked up the pistol. "Perhaps. The Ekhat would be a challenging foe, no matter how you are armed. You are so used to *ollnat*, to having an immediate solution to your problems, that you are angry when you perceive a failure. But to me, after hundreds of generations of Jao dying when confronting the Ekhat, this becomes an unsought-for answer to one of our greatest needs."

The governor carefully folded his hand around the grip of the pistol. "It is almost of a scale to fit a Jao hand. *Ollnat*, indeed." He handed the pistol back to Vaughan. "When we return to Terra, you will place these STI people in contact with me."

With that, Aille turned and left.

"I didn't take delivery of this until just before the fleet left," Vaughan said, almost apologetically. He picked up the magazine and loaded it in the pistol, worked the slide, then ejected the magazine to load the loose round before reloading the magazine.

"Not your fault, Flue," Tully said tiredly, running his hand down his face. "Like Aille said, *ollnat* happens where it happens."

"By the way," Vaughan said, "I don't know if the issue ten mil can make the shot, but two or three of these," he hefted the pistol, "at the base of the throat," he laid a finger below his own larynx, "took down four Ekhat for keeps." Sliding the pistol back into his shoulder holster, Vaughan concluded with, "Autopsy says there's a mass of neural tissue behind the neck right about there, so it may be like a shot to the brain."

"Damn, I wish we'd known that," Tully said. "That might just have kept some jinau alive."

There was a moment of silence, while the three of them thought about their losses.

"You've got to wonder, you know," Caewithe finally said.

"How so?" Tully asked.

"It's almost like the Ekhat have been designed to be killing machines. Why?"

Vaughan shrugged. "I can't find any origin stories for the Ekhat in either the Jao or the Lleix files. Maybe they did genetic modification on themselves. After all, they don't seem to have been shy on doing it on some of their slave species."

"Yeah," Tully said. "Or maybe, just maybe, there was somebody who came before them who uplifted them, just like they uplifted the Jao."

"But what would be the reason for making them this way, so crazy and violent?" Caewithe asked. "Why?"

"I dunno," Tully said. "Gladiators?"

"Oh, now there's a horrible thought," Vaughan said with another sour chuckle.

Tully tilted his head for a couple of seconds, then said, "Yeah, but it just might explain some things." He straightened up. "And how much did that sweet thing under your arm cost you?"

"You don't want to know."

"I was afraid of that. Caewithe, where's my cheese-burger?"

CHAPTER 87

Kamozh woke suddenly to find Shekanre shaking him violently. "Wake up, *Rhan*! You must wake up now."

"Enough, Shekanre, enough. I am awake."

With that Shekanre left off, but continued talking at a volume that Kamozh felt was entirely too loud for what felt like the early hours of the morning watch. "You must get up, *Rhan*. Lady Shemnarai has sent word that they need you as soon as possible in Shuttle Bay Blue 4."

"Urg," Kamozh muttered, uncurling from the pallet he usually slept on. He straightened out, stretched all four arms out wide, and yawned enough to cause his jaws to crack. With that, he rolled to his feet and midhands.

"What is the reason for the hurry?" he said, running his claws through his head fur. He looked up to see Shekanre directing Penshet and Zhebnikh, who were carrying in the clan lord robes he had worn a few days before. Now he was wide awake.

"And what in the name of all that's holy are you doing with that?"

"All I know is she said she needs you at the shuttle bay as close to now as we can manage, dressed in these robes, and as well groomed as we can manage."

Kamozh was thankful at that moment that he slept in nothing but his skin. If he was one of the more effete courtiers who wore complicated robes for sleeping, he'd be in a tangled mess at the moment. The young clan lord headed for what the humans called a bathroom. He eyed the shower with longing, but it would take too long to dry his fur. Kamozh settled for splashing cold water into his face, and using several of the cleansing wipes he had cadged from the medics to wipe down his fur. The scent they were imbued with had grown on him, to the point where he actually liked it now.

Feeling somewhat more awake, Kamozh stepped back into the other room. "Stand still and hold out your arms," Shekanre said, his hands full of robes. The clan lord did as he directed, reflecting on the times he had seen his own father standing in just such a manner for just such a reason.

For all that he was a weapons master, Shekanre had had more than one occasion to be involved with preparing his master quickly for a sudden audience or event. In fact, even as he admired the old retainer's skill, Kamozh seemed to remember that Shekanre had at least for a time served as his father's chamberlain at a time when relationships with another clan were tense. No wonder Shekanre had this under control, Kamozh mused.

It seemed but the work of moments and the young

clan lord was dressed. Shekanre reached out and tweaked the inner collar just a bit, then stood back to view the whole effect. "That will do," he said finally. "Penshet?"

The other retainer handed a small container of a stiff white substance to the weapons master, who scooped two fingers through it and handed the container back to Penshet.

"And what is that?" Kamozh said, drawing back a little as Shekanre drew near to him.

"Stand still," Shekanre said as he reached for Kamozh's head. "You keep your head fur so short that it needs something to make it look bulkier than it is; otherwise people will think you've been sick. I got this from one of the barbers on *Footloose* after we transferred. He says it 'will do the job.'"

Shekanre rubbed the substance vigorously into Kamozh's scalp, then stepped back beside Penshet.

"Towel." Penshet handed that over, and Shekanre cleaned his hands off.

"Comb." Penshet exchanged that for the towel, and Shekanre advanced on Kamozh again.

Shekanre worked for a minute or so. Kamozh winced as the teeth of the comb scraped across his scalp.

"What looks better, Penshet? This . . ." Shekanre stepped back for a moment, ". . . or this?" He stepped up and rearranged Kamozh's fur.

Penshet's muzzle wrinkled, and his hands wavered in the air indicating indecision. "I'm not sure either one is good. Try combing everything straight up."

Shekanre stepped in to drag the comb through Kamozh's fur again, then stepped back again. After a moment, he nodded. "Right. That will do. You may start a new fashion, *Rhan.* Just keep your hands off of your head."

A few more moments of attaching accouterments, last of which was the *Rhan*'s earring to dangle from the right ear.

"Right, that's got it," Shekanre said, clapping all four hands together.

The other retainers filed in, all dressed in the best they had. Shekanre stepped to the door. "Time, lord, to be about it." With that, he opened the door and led the way, as was appropriate for the weapons master of a clan. Kamozh followed, with the rest of the retainers marching behind.

"I feel like my sister's painted doll," Kamozh muttered.

"You're not that, not in the slightest," came a reply drifting back from Shekanre. "You are Lord Kamozh, *Rhan* of Clan Hoshep, and you have stood before Jao, humans, Lleix, and the Eleusherar Path as an equal. You have battled the Ekhat at their sides. You called the ships of the Khûrûsh to fly, and they flew. You, Kamozh are second to none."

The more he considered that, the more Kamozh thought his retainer was right. He straightened to his full height, and adopted a bit of a swagger; that is, until he heard Shekanre say, "Just don't get a swollen head about it."

And so it was that when Kamozh, *Rhan* of Clan Hoshep, entered Shuttle Bay Blue 4, he was barking laughter.

Third-Mordent arrived at Ninth-Minor-Sustained's great room. She was feeling a bit angry that the harmony master had interrupted her work on a variation of the grand canon that the harmony master herself had seen fit to introduce Third-Mordent to on the very day where they had met.

As she approached the private door to the space, Third-Mordent reminded herself, *Control*, and clamped down on her anger, squeezing it in until it vanished. Ninth-Minor-Sustained was not one to approach with that emotion tingeing one's harmonies.

The door irised open before her, and she stepped through to find that Ninth-Minor-Sustained was not alone. Seventh-Flat stood facing the harmony master, with three other Ekhat behind her. All were close to predator mode; their heads kept lowering, and their eyes were increasingly reddened. All were showing more than the barest edge of forehand blades.

Third-Mordent stopped behind and to one side of her ancestress. Her control tightened, and she suppressed the predator mode urge to enter her blade-dance focus.

Her posture changed slightly, leaning forward just a bit. She did not unsheathe her forehand blades, but she did position those limbs at particular angles.

Seventh-Flat did not react to Third-Mordent, focused as she was on Ninth-Minor-Sustained. The three standing behind her—members, so Third-Mordent supposed, of Seventh-Flat's subfaction—did notice. They tried to divide their attention between the harmony master and Third-Mordent, who judged they failed to succeed in either case.

"You have destroyed us again, harmony master," Seventh-Flat uttered in an almost atonal aria form.

Her voice was so distorted from its normal sound that Third-Mordent almost couldn't understand her.

"I?" Ninth-Minor-Sustained sang a bell-like tone, high and pure. "I did nothing."

"Spare us," Seventh-Flat intoned in bitter diminished downward steps. "You felt the nexus; you shaped the nexus; you caused us and so many others to send out ships to take or destroy the nexus, deny it though you may. And the nexus trembled, but it survived unchanged. The Melody has grown weaker, harmony master, the very Melody which should be receiving your prime service. And our ships, all of our ships, are gone, except for yours. There is no echo of them in the Melody. There are no notes from them. Where they were are nothing but blanks."

Seventh-Flat edged closer to Ninth-Minor-Sustained. "The Nexus strengthens, and we are, all of us, unable to act—except for you, harmony master."

"I do what is best for the Melody and for the Complete Harmony," Ninth-Minor-Sustained sang in a cold descending whole-tone fractal scale. "My skill, my authority, my judgment."

Seventh-Flat's forehand-blades snapped open and she leapt to the attack even as she shrieked "Traitor! Traitor! Traitor! Traitor!" in a stretto style.

Third-Mordent swept forward, forehand blades snapping open even as she sidestepped the first of the three Ekhat behind Seventh-Flat. She swirled down the side of the creature even as it attempted to spin. The spin failed because Third-Mordent had severed the major leg tendons on all three legs. The Ekhat crashed to the floor with a discordant screech as those legs collapsed.

By the time the second Ekhat understood what had happened, Third-Mordent had passed behind her and performed the same cuts on her rear legs.

This left the third Ekhat, who had not been entangled in the other two, and had spun herself to face Third-Mordent. She immediately launched a furious attack on Third-Mordent. She was good enough to challenge Third-Mordent.

She was not good enough, alas for her sake, to seriously challenge Third-Mordent. They danced one step, two steps, three steps according to Third-Mordent's plan, and then her forehand blades were swept out of line and one of Third-Mordent's entered her eye and sliced open her cortex while the other severed the great neck artery. White ichor spurted out and splashed across Third-Mordent's chest as she spun back to the two cripples. Two steps, two cuts with her forehand blades, and they were no longer cripples, but were imminent corpses as more white ichor flowed.

As she turned her attention to the dance between Seventh-Flat and Ninth-Minor-Sustained, Seventh-Flat executed a step that put her outside the harmony master's reach for just a moment—a moment that proved to be almost fatal. A savage cut crippled Ninth-Minor-Sustained's left foreleg, and the barest instant later an equally savage cut severed the harmony master's left forehand blade and sent it flying to land on the floor some distance away.

Seventh-Flat spun to face Third-Mordent even as she attacked to support her ancestress. Blades flickered faster and faster. Third-Mordent could place slashes on Seventh-Flat's tegument, but for every touch she made, the larger Ekhat made two. Nothing serious, yet, but Third-Mordent could feel the ichor oozing out.

Third-Mordent changed the pattern of her strikes, changing the rhythms of the dance as well as upping the tempo. Seventh-Flat kept pace with her for a short time, but the effort of having fought so intensely against Ninth-Minor-Sustained showed as the older Ekhat began to have trouble marching to the faster pace. More and more it was Third-Mordent who was making two strikes to the other's one. More and more it was Seventh-Flat who was being forced to give way, being forced to improvise counters to face the flashing attacks of Third-Mordent.

The end came when Seventh-Flat attempted the same movement against Third-Mordent which had ended so disastrously for Ninth-Minor-Sustained. It did not do so for Third-Mordent. She turned into the move, and a moment later both of Seventh-Flat's forehand blades were lying on the floor. As the older Ekhat shrieked atonally at the wounds and the defeat, Third-Mordent swirled down one side and crippled the legs so that Seventh-Flat collapsed to the floor on that side.

Third-Mordent stood poised for a moment, surveying the great room. Behind her she could hear her ancestress stirring a bit. Before her Seventh-Flat continued to shriek, mind lost in predator mode, as her legs pushed her crippled carcass across the floor toward a wall. The other three appeared to be well and truly dead, ichor spreading across the floor.

There was a sound behind her as of Ninth-Minor-Sustained trying to walk, dragging the crippled limb across the floor as she attempted the movement. Third-Mordent turned to face her ancestress.

Ninth-Minor-Sustained stood a bit unevenly because of the leg. Ichor dripped from the limb where the forehand blade had been severed. Her remaining forehand blade was unsheathed, but it hung to the floor.

"You will have to complete me," Ninth-Minor-Sustained intoned in a thin voice.

Third-Mordent simply looked at her, uttering no sound.

"You must complete me to attain your rise," Ninth-Minor-Sustained managed an aria form this time.

Third-Mordent still did nothing.

"Complete me!" the harmony master attempted a command in her full voice full tonal onslaught mode. If her voice had not cracked, she might have succeeded. "You must do it; else others will claim the victory and take that which should be yours."

Third-Mordent stirred finally, sheathing her forehand blades. "No," was her only response in a brief recitative mode.

"Complete me!" Ninth-Minor-Sustained shrilled in diminished descending steps, ironically echoing Seventh-Flat's final statement to her. She raised her forehand blade and lurched toward her descendant.

Third-Mordent waited until the last instant, then flashed her forehand blades open. A moment later, Ninth-Minor-Sustained's remaining forehand blade was lying on the floor, and the harmony master almost fell as her right-side middle leg suffered the same injuries as her left foreleg. With only four legs to bear her great weight, she could barely move, and with her forehand blades gone, she was no threat.

"Complete me," Ninth-Minor-Sustained whisper-sang.

Third-Mordent flicked her forehand blades to sling the ichor off of them, then folded them back into their sheaths. "No," she repeated, still in recitative mode.

Walking around the still shrieking form of Seventh-Flat, Third-Mordent stepped to the wall panel and raised a manipulator to the controls. When the response came, she fluted, "Send the creche masters and their attendants to this location."

CHAPTER 88

Vaughan sat down at the conference table. Also present were Aille, Fleet Commander Dannet, and Rafe Aguilera. "Thank you all for coming," he said. "This won't take long."

Tapping on his com pad, Vaughan activated a hologram floating above the table. It was a wireframe image of the *Lexington*.

"I told you, Governor," Vaughan began, looking at Aille, "that I would find out just how the Ekhat managed to break into the *Lex* so easily, and even more importantly, how they managed to find the command deck so easily."

Another tap on the control pad caused a yellow light to flare on one flank of the hologram model.

"The Ekhat boarded through the B weapons spine, after crashing their ship into an area already damaged from the battle. The ship's system records indicate that at that point, every crew or jinau member in the spine was either dead or incapacitated. Yet those same records indicate that the doors to the deck were opened from the spine side of the hull. Hold that thought."

Tap. A yellow line moved from the first light toward the prow of the ship.

"They left three Ekhat and several slaves to battle the crew and jinau who moved toward the boarding location. The rest headed forward. Now here's the interesting part," Vaughan leaned forward. "Ship's records indicate there was no wavering, no searching, no opening of doors along that path. They slaughtered every Jao or human they found in the corridor, but they didn't stop to open a door until they arrived at the command deck.

"Now here's the catch: based on all that, either there is a traitor among the Jao or human or Lleix feeding information to them, or they knew something about a ship they'd never seen before."

"Can't be the first one," Rafe spoke out immediately. "Even if we could talk to the crazy sonsabitches, no one would help them after what they've done to us. No one."

"Ekhat do not encourage traitors," Aille said. "Everyone who tries to approach them has been eliminated by the Ekhat. There are three kochan who no longer exist because of that."

"Right," Vaughan said. "What I thought. Which means that they found their way on their own, without mistakes, without fumbling around, without exploring other corridors."

"How?" That was Rafe again.

Tap, tap, tap. The hologram changed to a schematic of a door control. "So I did some more digging, and here's what I found out. All of these door controls are a Jao design. And right here"—Vaughan tapped to cause a component in the schematic to flash—"is a little fiddly bit whose only purpose appears to be to know three things: the number assigned to this control, the number of the control before it in the controller network, and the number of the one after it in the controller network. And it will joyfully pass that information to anyone who happens to ask it.

"Now—would you care to hazard a guess as to which number is assigned to the door controller of the command deck door?"

"One," Dannet said.

"Correct. And why is that?" Vaughan asked, a bit sarcastically.

"Because the command deck door is always assigned One," the fleet commander replied.

"And for how long has that been the practice?"

Dannet looked at Aille. Aille said nothing. Dannet looked back at Vaughan. "I don't know."

"It has been part of Jao ship design as far back as I can research. *Every single design document, no matter how old, has the command deck door coded as One!*" Vaughan sat back, breathing heavily. "Rafe, I hear you're a betting man. Want to lay odds as to whether or not the Jao did it that way because that's how the ships they took from the Ekhat when they revolted were set up?"

"I won't take that bet," Rafe said quietly.

Vaughan leaned forward again. "They walked up to the door, asked it for its number, and asked it which direction the next smaller number was. That's all they needed to know."

Tap tap. The hologram disappeared. "We did it to ourselves."

Aille looked at Rafe. "You will take this to the design teams when we return."

Rafe's eyes were narrowed and his jaw muscles were bunched. "Yes, sir."

Caitlin viewed her image in the mirror panel. Dressed in the best she had brought along. Hair okay. Makeup . . . she frowned. She never wore much makeup, so that didn't matter much anyway. Her eyes still seemed slightly sunken because of the dark circles around them. Restful sleep was still eluding her, and she didn't want to take the meds that the doctors kept trying to push on her.

Com pad . . . where . . . there. She picked it up and slid it into an inside pocket of the jacket.

Caitlin looked around. The room still seemed so empty, with Ed gone. Funny how it had never seemed that way during the years she had lived in one just like it aboard *Lexington.* But now, after just a few days of Ed being with her, it was like there was a large hole in it, where major parts of it had been ripped out of the picture.

All their things had been salvaged from *Lexington*, including what Ed had brought with him. Caitlin had placed his clothes very carefully in some of the drawers. At least once a day she would open a drawer and pick up a shirt and sniff it. She was convinced that the scent of him still permeated the fabric. It might be delusion on her part, but she still clung to it.

Time to get going, she thought. The planetary

representative would be arriving soon, and even though she was no longer part of Aille's service, he had still asked her to be there. She had almost turned it down, but in the end she decided that she owed it to Ed and to her dead to be there.

Caitlin bitterly regretted that the fleet had not stopped that last plasma ball from reaching Khûr-shi. Everyone, including Kamozh, said that they had done all that they could do. Everyone excused her. But she didn't excuse herself.

It was at least some consolation that by the time the shuttle that had picked her up from *Lexington* caught back up with *Footloose*, the last two Ekhat ships had been caught between *Footloose* on one side and *Pool Buntyam* and *Sun Tzu* coming up from the inner system, and were nothing more than orbiting debris. That, at least, had gone according to plan: all the Ekhat were dead. There was a very cold spot in her heart where she wished that for all Ekhat. Caitlin totally understood Kamozh's vendetta. Maybe humans really weren't as civilized as they thought they were.

There was a tap at the door. Caewithe, no doubt. Time to go. Caitlin looked around the room, tapped her com pad in its pocket, and opened the door.

The lights shut down a few moments after she left. No one else was there to keep them active.

Kamozh arrived at Shemnarai's side just as the nose of a shuttle began entering the shuttle bay. "What is so important that I need to be here like this?"

"Khûr-melkh Shmenkhat has sent someone."

A tingle ran through Kamozh's body. Every nerve

was awake; every hair seemed to be standing stiff. "Do we know who?"

That was a critical question. The stature of the person or persons sent would reflect the importance the Khûr-melkh attached to the issue at hand. The politics of the person or persons sent would reflect the views of the Khûr-melkh.

"No," Shemnarai said tersely, her fingers twitching in the manner of someone who wanted to make a sign but wasn't sure which one to make.

Now Kamozh understood Shemnarai's instructions to Shekanre. He tugged at the front of his robe. "How do I look?"

Shemnarai took a glance at him. "You'll do." She took a second, longer glance. "Nice hair."

By now the shuttle was fully in the bay, and settling to the deck. They waited for the propulsion unit to finish cycling down, then advanced a few steps to stand visibly in the open. Kamozh did a quick scan, then muttered, "I don't see anyone but us."

"They wait in the conference room. I asked that we be allowed to greet them first."

"Ah." Kamozh's mind raced through all the implications. "Indeed. Let us begin as we mean to continue."

"Precisely." Shemnarai's muzzle wrinkled slightly, and one midhand showed **<humor>** so briefly that Kamozh wasn't quite sure that he'd seen it.

They waited—impatiently on Kamozh's part—until the hatch opened and the ramp descended to touch the deck. His interest heightened even more. "Come on," he muttered when the hatchway remained vacant.

"Hush," Shemnarai whispered over Shekanre's low chuckle.

At that moment a figure appeared in the hatchway and strode down the ramp. "Oh, my," Kamozh whispered. Shekanre hissed.

"What?" Shemnarai whispered back, but there was no time to respond, for the person was upon them.

She—for it was a female—was in the briefest of robes; a uniform, really. And Kamozh recognized that uniform; oh, yes he did. The female stopped, placed her midhands on her lower hips, and showed **<peace>** with her left forehand and **<caution>** with her right. "I am Henzhre, Weapons Master to Khûr-melkh Shmenkhat."

Before they could respond, Henzhre reached out and tapped Shemnarai's Isha clan crest with a talon. "Nefreptah ar Isha, I assume?"

"My ancestor," Shemnarai said.

"His mother and his mate corresponded with the mate of Khûr-melkh Amozh. I have read them, and seen the pictures of the time. You favor him. You are . . ."

"Shemnarai, current leader of the exiles that are now in Khûr system."

"Shemnarai," Henzhre said with a sign of respect. "We will talk more later."

Henzhre turned to Kamozh. "And you . . . you I need no introduction. You are dangerous."

"You," Ninth-Minor-Sustained whisper-sang, dragging a step closer to Third-Mordent, "you are my progeny indeed. You will shape the Melody as none has before."

A moment passed.

"I have a request," the harmony master intoned.

Third-Mordent considered, then responded a motif of "Continue."

"Let me be last. Let me see Seventh-Flat taken," Ninth-Minor-Sustained sang in an elegiac form.

"Agreed," Third-Mordent fluted.

"And one final instruction, if you will. Do not implant everything you have in us. Save some to keep your mind in the highest mode."

That word from the harmony master gave Third-Mordent the final bit of knowledge she needed to understand how her ancestress had remained so strong, so controlled, so controlling, for so long. Carrying fertilized spermatophores affected the metabolic balances, she knew; now she saw that they strengthened the mental processes as well.

"I have a myriad," Third-Mordent intoned. "It was a good mating. I will have a plenitude even after implanting the two of you."

"My progeny, indeed," whisper-sang Ninth-Minor-Sustained.

The main door irised open, and three creche-masters entered followed by their servients.

Third-Mordent advanced on them. "Those three are offal," she sang, gesturing at the three motionless carcasses. "If they are not completed, make them so."

She gestured at the still shrieking Seventh-Flat and at Ninth-Minor-Sustained, standing nearby. "These two—can they be sustained for gestation?"

There was a long moment of silence, then the largest of the creche-masters intoned, "They can."

Ninth-Minor-Sustained dragged forward one step. "You, take notice, take witness, that Third-Mordent defeated both Seventh-Flat and myself. All that we have is now hers. All."

"Witnessed," that same creche-master sang as she

and her companions and servients all retreated toward the far side of the great room.

Third-Mordent gave way to *Spawn!* Her spinal column began to creak and shift.

"My progeny," Ninth-Minor-Sustained whisper-sang as the ovipositor began to rise.

"As are you," Kamozh said. "Commander of the Royal Guard, Weapons Master to the Khûr-melkh, and his half-sister as well. You are perhaps the most dangerous person in all the worlds of Khûr, which is undoubtedly why Shmenkhat keeps you so close." He dared to omit the honorific.

Henzhre barked a laugh, and clapped a hand on Kamozh's shoulder. "Your father always said you would be impressive once you came to rank. You bear him out, young *Rhan*."

That the importance of the issue to the Khûr-melkh was great had become very clear when Kamozh saw Henzhre on the boarding ramp. With those words the position of the Khûr-melkh Shmenkhat became equally clear. Kamozh's eyes widened, and he heard Shemnarai inhale sharply. Dead people could not be clan lords, and by admitting publicly that Kamozh was both alive and serving as *Rhan*, the Khûr-melkh was at least tacitly revoking the old law. Joy and triumph began to bubble up in Kamozh.

Henzhre noted their reactions, and crossed all four of her arms. "Oh, yes, Lord Kamozh, my brother has made his decision. Even if he had not been convinced by the sight of the fires of Khûr being dropped onto the heart of Khûr-shi; even if he had not been convinced by the sight of so many great ships fighting at the gate to prevent our destruction; even if he had not been of a mind that the old law was wrong even before this; even if the space forces and the military had not risen in protest to force the retirement of the old leaders and had not clamored for your return; even so, young *Rhan*, your speeches would have swayed him."

Henzhre spread her arms with a fourfold **<truth>**. "You claim not to be a poet, Lord Kamozh, and you are not. You are worse," she barked a laugh again. "You are an honest Khûrûsh-an whom our people consider a hero, and your every word will be considered an oracle from Khûr unless you misstep very badly."

With that she folded her hands again, and wrinkled her snout. "That is, outside the court. Inside the court, speak softly, walk softly, and keep this old warrior at your back."

Henzhre exchanged an arm-clasp with Shekanre. It hadn't occurred to Kamozh that the two would be acquainted, but of course, the weapons master of a major clan would be known to the weapons master of the Khûr-melkh.

Clapping her hands together, Henzhre said, "Well, take me to the meeting with the monsters. I am eager to meet those you defend so strongly, Lord Kamozh. But one thing," she stopped short and eyed them all sternly. "I speak for the Khûr-melkh; I alone. That is why I have no party, no associates, no attendants. I am the voice of my brother."

Kamozh understood the implications instantly. He was sure Shemnarai did as well. "It is as you say, Commander Henzhre."

"Good. Now let's be about it."

CHAPTER 89

Caitlin was with the others when the new Khûrûsh envoy made her appearance. Given what she knew of the Khûrûshil culture, she was quite surprised to see only one individual being escorted by Shemnarai and Kamozh and his retainers.

Granted, that individual was impressive by Khûrûshil standards, even in comparison to Shemnarai or Kamozh, neither of whom was exactly low-profile or self-effacing. It did throw Caitlin off-base a bit that the envoy was dressed so plainly. After the Lleix had compared Khûrûshil culture to that of Japan, and after seeing the robes that Kamozh had worn for the recent broadcast, she was expecting something elaborate and ornate. The reality was very different—almost Spartan; which gave her a new insight to the people of this system.

In the aftermath of the battle, the Terra taif ships had coalesced in an orbit around the point where *Lexington* and *Fancy Free* had almost ended their story. *Ban Chao*'s flotilla had joined up first, providing what aid they could until the support and logistics ships had made their way inward from the cometary fringe. They were joined by another squadron of attack ships and two more *Starcloud*-class ships sent by the Eleusherar Path.

The humans had held a memorial service for the dead. It had taken another full day to gather all the bodies, particularly out of the wreck of *Lexington*. The Lleix had been in attendance, as had been Kamozh and his retainers and Shemnarai with several others of the Khûrûshil exiles and D'mishri representing the Eleusherar Path.

The dead had all been taken into the star and released there to be instantly vaporized. While it had still been heart-wrenching to have to let go of Ed, Caitlin had drawn some comfort that his body was now part of a solar furnace which would keep lighting the sky of Khûr-shi for hundreds of millions of years to come.

And she remembered seeing Master Zhao Jiguang approaching Envoy D'mishri after the memorial.

"You speak of the Immanence as if it is God," Master Zhao had said after being introduced. "Is it?"

"That would depend on what you mean by God," D'mishri had responded.

Master Zhao had tilted his head a bit and looked at the envoy, then had smiled his big smile and said, "I foresee many enjoyable discussions between us. Do you drink tea?"

That memory caused Caitlin to smile for a moment as the introductions were being completed. Although she did not have *oudh* in what was about to transpire, she was still to be a part of it.

The core group was smaller than the initial meetings with the Eleusherar Path had been. Aille and Pleniary-superior Tura were the Jao representatives, since they had claimed *oudh*; Pyr, Ramt, and Helot stood for the Lleix, with Lim providing translation services for the Khûrûsh; and Caitlin herself and Gabe Tully were to be the humans involved. And it concerned her that Tully was not here yet.

They had commandeered the equivalent conference room on *Footloose* that had been used for the meetings on *Lexington* and set it up in much the same way. Just as the Khûrûsh envoy had been presented to everyone present, the door irised open to reveal Gabe Tully with Vikram Bannerji at his side.

Tully scowled down at the dress uniform he was wearing as he approached the door to the conference room. Bad enough that he was having to wear the monkey suit, but his left hand, wherever it was, was itching like crazy and it was about to drive him berserk.

"Okay, Lieutenant," Tully growled, "you can go play with your Trīkē now. I'm here in one piece."

"Nothing doing, Colonel," Bannerji murmured back. "Major Liang made it very clear that since Top is still in the body and fender shop, I am to be with you from the time you leave your room until the time you return to it. And I understand that Director Kralik had something similar to say."

"Hmmph," Tully said. "Did all of your Trīkē survive the battle?"

"They did, sir, the battle and the transfer to *Footloose*, both. Rather resilient little creatures, they've proven to be."

At that point, the door irised open and they proceeded into the conference room. Tully began looking for Caitlin.

"Colonel Tully," someone said in front of him. Startled, he looked up to see Lim approaching with a strange Khûrûsh at her side. *Must be the new envoy. Genius, of course that's who it is. Wake up, Gabe!*

"May I present Henzhre, envoy of Khûr-melkh Shmenkhat?"

"Pleased to meet you, ma'am."

Lim rattled off some Khûrûsh to the envoy, who nodded her head and rattled something back to Lim.

"She is pleased to meet you also, and wants to know if you are a military officer."

"Tell her what I do, Lim. You know it as well as I do." Tully smiled a little bit at that.

Lim and the envoy exchanged words some more. "She is very pleased to meet you, and wants to, ah 'talk shop' at some point. She wants to know if you were involved in the recent battles."

Tully hid the wince as he lifted the stump of his arm up into plain view. "Tell her, up close and personal."

The envoy's eyes darted from the stump to his good hand and back again. She stepped back a pace, made a complicated motion with her upper hands, and said something to Lim.

"She said she will definitely make time to speak to one of the heroes of this war. Please forgive her as we must continue."

"Any time," Tully said.

After they had moved on, Tully said, "Find me a chair, Vikram. I need to sit down now." He was beginning to think that Dr. Motlana just might have been right about doing too much, too soon.

"This way, Colonel."

After the introductions were completed, and as D'mishri was making some opening remarks, Caitlin moved to stand on the other side of Tully from his lieutenant. This gave her a remarkably good view of the room.

She had a good feeling about this, Caitlin decided. The right people were all there. And while she understood that the Eleusherar Path had thousands of years of experience at dealing with other races, she doubted they had anything like the experiences Aille and Tura had in trying to herd the Jao, so she suspected the sides would be pretty evenly matched.

Too, they all had experience now with the Ekhat. They all had an incentive to come together to defend against the madness of the Ekhat. Aille and Tura, she knew, would never lose track of that. Never.

For a moment Caitlin had a glimpse of a civilization that spanned across two galactic arms; that spanned across thousands of races; that united together to hunt down and crush the Ekhat. She smiled at that. She knew Ed would have approved.

CHAPTER 90

Third-Mordent stood at the window she had seen her ancestress at many times before. She looked out into the blackness, stark and unforgiving.

The creche masters had been quite careful in their care of her new hosts. Third-Mordent was certain that, as with her former mate, her former enemy and her former ancestress and mentor would receive the best of care in the creche until the surviving nymphs emerged. Unlike the last spawning, Third-Mordent had made no threats to the creche masters this time. The creche masters understood.

The creche masters had made sure that she had received all files belonging to both Seventh-Flat and Ninth-Minor-Sustained. The scope of their strategies and connections almost awed her, but she had absorbed much of it already. Assimilating the rest would not take long. Meeting and adjudging the lesser Ekhat of the factions and the leading servients was in process. That, too, would be concluded soon, with a minimal number of completions required. Third-Mordent did not want to waste resources, but she would not brook obduracy to any degree; alignment or completion were the only alternatives available to those who would come under her themes.

Third-Mordent could see her faint reflection in the glass of the window. It did seem very odd to not see or sense Ninth-Minor-Sustained in the glass or beside or behind her.

She could sense the nexus in the flow of the Melody. It stood there, obdurate, breaking wave after wave of Melody thrown against it. Carrying on as in the past would not resolve the problem, would not establish the Melody that the universe longed to sing. It would not establish the harmony needed to do the work of the Melody.

So, her immediate work was clear. And when it came to its cadence, then, Jao, anti-Melody that they were, would next be brought to completion.

Third-Mordent contemplated a universe without the discordance of the Jao, and found it pleasant.

Afterword

Eric Flint

I developed the plot for *The Course of Empire*, the first novel in the Jao Empire series, in the summer of 1997. My wife Lucille and I had gone to Alaska to attend the graduation of our daughter Elizabeth from the University of Alaska. Once that was over, we left Fairbanks and spent a week in the Kenai peninsula, most of it at the little resort town of Homer at the outlet of Kachimak Bay.

Lucille and Elizabeth went off on their own one day—shopping or hunting moose or bear-baiting; whatever—and I spent the whole day at a table in our hotel's little lounge developing the outline for a new novel based on the Roman conquest of the Greeks (and, although not to the same extent, the Mongol conquest of China). I thought it would be interesting to write a science fiction novel exploring the theme of an advanced civilization being conquered by one that was more primitive in most respects but had a superior political and military capability.

This is not a new theme in SF, of course. Christopher Anvil did much the same thing in his classic story "Pandora's Planet," and other authors have touched on it as well. But Anvil's treatment was lighthearted—almost comic, in fact—and what I had in mind would be a lot darker. My novels are oriented to an American audience, and while I generally approve of my countrymen, they have some characteristics that annoy the hell out of me. One of them is that Americans, as a people, tend to exhibit the same smug self-esteem found in so many rich kids. As the saying goes, *he was born on third base and thinks he hit a triple.*

So it is with my folk. Some—not all, by any means—of our good characteristics are ascribed to our own virtues when they are in fact simply the product of good luck. In particular, Americans tend to ignore the fact that we had the luxury of developing our new country and its institutions in relative peace and tranquility after we gained independence from Britain. We were not immediately subject to invasion by surrounding powers unhappy with the outcome of our revolution, as were most revolutions in history.

So, I thought it would be worthwhile to depict an America that had been conquered and occupied by a foreign power—in this case, a *really* foreign power. And I thought it would be still more worthwhile to depict an ensuing situation in which the correct political and military course of action was murky. The standard trope in such situations is to depict virtue as the property of revolutionaries against the tyrannical new order. (As, indeed, I've done myself in my 1632 series.) But I decided it would be more interesting to develop a situation in which the correct—it might be better to say, least incorrect—course of action would be to collaborate with the new dispensation.

That is, after all, what both the Greeks and Chinese did after they were conquered by the Romans and the Mongols. And within a relatively short time, measured by historical standards, it was impossible to tell any longer who had really conquered whom.

I developed the outline in great detail, in a single day of somewhat feverish work in Homer, Alaska. I swiped the title *The Course of Empire* from the historian Bernard DeVoto, who bestowed that title in 1952 on the last volume of his classic trilogy on the settlement of the American west, the earlier two volumes being *Across the Wide Missouri* and *The Year of Decision: 1846*. I always liked that title and since titles can't be copyrighted, voila. (What the hell, DeVoto probably swiped the title himself from the five famous paintings of that name done by the American artist Thomas Cole in the 1830s.)

And...

There things stood for a number of years. I was busy with other projects and *The Course of Empire* just sat on the virtual shelf, gathering virtual dust.

Then I read K.D. Wentworth's two novels *Black on Black* and *Stars Over Stars*. Those novels are centered on the hrinn, an alien race she created which I found superbly well-realized. I thought Wentworth might make a good co-author for the novel I had in mind, since one of the keys to making *The Course of Empire* work would be to develop the Jao into a well-rounded and complex alien species.

Happily, as it turned out, Kathy was out of work at the time and she readily agreed to the project. We decided that she would concentrate on shaping the Jao while I wrote the episodes featuring the Ekhat and the various battle scenes. After a first draft was finished, I did the final rewrite, making the complex social and political relations between humans and Jao work properly.

The end result—this is my opinion, anyway—was a novel that's one of the best I've ever produced. Kathy and I went on to write the sequel, *The Crucible of Empire,* which I was also very pleased with. We then began work on a third volume in the series, which we decided to title *The Span of Empire*.

But Kathy came down with cancer at that point. When she broke off from working on *Span of Empire* due to her illness, she'd done the rough draft of about four chapters in the book. After some rewriting and rearranging, the material was eventually incorporated into the novel that David Carrico and I produced. To the best of my knowledge, this is the last fiction that K.D. Wentworth ever wrote.

After struggling with her cancer for months, Kathy died on April 18, 2012. She was only sixty-one years old. The world lost a wonderful writer, and I lost a co-author and someone who had become a good friend.

By then, David Carrico and I had co-authored *1636: The Devil's Opera.* When he told me he was a fan of the Jao Empire series and would like to work on the third book in the series, I immediately agreed. David has his own strengths as a writer, and while he couldn't replace Kathy Wentworth, he did a superb job of expanding new areas in the setting that neither Kathy nor I had ever delved into. I'm very happy with the end result and I hope you are as well.

APPENDIX A
THE EKHAT

The Ekhat are an ancient species which began spreading though the galaxy millions of years ago, an expansion which reached its peak before the onset of what human geologists call the Pleistocene Age on Earth. That final period of expansion is called by the Ekhat themselves, depending on which of the factions is speaking, either the *Melodious Epoch*, the *Discordance*, or by a phrase which is difficult to translate but might loosely be called the *Absent Orchestration of Right Harmony*.

Three of the four major Ekhat factions, whatever their other differences—the Melody and both factions of the Harmony—agree that this period was what humans would call a "golden age," although the Harmony is sharply critical of some of its features. A fourth faction, the Interdict, considers it to have been an unmitigated disaster. The golden age ended in a disaster usually known as the Collapse. (See below for details.)

The era which preceded this golden age is unclear.

Even the location of their original home planet is no longer known to the Ekhat. They spread slowly throughout the galactic arm by use of sub-light-speed vessels, and in the course of that expansion began to differentiate into a number of subspecies, some of which became distinct species, unable to crossbreed with other Ekhat lines.

The Ekhat today are a genus, not a species, and some human scholars even think it would be more accurate to characterize them as a family. They are widespread throughout the galactic arm, but are not very numerous on any particular planet. That is partly because they are a slow-breeding species, and partly because they are still recovering from the devastations of the Collapse.

The golden age began when Ekhat scientists discovered the principles behind the Frame Network, a method used to circumvent the light-speed barrier. By then, they were already widely dispersed and the Frame Network enabled them to reunite their disparate branches into a single entity. Whether that entity was purely cultural and economic, or involved political unification is a matter of sharp debate. This is, in fact, one of the main issues in dispute among the factions of the Ekhat in the modern era.

It is unclear how long this golden age lasted. The lack of clarity is primarily with the beginnings of the era. There is much greater agreement about its end: approximately two million years ago, the entire Frame Network disintegrated in what is usually known as the Collapse (although the Interdict faction calls it the Rectification or the Purging).

The collapse of the Network was quite clearly

accompanied by (and probably caused by) a massive civil war which erupted among the Ekhat and quickly engulfed their entire region of galactic space. By the end, Ekhat civilization was in ruins and most Ekhat had perished. There was an enormous amount of collateral damage, including the extinction of many other intelligent species.

Slowly and painfully, in the time which followed, three different Ekhat centers were able to rebuild themselves and begin to reconstruct the Network. Two of them did so for the purpose of restoring the Ekhat to their former position (although one of them proposes doing so along radically different lines) and another wishes to prevent it.

The factions can be roughly depicted in the following manner:

THE MELODY

The Melody can be considered the "orthodox" faction. It believes the "golden age" was truly golden, an era during which the different strains of the Ekhat were working together toward the ultimate goal of merging and becoming a species which would be "divine" in its nature.

The Ekhat notion of "divinity" is difficult for humans to grasp, and can sometimes be more clearly expressed in quasi-musical rather than religious terminology. Each branch of the Ekhat contributes to the slowly emerging "supreme work of art" which is the "destiny" of the Ekhat. No faction of the Ekhat seems to have anything close to the human notion of "God."

The closest parallel in human philosophy is probably Hegel's notion of God-in-self-creation, except that the Ekhat see themselves, not some outside deity, as what Hegel would call the Subject.

The Melody advocates a pluralistic approach to Ekhat advancement. They are insistent that no single branch of the Ekhat is superior to any other, and that the "emergence of divinity" (or "unfolding of the perfect melody") will require the input of all Ekhat. In this sense, they are supremely tolerant of all the distinctions and differences within the genus.

But, while they tolerate differences, they do not tolerate exclusion or isolation. Since, according to them, the talents of all Ekhat will be needed for "divine emergence," no Ekhat can withhold themselves from the developing "Melody." In this, they are a bit like the old Roman or Mongol emperors: you can believe whatever you want, but you must submit to Melody rule and you must subscribe (formally, at least) to the Melodic creed. In short, they are uncompromising "imperialists."

On the other hand, the Melody is utterly hostile—genocidal, in fact—toward any intelligent species which cannot trace its lineage back to the Ekhat. All non-Ekhat species are an obstacle to the Ekhat's "divine emergence," considered by them to be static or noise impeding the "perfect melody." The Melody envisions a universe in which the transformed Ekhat are all that remains.

Scholars suspect the Melody's eventual goal is to exterminate all non-Ekhat life of any kind. The Melody believes the Ekhat were well on their way toward "divine emergence" when the sudden and unexpected treason of a faction which they call (translating roughly) the *Cowardly Retreat* or the *Deaf Lesion* launched a vicious campaign of sabotage which brought down the Network and collapsed Ekhat civilization across the galactic arm.

Human scholars believe that the *Cowardly Retreat* is essentially identical with the faction known in the modern era as the Interdict. What can be determined of current Melodic policy seems to substantiate that belief—the Melody is utterly hostile to the Interdict and will slaughter them on sight.

THE HARMONY

The Harmony arose after the collapse of the Network and can be considered the "revisionist" wing of the Ekhat. They believe the civil war which produced the great collapse was due to the anarchic and disorderly nature of Ekhat civilization which led up to it, an era they do not consider to be a "golden age" so much as a "bronze age." (Keep in mind that these are very rough human approximations of mental concepts which, in the case of the Ekhat, are difficult for other intelligent species to analyze.)

In the view of the Harmony, all Ekhat are not equal. Basing themselves on what they believe is a true genetic picture of Ekhat evolution, the Harmony ranks different branches of the Ekhat genus (or family) on different levels. All Ekhat have a place in the new "Harmony," but, to use a human analogy, some get to be first violinists and others belong in the back beating on kettle drums.

The Harmony ranks different Ekhat branches according to how closely they fit the original Ekhat stock. The closer, the better; the farther apart, the more inferior. Not surprisingly, they consider the Ekhat branch which inhabited the planet where the Harmony first began spreading as the "true Ekhat." In fact, they seem to believe that theirs is the home planet of the Ekhat (which no one else does and the claim is apparently very threadbare).

The Harmony advocates a genetically determined hierarchy, in which all Ekhat will have a place, but in which (for most of them) that place will be subordinate.

To complicate things further, the Harmony is split by an internal division of its own. The *True Harmony* believes the rankings of the Ekhat species are permanent and fixed. The *Complete Harmony* believes all Ekhat, no matter how lowly their genetic status at the moment, can eventually be uplifted into "complete Ekhat-dom."

This division, whose ideology is murky from the outside, does have a major impact on the external policies of the different wings of the Harmony. The True Harmony shares the basic attitude of the Melody toward non-Ekhat intelligent species: they are destined for extermination. The Complete Harmony, on the other hand, believes that non-Ekhat species have a place in the universe. The process of uplifting all Ekhat will require replacing the "sub-Ekhat" strains with other intelligent species to, in essence, do the scut work. The flip side of "improving" all Ekhat is to subjugate and enslave all non-Ekhat.

It was this wing of the Harmony which uplifted the Jao into full sentience.

THE INTERDICT

Of all the Ekhat factions, the Interdict is probably the hardest to understand. The closest equivalent in human terms would be something like "fundamentalist, Luddite reactionary fanatics."

The core belief of the Interdict is that the Network was always an abomination. Some human scholars think that the origins of the creed were scientific—i.e., that some Ekhat scientists became convinced the Network was placing a strain on the fabric of space-time which threatened the universe itself (or at least the portion of the galaxy where it had spread).

Whatever their scientific origins might have been, the Interdict, as it developed during the long years after the Collapse, became something far more in the nature of a mystical cult. From what can be gleaned from their extremely murky writings, the Interdict seems to believe the speed-of-light barrier is "divine" in nature and any attempt to circumvent it is "unholy."

It seems most likely that the Melody's charge against the Interdict is correct: it was they, or at least their ideological predecessors, who launched the civil war which destroyed the Network. In fact, that seems to have been the purpose of the war in the first place.

What is definitely established in the historical record is that it was the Interdict which freed the Jao. Not, of course, because of any concern over the Jao themselves, but simply to strike a blow at the Complete Harmony. It was they, as well, who provided the Jao with the initial technology to obtain control of a portion of the Network and begin to create their own stellar empire.

The fact that they did so—and still, in an off-and-on and unpredictable way, maintain a certain quasi "alliance" with the Jao—underscores the bizarre nature of the Interdict creed. The Jao, after all, are also maintaining and even extending the Network. Yet the Interdict seems not to object.

One theory is that whatever scientific underpinnings originally lay beneath Interdict ideology have long since been lost. What has come to replace the notion that the Network itself threatens the universe is a more mystical notion that the Network is "unclean." The danger is spiritual, in other words, not physical.

One contradiction this situation presents is that in order to destroy the Network, the Interdict must use it themselves. Indeed, in many areas of the galaxy, it is they who are rebuilding the old framepoints and extending new ones. Apparently, Interdict adherents go through some sort of purification rite which allows them to do so. As always, the precise tenets of the Ekhat creed are at least murky if not quite unfathomable to non-Ekhat.

APPENDIX B
INTERSTELLAR TRAVEL

The method of supra-light travel used by all intelligent species is usually called, by the Jao, the "Frame Network." The method involves warping space-time using extremely powerful generators positioned in at least three widely spaced locations in the stellar neighborhood. (Three will work, but is risky; four is better; five is ideal; more than five is redundant.) These "framepoints" must be at least three light-years apart, but are not effective if the distance between any two extends much more than eleven light-years.

Existing framepoints allow ships to cross the stellar distances between them in what is effectively an instantaneous transition. There is theoretical debate over whether the transition is "really" instantaneous. But from the subjective standpoint of any human or other intelligent species, the travel is instantaneous. The dispute is whether or not it actually requires a few nanoseconds.

In essence, two framepoints working together are

creating what can be called an artificial wormhole. New territory, where there does not exist a framepoint, can be reached in one of two ways. One way is to use sub-light exploratory ships. Once arrived at a suitable location for a new framepoint, the ship (or multiship expedition) can begin to create the new framepoint, which can then begin to participate in extending the entire Frame Network.

Of course, this method of extending the Frame is very slow. The other method is to use existing FP generators to create what is called a "Point Locus."

Triangulating (more often: quadri-angulating or quint-angulating) their power, these framepoint generators can create a temporary Point Locus at a distance. For a certain period of time, ships can travel to the Point Locus from any one of the FP generators which created it.

This is the normal method used for invasion fleets, since it is impossible to invade a framepoint held by an enemy. (They just "turn off" their end of the Network and the invaders vanish, no one knows exactly where.) Invaders from the outside can triangulate on an enemy solar system, create a point locus which is independent of the enemy's side of the Network, and send an invasion fleet that way.

The expense and risk involved is considerable, however. Point loci tend to be unstable over any extended period of time, so the window of opportunity for an invasion is limited. To use an historical analogy, each invasion is like a major amphibious assault during World War II. If a large enough beachhead is not secured quickly, the invasion will face disaster by being stranded and overrun. Moreover, because of the impossibility of matching loci in open space, the point locus must always be created within the photosphere of a star. In essence, the star itself serves the participating frame generators as a common target. But that obviously presents its own set of dangers.

How unstable and temporary a point locus proves to be, varies according to a wide range of factors. These include: the number of FP generators used, distance, and a multitude of more subtle factors involving a lot of specific features of the galactic neighborhood—dust cloud densities, nearby novas or neutron stars, etc. Creating a point locus is as much as art as a science, as well as being extremely expensive, and is never something to be undertaken lightly.

[illegible] and know how to be able to stop its schemes

[illegible] don't miss THE SHADOW OF THE LION [illegible]
[illegible] nate fantasies, written with Mercedes Lackey & [illegible]
[illegible]